Praise for David Nevin

"An intriguing overview of the fractious early days of the American public . . . tical tension, the grippin   inal moment in the infa   vell-crafted drama featu   his-torical characters."   *klist*

"David Nevin's colorful novel brings together all the figures, plus James Madison and Napoleon Bonaparte . . . and explains how the new nation survived discord and discontent, but also flourished."   —*The Dallas Morning News*

"What a book! It is a panorama of five crucial years in American history . . . told in David Nevin's inimitably personal style, giving readers fascinating and emotional insights into the great names of American history . . . hearts as well as heads were at risk yet the ending could not be happier. This is a book to treasure, to reread, to give to friends and relations."

—Thomas Fleming, *New York Times*
bestselling author of *The Officer's Wives*

"The stirring story of a young America's battle to remain a democracy . . . Nevin gives human faces to historical icons, Jefferson and Madison, Meriwether Lewis; Andrew Jackson and his beloved Rachel, and most noticeably Madison's charming, courageous, incomparable Dolley."

—*Kirkus Reviews*

EAGLE'S CRY

DAVID NEVIN

A TOM DOHERTY ASSOCIATES BOOK
NEW YORK

EAGLE'S CRY

A Forge Book
Published by Tom Doherty Associates, LLC
175 Fifth Avenue
New York, NY 10010

www.tor.com

Library of Congress Cataloging-in-Publication Data

ISBN 0-812-52472-1

First edition: October 2000
First mass market edition: October 2001

Printed in the United States of America

10   9   8   7   6   5   4   3   2   1

For Luci

I

ORIGINS

1

On the night of December 11, 1799, Gen. George Washington, retired now from the presidency of the United States for more than two years, sixty-seven years old and feeling older, saw a large, misty ring around the moon that hung over Mount Vernon.

"Coming on snow, General," Billy Lee said. They were on the front lawn. The big white house that stood for so much in Washington's life gleamed in the pale light. Billy was the general's manservant, huge, black, devoted, crippled in body now and hung on the bottle as well, but he'd seen the general through the war and all that had followed. His speech was blurred by the loss of his teeth, providing another bond; Washington's teeth were gone, his dentures painful, his speech necessarily careful. Which was all right—measured speech added to his gravity.

"Maybe not," Washington said. Billy would be free with a lifetime income to support him when the general was gone. He was a good man and loyal, but you didn't look to him for decisions.

In the morning the mercury stood at thirty-three, wind from the northeast wet and clammy, clouds hanging low.

"Don't look good, General," Billy said. They were in the stable, grooms saddling their mounts.

"You stay back, Billy—sit by the fire."

"Nah, suh. You go, I go."

"Well, I've never let a little weather stop me."

"Yes, suh, but—"

"I know—I'm older now. But that doesn't mean I'll roll over and die when I see snow. Now that's enough talk."

"Yes, suh."

They rode out of the barn. Temperature down, wind brisk, it *was* chill. He thought of the fire crackling in his study, quills sharpened and waiting on the gleaming desk. But he had rounds to make, fields and herds to examine, walls to check and foremen to query. That heifer in the far barn with the sore in her mouth, how was she doing? Hands expected to see the master as soldiers expected to see the general; you couldn't sit in your tent all day and pretend to be a leader. Presently it began to snow.

"I done told you I smelled snow," Billy said.

"That you did, Billy."

The snow eased into steady rain. He drew his greatcoat collar closer. He didn't want to see the day when rain could drive him from duty. But the balm he normally drew from the very sight of his land was lacking today. George Cabot's letter had disturbed him deeply and he'd scarcely slept, lying there listening to Martha's gentle breathing with awful visions of his country in trouble flashing in his mind. They were still there.

Listen to George up in Boston and it seemed the nation the general had nurtured was sinking in a tide of venom. Federalists attacking Democrats, Democrats snarling at Federalists. Damn all political parties anyway, shattering the American ideal! Of course, George did see things in extremes, but here he was talking of Thomas Jefferson and James Madison as handmaidens of the devil. The general knew that no more decent man than Jimmy Madison had ever walked, let alone one smarter, but George saw all Democrats as Beelzebub's minions. The blind conviction of his hatred told the story. Still, it wasn't just Federalists—Democrats were haters too.

He sighed, slouching in his saddle. The thing was—but then he saw a sagging fence. Better have Henderson get those posts reset immediately. He swung down and lifted the post straight, kicking dirt in around it. When he remounted he felt rather surprisingly winded. He was older, granted, but worse, he *felt* old; the world sweeping by him, the country troubled. But what had kept him awake much of the night was George's echo of a call that came more and more often: Come back, take command again, hold us together again lest we fly into fragments. But that was ridiculous, his time was past; John Adams was president now. Rescue us, show us the way, make us do right—they sounded like children acting up while the schoolmaster was out back relieving himself!

At the far barn Norris had set a fire, and Washington warmed his hands before turning to the heifer. She was standing, a good sign; he forced open her jaw and ran an experienced finger along its lower side. Yes, the canker was definitely shrinking. She rolled her eyes and bawled when he let her go. More of the blue ointment, he told Norris; keep after it.

Riding on, rain slanting against his face, he mulled over the nation's divisions. Hold us together, Cabot mewing like a pussycat.

"Why in the devil does everyone look to me?" He glared at Billy. "Answer me that!"

Billy had a chaw tucked in his cheek. He spat a brown gout to clear for speech. "Why, General," he said, " 'cause you knows what to do. Most folks don't know diddledum, but you got your head fixed on right. Most . . . well, look at me, hungering after the rum when I know it tears me up. But you . . ."

Well, it had been a rhetorical question anyway. He turned his horse to the path. But Billy was right; he'd always known what to do. Holding them together—the army, the country, the people—been successful too, until the rise of opposing political parties divided Americans who once had been a single people. At the start we were all together, in war, in striking a new Constitution, in firming the nation's place in the world.

His horse stumbled and he rose automatically in the stirrups. But once the new nation was on its feet, his own cabinet had split, young Alexander Hamilton, his favorite, really, off like a greyhound toward a future he could see more clearly than anyone else. And his other favorite, little Jimmy Madison, turned suddenly rabid in support of Mr. Jefferson, a man with whom the general had known from the beginning he would never be close. Tom and Jimmy had dug in their heels over a radically different vision.

He hadn't seen the split coming. They'd had problems and Alex had offered solutions. Tom and Jimmy saw dangers ahead, but Alex's solutions were immediate and real. But, now, looking back, what if Tom and Jimmy had been right all along? Alex was a near genius in finance, handsome, elegant, loyal—Washington felt him a sort of son. But that didn't mean he was always right. Sometimes ambition betrayed him, the hungers of a poor boy who has risen too fast, the arrogance of a mind that raced beyond others. But genius wasn't all that mattered. Heart mattered too.

A sudden image of Jefferson popped into his mind, tall, elegant of manner, rusty hair graying, head thrown back in that characteristic way when a thought struck him, saying, "Above all, trust the honest heart of the common man." *The honest heart.* Now that, George Washington well knew, was the plain truth.

Another memory . . . a column of his men, must have been in 'seventy-nine or maybe 'eighty, in there somewhere, the war settling into a terrible grind, the British locked into New York and Boston and holding hard. It was near dusk and he'd called a small attack and come out to watch the column go by, lean, hungry-looking men with rifles in hand, near empty haversacks slung, battered hats drooping over stern faces, rags tied around shoes that rotted on their feet. Marching out to fight, knowing that some wouldn't return, knowing that before the night was out they might be running in retreat before superior British numbers. The whole trick was to go in and hit hard, sting the enemy, throw him off balance, keep him on edge, and then slip away to fight him another day. It would be a long time before those men slept.

He'd stood and watched them pass, and as they went by they'd nodded. Nodded! "Evening, Ginral." "Evening, sir."

"How do, Ginral?" They would salute on the parade ground, but here it was one soldier to another, one citizen to another, men with honest hearts marching to war. Evening, Ginral.

His eyes blurred for a moment. He blinked rapidly. The rain slanted harder, occasionally flaking into snow; he should go back, he supposed. Yes, he was older now and intimations that he wouldn't live indefinitely were coming with disconcerting frequency. But he wasn't gone yet, and until then . . .

He knew why George Cabot's importuning disturbed him—it stirred the old call of leadership. He'd always been a leader. Born poor but of solid family, he'd molded himself so. Leading his men into combat for the British back in the French and Indian War—he'd been just a boy then, God, he'd been green, he'd had so much to learn. But some of his strength was the capacity to learn while holding poise and equilibrium. He'd made mistakes and sometimes they'd cost lives, but he never was flummoxed, never let his distress show, and he learned. His power wasn't in brilliant schemes nor seeing deeper than anyone else could see but rather in the capacity to grasp the whole, make the parts work, calm passions, hold control when things wanted to go out of control.

But now? Martha said sixty-seven wasn't old, but age is measured in more than years. It had been a long road . . .

He was home well before dinner at three, half hour at least.

"George!" Martha cried. "Didn't you take shelter? Look at you—you're all wet."

He frowned; he wasn't really wet.

"Flakes of snow in your hair! Oh, George! Your inner coat is damp too. Go and change; get something dry—"

All this maternal fussing! He couldn't help the iron in his voice, "That will do, madam." He was ready for dinner now. Actually he did feel a bit of a chill, but it was a little late now to mention the tickle in his chest. He took a long sip of claret and felt the act of swallowing, not a good sign.

After dinner, ignoring a half-dozen new letters, he read

the papers aloud and soon had Martha laughing over his comments. As concession to that tickle in his chest he went to bed early and in the morning decided not to go out. There was the new mail and swallowing his tea had been, yes, difficult. Why not cosset himself? After all, he wasn't as young . . .

Letters full of fear and foreboding from Fisher Ames and Timothy Pickering and Oliver Wolcott and one from Colonel Hamilton picking poor John Adams apart. John was having a troubled presidency, attacked by his own party as well as by Democrats and taking it hard. And why shouldn't he? The general himself took criticism like a bee-stung horse, and what was wrong with that? A man who'd molded himself into a leader wasn't likely to sit around with a smile as folks savaged him. And the Democratic papers had made brutal personal attacks in his last years in office, and if he could lay hands on a few of the worst editors he'd give them a taste of the horsewhip . . . except that that would be beneath his dignity.

When Cullie brought tea he asked her to add a little honey to ease his throat and say nothing to Mrs. Washington. A dull ache lay at the center of his chest. He sat by his window gazing over his grounds where three inches of snow had fallen overnight. He loved this place. As he studied it, he felt decision forming: those trees yonder did, after all, mar the view and should be cut. It was always his way, study as long as needed, then unshakeable decision and prompt action. He'd walk out later and mark the trees. Thus he had run army and country.

The letters echoed Cabot's call—come back, come back. It was a cry of anguish, but it was the wrong prescription. There was no going back, there never was.

On the other hand, that didn't mean there was nothing he could do. A leader must find his own way to lead. The problem was our divisions, the fear we would break apart or come to civil war. He shut his eyes, listening to the fire crackle, and it came to him that this new division of the parties really was but a metaphor for a struggle for the nation's soul. Who are we? What kind of country do we want? Maybe that query had been in the wings from the beginning and we'd been too busy winning independence and getting onto our feet to notice. Maybe it was maturity that brought it before us, lingering immaturity that made dealing with it so difficult.

But what could he *do?* A leader must rise above problems, see deeper and understand more than others. Parties seduced men into dogmatism—your way comes to seem the right way and then the only way and then the sanctified way, and opposition becomes first aberration, then evil, then treason. How to lift his people above that? He must find the kernel of truth, grasp it whole, turn it like a gem to the light, and make his people see as broadly as did he. He could do that— call for a big public dinner, let people know he had something to say. When he had everyone's attention, give them a talk or even a metaphorical toast that would guide quarreling men back to sanity.

But what would he actually say? He must be very careful, must think it all through as he once had done in war, for he knew he would get just one chance and then the force of his words would be gone. Think it through, ruminate across the years, see what they had wrought . . . and where they'd failed. He sighed, adjusted the chair's bolster at his neck, and let his mind drift back to the war where it all had begun. He'd been an ignorant Virginia farmer—he could see that now—and had learned about the varied country and its immensely varied people with not a few pratfalls. But his men stayed with him, they taught him, and he learned, and they went to war together. . . .

He'd never found decision difficult, but now with thousands of men awaiting his orders and a skilled army prepared to destroy him, he faced overwhelming detail. Everything— weather, food supplies, clothing and blankets, shoes, wagon stock and the animals to draw them, stocks of powder and ball, and when he could expect replenishment, how many ill or wounded and hence how many effectives, how to force feuding generals to work together, how to meld Virginia and

Massachusetts troops into units, scout reports on terrain and the enemy . . .

Stunning detail, long lists, piles of reports on his camp desk, he reading and trying to remember. Soon he began writing summaries, just extended lists at first, but the very process of writing produced such order, logic, and coherence that lists turned into essays. His pen scratched steadily down sheet after sheet of foolscap as the candle guttered on his desk and his camp bed remained smooth and untouched. Step by step the mass of information became a solid whole, and then, simply and clearly, decision took care of itself.

Was today so different? He felt the same confusion and clashes, same omnipresent sense of danger, the old calls to leadership renewed. How to respond? Surely as he had before—think it through, write it out—or, at least, think it out. Suddenly he was more content than he'd been in weeks: yes, review all that had happened till he knew the answers.

Martha leaned on the back of his chair. She put her hands on his throat. They were warm and he sighed. "You're not well, are you?" It was a statement and he didn't deny it.

"A cold," he said. "I'll shake it off."

"I *knew* you took a chill. I'll mix the medicine."

"No—you know I never take anything for a cold. Let it go as it came, without help."

"But, George, you're not as—"

"I know." He raised a hand. "Ask Cullie for more tea." There was a limit to just how much he would cosset himself. He was busy now . . . go back to the start, when things were simple. They had fought for eight fierce years; eyes shut, he let images of war roll in his mind. He had never seriously doubted they would win, and finally the British saw the reality and went home.

Ah, that November day in eighty-three! He'd grouped his troops just above New York City while the last British soldiers boarded ships off the Battery. Then, his big warhorse, Nelson, prancing under him—Old Nelson felt as proud as he did—he led the boys in. People lined the streets in awestruck silence and then burst into a stunning roar. Hats flew in the air, women rushed forward with hothouse flowers in thick bunches, Henry Knox's cannon on the heights opened in wild salute . . .

Flowery welcome speeches said no one but General Washington could have held it all together and made independence work. That was fair enough. He had a clear sense of himself: solid, strong, able, self-contained, intelligent—but, mind you, not brilliant, not even clever, never scheming, not the most rapid man in thought, not intellectual, not a wide reader, his real interests agricultural, all qualities that meant he understood his men and they understood him.

He knew himself very well. Slow to decide but unshakeable when he did; profound judgment proved over the years. He'd held them together, the boys suffering through winter after winter, gathering themselves for another awful forced march to another slashing attack and quick retreat—the men of the Revolution, great men, gallant, loyal, dangerous men with the taste of independence in their mouths.

Marched into New York to the boom of cannon and at four that very afternoon he summoned his senior officers to Fraunce's Tavern not far from the Battery. Looking at their familiar faces, lined now where once they had been smooth and young, he felt the tears start. Grew worse as he took each in hard embrace, whispering thanks and farewell and Godspeed. An hour later he was crossing the Hudson, heading south. It was over.

King George III, who had his odd moments but was nobody's fool, was reputed to have said that if General Washington gave up power now the American would be *the* great man of the eighteenth century. Well, he could have justified hanging on. Many men so urged, brimming with reasons, the country staggering out of the disciplinary grip of war, a weak and quarreling Congress, states that viewed themselves as separate powers, European nations looking upon us as a hawk looks on goslings. Men tried to push duty on him, told him he *owed* them a ruling hand. He remembered being infuriated one day, close to knocking the man down. . . . now he couldn't remember who it was. . . .

But it was clear he could have been king, and he thought about it. Power is sweet; he knew that who doubts that hasn't tasted it or is a liar. But he gave it up and went south in a great rattling coach with four horses that Simon Simcoe of Camden had loaned him, cheering crowds and cannon salutes and children with hothouse flowers all the way. The darling of the people. Tendered his commission to Congress with a graceful speech, tears standing in his eyes. Then he was free. . . . Mount Vernon and Martha awaited.

Even now, he remembered his contentment. He had been true to himself. He was a man of probity, above the slashing swords of ambition and desire and hence all sides could turn to him.

Meanwhile, he must mark those trees. He summoned Billy with the axe, wrapped a scarf around his neck in deference to a throat that now was worse than sore, and walked out, boots growing damp in three inches of snow.

"General," Billy said, "you look like something the cat drug in. You better stay inside."

"I'll manage," he said. He was very tired. Suddenly it seemed quite intolerable that people should call on him again—just too much!

Billy was holding the axe close to the head. "Show me which trees. I'll blaze 'em."

"*I'll* do it!"

"Suh—"

"Damn you, Billy, shut your mouth!" He was in a fury, hands shaking. He snatched the axe. Billy stared at him, dismayed but not cowed. It struck Washington that he must be sicker than he thought. . . .

"All right," he said at last. He touched Billy on the shoulder. "Maybe I'm not so well after all." It wasn't quite an apology. He passed over the axe. "You do the rest."

The pain in his chest expanded. He began to shiver, overtaken by a chill despite his coat. They walked back to the house in silence. He was searching for something to say to Billy when the big man said, "You'll feel better tomorrow,

General. You don't mind my saying it, you'll find a dollop of corn would go good right now."

The general smiled. "I believe you're right, Billy."

Inside, he asked Cullie to lace his tea with whiskey. He pulled off his boots and put slippered feet toward the fire before Martha could admonish him. His pipe had a foul taste, not a good sign. He was surprisingly tired, and he put his head back in the big blue chair, eyes shut, remembering. . . .

Home from war he'd seen immediately that a tottering confederation under a toothless Congress with no chief of state must fail. He remembered his surprise that it came as a surprise. There was just no focusing authority to hold states together. So he'd put into motion the steps upon steps that led to forming a new government.

There was a heat wave in Philadelphia that summer of 1787. Dancing on burning cobblestones and shedding coats in the stifling chamber reminded them of their common humanity, he felt, inducing humility. They met in the State House, in the same room where years before he had accepted command, and seated themselves at the same little tables covered in green baize. He took his place on a small dais between two dormant fireplaces faced with marble. He scarcely spoke; he was a commander, not an orator.

And he watched them unfold a miracle.

He jerked awake. Martha was standing over him, her hand on his forehead. She gave him a cup of thick pea soup that slid down his aching throat and said he must go to bed. In the bedroom she helped him disrobe. He made her face the wall when he pulled on his nightshirt—modesty holds to the end—and then sank into the feathers, exhausted. He let her spoon the potion of emetic, James powder and Peruvian bark, into his mouth.

"George," she said, "I forbid you to be ill." She sat on the edge of the bed and wiped his face. He brought her hand to his lips. She was stout now with jowls and double chin that accentuated her pointed nose, and her beauty of long ago had not faded but changed, gone inside, evident as ever through her eyes. She'd been a widow when he'd married her and well-to-do, not a small matter, and perhaps for both of them it had been as much arrangement as passion. He had known passions; now he wanted solidity, a woman who could manage a home and complete a life. And over forty-one years respect had deepened into profound love, and he was never quite so content as when she was near.

He lay there, drifting and dreaming and wondering, back in Philadelphia again listening to them build a new nation. They would have a president, and soon he saw they expected him to take the post and give it shape. Good enough. Sliding toward sleep, his breathing very shallow, ignoring the fire in his throat, he saw that *this* was why finding the way was so important. In Philadelphia they had created a form in which free men could live in peace, granting the rights of others while retaining their own. It was a noble document and it should live forever.

Indeed, it was proving itself out at just this moment of George Cabot's terror, when Alexander Hamilton was doing his best to crush the Democrats. Jimmy Madison had overcome the great pitfall of democracy, how to have majority rule while still preserving the rights of the minority. He'd crafted an intricate balance of powers between the three branches: Freedom within limits—divided legislature with staggered terms, each branch forced to yield to the others, two-thirds to impeach, three-fifths to limit debate. . . .

The general supposed Jimmy felt fully estranged from him now. Madison had left the Congress and was rusticating at his estate in Virginia, a great waste. Suddenly wistful, he thought how good it would be to see Jimmy again, see him walk in and flash that shy smile and hear his soft voice laying out logic in that building-block way of his.

And the general would say, my boy, you saved yourself and your people with that wonderful document. For as things had worked out, now Jimmy's own Democrats had become an angry minority that couldn't be silenced no matter how the Federalists tried. Good . . . as much as the general admired Hamilton he didn't like to think of a man with

Alex's instincts ruling without limits. Wouldn't be much different from that young devil Napoleon, now shattering the old orders in Europe, probably forevermore. Not that shattering the old orders was bad—open 'em up and let in air and light. But we needed no Napoleons in America.

Lying quietly on his side, swallowing only when he must, he searched those early days for hints of the trouble that was to come. Well, getting started had been the easy part. He'd been elected in an atmosphere of good humor. Hamilton as secretary of the treasury and Jefferson as secretary of state would be the key cabinet figures. Jimmy Madison was a congressman from Virginia and became the general's leading advisor.

Alike in their powerful minds, Jimmy and Alex were startlingly different in every other way: Hamilton handsome, vivid, swift of thought, clever to a fault, dashing with women; Madison modest, retiring, thoughtful, stimulating in quiet conversation, but downright dull in social situations. You never saw him with a woman in those days. But when he did stir himself to look at a woman, lo and behold, he chose the gorgeous Widow Todd, her husband swept away in the great yellow fever epidemic in Philadelphia.

Miss Dolley was as charming as she was beautiful, and when she began appearing on Jimmy Madison's arm the whole town took note and some of the racier lads made book on whether he would have the nerve to follow through. The general loved to dance with Miss Dolley—he danced with all the women, of course, a champion of the minuet, but she was special. Martha turned matchmaker: Had Jimmy spoken? She said Dolley looked ready to cry as she shook her head. Martha marched to Jimmy: This young woman was a prize and he'd better be sensible. The general was dubious about interfering in matters of the heart, but Martha pished him to silence and she proved right, for the wedding followed and they seemed supremely happy. That was in the easy days, dancing with Dolley before things turned harsh.

He was less familiar with Jefferson, who was just back from six years as ambassador to France under the old gov-

ernment. They'd gotten off to a poor start when Jefferson
had delayed accepting the appointment. Took a couple of
months to get a yes out of him, and the general heard that
Jimmy had had to make a hard case to persuade him. Jefferson had wanted to sit on that mountaintop he called Monticello—a pretentious name, really, not that that was any of
the general's business—but it was his business that a man
would hesitate when asked to serve at a crucial time. It embarrassed Jimmy; he and Jefferson were the closest of
friends.

John Adams was vice president. Fussy, good-hearted,
honest, more proud of himself than any man needed to be,
John was always ready to talk himself into trouble. He proposed the most god-awful kingly forms you could imagine
with a thirteen-word title for the president, his most exalted
etc. etc. The general never did get it really straight, but he
cut right through the uproar—his title would be president of
the United States and the direct address would be Mr. President and that was that! It had held so far; he hoped it would
hold forever. A good start for a democracy . . . but then,
thinking about it, he saw that the incident had foretold the
divisions of the future.

He snapped awake and knew instantly that he was much
worse. His throat was aflame, his breathing labored. All at
once breath stopped! Plugged! As if a hand clutched his
throat. Strangling, he raised himself with a hoarse cry.
Martha sat up, sleeping cap askew, horror in her eyes. He
stretched an imploring hand toward her and then miracu-
lously his passages opened and he took a rasping breath.

"I'll go for help," she said, throwing back the covers.
"We'll call Mr. Rawlins."

He stopped her. Rawlins took care of the people down to
the quarters and was expert with lancet and cup. Washington
knew he needed bleeding, he could feel the evil humors in
his veins, but if he let Martha wander the cold house she'd
be as sick as he was. He viewed this as pragmatic: Bleeding
could wait and he would need her before this was over. Yet
he also had an odd sense that nothing really mattered. The

suspicion that he was approaching the end was growing. They would call the doctors, but everyone knew that past a certain point doctors were helpless. He'd many times contemplated dying, doubtless everyone had, but never as an immediate prospect. Yet somehow he found the possibility not unduly disturbing.

He turned on his side and Martha held his hand in both of hers. He found that he could breathe through his nose and his throat eased a little and he slid into sleep. When he awakened he was dizzy, head whirling, and he lay very still, listening to Martha breathe. She was awake and he knew she was frightened, but there was nothing more he could say to her. He felt he was chasing something, a fragment forgotten, left undone. His mind dipped and whirled. A duty . . .

With an effort he remembered . . . he must put together a message and it must be exactly right. Recall their early enthusiasm. They were new and highly experimental, the only democracy in the world, moving on trial and error and struggling for balance. Now they must reclaim that focus. Somehow.

He lay in the dark taking careful, shallow breaths, afraid his throat would close again, asking himself if that original focus had really been so strong, since it faded when they faced real issues. It all began there, factions, clashing ambitions, rage bordering into hatred—still, he knew now that parties wouldn't go away because it was no accident that they had arisen. They represented the great philosophical schism breaking not on personalities but on opposite answers to that question, what kind of a country were we to be? He began to shiver and a cough tore his throat. Tears in his eyes, he tried to hold to his task . . . as soon they came to real things the question opened.

At the time he'd had no idea that the break was at hand. He wondered: if he'd been wiser, more prescient? Well, it didn't matter now. The problem was that they were broke, and the trouble arose in what to do about it. No nation can live long in insolvency. The trouble lay in those state bonds issued helter-skelter to finance the war and still outstanding,

interest unpaid for years. He'd passed out bales of them himself, payment to a gray-faced farmer for a dozen steers; payment to a wounded soldier for his service when real money
was scarce as hen's teeth. This debt now in the many millions undermined everything. What sayest thee, Mr. Secretary of the Treasury? Within weeks, Alex had dropped two
elegant designs on the cabinet table. Whence came Alex's financial genius? He was thirty-five, bastard son of a Scottish
planter in the West Indies, his only training in finance the
keeping of ledgers in an island store before he came to
America. Yet overnight he had put the national economy on
a sound footing—and it was only later that it became evident
that he'd also torn the cover off the philosophical question.

His eyes popped open—daylight. Rawlins was standing
by the bed, gazing down on him. Martha was up and
dressed. He'd slept but felt no better. Rawlins was quivering
with fear. He was a tall man with a permanent stoop who
was uneasy among his betters. Get on with it, Mr. Rawlins,
don't be afraid—but no sound came so the general pointed
emphatically at the big vein in the crook of his right arm.
Lips trembling, Rawlins drew up a stool and braced the arm
on his knee.

Martha watched from the end of the bed. "Not too much,"
she said.

Rawlins wiped the broad blade of the lancet on his sleeve.
Bracing the heel of his hand on the arm he made a swift, clean
incision, clamped his thumb on the vein above the cut, put
the cup in place, and let the blood run out of the instrument.
The general watched the cup filling with satisfaction. He felt
better already. Bleeding was just the ticket to relieve the
blood of the humors that caused the trouble. He'd used it for
years, swore by it.

When the cup was full, Martha said, "That's enough."

Anger forced open his throat. "More!"

"Yes, sir!" Rawlins placed a second cup.

"George, darling, you'll weaken yourself."

With a second cup gone, he nodded and Rawlins stopped
the wound. He felt suddenly weak and shut his eyes.

"Are you all right?" she said.

He nodded. "Better," he croaked. He wanted to sleep.

"Take a bit of the medicine," she said.

His throat had closed again, but he raised himself obediently and she poured in a spoonful. With his throat closed, the mixture had no place to go and suddenly he was strangling! He lunged upward, it was in his bronchial tubes, he was choking and coughing and his throat was tearing—he blew the medicine out on the bed and fell back in a near faint, the pain in his throat as bad as anything he remembered from a wound.

"George, darling—" But he raised a hand. Please, let me sleep. She sat on the side of the bed, her warm hand stroking his face. He heard her sweet voice, "Sleep, darling."

Yet the pain was too great—and yes, the sense of urgency. The way he felt now he doubted he'd be speaking to anyone. But somehow that made the quest more pressing, time narrowing down; he must find the answers. See that political parties won't go away so we can't let them destroy us. Keep them in bounds. . . .

But by thunder, he *still* thought Alex's plans had been wise. First, the new nation would take over the state debts, issuing new bonds, interest to be paid by taxes. Second, it would establish a *national* bank, quite an unknown critter here. Together, the two would stabilize the national economy, provide a new source of credit and a reliable currency, and assure foreign capital that it would be safe here.

It had seemed perfect, but immediately a storm of protest had arisen from men who scented royalist tendencies and cried that the bank was just like the Bank of England, which actually was one of its strong points. The government was still in New York then, in that ungainly building that later fell down or would have if they hadn't torn it down; the general hated inferior work, which he thought described the Democratic view. He remembered studying quarter-inch gaps in window frames as they talked. The quarrel had turned his Cabinet room into a battleground. He'd started to cut Jimmy off and then decided to let it rage. Madison and Jefferson were an effective team. He thought Jimmy provided the hard, analytical thought, Tom the flashing ideas and flights of rhetoric.

They listened as Alex presented the first leg, the bonds, and then Jimmy's icy question, "What about the original holders?"

"What about them?" Alex had a way of hunching his head down into his shoulders when he saw a fight coming.

Jimmy glanced at the general. "The original holders, mostly your soldiers, sir, plus the shoemaker and the gun-smith and the farmer who took these bonds for services; they haven't been able to save their certificates. Had to sell them off for what they could get in hard times. And who was buying? Speculators, paying as little as a tenth of the face value. Now, Alex, you know that perfectly well."

"Of course."

"Then for God's sake, take them into account! Give them some of the payment."

"Track them all down? Spend years when we're sinking right now? That's a baseless idea, all bleeding heart. Point is not to rescue little men but to save the country!"

The general remembered Jimmy's voice going flat, and he'd seen this would get no easier. "I see a plot," Jimmy said, "a design to give vast windfall profits to men who lit-erally stole from the little people who supported the war . . ."

A little later the bank produced an equal fight. Alex envi-sioned it as a treasury binding private capital to government. As the official repository for government money, its bills would be as good as gold, and we would have stable money at last. It would be tax-supported, but 80 percent would be owned privately.

"Privately? By whom?" Again, Jimmy moving to the at-tack.

The general remembered Alex's sharp, glinting glance, suspicious, a bit too surprised that anyone would be dull enough to ask, a manner that had reduced many antagonists to silence. Then in a rush, "Who do you think, Jimmy? Men who have money, naturally. They're the ones we need."

"But won't they shape policies of this bank of yours to suit their own ends? To the detriment of the common citizen?"

Something feral in Alex's expression, lips pulled back on his teeth. "Certainly—that's the point! Take care of people with money, and they'll take care of the country. Give them a financial stake in the country's success and it'll succeed." The general had seen immediately that the great question was opening. He'd sat back and let it unfold.

Alex pointed a quivering finger at Jimmy. "You know why? Because money is the real power in any country."

"No, sir! The people are the real power."

"My foot, they are! Men are creatures of self-interest. Damned little happens for love of country—save love talk for the bedroom, for God's sake. Money is what drives any country."

That was Alex, harsh, cutting, contemptuous of opposition. It made him effective, but it was a weakness too; someday he might pay for that arrogance.

"You're planning a cheat on the people," Jefferson said slowly. "Brutalize little men who have no recourse. It's a hoax to reduce honest American yeomen to serfs of the wealthy."

Their intensity shook the general a little. There was the division defined. What should government be? Tom and Jimmy said policies should help all citizens and especially the poor, since the rich took care of themselves. But Alex was rewarding the rich at the expense of the poor.

"General? General? Can you hear me?" Familiar voice, hand tugging his. He came swimming up from very deep under, Jimmy's words still loud in his mind, and opened his eyes to see Jim Craik at his bedside. Ah . . . good old Craik would know what to do. The very sight of the worn lines in Craik's cheeks swept him back to the forests of Kentucky in the French and Indian affair when they'd been together under Braddock, he the regimental colonel, Craik regimental surgeon. The doctor had been a new graduate in medicine from Pennsylvania Hospital, and he'd cared for his patients with the same loyal intensity that Washington gave his men.

The general's voice was a croak. "Bleed me," he said. He saw Jim had the cup in his hand.

"Mr. Rawlins already bled him," Martha said. He heard the uncertainty in her voice. "Two cups."

He tried to speak but nothing came out and he had a moment of panic, it was like awakening in a coffin, hearing voices outside but unable to say—with a convulsive effort that tore his throat, he ground out the words, "Bleed me," coupled with a command stare that told Jim Craik to get on with it! He could feel the evil humors circulating in his blood, affecting every part of his body, making him heavy and strained, blood rotten and useless. Drain it off and ease the pressure.

Not, actually, that he thought it would do much good. Doctors soothed more than they really helped. If they were caring, you felt better. Of course they did help sometimes, but he'd seen too many gut-shot solders die in agony while Craik watched, seen the benevolent pus that Craik sought in wounds and amputations turn into cascades that overwhelmed the patient.

Craik wiping the blade on a handkerchief, making the neat incision, blood running into his cup, ah . . . felt better already. Probably transitory, but welcome. He thought he was coming to the end and now, watching Jim wet his lips nervously, he thought the doctor was of the same opinion. He shut his eyes, suddenly desperately weak, felt he was whirling and whirling down into depths. He heard Martha's tremulous voice, realized Jim had stopped the blood, started to protest and was gone.

He'd had the key just before they'd awakened him, a grip on what it all meant. It had been oddly comforting. He'd been sitting at his camp desk with the long, white plume graceful in his hand, judgment taking hold with iron certainty.

He dug into his mind. He'd had hold of it there. . . .

Yes, yes, that was it! Alex insisting money is what powers any country; Jimmy leaping up in angry outrage. The fight wasn't about the bank or the bonds or any of the details. It was about who we were as a people. What did we care about, believe in?

Alex and most of his Federalist brethren wanted a tight, contained, carefully controlled government in the hands of the ruling few, everyone else taking orders. He would shape all policies to bind men of money power closer and hold little men in their places—limit their vote, reduce their capacity to rise, keep them subservient, make them glad to be of service at low wages to those who counted.

Jimmy and Tom wanted a diffuse government in which states were strong and the common man's voice ranked with that of the gentry. If the government were to be skewed, let it be toward the poor and the helpless.

Alex said Great Britain's system was the best in the world. Tom and Jimmy saw the British as oppressors and were sure Alex aimed at monarchy in America. That charge drove Alex wild. His slender face, handsome as a Greek statue, would go white and strained with ugly red blotches, all beauty vanished.

"Do you still not understand?" he cried. "We're bankrupt—no economy, no currency, no structure, no credit. We're the laughingstock of the commercial world. But I can give us structure, restore our credit, control inflation. Jimmy, I can put us on a par with any nation in the world."

"Nor do I doubt that," Jimmy said. "But, Alex, I think you understand finance too well and your fellow Americans too little."

"So you say, but what is there to understand? The common man is just that, common. He's a boor. Knows nothing. Captive of his emotions. Prey of demagogues. As witness the ear he gives all these dirty little Democratic rags attacking our financial reality."

Jimmy started to speak, but Alex shouted him down. "Captive of his emotions, sir! Swung by the last shout penetrating his piggy little brain. Of course he needs to be controlled, guided, shaped, held in line. He's a peasant! And peasants were made to be held in line, to touch their caps to their lords and ladies. This difference you see in Americans has about the width of an eyelash."

"You're wrong, Alex," Jimmy said. His smile was supremely confident, and it subtly ridiculed Hamilton. Alex caught it too, that flush riding up his cheeks again. "In fact, the common man is a lover of freedom. He possesses an innate wisdom, rough hewn at times but entirely real. He takes care of himself, he controls himself, his sense of right and wrong rings like a bell, he'll fight forever for his freedom. And he sees you canting government away from him—catering to the bosses, the money men, the merchants and owners. And sooner or later he'll make you pay, Alex."

The general had pushed back his chair. "That'll do, gentlemen," he'd said. Still, it had been illuminating and he was glad he'd let the argument rage, distressing as naked anger could be. He doubted Alex and the Federalists really wanted monarchy in America—the general had made that decision for them years before—but they certainly wanted the best people in charge and probably liked the idea of institutionalizing their role in a hereditary form, nobles in perpetuity. Once, much later, he challenged Alex to his face on this and Alex backed and filled, smiling boyishly, but he never denied it.

It wouldn't have mattered so much if this were just a cabinet quarrel, but in fact it swept across the country. The parties shaped ever more clearly around these opposite visions, newspapers hammered the issue, even the states split up, taking sides, New England strong for Federalism, South and West for the Democrats, middle states swinging. Federalists shouted that any nation must be run by the nobility, call it what you like; Democrats denounced an elite rewarded at the common man's expense. The general had judged the party break to be beyond repair.

The image of an old soldier swapping his certificate for a sack of beans was darkly painful, but in the end he'd accepted Alex's plan because he'd seen no alternative; we would have no standing in the world till we could pay our bills. But an estrangement arose between him and the two Virginians. This hurt, especially with Jimmy. Tom was brilliant, but there was something foolish about him too. Jimmy was solid.

A dream seized him. He'd plunged into a lake, didn't know why. The water's warmth was comforting and he'd gone down and down in search of something, he wasn't sure what, until his breath began to fail and now he was fighting his way back to the surface, lungs bursting. He popped awake and heaved a great gasp that broke things open enough—

Craik bent over him. With candle and mirror he cast light into the tortured throat. Craik's face was strained; the general read fear. There were more men in the room. He recognized Dr. Brown from over at Port Tobacco, and Craik introduced a Dr. Dick, Elisha Dick, new young fellow from Alexandria, who bowed deeply. He'd just finished medical school at Edinburgh, well known as the best in the world, but he looked very young. *Three* doctors . . . he must be as ill as he felt. He let Craik depress his tongue while Brown held mirror and light and they all peered. He felt about like that heifer he'd been doctoring.

"Quinsy, I think," Craik said. Pus engulfing the tonsils. The general nodded: That's what it felt like. Brown agreed. The young fellow hesitated, then said, "With respect, it could be inflammation of the throat membranes." Craik grunted, which told the general all he needed to know about the young man. Edinburgh was fine, but the lines in Craik's face made the real diploma.

Martha wiped his face. He asked for the two wills in his desk. Her eyes widened and she started to object, but he gave her his command stare. One was out of date: Burn it. The other went into her closet. She said he'd soon be better, but he raised a hand; he knew he was in a long slide toward the end.

Craik bled him again, Martha watching in alarm. Not

much blood came. Craik burned his neck with Spanish fly to bring blisters and draw blood from the throat. Fed him sage tea with vinegar, but his throat instantly closed and he was drowning until Craik lifted him. He fell back on the bed feeling more dead than alive; this was going to be harder than he'd supposed.

He spun off into blessed darkness, yet felt his mind was firing with its old force. Too late now to dream of the healing speech, but he didn't want to go into the dark night feeling his country was dying too. His brilliant young men had brought the issue to focus. Who are we? How will we define ourselves? Tightly held, narrowly based, men of wealth controling with lesser folk locked to place and class? Or open, fluid, moving, every man equal, with breaks as fair for the poor as for the wealthy, everyone limited only by his own capacities, free to be all that brains and grit could make him?

That was the quarrel out of which parties had grown. Now men seemed willing to war to the death over these matters. But how had we come to that? Eyes shut, motionless, taking shallow breaths, Martha's weight heavy on one side of the bed, he could hear them talking in low voices. But he held to the question—he must know!—and immediately saw how thoroughly the events of the last decade had pushed both sides toward extremes.

He remembered the day the news from France had burst—they were in New York, he and Martha still in the Osgood House on Franklin Square. There had been a clamor outside and he'd gone to a window to see shouting men running from the direction of the Battery. It was late fall and a light rain had kept up all day. An hour later Billy delivered a rain-spattered broadsheet headlined REVOLUTION IN FRANCE! the ink still wet. Commoners had taken over, all new laws proclaimed, the king acquiesces, crowds seize the Bastille, political prisoners stream to freedom. He remembered standing just inside the door, light pouring in from a high window, Billy pulling off his wet coat, and he'd thought instantly, this will be trouble.

It was happening too fast, the old thrown away too rapidly, wild mobs surging in the streets of Paris, and it was sure to get out of hand. Monarchies of Europe would resist it, and that could mean war and they would try to draw us in. . . .

Every ship brought fresh news. Americans took the French adventure as an extension of their own revolution. They thrilled to a glorious declaration of liberty, *Rights of Man and of the Citizen.* Crowds celebrated in American streets. Men wore the soft liberty caps affected in Paris, decorated their coats with tricolor cockades, sang French songs in theaters, dropped mister for citizen as a form of address. This enthusiasm swirling madly through the streets—he could feel it even as his stately carriage passed by—was infectious but a little frightening too. Everything seemed unstable.

Jefferson had been beside himself with joyous approval and infuriatingly patronizing to boot. On the basis of his ambassadorial years he explained it in moralizing little analogies for America, showing that the gentry should look for no special favors. When French affairs did darken, Tom seemed to see them as insignificant, the important thing being that the French movement stood for liberty.

The general had grown steadily more concerned. French radicals executed the king and scores of nobles, bloody blade clattering, heads tumbling to the basket. The mad zealot Robespierre opened a reign of terror that killed thousands; bodies must have been stacked like cordwood in France from the sound of things.

Americans enthused over revolutionary ideals as they lamented the excesses. It puzzled the general that events abroad that really were none of our business should so profoundly affect life here. Both sides were ready to fight. Democrats said all that mattered was that monarchy had been vanquished and democracy was on the march. Federalists said that France proved that democracy given free rein must destroy itself and all around it. Let Democrats push Federalists aside in America and next thing you know the best people would be dangling from trees.

Sure enough, war did flame in Europe. Surrounding monarchies attacked the revolution, which responded with evangelical fervor. Then Britain jumped in against France and, just as Washington had expected, both sides turned on the little United States. It had infuriated him then; and sick as he was, it still did, breath going short at the thought. Man abused you, you'd like to take a stick and break some heads. Both abused us, stopping our ships, seizing our cargoes, the British impressing our seamen, each trying to force us into a reluctant alliance.

The general had hoped this pressure would draw our own warring sides together, but no—the split widened. Never mind Robespierre's excesses, Democrats said, the French were fighting to preserve democracy against monarchial tyrants, and a fellow democracy *must* support them. Federalists called American Democrats slaves to the French, who would make us an overseas department of France. Rather, Democrats shouted, Federalists were using the war as excuse to tuck America under the wing of the British monarchy. At least, though, Tom quit talking about the nobility of the French after the Terror took hold.

"Tell me," the general remembered crying in exasperation one day, this when the secretary of the treasury and the secretary of state had stopped speaking, "do you really believe these extremes you're prating?" And both had nodded.

Papers had gone to new extremes. Congress rocked with charge and countercharge. Orators struck mighty blows for the British on one corner, for the French on the next. Some taverns were Federalist and some were Democratic, and it was as good as a man's life to go in the wrong one. In Boston a mob tarred and feathered a fellow who insisted on wearing a cockade and singing "La Marseillaise," the new French revolutionary song.

His eyes popped open. Someone had thrust a knife down his throat, or so it felt. There was haze in front of his eyes and then his vision cleared and he saw Billy Lee standing by his bed. Billy was crying, tears coursing unguarded down his cheeks. The general put up a hand and Billy took it and held it a moment. Then Washington's throat closed and he choked for air, his body bucking, and Craik was at his side holding him, and Martha was leading Billy away.

When he could breathe again, rasping, shuddering breaths, he told Craik to bleed him once more. The young doctor, Elisha Dick, raised a hand as if to protest, but Craik ignored him. The old doc milked the arm but almost no blood came and no relief. The general gasped, desperately sucking wind. The young fellow said something.

"He says your throat may close completely," Craik whispered. "Wants to try something new from Edinburgh. Open your windpipe below your throat so you can breathe through the opening."

The general was dubious. Speaking was torture. "Wants to cut me?"

"Yes, sir. Cuts into the trachea. Tracheotomy, he calls it. Says they preach it at Edin——"

"Has he done one?"

"No, sir, but he knows how. He says."

"Come on, Jim." The fear was back in his old friend's face and he whispered, his throat tearing, "Do we or don't we?"

Long silence. Jim sighed and shook his head. "I'm scared," he said.

That settled it. He didn't look at the young doctor. He took Craik's hand. "I die hard," he said, "but I'm not afraid to go. My breath cannot last long."

His secretary, Tobias Lear, knelt by the bed and took his hand. "I am just going." The general forced out the words. "Have me decently buried and do not let my body be put into the vault in less than three days." Lear, weeping, nodded.

"Do you understand?" Even now, it was the voice of command.

"Yes, sir!"

" 'Tis well."

He looked around for Martha. She came and sat on the bed. She held his hand in both of hers and after a while she leaned close and kissed him. He drifted away, conscious of her hand and her presence, drifting down and down into sleep, going away.

Dreams, flashing lights, but it was too late; he was hurrying now. Too late to grasp all the troubles, and did they really matter? The Whiskey Rebellion, those West Pennsylvania farmers bloodily protesting a tax. . . . He'd thought for a while there that scenes of France were to be replayed, but it had all passed. Finished his second term, the Democratic papers denouncing him in the vilest terms—too late to horsewhip an editor, but it didn't matter now—and John Adams had taken over.

More trouble with France, they treating us with vast contempt for no reason he could see, but neither was that cause for war. . . . But Alex wanted war, wanted to focus France as the enemy, wanted to link with Britain just as Jimmy had always said. That Jimmy . . . there was a man, frail in body, weak in health, iron in mind and courage and force of personality. And good John Adams resisted the Federalist clamor for war, may God bless him in heaven, the country more shredded than ever. . . .

And he was leaving, questions unanswered. . . .

Trust the honest heart of the common man. Only truly wise thing he'd ever heard Thomas Jefferson say. But maybe you only had to say one truly wise thing to be a great man. And maybe it contained the answer for which his soul was parched.

And that talisman memory returned . . . men you could trust passing in column, going to battle. It was before Trenton, he now remembered, dusk and already cold, their breath frosting in the air. They'd marched past, rifles in hand, slung haversacks nearly empty. He remembered those empty sacks. They were hungry, and they'd looked at him with level eyes, strong men, sensible, the taste of independence in their mouths, men you could trust to carry a battle, to make a country, to cut through the folderol of political clamor and do the right thing. Men of pride, of tradition; men who knew

who they were. They'd passed in a long, single line, given
him that appraising glance, and they'd nodded. Just nodded.

Said, Evening, Ginral. How do, Ginral?

He was leaving the country in good hands.

Goodnight, Ginral.

2

MONTICELLO, VIRGINIA, DECEMBER 1800

The news caught the Madisons at Monticello, twenty miles
and a day's span from their own Montpelier. A post rider
galloping from Charlottesville bearing a flyer from Richmond, hoofbeats coming up the hill. Tom led them out to the
veranda with its towering columns and there was Sint
Robertson, skinny as a rail, mustaches drooping to his chin,
sliding off his horse and shouting, "How do, Mr. J.—I mean,
that is, Mr. President!" Immediately he pulled off his
battered hat, but then elation defeated deference and he
shouted, "You done won, Mr. J.! Last return just come in.
South Carolina swung to you and you're in!"

Dolley wanted to whoop and yell and dance there on the
veranda that glowed with sunlight. They had lived in sus-
pense for days, the election of 1800 tied and hanging on a
single state. Sixty-five electoral votes for John Adams, all of
New England, New Jersey, Delaware, and split votes in
Maryland, Pennsylvania, and North Carolina. Sixty-five for
Jefferson, other halves of the split votes plus Virginia, Georgia, Kentucky, Tennessee, and the great Democratic coup in
New York. Aaron Burr had stolen its twelve votes right out
from under Alexander Hamilton's nose!

Only South Carolina's eight votes had remained in doubt.

She thought Tom took the news with remarkable calm. "Thank you," he said, taking the packet of papers that Sint dug from his saddlebags. "Put your horse away and we'll get you dinner and a pint of grog. It was a hard ride . . . you're a good man."

"T'wasn't nothing, Mr. J.," Sint said, obviously pleased. "And yes, sir, a bit of grog would sure cut the road dust."

As Sint led the horse around the house, Tom turned to them with a huge smile. Dolley felt suddenly abashed. Thomas Jefferson, their old friend, an odd and wonderful man given to lovely flights of rhetoric and intricate ideas that seemed to her to scurry about sometimes like mice running for their holes, was the new president! In an instant everything seemed different . . . so what was she supposed to call him now?

Jimmy put out his hand. "Congratulations, Mr. President."

Tom—the president, she'd have to get used to that—took the outstretched hand and drew Jimmy into a hard embrace. He stood nearly a foot taller than her darling little husband, but she never noticed it until they were side by side.

"We did it," he said. She heard the emphasis on the plural and was pleased, for surely the victory was as much Jimmy's as Tom's. Tom. Maybe she'd get used to calling him Mr. President, but she decided to take her time about it. For now, she put her arms around him and kissed his cheek.

It was a crisp day in early December and they would dine on the veranda. Tom laughed and cried, "This calls for champagne." He filled their flutes from a bottle chilled in the well.

Jimmy raised his glass. "To the new president."

Tom smiled and they drank. "And," Jimmy said, "to General Washington: It's precisely a year since he died."

"Hear, hear," she said.

Tom raised his glass but didn't answer. Then, as they seated themselves, he said, "It is symbolically interesting, you know. The general, representing the past, the old, dying as the century ended, our birth of a new way coming with the birth of the new century. May what we stand for live on through this century and the next and the next."

"Amen," Dolley said. But she noticed the distinction he made between himself and the man whose wisdom, in her view, had put the nation on track. And in a moment, his mouth twisting curiously, he said, "Though the general might not have welcomed this day, were he here."

She knew enough to keep her mouth shut at that. Jimmy said, "I think he might have been pleased. He was sensible."

Tom's smile was thin. Over his glass he said, "Perhaps. But he didn't much like me—I always felt that. He was in Alex's camp."

"Now, sir," Jimmy said, rather sharply, she thought, "that's much too strong."

She bit her lip to keep from adding anything. The old gentleman had tried so very hard for balance. He'd never sounded a Federalist to her. Balanced, steady, reserved—he wasn't a man to tell you what was in his heart. It had been a raw blow when he'd died so suddenly. She and Jimmy had gone to three separate memorial services, and she still grieved that she hadn't seen him again before he went. Life can be cruel that way.

"You're right, Jimmy." Tom smiled, his charm infectious. "I withdraw the remark. But there's a certain residual pain left over from those days, you know. He never got over his fear that Democrats, meaning especially me, would lead us into French anarchy if not aim to make the United States a satellite of France." He shrugged. "That's close enough to a treason charge for me to . . . well, remember it, anyway."

Dinner was served by Sally Hemings, Tom's housekeeper, an extraordinarily pretty young woman whom Dolley could see combined the best features of ancestry, both black and white. Confident of her own beauty, Dolley could afford to be generous. She noticed, as she had before, that Sally was profoundly self-assured; beautiful women had reason to be confident.

The quality of excitement still charged the air as they talked over the election, and she listened quietly, luxuriating in new success. First, there was Aaron's coup in New York, organizing the boys of Tammany Hall into a political force that gave him the weight to swing New York. She'd known Aaron for years and was very fond of him; he'd been a real friend when she needed a friend. His coup had thrilled Democrats and earned him a place on the ticket, running for vice president with Tom. He too had been elected, though they'd scarcely noticed in their excitement.

Aside from the importance of New York, it was clear that their narrow victory had turned on the French crisis and on the Alien and Sedition Acts. Both were excesses that she thought had doomed the Federalists. Their insistence that unleashed Democrats must run amok was so strange. Doubtless the guillotine's clatter did make some of the American gentry uncomfortable, but take Sint Robertson—he and common folk like him weren't likely to go ravening about stringing up leading citizens. That fear seemed ridiculous. American colonists had lived in essentially self-governing communities for two hundred years with no disintegration. And no matter what Tom said, she thought General Washington had understood that basic truth perfectly well.

The talk droned on and as a cat is drawn to catnip her mind slid off to the delicious dream that had been an indulgence and now would be reality. They would be moving and life would be starting over, moving from Montpelier to the new village on the Potomac to which the government had officially transferred two months ago. Her old friend Danny Mobry, whose husband had shifted his shipping business there from Philadelphia, told her the place was all joy because everything was new, handsome red brick homes springing up around new federal buildings. Of course the secretary of state must have a house—she could see it already, brick, white window framing and black shutters, three stories, porte cochere, kitchen separate for fire safety, stables in the rear . . .

And it would have the great advantage of not being Montpelier. Fine as the mansion was with its vast surrounding acreage and warmly as old Colonel and Mrs. Madison had welcomed her, life still was slow and far distant from the lovely bustle of Philadelphia. It was six years since she and Jimmy had married, and they'd spent the last four here, since he'd given up his seat in Congress. These years had given her ample time to explore the nuances of living in a home of which you are not the mistress. My goodness, yes, she was ready for the hustle and bustle sure to be found in a throbbing new capital!

She heard Tom saying the president and Mrs. Adams had moved into the new President's House, said to be gorgeous with its yellow sandstone walls painted a glowing white. "Poor John," Tom said, "I did want to beat him, but I know how hard he'll take this." Dolley bent an ear; this was more interesting. She knew Mr. Adams well and liked him, while his idiosyncrasies amused her. He was incorruptible, really an extraordinarily decent man, but he was fussy, prickly, usually in a huff, and able to find a slight in almost anything. Tom chuckled. "He'll be giving poor Abigail fits. He'll feel rejected, repudiated, feel nobody loves him when its so obvious that everyone should; he'll fall into one of his depressions, and she'll spend months jollying him out of it. Once I told her a boot in the backside might help on such occasions, and she didn't speak to me for three months. Loves him like a mother hen."

He poured a dessert wine and added, "Absolute antithesis of Alex. Something cruel in Alex, you know. I like to think I hate no man; but if I ever yielded to hate, Alex would head the list. Miserable man. Strange, too—and getting stranger."

Alex *is* strange, she thought. Undoubtedly brilliant, so everyone said, but too aloof, too remote, too proud. Liked women though. She remembered the first time she'd met him, when Jimmy was first squiring her about. She and Alex had danced together, and he had looked at her as a man looks at a woman. That was perfectly all right; but then he'd murmured something she didn't understand and flashed a look toward Jimmy in which she'd read contempt, and she realized he was suggesting he could serve her better. She'd come close to slapping him—*that* would have made a pretty incident!—and he'd read her expression. He stepped back, gave her a rueful acknowledging smile, and from that day to this had been charming but not familiar, and over the years she had come to like him.

But he'd ridden his hobbyhorse—the French are coming, the French are coming!—until the poor beast was collapsing. Driven by their fear of democracy in the hands of the common man and their hunger for a British connection, the Federalists had brought the nation to the brink of war with France essentially because France wasn't nice to us. Even now that sounded strangely in her ears, but how else to put it? The gentlemen in Paris were infuriatingly nasty, no question about that; but really, declaring war over irritations? At home in Virginia, out of the Congress since ninety-six, Jimmy watched in dismay as we titted for tats with the French and worked ourselves up to a frenzy.

The French finally realized we were taking all this seriously so they sent diplomatic word suggesting we talk it over. Defying his own party, Mr. Adams had dispatched a new commission and that had settled that. No war after all. But Alex still wanted his army! What could people conclude but that he intended to use it against them to support unpopular policies?

Then the Alien and Sedition Acts making disagreement with the government a crime, blowing the Bill of Rights apart, jailing editors, seizing orators off the street . . . Criticism equals treason? The Terror in France had executed thousands on just that basis.

Poor Alex, he just didn't understand plain Americans. Couldn't see that nothing would so energize the common man as the realization that he could be imprisoned indefinitely for sounding off in a tavern. And that was why Thomas Jefferson would be the next president. . . .

Tom was talking and laughing, freer than she could remember having seen him before. Sally brought a fresh bottle of champagne and he opened it, firing the cork off the verandah into a rhododendron. He was chortling over a turn in the election in Pennsylvania, and he was looking at Jimmy as he leaned across the table to fill her glass.

In one of those frozen slow-motion moments she saw the bottle tilting to pour and the mouth sliding away from the glass by several inches. Before she could move or speak, Sally leaned forward and deftly slid the glass under the bottle. As the glass filled, Tom looked at it and her for the first time, then moved to fill Jimmy's glass. The rescue was so smooth, neither man even aware that disaster had been averted, talk flowing unbroken, that Dolley was delighted. She glanced at Sally, their eyes met, and each had to suppress a mutual bubbling chuckle, as much at shared feminine complicity as at the situation. There was reassuring competence and authority in this young woman; she was profoundly confident of her position.

Dolley turned back to the talk, well pleased. As Sally cleared the dessert plates, Tom was saying, let's watch our wild eyes—arch-Democrats like John Randolph and Giles who were sure to take victory as license to throw out everything of the old and sweep the country leftward, to use the new French term.

Jimmy smiled. "The extremes of Federalism drove the voter to us; great pity if our extremes should drive him back."

What's more the victory had a disturbingly sectional tone. All New England to Adams. New York won only by maneuver. Middle states split. Only the South and the West holding to the proper course. She knew Jimmy considered this the supreme threat, much more dangerous than France or England. The North-South split over slavery had come close to shattering the Constitution before they finished writing it.

The talk slid to another favored theme—the West as site of the country's future. Her mind wandered. New England, New York, a way down the seaboard, represented the old and threatened, the West the young and new. Which raised the Mississippi, trade lifeline of everything west of the Appalachians and held in a death grip by Spain.

Old talk . . . but suddenly she remembered that everything had changed. They were no longer talking theory; the weight and responsibility for the nation had fallen squarely to them. The talk at this table would become national policy. She'd better pay attention.

". . . puts us on a collision course with Spain," Tom was saying. "Hold off long as we can—pioneers flowing west will give it to us ultimately anyway—but if the Spanish don't mind their manners in the meantime, we'll have to relieve them of Louisiana."

He laughed. He had a sudden boyish look, his faced flushed, and for a moment she thought he was tipsy, but then she saw he was excited by a thought. "What irony—all that talk about the French, but if we fight anyone it'll be the Spanish."

II

THE THREAT

II

THE THREAT

3

"Well," Anna said, lying on a sofa, thumbing Dolley's copy of *Mrs. Crowell's Philadelphia Commentator* with the latest in London and Paris fashions, "I hope nothing goes wrong."

"Why?" Dolley turned quickly. "Have you heard something?" Anna lowered the magazine. Dolley's baby sister was eighteen and on the cusp of womanhood, sometimes silly, sometimes wise and penetrating. "Just on the stage coming over. Passengers talking as if Mr. Jefferson was the devil incarnate. You could hear the hatred in their voices. They said they should have strung the first Democrats up to trees and settled it before it got out of hand. Talking about how the revolution in France ended up killing all the decent people."

"That's nonsense!" She knew she sounded more angry than she'd intended—that's what fear does. Anna looked at her, eyebrows raised, then returned to the magazine with a sniff. Dolley was packing her old leather trunk for the stage trip to Richmond where Jimmy, as an elector, would cast one of Virginia's twenty-one electoral votes, for Mr. Jefferson, of course. Electors meeting on the same day in each state theoretically reflected the popular vote, but things could always go wrong.

William, Colonel Madison's ancient body servant, tapped on her door. "Old Colonel calling for you and Mr. Jimmy." He saw her start and added, "He ain't no sicker today than yesterday, Miss Dolley. I done sent Jonas out to find Mr. Jimmy."

She hurried from their wing and heard Jimmy gallop up. He leaped from the horse, flinging the reins aside. "Is he—?"

"I think he just wants to see us."

He was breathing heavily. He was deeply devoted to his dying father; they feared the old man would be gone before they returned from Richmond.

But they found him sitting up in his blue brocade gown. He had a shrunken look, hair wispy and cheeks concave, but his eyes had the old force. Three glasses and a bottle of wine were on his table. His doctor forbade alcohol but Colonel Madison did as he pleased. He poured and raised his glass.

"To the *next* president of the United States!"

"To Mr. Jefferson," Jimmy said.

"No, no," his father said, "Tom's already elected. I speak of the next—James Madison of Virginia!"

Her eyes widened. The old man had lifted a line straight from her secret heart! Of course Jimmy should follow Tom! He'd earned his claim, central to the past and cocaptain of the new. Anyway, she thought it was Jimmy who provided the real weight in the partnership with Tom. Of course he should be next; to deny it was an abuse of modesty.

But Jimmy shook his head. "Succeeding Tom? That'll be Colonel Burr, surely, after being vice president."

"Burr won't make it," Colonel Madison said. "It takes moral fiber to run a country, strength of self. Look at General Washington, at Mr. Adams, a man of real quality even if we disagreed with him, and now Tom, men of stature all. Burr? No, he doesn't compare." A coughing spell overtook him and he set down his glass. "But the real point is this: You must be very careful. In everything, do you understand? This is a dangerous time; we could easily see violence."

In a phrase the old man had forced to the surface the fear she'd been trying to suppress for days. Violence? What, anarchy, civil war, those in power refusing to relinquish it? After all, they had all the tools of force. . . .

"Won't be violence," Jimmy said. His glance slid to her. "You're talking about a transfer of real centralized power to the people. That will terrify the former and could destabilize the latter."

"No," Jimmy said.

"James, there hasn't been a transfer of power from a closed inbred elite to the common folk without bloodshed in a thousand years. Read your history, Son. Men don't surrender power willingly."

"But we are different. We're a new people, we've built a new system, a government of checks and balances. Free men *can* govern themselves, Father."

The old man smiled, suddenly tired. "Just watch yourself, Son. Both of you."

Everything seemed darker as Dolley went back to the bedroom. She had been an inexperienced young Quaker woman when she married Jimmy, and she had moved into the highest circles of national life with studied aplomb—displaying much more confidence than she felt—and she hadn't managed that by being naive and foolish.

She continued packing. The storm was coming and they would be at its center, and yes, she was frightened.

When he walked into the bedroom, the set of her shoulders told Madison she was angry. Of course he'd seen her alarm, nor had his father told him anything new. Certainly there was peril in this discarding of an old philosophy for one that was new and untested, what Tom called the second revolution. But the men on the other side were honorable, despite their more restrictive view of democracy. They'd be all right so long as no new disruption shattered things and turned the genie loose. . . .

At last she spun around. "Why didn't you tell me you looked for trouble?"

"I don't look for trouble."

"Jimmy, don't tell me! Your father talked trouble; you didn't look in the least surprised. You knew it all along!"

She glared at him, fists on her hips. She was a stunning woman, her black hair full and striking, her eyes the color of

sky on a bright day, her cheeks always at a blush, which he'd
been amazed to learn was not entirely nature's gift, immense
strength in set of nose and modeled lips. In fact, he had
feared to alarm her, and he wondered if that were a form of
denigration.

"Don't shield me," she said. "My first husband died in my
arms and my newborn infant died the next day, and there's
hardly a dirtier death than yellow fever with black vomit and
bloody bile bursting from the bowels and the victim gasping
for water. The only blessing's that it's quick. I'm a strong
woman—I don't need to be shielded."

She wiped her eyes. "So," she said, smoothing her gown
down her sides, "if there's trouble, I guess we'll deal with
it." She blew her nose. "Now, didn't I see you turn your
horse loose when you galloped up? Let's go get him before
everyone decides he threw you."

She was the joy of his life and he took her hand as they
walked out into the sunny afternoon.

The man Burr sent from New York made a terrible impression. Madison didn't like him the moment he presented himself at Swan's in Richmond, where the Madisons had the
inn's only parlor and room, bouncing in like an absentee
landlord. His name was David Gelston, and he was a sleek
young businessman en route to what he described as unique
opportunities to be exploited in Charleston. Madison read
him at a glance: pale, overdressed, too eager, talked too fast,
and his open cupidity in describing his Charleston hopes put
a civilized man's teeth on edge.

"I'm here to tell you the New York view," he barked.
"This time Virginia must play fair. You betray us again. The
party will be torn to shreds." Madison fought to control
anger, though in fact there was validity in Burr's complaint.

In writing the Constitution they had left one fundamental
flaw, which was natural enough since that was before parties
emerged but now was very dangerous. The presidency

would go to the man with the highest number of electoral votes, the vice presidency to the runner-up.

No one thought in terms of a ticket then or of a running mate. That concept arose in ninety-six when the general was stepping down, and without much hope, Tom ran against Adams. In a loose relationship, forerunner of the ticket concept, Burr ran with him for the vice presidency. Things had been so informal then! As Madison remembered it, everything was casual. As it turned out, Burr drew far fewer votes than Tom, but it was the bare handful that Virginia gave him that he took as a special slight. He'd never forgiven Tom or Virginia.

But his ultimatum now raised a new problem. If electors voted two-by-two for Tom and Burr, each man would emerge with seventy-three electoral votes, and *they* would be tied. That would throw the election into the Congress, and the House still sitting was firmly in control of old-line Federalists consumed by fear of the new, and then anything could happen.

It was an immense danger but easily solved. Short Burr a single vote here, and there could be no tie. "Tell Aaron not to worry; we'll guarantee him a solid twenty votes."

But Gelston jabbed his finger. "We must have the full twenty-*one*. Nothing less will satisfy!"

"Look, young man," Madison snapped, "it has nothing to do with Aaron; the risk of a tie is what matters."

"Forget that," Gelston said. "We've already solved that—arranged for a couple of short votes in the North. Colonel Burr doesn't want an equal total; he just wants Virginia to pay him the respect that is his due."

"Does Aaron really endorse this claptrap?" Madison asked.

"Certainly, because he stands for New York, and New York, sir, is watching! Any fool can see that Virginia aims to rule or ruin. Biggest state, ran the war, ran the Constitution, ran the government. Adams not a Virginian, and we threw him out. Well, New York is coming up; we have our pride.

We don't intend to submit to Virginia, and you'd better believe it."

The young man leaned forward in his intensity, fist doubled and beating on his thigh for emphasis. "Look, Mr.
Madison, I can see you don't care much for me. Probably
you see me as a typical New Yorker, crass, competitive, not a
real gentleman. Well, I don't much like you, either, living on
a plantation with a passel of slaves to keep you comfortable,
and you're oh, so polite, so gentlemanly, drinking your tea
with your finger stuck out, darkies bringing you Madeira."

Gelston laughed without mirth. "It's time you got used to
New York, for we're coming into our own. Winning there
gave Mr. Jefferson the election, and that was Colonel Burr's
doing. So we want the honor due us. You slap us in the face
with a twenty vote and we won't take it!"

He stood abruptly and cracked his hands together. "You
go wrong on this, and I promise you you'll split the party
wide open. That is Colonel Burr's message, and it is totally
real. Please take it very seriously."

Madison stood. "Good day," he said. He didn't offer to
shake hands, nor did Gelston.

When Madison was troubled—and he was very troubled
now—he liked to put a good horse under him and take to the
country. He was trotting along a little used lane, passing
fields still covered with slash, fruit trees banked against
cold, a herd of cattle that would dress out, to his practiced
eye, at a hundredweight below his own cattle on Montpelier.

At a small creek he swung down and hobbled the horse to
let it drink and crop the abundant grass near the water. He
paced the bank. If he protected against a tie but raised the
specter of North and South at each other's throats on the eve
of triumph, what had he gained? And then, smiling sourly,
he had to admit that he wasn't all that selfless either. Now
that the prize was in sight, he *wanted* it!

So did Dolley. She hadn't said much, but he knew her
well. And Burr had another claim on them. He had intro-

duced them in Philadelphia and Madison recognized that as
a debt, for she had reshaped his life. She was gorgeous with
her robust figure and striking color. He was a gnomish little
fellow with a soft voice, a bit the looby in society, but a
beautiful woman loved him! He felt a personal triumph
when she turned heads. And so he was what he was and on
the whole was satisfied with that. He had a powerful mind—
a fact he had demonstrated too often for self-doubt—though
that was poor consolation when he was with men who were
tall, dashing, and touched with the gift of command. But he
made good decisions, if he always found many a pro and con
to weigh. Indeed, he doubted the competence of men who
saw issues as simple and made decisions in a finger snap. He
didn't decide things in any finger snap, you may be sure.

Anyway, the current problem was of his own making. Of
course they should have foreseen the rise of parties, which
are just vehicles to express different views, but they hadn't.
Failure of imagination then impaled him now. But he
wouldn't be deciding in any finger snap. A cold breeze
arose. He tightened the saddle girth and turned the horse toward Richmond, as chilled by the decision ahead as by the
wind.

At the inn's stables, he swung down and gave the groom a
coin to give the horse a good currying and brushing. Billy
Blackleg, so called for some presumably forgotten episode,
was a skinny man with hard, horny hands and rheumy eyes,
his drooping mustache gray at the top and stained brown at
the ends from the chaw always in his cheek. He lived in the
stables and he washed his shirt every week or so.

He slipped the coin into his pocket like a sharpster palm-
ing a card, pulled off the saddle, and said from the corner of
his mouth, voice very low, "Mr. Madison, I guess you're
watching out pretty good this business don't fall into no tie
between Mr. Jefferson and that New York feller."

Startled, Madison said, "We certainly don't want one,
Billy. What brought that to your mind?"

"Well, thing is, most rich folks ain't like you. They hold 'emselves special. They don't even look down on you."

Madison waited.

"Know what I mean? They don't even *see* you. 'Lessen you make a mistake. Then they act like you was a dog shat on the floor."

Madison nodded, waiting.

"So they talk in front of you, see what I mean? Now, most folks stay at Swan's they're going to be Federalists. I guess that ain't any news to you. And they come out for their mounts and they don't give me no warning, so I'm scrambling around getting them saddled and all and they go to talking like I ain't got ears, know what I mean?"

Madison nodded.

"And they're saying the electors—them that cast the electoral votes, ain't that right?"

"That's right."

"Well, they're saying the electors likely will cast votes two for two, see, every man for Mr. J. *and* the New Yorker. And then it would be a tie and they'd be on horseback."

"Horseback, eh?"

"They're saying maybe it ain't over yet—they get a tie and they say they can find some way to set it on its ear— keep the government in their own hands, see? So it seems like us Democrats would be smart not to let no tie develop. I don't know if you've thought on that or not."

"Billy," Madison said, shaking his hand, "that's very good thinking. I'm in your debt."

Billy gave him a grand smile. "Don't think nothing of it, Mr. Madison. We're all in this together."

Dolley watched Jimmy chew over the dilemma. She thought it incredibly selfish for Aaron to expose them to danger for reasons of shabby pride. Twenty as opposed to twenty-one would shatter the republic? Really! The tail wagged the dog.

Still, there was tension in the air. An old friend, a Federalist—which had never mattered before—set up a whist game that turned into an awkward disaster. The other women seemed to feel they were sitting with the devil's hand-maiden. In a millinery shop that same afternoon a fierce old woman in an expensive hat of apricot velvet put a claw on her arm and hissed, "I just want to tell you, we all of us, the sensible people, the right people, think it's *terrible* what you and your husband and the rest of them are doing!"

Men milled about the streets, laughing Democrats cele-brating victory with bottles in hand, Federalists with down-turned mouths. Several street fights became one with the whist game, the old woman, the newspaper venom, the vile accusations, the tomato someone had thrown at their car-riage, glares at the inn, a rude woman who'd brushed past her in the corridor . . .

It was like nothing she could remember since the early days of the Revolution when she was a child and all around her patriots and loyalists were dividing into blood enemies. And into this tinder Aaron had thrown a flaming torch. It struck her that she'd never felt he had much weight, clever and handsome and charming through he certainly was—wit-ness the way women melted in his presence. But that made her feel guilty and that made her angry. Would nothing go right in these ugly days? In fact, Aaron had been good to her when she'd needed help and she hadn't questioned weight then. She'd been half crazed with grief when the fever had taken baby and husband. She'd asked Senator Burr to guide her affairs and stand as guardian to her little boy in case the fever returned for her.

As a tenant in her mother's house he'd owed her nothing, but he had performed nobly. She'd felt so alone, this being after her Quaker father's business had failed in Philadelphia, and the church had expelled him for debt, and something broke in him—in the end, she thought, women were stronger than men—and he went to bed till he died while her mother opened for roomers.

Months passed and she'd put aside widow's weeds and looked about. And one day Aaron had told her that the great little Madison had asked to be presented. The request was so specific of serious intent that she was breathless, and that very afternoon he'd brought Mr. Madison around. Jimmy had been terribly nervous, his hand shook when he took hers, he murmured "You're very beautiful," and then was tongue-tied; and she had rattled on rather desperately, wondering if she were making a fool of herself, wondering if he were even interested; and then he stood to go and asked if he might call tomorrow and would she on the next evening accompany him to a dinner General Washington was giving?

He was a power in the House in those days and very close to the general, and she'd been swept into the highest circles of the capital in urbane Philadelphia and had held her own. Better than her own. Jimmy had glowed in her presence, many people told her she'd made a new man of him, and one day dear old Aunt Martha—whom Dolley could see was easily a match for the general despite her gentle manner—said she would nudge Jimmy along.

But nothing happened. Then, with the session ending and the time ever so clearly now or never, he sent a note: He had something to say. She wore a gown the color of roses that was cut as low as she dared, seated him on the sofa beside her, and waited for what she became sure would be bad news. He stumbled, his tongue twisted, she noticed a buckle coming loose on his shoe and he'd worn hose that were yellowing with age—not at all the picture of a man who'd come to propose marriage. She had an awful impulse to tell him she understood, he could go, *au revoir*—but no!—she would fight to the end. So she waited, smiling, encouraging him, and at last he blurted the question she'd been desperate to hear and she collapsed into his arms. Six wonderful years had passed, that no children had come the only shadow. She knew there was ugly gossip about this, which she could settle in a word if she chose. . . .

She wanted an afternoon walk and they set out, her arm through his, on brick sidewalks laid in sunburst design, past graceful stoops and saplings set in sidewalk squares and guarded by little iron fences. He still had a few days before decision and he was laying out the pros and cons, when an elderly voice hailed them. They saw an old man on a younger man's arm. Jimmy said it was Colonel Emberly, an old family friend, and his son. The young man, prematurely gray and wearing an army major's uniform, scarcely spoke and when he did his lips scarcely moved.

Glaring, the colonel cried, "I never thought I'd see a Madison betray his people. You've turned your coat, sir."

She saw a look of surprising vulnerability flash over Jimmy's face and then his expression hardened. "I've done no such thing, sir, and I resent your saying so."

It was so unexpected that she felt momentarily disoriented; then she saw the officer staring at her with angry intensity and all her instincts went on guard.

"Oh, do you?" the old man shouted. "Well, the people who matter, who count for something in this country, they understand what you're doing, the false doctrine you and your precious Mr. Jefferson are spreading. Common man democracy!" He spat the words out as if they had a foul taste. "Look at France, a monument to what it really means. What it's always meant. You let the rabble get control and they'll destroy everything—*everything*! Dragged everyone who counted off to that great bloody blade of theirs; you think that can't happen here? It *can*. You'll see. You think you're safe, but they'll turn on you too; you'll never be able to control the passions of your own followers—"

Listening to the old man rant, she saw the danger; he believed every word of it. Like the women at whist, the old woman in the apricot hat, he honestly saw Democrats as in league with the devil! No one denied that ideals expressed in our own revolution had spun out of control in France, the clattering guillotine taking revenge against centuries of wealth and privilege. And then Napoleon Bonaparte seized a broken country and imposed his rule—

"We're not the French, Colonel," Jimmy said. His voice was strong. It was the point he'd made again and again. The French peasant came out of feudalism, but the common man in America has governed himself for two hundred years. He won't lose his mind.

For a moment she felt reassured; but then, looking into the old eyes, she saw he hadn't even heard. "Do you have any idea how frightened people are?" he cried. "They look for mobs, riots, pillaging, burning. They're building walls, setting out buckets of sand, rigging two-man pumps at their wells. Laying out pistols and shotguns—"

The son interrupted. It was snakelike, his lips scarcely moving, and this stirred an atavistic fear in her.

"It won't come to mobs, because *we won't let it*! The army will be ready, cannon loaded with grape and bayonets fixed. We'll cut rabble mobs down like scything wheat!"

He whirled on Jimmy. "Take this as warning. You damned Jacobins aren't going to steal this country from us!"

"We're not Jacobins!" Dolley cried. The radical French clubs that led to revolutionary violence were nothing like American Democrats.

But the whisper went on, harsh as stones rubbing together. "The army stands for order, decency, stability. We destroyed the whiskey rebels, and I promise you we'll handle your democratic rabble just the same."

Oh, the whiskey rebels! Pennsylvania farmers protesting an unfair tax on what they made from their grain. There'd been a rough few weeks, but they'd dispersed in the end. But Federalists had mounted an army and saw the outcome as a great victory.

The soldier's hand came up slowly and he pointed a finger at her that was like a pistol. "So let me tell you, madam—and you, Mr. Jacobin Democrat *traitor*—you go one little notch beyond the straight and narrow and we'll *crush* you!"

She stared into his saurian eyes; her hands were cold and there was an icy flutter in her breast.

And Jimmy said, "Major, no one is talking mobs except you. Should mobs form, citizens can be deputized to control them. You are a subordinate officer of the U.S. Army, and what you are talking about is using the military to subvert the democratic process. Such action would be high treason, and such talk, sir, is a disgrace to your uniform!"

That told him—and yet, stating it so baldly increased her own sense of ground opening at her feet into a pit of danger. Now she saw what the stakes before them really were. They turned back toward Swan's and walked in silence. She clutched her shawl to her throat.

"Jimmy," she said after several blocks, "was he serious about the army? That it would come out; he's an officer after all. Could it block the election results?"

He hesitated. "Not—not on it's own, I'd think. But of course, any army is there to support what is, not what could be. It's conservative, resistant to change—"

"But would it come out?" she cried.

"On orders, yes. Soldiers do what they're told."

"Could Alex order it? Override Mr. Adams?"

"I—I don't think so. It would be quite illegal."

"But if someone tried, it would take a commander of real stature to resist, wouldn't it? A General Washington. And we're cursed with General Wilkinson, a rotten traitor."

"We don't know he's a traitor, not for sure."

"Oh, Jimmy, sometimes you carry fairness too far. Everyone says he's in the pay of the Spanish."

"But it's only suspicion."

"Well, when everyone suspects the leader of the army works for the enemy, it's a disgrace! Anyway, look at him! Gross, slimy, unctuous, obsequious—"

She had riveting memories of Wilkinson, uniform buttons about to pop over his belly, saber out like a rooster tail, toadying to her because her husband was important—

"How did such a creature land such a command anyway?"

"There's a type of man who's adept only at advancing himself, but at that he's very adept—canny as a fox and no more scrupulous, qualities more forgivable in fox than in man."

Her hand tightened on her arm. "Darling, let's keep this on a steady course. Can you imagine having your fate in the hands of General Wilkinson or that nasty major?"

She clutched the shawl closer. More than danger alone, she had a chilled feeling that something evil lay out there in

the dark like a sea monster swimming just beyond sight.
They dined in their room, emptied a bottle of wine, and still
she was cold. She sat on his lap, her head on his shoulder,
and whispered, "Take me to bed, Jimmy. Love me. Hold me.
I need to be held. . . ."

Still, things were brighter in the morning sun. She decided
she was weary of being worried and frightened; after all,
they'd won the election.

And then Rob Mustard banged on their door at the inn,
lively as ever. Said he'd left New York and was bound for
Charleston and heard they were here. She'd known him
since Philadelphia, where he had run a loud, vibrant newspaper that always made sense. Then he'd shifted to New York,
still publishing the truth as he saw it, which was as the
Madisons saw it.

He was tall and skinny, fifty or so, with a mop of wild,
gray hair, a big laugh, and a ready eye for the humor of human foibles. Nothing made his editorial wit and ardor glow
more fiercely than the missteps of government. But as he
nursed a glass of Madeira, she saw a difference in his eyes,
something haunted.

"So," he said, "they smashed my press and I'm wanted in
New York." His smile couldn't mask hurt.

"Wanted?" she said.

"Under indictment. Fleeing arrest. Sedition, you see,
which is defined as saying what people in power don't want
to hear." He laughed without mirth. "So I'm on the run.
Learned from poor Jim Callender—he waited till they came
and pied his type and wrecked his press and off to solitary he
went and lucky they didn't hang him." A wry grin. "You remember, I never minded calling a spade a spade when describing Federalist sins, but I'm not crazy brave. I slipped
away under cover of night. Peter Freneau promised me a
berth on his paper in Charleston, and I'm on my way."

"The only good thing about those evil acts was they gave
us the election," she said.

"Hurrah for the common sense of the common man!" Mr. Mustard cried. "Press side was the worst—imagine, smashing a paper, jailing a man for what he says—but the attack on aliens is about as bad. Friend of mine, John Finney, been here fourteen years, he remembers cheering on the sidewalk the day the Constitution was finished; he had something to say about a Federalist alderman in New York and a week later he was deported—home to Ireland where some folks are waiting to kill him, so he says. Poor devil. Still, attack on the press is the worst." He gave Jimmy an owlish look. "Pretty well blows your Bill of Rights to the devil, doesn't it?"

Jimmy nodded. "Only thing I ever really held against General Washington was his countenancing those acts."

Well, she thought, that's unfair. The general had been back in Mount Vernon by then, and Mr. Adams at the helm.

" 'Course, the acts have expired," Mr. Mustard said. "Seems the prosecutor in New York yearns to try me on the law that was. All unconstitutional, isn't it?"

She knew the question pained Jimmy—what was the point of a Constitution if the Supreme Court wasn't strong enough to enforce it?—and to deflect it she said easily, "One good thing, though—those acts told Americans where the Federalists wanted to take them more clearly than reams of Democratic rhetoric." She glanced at Mr. Mustard and smiled. "All but your rhetoric, of course; it was always potent."

She left unspoken her real fear—let a tie throw their victory into the Federalist Congress and they'd be right back in the land of excesses. As if he'd had the same thought, Jimmy asked about their New York visitor.

"Well, Gelston is a Burr toady, all right," Mr. Mustard said, "but he's making some sense too—New Yorkers are pretty sensitive about Virginia. You have to understand, when Aaron swung the state to the Democrats, his boys figured giving him a place on the ticket was the least Virginia could do; and they're not sure how willingly it was done. So they're watching."

"You've heard such talk?"

"Oh, it's real. Would they split over it? Maybe not, but a lot of hotheads are involved."

They went down for dinner, and Mr. Mustard drank three bowls of Mrs. Swan's peanut soup, downed a tumbler of whiskey, devoured a huge slab of roast pork, and called for more. His spirits bloomed and his voice grew stronger, his wit fiercer.

She was laughing when suddenly she noticed that he was acquiring an audience in the larger parlor for men adjoining the ladies' parlor. Talk there had stopped and she grew distinctly uncomfortable. Voice rising, Mr. Mustard abused Alexander Hamilton, who, he said, had ordered the arrest that he had barely evaded. She remembered Alex fondly despite everything. Oh, she said, he's not so bad.

"My dear lady," Mr. Mustard cried, "the Hamilton you remember has changed. Fine noble views he and his kind once held, but their vision became pinched and dark and full of fear, and the day came when they aimed no longer at the freeing of mankind to be its best—no, they turned toward control—*control!*—of the common man, binding him to the interests of his betters, teaching him to pull his forelock and knuckle down and take what pittance those in power might give him and be thankful, hats off, on his knees, thankee milord, thankee . . ."

From the adjoining room someone shouted, "You damned blathering fool! Hamilton *saved* this country when it was bankrupt, got no help from the bloody Democrats either!"

The editor leaped up, glass in hand. "A toast!" he roared, "to the big-mouthed gentleman of financial genius from whom we've been privileged to hear! It's all in the name of financial efficiency that thinkers like our good friend Mr. Genius feel that folks with money make natural leaders. Now, 'fess up, Brother Genius, don't you feel that men with money are a bit better'n anyone else—that God had rewarded them properly with coin of the realm? Eh? Eh?"

He emptied the glass and slammed it down. " 'Course you do! And that's your precious Mr. Hamilton's view. And what does that mean? Why it means perpetuating an establishment class, and what does that mean but a hereditary aristocracy, lords and ladies handing down their titles to their rotten offspring, and what's the natural outcropping of such aristocracy but monarchy?" There was an angry shout from the other room.

"Jimmy," she said.

"That's enough, Rob," Jimmy said. "Not another word."

The old Mustard smile reappeared. "I do like to bait 'em a bit. Didn't mean to embarrass you, Miss Dolley."

"Never mind that," Jimmy said. "Now listen. You're going to Charleston; you'll connect with Peter Freneau?"

"Promised me a berth on his paper—going daily, he is."

"All right. Suppose I pay you a hundred dollars in gold and send you straight through on the express stage, and you carry a message to Mr. Freneau."

"Sounds good to me."

"South Carolina electors will be gathering to vote. You tell him to make sure they hold back one vote for Burr. Eight Jefferson, seven Burr. Understand?"

Dolley sagged in her chair. After all her fears, Jimmy had chosen the danger of the North-South split over the immediate danger of a tie and hoped to patch it in Carolina.

"Can Mr. Freneau assure that?" she asked. She heard the anger in her voice.

"Doubtless," Mr. Mustard said. "They listen to him."

"Of course," Jimmy said. "Danger is, if they're not paying attention they'll vote two for two all the way."

"As I gather we will do here."

He gave her a very sharp look. "I don't know what we'll do here, Dolley. Whatever we do, won't hurt to drop one in South Carolina."

"But you've decided. I can tell."

"I have *not* decided—and I'll thank you not to try to read my mind!"

She glared, outraged.

Rob Mustard cleared his throat. "You want me to do that, I'd better get after it." He didn't look at her.

They went upstairs, Jimmy gave him the gold pieces and in five minutes he was gone. She sat on the sofa and opened her novel, her lips drawn tight as string.

Watching those lips, Madison was irked. She'd made up her mind on the course she favored and that was all very well, but he was the one who must decide. Anyone who'd sat through the writing of the Constitution knew of the raging passions dividing North and South even then—the endless fight over slavery, southern delegates threatening to walk out, more extreme northern delegates shouting at them to go and be damned. Even General Washington's great weight couldn't swing them. Abolishing slavery had been his proposal—count on a great man to turn to a great question—and it almost broke the convention. When Madison realized there would be neither Constitution nor country if this kept on, he eased them away from the brutal subject.

It had been deadly real then, to use Gelston's phrase, and it still was. He felt a stillness come over him; decision was fixing, not yet set but coming. Dolley sighed. She hadn't turned a page, and he realized she wasn't reading.

He put a glass of Madeira in her hand and sat beside her. "I've seen what the North-South split means up close. It can tear us to pieces." She nodded, but no smile.

He kissed her cheek. "Suppose you were deciding. What would you choose?"

"Why, the immediate, of cour——" She stopped in mid-word, eyes wide. Then, "I—don't know. . . ."

"Then we're in it together," he said. "Now give me a smile." And she did, that brilliant smile that exploded like a ray of light across her face, and then she set down the glass and turned on the couch and kissed him on the lips.

He decided as she had feared—Aaron would get Virginia's full twenty-one electoral votes. Jimmy said he relied in part on Gelston's promise of votes to be shorted in the North, in part on South Carolina, in part on the dangers of the split.

Her hands were shaking in her uneasiness, but in the end she did have faith in his decisions, which flowed from deep wells of instinct, intellect, and experience. Inner strength was the key to her husband. He was a superb horseman, though not physically strong; the feistiest mount calmed quickly after a moment of dancing and blowing. From her plantation girlhood Dolley knew that horses respond less to size or strength than to the iron they sense in the rider. Jimmy often doubted himself, but he was full of iron.

On the appointed day in the gleaming Capitol building that Tom in his architectural mode actually had designed— she supposed he was a genius when you got right down to it—the electors gathered to cast their votes. Afterward, Jimmy told her they were hard to convince, insisting that it demeaned the Virginia hero to pair him vote for vote with the slippery New Yorker. It had taken two hours to bring them around, but he'd gotten his way, as he usually did. But as he described it, an image flashed in her mind of Colonel Emberly's son, cold, saurian, ready to strike.

Jimmy was very quiet over the next few days as they awaited news. Every time the national count changed, the Richmond *Enquirer* published another penny extra. State by state the word came in, electors voting in lock step, two by two, Jefferson and Burr, the count standing equal. The last of the northern states reported, still two by two. Gelston's promise of votes to be held back did not materialize. Tennessee and Kentucky reported, and then only South Carolina remained. The count held equal.

At midafternoon they heard a newsboy shouting his extra. Jimmy ran down in his shirtsleeves. From the window she saw him toss the boy a copper, snatch the paper, and scan it. He whirled, threw up his arms in exultation, and came at a run.

Oh, thank God! South Carolina—eight for Jefferson, seven for Burr, one for someone else. Peter Freneau in

Charleston had scrawled a hasty letter to the *Enquirer.* Vote count seventy-three Jefferson, seventy-two Burr, sixty-five Adams.

He seized her and waltzed her around the room like a boy at a barn dance. She had champagne ready and he opened it, the cork putting a dent in the ceiling. Oh, she wished she had a cannon to shoot! They began planning a public party, invite everyone—

Extra! Extra! Extra!

They looked at each other. Jimmy went to the window. The same boy was there, hawking fresh copies of the *Enquirer.*

Jimmy put on his coat and went slowly downstairs. He bought the paper and returned without looking at it. In the room he unfolded it as if it might be a petard ready to explode.

Peter Freneau had written a second letter. He said his first letter was based on polling electors in advance; he had reported their promise. But the plan to stagger was forgotten when they voted; eight votes were cast for Tom, eight for Aaron. It was like a lead weight pressing on her heart.

Seventy-three Jefferson; seventy-three Burr.

Tie.

"Your goose is cooked, Mr. Madison," the fat man said, "and we're ready to eat it." He encountered them on the stairs and held up his hand like a traffic warden. "But we been figuring on a tie. Means the Congress will choose—and *we* have the Congress. You'll see. We'll appoint someone, master of chancery or something, keep the government in honest hands. You'll see."

Jimmy smiled as if he didn't have a care in the world. "No, that's just dreaming; you'd never get away with stealing the election. But it won't even come to that. Colonel Burr is an honorable man. He'll step back, take himself out of contention. They'll have no choice but Mr. Jefferson."

Of course. Aaron would step aside.

They picked at a light supper without appetite and went upstairs, scarcely speaking because there was nothing to say. Oh, Aaron, so much resting on you. What will you do?

Slowly her memory of that vivid day when Aaron presented Jimmy took on a different color. She'd been a vulnerable young widow and Aaron was friend, counselor, guardian of her child. One of the most prominent men in America had asked to be presented to her in a way that could only mean intentions both serious and honorable. But before Aaron even mentioned Jimmy, he undertook to seduce her. It had been amusing, even titillating, and after Jimmy's visit, largely forgotten. But now she saw that if she had yielded to seduction she would never have heard of Mr. Madison's request. She would have become another of Aaron's women, to be cast aside in due time. That was not the action of a friend. Aaron Burr looked out for himself.

Now, by accident, he stood head-to-head for the presidency of the United States. Would he step back? She had no idea.

"Come to bed, Jimmy," she whispered. "Today was exhausting and tomorrow probably will be worse."

4

NEW YORK CITY, MID-DECEMBER 1800

Aaron Burr was in his law office at No. 3 Wall Street when the news came. It was a small office near the docks, flanked by a bank and an insurance company, room for his two clerks in front with a large room for himself. A master of elegance in his several homes, a dandy in dress, a patron of the arts, a man-about-town whose perfection of manner no one could deny, he chose to make his law office puritanical in its plainness and attention to serious matters with solid oak chairs, a long table, a desk that in its size scarcely suggested the stature with which he stood before the New York Bar.

He had Hardwick's deposition in the Ernestine killing, the report from the captain of the *Mary W.* on the night of the collision, the bank's sworn statement that the failure of certain items to appear on the accounting was a mere slip of the quill . . . Bah! Who could think of such mundane things when the very future—the future that mattered, his own—hung on the news from South Carolina? How would the electoral vote go?

He heard Matt Davis's deep voice, always with that raw edge, greeting the clerks outside. Matt wasn't a gentleman, no other way to say it, but in real as opposed to ideal politics you needed a man who could knock heads together when necessary, and Matt could. And did. Burr put on his wire spectacles and took up the bank statement.

"Gentlemen," he said when the door opened. He removed the spectacles and blinked, a man emerging from deep concentration. Behind Davis came Peter Van Ness, tall and slender, a pale-eyed Dutchman, self-effacing but a wizard with the written word. Davis was a big man, wide, chest deep, the forty pounds hung on his belly putting weight behind his punch. His hair was black and spikey, his eyes meant for a smaller man, which made them hard to read, and he seemed to fill any room he entered.

"Report from Peter Freneau," Van Ness said in his precise way. He sat at the long table, carefully arranging his breeches. "The electors, he says they'll vote eight-seven."

"Ah." Not a flicker on his face, Burr was sure, but it were as if a sword had pierced his belly.

"By God, we tried!" Davis expelled his breath with a grunt and slumped against the table. Burr caught a whiff of rum. "Anyway, Virginia held the line. Twenty-one, twenty-one. I'll take some credit for that. I had Gelston primed for bear when he left here. I can just see little Madison squirming."

Burr actually was no taller than Madison, though heavier, but he rarely thought of this because he felt himself a giant.

"Madison made it work though," Van Ness said.

"After we put the wood to him. I met him once, you know—insipid as water. His wife, though—she's a pretty piece if I ever saw one." Davis grinned. "Makes you wonder how a man like that keeps her satisfied, know what I mean?"

"All right, Matt," Burr said. He didn't like such talk. "She's a charming woman. I introduced them, matter of fact."

Davis guffawed. "Eat my hat if you didn't first have a run at her yourself."

"That'll do, sir!" After an uncomfortable silence, Burr said, "You assured Mr. Madison we'd lose a vote elsewhere?"

Van Ness grinned. "Gelston didn't know where, but we had our people in Rhode Island all prepared."

Burr nodded. Rhode Island Democrats had a snowball's chance on a hot griddle, but they'd met the letter of the law, which is the nature of maneuver.

"It mattered too," Van Ness said. "If Virginia had held back like last time, John Adams would be vice president."

And Davis said, "Those bastards in South Carolina give eight to eight like they should; we'd have put it over, by God!"

Aye, there was the pain that Burr felt gripping his heart. He smiled. "We weren't really seeking a tie," he said. Which was a lie, which he knew and they knew, but a lie that needed to be said. It had been so close too, and now it seemed one rotten vote in Carolina was to unhorse the dream. He sighed. He'd let himself obsess a little, he supposed, about what a tie would mean, how those damned Virginians would scurry around clucking.

It would have been comforting revenge for the grossness of the insult last time. He would never forget the sting when the Virginians spat in his face. His way now had been the more clear because Alexander Hamilton, not as slick as Burr

but very slick nonetheless, had worked a similar effort to try
to unhorse Adams back in ninety-six. That's where Burr had
gotten the idea.

It wasn't anything against the Madisons either. They were
friends. No, it was Jefferson, how he repelled with his
holier-than-thou manner, his oh, so elegant elegance, letting
you know by his very bearing that he felt himself a prince
among lesser men. He was able, no doubt about that, but erratic, possessed of odd ideas, charming but vague, and always that maddening superiority. Wanted office but you
could tell he looked down on politics and its practitioners.
Vulgar, you know. Surely no man was less vulgar than
Aaron Burr, the Chesterfieldian gentleman, but Burr understood that politics is practical, one vote at a time. . . .

"Well," Van Ness said, "I wouldn't have minded a tie.
They're reaping when we sowed. *We* won this election."

"Damn right," Davis said. "Those lace handkerchief boys
from Virginia don't know a shitting thing. Let 'em go down
to Peck's Slip with me and try to get aholt of those dock wal-
lopers."

Burr frowned. Matt knew he didn't like vulgarity, but the
point was well taken—go down to Peck's Slip hard against
the East River, where the newest and hence poorest immi-
grants lived stacked atop each other like cordwood, try to
make 'em see the wisdom of voting their interests, try to get
them to quit going home with a gutful and beating the wife
and kiddies, never forgetting that the wife and kiddies didn't
vote. . . .

"I bought a plenty of beer around Peck's Slip," Davis said.

Van Ness grinned. "Drank one for one yourself, I'd
guess."

Davis forced a belch. "Gotta keep up my strength."

What did Jimmy Madison know about the reality of
things? You wouldn't catch him buying buckets of beer. Burr
had taken Tammany Hall when it was a little social club and
made it a power! Law said you had to be a property holder to
vote? Fine. He'd bought houses in the names of a hundred
owners each, every man a voter. All legal, mind you. Alex

Hamilton and his Federalist pecksniffs would catch him up if it wasn't; made every owner of record put up a dollar, gave him a participating deed, paid him a bonafide share of rent, and sent him out to vote.

And even then, so loaded against the common man had the Federalists arranged things in New York, it took real guile to carry the election, a quality with which Burr fortunately was well equipped, if he did say so himself. Did the lace handkerchiefs below the Potomac imagine it was their excellence that swung matters? Burr could sing the Democratic song with the best of them, but down at Tammany and all along the wharves they didn't talk a lot of Constitutional folderol. They wanted to know who was buying. But, by *God*! the boys had turned these louts out on election day, and even then, they'd carried the city by only a few hundred votes.

Put Alex Hamilton's nose way out of joint too. Burr had waited, letting Alex pick his slate first. Naturally Alex chose nonentities; no one wants someone in office with ideas of his own. But this time Burr dragooned leading Democrats, names everyone knew, prated democracy till he sounded like Madison and Jefferson combined, promised he would do all the work, write all their speeches, and their weight had put the ticket over. He and the boys had bumped into Alex at a polling station on the Battery, and Matt had bellowed, "Stepped in shit, huh, Mr. H.?" Smoke was coming from Alex's ears.

Strange about Mr. Hamilton. Maybe it was that he took everything so seriously. He seemed to burn with his political passions. That made it a joy to whip him, but in the end when the votes were counted and a new day was born—or wasn't—it was time to sit down to a bird and a bottle and move along. That was life and politics as well. But Alex seemed to *hate* him. Strange. They'd practiced law in the same city, been cocounsel on a couple of big criminal defense cases, and Burr had supposed them friends. Opponents, of course, that's the nature of law and politics; but Alex was becoming a humorless zealot.

But clearly it was that day in the New York City spring when they beat Alex to the ground that won the national election. New England was for Adams, South and West for Jefferson, Pennsylvania and Maryland divided, New York in the balance, the legislature split. New York City Democrats swung the state; the state swung the nation. Damned right we won it!

They hadn't been wrong to seek a tie either, not after the way Virginia had handled him last time. Anyway, was he less the Democrat, less sincere, less able than the sainted Tom?

Well, what the hell . . . so it hadn't worked out, but he might as well milk a little good will from it.

"Peter," he said, "draft me a letter. Make it to . . . Sam Smith, I guess." Sam was a Maryland congressman, a pompous fellow sure to enhance his own importance by publishing the letter.

"And it should say?"

"Well, take note there's been talk of a tie, say something like, oh, that it would dishonor my views and insult my feelings if my friends supposed—make it suspected—I would permit myself to be instrumental in counteracting the wishes and expectations of the nation. Some such."

He shrugged. What would he have done with a tie anyway? It would have thrilled Theodosia, that was all. His darling daughter, as beautiful as her gorgeous mother whose death remained a wound that couldn't heal, had dreamed of a tie as no less than their due. That Father could do no wrong in her eyes warmed his heart and suffused him with love. She probably would marry soon, to a fine young man who already regarded him as a father—she had made that a condition—and a tie would have been like a, well, like a wedding present!

Theodosia Burr knew herself to be an accomplished, sophisticated young woman of eighteen, and she knew that much of the polish that made her stand out and that seemed so to attract Mr. Joseph Alston of South Carolina, whom she might or might not decide to marry in the next few weeks, was the result of her father's rapt attention to her education. Mr. Alston expected in due time to put aside his rice fields along the Waccamaw River and assume the governorship of South Carolina; and thus, if she were, in fact, to decide that she could stand the ennui of life along the Waccamaw, she would be the governor's lady. She was comfortably aware that Papa had prepared her for no less.

Yet Burr's real gift, which she reciprocated in full measure, was the bath of warm, unqualified love in which she'd been immersed since before she could remember. It had cushioned the loss of Mama, for whom she'd been named and whose years of illness and lingering death had been a cloud over her childhood. Papa understood how her world had tumbled in on her in Mama's last days because the same thing had happened to him when he was a little boy. But like a colossus of old he had stood over her and through sheer strength had thrust her world back into place. She knew objectively from seeing them together in mirrors that she was substantially taller than her father, but she never really thought of this because he so clearly towered.

Now she sat in the projecting bay window of their town house on Fulton Street watching for his sturdy form, knowing he would be along soon. A carriage passing before her house collided, or nearly did, with one entering from Church Street. One of the horses fell, the drivers screamed at each other, and one struck the other; but she ignored this, her gaze fixed on the sidewalk beyond. Ah! There he was, silver-headed stick in hand, his black suit neat as always, hose gleaming white, sun catching the buckles on his shoes.

But then he stepped around a drayman unloading barrels on the sidewalk and she saw instantly from the cast of his shoulders that he had taken a heavy blow. He never revealed anguish, but she knew him so well and loved him so fiercely that the slightest nuance alerted her, and she flew to him as he entered, placing hat and stick on the balustrade.

"Ah, my darling girl," he cried, as she embraced him, but when she stepped back she saw the sadness in his smile.

"What is it?"

"News from South Carolina." She gazed at him and he added, "Mr. Jefferson will be president."

"But what about—"

"It seems the electoral vote will be eight-seven."

"They *shorted* you?" She felt dizzy with anger. "They *owed* it to you. *You* won the election, *you* put them in, how dare they—oh, *damn* them!"

For a terrible moment she thought he might weep, but then his face cleared. "It's nothing," he said. "It would have been like—oh, I don't know, an honor, I guess." He shrugged. "After all, presumably I'm no less a leader than the Virginia gentlemen purport to be."

"Why, you're more!"

"So—and I'd never admit this to anyone but you—but yes, I suppose I'm a little disappointed."

"Oh, Papa!"

Someone turned the bell in the door, and when he opened it she saw over his shoulder the dense black beard decorating Mr. Alston's face. It wasn't really the best time for Mr. Alston to appear, but then she noticed his vivid smile, the unusual brightness in his eyes, and he was bowing over her hand, to which she dropped a perfunctory curtsey; and he turned to Papa and cried in that slurred accent that still sounded strange, "Have you heard the news, sir?"

"We've heard, Joseph," she said, not bothering to disguise a certain tartness. For Joseph to discuss this disaster in terms of good news seemed more than she could bear.

She watched the gentleman's smile fade. "Excuse me," he said. "I thought Mr. Freneau's second report was good news."

"Second report?"

"Of the actual electoral vote in South Carolina; it came in only an hour ago. Eight-eight. Seventy-three for Mr. Jefferson; seventy-three for Mr. Burr. It's a tie, sir."

"Oh!" She felt she might faint.

"Thank you, Joseph," Papa said. "That's most interesting." He looked as unruffled as if he'd been given the time of day, but she saw the lift in his shoulders, the sudden brilliant flash of eye, something wild and joyous tumbling in its depths. . . .

But perhaps Mr. Alston had caught it too, for there was a knowing quality in his smile as he said, "It faces you with a bit of a decision, doesn't it, sir?"

Of course he couldn't display the wild elation he felt, not even to Theodosia, let alone to her young man, so shortly he was on the street, walking swiftly up Fulton toward Broadway, stick swinging, heels tapping on brick walks. . . .

By, *God!* He'd done it—nailed it down, matched that pompous gentleman from Virginia! Let no one—no one!—look down on Aaron Burr. He spun left at Broadway, the day chill but sunny, stepping along at almost a trot, feeling as he did when the jury walked in and gave him the smile that told him he'd won.

He saw the Aubreys ahead, John and Matilda, ready to congratulate him, John reserved as always, Matilda gushing. He bowed over her hand, squeezed it more than necessary, felt her answering pressure, looked into her eyes, and saw what he wanted to see, shook John's hand and walked on. The next time he heard John had gone to Albany he'd send Matilda a note. . . .

At Park Row he turned into the green on impulse and marched along gravel walks, new little maples banked against the cold, the hurdy-gurdy and the puppet show shut down. . . .

"Aaron! Aaron, darling!" It was Gertrude Heinz, much too heavy and much too loud, who burned with unrequited hope that he had every intention of keeping unrequited, walking with her grim old maid sister, both draped in fur.

"Ladies," he said, bowing, not quite stopping until Gertrude caught his arm.

"It's so thrilling! I can't believe I know someone of such position. Vice president! And the tie! Oh what an honor! Of course you'll step aside for Mr. Jefferson, but just to think—"

Burr bowed. "Good day, ladies." He marched on, aware of their startled expressions as they gazed after him.

How dare they! At the moment of his triumph when he'd had but an instant to savor the wild elation of it all, this cretinous puddle of lard should—oh, certainly, he can't wait, just can't wait, to step aside for the sainted Mr. Jefferson. . . .

His mood now darkening, he frowned when he saw Simmons McAlester ahead. Simmons was walking with that rolling gait he seemed to feel appropriate for a man who owned ships, though he never actually went to sea. An ass, really, but useful. Burr owed him almost three thousand dollars.

"Sim, my friend," he said, shaking the other's hand. "How are you? Heard the news, have you?"

"Absolutely delightful—a great honor for New York too. Goes to your image of yourself, I'm sure, patron of the arts like you. A regular Medici, supporting painters when no one wants their stuff." Burr ignored a tinge of mockery in his smile. "Warms my heart to have been of some little assistance; makes me a patron of the arts once removed!"

"And you know how grateful I am too," Burr said. That was the trouble with debt, a problem he understood very well, you had to express gratitude so often to so many.

"Now, Aaron, you'll have expenses and I know you've been neglecting your practice on behalf of this election; I'd be more than happy to help."

"Sim, you're a wonderful friend. Yes, now that you mention it, I've been a bit concerned—"

"Say no more. Five hundred? Seven-fifty? Send your note around tomorrow; I'll send your man back with gold."

"You're a prince, Sim."

"A suggestion, Aaron. Don't be too quick to withdraw in favor of Jefferson. There might be advantage in waiting. Eventually, of course, you must, but—"

"Oh, I don't know," Burr heard himself say. The thought startled him.

Startled McAlester too. The merchant's mouth twisted. "That's foolish talk."

At once all the dark mood, the day's turmoil, the terrible pressure he'd felt came boiling up and he cried, "Take care, sir. I don't appreciate being called foolish."

McAlester leaned toward him and Burr was suddenly conscious of the man's size. "Don't get high and mighty with me, Brother Burr. I can put you in bankruptcy anytime I choose."

"That's right," Burr said, back in control. "But you won't. It would cost you much too much."

McAlester smiled. "We understand each other. Send your note around in the morning."

As Burr walked away, his mind pushing aside the real question, he felt the sting of that Medici remark. Yes, he supported certain artists and writers, men whose talent was still unrecognized. He maintained the house on Fulton Street and the country place at Richmond Hill, a hundred wonderful acres and a manor house on a bit to the north, just below the village of Greenwich. When the great Talleyrand toured America, being temporarily persona non grata in Paris, he'd spent his whole New York visit at Richmond Hill, lauding Burr's table and cellar. Nothing wrong with a taste for fine wines, excellent tailoring, the latest books from London and Paris, and entertaining well. It cost him, but what did that matter? There was no shortage of McAlesters ready to help; and when one tired, three others stepped forward, thrilled to be useful to a great man. He chuckled: What McAlester didn't know was that there were twenty men or thirty or more who could put him in bankruptcy. But none would dare; Burr's influence made him much too important.

Interesting how surprise had snapped an unexpected answer out of his mouth. He felt the blood in his face again. Damn them, why must everyone assault his moment of triumph with the earthy reminders that it wasn't such a great triumph at that, required as he was to step back, throw away the prize, bow to the Virginian? No doubt that was what he would do in the end, but he wasn't at that bridge. Why must he cross it now?

And what did it really mean? He had, after all, received the same number of electoral votes as had Thomas Jefferson. Was it so clear—would it be so clear when Congress voted—that Jefferson would be the better president? Did it mean that it was Virginia's destiny and not New York's to produce presidents? As a matter of plain fact, Burr knew he would be a stronger president than the Virginian because he knew politics, he was a mover, an arranger, yes, a conniver, and there was nothing wrong with conniving; he knew when to pull the levers and when to leave them alone.

What did Jefferson know? He'd sat out the election in that hilltop house of his, Monticello, not even an American name, standing above it all, while Burr had sweated in the trenches. Did the sainted one feel he had won it with his noble rhetoric and his high ideals? Well, Burr could tell him differently, by God! The election had been won right here in little old New York, where they knocked heads when necessary and Tammany poured enough beer on election night to float the USS *Constitution*!

And what now? Vice president was all position and no power. The Virginian would be president, and he'd make it a lifetime role. He'd never step down. Sure, Washington had quit after a couple of terms, but that was because he'd hated the job. The Constitution was silent on the question. But Burr could argue equally well—he brushed aside the inconsistency—that Jefferson would botch things so badly that the Democrats would be discredited and the Federalists would come dancing back into office in four years to minuet music!

So yes, doubtless he would withdraw, step down and back, be noble and self-sacrificing. But, by God, don't just be taking it for granted; don't be waving it in his face like a bloody insult even as he savored the joy of standing toe to toe for the presidency of the United States! And he slammed fist into palm.

It was dark now and he wasn't sure how long he'd been walking. Glancing about, he found he was near Fraunce's Tavern, which reminded him. He drew a turnip watch from his waistcoat pocket; he was an hour late, but still, why not?

In the tavern, Pierre, the headwaiter, greeted him with rapture. After election felicitations from a half-dozen men, Pierre walked him to a private dining room.

He opened the door to find Arabella half-reclining on the long sofa. The table was set for two, and he saw she'd finished the first bottle of wine and had started the second. She held out her arms. "Aaron, you naughty boy, you're late. Come give me a kiss, darling, and tell me your triumph!"

A week later he dined at the Bull's Head with his old friend, Jim Wilkinson. "I have a message for you, Aaron," Jim said, "from people who count in the Congress. Federalists, you understand—they can be the key to your future."

He admired Wilkinson; by stealth and guile and a terrier's willingness to snarl and scrap when aroused, he had made himself commanding general of the U.S. Army. He was a natural conniver, which often was the key to getting things done. They had been young officers in the Revolution, both drawn naturally to staff duties where skill in arranging is a quality much prized, and they had remained friends when Wilkinson went out to Kentucky and cut a wide swath as merchant, trader, speculator in that wide-open climate before the lure of duty—if that had been the lure; you never could tell with Jim—had drawn him back into the army.

He had set aside his uniform in favor of street clothes now, but even so he drew the alcove curtain closer and turned his bulk farther to hide the letter he took from an inside pocket and slid cross the table.

"From Harper of Maryland, and I happen to know he speaks for a good many. Hold back, say nothing, give your

friends in Congress a clear field, and the results may please
you."

This had been a difficult week. He'd found himself torn
by hungers, fears, dreams that had been as surprising as they
were disturbing. Yes, he'd wanted the tie—mainly to assure
the second position, but for a certain vindication too, a sign
that he stood equal among giants—but he hadn't actually
considered it much further.

Then the lightning struck. Doubtless he would step back,
and yet that easy assumption had roused a visceral fury that
had stunned him. All week he'd wrestled—one moment
seeing the good of the party, the common expectations, the
need for a stable transition if the new open democracy were
to flourish—and then, like the roll of drums in his heart, why
he? Was he so clearly inferior? Jefferson and his superiority the automatic leader? Did having equal votes count for
nothing?

"Have you told anyone your plans?" Wilkinson whispered.

"No." Burr didn't add that his turmoil had been so great
he hadn't dared speak.

"Good. Good. Aaron, I tell you, you can *soar* out of this.
It can be big. Big!"

"What the hell are you talking about?"

"The Federalists see huge opportunity here. You can
imagine how the idea of Jefferson—and you, of course—
taking office just shatters them. Not one in ten believed it
would happen. Right until the last minute when our side—"

"Our side? Since when were you on anyone's side?"

Wilkinson winked. "The winning side is my side, Aaron,
always has been. Know why I'm a Democrat now? 'Cause
they'll open the West and the Federalists won't."

"You've become a western patriot?"

"Shit! Don't be ridiculous. There are fortunes to be made
in the West, fortunes that easterners can't even imagine. It's
a place of empire. The Mississippi controls the very heart
and soul of the continent, you control that river, and—"

He broke off, grinning sheepishly, his fat, round face creasing into joviality. "My, I wax enthusiastic, don't I?"

"Does sound exciting."

"It is, it is. Unlimited future; everyone agrees."

"Which the Spanish at New Orleans control." He eyed the fat general. Rumor had said for years that Wilkinson was in the pay of Spain, and Burr thought it well could be true. He knew Wilkinson would consider it quite innocent, treason in name only.

Wilkinson smiled and waved off the Spanish with a flick of his puffy hand. "To business, dear Aaron. These Federalists are serious. They're thinking of improving the opportunity the tie has given them, as they put it, rather quaintly, I thought. They think they can tie up the election in the Congress, they'll vote for you, the Democratic states will hold for Jefferson, stalemate will stretch past the inaugural date, and they can appoint a protem president, caretaker figure, what have you—point is, they'll still be in power, and that's what counts."

"They want to use me, in other words."

"Of course. Doesn't everyone? But look, you can use them. Play your cards right and they'll swing to you in reality. Stick with them and you can push Mr. Jefferson aside yet."

Burr found it stunning, as if the devil had opened his head, pulled out thoughts he hadn't even dared voice, and dropped them on the table like dead fish. To cover his confusion, he blurted, "Is that how you got rid of Mad Anthony?"

Anthony Wayne—Mad Anthony, for his wild exploits in the Revolution—was commanding general when Wilkinson had reentered the army. Everyone knew that Wilkinson had waged a violent internal attack on Wayne, turning officers and political weight against him; only Wayne's early death averted a showdown, whereupon Wilkinson slid into Wayne's position slick as a greased pig.

Burr had spoken half in jest, expecting a cynical witticism in response, but Wilkinson's little eyes went hard as stone, his fists curled on the table. "Aaron," he said, his voice a rasp, "mind your tongue. You're an infant in these matters. I don't like such talk, and I'll destroy any man who makes it."

Burr had a sudden understanding, very startling, that his old friend was dangerous. And then the general relaxed.

"Come, come, let's not have such talk. I'm giving you a friend's advice: Listen to what these Federalists say."

"And what's in it for you?"

Wilkinson chuckled. "In having a dear old friend as president? Oh, I'd find some advantage or other."

"There's talk on the street that the administration in its waning days might call out the army to set aside the election. What do you think?"

Wilkinson sat back, his expression lazy. "If it came to that, I suppose I'd have to assess my options." He shrugged. "See what's in it for me. But you, now . . . play the hand that's being dealt you and that won't happen. *Comprende?*"

Burr smiled. Infant in such matters he might be, but not so innocent that he would answer that question.

Burr rode the stage into Philadelphia on the evening of the day Sam Smith had expected him in the morning and met Sam the next morning, a mere twenty-four hours late. Which was all right; Colonel Burr was a presidential figure, after all. Still, when he saw Smith in the hotel lobby the next morning standing with Hichborn, whose first name he never remembered, the older man looked ready to erupt.

Smith was a burly fellow from Baltimore who'd made pots of money in business and shipping before going to Congress. He was important in Baltimore and thought he was important nationally, a faith that Burr felt ranked somewhere between illusion and delusion. He also was an inveterate busybody, which was why Burr had written him in the first place.

"Sam!" he cried, shaking the other's hand and treating him to a big smile, probably the last to be seen this morning. He gave Hichborn a languid hand.

"Good morning, Aaron. I thought yesterday was our day—"

"Tied up in New York," Burr said with an airy wave of his hand. Smith was lucky he was here at all.

"Anyway, you're here, so tell me what the devil—"

"Hold it." Burr raised a palm. The hotel was full of men. "I don't care to have every mountebank in Philadelphia listen." He led the way outside, found a bench warmed by a shaft of sun, sat at its center, and turned toward Sam as the bigger man sat. That left Hichborn the opposite end, facing Burr's back, which was about where he belonged.

"Now, Aaron," Sam said, at his most portentous, "I want to know what the devil is going on."

"I suppose the Congress will choose a president."

"Goddamn it! Don't toy with me, Colonel Burr. You put me right in the middle of things with that letter. I published it and everyone heaved a sigh of relief: Good, Burr will do as he should, and since then not a word from you!"

" 'Do as he should.' Now what does that mean?"

"What the hell do you think it means? That you should make it clear you won't contest, that if these Federalists in Congress should manage to elect you, you would refuse to serve. Nobody voted to elect you; they voted Tom, and you were along for the ride!"

"First, Sam, you made a serious mistake in publishing a private letter."

"Private, my foot! Don't tell me that wasn't intended for more than my eyes!"

"I sent it to you as a casual comment to an old friend. I regret you saw more in it. Now as to my making some more definitive statement, yes, I considered it. But I found a peculiar view that you apparently hold too. Everyone assumes I will back away. Why do they so assume? That I'm incapable? That I would be a worse president? Inferior to the Virginian? Frankly, sir, I find that insulting. Having reviewed the matter carefully, I believe it is my duty to my party and to my country to do nothing to influence the congressional decision."

"Why, you damned fool—"

"Fool?"

"Fool!" Smith said it with such force that Burr was momentarily silenced. "They're trying to use you to steal the damned election. Think they want you? They don't want you. They want to tie it up so they can keep it for themselves, name a president protem, steal it!"

"They know they can't get away with that."

Smith gave him a speculative look. "But you think they might swing to you as more palatable somehow. Fat chance with Hamilton denouncing you right and left. How hungry you must be, willing to betray your friends."

Trust Smith to seize such an interpretation! In fact, Burr had worked it out fully in his mind, and the news that Hamilton was attacking him only solidified his conviction. Hamilton was making himself an enemy. So be it. Burr could well live without Mr. Hamilton, and he could deal with him whenever he chose. But in this situation there certainly was no betrayal, and he said so emphatically. He stood as the very personification of honor, remaining aloof, above all interests, influencing nothing. He would answer no messages, from the Democrats or from the Federalists. That was the utterly honorable course, one he had thought out with great care.

"So what do you think will happen?" Smith asked.

"Congress must choose a president."

"And if they choose you?"

"So be it."

"But, Colonel Burr," Hichborn squalled from behind him, "Who would be vice president?"

"Why, Mr. Jefferson, of course."

He was walking rapidly down Broadway, heels hammering on brick, stick clutched so hard his hand hurt, heading toward a supper he didn't want with a woman he couldn't stand. Sam Smith had abused him, called him a betrayer, said he was selfish, his very conscience in question, asked if ambition so ruled him. Sam had come dangerously close to the point of a challenge. They had parted without handshake or salutations, and Burr had returned in a white heat that hadn't yet abated.

Ambition did not rule him! He had thought this out carefully, had seen the insult in the blithe assumption that he would immolate himself on the Virginia pyre, the decent and honorable course becoming evident, what he owed himself, after all, and Theodosia, to stand above it all, aloof, silent—honor beyond challenge that sought nothing for itself!

Ambition, they said. He was ambitious as was every man, but it didn't blind him. His breath was ragged. That was God's truth, but still, there was that vaulting fire within that could shake him as a terrier shakes a rat. Even now, hammering down Broadway, he felt the surging force of desire at the very thought, Aaron Burr, third president of the United States! Oh, it was there, all right, and he was a big-enough man to make that admission to himself, but control him? Not at all. He was acting with honor, propriety, decency—

A figure lurched out of an alley, an old man with a long beard; it was dark now, no one about, dim light of an oil lamp a block away. A footpad. Burr raised his stick.

But in a rolling voice that might have come from a sepulcher, the figure cried, "You're doing wrong, boy. Wrong, wrong! I'm the Reverend Whitney. I knew your father well, admired him and loved him—him snatched off in the very prime of his life, him and your maw too—and I say to you on this night, he must be rolling in his grave! Spinning at the sight of what his son has done!"

"Get away from me, Goddamn you!" Burr cried. "Get away from me!" He hurried on at a near run, breathing in gasps, hearing the old devil shuffling behind him. Where in God's name was that tavern where there were lights and he was expected and everyone welcomed him; but he saw he had wandered down into a dark area near the East River, no one about, and he hurried on, hearing the footsteps behind him.

How dare the old man invoke his father? Burr came from

a fine family, the best, the great preacher Jonathan Edwards his grandfather, the first Aaron Burr a minister of note who had started the college at Princeton where he and Madison had been classmates.

And his father had betrayed him. As had his mother. How dare the old devil throw his father up to him after what his father had done. There were sudden tears in his eyes. He didn't hate his father or mother; it was just that it hurt so. And it had been years before he'd even understood what yellow fever was, how the sick miasma festered in low-lying areas and swept out to fell men and women by the score. He'd been six when they went. He'd cried himself to sleep at night for years; but sometimes he'd cried with hate too. They'd gone off and left him, except he didn't really hate, he loved—

"Aaron Burr," the roaring voice from behind cried, "harken to my words. You are destroying yourself. Oh, my son, I see you stepping toward perdition, wallowing in the sin of pride and ambition, betraying your heritage. You are blinded by lust for power and glory and position. Repent now, while you still can. Your father—"

It was more than Burr could stand and he whirled, stick raised, and the bearded figure stepped into an alley and was gone. Burr stared. Had the old man been there at all? Could he have been an apparition? Burr peered into the alley, saw it was empty, turned and hurried on, stick now raised as for a weapon, and the old devil's voice echoing and reechoing against the dark and silent buildings.

5

MONTPELIER, VIRGINIA, JANUARY 1801

He was a hunchback, this little man, his linen was soiled, he needed a shave, a long queue hung down his back with a twist of leather at the end, he spoke with a slight burr of Scotland in his voice, and he had lived with the Indians as a trader off and on over the years. He had no family or settled home, and he could be forty or he could be sixty. He used a half-dozen names and Madison doubted any of them were his own.

All that on the one hand. On the other, that perhaps a dozen men, all merchants of power, all Democrats, used him to carry messages and he had never been known to betray a confidence or err in what he said. He'd carried gold and letters and verbal messages too sensitive to put on paper. If a shipment disappeared he knew where to look; if bribery was afoot he could sniff it out; if threats had been made, he could arrange retaliation. 'Twas said that he'd killed or caused men to be killed, but of course there never would be a record of that, and those who employed him wouldn't want to know. If you wanted him, you left word at one tavern or another and after a while he appeared.

Madison had never seen him nor had use for him, but he understood instantly who he was. The fellow had appeared at Montpelier; the plantation manager was ready to throw him out on appearances alone, but something in the other's expression changed his mind and he sent the visitor on to the big house. Madison saw him in small room off the main salon. A maid named Suzanne, a slender girl with long, taper-

ing fingers whom Sukey was breaking in, served beef and
bread with a pot of butter and a tankard of ale brewed on the
plantation, giving the visitor a supercilious look.

"Nigger don't care for me," he said, grinning.

"Let's say you're an unusual visitor, Mr. Dinwiddie."

"Dinwiddie ain't my name. I had to tell that nosy bastard
manager of yours something. You know who I am?"

"By reputation, I think so."

"Good. That's enough." He cut slabs of beef with what
looked like a fighting knife and stuffed them in his mouth,
licking his fingers and gulping the ale.

"Now, Mr. Madison, I come from Sam Smith." Madison
wasn't surprised. The Maryland congressman had published
the letter Aaron had written, which seemed on its face to remove him from any competition for the presidency. But
Madison had already concluded that Aaron had written on
the first report from South Carolina before he knew there
was a tie. And there had been nothing since.

The man drew a clay pipe burned nearly black, shaved
plug tobacco with that big knife, turned the pipe down over
a candle and filled the room with pungent smoke. Madison
swallowed a need to cough. He said nothing, waiting.

"Now," pointing with the pipe stem, "Mr. Smith wants
you to know two things. First off, Burr ain't going to step
back. He met Smith in Philadelphia and seems like he said
the Democrats could kiss his ass. Said in so many words
he's in it to win. Says Mr. Jefferson would make a right fine
vice president."

The effrontery! Madison knew he'd masked his fury, but
his breath was short.

"The other thing is, the Feds got the bit in their teeth.
They'll back Burr to the hilt. Way it works out, Jefferson'll
have eight, Burr six, two split even and not voting."

Sixteen states in the Union, each with one vote in the
House, that vote to be decided by a majority of each state's
congressmen; Tom needed nine states to win and was one
short.

"You understand, they don't give a fiddler's fuck for Burr.

Mr. Smith has it straight. Says they're looking for stalemate. They'll hold it frozen till March 4 when the current administration ends; then they'll appoint themselves a caretaker president to run the country—run it their way.

"And you know what that means?"

Madison raised his eyebrows.

"Means you can take the Constitution to the outhouse and use it for ass-wipe. That's all it'll be good for."

"I don't really need a constitutional lecture," Madison said.

The other grinned. "I expect that's true. Mr. Smith says you about wrote the blamed thing. But his message is, you'd better get off your ass and take a hand in this game. Didn't put it that way, exactly, but you get the drift. See, the boardinghouse where he lives in Washington City—Conrad and McMunn's, you know the place? No? Well, don't matter. Point is, Mr. Jefferson stays there too, Mr. Smith sees him every day, and he says the man won't lift a finger in his own defense."

Tom was adamant: He would not bargain for the presidency, would not accept it as a deal. Madison was pretty well bound by those strictures too. Still, he wasn't running for president. He was just a citizen. Bound he might be in a public sense, but there was always the private sense too.

"You want me to carry a message back?" The fellow's pipe had burned down, and he knocked the dottle into his plate.

"I don't think Sam Smith expects an answer," he said.

"I think that is an answer," the fellow said, and he was up and gone, leaving Madison still at the table, lost in thought.

The rotten Goddamned scoundrel . . .

James Madison rarely cursed and disliked crude talk, but now anger greater than any he could remember swept him in waves.

Dawnlight glowed across his fields. He'd awakened long before light, saddled a big buckskin gelding himself, and now had the horse pounding along the turnpike, the flexing rhythm beating against the waves of anger.

Burr had aimed to steal the election! Sent that miserable creature Gelston—God! he would slap Aaron's face if he could reach him and if that led to the dueling field, he would doubleshot his pistol!

Sent Gelston to assure him they had cured the tie danger and to focus the North-South clash—all a trick. They knew electors would tend to vote for both president and vice president and that Madison would see the danger and block it. They'd set out to neutralize him, to use against him his instinct to take men as honorable until they proved otherwise. Tricked him . . .

He slowed the gelding, whose heavy breathing was making steam clouds in the chill air, and slowed his own racing heart. The eastern sky was taking on an orange glow. Fury was an indulgence and Madison didn't often indulge himself, but he would not forget the corruption inherent in Burr's act.

For it jeopardized the great democratic revolution, the turning of the nation from narrow elitism to the broad belief that free men have the capacity to govern themselves wisely. He thought it the most dangerous time since 1776. The great Federalist fear was that, as in France, the passions of free men must overcome their senses and lead to chaos. But the people had put their trust in the Democrats, said by their vote they believed free men were responsible. Not overwhelmingly, however, it was a narrow majority that had said, all right, we'll try you once, we'll see; but foul your nest and we'll go back to the safe and the true because maybe, after all, free men do go out of control. We'll have to wait and see, won't we. . . .

And here was Burr spinning it into chaos before they could even start! One hungry man willing to destroy the future in his search for self-glory. . . .

"By God, sir," he cried into the cold morning air, seeing Burr's pasty face before him, "you shall not succeed!"

"De old colonel calling for you, Mr. Jimmy."

Madison hurried to the sickroom. His father was rarely out of bed now, clearly but slowly dying. The bony old hand searched for his, clinging, the feeling of a drowning man.

"I'm going to go, Son."

"Yes, Father."

"I can feel it, waiting to take me. So I wanted to tell you, you must . . . you must . . ." The wavering voice faded away. Then, stronger, "Damn, I forgot."

"About the farm, Father? You've given me my instructions."

The hand tightened on his. "You must see to it, James. It's your sustenance, your life blood, it will see you to the end . . . take good care of it. . . ."

He was asleep. Madison disengaged his hand and went back to his desk to sit there, tapping his pen knife lightly on the blotter. Another messenger had come this morning, this one from Richmond. It was time for action.

Running north from Montpelier on a rattling stage that managed to find every lurch and pothole on the dirt high road, Dolley rehearsed what she would say and to whom she should say it. She had a message to deliver—Jimmy had emphasized that. "You're not negotiating," he'd said, "don't let anyone put you in that position."

This when she had protested that women didn't negotiate. She chuckled, remembering his response. "Do all the time in Europe. Tom says in Paris all the important messages are delivered by mistresses."

"Oh, is that so!" she'd said, laughing. "Well, I'm not your mistress, thank you."

And he'd said, "Mistress, lover, wife, best friend, shining light of my life, answer to my prayers, guarantor of my happiness—sweetheart, you're everything!"

She sighed, lonely already. He was a darling man. He'd whispered, "You do brilliantly what mistresses do best," and she had said, "You dirty dog," and kissed him, and the evening had gone on from there.

When the stage stopped on the south bank of the Potomac across from the shining new city, she was still nervous, but she didn't let that quiet her lively anticipation. She'd been dreaming of Washington and the role Tom had asked her to play for a long time, and now, the town drawing close as the ferry worked across the Potomac, she was there. Tom was a widower; he had asked her to serve as his official hostess at state dinners in the President's House, and already she was planning.

Her old friend Danny Mobry awaited her on the bank, a tall, pretty woman with her face framed in black curls, wearing a brocaded gown the color of oysters. She was standing by a gleaming landau, a big black man holding the horses. As Dolley stepped ashore, Danny enveloped her in a hug.

"What a sight for sore eyes!" she cried. "Dolley, you'll love it here—new houses started every day. Come along, we'll have a grand—" She broke off, forehead wrinkled. "Sweetie, what's the matter? You look downright strained."

"No, no. Just a long trip."

"I suppose, but no, there's more to it than that." She slapped her forehead. "But of course! You hardly came all the way alone just to look at houses. You're up to something; I can see it in your face."

"Danny, really!"

"See, I knew it! Edgy as a cat. And why not? Country's trying to blow itself up, and Jimmy sent you to work some alchemy—"

"Danny! That's enough now. I mean it."

Danny bit her lip. "All right, dear. I'm sorry. Come along; we'll tour the new capital city. And Carl and I will help if we can or stay out of your way. . . ."

She introduced the big coachman as Samuel Clark and said he once had been a slave on her father's plantation. Carl had purchased his freedom and that of his wife, who ran their household. The big man bowed and Dolley nodded, but what struck was the force of character she read in his squarish face, the authority. She was surprised and then a little ashamed because she was surprised. She didn't pay much attention to the black people at Montpelier, except for the house servants.

Montpelier was a benign plantation, as benign as slavery could be; the old colonel and now Jimmy made sure their people were not mistreated, though she supposed the overseer did discipline when necessary and that meant flogging. It all was deeply disturbing. She'd grown up a Quaker on a slave-owning Virginia plantation. Her father had lived out his convictions, freed his slaves, and consequently had to sell the plantation, there being no white labor available in slave country. Someone else bought the land and bought slaves to work it and all went on as before. And the Paynes moved to Philadelphia and failed in business and everything collapsed. . . .

Inside the carriage Danny said, "I'll tell you their story someday, Millie and Samuel. I grew up with Millie. She was my nurse from the day I was born. Just a girl herself then, eleven or twelve. I taught her to read, and don't you think *that* kicked up a rumpus at home!" She sighed. "Now I don't know what'll happen; they're so on edge here. Philadelphia was fine—it's the center of the Quaker abolition movement—" She broke off, laughing. "Forgive me, *I* should be telling *you* about the Quakers?"

"But why? You said they were uneasy here."

Danny gave her an odd, sharp glance. "Washington is a slave city, you know. Auctions down on the Eastern Branch couple of times a month. You see coffles, men in chains and women chained right with them. Not very attractive in a great nation's capital, seems to me, but it doesn't make you very popular to bring it up. But you can see that it would make free Negroes nervous, papers or no papers."

She laughed suddenly and covered Dolley's hand with her

own. "Enough dark talk. You're here at last. I can't wait to show you your new city. Oh! There's a house just going up that you must see; I promise you'll love it. . . ."

It was like coming home to encounter Danny's exuberance again, though she'd hardly realized that her own tensions were so obvious. Still, Danny knew her very well. They'd been close for years. Dolley's first husband had been Carl Mobry's lawyer, and after the yellow fever it was Danny to whom Dolley had turned for comfort. And Aaron had been her friend. . . .

Danny's dark eyes were highly expressive and something in their depths gave Dolley the impression she was deeply interested in what went on in the bedroom, though they had never found reason to discuss such matters. She came from New Orleans, still a French city despite years of Spanish rule, and Dolley had always supposed her a Frenchwoman. But she was Irish. She'd been Daniella Clark, named for her uncle, Daniel Clark, the Irishman who'd made himself the merchant prince of New Orleans. She'd been sixteen when Carl found her, and Dolley imagined she had had an irresistible bloom. He'd sailed his brig up the river looking for sugar, found his way to her father's plantation, and sailed away with sugar and a bride.

They set out, the carriage lurching with creaks and groans, dust eddying up through the floorboards. She braced herself against the door.

"It's nice here even if coaches do turn into kindling wood overnight," Danny said. "It's vivid—full of life, people bustling about. Of course, they're pretty worried."

"About the change?"

"That there'll be trouble over it. Those with government jobs fear they'll lose them, those without hoping they'll get one, everyone wondering if there'll be riots."

"Why should there be riots?"

"Well, they don't know what to expect. Congress is in session, the Federalists are trying to steal the election, the Democrats surely won't stand for it, new rumors every day."

Washington struck Dolley as mostly wilderness. She had

a confused impression of forests through which rough roads had been hacked, stumps left in roadways. They crossed open spaces that Danny said would be squares and circles, saw lanes called New Hampshire Avenue and Massachusetts Avenue. Occasionally there were houses, quite handsome individually but separated by cornfields in which dried stalks still stood after the harvest.

Clusters of houses stood around Capitol Hill, which Danny said had been Jenkin's Hill till the other day. Like an awesome crown, the unfinished building stood amid piles of stone separated on lathes, stacks of brick, six-by-six timbers laid in square towers, cement mixing boats, ladders, tool-sheds, planks laid as walkways over mud. It was such a work in progress as to be amusing, and yet it had a grandeur too, if only grandeur of intentions. What a magnificent conception this someday city was, the ceremonial diagonal avenues piercing the streets, squares, and circles every few blocks; the great open mall stretching in imagination from the hill to the river. It was a tangle of trees and elder bushes now, with cornfields and a creek winding through marshland alive with ducks and geese, but in imagination it all leaped to life. This was a town she could love.

With a sudden tremor deep in her gut she remembered why she was here. This brave experiment, the town created overnight from open farmland, the nation created overnight in the radical idea that free men can govern themselves, was it all to be shattered before it properly began? Danny was chattering away and all at once Dolley realized her old friend was trying to distract and soothe her and she began forcing calm on herself. She took several deep breaths, saw Danny glance at her, and smiled reassuringly. She was all right.

They meandered along Pennsylvania Avenue. The carriage gave a great lurch that threw Dolley against Danny, and she swore to herself that she would make Tom give this miserable street a cover of crushed stone. In time they came to another cluster of houses. Then, as they turned a corner, Danny said with something quite like pride of ownership, "There! What do you think?"

With a jolt, Dolley recognized the President's House from drawings. She'd given a lot of thought to making this building the social center of the capital, and now she saw that with its yellow sandstone walls freshly painted in glistening white, it triumphed over an unfinished setting. Though a half-dozen saplings had been planted, the muddy ground was rutted and littered with wood scraps and debris. Several piles of lumber weathering gray looked abandoned. Yet that scarcely detracted from its beauty.

"Poor Mrs. Adams," Danny said, "says there is scarcely any furniture, the bell pulls haven't gone in, only a room or two has been plastered, the big ceremonial East Room has hardly been touched—she hangs the family wash there."

Dolley didn't answer but she thought such talk unnecessary. Mrs. Adams had only been here since November and was said to be even more bitter than her husband over the election. This was a great national house, and it deserved loving attention. Moving beyond the first impact, she saw it did have a faintly shabby air that she was immediately determined to correct. She would see to everything: decoration, colors, finishing, furniture, all the things that shape a shell into a national home. And someday, though she kept the thought to herself, she too might live here, with plantings everywhere and trees growing sturdy, a formal garden in that square across Pennsylvania Avenue that now was a cornfield. . . .

"Let's stop and walk a bit," she said on impulse. "Get a better look." In truth, she wanted to savor the place. She was thinking of Colonel Madison's prediction for his oldest son. Tom wouldn't be here forever. . . .

6

He boarded the stage at Annapolis and found one other passenger, a heavy man with gray whiskers to his jaw line, his bulbous nose mottled with broken blood veins.

"Well, young feller," this worthy boomed as the vehicle lunged off, "looks like we got the Washington stage all to ourselves. My name's Thomson Tolliver."

"John Adams."

"John Adams! But you ain't the president, I reckon." An explosive laugh. "Not that he'll be president much longer. Poor John, I really admired him. Fine, honest man. Loved the British a little too much, but what the hell. I seen him once, you know, passing by in a stage, and I saluted him. And by God, he saluted me back! I always remembered that."

Mr. Tolliver settled back with a contented sigh. "This election, you know, it wasn't just an election. No, sir! It was an earthquake like they have across the water, buried Sodom and Gomorrah or whatever that town was. We was bound down the wrong road going hell for leather and the people put up their hand and said, Whoa! We ain't going that path no more! You know how you drop an egg in the frying pan and the yellow's looking up at you, and then you flip it over and it looks all different? Same egg, see, same country, but all different. But it's too bad Mr. Adams had to pay the price, for he's a damned fine man."

With which he folded his arms, wedged himself in a corner of the lurching stage, and went immediately to sleep.

John Quincy Adams, son of the president, diplomat returning from six years abroad, equally concerned for his father and for his own rapidly dwindling future, rather dreading the bitter anger he was sure his mother would be focusing on their old but no longer admired friend, Mr. Jefferson, opened his traveling copy of Thucydides. But the Peloponnesian Wars failed to grip him, and with his finger holding his page he rode along gazing out on a dense forest of hardwoods broken here and there by a farmhouse behind a rough rail fence, hogs rooting in bare yards, dogs barking at the stage.

He'd been at his post in Berlin when dispatches gave him the stunning election news. It was shattering in a peculiar way; he'd always seen his father, great patriot and ranking intellectual, as invincible. That he would be cast aside amid electoral detritus was always possible, of course, but John Quincy had never imagined such a thing. A flashing image of how his father would be feeling had struck him, eyes moist, mouth twisted at this new evidence of failed appreciation for a lifetime of public service. The dear old man! They were profoundly close. Over the years their conversations had stretched toward dawn, with the older never condescending to the younger, and much of what the son was today had grown from that intellectual nurturing. And from his powerful mother too, with her incessant demands for excellence.

But it had been six years since he'd been home. . . . Nabby, more boon companion of his youth than sister, had married and his brothers had gone their ways, and my goodness, he himself had changed quite radically. Married to Louisa three years—he'd resisted, but what joy the wedded state had proved to be. He was deeply in love with her. That Louisa was American, daughter of the U.S. consul in London, had relieved the Adams, but tensions still swirled around his temerity in choosing without family—meaning maternal—guidance. His lips tightened at the thought. He was thirty-three, for goodness sake, if he'd awaited Mama's total approval, he'd still be celibate at ninety!

Louisa would come later, in more leisurely comfort; John Quincy had set out at once, by stage and horseback and small boat and a brig that seemed ready to disintegrate in heavy seas, and finally the long run up the Chesapeake, and now this stage creeping along a road more notable for its holes than for its surface. He was nearly there and should be concentrating on the agony of rejection he knew his father was feeling, but Mr. Tolliver slept on and Adams's mind circled back to the contemplation of his own dismal future.

The law . . . back to Boston, back to a hated practice, rooting among assizes and assigns in search of a meager living, far cry from the promise of his golden youth. He remembered boyhood days in Paris and later in London and, indeed, across Europe when he'd accompanied his father's diplomatic travels. He'd been warm friends with Mr. Jefferson in the palmy days before that gentleman betrayed his old friends with weird ideas, he'd associated with international statesmen, his French had been better than his English, he'd tutored important men in both languages, and he had forged for himself a lifetime career as student of classics and languages. Quite enough to turn a young lad's head, though the hammering admonitions his mother sent in every post from Braintree had saved him from that failing, so he felt. He'd entered the magnificent University of Leyden for profound studies, then enrolled in Harvard when his parents insisted he have American training. Harvard was rude and raw, but he'd managed to dig out a few nuggets. Finally—one did, after all, have to earn a living—the dismal law, three years of reading in a good firm and then to Boston, scratching in the courthouse for a miserable living like the guinea fowl in yonder yards. And he'd been single then!

Rescue from this limbo had come when General Washington named him envoy to The Hague. The general had assured him that his own analytical writing, not his father's vice presidency, had earned him the post, and off he'd gone to Holland with a light heart. From The Hague and then from Berlin he'd soon been monitoring all of Europe from a ringside seat as the French Revolution changed the very na-

ture of the continent. Ah, those were the days, ample time
for obsessive study, frequent travel to Paris and London, a
salary on which he could marry and still manage to save,
nightly forays to the theater that he savored above all the
arts—and now this! Boston and hustling for clients, lurking
in courtrooms hoping something would come his way!

The ride ended at Stelle's Hotel in the shadow of the massive
Capitol. Adams reclaimed his old leather satchel from the
boot and paused to examine the building. Far from finished,
its muddy grounds still littered with building materials, it
nevertheless was impressive, though that was a relative term
for a man who'd seen Versailles. He set out along the gravel
walk beside Pennsylvania Avenue, dodging the mud
splashed from passing carriages, sighing when the gravel
walk ran out after a block or two and left him stepping
around mud holes. From the jungle to his left he saw ducks
scattering, wings glinting, and heard a distant shotgun. A
passerby told him that was where L'Enfant envisioned a
great mall that would stretch to the Potomac. You had to admire—and perhaps question the sanity—of a man who
could dream so magnificently from so pedestrian a start, for
there was nothing at all magnificent about the new little
town's physical setting. A misty sun glowed in haze and the
air felt damp and warm. Soon he was perspiring and his
mood was not high when a voice cried his name.

"You there! Haw! Rushed home to commiserate with the
old man, eh?"

Timothy Pickering came bearing down on him, eyes
alight with malice. The tall, skinny Bostonian, sour as a
quince, had been secretary of state and, hence, John
Quincy's nominal superior until the president had cashiered
him. Cashiered the whole cabinet in one ferocious sweep—
oh, that had set tongues to wagging! But in doing so the
president had saved the nation from war with France. Indeed, John Quincy felt it was not self-aggrandizing to take
quiet satisfaction in the fact that he himself had had a signal

hand in easing that war danger. His actions had not endeared him to the secretary of state, but there was little love lost between them in any event.

Now Pickering hurried toward him, stumbled, stepped into a deep puddle and jumped sideways, cursing and shaking a foot. With a tortured smile he said, "Well, a son should commiserate, I suppose, but your father's a foolish man. He threw everything away when he sucked up to France. Proved to be a mere Gallic tool like that dandified oaf Jefferson, who's naught but a lickspittle to the Frogs. Mark my words, the French'll be our destruction, we give 'em a chance!"

John Quincy bowed. "Mr. Pickering, one can count on you to run true to form."

"Certainly, sir." The older man stopped, peering suspiciously. Had he been insulted? "Well," he said, "consistency is a virtue and so is speaking against John Adams, you like it or not. But we ain't lost yet. Colonel Burr will turn things our way."

"Colonel Burr?"

"You ain't heard about the tie?"

Adams's mouth fell open as the older man sketched the situation. "But Burr will withdraw, won't he?"

"Hell, no, that's the point. He's contesting! Puts it all back in our hands; we still have the House, you know."

"You'll give it to Burr, you mean? That's—"

"Keep it to ourselves. Appoint a caretaker for now, then a new election, bring the people back to their senses."

"My God, sir!" The words were torn from Adams. "You'll shatter the Constitution."

"Shatter, my foot! We're *saving* it. How long do you think it'll last under Jefferson? He'll sell us out to the Frenchies the moment he gets in office. Been his plan all along. You squint your eyes and what do you see—Robespierre!"

Jefferson as Robespierre . . . ridiculous! He remembered Mr. Tom taking him in hand as a raw boy, polishing his language, leading him on long walking tours of Paris and London, making him understand painting and sculpture and the soaring cathedrals that were both art and worship. Weird and

dangerous ideas seemed to have overtaken him, but he still
was not to be traduced.

"Mr. Pickering," he said, "I've known Mr. Jefferson all
my life. He's no Robespierre."

"So you say. But you're not much 'count. Don't think I've
forgotten it was you who overturned what the country
needed so desperately, to settle things with France. Don't
think anyone will ever forget!"

Adams smiled. "That I helped avert war? I take that as an
accolade."

"God! You and your father are fools alike!"

Still smiling, Adams said, "Now, sir, you criticize my father, and in one respect I do too. He should have cashiered
you years ago." He bowed. "Good day, sir."

The thing that really struck him was the pain in his father's
eyes and that drove all thoughts of Mr. Pickering and
Colonel Burr from his mind. Of course, first there were rap-
turous greetings: "Oh, Johnny," his mother crying, "you're
all grown up!" and then treating him as a child, fussing over
his failure to write more often, dubious about his marriage.
He assured her she would love his beautiful young wife as
he privately measured wife against mother and decided
Louisa would have no trouble holding her own. There was
the quick tour of the sadly unfinished mansion, its interior
streaked and scarred—apparently the roof leaked even
though it was new.

But it was that look in his father's eyes . . . his face had
taken on a wizened quality that John Quincy had never seen
before. Of course, he was older, sixty-five now, but it wasn't
that. During dinner, the sun slowly settling as they lingered
at table, purple dusk stealing across the field below, herds-
men rounding up the goats who grazed there, the reality of
his father's manner dawned on him. He'd seen kings deposed in the wild turmoil of Europe today and they had
looked . . . diminished. So did his father. His mother
launched a furious tirade against Jefferson, whom she

seemed to see entirely in terms of betrayal of their long friendship—"He *turned* on us, Johnny, he was the asp in the bosom; he'll carry that to the end of his days!"—while his father said little, that look of pain deepening in his eyes.

At last his father said that he and Johnny would go off to his study to chat a bit, and she smiled and put her hand on his with such a look of devotion that the son felt sudden moisture in his eyes. He knew that her rage against Thomas Jefferson was simply that he had caused John Adams pain; in defense of her husband she was a warrior.

Parsimonious to the core, his father lighted a single candle and set it on the desk between them. Clouds had comes abruptly with the night and thunder burst outside. A flash followed and then a quiet but steady rain began to fall, ticking softly against window glass that threw the candle's flicker back into the room. John Quincy felt the little room reflected his father's modesty; he might dream of titles for his country, but he was himself an unpretentious man. The wainscoted walls were bare of pictures, and he supposed now none would be hung. The candlelight glinted redly on the Madeira, flashing now and again on cut-glass facets as they drank the wine.

"Probably I was never right for the presidency," his father said. "Too fussy, too particular, too concerned about details. Talking truth instead of politics."

"No!" John Quincy banged a fist on the desk. "Remember, you succeeded a man who had assumed near-deity status. All the criticism they hesitated to put on him they heaped on you. I'd say you managed it brilliantly."

His father smiled, liking what he was hearing but too wise to accept it. "That's why they rewarded me with a thrashing."

John Quincy refilled their glasses and settled back in the chair. Now he saw that, indeed, a single painting had been hung behind the desk, showing the farmhouse at Braintree to which the Adams would be returning and which he knew a part of his father's heart had never left. He smiled. "You tell me why they so rewarded you. After all, you saved them from a disastrous war. Did they hold that against you?"

"No, that was popular. But you know my mistake? I should have started afresh with my own cabinet—men loyal to me. But I—oh, I don't know—I guess I hadn't realized how party had come to dominate. I was a vice president moving up to president—it seemed an extension rather than a new administration—seemed logical to keep the same cabinet members in place . . .

He talked a good while in this vein, somewhat obsessively, the son thought, but the gist was the unexpected strength of party division. Hamilton had been out of the government by then, practicing law in New York, and what the president understood only too late was the cabinet's fealty to Hamilton and Hamilton's blind determination to control from afar.

The president—he was still the president, though from his manner his son could hardly be sure—seized a coal from the fire, lighted his clay pipe, and passed the tongs.

"So my government was answering primarily to Alex, and Alex wanted war. Madly fearful of the French, sentimental to a fault about the British even after the Revolution. Maybe growing up on a British sugar island inculcates that. Of course, this revolution in Paris scared a lot of people. Scared me too."

"Scared everyone," John Quincy said. "It was violent, dangerous, murderous at times, far beyond rational control for a while. Personification of good gone wrong."

"Maybe that kind of violence is inherent in democracy after all," his father said in a small voice.

"Oh, Pappa! I just don't think so. I've seen it up close; it doesn't translate to America."

"Really? That's encouraging. Jefferson as Robespierre is an article of faith with a lot of people."

With, for example, Mr. Pickering. He had told his father of the encounter. Now he said, "Oh, Mr. Jefferson is not—"

"Yes, yes, I agree. But remember, Robespierre was the end, not the start. Good men were full of hopes and dreams at the start, and then they were swept away and things got worse and worse. Executed the king and then started killing the nobility, and then the men who'd started it were insufficiently radical and Robespierre came up like a shark after chum and gave the world the Terror. And then military dictatorship and Napoleon—if it came here, Jefferson would be just the start; he'd soon be swept away and the evil men would rise. . . ."

John Quincy dug the dottle from his pipe and refilled it. He was very content, sitting here with his father. "You'll see," he said. "We're growing from such a different seedbed here from what I see in Europe. Mr. Jefferson won't be able to ruin us."

"Well," his father said slowly, "we won't ruin easily. But Jefferson's ideas are so bizarre it will put us to sore test." He sighed. "To think we were once the closest of friends."

"Do you feel he stole it?" John Quincy asked softly.

"Yes." He stopped. "I wouldn't admit this to anyone, not even your mother, but in my heart of hearts, I see him creeping up under cover of friendship and—" He stopped, his mouth working, then shook his head and said in a whisper, "No, I don't like thinking such things; it's not good for me. . . ."

There was a long silence and then he said, "Well, it's not just me personally. Tom will put the whole country under attack. His ideas are strange, something has happened to him, he's dangerous—he'll tear things apart. He'll throw away the national bank and it's obvious we need it, he'll reduce privilege and make enemies of men of power without whom the government can't really work, he'll kill the navy and shrink the army to a border constabulary—Oh, Johnny, I fear he'll be wild!"

"Only consolation," John Quincy said, "in four years the people will be so sick of the mess the Democrats make that they'll scream for the Federalists to come back."

"The fools," his father said, and John Quincy knew by instinct that he referred to Hamilton and the cabinet. "They're the ones put us in this mess."

The story poured out. It was not unfamiliar, but there was a special poignancy in listening to his battered father tell it.

It boiled down to the French in their revolutionary arrogance demanding we swing to their side against Britain and erupting in fury when we held to our neutrality. They did treat us with abominable rudeness, as they were treating everyone, and we took bitter offense.

"The XYZ Affair," he father said, lips tightening.

"Oh, well," John Quincy said, "that was just Talleyrand, obnoxious and outrageous as always."

John Quincy himself had smarted under the French foreign minister's sarcasm—Talleyrand left no one untouched and was corrupt to the core, but his brilliance invariably overcame the trail of outrage he left behind him. He had refused even to talk to an American delegation without payment of a bribe, sending three agents whom the Americans later labeled X, Y, and Z. They'd reported the insult, and Hamilton began beating the drums for war.

John Quincy chuckled. "The story I heard was that Talleyrand was amazed when the Americans stormed off. *'Sacrebleu!'* he's supposed to have said. 'The Americans don't know how to play the game."

"The devil! What were we supposed to do?"

John Quincy saw his father was getting angry, but he said quietly, "Offer him less, pay him less than you offered, write it off to expenses, and move on."

"Johnny! That's not the American way."

"Europe was amazed when we talked war over that."

"Here it was a deadly insult. I guess it really was that the world wasn't taking us as seriously as we took ourselves. Of course, they were abusing our trade and seizing our vessels in the sugar islands; it wasn't just talk, you know."

Well, finally it wasn't. It came very close to war, Hamilton and the press he controlled beating the drums, new warships on the ways, militia polishing weapons . . . and John Quincy had found himself thrust into epic events. He'd gotten to know a minor figure in Talleyrand's diplomatic establishment named Louis Pichon during a three-month tour in Paris. They had taken a shooting holiday together in the south of France and had become fast friends.

Then Louis appeared suddenly in Berlin. After dinner—
Louis was absolutely gallant to Louisa, which pleased her
inordinately—the two men settled down to talk. Just as John
Quincy had suspected, it seemed the French had never
wanted war; they were just playing with the uncouth Americans. Now the game was getting out of hand, so the message
Louis brought was to send a new delegation and there would
be no more XYZ foolishness.

The American thought this over for a few days. If he reported it to the secretary, it would be shot to pieces before a
real decision could be made. Finally he ignored his nominal
superior and sent it directly to his father in a confidential
dispatch. The president presented it to the cabinet. Ignore it,
those worthies said unanimously, it will only lead to further
demeaning humiliation. Hamilton was in a froth. But the
president sent a new delegation, peace with France was
quickly concluded, and war talk collapsed. Just before leaving Berlin John Quincy had had a note from Louis: In reward Louis was being posted as envoy to America.

"Sending the new delegation was the right thing," his father said, "but by then, you see, war had the bit in its
teeth—huge army building, big navy, new taxes to pay for
it, heavy borrowing from financiers who were licking their
chops at the interest rate, fifty thousand militia authorized—and then no war to justify it all. And the Alien and
Sedition Acts. Well, we were all worried about the vitriol
the Democratic papers sprayed on the government, on
everyone, you see. Painted me as black as they painted
Hamilton and the most extreme. So we were jailing editors
and lurking in barrooms to catch men blackguarding the
government. It was like dogs snarling in the pit, everyone in
a fury—and the people were moving to the Democrats in
droves.

"And then on top of everything, Alex writes this stupid
letter to party leaders, trying to get them to shift support
from me to General Pinckney—running for vice president
with me, you see—and Alex wants to install him in my
place! Says that in failing to attack France I'd knuckled un-

der to the tyrants and had betrayed the country and so forth and so on.

"Naturally it splits everything wide open. And you can't keep such a thing secret. So none other than Aaron Burr ferrets out the letter and publishes it, and the whole country knows we're fighting harder with each other than with the Democrats. Voters sliding away like tilting a table."

His father chuckled sourly. "And now that same Colonel Burr has triggered off the instability that wise men long have seen as inherent in Democrats. Ha! Before they can even enter office they're already breaking up, attacking each other; why, they're so many fishwives with gutting knives at the ready!"

That wizened look of age and disappointment now was striking in his father's face, accentuated by the dark hollows left by flickering candlelight, and the son saw he was revealing fully how hard the election had hit him. It was profoundly sad, but John Quincy knew better than to voice the thought.

Instead he said, "It doesn't speak well for the Democrats, granted, but the situation is easily enough settled. Let the Congress give it to Jefferson over Burr; that clearly was the people's intention. It should have gone to you, but between Jefferson and Burr there's no question. But Mr. Pickering talks as if they intend to overturn the election."

"They may do," his father said, voice frosty and distant.

"It's really very dangerous."

"Aye." Not another word. His father puffed on his pipe.

"Would you support Burr?"

"Over Tom, you mean? No. Jefferson is misguided but honorable. He's no friend of mine—he betrayed me—but he *is* a decent human being. Burr is . . . well, slippery. Decidedly slippery. No force of character. I could never support him."

"Have you said so?"

"In public? No. It's not my place. The people have rejected me. No one wants my thoughts."

"Father! That's not true."

"They voted. Let them see what they get."

"You're immensely respected. This tampering with the election sounds like a tinderbox ready to go up. Surely a word from you would—"

"No! If I'm asked, I'll say what I think. But I'll take no public position, write no letters, advance no opinions."

"Pappa—"

"Son, I have been in public life since seventeen and seventy-five and very little has been the recompense. Now, old, broken in body, my purse flat, I go home to Braintree not sure if I can support my wife and household. I haven't been able to save a copper in office. It's too late to return to the practice of law. And what has been my thanks? Satisfaction of a job well done, perhaps, but nothing from the people I served. They flung me on the ash heap, bag of bones too old to be further used.

"Now, then, sir, in the face of that, when they have said so clearly my voice counts for nothing, why should I thrust myself forward and cry disaster, though surely Burr's attempt to seize the presidency is a disaster. But why should *I* speak?"

There was a long silence. John Quincy refilled their glasses and pressed a new coal to his pipe.

"Tell me about Nabby, Pappa. Has her baby come yet?"

7

WASHINGTON, JANUARY 1801

The door on the street banged open and Dolley heard Carl Mobry's heavy tread on the stairs. Danny jumped up as he strode into the room, a massive man standing well over six feet with a huge belly, a leonine ruff of gray hair around a bold face, a seabag on his shoulder. He was twice Danny's age.

"Hello, Princess," he said, with a smile so full of love and trust that Dolley turned away as Danny flew into his arms; it was like looking into a man's soul.

"And Miss Dolley!" He took her hand. "We're honored."

He threw the seabag in a corner. "Millie! It's teatime! Sailor's home from the bounding main. Let's eat!"

A tiny black woman leaned into the room. "We got gumbo, Mr. Carl."

"Damn me, that's what I like about coming home!" He glanced at Danny and winked. *"One* of the things."

The gumbo was New Orleans style, heavy with shrimp and oysters, plenty of okra, enough pepper to make Dolley's eyes water—a very solid tea. Through a front window she could see the massive Capitol looming over its bedraggled grounds.

"Philadelphia's all in a dither since the government left," Carl said. "They knew it was coming but it still seemed like an insult. Oh, and Henderson's warehouse burned—terrible mess."

"With our goods only half-insured?"

"No, no,—*Sea Sprite* loaded and cleared two days before."

"Thank God!"

"Captain Thompson brought the *Mary Weatherly* in a week ahead of time. Cracked mizzen and she'll need a new suit of sails."

"Carl, we just outfitted her a year ago!"

Millie brought Carl a fresh bowl of gumbo without being asked. Dolley noticed Danny frown. "Well," Carl said, "Tommy's a driver, you know."

"He'll drive that ship right under one of these days."

"But he makes the best time of any skipper we've got."

Dolley knew that Carl involved his wife in every aspect of the business. It was most unusual. They had a dozen vessels, each with a trusted captain, warehouses in New Orleans and Philadelphia and Baltimore. He was in Washington because government was crucial to shipping. Export-import duties, the need for a strong navy to protect against pirates . . .

"Why," he said, cackling, "I talk like a Federalist."

"But you're a Democrat," Dolley said.

"Yes! A rebel—or a traitor to my class. But I put country before profit, though mind you, there's nothing wrong with profit. But the Federalist hull is full of worms. Any day now they'll bore through and she'll go down like a stone! Every sensible man is a Democrat! Millie! Any more gumbo?"

"Carl, for goodness sake," Danny said.

He raised his hand. 'Pon my word, haven't eaten since I left."

"Go on. In Philadelphia and no scrapple?"

"Well, scrapple. Yes, a little."

"Fried in ham grease?"

"Bacon, actually. God, it was good!"

"Four helpings, I suppose?"

He looked wounded. "A couple only. Maybe three."

"Oh, darling," Danny said, "I do fear for you."

"Princess, Princess, I'm healthy as a bull!" He turned to Dolley, eager to change the subject. "Do you bring us news?"

"We're hearing terrible things," she said.

"So are we. What say they in Virginia?"

"That federal armories are being stripped of powder and weapons, arms taken into hiding, maybe to keep Democrats from using them to attack, maybe actually for use against our people. Army officers making threats—" She stopped, remembering Colonel Emberby's son. "Federalist papers insisting *they* are trying to save the nation against the hordes. Democratic editors under arrest. That frigates may sail into southern ports and run out their guns. All rumor, of course, but imagine! That we'd use our ships on our own people. It's unthinkable!"

"Tallies with Pennsylvania," Carl said. "Rumors, rumors. That they'll use the army against us. That General Wilkinson, that toadying sycophant, will lead troops if Democrats get out of line. That Pennsylvania armories are being stripped. That troops are being called in from the West to ring the Capitol when voting starts. We heard the navy talk too. Looks like Mr. Burr has kicked over the milk pail, don't it?"

Old Colonel Madison's prediction coming true. She was surprised to find she wasn't angry. It was just Aaron being himself, and she found she did still like him, though it wouldn't do for his selfish solipsism to destroy the country.

"Carl," she said, "I must deliver a very private message to the Federalists."

Danny's head snapped around, but she didn't speak. Dolley saw a sudden intensity in Carl's expression.

"Jimmy thinks Mr. Bayard would be the logical choice."

Carl nodded. "Bayard of Delaware—ships with us out of Wilmington. Strong Federalist, but his probity is unquestioned and he carries great weight in that party. And then, Delaware has just one congressman. He can swing his state yea or nay without a word to anyone. Gives him great power."

"I want you to go with me," she said.

That glitter of eye again. He has an interest of his own, she thought. But she needed him; women didn't go about on matters of state, no matter what Jimmy said about European mistresses. Not that Jimmy really knew; he'd never been to Europe nor had he ever had a mistress, or so she liked to believe. She didn't need Carl's support; he would learn what was afoot when Mr. Bayard did. But Jimmy had agreed: A woman alone could so rattle the man as to block out her message.

"My pleasure," Carl said.

Dolley worked out the arrangements with Margaret Bayard, her young friend from Philadelphia who had married a Mr. Smith and come to Washington, where they would publish the *National Intelligencer.* They were solid Democrats, though the Bayards of Philadelphia were famous Federalists. Indeed, young Mr. Smith had come on Tom's express invitation to be sure there was a paper in Washington to give the truth as Democrats saw it, and Maggie was said to be absolutely enamored of Tom. Mr. Bayard was Maggie's uncle or cousin or something, Dolley thought; at any rate she quickly agreed to provide the setting and make the arrangements for what she obviously saw as a dashing bit of political intrigue.

Willowy and bright with the glow of the newly married, Maggie welcomed them at ten in the morning. The ring of hammers came from the nearby Capitol. Mr. Bayard bowed, a cool, austere man in his middle years, round in body, small beside Carl's bulk, and Dolley responded with a brief curtsey.

Maggie led them to an alcove in her drawing room and settled them at a polished whist table on which she placed a tray with coffee and a platter of morning breads studded with raisins before leaving them alone. Bayard gazed at the breads, and Dolley saw that he expected her, as the woman present, to serve. Amused, she decided to oblige.

Bayard turned to Carl. "We've done business for years, and you know I respect you, but this is extremely irregular."

Dolley cleared her throat. "Mr. Bayard, I am the one who asked for this meeting. And it is irregular because these are irregular times." She explained the circumstances that led Jimmy to send her to deliver the message in his place.

"A letter might have sufficed," Bayard said.

"There are things best not committed to paper."

"Ah." His smile was clearly patronizing. "We enter an era of mystery."

"We are in an era, sir," she snapped, "when men who can't win at the ballot box seek to win by other means." And bit her tongue: she was here to deliver a message, not to debate.

Bayard put down his cup with a clatter. "I assure you, madam, that's not so. We seek to preserve the Constitution."

"Preserve?" Carl cried. "Pulling weapons from armories, calling in troops, readying ships—this to block an election already lost? Let me remind you, sir, the whole thing is a mere accident. There was no tie. Jefferson clearly defeated

Adams. That by accident he tied with his own vice presidential candidate is a mere quirk."

"But most of life is accidental. We must deal with things as they are."

"Which means using the army on your fellow citizens to seize the advantage you find in an accident?"

"That's newspaper talk. I know of no such plans."

"Mr. Bayard," Dolley said, "are you saying there are no such plans or that you know of none?"

He hesitated, face reddening. "I know of none, madam."

But of course, he wouldn't. A moderate, he was decent to the core by every report. As was Mr. Adams and certainly Alex Hamilton and, so she supposed, a host of other Federalists as well. But the problem was with the radicals.

"Anyway," Bayard said, "if troops were called, it would be to control democratic mobs. It's preservation, not usurpation. We know what the Democrats want. Even assuming mobs won't form on the French model—a dangerous assumption—it's clear that the new people will ruin everything. They'll destroy army and navy because they fear that troops lead to oppression. They'll repudiate the national debt, and that'll destroy credit markets and trade, make us the laughingstock of the world. They'll break up Mr. Hamilton's bank, which has been our deliverance. And they'll throw out honest government workers so as to replace them with their own people full of crazy ideas. And then you'll have chaos and disaster. Oh, I *fear* for the future!"

How madly fervid!

"I've heard no such planning," she said.

He pounced like a cat. "Do you speak for your husband in making that statement?"

"I do not, sir! You know better than that. I bring a specific message, that and no more."

"And pray, madam, what is that message?"

"Governor Monroe of Virginia wants the Federalist Party to know that he will call out Virginia troops to march on the capital the moment it's clear that usurpation is taking place—men with arms to be sure that government is not stolen."

Bayard rocked back in his chair. "My God, madam! March? Attack, you mean? You come here and threaten civil war?"

"I tell you the consequences of theft of the election."

"Don't prate to me of theft—coming as you do to talk of taking the government by force. Perils of sending a woman to negotiate; you can't tell her she's a damned scoundrel!"

"Mr. Bayard," Carl said, but Dolley held up a hand to stop him and said, "Sir, you may speak to me precisely as your measure as a gentleman may suggest. What you may not do is accuse me of negotiating. I am a messenger, and I have given you the message."

"Just what one would expect from Virginia." His eyes were glittering. "Why everyone distrusts her influence; she has a rule or ruin mentality. Threatening this way, willing to destroy everything to have her way. Stands alone too. I'll wager other states won't support such mad hubris."

"In fact," Carl said, "other states do."

Startled, Dolley turned to stare at him.

"Pennsylvania, Governor McKean, asked me to give you what proves to be an identical message. He will call out militia and lead the march on Washington himself if usurpation takes place."

"McKean? No. I know him well. He wouldn't . . ."

"Yes, he thought you might doubt me. So he told me to remind you of something he's never told another soul."

"And that is?"

"When you and he were in a duck blind together and you were relieving yourself just as the ducks came in and in the excitement you wet down everything in the blind—"

"All right! My God, that's enough." Dolley bit her lip to keep from smiling as Bayard said, "Now, Mr. Mobry, I swore McKean to secrecy, I'm sorry he told you that story, and I demand—"

"You have my oath, sir. Not a word of it."

Bayard glanced at Dolley. "Good Lord," she said, "I hope you don't think *I* would repeat such a tale?"

"Good." Bayard was breathing heavily. "So, Pennsylvania too. This is more serious than I thought."

Dolley said, "I was to say as well that Governor Monroe is urging states both to the south and the west to consider parallel action. An army of citizens, sir, to reclaim their government."

"And you come to me because . . . ?"

"Because you have a reputation for good sense," Dolley said. "Because this is information Federalists must weigh."

"And," Carl said, "because you can swing Delaware's vote on your own."

Bayard sighed. "You've come to the wrong man," he said at last. "I couldn't vote for Mr. Jefferson. He's a traitor. He would destroy the nation, all we've built, all we stand for in the world."

Carl said, "Isn't it true that your associates see Burr as a heaven-sent opportunity to disrupt the Democrats? And you're playing him like a fish on a line?"

"Some of our people, perhaps. I'm not. And Hamilton is mounting a powerful campaign against him." He noted Dolley's surprise. "Surprised me too. He says Burr is a man of expediency, which I wouldn't doubt, and Jefferson a man of character, which is a total mistake."

Oh, Alex! On the wrong side of the great equation but honorable to the core! Arguing for a man he hated because he placed country ahead of all. He had been their friend and someday she would bring them together again.

"Mr. Hamilton is offering sound advice," she said.

"Vote for Jefferson? No, never."

No added argument could shake him. He agreed to present the danger as real to his fellow moderates, but that was as far as he would go. As for Delaware's single vote, which he was free to cast as he liked, yes, that was key to the whole heartbreaking mess. But it was a key that he would not turn.

She walked away with a profound sense of failure. Jimmy

had been sure that the cold reality of the threat would bring moderates to their senses, and it had not.

For the first time, she felt her faith flagging. Perhaps this wonderful experiment in democracy, the passionate belief that free men could stand responsible for their own destiny, really was doomed. If men in the saddle were so headstrong, if their hatred and fear were so powerful, if they truly were blind to any reality but their own, the noble dream could collapse. There was, after all, an inherent fragility standing alongside democracy's deep-rooted strength. If free men lacked the discipline to live by the rules they set for themselves, then freedom itself must vanish.

Dolley took the southbound stage and rode for unseeing miles, willing away tears.

8

NASHVILLE, TENNESSEE, JANUARY 1801

Andrew Jackson packed his saddlebag before dawn, before Rachel stirred. He was off again and his going would hurt her, it always did, but he could feel the nation calling. This mad Federalist plan to steal the country like so many highwaymen—it came to that, he would rally Tennessee men, they'd march six hundred miles, come up the Great Valley, and be there in a month to fall in beside Virginia and Pennsylvania men and the others who wouldn't let the government be stolen.

Rachel stirred and murmured, and he stepped quickly from the bedroom and dropped the saddlebag on a chair by the front door. Fat old Hannah had the kitchen fire going and the wooden-handled coffeepot bubbling on the grate. He reached into the fireplace to pour himself a cup and stood by the window of his handsome house, damn near the only frame house in Davidson County, watching dawn brighten his fields.

He heard Rachel moving about the bedroom, dressing, and remembered the first time he'd seen her. He'd been a young lawyer then; he had read the law with Spruce McCay back in Salisbury when the west end of North Carolina was the West and Tennessee was still wilderness. Studying law with Spruce McCay meant just about whatever Spruce said it did, from getting the fire going in the morning and the teapot simmering to sweeping out the office to running notes down Salisbury's single street to the courthouse to interviewing witnesses to—once in a while—learning some law. Then, drifting west, he'd trained a little more under Col. John Stokes, who was much man and about the smartest lawyer in all the Carolinas. The colonel had lost a hand at Buford's Defeat—it seemed Ma actually had nursed him, that was before she'd gone on the prison hulks the bastardly British kept in Charleston Harbor, gone to nurse our men captured and held there, and died herself of the ship fever. Dear old Ma. It still hurt that she'd left them to go serve her country. He had been still a boy and the others even younger, but he'd been so proud of her. Anyway, Colonel Stokes wore a silver knob in place of the hand, and to emphasize his points he banged the knob on the table and everyone from the bailiff to the judge bent their ears. Suited Jackson's style.

So when he'd learned the law pretty good, he'd headed on west, packing a letter from a friend who said he'd been named judge for the Western District of Tennessee, and did Jackson want to be prosecutor? Did he! And now he was himself supreme court justice for the Western District of Tennessee, riding circuit through all the far-flung settlements.

So that was how he'd found his way to Nashville, and he remembered how much he'd liked it right from the start. Plenty of rough-handed men who looked the sort to make work for lawyers, two taverns—both natural business producers—a distillery that was sure to help, a couple of stores, a courthouse. It was the end of the line in those days. No white settlements to the west, but that wouldn't last long. People were surging westward, and Tennessee was talking already of separating from North Carolina. He'd been right at home.

In those days Indians raided at will, and you went out at night you'd better be well armed. He rented an extra cabin in the Widow Donelson's stockade and took to the widow immediately, a round-faced woman with gray hair pulled back in a tight bun, the severity at odds with her gentle manner. Met her daughter that same day, a bright-eyed, laughing girl named Rachel, who spun out a good story about as well as anyone he'd ever heard. A mane of chestnut hair, a figure that a man could appreciate, a pretty face with a certain strength that grew quickly into beauty, a way about her . . .

"That is a fine-looking woman," he'd said later to little Johnny Overton, who was about as good a friend as a man could want, then and now too.

"Yes," Johnny had said, and then stopped. Jackson still remembered that pregnant moment of hesitation, and then Johnny had said, "But she's married, you know."

"Oh." It had been a draught of cold water to his face. Surprised him how it had hit him, but maybe he'd known even then, at first glance.

"To a fellow named Robards," Overton said.

"Robards?" Another dash of cold water, and Jackson had cried, "But I met him this afternoon in the tavern. Why, Johnny, he's a sorry son of a bitch; you can tell that in the first five minutes talking to him."

"That's exactly right," Overton had said, "but he's still married to her."

Yes, Jackson had thought, and she's still fine looking. He'd walked out into the stockade yard. He was exactly where he wanted to be—in country where a man's dreams could range without limits. The back door of the blockhouse opened and Rachel stepped out with a pan of soapy water that she splashed across the yard. Saw him and smiled, and he'd doffed his hat and bowed. Yes, then and now, a fine-looking woman . . . damned fine.

• • •

Rachel Jackson could feel the distress mounting, her breath getting wheezy the way it did, the trembling in her hands. Andrew would leave within the hour. She knew him so well. He wouldn't put it that way, but he was going to rescue the nation. That could take him far, far away and into the gravest danger. Would the Lord follow and protect him all the way? She shivered.

"It's the Sabbath," she said, a quiver in her voice. "It would pleasure me if we went to service first, knelt down to Jesus . . ." The thing was, if he prostrated himself before the Lord, maybe the Lord would keep a closer eye.

Where was the laughing, dancing girl of long ago, back in those stockade days, trapped in a bad marriage, rescued by a Galahad with red hair and a lawyer's license, who had saved her then as he stood ready now to save the nation? Buried by scandal? Destroyed? Perhaps . . . but no! No, she wouldn't accept that, and she straightened and was strong again. It was what she had had to do to live through the disaster that nearly crushed her and that brought out all his mad, fighting instinct.

She shook herself, standing straighter, knowing he'd noted her tumult from the quick look he gave her. He was tall while she wasn't, rail thin while she was growing heavy and short of breath, gray overtaking the red in his hair though he was only thirty-three; and he moved with a quick, decisive vigor that made it clear he knew his own mind on anything and everything and would brook no resistance.

Now he put his arms around her and she sighed and laid her head against his chest and let the comfort of his confidence flow into her like fresh blood in her veins.

"I called the meeting for noon, love," he said. "It's a two-hour ride and then some. Jack will be along any minute."

Their home, Hunter's Hill, he liked to call it, was near a dozen miles from Nashville. It was a lonely road, and while the Indians weren't the threat they'd been and there hadn't been a real war party through in some time, she was glad

Jack Coffee would be with him. He was gone so much. A superior court judge rode circuit, town to town on horseback, with law books on a pack horse, dealing with folks who'd bitten off someone's nose or snuck away with title to some wilderness tract none of them had actually seen. . . .

"You'll be back before nightfall, won't you?"

"I don't know, love." She heard that patient note in his voice. "I may have to stay over. This is serious business." For the first time she noticed the saddlebag on the chair by the door. He *expected* to be gone. But it wasn't that he wanted to be away; he loved her and he loved the farm, the mares in foal, the new colts in the spring, the young wheat and corn and the new crop, cotton, when green shoots first broke the tilled ground. It was just that the world called, and he answered, which was his nature. It had been so from the beginning and she knew it always would be so, but there still was the anguish when he left . . . and the fear.

Jack Coffee came up the lane and swung off the massive gelding he rode. He was a huge man, younger than Andrew, their best friend, loyal, steady, taciturn, always there when called. He was courting her niece and she thought they would wed, though Mary had a contrary way about her that a steady man like Jack didn't deserve.

"Aunt Rachel," he said, when he came in, pulling off his hat. Andrew went out to see to his horse; she noticed he scooped up the saddlebag as he opened the door.

"Jack," she said, "this meeting—"

"You know they're trying to steal the government?"

She nodded impatiently. Andrew had talked half the night on how Democrats, which certainly included just about every breathing soul in West Tennessee, had won fair and square, and now the Federalists wanted to appoint their own president and keep the government. They would defy the will of the people, shatter the very soul of democracy! Andrew pacing the floor, beating fist into palm, pale with rage. By *God,* they weren't going to get away with it, and she'd told him not to use the Lord's name so, but her heart hadn't been in the remonstrance, he'd looked so violent.

"But why you?" she'd whispered. "It's not a court matter." But she knew the answer. "I'm the leader." He straightened. "I speak for West Tennessee. Everyone looks to me."

It was true, too, had been since the beginning. Now, to Jack, she said, "This meeting, it's the kind of thing that can make trouble."

"Yes, ma'am. I'll keep an eye out."

Then Andrew was ready, that look of power sweeping his face, hair standing stiff as a brush as if it felt his intensity, his mind already far ahead, and she threw her arms around his neck and held him and then stepped back and watched them ride out. At the gate he turned and waved. He didn't forget her, he never did, but he always left.

The hoofbeats faded, the stillness became acute, a distant birdsong clear and sweet proving no consolation. She turned back to the house to dress for church, wondering as she often did of her terrible loneliness when he was gone cast against her undoubted competence in everything else, in church affairs, in seeing to widows and orphans for miles around, for keeping the farm steady and ever more prosperous. Andrew didn't run the farm; she did, while he was off judging and legislating and running the country, or at least wanting to. She made things work here. They had their people down to the slave quarters whom she must see to, and 640 acres to manage, horses and cattle, smokehouse and birthing barn and training paddock for the racing colts—it kept a body busy, and she did it, Andrew lavishing compliments on her. When you got right down to it, that this is what freed him to go was just plumb ironic.

Yet she knew the source of her distress, no question about it. The flames of scandal had seared her, the explosion had scarred them both, for life she understood now. The blue gown, she decided, the one with puffed sleeves and slender gray stripes. Blue was Andrew's favorite color and the gray stripes suited her mood. She was lost in thought and Hannah, sensing this, laced her up without a word.

Seven years past now, and it still was like yesterday that little Johnny Overton had come to tell them they weren't married. Not really, not legally, after two years of living as man and wife. She remembered Andrew denying it, face red and then white, it couldn't be, they'd been married proper, had the papers to prove it—and Johnny pounding it home, word coming down from the court, whole community knows, they're talking of nothing else, calling it adultery.

Adultery!

Sam was waiting by the front door with the carriage. He'd loaded the three cakes, both cobblers, the tureen of succotash she'd made with her cheese dressing—church was more or less an all-day affair and the big covered dish dinner after the service and before vespers was the social event of the week.

The carriage ground down the long driveway. Adultery . . . Two days later, sick with humiliation, they'd—again! —taken license and sworn vows and become man and wife—again!

She had to be careful here. She clamped her hands on her umbrella; she could go to shaking as with the ague when she thought about Lewis Robards. Shaking with pure hatred, just what our Lord Jesus warned against, right there in Mark he said that after loving God, next was to love thy neighbor, and she calculated that meant folks everywhere and that must include Lewis Robards, but she had to be often on her knees praying for strength not to hate, sweat beading her forehead.

He'd been nice as pie, Robards, till she'd married him, at which moment his kindly good nature fled and he became jealous, domineering, abusive, unfaithful—out to the slave cabins every night; didn't even try to hide it—and he'd have beaten her but for Andrew showing him that fighting knife he carried and telling Lewis he'd kill him if he saw a bruise on her face. They were all living in the big compound Pa had built around the main blockhouse, the Indians so bad no one dared spend a night outside.

Lewis going out to the slave cabins at night. What did those black women feel? She didn't like to think of it, but it had a way of sneaking up on her, making her look at things she didn't want to look at. Did they welcome him? Why would they? Lewis wasn't offering them love, he didn't know how to love, he'd long since proved that. He just used their bodies and that sounded like the worst sin of all to her. Now she and Andrew kept slaves, which meant holding off some uncomfortable thoughts, but the good Lord knew that at least no white men went down to the slave quarters at night. Andrew saw to that. He worked their people and punished them when necessary, but he saw to it that no one abused them. They married, they had families, no one tampered with that. . . .

Another mocker's fluting notes filled the carriage and her eye automatically picked out the bird, perched at the crown of an ash singing his heart out, not a care in the world. Andrew would be approaching Nashville by now; she sent heavenward a brief prayer for his safety.

She remembered the first time she'd seen him, he at her mother's blockhouse, come to rent a cabin in their compound. Tall, skinny, brush of red hair, something about him like a pistol on cock: tense, ready. He'd said the right things when Ma introduced them, all very polite, but the way he'd looked at her—she'd recognized it all right; a lot of men looked at her that way and she uniformly resented it—but this time she didn't, not at all, and she'd had to turn her head and still her fierce heart. This was after Robards had left her in spirit, they hadn't had relations in months, and she had looked at Andrew and felt that stirring and felt at the same time the weight of his strength and character, all the qualities her husband lacked. Saw him again later that same day and he'd smiled and she'd smiled and she knew right then something would happen.

And that damned Robards (a word she used only in her mind and accurately enough at that, for she believed the good Lord *had* damned Lewis Robards for what he did out of pure malevolent spiteful hatred). Well, Lewis had gone back east to get him a divorce, which could only be had by an act of the Virginia legislature, he being a Kentucky man and Kentucky still part of Virginia then. One day the rumor swept Nashville that he was coming back to take her with him by force, and Andrew had bundled her up and carried her off to Natchez in Spanish territory. They rode a flatboat with Colonel Stark's family down the Cumberland to the Ohio and the Ohio to the Mississippi, and the colonel testified all was as it should have been. Andrew went back to Tennessee, and when word came down that Robards had his divorce he rushed back to Natchez and they were married, everything proper.

Two years later they learned the legislature hadn't given Lewis a divorce; it only had given him permission to file for divorce. And he'd waited two years to act, sure they would assume they were clear to marry, and then had filed, charging his wife with adultery! The hateful word had swept West Tennessee like so many lightning strokes. Everywhere they turned people spoke to them or didn't, rolled their eyes or looked away, offered sympathy soaked in self-satisfaction. Oh, you poor dears, thank God *my* marriage is sound. . . . She shuddered and the involuntary movement of her arm nearly spilled one of the cobblers.

Of course they should have delayed marriage till they knew the divorce was final, Johnny Overton had argued to wait, but there was no slowing Andrew. It would have taken months, even years, to check it. Nowadays mail came on a regular route, what they were calling the Knoxville Post Road, but in those days a letter went by your asking a traveler to carry it, same on the return trip, and Andrew hadn't been going to hang his whole future on a scrap of paper in some scamp's saddlebag! Suppose Indians got him or he swam his horse and soaked the letters or he turned off to Kentucky—what then?

The awful weight of scandal had crushed her. She had turned to Jesus with new desperation. She'd understood at last what Savior *really* meant. For months she hadn't wanted to show her face, she'd knelt in the last pew, covered with veils, feeling the scarlet letter blazed on her chest in fire. Thank God for Andrew! He had rescued her.

For his reaction was the opposite. He went everywhere,

faced everyone, always ready. Sometimes she'd be with him
and he'd see that smirk, the raised eyebrow, the greedy stare,
the whispered comment, and he'd walk up to the man, his
whole body stiff, and ask if the fellow had anything he
wanted to say, the cold whip of his voice making it clear that
the fellow held his life in his hands at just that moment; and
men would back off like curs dodging a kick. And when
women did it, Andrew would seek out their husbands or
their fathers. . . .

It had made him stronger, fiercer, more commanding; and
he had provided a shelter in which she could live. Deep
down, she knew that was why it bothered her so when he left.
But there was another reason too. His ferocity seemed to
grow stronger even as the need for it shrank. He'd long since
surmounted the adultery charge and was widely recognized.

My word, in the four years Tennessee had been a state, Andrew had had one honor after another. Tennessee's first congressman; quit that and came home and was appointed to the
Senate and gone again to her dismay; quit that and came home
and accepted the circuit judgeship and he was off again. . . .

He was a leader, just as he'd said, and it was time that he
broaden, strengthen, deepen, and step back from violence.
Someday that willingness to fight in which she sensed something that salved some burning need within him could get
him killed. And she didn't think she could live without him.

They turned off a dirt lane and there was the church, balm
to her heart. It was of logs, lovingly adzed square and
notched. Andrew had pledged to build them a church of
brick when he could; meanwhile they had added a wing that
also faced the altar.

Mary Bainbridge rushed toward her as Sam handed her
down.

"Oh, Rachel, the most awful news. Susan Peabody is
worse than poorly—they say it's the consumption."

"Poor dear," Rachel said. There was no cure for consumption but rest for months, maybe years, and even then the battle usually was lost.

"She has those darling little girls," Millie said. "Can't

keep them to home of course. I could probably take them later, but I have three little ones sick now and another on the way." She patted her extended belly and Rachel felt a stab of anguished envy. Sometimes she thought her own barren womb was God's punishment for the Robards sin, not that it was really a sin, not really, but still. . . .

"Of course," she said. "I'd love to have them."

Millie hesitated. "You reckon Mr. Jackson—"

"He loves children. He'll be tickled."

Jack Coffee was a good man to ride with. He didn't talk much, never unnecessarily, but you could count on him. So they rode along toward Nashville, fording shallow streams, bowing from the saddle to the occasional traveler, leaning on a stirrup to clasp a hand, Jackson's practiced eye ranging over his neighbor's fields, the state of their barns, the quality of their herds.

The infuriating word that the Federalists intended to steal the government had come down from Senator Fleming in the new capital village on the Potomac, which Jackson had no desire to see. His two tours in Philadelphia had been more than enough: the narrow streets crowded and noisy, the air heavy with smoke, the weather nasty. Of course, the senator's official message had gone to Governor Sevier in Knoxville, but good old Fleming hadn't overlooked West Tennessee. Right now East Tennessee had more people than the west end of the state, which stopped right after Nashville, but that was a temporary status and Fleming knew it.

He said Governor Monroe of Virginia, whom Jackson considered about as strong a Democrat as you'd find anywhere, and McKean of Pennsylvania would call out the militia and march on Washington if the Federalists tried to appoint one of their own after Jefferson and Burr won the election.

It was the theft that mattered, tearing up the Constitution, shedding democracy like a snake shedding its skin—outrageous! As to the tie, so long as they chose one of the winning Democrats, it didn't matter much which one. Burr was a gentleman and an undoubted friend of the West; during Jackson's unhappy stay in the Senate, flopping around like a trout tossed on the bank, it was the urbane New Yorker who'd gently taken him in hand. Jefferson, on the other hand, was cool; when they'd met it was the Tennessean's impression that the Virginia gentleman was looking down his nose at the rude frontiersman. He remembered a time he'd been so angry that words had failed him and he'd seen the Virginian's face swept with disdain at which his own fury doubled. That was the day he'd decided to go home when the session ended and not come back, but by God, he hadn't forgotten the look the tall Virginian had given him.

Burr would make a hell of a good president, proven friend of the West that he was. The West needed friends too because the Spanish were pressing again, and the time was coming when if the national government didn't do something about those rotten dons in New Orleans strangling American trade, frontiersmen would rise and march down and throw 'em into the sea, and Jackson might well lead that march his own self!

Burr's instincts were right, he was practical, he understood how the Spanish stranglehold on the river hurt the West. Sooner or later the rivers this side of the mountains flowed to the Mississippi, while those same mountains, fold upon fold, blocked trade to the East. That's what that whiskey rebellion in western Pennsylvania was all about; only way you could haul corn over the mountains was to distill it down to liquor. Special tax on it just wasn't fair. No wonder they marched; he'd been up there, he'd have grabbed a piece and gone with 'em. The Federalist fear and outrage showed the real eastern attitude.

Between mountains to the east and Spanish to the south, this whole region, Tennessee and Kentucky, Ohio pushing for statehood, settlement moving ever farther west, the whole shooting match was locked in place like a bull with a ring in his nose. But the West was going to boom; It was alive, vibrant, growing, hungry for more, new fortunes being made daily, at least in potential. One of these days settlement would fill everything this side of the Mississippi, and it couldn't do all this with a ring in its nose that the Dons could twitch any old time they felt like it.

Democrats understood that, and the West was their natural ground. Hell, it was easier to find a snipe on a snipe hunt than to find a Federalist in Tennessee. And why? Because Democrats stood for the rights of the common man against the bosses and that was the heart of things in the West. Man didn't like getting pushed in a Boston factory, he packed up his family, put his goods in a wagon, and trekked west—more coming every day and Democrats to a man. They didn't find property qualifications for voting when they got here, by God!

Which made it the perfect place for Andrew Jackson; and you wait and see, he would leave his mark on the West. He burned with an inner sense of capacity, had for years, sometimes it was so strong he wanted to throw up his arms and shout. He *knew* he had the power deep in sinews and mind and soul; command came as naturally as breathing; men had wanted to follow him ever since he could remember. Not as senator or congressman, he'd tried that, not as governor in constant compromise with a legislature. The military was the answer, on a white horse, saber held high, leading the charge! Wait and see. One of these days . . .

The only dark side to this bright glow in his mind—this sheer confidence that he could daunt the world—was Rachel's pain when he left. She had never really recovered from that miserable Robards business, and maybe he hadn't either, except that in him it had turned outward into force and in her inward into pain. And yet she was the center of his life; she was the stabilizer that held him together, when they were apart he needed her—right now, riding to Nashville to make sure that West Tennessee understood the stakes and would be ready if the situation made it necessary to march, he looked forward to getting home and seeing her relieved smile. But the power nevertheless burned within him, the power of capacity, and he felt himself but a tool in its hands.

Toward town he saw more riders and the dirt streets cross-hatched in the Great Bend of the Cumberland seemed to

throb with repressed excitement. Immediately his own blood
quickened, and he put his mare into a canter. A good hundred
men were already on the square before the little log courthouse and more were coming. A half-dozen had climbed
onto the roof of the jail, the whipping post and stocks in
front now empty. Several strangers were on the courthouse
steps, and he saw travel-stained horses tied to a rail.

Phelps Austin hurried toward him. "Judge, fellow here
from Knoxville, says he comes from the governor? He
wanted to address the boys, but they voted to wait for you."

A tall, rather imperious-looking man in his middle years
approached, stout, graying, his expression impatient and
somehow superior. Jackson felt a stirring of dislike.

"I'm Sam'l Horsby, Knoxville. Representing the governor."

"Judge Jackson." The handshake was perfunctory.

"Governor sent me to speak to folks hereabouts, and they
seem to look to you. But you have no objection, I'm sure, to
their hearing from the chief magistrate of the state."

That was close enough to impudence to get Jackson's attention. He stood on a step above Horsby and told him to go
ahead. When he saw no one was listening, he shouted, "Give
him an ear, boys! He's right proud of himself, coming from
the governor and all."

Horsby's head snapped around at that, but Jackson
grinned and said, "Talk on, brother."

The man wasn't a bad talker. He sketched in the crisis,
Federalists talking about stealing the government, Virginia
and Pennsylvania ready to march, other states fixing on following . . .

Pete Olive cried, "We're Goddamn ready to go!" There
was a roar of approval.

But Horsby's face went red and he shouted, "Now, that's
commendable, and we'll be calling on you if the time
comes, but that's just the point. Action now is precipitate."

Jackson saw that most of the crowd didn't know the word.
"So let's go!" Pete bawled.

Horsby flushed redder. "No! Governor Sevier will decide

when we go and how we go, and then—and not before—he'll call on you. They haven't stolen nothing yet, don't forget, and last thing we want to do is run off half-cocked."

Half-cocked! With Andrew Jackson at their head? He felt like booting Horsby in the ass.

Now, the truth was that just the mention of John Sevier's name got Jackson's hackles to rising. Yes, the man was a great hero and all that; but, Lord ha' mercy, he'd been trading on it for twenty years. Led the Tennessee mountain boys who whipped the British at King's Mountain and saved the West. No small matter either. Jackson had had his own taste of the British as a boy in South Carolina and there was a scar on his head to prove it. As for Sevier, he hated Jackson, which showed you right there what a pig-headed old bastard he was, for he had no earthly call to hate, whereas Jackson had plenty of reason to hate him, the damned scoundrel. . . .

Pete Olive was on the front row listening to this twaddle-merchant from Knoxville. Had a bottle in his hand and from his face Jackson judged he'd not missed any opportunities to drink. "Well, how about that?" Pete yelled. "Ol' Sevier wants us to lay back, do he? Sounds like you boys in East Tennessee have gone just a leetle soft. Hell, man, you're in *West* Tennessee now. Out here we talk with the bark still on; out here stealing the government from good democratic yeoman just ain't done!"

Over a roar of laughter, he shouted, "Let's hear what the judge has to say."

Jackson stepped forward, arms raised to quiet them. "Well, boys, don't matter much what the governor says—"

"Now, see here—" It was Horsby.

Jackson spun on him. "That's enough out of you, sir! Hold your tongue while I speak." Horsby stared but didn't answer.

Jackson's voice went shrill when he was excited, but one thing for sure, no one had trouble hearing him. "Now, boys," he shouted, "what matters is how you feel about them Federalists running our lives! These are the fellers who gave us the Alien and Sedition Acts, throwing folks in jail for their words or their ideas. Aliens, now, they're the enemy? Is there a man here older than ten who didn't come from Carolina or Virginia or someplace? We're all aliens.

"So who are these men back East trying to steal the election we won fair and square? Why, they're the same folks who fought like dogs trying to deny Tennessee statehood. Remember?"

There was a roar. He was warming them, and my Lord, out here in Tennessee, the Federalists were easy targets.

"Same folks who denounced us when we had to fight Indians: Same folks talking about sticking with the original thirteen and cutting the rest of us loose! And those Dons down in New Orleans, Don Diego and Don Felipe and Don Fat-ass, strangling our trade, seizing our produce if we dare go down and ask, please, *seen-yor*, can we ship out a little wheat to starving Europe and hope to make a couple little pieces of gold—now, boys, you tell me, you hear anything from these Federalists about how they'll stop such outrages? Go down the river, maybe, and clean the Dons out, drive 'em into the sea, let 'em swim to Cuba? Hear anything like that? These are the folks trying to steal our government."

When he got going in a red meat speech, he could fire the boys right up. They were laughing and yelling, and he saw several bottles moving hand to hand.

"Tell you what else too. These are the same folks rolled out the red carpet for Mr. Gardoqui. You remember Mr. Gardoqui, don't you, *Seen-yor* Gardoqui, Don Something-or-Other Gardoqui, come to offer a deal the Federalists in the East just couldn't pass up, all the rich trade they could handle, stacks of gold in their countinghouses you couldn't see over, and all they wanted was the right to close the Mississippi to our trade for twenty-five years—twenty-five years! Button it up and destroy the West, let it wither away to nothing, die on its feet, ripe for Spain to pick it off and make it her own.

"And what did they say back east? Remember? Why, they said, this is better'n a hot toddy in a snowstorm: And it went to the old Continental Congress, bless 'em, and seven states—*seven states!*—voted in favor; and thank God it took nine to carry anything in that august body or we'd have had to fight Spain ourselves years ago. And that's the attitude of New England and the Federalists and the same men who want to use a simple tie between two good Democrats as an excuse for denying the prize to either and keeping it for themselves; and, boys, what I'm here to say is that I don't intend to stand for this. They try it, and I want to know right now if you're with me or agin me!"

They were whooping and yelling and shouting, "Amen," and "That's right," and "Let's go stick a bayonet up their ass," and "We ain't going to leave it all on Virginia and Pennsylvania to clean up the mess. When do we march?"

Then Horsby bounced forward, almost pushed Jackson out of the way. He was waving his arms and shouting. "You men, listen to me, listen! They haven't stolen anything. Talked about it but haven't done it. They do it and believe you me, Governor Sevier will be more than ready to take action, and he'll call on you, too, but it'll be done in an orderly way."

"You hear that, boys?" Jackson shouted. "Now *we're* the disorderly ones, not the damned Federalists. And let me ask you something. You don't suppose our good governor is being so cautious 'cause he's got Federalist money backing all his land deals, do you?"

"Oh," Horsby cried, "that is outrageous. Obscene. I'll have to report that." He pointed at Jackson. "You are a master of wild irregularity, sir, you're famous for it, you—" He broke off, staring, as Jackson slowly turned to him.

Turned, his head sinking into his shoulders, filled with horror and amazement—

Irregularity—

Did he mean, could he *presume*—

Did he raise the terrible issue?

Did he *dare*?

Slow steps toward the scoundrel, head down and thrust forward, hands curling into fists, the pistol in his belt suddenly heavy against his belly. . . .

"Judge! Judge! Hold on." It was Jack Coffee.

"Eh?" he asked, his throat swollen, felt as if he were strangling. . . .

"I don't think he meant nothing personal." Horsby was stepping backward. "You didn't mean nothing personal, did you?" Coffee said to him. "Talking about this meeting, weren't you?"

"Of course. The meeting is most irregular. It's the governor's prerogative to call out troops. Nothing to do with the courts."

"See, Judge." It was Pete Olive, suddenly sober. "He didn't mean nothing."

Horsby looked one to the other. "What are you talking about, personal? I didn't say—" He broke off, suddenly pale. "Oh," he said. "Oh."

He put out his hand. "I give you my word, the reference was to a meeting I consider irregular if not extralegal."

Jackson stared at him, the thrumming in his ears dying down, the taste of metal in his mouth bitter as gunpowder. He nodded, took the proffered hand, cleared his throat, and said rusty-voiced, "Extralegality *is* in my province, and I judge it does not apply to this meeting, nor is it irregular for free men to determine to defend their freedom. West Tennessee will march when it chooses. Kindly pay our respects to the governor and convey that message. Now, begone, sir."

"Boys," he said, the fire gone out of his voice, steady and collected, the voice of leadership, "we'll march the minute we hear the Federalists actually try to appoint their own president. Soon as Monroe moves his troops. I want a solid one hundred men ready to march on twenty-four hours' notice, rifle, sixty rounds, blanket, three day's rations. Wagons to carry supplies. Two doctors and a chaplain. We'll strike the Cumberland Gap, then north into the Great Valley—six hundred, maybe seven hundred miles all told, four to five weeks.

"And we'll take back our government."

III

THE TEST

9

Danny Mobry, alone in her drawing room with the view of the Capitol, studied and restudied the letter that quivered in her hands. She needed Carl for this and he was away, gone to Annapolis to test a new vessel with a new captain. The letter was terrifying, for it would shift her from spectator to participant in an insane national drama.

It seemed a mad dream that now, after all the storm and bombast, the vote in Congress that would choose the next president was only two days away and nothing had changed. Jefferson still had just eight states, one short of election. Six were for Burr. Two were divided, their votes canceled. Of course the six didn't really want Burr; they wanted to hold fire till President Adams's term ran out and then appoint their own president. Steal what they'd lost at the ballot box. One of the six was Delaware, controlled by the vote of its single congressman, James Bayard.

The letter quivering in Danny's fingers surely came from Dolley, though it was not in her hand and was unsigned. But who else would write so, speaking for men bound to silence? Mr. Madison was pinned in Virginia at his father's deathbed. Mr. Jefferson was here at Conrad's boarding-house, talking freely of government policy but silent on election issues, determined not to win office by making deals.

She reread the letter for the fifth time. It instructed her to see Mr. Bayard as the key figure. So great was his reputation for good sense that Federalists in both the undecided states, Vermont and Maryland, had agreed to act in concert with him. Combined with his own state, this put three votes in his hand.

The sheets of paper seemed charged. Make him *see* the consequences, citizen bayonets ringing the Capitol. Ask him, it added, the following questions. Every time she read them her heart began to thunder. She, an anonymous young woman, should seize Mr. Bayard by the lapels and shake sense into him? It was terrifying, and yet she realized it made perfect sense. There are things that must be communicated unofficially, without records. Perhaps it was fitting that she, a nobody, should be the hinge point on which great events would turn. Carl had done enough business with Mr. Bayard to assure that he would meet them—and, perhaps there always was such a person as she who carried the message or made the point or applied the pressure in the midst of crisis and then disappeared unheralded.

She studied the letter for an hour and then, as instructed, touched a corner to a candle's flame and watched it burn.

She was calm again. Anonymous she might be, but she had been appointed and she had a mission of high trust. And it struck her how far she'd come in the ten years since Carl had plucked her off the plantation. She'd been the princess of Bayou La Fouche then and confident she knew everything; and since had found she'd known almost nothing, as Carl brought her along step by step.

There was a power in her massive husband, authority of manner, wisdom, and judgment without which you didn't succeed in the shipping business. He'd had his own brig on the Atlantic run when he was eighteen; now he had a dozen ships. Someone had sketched him then and she'd been surprised to see a slender boy grasping a ship's wheel. Now he stood at three hundredweight and puffed when he walked, though he still moved and talked and thought with the quick urgency of the boy he had been.

So she was ruminating when she heard the front door crash open and his loud voice calling on Millie for beef and beer and a loaf of her fresh bread with a crock of butter and hustle it on up to the family parlor, lickety-split. But when he burst into the room she felt a sudden fear. He stood with a slump, his face looked gray and exhausted, his hair floated in wispy strands like an old man's; his fist was pressed to his chest.

"It's nothing!" he roared. "Nothing that a pound of beef and three or four tankards of ale won't cure, my dear. You know me, hearty as a damned goat; they'll never kill me off." He laughed that big laugh of his. "Why, what a waste to fold my tent and leave a wife like you behind. Give me a kiss, milady, and after a meal I'll take you to bed and you'll see"—he winked—"*feel* my enthusiasm."

"Oh, hush, Carl," she said as Millie came into the room with a tray. "You look awful. Here, sit down, tell me—"

"Nothing much," he said, tucking a napkin in at his collar and taking a draught of ale. "The new brig's a sound vessel, but she wasn't fully outfitted. It was just a trial and then we hit one of those freak Chesapeake storms and had to run all night on a staysail till it blew itself out."

"I hope you were under shelter."

"Well, actually, the new skipper won't do. Lost his nerve. God, I thought he was going to *weep* when it got bad. It was infecting the crew, mostly new boys, you know. We'd already lost some rigging, we got the staysail set, and here comes some fool in a sloop running wing and wing before the wind and damn near rams us. When he's alongside, his mast goes, sounds like a cannon, his rigging's overboard, and then he's gone in the gloom. I look around and my captain is all white in the face and shaking: Can you believe it? So I backhanded the silly bastard into the scuppers and took the wheel myself and ran through the night. Eased off around dawn and we brought her on in."

"For God's sake, Carl, you had the wheel all night?"

"It was fun—like the old days. A little cold though, taking green water over the bow, spray riding a winter wind. Yes, it was cold, all right. Ice forming on the wheel, that sort of thing. But not really bad—"

He coughed heavily, hand pressed to his chest. "Touch of pleurisy, I'm afraid, bit of ague, what have you. Nothing to it. C'mon upstairs. I'll prove I'm in top form."

"Oh, Carl," she said, but she had to laugh. Still, he was so big and now, wolfing his slab of beef, smearing butter on Millie's soft bread, washing it down with ale and calling for more, he'd gain a few more pounds. Where would it end?

When she told him of the letter his face took on the firm, rather calculating look he had when dealing with their ships. "Bay Bayard will meet, I'm sure. He's too smart to pass up any overture. But he won't give you much satisfaction; listen but keep his own counsel. Plays 'em very close to his vest."

"If he listens, will he act?"

"Well, he's not at all a fool. I guess it depends on how hard Federalist fears and ideology grip him."

"When you and Dolley talked to him—"

"He was courteous, not cordial. Didn't like having a woman lecture him. But that was a month ago; there was still plenty of room for maneuver then. Now . . ."

In a flurry of notes hustled about by messengers on foot, Maggie Smith offered her living room as neutral ground once more, and Mr. Bayard said he would make time to come. Carl still had that gray look and she wanted to take the carriage the four blocks to Maggie's house, but he insisted on walking.

Sam Smith emerged from Conrad's boardinghouse as they passed. He was cleaning his teeth with a gold pick that he hastily slipped into a waistcoat pocket when he saw them. Sam had been a commercial power in Baltimore before Maryland sent him to Congress, and they did even more business with him than with Mr. Bayard. Danny liked him. He always bowed over her hand and clicked his heels, which reminded her of those elegant Frenchmen at home in New Orleans but amused her because he so clearly wasn't an elegant Frenchman. A hearty, solid man with pale hair and pale blue eyes, he radiated power. Now his full hatred was turned on Burr for repudiating that first letter after Sam published it. He willingly joined their visit to Mr. Bayard.

Danny had met the Delawarian but wondered if she would have recognized him on the street; now, sitting around the polished whist table in Maggie's drawing room, a plate of cakes and glasses with a sherry decanter in place, she saw why. He was nondescript, remote, somehow inconsequential.

"Bay," Sam said, "do you remember Andrew Jackson?" Bayard shook his head and Sam said, "Served a term as a Tennessee congressmen, I believe, and sat in the Senate for a while. No great shakes as a legislator, but a fiery young devil and a born leader of men, I'd say."

"Yes, by George, I do remember him! Tall, skinny youngster? Wild-eyed frontier Democrat, I recall. Seems to me he even voted against a resolution of thanks to General Washington. Said it was too royalist. Imagine that!"

"Well, Enoch Bass of Tennessee tells me Jackson has pulled a small army together in real military style and has 'em on standby and ready to march. If election theft goes forward."

Bayard frowned. "Yes . . . that could be very dangerous."

It was time to assert her own role here. Without much thought, Danny said, "That's just why I asked you—"

He wheeled on her. "I *understand,* madam. That's why I'm here." He looked at her with a force quite unlike his remote manner so far, and with a jolt she realized she had seriously underestimated him. This man was a major personality; at once she understood why Vermont and Maryland had chosen to place themselves in his hands.

"So, madam, just what did you have in mind?" His voice was harsh as if pressing an advantage in debate, and at this her tremors passed and she was very angry. She stared at him till his eyes fell; then she described the letter.

"Anonymous?" Bayard said.

"Unsigned."

"So you don't really know . . ."

"Don't be silly, Bay," Sam said. "I can tell you it describes democratic sentiment perfectly. You're sitting on a powder keg, my friend, and I hope you can persuade your colleagues to smoke their pipes elsewhere."

Bayard sighed. "You know," he said, "some of us aren't so radical. Jefferson could yield a little, give us a few guarantees, and maybe he could swing it."

Sam shook his head. "He won't bargain for the office. That's Mr. Burr's style."

"Burr isn't so stiff-necked, you mean."

"I mean the man is a mountebank:"

"Oddly enough," Bayard said, "that's what Hamilton says."

Alexander Hamilton's face, with its fine features, flashed into Danny's mind. She'd danced with him one night. He was secretary of the treasury, and Carl had just fetched her from New Orleans. She was seventeen, perhaps, or eighteen, green still but not so green she didn't recognize the way he'd looked at her. He was striking and danced with a muscular power, and she'd felt herself being swept toward him. Shaken, she'd sought out Carl and stayed close to him through the evening, and when she'd seen Mr. Hamilton a week later he'd merely bowed and passed on. But she hadn't forgotten that vivid force.

"He's a New Yorker," Bayard said. "Ought to know Burr if anyone does. Says Burr has no character and Jefferson has too much. He may be right about Burr, but he's wrong on Jefferson. It would tear my heart out to vote for that man. It's not that he doesn't love his country—he does—but he's a zealot entranced with the dreams of France and its revolution, unable to see the disasters that would follow when he imposed it here, blinded by arcane philosophy."

Danny snorted. "Democracy is hardly some arcane philosophy. Seems to me Alex knows both men a bit better than you do."

Bayard stiffened. "I know Mr. Jefferson well enough. Don't waste advice on me; advise Mr. Jefferson it's time he showed some Burr-like pragmatism."

It wasn't Danny's place to argue such a point, but Sam said, "He won't do it. And he shouldn't. He must enter office with a clean slate; no bargains, no deals. If your people are willing to destroy the Constitution over this, so be it."

Danny hesitated, feeling in very deep water. A tremor in her voice, she said, "I was sent here to ask—"

He whirled on her. "With all respect to Carl, I doubt you have any real authority."

Oh, is that so! Immediately her trepidation vanished. "I speak for very highly placed persons, sir! Informally, yes, but informal communication is common when great issues are at stake."

"Pshaw!"

She felt calmer and stronger every minute. "I'm only a messenger," she said, "but wise men listen to messengers."

That jolted him. He was silent as she sketched the dismal facts. Armies forming to restore democracy! Didn't he already know this? At last, mouth twisting, he nodded.

"Then, sir," she said, "let me ask what I was charged to ask. When the soldiers of democracy come, who will fight for you? Will Federalist supporters come out to die so you can steal the presidency?" Her raised hand stopped his protest. "Will the army fight for you? How big is it now— three, four thousand men, mostly on the frontier? They'll be anxious to fight armed citizens who are only trying to preserve democracy? Will they follow General Wilkinson? Can you trust him? Do you doubt he'll make an arrangement to his own advantage?"

She drew a deep breath. "If you take it by guile, you must keep it by force. Oh, sir, do you have that force at your command?"

Bayard's eyes glittered with anger. "Carl," he said, "I see you have married an orator."

Carl had been coughing into a handkerchief. He looked up and said, "Well, sir, the truth gives her power."

There was a long silence. Then Bayard stood, bowed, and left without another word.

Danny was crushed. "I made a mess of it, didn't I?"

"Actually," Carl said, taking the handkerchief from his lips, "I thought it went rather well. Sam?"

"I thought so. You punched him with some ideas he has to think of. They were already in the back of his mind; you got them up to the front. Not much more you could do."

He excused himself and hurried off to the Hill.

Carl didn't move. "I was proud of you, darling. Very proud," he said. She glowed. Then he said. "Let's send for our carriage. I really don't feel like walking. . . ."

The Capitol would be an extraordinarily handsome building when it was done, which might take a decade or two; certainly the finished parts, which included the House chamber, were magnificent with rich marble, carved and polished mahogany, scarlet drapes fringed in gold, an eagle of wood and plaster over the speaker's chair. Today, the great vote at hand, it was closed to all but members, but Danny had seen it from the visitors' gallery. Here as in Philadelphia attending the more important debates had become a major pastime; sometimes dozens of women were in attendance, which often had a galvanizing effect on oratory, flowery allusions thick as swallows in flight.

But the rest of the Capitol didn't exist; foundations laid or at least pegged out on the Senate side, marking string grayed with rain-soaked dust, stone floors of the rotunda laid but the roof crude timbers and canvas, a lone bust of General Washington executed without distinction standing as sort of an initial payment on decorative intent. As the closest place to the closed debate, the rotunda would fill early, and Danny insisted they set out a bit after dawn. Carl fetched a canvas sling chair for her but they captured a stone bench and she made him take the chair, not liking his gray color.

A buzz of excited talk filled the big room. Two large fireplaces were ablaze, and there was the companionable odor of frying meat with the cries of venders selling bottles of syrup water and beer, sausage wrapped in a dodger, sweet

breads and tea and hot chocolate. A dog wandered through
and she scratched its ears. When she stopped, it nudged her
impatiently: more.

So she was scratching a mongrel's ear when the hundred-
odd members marched up from the Senate chamber, the formality of the official opening of electoral votes behind them.
Guards posted themselves at the door but left the doors
open. She heard the House called to order. Mr. Bayard had
avoided her eye when he passed, whether by chance or intent she couldn't tell. He looked stern and strong but very
tired, the weight of Delaware, Maryland, and Vermont a formidable burden.

Two men bearing a third on a stretcher, a doctor walking
alongside, passed into the chamber. A round of whispers
swept the rotunda: a Federalist member at death's door but
carried in to anchor his vote against the hated Democrat. The
doctor was allowed to remain on the floor.

The voting started. "Connecticut," she heard the clerk cry.

"Connecticut for Mr. Burr," the guard said to no one in
particular. He was a tall, heavy man of boiled beef English
stock, face red as a carrot, a shock of white hair and a fine
white mustache. She'd noticed the members speaking to
him, his response in that curious mixture of gracious subor-
dination and lofty superiority that mark the truly secure
functionary. "Delaware." Pause.

"Mr. Burr."

Bayard had held his obstructionist vote for Burr! Her face
stung with mortification. After all she'd said, he whose single vote could end the terrible charade in a moment had
walked away in a huff, unmoved, uncaring. Tears formed,
fell, streaked her cheek. Carl squeezed her hand; he'd been
pressing a handkerchief to his lips and he passed it to her to
dry her eyes.

She listened to the rest of the vote, called in the same unconcerned way by the big guard. Georgia and Kentucky for
Jefferson. Maryland divided and not voting. Massachusetts
and New Hampshire for Burr. New Jersey, New York, North
Carolina, and Pennsylvania for Jefferson. Rhode island,

Burr. South Carolina, Burr! What irony. Carrying South
Carolina had given Jefferson the presidency over Adams and
now its delegation had voted against him. Tennessee for Jefferson; thank God for the West. Vermont, divided, not voting. Virginia, of course, for Jefferson. So it was unchanged:
six holding for Burr, eight for the Virginian, one short of victory.

They took the vote again. Same results. Again and again
and again. No change. Again. She lost track of the number
of votes. At midnight someone said there had been nineteen.
No change. The diehards were holding, Bayard among
them.

Carl was sunk in the sling chair, his face gray, mouth
slightly open. She thought he was panting. He said he
wasn't.

"Let's go home," she said. He shook his head.

"Carl, you don't look at all well. Really, darling, we
should—" He shook his head.

Vote starting, the guard said.

Connecticut. Mr. Burr.

Delaware. Mr. Burr.

Carl fainted at three in the morning. His head rolled, his
legs went slack, the chair tipped and dropped him face first
on the stone. She screamed. The guard fetched that doctor
from the floor. Carl awakened with a wide-eyed, frightened
look. The physician laid his ear to Carl's chest; there was
something odd in his expression when he turned to her.

"Take him home, madam," he said. "Get him in bed."

Their own doctor visited Carl in the morning, debated bleeding him, settled for telling him stay in bed. A special edition
of the *Intelligencer* said voting had gone on till noon, results
unchanged. A new rumor raced through the streets: stalemate to March 4, then John Marshall, the new secretary of
state, would become president. And, Danny thought, the
South and the West would march. She remembered Jackson.
She'd met him a couple of times, and given his reputation,

she'd been struck by his graceful courtesy. She had an image
of those Tennessee long rifles, lean, hungry men with pieces
in hand, boots worn by six hundred miles, swinging along,
ready to fight—and when all was done, what would be left
of their country?

A new rumor: Mr. Bayard would change his vote! So he *had*
listened!

She made Carl promise to stay in bed and hurried up the
Hill. Her bench was taken. She leaned against a marble pillar near the entrance.

Vote's starting, the guard said.

Connecticut: Mr. Burr.

Delaware: Mr. Burr.

She reeled away from the pillar afraid she would vomit.
She found an open bench and took it, gasping.

An immensely fat woman in a magenta gown, the bench's
other occupant, turned to Danny and said, "Mr. Burr's in
Baltimore."

"I beg your pardon."

"Well, what's he doing in Baltimore if he don't intend to
come over here and take it by storm? Any minute now he'll
come walking in, go right on the floor, give 'em a speech to
knock their hats off, and they'll swarm all over him. Have
'em eating out of his hand. You ever see him? Handsome
devil. I'd eat out of his hand anytime, I'll tell you. Anything
else he wanted too. Any minute now, right through that
door." She raised a fat arm to point, flesh sagging.

The House recessed, members poured out, and she saw
Mr. Bayard coming straight for her. "Madam," he said without preamble, a harsh crackle in his voice, "since you seem
to be the democratic messenger, kindly get word to Mr. Burr
in Baltimore that it's now or never. He should get over here
and make his case—now!—or he should forget it."

"Mr. Bayard," she cried, "don't count on me to deliver
such a message."

"Oh, I don't. Many messages are going. Since you are a

beautiful woman, knowing Burr, I thought he might pay attention to you."

"Sir," she said, "that is a crude and insulting thing to say. You should be ashamed."

He bowed. "Good day, madam."

"Well, I never," said the woman in the magenta gown.

Aaron Burr paced up and down, up and down, before the hotel, Baltimore's finest but nothing special at that. He paced and paced, swinging his ebony stick, slashing grass spears, his baleful stare forbidding any trespass on his silence.

It was insane, they'd had six weeks to work it out, they'd stalled, done nothing, and now they wanted him to come in person, seize the ground, exhort, demand, beg. What fools!

He'd been drawn as a moth to flame, drawn as close as Baltimore, but he could come no closer. The Federalists wanted him to come and give them a sign that as president he'd see things their way. But for what? He already had the Federalists; begging would gain no more. What he needed was obvious; three states now voting for Jefferson must be persuaded to shift. It shouldn't be so difficult; after all, he was a good Democrat. Better him if they couldn't have the sainted Tom, and obviously they couldn't; better him than the raging Federalist John Marshall as caretaker president, with the shards of the Constitution scattered at his feet.

Like the tongue to a sore tooth, his mind darted off to Hamilton and his vicious attacks. He couldn't understand it. He and Alex had been friends, more or less. They'd been co-counsel on important cases; and while they were political opposites now, he didn't hate Alex and was amazed to find that Alex apparently hated him. Add that to the ridiculous Federalist urgings when the solution was obvious. Really, it was the perfect solution, for in fact he *was* a good Democrat, a fine Democrat. There had been talk that he should have stepped aside, but he'd brushed it away. He had been rigidly proper; indeed, he was proud of himself. He had done nothing—not one thing—to advance his cause or thwart Jefferson or challenge the will of the people.

He walked and walked, swinging the stick in a blurred arc, scarcely noticing the wide berth passersby gave him. His position was strong, he saw, looking at it realistically. He might yet be called. But if he weren't and it went to usurpation, he would lead troops on the attack, being no mean military man himself. And if it turned around and went to Tom, he would be second in command, an honored member of a new administration, crucial to holding all-important New York.

His position, he decided, clipping grass so hard the cane whirred and vibrated, couldn't be better.

It was Tuesday, six days since the voting had begun. Repeated ballots had produced no result, but the talk was that it would be settled today. Hold for usurpation, chaos, and war or shift three democratic states to Burr.

She awakened to find six inches of snow glittering on the ground. Boys played on barrel stave skis on Capitol Hill. Service as a messenger had made Danny part of it and she had to witness the climax. She was pulling on her boots when Carl said he was feeling better and tired of bed and would join her. When she fought him he got that stubborn look she knew too well.

"All right," she said, "the snow and all, let's not go. Doesn't matter. We'll learn soon enough. . . ."

That look again. She saw that somehow she had challenged him. "Fine," he said. "You stay here. I'm going."

They went slowly, stamping a path through unbroken snow, and arrived early. The bench near the door that she regarded as their own was empty and they waited quietly.

The guard knew them by now.

"Mr. Bayard will change his vote, they say."

Presently: "Mr. Bayard is taking the floor." She heard voices, then one clearly orating, words unintelligible.

"Says he won't let it go to stalemate. Says he won't count—count—"

"Countenance," she said.

"That's right. Won't let it go to stealing it."

Thank God!

"Says he'll grit his teeth and vote Jefferson."

"Mr. Speaker! Mr. Speaker!" A high, clear, Yankee voice, very loud.

"Mr. Morris of Vermont," the guard said. "Federalist."

The Yankee voice went on and on.

The guard nodded. "Mr. Morris will withhold his vote." Vermont's two congressmen had been split, each neutralizing the other. Now Mr. Morris would let his democratic opposite prevail.

"Vermont in Mr. J.'s column," the guard said.

Maryland, evenly divided, four to four, took the floor. The four Federalists would withhold their vote; the four Democrats, among them Sam Smith, would carry the state.

Sure enough, as agreed, they were following Mr. Bayard's lead.

Shouts from the floor.

"Motion to make it unanimous for Mr. J.," the guard said.

More shouts, raw anger vibrating through the now utterly silent rotunda. One voice began to dominate, loud, strident.

"Mr. Esmonds of Connecticut says he'll die before he'll vote for Mr. J."

The voice went on and on.

"Says Connecticut will secede before it casts a vote of perfidy. Won't be party to the chaos and ruin Mr. J. will bring."

Someone called the guard from within, and he disappeared. A taciturn man with a hank of black hair and a long, black truncheon took his place, legs spread, both hands gripping the club. No information from him.

Danny was on her feet hopping up and down, trying to see over the brute's shoulder. Shouts and screams echoed from the floor. The chair howled for order, the gavel ringing like pistol shots. She jumped up and caught an image of a fist flying toward a face that disappeared. A roar of disapproval.

"Order! Order! Order!" the chair screamed.

The excitement inside infected the rotunda. Men and women were standing, on benches, on boxes, waving their arms and shouting. They surged around the entrances, blocking her view. She was in a fury; she pushed and yelled—

Someone burst from the floor, member or clerk, she didn't know, and bellowed, "It's busting wide open!"

"Danny . . ." Dimly she heard the voice.

"Danny!" She whirled. Carl sagged on the bench, both hands pressed to his chest, a desperate look in his eyes, a look she recognized with sheer horror as that of a wounded animal.

"Carl! For God's sake!" She got an arm around him just as his head rolled back and he made a terrible choking noise. He sagged against her and started to fall forward. He was more than twice her weight, and as he tumbled to the stone floor the best she could do was cradle his head.

She screamed for someone to fetch that doctor from the floor. She tore open his cravat, buttons flying from his linen shirt. He panted, his eyelids fluttered, and a long, desperate moan burst from his lips.

"God, it hurts, it hurts!" he gasped.

"Where is that damned doctor?" Her scream was drowned in the tumult. She stroked his cheek. "Carl, Carl baby, don't, don't . . ." But she couldn't say it.

Dimly she heard the roll call going on and on; and then, as Carl Mobry gasped and choked and his breathing slowed, she heard a roar.

"Jefferson wins!" someone shouted. "Jefferson is president!"

The rotunda rang with cheers. "Jefferson! Jefferson! Jefferson!"

The noise made sort of a shield that wrapped her in her horror like a shroud as she watched her husband die. She put her head on his massive chest and sobbed, and the celebration roared on and on all around her.

10

Anchored to Montpelier by the old gentleman's stubborn grip on life, though he was rarely conscious, the Madisons awaited news of the vote with increasing anxiety. The relief when word came was like a dam breaking. Ecstatic letters from Albert Gallatin and Sam Smith, more measured remarks from Tom, rapt accounts in half a dozen friendly papers—and a shocking letter from Danny.

Now, a month later, opening another letter from Danny, Dolley felt still the sudden shock of the last: Carl dying at the very moment of their success. How life can change, turn upside down in an instant, dreams canceled, demands and responsibilities and pressures crashing around you, and not a soul to really help. She looked at Jimmy, who was reading a report forwarded from the State Department. They were in their bedroom, he lying on the big bed, pillow doubled under his head. It was nearly three in the afternoon. Dinner had been served at two. She was in her chemise, folded into a love seat with a new novel from Paris. Jimmy was older than she and sometimes he looked dangerously weary. She didn't want to think of life without him and decided she must take better care of him. . . .

By now they had had a dozen reports on the inauguration from newspapers and letters. Dolley had repeatedly to stifle something rather too much like anger; they should have been there. It was a great national pageant, and they had earned the right to be part of it. But Jimmy wouldn't hear of leaving his father to die alone.

Sighing, she settled deeper into the love seat and opened

Danny's letter. But in a minute she looked up. "Listen to this, Jimmy. She's going to keep the business!"

"But not run it herself?"

"Says that's what she intends."

"Can she do that?"

"She's clever, quick, smart as can be. And Carl taught her all about it."

"Yes, but a woman alone . . ."

"Well, some women have businesses. A few. And Danny is strong."

"She remarries; her husband will own it."

"Maybe she won't remarry."

"Well, she'll have lots of opportunities. She's a very attractive woman."

She glanced at her husband, a little surprised. He rarely seemed to notice women, but of course he did; all men did.

"Lots of detail on the inaugural; you'll want to read this. Hah! Says we were sorely missed—well, I should hope so!"

She turned over a page. "Why," she said, "Mr. Adams wasn't there. He refused? What—oh, here it is. Seems the Adamses packed everything in a wagon, called their carriage at four on the morning of the inauguration, and drove away. What was he thinking of? Isn't the outgoing president supposed to be there?"

Jimmy had put down the report. "It is strange. I don't suppose there's any rule, but you'd think . . ." His voice trailed off. "Bad form, really," he said in another moment. "He owed Tom his presence, and he owed it to the image of orderly transition. But you know, poor old devil, it tells you how hard this loss really did hit him. You remember he was always having his feelings hurt, slipping off into depression, agonizing over things, some new fuss cropping up regularly. I suppose he couldn't see this loss as just one of those things; maybe nobody could. But on the evidence of this breach of etiquette, I'd say he's going off a wounded man . . ."

"Must have hurt Tom too," she said. "They're the oldest of friends, aren't they?"

"From the beginning. From the time I was still learning my letters. Tom is hoping to smooth things over, but I'll wager he's not so sanguine after this." He sighed and added, "Though given the way Mr. Adams packed the courts before he left office, I don't know why I'm wasting sympathy on him."

It had been the small act of a desperate man terrified of a future under a new theory of government. President Adams had created dozens of new judges, Federalists all, in a series of midnight appointments in literally the last hours of his administration, saddling the new administration with hostile judges sure to fight the new government's every move. And then he'd packed his bag and gone off to Braintree in Boston's shadow, leaving his one-time friends to deal with the tangled mess of appointments he had created.

Jimmy returned to his report and she resumed reading, but in a moment she interrupted again. "Listen to this! Danny says she saw Aaron after he was sworn in as vice president, and he seemed all out of sorts. Said Tom had cut him dead. Said he went to offer congratulations and pledge he'd do all he could to make the administration successful and so forth and so on, and Tom barely touched his hand, gave him a faint smile, and turned instantly to someone else. She says Aaron was quite dismayed. Says—my, this is odd, too—she had a momentary sense of a child about to cry and then Aaron was his old self, offering her condolences even as he managed to imply that he would be more than willing to help assuage her pain."

"Really? She says that?"

She nodded. "Aaron being Aaron, you know. But Tom cutting him—"

"Well, of course. Burr destroyed himself with that little trick."

"Oh, Jimmy—"

"What? He can't be trusted, that's all. He's self-focused to the core. Sacrifice his friends, his country, everything to his own selfish hopes. You can't trust such a man."

That was Aaron's great flaw, all right, but she thought Jimmy was making much of it and said so.

"Oh, do you!" He leaped off the bed, standing with legs spread, staring at her with startling anger. She was amazed.

"He's a scoundrel. Sent that damned oaf to trick me, gambling that no one else would see the danger in time to block the tie. All purposeful, you know. And then, with the tie, he refuses to step back, he tries to steal the presidency of the United States! As if it has no more significance than the presidency of some whist club. Nobody voted for Aaron Burr for president, nobody! But he tried to steal it."

"Yes, but—"

"Dolley, damn it, there aren't any buts!"

She thought she'd better not let this get out of hand. With more asperity than she felt, she snapped, "Mr. Madison, don't you yell and curse at me!"

"I didn't curse at you."

"You said damn."

"I didn't say damn you. I said damn *it,* the whole miserable imbroglio that cost us such agony. Look, what was the opposition saying all along—that the full practice of democracy must end in mobs and violence, that the common man can't control himself. And what happens? We win and we can't control ourselves. Before we can even take office, one of our own tries to steal it all. Good God! Must have seemed we were proving their nastiest point. Now the public will be watching us twice as closely so we'll have to be twice as careful."

"Really, Jimmy."

"Really, my foot! Aaron Burr ruined himself with that action. He proved my father right. High levels of any calling demand force of character, and Mr. Burr proved he lacks that. He might as well be dead so far as this administration is concerned. No one will trust him. He's finished before he starts."

Poor Aaron. Jimmy was right, she was sure, both to the justice and to the wisdom of keeping the new vice president at arm's length. She wouldn't trust him herself on anything that mattered. But it was sad. He was a man of charm, of striking intellect, of real ability, all fatally flawed by self-focus. She could hear him making his subtle approach to Danny, self-serving to the end, Aaron being Aaron. She smiled. He was an old friend and he'd been a very good friend when she'd needed one. Jimmy and Tom might write him off, but she knew she wouldn't.

11

NORTH OF THE OHIO, APRIL 1801

Capt. Meriwether Lewis, U.S. Regular Army, First U.S. Infantry, a tall, rangy man with heavy wrists and big fists, on duty now as regimental paymaster commanding a squad of five men and an iron-fisted sergeant, a sack of banknotes lashed to a separate pack horse—pay for who knew how many soldiers scattered at their lonely forts through the vast forests north of the Ohio—rode along a lightly defined trail feeling supremely pleased with himself and his duty and life itself. It was April and spring had come to the Ohio woods. Tall hardwoods, oak and elm, ash, and here and there a shagbark hickory, were dusted with green fuzz that made them look new and innocent and somehow pure. The clean odor of earth still damp from snowmelt combined with that of new grass. Deep in the forest floor he saw flashes of color, first wildflowers, and he could hear woodpeckers boring holes from which fresh sap would dribble to catch the no-see-ums soon to appear.

It seemed to Captain Lewis that he was born to ramble. Ma wanted him back to run the plantation and maybe he'd go someday, but he had many a mile of trail to cover first, many a far-off place to see. Nowhere in the world, so it seemed to him, was he more at home than on the trail, in un-marked forest, sign of game wherever you looked if you knew how to look, long satisfying days as the sun lowered, then a rude camp, beans and bacon in a pot over a fire kept low so as not to signal everyone in creation you were there, sourdough browning in a skillet, coffee heavy with sugar in a tin cup, and then a pipe, take the first sentry rotation your-self and then roll in a blanket to sleep dreamless sleep. Maybe someday he'd go back to the plantation, but not to-day and not tomorrow.

He rode about fifty yards ahead of his men, beyond their tiresome badinage but within easy hailing distance, aware of the gentle rhythmic sound of hoofs on damp soil. Presently they came to a settlement, eight or ten houses and a store with a barn and a corral alongside.

He drew up by a community well with a horse trough. "Get a drink and water the horses, but keep the boys to-gether. We'll be moving right on."

"Yes, sir."

He headed for the store, noting a heavy man sprawled on a bench, nose crooked on his face. A horse was tied to a post and two or three others were hitched to the top rail of the corral. The near horse, a roan mare, stood with right rear hoof turned up on the toe, weight cast on her other side. Something odd there.

"Loose shoe, I think," he said, nodding toward the horse.

The fellow looked at him. "That so? 'Taint mine." There was lazy insolence in his voice.

Lewis went inside. The storekeeper was a round little man with small eyes. He wore a leather apron.

"Well," he said, "rider through here yesterday; he said that wretch Jefferson done been inaugurated. Reckon the coun-try'll go to hell now."

"I don't think so," Lewis said. "And I wouldn't call Mr. Jefferson a wretch." He could feel his heat rising.

"Well, hell," the storekeeper said, "my own personal view, he's about as fine as they come and it's high time some new blood turns the country around. But you're the first army officer I ever met who thinks like I do."

Lewis bought a half-pound of chocolate, paying more than he liked, broke it in pieces on the well cover, and passed it out to his men. Chocolate was some treat on the trail. The man with the crooked nose was gone and so were the horses.

"Which way did they go?"

"Way we come, sir," the sergeant said, pointing. His name was Rollo and he'd been with General Wayne at Fallen Timbers and he was nobody's fool. "I had my eye on 'em, but they went opposite to us."

"Good."

Riding along at their easy pace, trot a mile, walk a half mile, pause for water at every stream, he thought about the storekeeper. Damned if it wasn't true, army officers seemed Federalist to a man, especially the new ones coming in over the last two or three years when Mr. Adams was packing the army—

There! Fresh hoofprints appeared on soft dirt. He reined up. Yes, cut in from the left, way he would have gone if he'd wanted to circle the town. He followed along, studying the sign. Three horses—no, four. One favoring the right rear hoof. Within a half mile the loose shoe was evident, and in another half mile he came on the shoe itself. He glanced back. Sergeant Rollo was studying the sign, bent over in his saddle.

At a stream Lewis swung down.

"Sergeant, you and Jenkins come with me. Rest of you stand by here. Tie that pay-sack horse to a tree—I don't want him straying. Full alert, pieces primed—let yourself be surprised and you'll answer to me."

Rollo and Jenkins following, they tramped a mile in silence, climbed a hogback, came down its far side step by careful step, and saw them where he'd expected to find them, positioned for ambush in an old windfall, trees tangled and graying.

His men shook powder in their pans as Lewis drew his heavy pistol. He checked flint and priming. They were quite close when the man with the crooked nose sensed them and turned.

"Lay down your pieces slow and easy," Lewis said, voice brassy and loud. "Now, boys, you waiting for someone?"

"Why, no, Cap'n, no we wasn't. Just resting a bit. See, we're going on right now—"

"You lying son of a bitch, you were dreaming on robbing the U.S. Army, and I'm here to show you that ain't near as easy as you had it figured."

"No, that ain't it at all—"

"Jenkins, wrap their pieces around that tree."

Jenkins seized each rifle by the muzzle and swung it against a young oak. He dropped the bent barrels in a clattering heap.

"Sergeant, give this ugly bastard a kick in the balls; I want him to remember us."

The fellow cupped his hands over his groin and Rollo stepped in with an overhand smash that broke his nose with a sound like kicking a melon, and blood sheeted down his shirtfront. Rollo hit him twice low in the gut and then smashed the nose again. The bastard screamed and fell, and Rollo put two solid boots to his ribs before Lewis called him off.

"I want him alive, Sergeant."

Rollo laughed. "He'll think about us every time he breathes for a good six months."

So, Lewis thought, riding on, the men strung out behind him, couple of hours to go before camp, *Mr. Jefferson is president. Imagine that.* Lewis's plantation was two miles from Monticello and Mr. Jefferson bought all his hams from Ma's smokehouse and Lewis had lavished a case of hero worship on Jefferson for just about all his life. At least ever since his own daddy died in the Revolution, and he was only a tad then.

After a while Ma had married Captain Marks and they'd gone off to a place he had in the Carolina wilderness, and

Merry had spent most all his time in the woods, packing a rifle longer than he was, cornmeal in a sack and a piece of sowbelly, old skillet dangling from his shoulder bag, living off the land. But the plantation was his by right of being firstborn, and when he was thirteen he decided he was man enough to run it so he came home and did a right creditable job, the guidance his uncles gave him less necessary year by year.

He would go visit Monticello whenever Mr. Jefferson was home, and my, the things he learned about scientific methods and what made the weather act like it did and why tobacco wore out the land and how to use the plow with the curved moldboard Mr. Jefferson had invented and how an animal's biology wasn't all that different from our own and what books an educated man should know. Loaned him books right out of his own huge library too.

Nor was it all one way. Mr. Jefferson had never been west of the Blue Ridge, and he listened respectfully when Merry talked about tracking critters through untouched woods and dressing out a pelt for the ants to clean and how to tell the plants apart and the new plants he'd found and reading what Mr. William Bartram's wonderful new book said of his travels in the forest and going him one better, finding a plant that it looked like even Mr. Bartram, the great naturalist, didn't know about. And one day Mr. Jefferson said with a note of wonder in his voice, Why, boy, you are a first-class naturalist, self-taught and that's the best way. I believe you can match anyone in America.

Well—he was some proud!

And that's why he'd worked up his nerve and asked Mr. Jefferson—

But that brought Mary Beth Slaney to mind. He'd been nineteen then and Mary Beth eighteen, hair the color of honey, freckles all over the place, changeable eyes going green to gray, and you could never tell what she would say in that low voice that was like a fiddle when it was crying. He'd been over that night a hundred times, a thousand times. She'd been sitting on the steps of the turnstile that led to the orchard and he'd been standing, restless as always, and the quarter moon had cast just enough light to see the intensity of her expression. . . .

He'd been rattling along—she'd always said she loved to listen to him—and he'd been telling her the wonderful news he'd heard. That Mr. Jefferson, him secretary of state then way up yonder in Philadelphia, this was 1793, Mr. Jefferson wanted to send an expedition for science and whatall out into the wild unknown Far West, on to the Stony Mountains said to be as high as the Blue Ridge—and the Blue Ridge was four thousand feet in places, so he'd been told—on past the Stony Mountains and right on to the salty shores of the Pacific Ocean!

Her smile was gone; he could feel her drawing away. . . .

"And you want to go along," she said.

Her voice was small and distant, he remembered now; then he'd scarcely noticed.

"More than that—lots more. I intend to *command* it."

At which she laughed: Loud, musical laughter, bright as a bell, infuriating as a lash across his shoulders.

"Oh, Merry, sweet Merry, you can't go commanding things. You're just nineteen; no one would—"

"Why in tarnation not?" He was choking on anger. "I know the woods good as any man. I know plants and trails and tracking and the way the animals do. He said so himself!"

"Yes, but—"

"And I run the plantation and folks mind what I say. I reckon I could lead men; they'd do what I say or get a fist in the mouth. And the Indians out there, I've dealt with Indians, got along all right, I reckon I could handle—"

Abruptly his anger fled. "Oh, Mary Beth, don't you see? Across a whole *continent*! Think of it—going where ain't nobody but Indians gone and not many of them, opening hundreds of miles, maybe thousands of miles nobody knows a thing about. Why, it would be—"

She was crying. He stopped and swallowed, staring at her. "What—what's the matter?"

Then she was off the stile and in his arms. At once he was wildly excited and so was she, her mouth open and lifted to his, arms locked around his neck, her body thrust hard against his, her sweet breath warm on his face, and he ready to burst. "God, I want you, Merry. Don't talk so. It frightens me bad. Let's get married. I want you—I wake up in the night wanting you. I dream you're inside me—"

She laughed, wild note in the still night. "Listen to me, way I'm talking. Ma would kill me. But it's true. Oh, Merry darling, let's get married and make love and have wonderful children and teach them all you know—"

But he couldn't imagine giving up the great dream, and they walked back in silence; didn't even speak when they, reached her house and she walked steadily up the path to the door and she never looked back once.

Next day he wrote Mr. Jefferson asking for the command. There was no answer. Much later he learned that Mr. Jefferson had chosen some Frenchman, scientist of some sort; and then it turned out the Frenchman was a foreign agent sent here to subvert the government or somesuch and it all was canceled. Not another word about going to the Pacific.

He rode along now, thinking of Mary Beth Slaney. What would it have been like? He'd joined the army the next year, and he was happy. Ma wanted him to come back. Captain Marks had died and she'd come back from Carolina, but he had a sight of rambling yet to do. He'd decided it was a Meriwether trait, from Ma's side of the family. That's what she got for giving him the family name; it meant he was pre-destined for rambling.

But even today he could feel Mary Beth Slaney's breath sweet on his face. Still, if he'd laid her on the moss and taken her right then, she achingly ready and willing, he'd have been lost. He'd be on the plantation, locked in place, his rambling hunger stifled. Yes, and he'd be mounting Mary Beth most every night, and he'd be a man of importance in the county with a significant plantation and a family coming on. He was happier now, riding the trail, rambling, sleeping on the ground. He sighed. Mary Beth had loved him since he was thirteen; he could see that now. Lately he'd found himself thinking of having a woman for more than her body, though he liked that part of it too, but a woman for her company, for the way she saw things, for the empty place in his soul or his heart or wherever such ideas might lodge. . . .

He shook his head and at last gave rein to the thought that had been in his mind for hours. As soon as it was clear Mr. Jefferson would run for president, Lewis had thought, if he's elected, he'll have the power to *order* an expedition to the Stony Mountains and on to saltwater. And now he was elected. . . .

And it seemed to him that they were far behind, and it was long since high time they moved. The Spanish weren't the threat in the Pacific Northwest, though they kept sliding up the coast from Drake's Bay as if that's how they fancied themselves. But in fact they were weak and getting weaker. Said they controlled everything from New Orleans to San Francisco Bay, but they didn't have the faintest idea what to do with it. Look at how they'd backed down when they'd seized British trading ships on Nootka Sound above the forty-ninth parallel and the Royal Navy had run out its long guns. The Spanish couldn't wait to draw in their horns, a dying empire that before long we must gird ourselves and brush aside.

No, it was the British who posed the danger. Arrogant devils. Only now were they vacating the northwest posts up around the Great Lakes; redcoats there for years in direct violation of treaties. But in the Pacific Northwest they were free to do as they pleased, for we weren't making any real effort to claim that country.

Oh, New England merchant brigs were calling regularly, trading for sea otter pelts they carried on to China in round-the-world voyages of two and three years. But the British had the Royal Navy there, *exploring*. Captain Cook's voyages, George Vancouver's little fleet. Laying down charts; and out of charts, roots.

And the Northwest Company was striking overland from Hudson's Bay. This fellow Mackenzie, Alexander Mackenzie, he'd made it most of the way across the continent, coming down on a river he claimed was the Columbia. Well, that was *our* river, claimed by Captain Gray in the merchant brig *Columbia*; and if Mackenzie had actually reached it he'd better be right smart in vacating it, for Captain Lewis didn't suppose the United States of America would long tolerate a jackleg merchant from Hudson's Bay on its river, no matter what the Royal Navy might have to say!

Wasting time. General Washington too busy to look west, Mr. Adams too ignorant, but Mr. Jefferson knew the Far West and long had wanted to go there. . . .

The sentry at the cantonment gate in Pittsburgh stopped him. "Sir, General's had an order out for a week—checks every day—you're to report to him minute you arrive."

"General Wilkinson?"

"Yes, sir. On the double. That's what he said."

Tom Sutton was officer of the day. "How'd it go, Merry?"

Lewis fluttered his hand. "Sixes and sevens, Tom. Nothing special." He was trail whipped. He could use a bath, a fresh shave, a clean uniform. On the other hand, on the double meant on the double. He crossed fresh-scythed grass, passed the flag limp on a recently peeled pole, and entered headquarters, a long building of neatly squared logs.

"Captain Lewis, reporting as ordered."

The clerk, a corporal, went in the general's office, emerged shortly, and sat down. After five minutes he said, "You can go in now, sir." There had been no signal; the general had kept him waiting on principle. Which was all right; though he didn't like Wilkinson, he took this as the way of generals.

He stood at attention. Eventually the great man looked up.

"At ease, Lewis. Take a seat."

The general seemed to have gained another twenty pounds. His cheeks were puffy and mottled with broken veins, his eyes currents in a fat bun. He wore a heavy ring on fat hands, and the special uniform with its showy epaulets, which he obviously found elegant and Lewis found ridiculous, strained across his belly.

He tossed a letter across the desk. "This came for you." Lewis stared at him; the general was delivering mail?

"Open it!" Wilkinson said. His eyes glinted and Lewis saw he was angry. "Read it."

Of course he recognized Thomas Jefferson's hand in the address, but this all seemed damned mysterious. Then, stunned, the pages trembling in his hand, the full import of the letter dawned. The President of the United States was inviting him to Washington to serve as his private secretary. His jaw tightened. Private secretary: What the hell did that mean? Writing letters, filing papers, running errands to the Congress and the cabinet. Playing the same role to the president the corporal outside played to the general! God Almighty, next thing Mr. Jefferson would want him for a body servant!

For this he was being pulled off the trail? He studied the letter. It said he would retain the rank of captain and order of promotion in the army. As for letter writing, Mr. Jefferson wrote his own. He needed someone he could trust who had knowledge of the army and of the western country.

And then, of course, it struck him like an explosion. The western country! He planned the expedition to the Far West, he'd never given it up, he hadn't forgotten that long-ago letter from a nineteen-year-old neighbor, only now the boy was grown, a proven soldier, a leader of men!

He looked up, trying to hide his excitement. Wilkinson was staring at him, his expression a curious mix, anger giving way to envy and then to caution. Lewis at the president's elbow could put in a good word for him. Or a bad word.

"I know the contents," Wilkinson said. "He explained it all in a cover letter. So will you take it?"

Lewis shrugged. "Not much choice, I suppose."

" 'Not much choice,' " Wilkinson said, in ugly mimicry. "You're mighty calm about it. President summons a line captain, nothing very special about that. Happens all the time. I take it you know him?"

"Yes, sir."

"And you're not going to say how."

"Boyhood, sir. My family's farm is near his place."

"Constant companions, I suppose?"

"No, sir, but I knew and respected him."

"And I reckon he respected you."

"Yes, sir. I guess."

"So you were expecting this. No surprise."

"Not at all, sir. I'm surprised in the extreme."

Wilkinson was silent, conflicting emotions sweeping his face, sheer outrage that a mere line captain should vault effortlessly to the very center of things coupled with inherent cupidity—what could he do for me in that position?

"You're a funny bastard," the general said at last.

Lewis stiffened; no one called him a—

"Easy, young fellow," Wilkinson said. "As used, that's an affectionate appellation. Why the men use it on me all the time. They're always saying, 'He's a good old bastard.' "

Lewis didn't answer. The general was correct on the noun; they called him a bastard, all right. They hated him. He was arbitrary and often cruel in matters of discipline; he demanded subservience that, if you weren't careful, made you a toady; he was a political general at home in the halls of Congress but at a loss in the field, a sneak who had steadily undermined one of the great generals, Mad Anthony Wayne. . . .

And by repeated rumor, a traitor long in the pay of the Spanish, who controlled New Orleans and kept the West in a state of constant turmoil. Lewis didn't know if the rumor was true, but there was a hell of a lot of smoke for there to be no fire.

Wilkinson leaned back in his chair and talked at length of how strongly he supported Mr. Jefferson. The Democrats were no less than prayers answered. Lewis could assure the president that the army under Wilkinson would work day and night for him.

Lewis nodded dutifully; through a window behind the general he could see a prisoner in stocks. The figure was writhing, the pain in his back growing excruciating. A corporal came out of the guardhouse, shouted something at him, and went back inside.

"Well, congratulations then," Wilkinson said. "See the remount captain; I'll authorize two mounts and a pack horse. I want the president to know I sent you off in high style."

"Thank you, sir. You're very kind."

He walked out floating. The magnificent dream coming true! He'd wanted this, yearned for it, dreamed of it, plotted it, and almost given it up, ever more sure that the dream had passed him by. Now it was his! Or almost, he was certain of it. Why else would the president invite a frontier captain to be his secretary? What the hell did Meriwether Lewis know about being a secretary? Government was full of experienced men. President wanted a secretary, he'd know where to find him. But no, he reaches out to the far frontier, man who has spent years on the trail and not a moment in capital drawing rooms, and there could be just one reason, just one!

It wasn't much beyond dawn when he rode up the familiar winding path to the great domed house called Monticello. It was a month since he'd had the president's letter; he'd sent an instant acceptance and then had hurried east. In Washington he'd found a message telling him to follow on and plan to see his own family while he was here.

As he swung out of the saddle, the door opened and Mr. Jefferson emerged with a wooden case under his arm. He was wearing loose cotton trousers and muddy boots and looked little changed, tall, angular, something gentle in his demeanor, sandy hair, more gray than Lewis remembered, clubbed loosely at the back. He came down the steps with a huge smile.

"Merry, my boy!" He grasped Lewis's hand fiercely. "I was delighted with your letter. Welcome to my official family!"

"Thank you, sir. I—"

"Glad you got here today. Go right inside. Mr. Madison is having breakfast and you can join him. He'll discuss the problems and issues we face. He's riding back to Montpelier today; you can accompany him as far as your place. I sent your estimable mother a note saying you'd be along soon; I know she can't wait to see you."

It was dawning on Lewis that Mr. Jefferson didn't intend to talk about the expedition. Wasn't even going to mention the Pacific Northwest, Lewis wasn't sure what he'd expected, perhaps not immediate talk of logistics and travel problems and ultimate objectives, but a remark, at least, that would establish the base of what they were about. On the long ride from Pittsburgh he'd been over and over what he'd need, the approaches he'd take, personnel, supplies, boats, and an idea he had for a forty footer so light two men could carry it, plans revised and rethought a dozen times, pockets full of notes he was ready to spread before the president. He'd envisioned a month or two of study, analysis of plans, modifications as problems and issues arose, before he set out on the great adventure.

"Mr. Jefferson—I mean, Mr. President—"

"Run along inside. Mr. Madison will make you aware of the nuances. I'm off. Scientific rounds, you know." He tapped the case under his arm, which Lewis supposed contained instruments. "Dew levels, soil moisture content, soil temperature, all of it." He shook his head. "Records go straight to the devil when I'm away, so I must be all the more diligent when here. My! Good to see you. I'm looking forward to your assistance."

With that the president wheeled and hurried down a path toward the fields.

A young woman in housekeeper's apron opened the door. "Welcome, Captain Lewis," she said.

His surprise at her use of his name was swept away by the sudden realization that this was a beautiful woman. She was of mixed ancestry, clearly combining the best of black and white, and he supposed she was a slave though there was nothing subservient in her manner. But immediately, though she was cool and proper, a surge of desire struck him a near physical blow. His mouth fell open and he struggled for composure, off balance and embarrassed.

Just then a little boy with long, blond curls and sharp features bounded into the room. "Ma, Ma! I want a cookie and Tillie says I have to ask you."

She leaned down to put a hand on the child's head. "Beverley, you know you're supposed to stay in the kitchen. But tell Tillie it's all right."

She turned to Lewis as she opened the door to the dining room. "Please come in and have breakfast."

Suddenly he remembered her. Sally, Sally Hemings. He thought she'd been companion and nurse to one of Mr. J.'s daughters when he'd last seen her. He started to call her by name but so dignified was her carriage and so clearly was he struck by the sudden conviction that she had read his reaction only too well that he was abashed and merely murmured, "Thank you, Miz Hemings," as he followed her into the dining room.

There he found Mr. Madison absently drinking tea and reading the Bible. He appeared to be deep in the Old Testament. He was a small man, something ineffably gray about him. Lewis had met him casually several times. It was said that he had married a striking woman, but how striking could she be if she had married this little man?

"Why, Captain Lewis," Mr. Madison said, standing to offer his hand. "What a pleasant surprise." Perhaps he had overheard the talk with the president outside, for he launched without preamble into the tie that he described as precipitated by Burr. He assumed Lewis knew the rough outlines but did he understand that it had constituted the most serious threat to the democracy yet to arise? Burr, he said, was no friend of the administration, which was startling—as vice president, Burr was *part* of the administration. A viper at one's bosom apparently.

Still unsettled by his unexpected reaction to the woman outside, Lewis struggled to focus on the little secretary as he served himself eggs, bacon, hotcakes, and poured hot tea.

"Now, Captain," Mr. Madison was saying, "the immediate problem is that Mr. Adams in his waning days as president undertook to pack the courts and the officer corps of the army with Federalists. Hoping to prolong their philosophy even as the people rejected it, you see. We must undo this—restore some sort of balance."

He paused to refill his cup. Lewis mopped egg yolk and took more bacon, his mind now focused as he wondered what all this had to do with him. Immense planning would have to go into the expedition. He would need a dozen men at least, probably more, and that would mean a sizeable appropriation, which he would have to defend before Congress with carefully developed facts and projections, but Mr. Madison seemed quite unaware of plans for an expedition.

If there were, in fact, such plans. A familiar chill was settling on Lewis's spirits.

"We'll deal with the judges," Mr. Madison said, "but we look to you for the army. The president intends to reduce it by half—the crisis with France is well past—and he'll want your guidance on cutting the officer corps."

"He'll drop the Federalists?" Lewis was feeling disoriented and a little stupid.

"No, no—indeed, that raises a critical point. We must be fair in what we do. The people turned to the Democrats because they were willing to try the new vision. Now they're waiting to see what we do, and they don't expect us to turn the government upside down. Some of our own people do expect that, frankly, sort of a wholesale housecleaning: Sweep out all Federalists on the grounds that Federalists are bad per se. That attitude is a bit of a problem, actually."

He sighed, drained his cup, wiped his mouth with a cambric napkin, and pushed back from the table. "So it must be steady as she goes. But the last-minute packing must be corrected; and then in cutting the army, while we don't want to treat Federalists as targets, we must be sure we're not unfairly cutting good Democrats. You see the issue, of course. The Federalists present us as revolutionary radicals, and we must show the people that that is false."

The secretary of state was still talking in this vein as they parted at the lane leading to the Lewis plantation. There had been not a word, not a hint, on the only thing that really mattered.

• • •

Ma made a splendid dinner of ham and yams and fresh pork and succotash and corn bread and the first gleanings of the garden. She served it at two in the afternoon, all the family gathered, and it was near four when they finished the deep-dish apple pie floating in cream.

At last he rose, stretched, said as casually as he could manage, "I believe I'll ride over and see Mary Beth Slaney."

There was abrupt silence in the room.

"What?" he said.

"Well," Ma said after a moment, "you see, Mary Beth, she got married a while ago. One of the Slocum boys. Their first baby came last month."

"Oh," he said. "I see. Well . . ."

They were all watching him as if some damned calamity had overtaken him. Hell, it didn't make any difference to him. My God, she was just some girl he used to know—

"C'mon, Reuben," he said to his brother, voice rougher than he'd intended, "let's walk around, show me what you're doing with the farm. . . ."

12

WASHINGTON, FALL 1801

"Well," Jimmy said, smiling as he unfolded a letter, "It seems that I'll have seven clerks to run the State Department."

"Seven?" Dolley said. "That's all?" She liked his easy manner, so different from his tension during the Burr trouble. They were taking tea on the third floor of their new house on F Street. They had just moved in, shifting at last from Montpelier after burying poor old Colonel Madison. The dear old man had lasted too long; at graveside she had watched grief and relief wage cruel contest in Jimmy.

Now she luxuriated in the afternoon sun slanting through the open window, the tide of cool, dry air, fall's blessed relief sweeping away the miasma of summer. The village on the Potomac was coming to life, government figures reappearing, congressional session soon to begin. "Seven clerks to deal with the foreign affairs of a great nation?"

"Actually, we'll probably drop one. The president is determined to cut expenses."

"Jimmy! That's all very well, but he's doing it on your back. He won't expect any less work to be done, you know." Tom was a great man and a genius and all that, but in her view he had scarcely a practical bone in his body. He looked to Jimmy for good sense, and here he was adding to burdens already heaped to the ceiling! "Tell him you need your seven clerks and more!"

He laughed. "It'll be all right, sweetheart. They're exemplary clerks. Listen to this." He had that sly, sweet smile that came when some irony struck him, his blue eyes glinting with pleasure. She loved him most at these moments when his wit came bubbling up, his real self blessedly free of restraint.

He waved the sheet. "From Duane of the Philadelphia *Aurora*. He says the top three clerks are complete picaroons."

" 'Picaroons'? Pirates, he means? Thieves?"

"No, no. Adherents of Mr. Pickering."

"Ah. The maddest of mad dog Federalists."

"Dolley! Do you speak so of my predecessor?"

"Darling, Mr. Pickering leaves you nowhere to go but up."

"I'm to have help though. Mr. Duane says the other four clerks are varied, one a Hamiltonian, another a nothingarian—I do like that, a nothingarian! I shall keep him for the sheer elegance of his description. Then, let's see, another is a nincompoop, the last a modest man. If one must go, I suppose it should be the latter."

She poured now cold tea and took the last cookie. "Seriously, Jimmy, will you have to root them all out?"

"I don't know. God knows, the pressure is awful. Our people want them out; they'd draw and quarter 'em if they could get away with it. Say that Jacob Wagner, the chief clerk, is author of all old Pickering's mischief. Everybody wants his scalp. It's important, you know, chief clerk—more undersecretary than clerk, really. Runs the staff, sits in when I'm away, supposed to be my chief advisor. And by every account, he's a hot-blooded Federalist."

"So you'll have to let him go."

"So we'll see." He leaned over and took the cookie from her hand. "Give me the last bite; you've eaten them all!"

"We will be closing the bulk of our embassies, Mr. Wagner—Lisbon, Venice, Berlin, Saint Petersburg—they'll have to get along with chargés or consuls. Ambassadorial level only in London, Paris, and Madrid."

"But why, Mr. Madison? Berlin, Saint Petersburg, they do important work."

"We are ordered to reduce costs."

"Such closings aren't wise, sir. I wouldn't recommend—"

"I'm sure you wouldn't. But the decision has been made."

"Very well, sir." Wagner sighed and settled back in the wooden chair facing Madison's desk, which in fact was only a plain table. This square brick building flanking the President's House that State shared with the War Department was newly opened, the smell of varnish and new wood still strong, the ground outside littered with lumber scraps, weeds the only greenery. The grounds were mean and the building meaner; at least it would demonstrate to diplomats of great nations the democratic spirit now required after Federalist pomp and ceremony.

Wagner sighed again and glanced around with evident distaste. These were nothing like the elegant rooms he'd known when the government was Federalist and in Philadelphia; the change from both, he clearly thought, a great misfortune. He was a tall man, graying, with a distinctly intelligent expression; he wore black, as did Madison—really the only proper color for a gentleman no matter what Dolley said about style—the suit a bit frayed, white cravat plain, hose cotton instead of silk, shoes scuffed with dulled pewter buckles. Quite appropriate. . . .

"I've written Rufus King in London," Madison said, "asking if he'll stay on as our ambassador to Great Britain."

"A very wise choice, sir. Mr. King is exemplary."

"An ardent Federalist, but he seems to represent country, not party, in London."

"As he should, if I may say so."

"Ambassador to France will be Robert Livingston. You know he was secretary of foreign affairs under the old Continental Congress, as well as chancellor of the state of New York. Strong Democrat."

"But an excellent choice nonetheless—" He stopped short.

Madison chuckled. "You'll find, I hope, that being a Democrat is not incompatible with excellence."

A wintry smile. "Forgive me, sir. I meant Mr. Livingston is a man of recognized probity and excellent judgment."

"Part of his duties will be to disabuse France of any notion it may have from Federalist rhetoric that we intend to turn the United States into a French satellite. Not true at all."

Wagner's eyes widened. "But—"

"I know. That we would bow to France and align against Britain was an article of Federalist faith. But it was false when said, and it's false now. Understand?"

"Yes, sir. May I say . . . well, that is excellent news."

"You were expecting something else?"

"Perhaps 'fearing' is the better word."

Madison smiled. "Fear no more. Now I'd like you to give me your perceptions of the nation's foreign affairs."

Wagner had been agent if not architect of all the foreign tomfoolery that had so offended Democrats, the belittling attacks on France, the disgusting tail wagging to Britain, the sheer recklessness of shaping foreign policy to ideology; but quite to Madison's surprise, he gave a well-balanced commentary on nation after nation. Russia, the Baltic states, Prussia, France, Spain, Portugal, the Italian states, the Barbary Coast. He was a professional, a seasoned diplomat. He talked half an hour without notes, and Madison was impressed.

Then Madison saw a subtle change in his expression. "Sir?" he asked, and stopped. He clasped his hands to stop a tremor.

"What is it?"

"Will you, then, be wanting my resignation?" His lips quivered.

"We'll see," Madison said, "we'll see."

"Well, Mr. Madison," said Mr. Bayard of Delaware, "welcome to the Hill." They were on the Capitol steps, Madison on his way to see John Randolph, Chairman of the Committee on Ways and Means. A fine, cool breeze made sun-warmed stone comforting to the touch.

"Thank you, sir," Madison said. "It is a matter of, shall we say, nostalgic interest to see you again."

"I regretted your leaving the Congress," Mr. Bayard said. "Baiting you was one of the pleasures of my life."

"Yes, a fault of mine; I've always been quick to challenge intellectual inconsistency."

Bayard laughed. "Well, well, tit for tat. Not bad, not bad at all. See the pleasure we deny ourselves? Now to more serious matters, since I've chanced to encounter you."

This immediately made Madison wonder if the encounter *was* by chance. Bayard hadn't shown the least surprise at seeing him. He took Madison's arm and drew him into the shadow of a pillar and spoke in a low voice.

"I had a hand, you know, in Mr. Jefferson prevailing."

Madison nodded.

Bayard sighed. "Parenthetically, I might say, this fellow Burr is an ass. Could have had it. God knows, I held the line for him as long as I could. He'd have been much more to our taste, but damned if I'd let it go to usurpation—and civil war! But if Burr had come forward . . ."

"Ancient history now," Madison said. It had been deadly—it could have unhorsed democracy—but it was over now.

"Exactly," Bayard said. "But the point is, we did come your way. Now we're counting on you not to tear up the pea patch. We're ideological opposites, granted, but neither of us is a fool and both, I fancy, are patriots."

"Certainly, sir."

"You'll change things, yes—the prerogative of the winner. But I caution you, restrain your maddest of impulses. Not all that the Federalists have done is bad; don't throw away the good with what you see as the bad. Don't shatter our international reputation with wild and sudden changes. Most sincerely, I urge you to keep Jacob Wagner at your side. He understands our foreign connections better than any man in America. Far better than Mr. Pickering did, I might say. If you throw him out, you'll confirm the worst Federalist fears; if you keep him, you'll give us hope. I think that's important."

"Thank you, Mr. Bayard," Madison said, and offered his hand.

Inside the Capitol, Madison was impressed again. It was a fine beginning on a building for a great nation-to-be, a building for the ages. Pillars of marble, steps of stone, polished wooden floors, paneling of walnut on corridor walls, velvet ropes on brass stanchions blocking certain passages. Of course, it was a work-in-progress projected across years to come, the Senate side not even begun, the rotunda still under canvas. To reach the entrance he'd wound among stacks of lumber and a pile of stone, but the inside was reassuringly well done.

The chairman's office was suitably grand. French windows were open to a view that swept down the hill to the Potomac in the distance; a swirl of geese rose from the creek that cut the intervening swamp and he heard faint reports. John Randolph's three hounds sprawled on a Persian rug;

one raised his head and growled and Randolph rapped the desk sharply with the whip he always carried, which now lay across his blotter.

He stood, tall, thin to the point of emaciation, a tautly drawn spring in his manner though he spoke in the cultivated drawl of upper-class Virginia. Randolphs had been central to Virginia history; Madison had grown up on tales of the family, though he didn't know John well. Perhaps John Randolph was unknowable; boiling inner tensions seemed to separate him from other men, and he was given to wild tirades on the floor of the House that came dangerously close to tantrums. A strain of madness was not unknown in the family, and Madison remembered times when John looked as if his mind had fled; but he was immensely effective both for powerful intellect and his willingness to savage opponents with slashing rhetoric.

So it wasn't surprising that House Democrats, newly in the majority, gave him the committee. Of course the speaker was in charge, but he was a self-effacing man and chose to have Randolph out front. And the gentleman with his hounds and his whip on the House floor would be crucial in steering Democratic legislation. They must do something about the way Mr. Adams had packed army and courts with Federalists.

"Now, James," Randolph said, after a little courteous chat, "let's get to real things." He leveled a finger. "I'm hearing damned little about removals. Damned little! Let's get rid of these Federalist scoundrels; throw 'em out on the street in droves. Let's clean up our government, remove all taints of evil, out with these bastards, every damned one!"

"Well—"

"And start with that miserable damned Federalist traitor, Jacob Wagner; been flying the Federalist banner on the tip of his lance for years. It was he who did the dirty work, you know—led Pickering around by the nose. Pickering was a fool, never had an original idea, I suppose you know that; he didn't fart but what he asked Wagner how to manage it!"

"John—"

"So why isn't Wagner gone? Mr. Jefferson should have lowered his hand from taking the oath, pointed it at Wagner, and said, 'Git!' " The chairman was on his feet now, pacing, waving his arms, the dogs watching him alertly. "He's your man now, chief clerk in your department. Never mind why you haven't booted him yet; just tell me when, how soon? This afternoon? Tomorrow morning? For God's sake, let's get on with it!"

Madison felt a burst of rage that he forced under control. His hands shook. Randolph raised everything to fever pitch, made everything a crisis, there was no *talking* to the man.

"I haven't decided. There are crucial issues here—"

"Haven't decided! Why—"

"One moment, sir!" Madison slapped the desk so hard the lid on Randolph's ink pot flew open. One of the dogs stood. "I haven't finished, and I don't care to be interrupted!"

Randolph gazed at him open-mouthed, then dropped abruptly into his chair. "Say on," he said, anger glittering in his eyes.

Randolph was an ideologue, that was the trouble. Young Captain Lewis had absorbed the same points with sure grasp, while Randolph shouldn't have to be told. It was so simple. The electoral shift wasn't unqualified endorsement; it was a we'll-give-you-a-try move and could turn overnight. And nothing would make that turn more rapid than treating public office as spoils for the victors. In fact, they were themselves on trial. . . .

Randolph's voice went silky, the sort of turn that made him formidable in debate. "You're confused, dear friend. We had a trial, what we call an election, and we won it. Remember? People *want* us to clean house." He stood abruptly and leaned forward, both fists on the desk, whiplash in his voice. "Now, let me tell you, Mr. Secretary of State, those of us who really care about this democracy want that scoundrel Wagner out by the close of business today. Today! What is your answer?"

Madison's mood shifted; he had to struggle to avoid laughter. He stood and stretched. "Well, John, it'll be evident by the close of business today."

"Mr. Wagner," Madison said, seated at the plain table, "do you consider yourself a professional?"

"I do indeed, sir, and I try to conduct myself accordingly."

A candle guttered on the desk. It was after six, growing dark outside, supper delayed, Dolley probably worried, the other clerks long since departed. Ruefully it struck Madison that the three-block-walk home in the dark on muddy streets innocent of either sidewalks or lights would be no great pleasure.

"You're aware that you're regarded as the architect of all Mr. Pickering's excesses?"

Wagner smiled. "So I've heard. Mr. Pickering liked to use me as a lightning pole. Is that correct, Mr. Franklin's invention?" Madison nodded. "But Mr. Pickering ran the ship of state to suit himself. I carried out his orders. In fairness, I agreed with most of them." He hesitated, then added, "Should I stay on, sir, I expect I would continue to think as I do."

"The question is how you would *act*. Things will be different, not extreme but different. Can you carry out orders whether you agree or not? Give me honest advice toward what I want done, not what you may think proper?"

Wagner seemed genuinely surprised. "Why, of course, Mr. Madison," he said. "I'm a professional."

Madison gazed at his clerk. Randolph's vehemence had shaken him more than he liked, for it suggested deep divisions among Democrats that in time could become dangerous and treacherous. Yet Madison was sure—he and Tom had talked endlessly about, it—that it was crucial to set a steady course and follow it. Still, Mr. Wagner was just one man and was a huge burr under a lot of saddles among extremist Democrats. Must Madison really pick a fight even as he started?

He sighed. So be it. . . .

"I think, Mr. Wagner, that I'll not ask you to resign."

13

Dolley was on her way to the President's House for a showdown. The social season was just beginning, and Tom was
counting on her for a major diplomatic dinner he planned.
But he also had hired a professional steward from France
and had made no attempt to connect her to this worthy. She
hadn't even met him.

Taking a Frenchman in hand seemed an unlikely beginning, but then she hadn't supposed the mansion would be in
such a shabby state either. She had more sympathy now for
Mrs. Adams's laments, for the big house was essentially an
unfinished shell, beautiful on the outside where Tom had, at
least, ordered the construction debris removed, but bare on
the inside. Well, she would see about that. . . .

As she started up the mansion's walk the front door
opened and Captain Lewis emerged. The figure in the doorway, small in the bare front, made her see again the need for
a portico or wings or outbuildings or a pool . . . anything to
break that plain expanse.

Lewis wore a black suit of rakish cut with boots. Not quite
handsome—there was an angularity in his face—but he ex-
uded vigor, intelligence, force. Too much of the latter, perhaps; there was an intensity in him that seemed to crackle.

He bowed over her hand just as her little sister came dashing up the walk after her. "Dolley! Oh, I'm so glad I caught
you!" Anna's clear young voice was highly musical. She had
turned nineteen, had Dolley's coloring, and her figure already was full. Dolley felt a little outclassed though Jimmy
said that was ridiculous; Anna was just youthfully pretty

while Dolley was beautiful, and she certainly wouldn't argue with him.

She presented Captain Lewis and was startled to see on his face the look of a man smitten if not poleaxed, lips parted, eyes yearning. Force seemed to flow off him like heat rays. But even as he bowed over Anna's hand, her sister was saying with that snap in her voice that made her so popular, "There's a big picnic at Great Falls, Mr. and Mrs. Douglas are going as chaperones, they invited me. You don't mind, do you, Dolley?"

The captain's face shifted abruptly to dismay as Anna went on heedlessly, "Oh, and I met the nicest young man. A Mr. Cutts, a congressman, I think. The Douglases invited him too. There'll be twenty of us or so. I rather liked him . . ."

Seeing Lewis's stunned expression, Dolley thought, Oh, this is just too much. "Well," she said, "enjoy yourself, dear," and fled toward the mansion, shaking her head.

The single guard touched truncheon to hat brim; inside she saw a new streak on roughly plastered walls and realized the roof, faulty from the start, had sprung still another leak. Visitors were in the oval drawing room beyond the entrance hall. A child brayed with laughter, pointing at something out of Dolley's sight; and a man sprawled on a sofa, boots on the brocaded blue cover. It was part of the president's democratic philosophy that the mansion be open daily to the public. . . .

Still thinking of the captain's poleaxed expression, she went down a flight of stairs and along a vaulted passageway, massive stone groins overhead, to the big kitchen. Only one of two cooking fireplaces was in use. Chef Julien, whom she'd met, was tasting soup. A smallish man with waxed mustaches sharply pointed, cravat but no coat, soup spot on his shirt, bounded up from a desk, his expression fierce, and babbled in French. She smiled. He switched to halting English.

"*Madame, madame,* please, here is not for visitors, no, no—"

"You must be Mr. Lemaire. I'm Mrs. Madison."

His eyes widened. He was new, but she saw he'd learned cabinet names. "Yes, *madame*, but what—what—"

She switched to conversational French. "The diplomatic dinner," she said. "We must go over the details."

"Details? What details?" He frowned. His French was fluid and very rapid. She struggled to keep up. "I will design the dinner, oversee its preparation and its service. The president chooses the wine." He clucked his tongue. "I disapprove, but so be it. Nothing else is needed."

"You know the president asked me to serve as hostess?"

Lemaire sniffed. "He mentioned something to that effect. You're to charm the guests, I suppose. Make everyone welcome."

"Perhaps I should review the planning too."

"*Madame!* It is in the hands of Etienne Lemaire of Paris! Everything will be to perfection!"

She smiled and switched to rapid English. "Why don't I just tell the president that Mr. Lemaire sees no need for a hostess?"

He leaned forward, struggling to understand. "Eh?" he said. "*Pardon?* The president?"

"I'll tell him you'll brook no interference. Settles everything."

"No, no." He returned to French, but sharply slowed. "Please, *madame.* I will . . . ah, appreciate your participation."

But she saw Chef Julien smother a smile.

"*Merci,*" she said. "Tomorrow, then. But, Mr. Lemaire—hereafter we will speak in private."

His glance flicked to the others. Chef Julien was peering at the soup.

"Thank you, *madame,*" Mr. Lemaire said.

It was a good beginning.

Lewis set his mount at a swift trot down Pennsylvania Avenue toward the Capitol. Rain the day before had left churning mud that splashed his boots. Mrs. Madison was charming. She was damned handsome herself, and she had a kindly quality that made you want to sit down and talk with her—but Anna, oh, my God, what a woman! The look she'd given him even while talking about some man she'd met, a fop, probably, this Mr. Cutts. One of those fancy Dans who drew women but couldn't keep them, lacking the solid virtues of someone like, well, like Lewis, for example. He'd scarcely gone a block before he'd worked up a substantial hatred for Mr. Cutts, whoever he was.

But the *look* she'd given him—sudden, fierce as a lightning bolt, right into his eyes, clearly for him alone. Oh, she'd been attracted, all right; for an instant he'd had her full attention, her whole force of being concentrated just for him—he wouldn't forget that very soon. She was so, so—*alive*, that was the word, beautiful, yes, but that vitality . . .

And then, oddly, Mary Beth popped to mind. Which made him think of the expedition, on which not one word had been said, not one. He slowed climbing Capitol Hill, circled the unfinished building, tied the horse to a sapling. Not a hint. It seemed Mr. Jefferson really did want him as a glorified errand boy. When did men of power ever care about the dreams of underlings?

Underling he was, important for whom he represented, not for himself. A captain in the U.S. Army had a clear position, one widely respected too. He'd go back anytime, maybe soon if there was to be no expedition. He'd tell Mr. Jefferson he wasn't cut out for this, damned fish out of water; he was going back where things were clear and men were men and a captaincy meant what it meant. He scraped mud from boot soles and walked into the big building, trying to look as if he belonged when he knew every fool could tell he was a rank outsider, adrift in the halls of Congress. He pulled a kerchief to wipe his boots, thought better of it and decided to find the Ways and Means chairman's office on his own rather than humiliate himself by asking.

His mood, therefore, was less than sunny when he found the ornate door. Inside a slender youth, delicate in look and manner, stood by a bookcase examining a volume.

"Yes?" the high-pitched voice was rude and impatient.

"I'm Captain Lewis. I have a message for the chairman from the president."

The youth tossed a hank of black hair out of his eyes. "Drop it on the desk," he said, and went back to the book.

"No," Lewis said. "It's for the chairman."

"Just leave it." The youth gave him a glare. "He'll see it in due time."

Lewis took a step forward, fists unconsciously doubling. "You seem hard of hearing. This is a message from the president of the United States and it's not to lie around on some desk awaiting the pleasure of a skinny clerk! It's to be put in Mr. Randolph's hand and I'm to put it there."

That considerably exceeded his instructions, but by God, even errand boys must maintain some position. He took another step. The wretch dropped the book and stepped behind a desk. He picked up a paperweight to defend himself.

"Get away from me!"

The inner door opened and a slender man with an imperious eye appeared. He was emaciated, couldn't weigh much more than a hundred pounds, but he radiated authority.

"What the devil's going on?"

"I told him," the clerk squealed. He glared at Lewis. "Mr. Randolph doesn't like to be bothered. When he's ready he *asks* for his messages."

Lewis ignored him. "I'm Captain Lewis," he said to the chairman, "the president's secretary."

"Oh, yes. The soldier. I rather distrust soldiers."

Lewis thought that not worth comment.

"So you've brought army ways to Washington."

"Not necessarily, sir. But the president deemed the message important. It's his position on repeal of the Judiciary Act."

"And he told you to come up on the Hill, browbeat my clerk, ram your way into my office, and slap me in the face with his message?"

"Of course not, sir—"

"Tell me, Captain, have you heard of the separation of powers? Tripartite government? Independence of each branch? Not the army way, granted, but then, this isn't the army. Here the president rules the executive branch—not Congress or the courts. My goodness, when I see him next I'll ask if he's forgotten all that. He—and Mr. Madison—have already decided to keep that scoundrel of a Federalist clerk, Mr. Jacob Wagner, a hound of hell if ever one walked, keeping him against the express advice of the Congress. Now perhaps he expects to rule the Congress as well, sending his military clerk up here to abuse, threaten, demand, crash open doors, ignore all norms of gentlemanly conduct. Perhaps flying in the face of the Congress on the question of that arch picaroon has so emboldened him he now plans to rule the Congress through his ferocious soldier-clerk—"

It was ridiculous, small-minded beyond belief. For an instant it was funny and he smiled, and then a tide of anger gripped his throat. But Mr. Randolph pounced.

"You laugh, sir. You are amused. You find it a matter of comedy that the U.S. Congress should defend itself against the encroachments of the executive branch?"

Lewis stepped forward. "Mr. Chairman, a message from the president of the United States." He thrust the envelope forward and the chairman, startled, took it.

"Good day, sir," Lewis said, and left the office, fearing in another instant he would lose control.

"Ah, Merry," the president said when Lewis recounted the incident. "I take it you learned a lesson." He smiled that gentle smile that Lewis had known since boyhood, kindly, almost sweet, and yet never lacking in authority. When he was with Mr. Jefferson all his angers seemed to flee, though an insistent voice in the back of his mind told him still that this was no place for a soldier.

"I fear I did, sir." They were standing on the circular balcony looking south; in the clear air he could see Alexandria bright in the distance, the river a glittering ribbon. The president put a hand on the marble balustrade.

"Well, for the record, we're far from the frontier. Force per se doesn't work in politics. The army is behind you now, if only temporarily. But I suppose you understand."

"Yes, sir."

"When Mr. Randolph speaks to me—and he will, at the first opportunity—I'll tell him I gave you a hiding that made all he said seem mild. That should satisfy him as to lèse-majesté and at the same time irritate him, since he feels no one speaks with more force than he."

He turned, hip against the balustrade, and gazed at Lewis. "We are working tremendous change here," he said, "quietly, ruffling as few feathers as possible. But this is truly a revolution, just as that of 1776. Make no mistake. The nation was moving to a centralized system of elitism, power in the hands of the few, the wealthy made part of the government, the common people cut out, dissent literally criminalized, hereditary aristocracy in the wings, monarchy itself looming in the future. You understand this?"

"Yes, sir."

He gazed at Lewis, thumb under his chin, forefinger on his lips, pensive, thoughtful. They were of equal height, eyes on a level. Then, as if taking a plunge, the president said, "Yet, you know, it's deeper than any single nation, single society. I believe we are at the turning point of a vast transition in human society. We're moving from highly centralized and tightly controlled monarchy to a broadly diffuse form of democracy, shifting power from a wealthy elite to a broad base of the common man. We did this, here in this country, with revolution followed by a Constitution that institutionalizes the rights of the common man. The French Revolution shook the world because at the crucial moment it symbolized and articulated all the glorious possibilities of human freedom in this new form. And in its outcome it illustrated with equal force the profound dangers of loss of control and chaos that are inherent in men governing themselves as opposed to naming a king whose function, after all, has been to control them when they couldn't control themselves."

Lewis stood transfixed, thrilled by the depth of ideas. Once again Mr. Jefferson had led him into deeper waters than he'd ever experienced. He felt humbled.

Mr. Jefferson smiled. "Given all that, such change and the

changes we are making is noble work. Bigger than any of us. Never forget that. Now, we count on Mr. Randolph to move matters through Congress. We need him. We can't do it all by ourselves. We've already offended him on the Wagner matter, but I think Mr. Madison is right on that. We can't be blatantly throwing out men whose only sin was being part of the old. Same with your work in helping trim the army; we must be fair. Now, Mr. Randolph can be extreme—"

"Yes, sir. I noticed."

The president chuckled. "But we do need him. We may lose him someday—we're on a middle course and he rides out to the far edges—but let's not do so casually. In short, let's mind our manners on the Hill."

"Yes, sir." Lewis thought he'd never felt quite so profoundly a horse's ass.

14

WASHINGTON, FALL 1801

Two nations were supremely important to the young United States—Britain and France. They were the world powers before whom all other nations trembled. They were locked in war and each struggled to bring other nations to its side. Those that neither side could coerce, both sides abused. It was the duty of the new secretary of state to try to retain shreds of national dignity in the midst of war.

Britain and France. Madison decided to take them in order and invited each envoy to call. First came Edward Thornton, handsome young chap of thirty or so, the British chargé. He entered the modest State Department offices with riding crop and gloves in hand, bowed, seated himself, and crossed his legs, polished boots reflecting a shimmer of light. He was gracious, relaxed, his blue eyes direct but mild, his mustache not quite military. Yet beneath a genial, even gentle surface there was a hardness. He would be a bad man in combat, Madison thought, surprising himself a little, and probably in the diplomatic wars as well.

"Now," the secretary said, "please understand that the attacks on Britain in the Democratic press do not express our policy." He smiled. "The bark far exceeds our bite."

"Welcome news, Mr. Secretary," Thornton said politely.

"Next, I know you have been romanced by Federalist society." No flicker of response in Thornton; the man was cool. "But you should understand that to place weight on what they tell you will sever you from reality."

Thornton bowed in his chair. "I stand admonished, sir."

"Now to the real issue. High as we place our relations with Great Britain, even higher do we place our own national honor. And that honor is sorely tested by the Royal Navy's continued abuse of our trade and our ships." He watched Thornton settle deeper in the chair. It was an old issue, and he had a hunch it would bring the United States to war with Britain someday, but he wanted that date as far off as possible.

Claiming an arbitrary wartime right, Britain had fixed unilateral rules under which it already had seized American goods worth millions and doubtless would seize millions more. The United States built the best ships in the world—it was forest country; the choicest of timber was always available—and its seamen ranked with the best. It was a powerful trading nation—indeed, it already was the largest neutral shipper. Britain tried to bend that trade to its own use, and what it couldn't bend it often seized.

But even more arbitrary and outrageous, it stopped our ships on the high seas to board press gangs that simply kidnapped likely sailors to serve on its warships—pressing them into maritime slavery in a navy famous for its brutality.

"They stop your ships to search for their own deserters. Surely that is their right, sir," Thornton said.

"But for every deserter recovered, they steal ten of our men. It's clear they seize anyone they think they can use."

"And return them when an accidental seizure is reported."

Madison laughed. "Please. You have taken more than two thousand of our young seamen—scarcely a third have been returned—and that after they've given your navy years of the most brutal service."

"But surely, Mr. Madison, you understand, Great Britain is engaged in a war of great consequence with a mad tyrant—"

Madison held up a hand. "Mr. Thornton! Kindly remember that it's your war, not ours."

"Sir, with all respect, it should be the war of every man who loves democracy. Napoleon is a dictator."

"Be that as it may; studied neutrality is our policy. Certainly the president admired France in the past, but he has no illusions about its government today. But seizing our goods and kidnapping our men is not acceptable."

Thornton shifted uncomfortably on the hard chair. "But, sir," he said, "you must know that I am without authority to negotiate on such matters."

Of course that was true, nor had Madison expected more. They parted courteously but not cordially. Madison stood by the window watching the young man mount a fine mare. The horse heard a noise in the street and snapped her head around, moving away from the man as she did so. With one foot in a stirrup he was forced to hop along on the other foot. He glanced over his shoulder, and Madison stepped back from the window so that the envoy might feel that this loss of dignity had gone unobserved.

Would Thornton be wise enough to pay less attention to Federalists who revered his nation despite the abuse it meted out to its erstwhile colonies, Alexander Hamilton calling its system the best in the world and urging the United States to emulate it? Erstwhile colonies . . . that was it. The British had never forgiven us, less for turning on them, than for whipping them when they tried to do something about it. For years they had refused to honor the treaties ending the war, holding onto those forts up around the Great Lakes and arming and supplying Indians for attacks on settlers. In this and

other ways they'd abused us with a peculiar air of contempt,
as if it were somehow personal.

But stealing goods from our ships on slender pretext of le-
gality and kidnapping sailors into brutal bondage, these
were the actions of the powerful against the weak. What
made it even more difficult and irksome was the simple reality that what was so important to us was but a pinprick to the
great nations locked in war. They paid us almost no attention
except when moved to use us. Our envoys waited months for
audiences that rarely produced the courtesy of a direct response. Of course, Madison must protest, bluster, threaten—
but he knew British hostility was not likely to ease.

He watched Thornton's mare—God, that was a good-
looking horse—turn onto Pennsylvania Avenue and break
into a canter at a touch of the spurs. Sooner or later, he
thought, we'll have to fight them. . . .

France, in Madison's estimation, should be easier. We were
friends, sealed in writing by the new treaty that had solved
the problems of the last few years, problems that Madison
felt were largely caused by Federalist desires to take
Britain's side in the brutal war. French arrogance and the
greed of the strange little foreign secretary—imagine Monsieur Talleyrand demanding a bribe before he would even receive our envoys. Britain might abuse us, but it didn't
demand bribes.

But when Talleyrand saw he couldn't get away with such
effrontery and the United States was ready to join Britain he
switched to an improved tune and the friendship with France
that never should have been in question was quickly restored, John Adams having the courage to fly in his party's
face.

Louis Pichon, the recently arrived envoy from Paris, was
in some indefinable way a more modest man than Mr.
Thornton. He appeared at the appointed time, suit impeccable, linen fresh, buckles on his shoes gleaming, hair in a neat
queue, all quite beyond fault. But his features were nonde-

script, his eyes pale neutral in color, his manner very quiet. Yet it was Pichon whom the French government had sent to Berlin to let young Mr. Adams know that tomfoolery was over and the French wanted peace. A note from John Quincy Adams had so informed Madison, startling him profoundly. It explained so much about President Adams's turnabout. He'd been willing to defy his party because he knew he could trust the latest overture: It came from his son.

Pichon clearly had to be taken seriously, but that made it the more important to get things straight. Madison said firmly, "You must understand, my dear sir, that while Democrats have been friends of France, our policy remains one of total neutrality. In short, we will take no sides in your conflict with Britain, and we will permit no trespasses—specifically, French privateers will not be permitted to operate from our ports."

Pichon looked chastened. "We have always thought of Mr. Jefferson as our friend," he said tentatively.

"We are the best of friends—but within that framework."

In fact, Tom had clung longer than most to the rapt faith that the revolution in France represented a new glory of human freedom and possibility, but the Terror, the clattering guillotine, the slide into military dictatorship long since had quenched his enthusiasm for France as it stood today.

Pichon cleared his throat. "Sir," he said, "it is on that profound base of friendship that Monsieur Talleyrand counts on the United States to assist it in dealing with that evil rebel, Toussaint L'Ouverture."

"Ah, yes," Madison said. "Santo Domingo." He was surprised. Things on the Caribbean island of Hispaniola had seemed quiet. Toussaint was a political and military genius who had risen to lead his fellow black slaves in a wild revolution that had proved unstoppable. He had seized Haiti, the east end of the island, then swept across the Spanish end, Santo Domingo, ejecting all European troops and establishing an apparently benign rule over a half-million blacks, fifty thousand whites, and a like number of mulattos, the native-born long since having been killed or absorbed. The world expected quick retaliation, but Napoleon had had his hands full smashing the Second Coalition and dismembering the Holy Roman Empire; meanwhile Toussaint declared himself a loyal Frenchman and the island still a French colony. So Napoleon had named him captain general of the French army to command Santo Domingo.

Well, well—Pichon seemed to be saying that Toussaint's affection for France was not reciprocated after all. He had said he considered himself Napoleon's brother since they both had come to power in the same way. Perhaps that had not been well received in Paris.

"What do you have in mind, Mr. Pichon?"

"We intend to starve him out. We want the United States to cease all trade with him. He can't survive without food supplies and manufactured goods. Soon his people would turn on this black tyrant and welcome the return of honest French governance."

That was preposterous enough to endanger Madison's composure, but he managed a quiet response. "Well, Mr. Pichon, we have developed regular trade relations with Santo Domingo. You can see we can't abrogate them without cause."

"But, Mr. Secretary, they're blacks. Niggers. Slaves! In revolt against their masters. Surely, sir, that gives pause for reflection in your own southern states, in Virginia itself."

"That doesn't concern us," Madison said. He knew his voice had gone harsh, and he knew Pichon didn't believe him. Of course a successful slave revolt just offshore had shaken the slave-holding states to the core. Shaken Madison too. Slaveholders lived in ever-present terror of slave revolts—we always fear those whom we abuse and why not? None are slaves by choice, and many would be willing to kill us. You couldn't say that black men and women in America weren't abused; someday the ugly institution would die but meanwhile . . .

Well, that's why slaveholders resisted slaves who read, though Madison allowed reading on his plantation and was angrily criticized by other plantation men. Slaves who could read, absorb ideas, get the news, talk to their fellows—that was where organization started and organization led to revolt. That was Toussaint's story. He had a genius capacity to organize, and once he could mobilize numbers he couldn't be stopped.

"I mentioned this over tea to the president," Pichon said cautiously, "and he seemed amenable. . . ."

Well, Tom did feel even more strongly the perils of a slave revolt, and there wasn't much question that a successful black revolt off our shores would fill our own blacks with hope. And then a great many people who met with Tom when he was in his genial mood came away sure that he agreed with them. Madison feared a slave revolt, but he didn't intend to let that fear drive American foreign policy.

"We don't plan to recognize Santo Domingo nor have we been asked to do so," he said. "But we have reciprocal trade agreements, and we will maintain those."

"Ah, sir, my government will be gravely disappointed."

Madison stiffened. Did that suggest a threat? Perhaps. He stared at Pichon and found no trace of give. The Frenchman was tougher than he'd thought.

"Well," he said, his voice casual, "I'm sure our friendship in many other areas will quickly overcome disappointment."

15

WASHINGTON, FALL 1801

Matt Davis was whining again. You couldn't blame him, either; he'd been treated abominably. They were in Burr's parlor-and-room at Pensee's boardinghouse. It was the establishment's only suite and more than Burr really needed, but he always had the best even if he had to juggle accounts from time to time. He was a gentleman, after all. He had ar-

rived on a late stage and Matt had come lurching out of the
shadows and started to complain before Burr could open his
grip.

Poor Matt. Big, a bit rough in speech and manner, he was
a jewel too little recognized, his ability beyond question.
Burr had asked very little of the new administration, a mere
five federal appointments in New York City to take care of
Matt and David Gelston, and three key workers. How the
devil did Brother Jefferson suppose he'd won in New York
City, which gave him the state that gave him the whole kit
and caboodle and put him in office, but that some folks in
the city had extended themselves? And they should be rewarded, surely, could anyone disagree with that? Certainly
the Federalists now occupying the posts should be tossed out
on their ears, matter of principle.

Burr had submitted his list months ago, five names only,
mind you, reserving a plum for Matt, naval officer at the
Custom's House, one of those sinecures that paid well and
demanded little. Not a word of response. He'd written to inquire. A cool note from an underling answered; nothing had
been decided. Poor Matt had been beside himself; he'd come
to Washington and gone on to Monticello to beard the winner in his den.

"He was cold as ice," Matt said. "Looked down on me as
so much scum. Kept talking about New York and what a
quaint place it was. 'Quaint,' that was the word he used. I
told him it was a place that had worked its ass off to get him
elected."

"Yes, yes, but did you tell him why you were there?"

"Of course. He looked at me like I was dirt. Said I would
hear about it when others did. Threw me out, he did."

Burr was shocked. "Ejected you?"

"Naw, not literally. Killed me with kindness, you know,
but wasn't nothing left for me but to go." His mouth worked.
"I thought sure if I went down and explained how bad I need
an answer, he'd about have to say all right. I told him it
wasn't like I'd come in from the moon or some place; the
vice president had recommended me. Didn't cut no ice."

He gazed at Burr, something strange in his expression. "I mean," he said slowly, "you *are* the vice president, ain't you?"

Burr froze him with a glance. "That'll do, Matt," he said, and stood in dismissal. "See me when I return to New York."

"Aw, I didn't mean nothing, Aaron, please."

"Good evening, Matt."

The next day, walking two blocks to the Capitol, Burr reflected on Davis. That remark hadn't been accidental. He'd had the oaf figuratively on his knees begging forgiveness before he'd finally told him to go, but the point had gone right to the heart of things. If he couldn't deliver on a rotten five appointments, what did it mean to be vice president? Was he part of a new administration, or was he a political eunuch? This world operated on power; strip a man and the political wolves would take him overnight.

He'd been consulted on nothing. Not a word. Cabinet chosen, ambassadors appointed, his opinions not sought. Robert Livingston named to France; patriarch of the up-Hudson family, good man and good Democrat, but Burr would have been glad for some say. Point was, Burr ruled the Democrats in New York City but not in the state. The Clintons were rulers in the state, old George and his son, De-Witt. They were allied with the Livingstons and hated the Schuylers, who had been Burr patrons before their power faded. So Livingston meant trouble for Burr. He should have had some say. Should have heard of it before others did instead of learning in public what he obviously didn't know, a slap in the face much remarked upon in New York.

He climbed the long steps and passed into the rotunda with its hubbub of voices, odor of meat braising on charcoal, sour smell of beer. A dozen men stood about, voices echoing. He spied Chairman Randolph at a stand buying sausages for three sleek hounds on leashes and advanced with hand extended.

Before he could speak, Randolph leveled a finger at him and cried in a piercing voice, "Ah, the grand master of theft honors us with a visit. The betrayer, the Judas of our world, here among us! Porter, porter! Where is the damned porter?

Bring swabs, won't you, to mop the floor after the honorable *vice* president of the United States! Wherever he walks he leaves a trail of slime."

Burr stopped, appalled. The rotunda went silent, men staring. "Sir," he said, but Randolph rode him down.

"Or is it not slime at all but tears? Tears of regret, tears of loss, laments of the failure of the grandest theft since Sinbad went after the jewels of the Kublai Khan"—his voice rising to a near scream—"tears mixed with slime, sir!" The dogs, excited by the tone, were lunging and snapping.

Burr tried to get his breath. The man must be mad! "How, how dare you, sir?"

"Why, Mr. Vice President, Mr. Genius of New York, I have it on the best of authority. My old friend Samuel Osgood tells me he can prove you tried to steal the election from Mr. J."

Osgood! He was one of the great names, former postmaster general of the United States, Burr had persuaded him to stand for the New York legislature in the coup that swung the election—could he now be saying—

Burr reeled out into the sunshine, walking, walking. But it wasn't true! He'd done nothing! How could Osgood say— What proof? There was none, Osgood must be crazy. Yes, they'd pressured that miserable little Madison a bit, thought a tie would be an interesting situation, more an experiment than anything, but once it happened, he had been impeccable, he'd done nothing whatsoever to influence outcome, let them choose honestly, Burr or Jefferson, and they'd chosen and it all had been honest, honest, he hadn't made a move—

Cold anger settled over him and he walked steadily, swinging the stick like a boulevardier on the banks of the Seine . . . but with his heart racing. At the boardinghouse, hours later, an invitation from the president. Would he dine on the morrow at half after three?

So! They would sit down after all, doubtless tête-à-tête or perhaps with little Madison and the Treasury secretary, Albert Gallatin, and they would go over plans, appointments, legislation needed, Federalists to weed out . . .

But six congressmen were there, three from each party, James Bayard among them, and no cabinet officers. The conversation was general and, to Burr's ears, banal. No real talk of politics beyond a bit of joshing, Jefferson entertaining them with flights of rhetorical fancy that Burr felt didn't make much sense, the dinner soon over, the president turning them into the hall, bidding them a collective good day, disappearing . . .

One of the Democrats drew Burr aside, an upstate New York congressman whose name he'd forgotten. "Haw!" this worthy cried. "Looks like you ain't the biggest wig in New York after all. You hear about our host's letter to DeWitt Clinton?" He laughed. "I see from your eyes you haven't. Well, seems the president wants old DeWitt's ideas on appointments, plans, what matters to New York State." Burr saw raw malice in his grin. "Says no one's opinion would he value more on New York matters."

"Oh, I doubt he said that." The remark was torn from Burr's throat; instantly he regretted it.

"I seen the letter," the other crowed. "I seen the letter."

They paused at the door, Burr scarcely aware that heavy rain was falling. The president going to DeWitt Clinton? Livingston named without a word, and now the president was telling Clinton—who really was Burr's enemy at home—that he would value no opinion more? His throat was tight. He felt circled by enemies. Could the Virginian's jealous rage be so out of control that he aimed to destroy his own vice president? It made no sense. Or did it? No, not really, but. . . . There was a quiver deep in his chest. He locked his hands together. Calm, calm.

Bayard took his elbow and invited him to share his carriage. Burr accepted without thinking but was immediately sorry, for the moment they started, Bayard said, "Why didn't you come when I called? You were in Baltimore."

That again! With an effort, Burr focused his attention. "First, I swore I would do nothing to influence the outcome. I'm not a thief, sir, of elections anymore than of gold. Second, it was ridiculous. The point was not to persuade Federalists; they already were persuaded. Point was to show Democrats that I was the one of their own who could win."

Bayard threw back his head. "Had the Federalists, did you? Ho, ho. Maybe you could have a career on the boards with such pitter-patter. No, my friend, after what Hamilton had to say, they were deserting you in droves. He was mounting a major campaign against you, and I do mean major."

Alex? My God, was the whole damned world against him? Why would Alex attack him? They'd been adversaries, of course, political adversaries, but that was like appearing against another lawyer in the courtroom; it was part of the game. Yes, he'd stolen New York City from under Alex's nose, that was politics, maneuver and counter. His breath went short. Alex abusing him, the president, that impudent wretch Randolph, Matt Davis whining and complaining; by God, he'd had about enough!

He heard his own voice go soft and deadly. "What was Alex saying?"

"Suffice it to say that he considered you not qualified for the presidency."

Burr caught Bayard's arm. "What did he say, damn you; to so alarm your brethren? Did he call me despicable, dishonest, a cheat, a liar?"

Bayard jerked away. "Oh, no you don't. You shan't use me as a vehicle for a duel. You want to challenge Alex, challenge him, but don't try to use my words."

Burr beat his stick against the carriage roof. "Stop! I'll get down here."

He walked on, scarcely aware of chill rain soaking his coat. Everything, everyone, standing against him like some great malign conspiracy to destroy him when he had done nothing but work his heart out, he had won the damned election single-handedly and put that rotten Virginia blueblood in position to—

"Aaron! For Christ's sake, get in here before you drown!" It was good old Jim Wilkinson in a big carriage, two mounted soldiers looking miserable to the rear, two to the fore, coachman holding the reins and staring straight ahead. Wilkinson did know how to handle a general's pomp; he had an air about him that was fit for a ruler.

"You look as if you've lost your last friend and are coming down with consumption to boot. Let's go have a half-dozen boiling hot toddies and talk of dreams and empires."

Dreams and empires! By God, Burr thought, he could use a little such talk. His heart soared at Wilkinson's warm welcome.

"Let's," he said. "Yes, let's."

"Roughing you up, are they, Aaron?"

They'd had four hot toddies and were working on oysters wrapped in bacon rashers and broiled. The general speared another oyster and held it high. "Well, my friend, they're scum. You're one of the great men of our time, Aaron, and throwing you away indicates their pygmy scale."

He held thumb and forefinger a half inch apart. "Miniscule men, Aaron. But you wait and see—the future will belong to men of power. You stand high in that rank and so do I." He popped the oyster into his mouth and chewed noisily.

God, what a hell of a good fellow old Jim was!

Madison took the chair before the president's desk that gave him the long view down the Potomac to Alexandria. He liked this big sunny room on the southwest corner so that morning as well as afternoon sun poured in through near floor-to-ceiling windows. One was open and errant breezes fluttered voile curtains. The room was big enough for separate work stations, each heaped with the materials of a particular interest. Madison thought it was a form of genius that allowed Tom to master so much—science, astronomy, medicine, agriculture, exploration, statecraft, more expert than most experts. His own mind was nothing like that. His was deeply penetrating and drove fiercely to conclusions. Jefferson insisted that together they were a perfect team.

Albert Gallatin hurried in, quite out of breath. He was slender and saturnine, bald as an egg, a smallish man from Switzerland whose years in Pennsylvania hadn't touched his heavy accent. His mathematical brilliance far surpassed that of anyone Madison knew except Alexander Hamilton. Albert understood Alex's mysterious financial measures perfectly, and though Federalists hated him and used his accent to insist on dark foreign intrigue, anyone else as secretary of the treasury would have been unthinkable. Indeed, Bayard had warned them not to tear up Hamilton's pea patch and he should be pleased, for Albert was holding the Hamiltonian financial structure on a steady course while softening its impact on the common man and lessening the advantages Alex had lavished on the wealthy.

"Now," Albert said, after twenty minutes of parsing numbers that made Madison's head swim, "we really should turn to Mr. Burr." Albert liked Burr. They had been allies when both were congressmen. But he never left any doubt as to his loyalty.

"This person Matt Davis," Albert said. "I admit he's rude and crude, but he's close to Aaron and valuable in New York."

"Disgusting fellow," Mr. Jefferson said. "Came to my *house* seeking office. Imposed on my hospitality. Blustered about New York's significance, as if I needed lessons in counting votes."

Albert grinned. "Did you throw him out?"

"I smothered him in kindness. So polite he couldn't stand it and soon fled. And very good riddance."

Madison chuckled, but he remembered Gelston's biting comment on what New Yorkers thought of Virginia manners.

"Well," Albert said, "Burr clearly will take failure to name Davis as a declaration of war. That's all right, but it raises two questions. First, Mr. President, do you intend to support Burr as your successor whenever you decide to leave office?"

Madison felt a strange little jolt. He'd always said he wasn't ambitious and did feel that he lacked command qualities, though lately he'd begun to wonder. He dismissed the idea, yet found his heart beating more rapidly as he awaited the answer.

"And the second question?" Mr. Jefferson asked.

"Well," Albert said, "assuming you run again, do you even want Burr on the ticket?"

There was no danger of another tie; a constitutional amendment now in the works would obviate that problem.

"Interesting questions," the president said, after a pause. "Well, gentlemen, thank you for coming in."

Afterward, Albert said, "Those questions deserved answers."

"I think they were answered," Madison said.

16

WASHINGTON, LATE OCTOBER 1801

"Millie," Samuel Clark said, "she ain't going to make it."

His wife had a stern look. "Don't you write off Miss Danny. She know what she's doing."

"Woman, it's *me* what's hauling her about, and she ain't making no headway. No one wants to deal with a woman. You know what that means?"

"That's fool talk," Millie said, but her voice was small.

"Means," he went on, "she won't survive in business, and sooner or later she'll marry. She's a pretty woman. You ought to see how the mens look at her. And where'll that leave us? With Mr. Carl dead—I tell you, Millie, him going off like that so sudden, that's the worst thing ever happened to us."

"Bad for Miss Danny too," Millie said. His wife was sitting up in bed, the blanket drawn to her chin, and he saw she had that stubborn, half-angry look that told him to walk softly. But he'd been thinking hard on this and it needed to be talked on, she liked it or not. He was in his nightshirt and his old cloth slippers, pacing back and forth along the end of the bed. It was chilly, stars crackling out the window of their third-floor room with its view of the Capitol dome. The first norther had gusted in that afternoon, sign there'd be winter someday.

"This is a slave town," he said, "and don't you never forget it. You ain't out a lot, you get treated real decent in this house; but I'm out every day and let me tell you, they treat niggers like dirt. Always eyeing you, always a chance some slaver'll grab you, clap you in irons, sneak you away. Your freedom papers don't mean a thing then. You hear about it all the time. Those slave auctions down on the Eastern Branch. I been driving Miss Danny to the docks down there and you can hear 'em chanting, see some poor black devil ain't no different from you and me 'cept he ain't free, he's standing there trembling so his chains rattle, sold like a damned hog, got no more rights than a hog.

"And those bastards look at you. You can always tell a slaver; look at you like they was figuring a hog's weight. Looking in the horse's mouth—he still got his teeth? That's what they think about a black man."

"Oh, Samuel," Millie said, tugging the blanket tighter to her throat, "you fixing for trouble."

"Mr. Carl dying, that's what fixed us for trouble. He was a figure in this town, everyone respected him; and yah, lots of 'em feared him too. He wasn't a man to cross. You Mr. Carl's man, slavers didn't give you no trouble nor anyone else long as you didn't start up a fuss. But it's all different with him gone."

"Well, she'll keep the business going. That's what she said, and who can stop her?"

"Who? Everyone! Damn, woman!"

"Don't you curse in our home, Samuel Clark!"

Millie was fierce and it didn't do to cross her. "I'm sorry," he said, softening his voice. "But you don't know. A business can't go on without customers, and Mr. Carl's customers, they don't want to deal with her. I take her to some office atop a wharf and she goes up the steps all perky and bright; she comes out in ten minutes looking like she done been whipped . . ."

"That don't mean—"

"I hear it on the docks. Slave dockhands know what's going on, they listen, they don't say much but they know—"

"Sure enough," Millie cried, "they do, do they? They don't know nothing!" She slapped her chest with her doubled fist. "I *know* this girl, and she ain't going to be put down easy—"

"All right, all right, she ain't. But the weight's against her, and if she loses where does that leave us, here in this miserable city? I knew when Mr. Carl said we was coming here it was a big mistake. Philadelphia, it was different, black man didn't walk around with his breath going short all the time." He threw up his hands. "Imagine a great country like this, way it talks freedom and independence. You can look out the window of the Capitol itself and see slave auctions. Hear 'em too."

"Well, what are you saying? She ain't easy to beat, never was. Little girl she was already strong; stood up to her ma and pa—"

"We gotta think about going north, out of slave country, that's what I'm saying. I been talking a little. They say they don't have no blacks, or not many, and no slavery, you go far enough north."

"How far?"

"North end of Massachusetts. What they call Maine."

"That's crazy talk, Samuel. We'd freeze to death."

"But we'd be free."

"We free now. That's what Mr. Carl did for us."

"That's right, and I want to stay free."

"Samuel, this is ugly talk. I don't like to hear it. We ain't leaving Miss Danny no matter what happens. Now you shut your mouth and come to bed."

He judged he'd said enough—more, really, than he'd intended—he should have broken the idea of going north a little more gently. He was downright cold now, arms crossed to hold a little warmth to him, and he climbed in beside her and pulled the blanket close. Her back was to him and she didn't turn. After a while he put his hand on her hip. "I love you," he said. She didn't answer, but she covered his hand with hers. He was awake a long time and felt that she was too. At last her breathing steadied and he lay with hands laced behind his head, staring into the dark.

When Millie was sure Samuel slept, she got up cautiously and went to the kitchen. She thrust a straw into the banked fire, lighted a candle, and brewed a cup of tea. The house was very silent. She wondered if Miss Danny were crying herself to sleep, but it wasn't something to ask. The moon had risen and light flooded into the kitchen. She snuffed the candle and sat in the dark, both hands around the cup.

Samuel had frightened her, opening dangerous vistas that she knew were true. This *was* a slave city. She saw the coffles, men and women in chains marched from ships and into auction barns, marched right along city streets, heavy white men with whips driving them. Made you shudder. But for the grace of the good Lord and Mr. Carl and Miss Danny, she and Samuel could be in those coffles, marching in chains. He was right about that.

But she couldn't leave Miss Danny no matter how uncomfortable they might be. She'd been just ten herself when Danny was born on the plantation, and she'd been assigned as nurse and playmate and nanny and servant. The baby had seen a sight more of her than of her own ma and, Millie quickly divined, liked her a lot better. Indeed, she had to caution the child as the years went on—if it seemed she liked Millie better than Ma, Millie would be sent away. It was their own secret, like a little conspiracy that Ma never figured out.

Danny was six when Millie married Samuel. He was a field hand, big powerful man whose gentle manner was in contrast to the potency of his stare. No one wanted trouble with Samuel. She'd seen an inner goodness in him, and the years had proved her right. He had a way with horses; and when Danny learned that, she'd talked her pa into assigning him to the stables.

When Danny was nine she was surprised to find that Millie couldn't read and set out immediately to teach her. Millie was frightened but Danny insisted, and the process of learning proved easy and very pleasurable. Opened the whole world to her, slave woman though she was. At night she taught Samuel, and the speed with which he grasped it all amazed her. She taught him and her sister, Junie, as well. She warned Miss Danny to keep quiet about it, but after a while old Mr. Clark figured out what they were doing and he'd been some mad about it. She could still hear him yelling all over the house.

"Slaves ain't supposed to read. Gives them ideas. They'll go to putting on airs, next thing you know, you have to sell 'em."

"Sell?" Danny's slender little voice.

"Well, Daughter, you can't keep a troublemaking slave . . ."

Millie had an idea it was the first time Danny had had a clear grasp of the separation of the races. Her daddy rattling on about how a black nigger was like a piece of livestock; you owned 'em, worked 'em, fed 'em, but you didn't teach a horse or a hog to read. Millie in the next room, one part of her not wanting to listen, another part straining to hear.

Fairly soon after that Danny had lost her temper—she had a sharp temper then and did to this day—and shouted, "You're just a nigra—you're a slave. We *own* you. You *have* to do what I say!"

It had been a crucial moment. Millie remembered how she had stood still as a tree rooted in the ground, staring at the child, and then she'd said, words like pieces of falling stone, "Yore daddy can whip me, he can sell me, even kill me, I reckon, but he don't own me. *I* own me. My heart, my mind, they are *mine*. Don't nobody own them. Now you think on that."

God surely knew how hard it was, Millie turning her back

on this child she loved like her own and walking away, back
straight, shoulders squared—

"Wait! Wait, Millie." The child's voice was high and
frightened. Made her heart bleed, but she didn't turn.

"Millie—please!"

She turned then. "What?" her voice cool and remote.

"But—but you still love me, don't you?"

Cool little smile. "I reckon I do, but that don't mean—"
but Danny ran into her arms and hugged her. "I love you,
Millie."

So when Mr. Carl showed up on the plantation and went
to courting her, she said, "We can take Millie and Samuel,
can't we? I think Daddy would let 'em go. Like a wedding
present . . ."

"But, Princess," Mr. Carl said, and Millie, by chance in
the next room, felt her heart freeze. He didn't want no
slaves. And Miss Danny was going to go off with him, you
could see it writ all over her face, and she was like Millie's
own child. The more so, Millie understood, because no babies of her own had come no matter how hard she and
Samuel tried. Wasn't even that she swole up a bit and then
lost 'em, that'd make you think that someday . . . but nothing. She bleeding regular as the sun coming up.

"You see," Mr. Carl was saying, "This is slave country
and down here I don't judge folks, but I myself, I don't keep
slaves. Don't hold with the practice."

"But—but who does the work?"

"White folks, black folks, it doesn't matter. I pay 'em a
wage, they do the work, they don't I get someone who will."

Millie was edging closer to the door; she couldn't help
herself. Danny's voice was so soft and hesitant that Millie
could barely make it out. "We could set 'em free, couldn't
we? If Daddy gave 'em to us."

"I don't like it," Mr. Carl said, and Millie near fell on the
floor. Her heart was ripping and roaring in her chest. "Tell
you what," he went on. "See, no man should have the right
to tell another he's free or he ain't free. Makes him like a
god, don't you see? Here's what we'll do. I'll talk to your

pa; and if he'll let 'em go, I'll loan Samuel and Millie enough to buy themselves free. They'll both sign on the note. When we get to Philadelphia I'll hire 'em. Half of what they earn they'll get; the other half will go to pay off the note they sign to me. They'll be free, they can go, but I can come after 'em for the amount of the note. See what I mean? Then it's a business arrangement; they're working for what they get. And we won't own them."

And Millie heard Danny say, her voice stronger, "Well, nobody owns them, really," and it was all she could do to keep from dropping her broom and rushing into the room to kiss that sweet girl's cheek.

So it had been, she and Samuel had come to Philadelphia free man and wife, and three years later they'd paid that note and didn't owe a red copper, and since then they'd been putting money away in the Bank of the United States, looking to when they might buy Millie's sister, Junie, free. Junie had married Joshua, who was Samuel's brother, and they already had three children and every time they had another the cost of freeing them went up some more. But children were a blessing from God.

She sat there in the dark, watching the moonlight track across the floor, cold but not wanting to move, thinking on the barrenness of her womb and wondering if it were some kind of punishment. The prophet Isaiah made it clear the Lord God could be as swift in vengeance as in generosity and you just had to love God and pray and do your best.

She bowed her head, hands clasped around the cold cup, and went to praying as she always did, for a baby, of course, but that said, asking Him to look after Samuel. You had to watch Samuel. Good though he was, his very strength led him to strong positions, the sort of thing a black man in today's America just couldn't afford. Take this business of Santo Domingo, this Toussaint person. Samuel was thrilled, for a while he couldn't talk of nothing else, what a hero that great black man must be, pulling the slaves together, driving the whites away. Black men turning on their masters, coming in the night with machetes—way the slave folk here in

Washington talked sounded like the rebels cut off heads and gouged out eyes, taking revenge with blood flowing like rain in hurricane season. Made you shudder to think on it and yet it gave you a thrill down in your guts and down below that too, at the center of your being where your man came to join you, the idea of black folks rising up in the might of right, taking their own. . . .

Millie did much of the shopping and she talked to other black women on market day, some free, most slaves. Santo Domingo was frightening too. You wanted to hear about it, but at the same time you didn't. There was fear in the way the women talked, looking over your shoulder, turning all around, making sure no white folks were near. Revolt, maybe it was good for blacks in Santo Domingo, but she'd long since decided it was bad for black folks here. Made the whites jumpy, watchful, suspicious. They saw slave conspiracies everywhere. Two black men talking about the weather or a horse or a woman and along would come a white man. What you boys talking about? You plotting some deviltry? You move along now. We have an eye on you black scoundrels and don't you never forget it. . . . Samuel would come home shaking with rage, and it would be late before she could get him to sleep.

Heroic black men didn't sit right with whites. 'Course, good white folk like Mr. Carl and Miss Danny, like the Madisons and most of Danny's friends, but not all of them, mind you, they didn't seem to suspect every black man and woman they saw, or if they did they kept it well hid. But wasn't a one of them that would cotton to a slave revolt, who wouldn't see an uppity nigger as on the road to mayhem and murder. It made these dangerous times for black folk, free or slave, and with his admiration for Toussaint and his machete men, Samuel was at risk every time he went out.

Her hands were stiff around the cold cup and only a sliver of moonlight was left. She shook her head. They couldn't leave Miss Danny; they owed her too much and Millie loved her. But she knew Samuel was pretty close to right about the danger. Last thing he'd said before drifting away, Well, if she marries, we going to be under God knows who's thumb. We got to go.

Now, single shaft of moonlight cold as an icicle, she knew Samuel was right. If Miss Danny married . . .

17

WASHINGTON, FALL 1801

"Mr. Wagner," Madison said, "how do you assess our relations with Spain?"

"Tedious, painful, often the captive of small-minded men in New Orleans who violate treaties. But all told, more irksome than serious."

"You don't regard an open Mississippi as serious?"

"It's desirable, and naturally our western folk care about it. But they are relatively few in number, and by hook or crook what they ship usually gets through."

From the beginning there had been trouble over the lands to the south and navigation of the river. Indeed, Spain had tried to maneuver a deal closing the river to American commerce for twenty-five years, obviously hoping to split off everything beyond the Appalachians and attach it to Spanish Louisiana.

By 1795, we were strong enough to demand a treaty that moved the southern border below Natchez and opened the river to American trade. But Spanish officials in Louisiana took years to comply, and Americans still were harassed and never sure their shipments would pass.

"Mr. Wagner, get clear in your thinking that an open Mississippi is vital to the West, and the West is absolutely vital to the United States and the democracy we're building."

"Yes, sir, but—"

"No buts, Mr. Wagner. We don't carry a lot of international weight now, but we'll be a power in time, almost certainly a continental nation, and I believe our democracy will be a beacon that lights the world."

"Yes, sir, I'm sure, but meanwhile—"

"Save your doubts, sir! And understand, you and I could run aground very rapidly here. I know the line of thought that argues for cutting off the West and limiting the nation to the original thirteen. Disabuse yourself of that notion; it will never happen. Never. Now, sir, I want a report on our dealings with Spain and recommendations for improving them."

Lewis popped out of the mansion at a half run, decisions on cutting the army piling up, another damned errand of no importance, and heard someone call his name. He spun about and saw it was that tedious Mr. Wagner with the ramrod up his backside bolting from the State Department and waving his arms. Lewis had long been tempted to drag the gentleman off to a tavern and see if a glass of stout wouldn't relax him a little; they were both clerks, after all. Wagner was in shirtsleeves and a cold wind was cutting from the north. He was shivering.

"Jesus, man," Lewis said, "get over here in the lee of the building; you'll take your death."

"Thank you," Wagner said, clasping his arms over his chest. "I just wanted to ask you, you're experienced on the frontier, did you find the Spanish hostile?"

"Of course." What an odd question! "Arrogant bastards, still believe they can peel the west off this late in the day, had an encounter with a Spanish captain in Saint Louis—"

Wagner seemed to be turning blue and Lewis decided he'd better hurry. "I'll just say that it was damned unpleasant and entirely unnecessary. I was ready to teach him a lesson, but I was on his territory, so I backed off. Sum up, they're hostile as hell, and they expect to take the West from us."

"Thank you, Captain," Wagner said.

What an odd duck, Lewis thought, drew his collar closer, and hurried on.

Still, the older man's question lingered. Did it suggest the administration might be looking westward after all? Lewis had had the feeling lately that he was the only man in Washington who understood that there *was* some of the nation west of the Appalachians. In fact, the Mississippi was crucial to the West; everything depended on having it open—and not just open for the moment but securely, permanently open! It was high time to bring the Spanish to heel, and after that, the British, at least as far as the American West went. And that included the Pacific Northwest, by God, whether anyone here understood it or not.

Damn it, *that's* why it was so important to get moving. For the thousandth time he wondered if Mr. Jefferson had the faintest idea of what really was involved in moving a body of men across a continent. He hoped they wouldn't spring it on him one day and say be ready to go the next, though he'd rather hear that than the nothing he was hearing. Point was, it was ridiculous to delay. Made you wonder if they really were serious men despite all their gravity.

He was still thinking of this when he stepped into into Sim's Tavern, marking it immediately as surely the meanest hole in Washington. Yes, there was the man Mr. Jefferson had sent him to see, a fleshy fellow with a hank of black hair hanging over his eyes and a purpling complexion, crouched at a small table scribbling on foolscap with a stub pencil, left hand cupped secretively to protect his writing from others' eyes. It had been five or six days since he'd shaved and, from the look of it, since he'd changed his shirt.

He saw Lewis and his manner changed. He crouched lower, looking about as if for allies, at a window as if considering flight. He wadded the foolscap and thrust it under his coat.

"Mr. Callender?"

"I'm not—I'm not wanted! You can't do anything to me!" Voice high and squeaky.

"For God's sake, calm yourself," Lewis snapped. "I'm Captain Lewis, President Jefferson's secretary."

"Oh," Callender said, "oh." His head rolled back, his shoulders moved, tension fleeing. He grinned, the change in expression not an improvement. "So," he said, "sent his lackey, did he? And about time, too, about Goddamned time!"

He slapped the table with both hands. "Ellen!" he bawled. "Porter!"

A pretty girl with yellow braids crossed over her head and bare arms said, "Now, Mr. Callender, I told you—"

"It's all right. My friend's buying."

She glanced at Lewis. He nodded. She set a foaming glass on the table. Callender downed half with a swallow, set it down with a crash. "Ellen! Another!"

Well, Mr. Jefferson had said the man might not be in very good shape. James Thomson Callender was an editor with a roaring style that he employed heart and soul for the Democratic persuasion, struck Federalists hip and thigh to the cheers of his fellows, so the powers that be convicted him of sedition in arrant violation of the Constitution, imprisoned him for a year under the harshest possible conditions, and fined him two hundred dollars, a fortune for such a man. Paying it had stripped him of press and all he owned.

Unfortunately he had served the whole year before the Democrats were elected, so the most the new administration could do was refund the fine. The president had ordered it repaid immediately, but the marshal in Richmond, an arch-Federalist who had jurisdiction over the monies, was relying on a technical reading of the law to resist the order.

"He had a real grievance," the president had said, "but the trouble is it's gone rather madly to his head. He wants repayment immediately, which obviously I can't order until the law is sorted out. Worse, though, he wants an appointment. Postmaster of Richmond! He's totally unsuited, and the Federalist holding the position has done nothing to warrant discharge. Anyway, he's doomed to disappointment. It seems he has conceived a passion for a young woman of social position and feels that as postmaster he'll have a chance for her hand. I happen to know her father; he wouldn't let Tom in the door."

The president had tossed a small sack across the desk. "Here's fifty dollars in gold out of my pocket. Take it to him as a gesture to tide him over and explain the situation."

Now, watching this gross, unshaven man drain his glass at a swallow and belch thunderously, Lewis thought how sad that such a creature should fix on a society belle of Richmond as his ideal wife. This innate sympathy vanished, however, when Callender opened his mouth. "About time, by God. Did you bring me my money?"

Lewis started to explain.

"And the commission," Callender said, not listening. "That's what counts. I told him what I wanted, sent a letter; and by God, I expect to get it. Y'understand? Ellen! Another!"

Lewis returned to the explanation. Nothing had been decided on appointments, but the postmaster in Richmond probably would not be changed unless malfeasance on his part could be proved. As to the money, the president was advancing from his own funds a sum to ease Mr. Callender's discomfort until the fine could be remitted. He drew the sack from his pocket and Callender snatched it from his hand and shook its contents onto the table.

"Fifty dollars! Hell, man, that won't do. Fifty dollars ain't going to solve my problems." He shoved the sack into his coat pocket. "Now, you listen to me. I've earned what I want, I've paid for it, I suffered, Goddamn it, a year rotting in prison, year out of my life, year of suffering like you can't Goddamn imagine. I've paid the price and now I Goddamn well want what I want. Now! You got my commission in your pocket, good, give it to me. You ain't got it, you better get on your horse and go tell your master if he knows what's good for him, he'll—"

" 'If he knows what's good for him'?" Lewis asked.

A look of intense cunning. "Damn right. I know plenty about him. He ain't so damn noble; he ain't so perfect. Folks talk like he's some kind of god or something. Well, I can tell you he's mortal man. I know things and I can put 'em out, too. I'll publish the whole rotten story if I don't get what I want! Fifty dollars! Just a down payment on keeping me quiet, you tell him that—"

Lewis reached over and caught his shirtfront, lifted him half across the table, beer glasses crashing to the floor, drew back his fist to smash this rotten bastard into oblivion—

And stopped himself. Callender was squalling, patrons were staring, he saw the girl with the braids duck into a back room to call the owner. What, the president of the United States sent his secretary to a public tavern to thrash somebody? This was the new administration's style?

"Mr. Callender," he said, "you'd do well to watch your tongue. And I think you can forget hopes of an appointment."

Callender crouched in his chair, glaring like a rat. "I'll make him pay," he hissed. "You tell him, I'll make him pay."

Lewis walked out. He needed to wash his hands.

Mr. Jefferson got a look on his face that reminded Lewis that he was the president of the United States. There was a gentleness about him usually, an easy good humor, a kindness. It wasn't that you doubted his authority but rather that you didn't think much about it. But now it was beyond doubt. Lewis had reported on his meeting with Callender.

"Strange," the president said at last. "The old adage that good deeds make enemies seems to prove out. He'll make me pay? Who knows what he means—I suspect he has a very twisted mind, not improved by a year in Federalist jails. At any rate, that ends our efforts to help him. Have nothing further to do with him. If he calls on you, grant him no audiences. Understand?"

"Yes, sir!"

In some obscure way Lewis was relieved; but as he left Mr. Jefferson's office, the familiar darkening took hold. He felt lonely, as if he understood no one and no one understood him, and the world was sweeping along and leaving him untouched and perhaps a bit baffled, which somehow seemed his fault though he knew it wasn't. It was a cruel feeling and he knew too well that he couldn't afford to let it take real hold. His boots echoed on marble floors, and his hands were clenched into fists.

Then at the center hall of the mansion he spied Mrs. Madison sitting in the sun on the south balcony overlooking the swamp and the river. On sudden impulse he decided to join her. He liked Miss Dolley. She was kindly, wise, good humored and he always felt better about things when he talked to her.

She said she was tired; she'd been planning the big diplomatic dinner to be held next month, and Mr. Lemaire was finding her role a bit difficult to accept.

"The Frenchman?" Unconsciously Lewis's fists doubled. "Maybe I should speak to him."

She glanced at him quickly. "Ah, Merry," she said, "no, that won't be necessary."

Clearly changing the subject, she asked if he liked his role as the president's secretary.

He started quietly enough, of course he was honored and all that, but then like a field dike giving way in a freshet it all came tumbling out, wrath and longing and sort of a grief. He didn't belong here, didn't fit. He didn't understand the way people talked, what they meant. There were always implications that seemed to escape him. He was direct, a soldier, he expected things to be as they were and to deal with them. He missed the trail, deep woods, eye cocked on the weather, watching for sign, touch of danger in the air, never knowing what might happen, and then, quiet things too, the way the camp was at night when he walked the perimeter in the dark and checked the sentries. That's where he wanted to be, in the West, in the open—

And then, much to his surprise, he found himself telling her of the expedition, how Mr. Jefferson had planned one back in 1793 and he'd supposed when the call came this time that that was what was afoot. Imagine, walking a couple thousand miles into the unknown, land no explorer had

ever seen, it would be like Columbus casting off from
Genoa, Marco Polo striding across Asia! A magnificent
dream . . . but there hadn't been a word.

Then, a real fountain he was, pouring out his heart, how
he'd proposed himself to command that early expedition,
how he'd told Mary Beth Slaney and she'd laughed . . .

"Well," Miss Dolley said, "she was just a girl."

"Yes . . . she's grown now. Married. Has a baby." He wondered if he'd betrayed anything, for Miss Dolley gave him a
sharp look at that. He hurried on. "So you see, when I got his
letter, I figured—well, I mean, he wouldn't put plans like
that in a letter, you know, that anyone might see; but I figured why else would he ask me? I don't know nothing about
being a secretary."

"Well, maybe he does plan an expedition. I know he's interested in the West. Talks about it all the time."

"But then, why don't he say so?"

"Maybe for a national expedition the leader needs a—oh,
how to say it? Like a national point of view, so to speak. National attitude, comfortable dealing at the national level."

"Waiting for me to prove myself, you suppose?"

"I don't know, but it's reasonable, don't you think?"

He felt a boundless surge of energy and had to be off, and
in a moment he was walking fiercely along a rough path toward the river, boots ringing against stone. By God, it could
be! The president wasn't going to send a damned novice out
to cross the whole continent, not the sort of fellow who
didn't know any better than to go up on the Hill and threaten
Mr. Randolph's clerk, for goodness sake. You're going to
send a man across the continent, you don't know who he'll
meet and you better be able to count on him not to act the
horse's ass.

Faster and faster he walked, the river gleaming up ahead.
He always felt better when he talked to Mrs. Madison.

18

"There's going to be trouble," Andrew said. Rachel Jackson didn't answer. She saw he had that grave look that meant bad news; and for her, as he well knew, there was only one kind of bad news that really mattered: his departure.

"Spanish are acting like mad dogs," he said. "Word's coming up that they're fixing on closing the river again—stopping our trade, bottling us up like flies in amber." He smacked fist into palm. "Idiots! They still think they can split the West off from the East! Can you imagine us a separate nation, pulling our forelock to the Spanish crown so they'll let us use a river that's rightfully ours in the first place? It'll never work. So I've been thinking . . ."

She started getting that frantic feeling. He was going away, she was sure of it, she could see the signs even in the restless way he paced. The next round of circuit court was a month away; she'd been counting on that month to get herself ready. But now she was sure he would tell her something had come up, some new crisis, this time with Spain apparently, and he must go in a week or, worse still, tomorrow. Her heart began to beat rapidly and she pressed her hand to her chest. He gave her a sharp look, and she shook her head and managed a shaky smile.

Obviously the pressure on her soul went back to the terrible scandal, but why baffled her. It wasn't that anyone would say anything now, years later; and she knew she'd made a sterling reputation of her own for kindness, repaying Jesus for her rescue. But those days had torn her heart.

She was sitting in her wickerwork chair on the brick

courtyard Andrew had had laid for her between house and
her garden, which now was carefully banked for winter,
seven varieties of roses, and that just the start of the flowers.
The teapot was empty, its flame snuffed, the platter of sugar
bread bare. Early morning sun gave a golden cast to the
white planks of the house, laid vertically, seams covered
with narrow lathing. Hunter's Hill was a marvel of elegance
and luxury, as one of the few frame houses in a country
where logs were still the standard. Andrew paced and talked,
his body long and lean with that deceptive strength of the
mountain man. . . .

Did she remember David Allison coming down from
Philadelphia and whirling through like a dust devil, buying
land and selling it to speculators at home, prices rising from
the sheer energy of his purchases? He'd seemed so happy,
always laughing, looking ready to dance. He was as golden
in Tennessee as he had appeared to be in Philadelphia.

But she knew the story, for she kept the books, one ledger
for the farm, another for their land deals with location and
cost per acre and offers they'd had and rejected. Land was
the heart and soul of business in the West. Everyone dealt,
looking for prices to rise, profit in spinning parcels here and
there, swapping this for that with something to boot, buy on
credit at five cents an acre for land out in the forest and sell
on credit at ten cents. Before too long that land would be going for three and four dollars, cleared and plowed and
fenced with split rails.

Rachel Jackson knew her value in this equation, for the
home place she ran was the base on which all else stood. It
ran well because she saw to it. Sowing and reaping were
timely, yields were high, cotton was coming as a new money
crop since Mr. Whitney invented the gin over to Georgia.
They had their own gin now, doing cotton for their neighbors too. Her vegetable gardens fed the plantation; now was
canning and drying time. The hickory odor of the smokehouse lay on still morning air. They had milk cows and beef
calves for slaughter and sheep for wool and were known for
breeding stock. Fine hogs ran loose like dogs.

It was a good frontier farm; she reckoned Pa was proud of her, looking down from heaven. He'd been a great frontiersman. He'd led the first party into West Tennessee, sited Nashville on the Big Bend of the Cumberland when the Indians controlled the land and a settler had to struggle to hold his own little homestead with blockhouse and stockade, and she could see him nodding his big head when she told him that for all the luxuries Andrew showered on her, all they really needed from the outside was salt and tea and bar iron.

The mercantile business Andrew had started with Jack Coffee was more complex. They had a store at Clover Bottom hard against the Cumberland, where folks swapped their produce for strap leather, axes and knives, gunpowder and lead and the weapons to use them, factory-made calico and bonnets, pins and needles and medicines and salves and ointments, tea and coffee and sugar and salt, and all the things people got to hankering for when they built their places up to do more than just keep them alive.

There was frightful expense in bringing in such items—purchase in Philadelphia, wagon freight to Pittsburgh, flatboat down the Ohio to Louisville, overland to Nashville. Goods selling at three times Philadelphia prices still left little profit. Receipts were in barter, hard money being a precious commodity out here on the western edge of the nation. People brought in cotton, wheat, corn, tobacco, pickled pork, skins, furs, and all else for which a market might be found.

All this must be loaded on flatboats and sent down the Cumberland to the Ohio and then on to the great river for the long float to Louisiana. The boats would hold at Natchez, and if they could get through the Spanish officials they'd float to New Orleans, doorway to the world market. Some produce went to states back east and some went on to England and Europe, Tennessee wheat and corn feeding armies locked in slaughter in places with names she couldn't pronounce. Which was all right. They were far from Tennessee; she didn't have any trouble pronouncing names here.

The firm built its own flatboats, forty feet by twenty-four; downriver the boys broke them up and sold the lumber. She imagined half the houses in New Orleans were built of Tennessee flatboat lumber. Then the boys walked home, six hundred miles on the Natchez Trace, each man with his own piece and always in large groups. It was as good as a man's life to walk that Trace alone or with two or three; and you wouldn't never know if it was Indians or highwaymen, white of face and black of heart, that got them. Every bit of this had to be paid for. A shipper never made much profit, but worse, could be badly hurt if the Spanish made trouble, which one way or another they usually did, slapping on new tariffs, palms out to be greased, some miserable little official with his britches frayed waylaying honest folk with honest goods. It just made your blood boil!

That was the Spanish problem. If the river really were closed, land prices would collapse, ruining them and countless others, and there would be no market for her careful husbandry. Of course, the very idea of such a threat came to Andrew as a challenge, a call to duty. He had burning dreams and the sense he was destined to lead, Tennessee and maybe more too. The idea horrified her and yet she could hardly doubt it. He'd done so much already—congressman, senator, judge—everyone out here on the far frontier looking to him. It distressed her but it reassured her all at the same time.

Anyway, this was the man who had defied all convention to take her to Natchez when Lewis Robards had threatened her, who'd come galloping down the Natchez Trace to wed her the moment word came of the divorce, who'd stood like an oak against the storm of consequences to save her life and her sanity. Did she really expect him to see naught beyond a 640-acre fenceline? He was a national man. . . .

Yes, she remembered David Allison. Andrew had gone to Philadelphia to offer seventy thousand acres, bottom price twelve-and-a-half cents an acre. David offered twenty cents but payable in notes. Andrew took the notes over to the John B. Evans Company and endorsed them in payment for supplies to stock the store. But scarcely was he home before word followed that David had failed, his empire had col-

lapsed, he was in debtor's prison, the notes were due, and
Andrew must pay. It had been an agony that had possessed
them both and left them still in debt. Allison had died after a
year in debtor's prison, poor sad man who'd made such trouble for so many, might he rest in peace.

Andrew was coming to his point, and now she saw that
leaving wasn't the issue. He wanted to sell their holdings,
some forty thousand acres out to the west they'd collected so
painfully, and clear their debts. She nodded, liking talk of
clearing debts. And then . . . did she remember that tract
they had over by Stone's River? How choice it was: 450 very
favorable acres with two log blockhouses, holdover from the
old days but still in good shape; with a minimum of fixing
they'd be—

She stared at him, the place emerging from memory,
blockhouses like what her father had built so long ago.
Ma, God rest her soul, had done well there after Pa was
killed. Blockhouses were warm and comfortable, the top
floor bigger than the bottom so that in an attack you could
fire down as well as out, and she'd smelt the powder smoke
in their blockhouse more times than she wanted to remember. The screams and shrieks and war cries of painted men
come to kill them, terror gripping her throat like a strangling
hand, men slithering close like snakes with murder in their
faces. She shuddered. If she lived to ninety, she'd never forget that terror, her throat tightening at the very sight of an Indian. Back in those not so long ago days where she and
Andrew had started, in the log-walled compound where he'd
looked at her that day and she'd felt it all through her body,
and the next time she'd seen him she'd smiled. . . .

So he came to his point. He wanted to sell Hunter's Hill,
clear the last of their debt, and live on the smaller property.
Yet something was missing and she waited and then the answer to her last question came with the name he proposed
for the new property: *The Hermitage*. It would be a refuge; it
would protect them, it would draw him back from all his
wild wanderings, back to her where he belonged.

"And," he said, "we'll clear the decks for action." He

meant against the Spanish, and she felt a shiver of apprehension. But whatever happened then would be later, not now.

She stood and put her hands on his shoulders. "All right," she said.

"They say the militia election's set for February," Jack Coffee said. "Conway's stepping down—seems he ain't well. Some of the officers are talking you up for major general."

"Well, we want to be a mite cautious there," Jackson said. He was saddling the bay mare; he and Jack were going to the store to meet their factor who'd come up from New Orleans. Rachel had kissed Jack's cheek and gone inside.

Jackson was proud of the calm in his voice, for in fact the very idea set off a flash of desire. The notion that destiny had singled him out for great things made him sound like his head was too big for his hat, but it was true just the same. It burned in him like those rockets he'd read about in the French wars, white heat, tail of flame, riding mind and heart. Felt destined, and not just in Tennessee, either . . .

The military was his answer. He liked action, knew his own mind and didn't hesitate; something needed to be done, he'd issue the orders and lead the charge. Men had always been willing to follow him. Major general, Tennessee militia, would be just right; but that didn't make it easy.

Jackson's mind was ablaze when they rode out, which didn't prevent an appraising look at his acres, fields in dry stubble after the harvest, corn stalks to be gathered for fodder, cows grazing comfortably in the far pasture, fruit trees strawed for winter. A promising colt galloped along the rail fence as if it wanted to race; a good sign, horse that wanted to run.

It was a fine place and he hated to let it go, but it was time. That clearing the decks business, he hadn't meant to say that, though the truth does have a way of popping out. But he was always careful of Rachel. They had paid a heavy price for what would have destroyed people of less strength. His natural instinct to fight had sharpened to what in calm moments he could see was a sort of mania. And her wild discomfort in his absences was sort of a mania too.

But trouble was coming, and if it didn't come on its own he might make it himself. It was no time to be overextended, debt leaving a man vulnerable, for with this Spanish pressure, sooner or later things would pop like a stopper from a bottle left in the sun. Settlers were pouring westward, over the Cumberland Gap, down the Ohio from Pittsburgh, new state of Ohio demanding admission. Vast new areas were being broken to cultivation as Indian titles were extinguished by treaties that, right or wrong, probably would soon be violated.

Well, wrong, he'd agree to that, but the treaties made promises that there wasn't no way of keeping. Can't keep settlers from coming on for good land lying fallow. Yes, it was hunting land for Indians, but could you really keep land open for naught but hunting with settlers coming over the Cumberland Gap in ever greater streams?

The Indians whose wild attacks at dawn had driven them into blockhouse walls in the old days were mostly gone now, gone south, down to Alabama country where there was still plenty of hunting range. They brought in pelts from time to time, and he traded with them and liked them well enough. They liked to laugh, and sometimes they made him laugh too. But friendly as they could be when well separated, there'd been too much killing on both sides, too much hatred deep ingrained. Man with any experience in the West saw an Indian, he remembered his own brother killed when just a boy, his auntie wearing a bonnet day and night after the Indians took her hair, and she thanking God every day she survived at all. No, settlers coming was the way of the West, and Jackson's own experience with roving war parties told him settlers and Indians would never live together without trouble.

The road was deep-rutted clay, the horses daintily picking their way. Presently it plunged into a mile of dark woods, hickory, mostly, with a good sprinkling of chestnut and some poplar. It was natural ambush country. He didn't ex-

pect trouble, but he eased his pistol and made sure the carbine in the boot was clear. He saw Jack touch his own pistol.

Once it had all been forest like this, settlers downing a few
trees for room to scratch out a cornfield and living mostly on
game. Now countless fields like his own funneled produce
down the river; fifteen years ago a half-dozen flatboats made
the run but near five thousand had gone last year. The river
opened the world to the American West. The Spanish were
crazy to think they could stop this flow like corking a bottle.

Jackson was some disappointed in the new administration. He was a Democrat to the core and had been ready to
march when the Federalists backed down. But since then
you couldn't hardly tell that a new philosophy had come to
town. Same old business, so far as the frontier was concerned. Whatever happened to that 1795 treaty with Spain?
The Spanish took years to vacate treaty lands and still closed
the river whenever they felt like it. Any pissant official could
hold you up for days, and you had no recourse. It was all international too, Spain still dreaming of peeling off the American West into a neutral buffer state supported by the
Spanish crown. Maybe something was in planning up to
Washington, but if so they were taking their time. Still, that
little Madison was tougher than he looked and was a friend
of the West; he'd stood shoulder to shoulder with Jackson
when Tennessee was fighting for statehood in the Congress.
So there was still hope.

But Tennessee was the closest place to New Orleans, and
Jackson figured that put it on the front lines. If the United
States took action, it would call on Tennessee; if it didn't,
Tennessee might take action and call on the United States.
Find out if they had any guts in Washington. . . .

He needed that major generalcy in short, but John Sevier
stood squarely in his way. The bad blood between them went
back six years. Sevier had commanded Tennessee militia for
years, he the hero of King's Mountain, won the Revolution,
and so forth, long, long time ago. But then he was elected
governor and that threw the militia post open and Jackson
stood for election. He was twenty-seven years old at the time

and that looked plenty mature and seasoned to him. But Sevier had taken offense at his youth, it seemed. He'd jumped all over Jackson, said he was young and callow, and labeled him an upstart because he had no official military experience, though he'd led the boys into the deep woods on plenty of retaliatory raids to teach Indians they couldn't just raid settlers whenever they wanted and he'd never lost a man. But Sevier, he just acted the dog in the manger, no other word for it. He put up a nonentity, George Conway, amiable but no military flair and no national view. Figured that would leave old Sevier himself still Mr. Tennessee Military. Governor wasn't enough, you see. Like he owned the military. Finally he'd made it a test of his own reputation, and Jackson went down to humiliating defeat and that sort of treatment don't sit well. Jackson wasn't done with Sevier, not by a long shot.

Rachel said it hit pride harder than reputation. Maybe, but it was different now. He had made himself a power in West Tennessee and to be brushed aside again would be dangerous and perhaps even fatal to his hopes. Yet it was a tricky election, with scarcely a hundred senior officers voting and their interests sharply different from those of the people at large.

It was a time to think carefully.

"What I hear," Jack said, as if unburdening himself, "is that Sevier plans to run his ownself, now that his three terms as governor are over. Wants his old job back."

That was bad news—for Jackson and for Tennessee. Things were hotting up, and it would be at the national and international level. But Sevier couldn't see an inch beyond state borders. Jackson's vision was broad and sweeping; he was an American and his country was in danger. And Sevier was old, way up in his fifties someplace, and soft from sitting around for years being important. A day in the field would probably finish him. He would be a critical mistake for Tennessee. Reputation only carries you so far.

But he was still formidable. And there are many ways to serve; could Jackson risk a destructive defeat?

"Drover come in from Louisville yesterday says the talk

there is same as here—Spanish gonna close the river again,"
Jack said. "Seems they figure if they punish the West, the old
Spanish conspiracy talk in Louisville may get going again—
split the Union talk."

"Bastards!" Jackson cried. "I hate that conspiracy mouthing." Before Kentucky and Tennessee were admitted, some
of the boys flirted with Spain in hopes of getting the river
open; but now talk of separating the West on behalf of Spain
was treason! Leave it to him and he'd string a few of 'em up
to a stout oak limb and put an end to such chatter. He had his
suspicions that that scoundrel General Wilkinson was ped-
dling the same dream to the Spanish, knave selling his country for gold. By God, he ever got a chance to prove it, he'd
have the fat general dangling from the same limb!

Jack grinned. "Good thing you don't talk that way from
the bench."

Jackson calmed. The outburst had done him good. "They
hear it with the bark still on in my court," he said. "But I'll
tell you, Spanish close the river, never mind separating from
the Union. We'll go down and separate Spain from New Orleans. Throw 'em in the sea, by God, let 'em swim to Cuba!"

"So," said Jack, "I guess that election matters, don't it?"
Jack didn't say a lot but he was a pretty smart fellow.

"I'll think on it," Jackson said.

Daniel Clark was *the* merchant capitalist of New Orleans,
and every year he sent a factor north to Nashville and on to
Louisville and Cincinnati, lining up cargoes for the seagoing
brigs that came up the Mississippi. The factor this year,
whose name was Umbrick, proved to be a laconic fellow
with a gotch eye and Tennessee in his voice, probably a flat-
boatman who'd found a home with Clark. He was explaining what Jackson already knew, that Clark was the soul of
honesty but no one could guarantee that any shipment would
get through. They would take all Jackson could send, but he
would send at his own risk, not their problem until it cleared
the Spanish and was in their hands.

That alone told you how outrageous the Spanish really were, and there was plenty more in the way of outrages. You'd think a fellow as smart as James Madison could grasp the peril of the Spanish thumb on the western jugular.

"Carl Mobry died," Umbrick said. "Word come awhile back."

Jackson was sorry to hear that. He'd been shipping with Mobry for years and liked him personally. He was square. Umbrick said he'd gotten heavy, which made Jackson think of Rachel pressing her hand to her chest. Sometimes her heart went to fluttering something fierce and she was getting heavy too, though she struggled with it.

After a bit of polite palaver, Jackson asked what this would mean to his goods.

Umbrick shrugged. "I understand his widder woman plans to run the company."

"A woman? I don't know . . ."

"Me neither. She's a New Orleans girl, relation of old Dan'l somehow. I understand she's coming down. But I can find you a different shipper."

"Sounds like she's got guts," Jackson said. Rachel was all courage and ran things perfectly well. "I'll give her a try," he said, "but she'll have to be tough."

"You bet, what with the news. You hear the French are coming back? Taking over Louisiana?"

"French! What the hell are you talking about?"

"They say Spain has done signed a secret treaty to give Louisiana back to France."

"That's supposed to be for sure?"

"Hell, nothing's for sure in New Orleans. Rumors every day. But a lot of folks are listening to this one."

Jackson pondered on that after Umbrick left. It did make kind of an awful sense. New Orleans was French through and through. France had owned it for a hundred years till England took it in the French and Indian War forty-odd years ago and gave it to Spain. The dons hadn't yet made a dent in its Frenchness; you met a New Orleans man, he couldn't wait to tell you he was French, not Spanish.

Until now, at least, Jackson had admired Napoleon for his military manner and his decisive use of force, to say nothing of the fact that he was fighting the British for whom Jackson had no affection; but now, by God, the man was beginning to resemble one of those octopuses they said would come out of the sea and wrap themselves right around a ship and carry it down. He'd fought the continent to a standstill and was building up his forces for more. And you could figure losing Louisiana even forty years ago would be a burr under such a man's saddle. Big men think about righting national wrongs, and Napoleon was big.

France astride the western jugular . . .

"That could be a disaster," he said.

Coffee grunted agreement.

The thing was that while the Spanish made trouble, they actually were weak. Their colonial army was small and scattered thinly along the river clear to Saint Louis. A brigade of Tennessee militia could deal with them, though it would make a hell of an international fuss. But France was a major power and had been victorious all over Europe. Napoleon's blooded troops wouldn't worry about a Tennessee brigade.

"The French get in solid, we'll never get 'em out," he said. Clouds had been building. A cold rain began, and they went inside the log store. The river had turned slate gray, matching his sudden turn of mood. "We'll have to fight if they come. I mean, really fight. Have to get the nation behind us."

He sat in a wooden armchair, stretched his feet toward the fire, and stuffed an old cob pipe. When it was drawing right, he lighted it with a glowing coal and filled the room with fragrance. Napoleon astride the American West's lifeline? If it proved true, it would be fatal to the future. Tennessee had to get ready, and that meant that he had no choice.

"I think I'll throw a Christmas barbecue," he said. "At the new place. Butcher two or three steers and as many hogs and get 'em on the slow fires. Kegs of beer, plenty of whiskey punch. We'll lay down a floor and get the fiddlers in and have a dance, Rachel's choir for some good gospel singing. No preaching though. I'll invite all the voting officers, them and their ladies, we'll put them up all around, and we'll have one hell of a party."

He pointed his pipe stem. "And before they get too far gone, I'll talk to 'em. Tell 'em about the French and what that means if it happens and where the nation stands in the world and Tennessee stands in the nation. I'll show 'em we're on the front lines, and the day will come when the whole country will look to us to lead the way. Show them what will happen to them and their farms and their families if this comes and we knuckle under and let it stand."

He nodded to himself, mulling this over, liking it. "Now," he said, "old Sevier don't talk like that. I've heard him. His vision is about to the end of his thumb. He'll tell them how he won the revolution at King's Mountain and how he loves Tennessee and they ought to vote for him 'cause it's his right."

He was up and pacing, the excitement of it fierce in his blood.

"But I'll be telling them about real things, and I believe they'll listen. I can beat Sevier; and by God, I'm going to do it!"

And he had a secret weapon he might use, but he didn't tell Jack about that.

19

NEW ORLEANS, FALL 1801

The *Cumberland Queen* lay on the hook at English Turn, the great looping bend in the Mississippi some twenty miles below New Orleans that vessels could take against the current only when the wind was right. Danny Mobry stood at the taffrail watching mud brown water suck at the stern with an insistent chuckling noise as brown pelicans wheeled and plunged to snatch fish from the water. The *Queen* had been on anchor four days, no sign of the wind changing; a dozen ships were anchored within view.

Danny had heard of English Turn all her life; legend said it was so called because in the days when the French still ruled the Mississippi, a British warship poked its way that far up the river. Frenchmen in pirogues appeared and told the English captain that he couldn't get through, and if he did, shore batteries would blow him apart. So he turned and fled the hundred miles back down the river to the sea, while the French chuckled. New Orleans loved that story. But then, New Orleans was definitely, certifiably, everlastingly French.

Captain Mac used the time to square away his vessel, scrubbing decks and fo'c'sle of salt accumulated in a rough passage from the Chesapeake, savage water off Cape Hatteras and the tail of a hurricane in the Straits of Florida. Men deftly spliced new lines to repair frayed rigging. Spars were scraped and varnished, brightwork polished. One by one sails were laid on the deck and scrubbed, hosed down with river water from a two-man pump and hoisted to dry, snowy in the sun.

Carl had always said that Capt. William McKeever was a sound man who ran a taut ship and could be counted on to carry a cargo to Le Havre, negotiate a price, find a return cargo, and come in on time. Faced with the reality of running a shipping company alone, mistress of a dozen ships crewed by men who ranged from rough to dangerous, she had turned first to McKeever.

Shaking aside terrible memories—she thought she would never again go to the rotunda with its awful echoes—she had dressed in widow's black and set out. Samuel had driven her to the quay in the Eastern Branch where the *Cumberland Queen* was moored in the shadow of the massive frigates at the Washington Navy Yard. She knew the vessel well, but now it seemed different and almost threatening. It was a merchantman riding high in the water with its cargo discharged, a brig square rigged with two towering masts and slender three-pound guns fore and aft to ward off bumboat attack. McKeever was a stout man of about fifty, sandy hair giving way to a bald spot, blond hair matted on his arms, with a tiny wife named Molly who sailed with him on every trip.

He set out a small table on the quarterdeck near the highly varnished wheel, while Molly McKeever offered thick Turkish coffee in tiny cups that Danny understood was a welcoming ceremony. She sipped cautiously, admired the care he'd given the ship, and told him that Carl had left the company to her and she intended to run it. At that Mrs. Mac, as she said she liked to be called, sat up straight and gave Danny a dazzling smile of approval.

Captain Mac nodded. "We figured so, and I don't see why you can't do good. Carl thought you was right smart—you could tell that." That Carl had made his feelings so evident surprised her, but she said nothing as he continued, "So, yes, ma'am, I'll be right honored to sail under your orders. Carl always treated me good; you do the same and we'll get on fine."

The other captains were different. Obviously the very idea of working under a woman's direct orders disturbed them. Three flatly refused, one with a string of obscenities. She sent McKeever with his first mate and a couple of ordinaries to make sure this one didn't fire the ship as he left. She found she could rely on Captain Mac and decided to make him a 10 percent owner of the *Queen,* a share that could rise in time.

"Oh, Miz Mobry," he cried, "that's mighty fine of you. Maybe we better see how we get on."

"We'll draw the papers now to take effect in six months if all goes well."

The real difficulty was with the shippers on whom she must depend for cargoes. Many were friends and she knew others as customers, but one by one they refused to do business with her. They were full of condolences for Carl, and they urged her to sell and settle down to comfortable widowhood. She rejected four offers to buy the firm, two of them decent. As to placing cargoes with her, they really didn't think a woman alone could run such a company. They said it would all fly apart, crews would dissolve, cargoes would be stolen, in a year there would be nothing left. The losses they could suffer if she collapsed and their cargoes disappeared could put them in debtor's prison.

She felt she'd climbed the stairs over every wharf in Washington and a good many in Baltimore; it got so it took all her courage and nerve to walk up, all her strength to come down after another refusal with her shoulders squared and her chin high. Some were hostile because they felt running ships wasn't a woman's place, but most were just plain worried. Many said that if she lasted a year, then maybe . . .

A year was forever. She sat alone in the big house with its view of the Capitol and knew she was at the crisis point of her life. Selling the ships, the warehouses, all that Carl had built in thirty years seemed like killing his memory, which was all she had left. Darkness came; the building glowed in violet twilight. Tears started and she checked them. For a moment she had an overpowering desire to open the rum that Carl had liked and drink and cry, but she didn't move and the yearning passed. The building loomed in the window, now bathed in moonlight.

Gradually her sense of the Capitol changed. The image of echoing voices in the rotunda as her husband died in her arms faded toward a new perception. For this building also was a tower of bravery, crowning a hill that just the other day had been a cornfield, anchoring a city that hadn't existed, focusing a nation cradled in revolution and nurtured on dreams, all of it testament to courage and faith and conviction. In the shadow of such a totem, could she be less?

Sometime before the moon's gleam passed from the looming dome, a plan came to her. If she could find just the right customer, someone entirely new . . .

Doing so took two months of calculating, arranging, planning and proposing, including a trip by stage to Boston and back that ate up agonizing days. On her return she sold three ships for capital and loaded the *Cumberland Queen* with finished goods likely to find a market in New Orleans; hardware, notions, luxuries, French wines, satins and silks. Then, making sure Mrs. Mac was aboard and taking Millie and Samuel with her, she set out for the one place in the world where she had blood connections.

She remembered her uncle with awe. She'd been a girl when Carl snatched her away and Daniel Clark, for whom she'd been named, was a businessman of great weight. He was a master at dealing with the Spanish overlords who often made trouble for shipments from the north but for whom his trade nevertheless was a chief source of income in a province that never paid its own way to the Spanish crown.

But he hadn't achieved such eminence by being soft, and she sensed that blood ran as thin as did friendship in matters of business. He had succeeded the original Daniel Clark, founder of the business, and she remembered mainly his austerity and the firmness with which he had eliminated Ireland from his accent. Now, older herself, she could see that a certain harshness of manner probably was essential to a successor taking control, but it had become his persona. So would he be moved to help her? As factor for upriver clients, he had plenty of cargoes to place, but would he risk losses for which owners would blame him? Unlikely, she thought. But she had something to offer.

Overnight the wind shifted. Chanting sailors on the windlass hoisted the anchor as sails bellied. They made English Turn in three tacks and late that afternoon moored to the levee at New Orleans. The turrets of the cathedral were visible over the top of the levee, bearing a startling force of memory. She sent a message to her uncle: She was here with urgent business; could he see her tonight?

She sat in a folding chair on the quarterdeck watching the evening sun give a golden cast to the levee and the figures along its crest and the fishermen unloading their catches on narrow wharves lying lengthwise. Someone was cleaning fish, hurling offal into the river, where it was snatched by gulls and seabirds that fought for dangling prizes in midair. The distinctive odor of alligator musk swept over the water from the swamps beyond. It had been years since she'd been here, but the familiarity of it all brought tears to her eyes. But even wiping her eyes, she knew that this wasn't home; her mother and father were dead and she'd never been close to her older brother, who had taken their small plantation and would not welcome her. Home was the new capital of the United States.

Presently she saw a tall, slender man wearing a planter's hat and a coat of rakish cut come down the levee steps, moving rapidly with an easy grace. He mounted their gangway and tossed a salute to Captain Mac.

"Splendid-looking vessel, Captain! You bring honor to our port." His voice was clear and bright; it flashed through her mind that he probably could sing. "Madame Mobry is here?"

Captain Mac led him up to the quarterdeck.

"Daniella!" he cried. "How wonderful to see you!"

She was startled. "Do I know you?"

"Ah!" He laughed, a quick bark. "What a blow to masculine pride! You don't remember me, and I was sick with love for you. But that's the way of all tragedy, you know, the fate of the ardent lover to be cast aside on life's cruel dust heaps. I'm Henri Broussard."

"Henri?" Dimly she remembered, a tall, skinny boy with dreadful pimples who'd been a pest, often near, rarely speaking. "But—but you were just a child."

"A child! Madame, forgive me, I am two years your senior."

"You couldn't be! I was sixteen when—"

"I know too well. When Mr. Mobry swept you away to the United States, which I have detested on principle ever since. I was eighteen." He struck a gallant pose. "And passion never beats more fiercely in a man's heart than at eighteen."

When she didn't answer, he said quickly, "Forgive my chatter. I am commissioned to present you at Uncle Daniel's house at nine. It's only seven; I suggest we stroll in the twilight and reacquaint you with what once was your home."

They climbed the steps to the top of the levee, which was a promenade, wide and paved with crushed shell, orange trees in orderly rows. Couples strolled and vendors offered small glasses of lemonade and little cakes arranged fetchingly on sheets, some with languid fan overhead to drive off flies. Broussard led her along the pathway, bowing occasionally to acquaintances but not introducing her. He continued to expound on the passion he had felt for her long ago until she grew exasperated.

"Really, Henri, don't you see I'm in mourning?"

"Forgive me, Daniella," he said. "It is a joy to see you, but I do understand grief."

He said this with such feeling that she glanced up quickly, wondering if he was playing with her, but he looked quite guileless. He also looked quite startlingly handsome, his face lean, his profile dramatic. She glanced down quickly, feeling disoriented and somehow inappropriate, and immediately noticed the strength of his wrist, held before him to accommodate her arm through his. It was thick and powerful; she thought he could break things with his hands, and she noticed curls of dark hair lying against his knuckles. She was shaken in some way that she couldn't have imagined and didn't like. She looked away from him, drinking in the familiar look of what had been home and was—definitely—home no longer.

The cathedral bells were tolling for evening worship, the windows of the Cabildo were dark, government foolscap put away and workers fled. Presently they came to the market on the levee, tables under awnings loaded with fresh fish, vegetables, cuts of beef and pork; hawkers sold cups of gumbo, braised meats on sticks, bottled beer cooling in tubs of water, rum in what looked like pewter thimbles . . .

Just short of the market Henri turned down the levee and they were in the great square, with more people hurrying toward the cathedral doors that now were closing. Others strolled, laughing, men holding women close, women looking up with promise in their eyes, boys skipping and yelling and sword fighting with sticks. There seemed music everywhere, drifting on night air, fifes and fiddles and banjoes and here and there a mouth organ, plaintive and sad. Couples danced impromptu little turns to this music, rolling right into the dance and back out on walks made of crushed oyster shell, tossing coins to the players. The rhythm of it, the laughter, the careless abandon of the flow into the dance to emerge rejuvenated, invaded Danny's mood for a moment, and she too wanted to dance and then remembered and then feared Henri would forget and turn to her. But he walked on and she walked beside him, as calmly as if her heart weren't churning. How many times in her girlhood she had strolled here, noticing every hot-eyed glance from almost every man and boy she passed and acknowledging none, until Carl had swept her away to a new life.

New Orleans throbbed like a great city; she thought it more lively than Philadelphia though with eight to ten thousand people it was scarcely a sixth of that city's size. Maybe it played a city's role to the hilt because there was no other for a thousand miles in any direction. It was civilization's outpost deep in a swampy wilderness.

It was dark now, but Henri said there was ample time and steered her into a *limonadier's* shop for a glass of the sweet-tart drink that nauseated her as if in reaction to the gaiety. And then she realized it was because this was an interlude of play before the business on which everything depended.

Henri said that his mother was Daniel Clark's second cousin and so his use of uncle for Mr. Clark was a title of courtesy. Hence he and Danny were scarcely related, which seemed to please him and, oddly, pleased her too. He went on recalling the sunny days of youth, and to break from too personal a turn she asked him, what, then, had he never married?

"Oh, yes," he said, and to her surprise and mortification, she felt disappointed. He gave her an appraising glance— Was she so evident?—and continued, "Do you remember Madeleine Bercy? Very beautiful, hair like spun gold?"

Danny was suddenly conscious of her own dark curls. She nodded, growing angry with herself.

"Two lovely little boys, now five and six," he said. "I am raising them."

"You make that sound—"

"Madeleine died. Yellow fever, four years ago."

"Oh, Henri, I'm so sorry."

"As I am for your loss. We understand each other."

It passed through her mind that she wasn't entirely sorry for his loss, nor was he for hers. And that was most disconcerting of all, and she stood abruptly and said they should go. They walked on, past taverns and dance halls and a sign announcing a Quadroon Ball and the opera house where *Sylvain* by André Grétry was playing and neither spoke again.

Samuel and Millie Clark stood on the forepeak of the *Queen,* watching Miss Danny cross the levee with the handsome man and disappear. They were anxiously awaiting their own family. Samuel's brother, Joshua, and Milly's sister, Junie, who had married and now had two children. Miss Danny had sent a message to the family plantation asking her brother to give the couple a pass to town. It was too dangerous for Samuel and Millie to leave the ship; manumission papers in English wouldn't count for much in New Orleans.

Then Samuel spied his brother atop the levee, face achingly familiar but heavier, stronger, older. The difference startled him, and then watching the now thickset figure coming down the levee he saw that his little brother had grown up and looked to be a man it would be dangerous to cross. Junie, no bigger than Millie, was behind him, apron not hiding her swollen belly, her bonnet cast back on her neck.

They weren't entirely severed. Millie had taught Junie to read and write and she had taught Joshua, and every year or two a smuggled letter got through. But they needed a wealth of catching up and in the babel of words it struck Samuel as pure joy to hear the guttural French patois from the plantation. It made him see how long he'd been away and how far he'd gone and it made Maine a distant chimera, the patois and the smells of the river and the sounds of music and laughter from across the levee the reality.

Even as these impressions registered, his brother drew

him aside with startling urgency. He caught a glimpse of Junie looking near tears and then Joshua whispered in a tense voice, "You heard about Santo Domingo?"

He was surprised. Of course it was wonderful news—black men rising, forcing whites to yield, slaves no more—but then he heard his brother's hoarse whisper. "I'm going there, Samuel. Going to fight for my people."

"I thought they won the fight," Samuel said. He felt stupid and disoriented.

Joshua looked around, being sure they weren't overheard. "French'll be back. You don't think white men will roll over for black men, do you? But we'll whip them again when they come. Toussaint, he'll never give up. He's the greatest man in the world. And he needs my help."

Samuel had his wits back. "You got two little babies, and Junie looks like she got another one coming." Joshua nodded. "*They* the ones need your help, brother."

But no, Joshua intended to live free and get them free too in time, and any sacrifice, for him and for them, even up to death itself, was worth it to live free. He would steal a pirogue and run through the swamps where no white man could keep up with him, and he'd fetch up in Barataria Bay and get on one of Jean Lafitte's ships. In Barataria they don't worry about a man's color.

"Pirates," Samuel said.

"What's the difference? They prey on white folks, and white folks prey on us." He said the freebooters call regularly at Santo Domingo to fill their water butts.

"You're crazy, Joshua. You'll get caught, you'll hang."

"Nah! You should come with me. Where else a black man really free?"

"I'm free now," Samuel said, but he knew his brother had heard the hesitation in his voice.

"Is that so? You walk around free as a bird; don't doff your hat to nobody? That ain't what I hear."

"Well," he said, thinking of the streets of Washington, "a black man has to mind his manners, that's so . . ."

When they left, Millie was sputtering with indignation.

"He's crazy—leaving his family, sure to get killed. Junie about to lose her mind; figures he's already lost his."

Samuel agreed, but still he understood his brother's yearning. Santo Domingo . . . imagine black men rising and driving the oppressors into the sea. Made him hunger to be part of it too. He didn't say as much to Millie, but he understood his brother all right. . . .

It was all so familiar, Daniel Clark's home, the iron-studded oak door swinging open, the bowing black face, the interior garden with its pool and its fat goldfish, the ballroom-sized gallery straight ahead. For a moment Danny was swept back across the years, but then Henri turned her to the right and she found herself in a small study she'd never seen before. Her uncle came through a door and embraced her. He was slender with aquiline face and hard eyes. A small gold ring in his right ear made him seem a corsair. But she dismissed the thought. He kissed both her cheeks, murmured condolences, led her to a chair and pressed a glass of champagne into her hand, but she sensed his wariness. This was just what she had expected, and its effect was to firm her mood and collect her thoughts.

She laid out the situation. Mr. Clark was sympathetic but said she should sell; a woman could hardly command men of the sea who went to whores and drank themselves blind when ashore.

She put iron in her voice: She would keep her business.

"So I expected, my dear. You are a Clark. But you seek my help and I have none to give. You need cargoes and I have much to be shipped in bond for men upstream. I can't put their goods at risk, and I must tell you I think you'll fail. I had a man up the river—Umbrick, do you remember Umbrick? No? Well, I had him inquire. One man, one only, a judge in Tennessee, authorized him to ship with Carl Mobry's widow."

That was worse than she had expected. She glanced at Broussard, who was watching her with a peculiar intensity, fingers locked around one knee, his strong wrists—she jerked her eyes back to her uncle.

"Monsieur Boré is still active?" she asked. Five years before Etienne Boré had developed Louisiana's first system for mass production of sugar from cane. The process could mean real commercial sugar production, but so far that had not happened.

Clark shrugged. "He's producing and others would too, but there's no market. Our Spanish masters are trying to preserve the sugar market for Cuba, and they don't welcome ours. They threaten to withdraw their product from anyone who takes ours."

"I have a new market for sugar, Uncle," she said.

He stared at her. "You do?"

"It's not dissimilar in America, you see. Rum distilleries in Massachusetts rely on sugar from Cuba and the islands. But they also are the market, and they will freeze out any supplier who deals with their competition."

Mr. Clark smiled. "And you have a competitor?"

"Someone who wants to compete. If I can guarantee sugar, he'll build a new distillery. There's a huge market for rum and he'll have no trouble selling what he produces."

"We can supply the sugar." She saw his quick glance at Broussard. He paused, as if to consider, then said, "Yes, I can assure that. The Spanish are troublesome, you know; but in the end, when it matters, they come around. Time to time, they get a wave of alarm as they see the American West growing and they shut down the river and ruin a few men upstream, whose produce rots. Drives the Americans to fury but it doesn't hurt us. I don't accept an American shipment till the Spanish have cleared it."

He laughed. "In a way the Americans themselves cause their own problems. The Spanish aim has never changed, you see; they want to split off the American West into a separate state under their control. And this man Wilkinson keeps them convinced that they can do just that."

"Wilkinson, the American general?" She was surprised.

She'd met him at parties, an unpleasant fellow toadying to superiors.

"Yes, he's been feeding Spanish dreams for years."

"Do they pay him, Uncle?"

"I assume so, of course."

"Isn't that high treason?"

"If I were the American government, I'd hang him. Instead, they give him command of their army. Tells you about Americans, don't you think?"

She let that pass; this wasn't the time to quarrel. Avarice gleamed in his eyes as he laughed and said, "So, yes, I may have to grease a few palms, but I can supply all the sugar your man can use."

"And I have the ships to transport it," she said.

"Well, well, well!" He clapped his hands together. "This does rather change things, Daniella. This gentleman distiller of yours, my dear, who is he and where is he?"

She smiled. "Oh, Uncle, it is so fine to see you again. And to be in New Orleans. My, Henri walked me about and it was as if I had stepped back in time and was a girl again. But I am no longer a girl and I have come a great way at great expense and I have done so in utter faith that you and I could find a way to deal. And now I think you must have a little faith in me."

At which Mr. Clark threw back his head and laughed. "Child," he said, "you will do well—very well. My advice to give it up may have been quite mistaken. So, I will supply all the sugar you can carry. It will cost you nothing, but you will then repay me in manufactured goods to my order, which I, in turn, can sell here and as far up the river as Cincinnati."

He stood, bouncing on the balls of his feet with a vigor that surprised her. "Come, we will shake hands like business associates." But then, holding her hand, he said with a sly crinkle of his eyes, "But what will you do if the French come?"

"The French?"

"There is a rumor—and it seems to have a bit more prove-

nance than most rumors—that this fellow Napoleon is forcing Spain to return Louisiana to France. And why not? Forty
years of Spanish rule have scarcely dented its Frenchness,
you know; even today the Spanish are tolerated as temporary inconveniences. And the Spanish power of a century
ago is gone. They're weak, while the French are strong and
wealthy. They can take charge here and drive their empire
right up the river to Canada. Of course, that's their real
aim—to reclaim Canada."

"And how do you feel, Uncle?" she asked, conscious of
her hand still in his.

"Well, there'll always be trade, and where there's trade
I'll prosper. And then, I'm too old a fox not to understand
that the affairs of individuals are but chips on the current of
grand affairs. One can only drown if he fights such current."

He smiled and released her hand, giving her the odd sensation of being cast adrift.

"But as for you, Daniella, if the French do come, surely
they would limit shipping to their own bottoms. And then,
my dear, all your dreams must die."

She saw that he had saved this for the end and was
amused. Which was all right, for it told her exactly where
she stood.

She smiled. "Get me the sugar, Uncle, and we will prosper together. As for the French; don't give them another
thought. The Americans will never allow them on the Mississippi."

"The Americans!" Henri cried. "Why, they can't do anything. They're weak. They can scarcely stay afloat as a nation. France won't give them a thought, and rightly so."

"I'm afraid Henri is right, Daniella," Clark said. "I deal
with the Americans—even took out citizenship a year or two
ago to smooth my relations upriver. But it makes sense for
France to reclaim its American empire, and Napoleon will
brush American complaints aside as a horse flicks flies."

"Get me the sugar, Uncle," she said. "You will find that
the Americans will surprise you. I know them well, you see,
for I have become an American."

20

"Tell me, Mr. Pichon," said the president of the United States, "should we be concerned about the rumors that France intends to reacquire Louisiana in retrocession from Spain?"

Dolley Madison was startled and pained. The question seemed blunt, crude, quite uncalled for at the president's first entertainment of the diplomatic corps. It was the day so long planned on which she had worked for weeks with Mr. Lemaire, carefully weighing the nuances involved in bringing together the representatives of England, France, and Spain. Mr. Jefferson already had overruled her careful seating plan and now this untimely question.

They had just started the chestnut soup over which she'd fought Mr. Lemaire for three days and which, she noted in passing, was superb, just as she had expected. Apparently as shocked as she by such undiplomatic bluntness, the guests had paused, their spoons aloft like so many soldiers presenting arms.

The French attaché lowered his spoon and said, "Mr. President, of course I'm aware of the rumors, but my government has given me no intimation of such intention."

"Thank you, Mr. Pichon. I'm gratified to hear that. Mr. Yrujo, the rumors concern your country as well."

The Marquis de Casa Yrujo, Spain's ambassador to the United States, stiffened and bristled. Dolley held her breath. He was a startlingly handsome young man, member of a noble house of Spain, immensely wealthy, and to Dolley seemed somewhat consumed by a pride that was not quite appropriate in this most democratic of nations. But he had married her old friend, Sally McKean of Philadelphia, the governor's daughter, who seemed to adore him. Dolley darted a quick glance at Sally, fearing they were offended, but Sally was gazing rapturously at her husband.

"I have no instructions on such a subject, Mr. President," Yrujo said in his rather heavy accent, "nor knowledge of such a move. But with the greatest of respect, I must nevertheless assert it is my country's right to take such action as it may see fit without notification to any third party."

Third party . . . Dolley's uneasiness grew. The young Spaniard had skated on the edge of rudeness. But then, Mr. Jefferson's question had hardly been a model. She glanced at him; if he were offended, he concealed it.

She saw a faint smile on Jimmy's face and realized something important had transpired. The president talked on easily, pronouncing her chestnut soup a great success, reflecting on the various uses made of chestnuts and their role in the life of the black bears of Virginia. And, he asked, were his guests aware of the significance of berries ripening in the fall in preparing bears for hibernation? Soon he was developing his view that the life habits of bears simply followed circumstances of berries and falling chestnuts, for surely nature was interdependent, with little left to chance. Man, he said, who bent nature to his requirements, was the exception that proved the rule. She feared he would ramble indefinitely on biology, another of his catholic interests but poor dinner talk, when he shifted smoothly to the soup, in which he said he detected a haunting flavor of hickory-smoked bacon that must account for its perfection.

She was pleased, in part because she had gone to great lengths to get the right bacon, in greater part because it seemed no diplomatic contretemps would mar her first dinner. . . .

She had spent much of the last month on preparations. It was surprising how complex a big state dinner could become. Entertaining in her own home hardly carried the significance of such a dinner as this. By now she had won over Mr. Lemaire completely; the soup argument had been hard fought but good humored. She had made herself a buffer between him and the president, and had persuaded Mr. Jefferson to let Mr. Lemaire choose the wines, subject to approval. This had restored the Frenchman's sense of the fitness of things, and indeed, Mr. Jefferson had only overruled him once, and that on the grounds of personal preference. Dolley never let him forget the value of an ally.

But there had been so much to do! There would be three meat courses, venison, Virginia ham, and a fine veal from Pennsylvania. For the fish course, she'd arranged mountain trout from the Blue Ridge; and for appetizers following the soup, delicacies from the Chesapeake, spoon-sized crab cakes and soft shells, and tiny oysters in a sauce. . . .

Of course there was a different wine for each course, and she'd established a washing station in the basement to be sure they didn't run out of wineglasses. Mr. Jefferson had brought his own tableware from Monticello, purchased in Paris during his ambassadorial residence there, and it was excellent. Each plate was polished and checked for blemish. The table linen, inset with Flemish lace, had come from the same source; she'd had everything washed and pressed.

The table would be superb, but the building itself was another question. Its shabbiness dismayed her. It simply wasn't finished and they must do something about it before long, but she knew now wasn't the time to broach it.

The day dawned bright and clear, air crisp but not really cold. Congress was in session, and the Washington season now was in full force. The invitations were set for half after three, the usual dinner hour, and winter sunshine brightened the room. By five it would be coming on dark, and she made sure new tapers were ready in the polished girandoles.

She and Jimmy were on hand with Anna in the oval drawing room as guests began arriving. Albert Gallatin, their dour but brilliant Treasury secretary came first with Hannah, a New York City belle with whom Dolley had become close. She was greeting them when Maggie Smith walked in with her husband, Samuel, whose *National Intelligencer* could be counted on to portray things honestly with a clear grasp of the administration's intent. Maggie, whose relationship to Mr. Bayard Dolley still didn't quite grasp, was enamored of Mr. Jefferson. He bowed over her hand, holding it overlong. Danny was still in New Orleans, or she would be here.

Dolley saw Sally McKean, as she still thought of her old friend, coming in just ahead of her new husband. Mr. Jefferson hurried to greet her, remarking on Governor McKean saving democracy the day he joined with Mr. Monroe in willingness to call out troops to enforce the Constitution. He gave warm greeting to the ambassador, who in turn clicked his heels and brought Dolley's hand to his lips. Mr. Yrujo wore an expensive suit cut in the latest fashion—she wished she could get Jimmy to pay more attention to fashion—and was scarcely older than his wife. He was almost beautiful really, with curls of light brown hair cascading down his forehead, all marred by a supercilious note in hooded eyes and finely modeled lips. Dolley saw he didn't intend to be impressed.

Young Meriwether went straight to Anna when, of course, he should be circulating among the guests. Louis Pichon arrived with Madame Pichon. He struck Dolley as earnest and friendly but uncomfortable with small talk. He presented his wife, a slender, somewhat remote woman with little English. Mr. Jefferson welcomed her in polished French, at which she brightened; and soon Dolley saw her talking to Albert Gallatin, who, though Swiss, possessed French almost as a primary language.

Dolley barely had time to nudge Merry and tell him to talk to other people when Edward Thornton, the young British attaché whom Dolley found interestingly handsome, with soft brown hair and blue eyes that despite a cultivated languor were rather sharp and searching. She liked Ned and chatted with him a moment, noticing that Anna was holding Merry in vivacious talk. That sister of hers!

No one remarked on the vice president's absence. She had proposed inviting Aaron; one sharp shake of Jimmy's head answered her and she'd let it go, her own feelings mixed.

With the guests chatting over wine from trays waiters passed among them, Mr. Jefferson drew her to one side to compliment her. But she saw Mr. Lemaire approaching from the dining room and whispered urgently, "Mr. President, it's nearly time. You really should take Mrs. Yrujo in. He's the only one of full ambassador rank, and Sally's father—"

"Perish the thought, Dolley, pell-mell shall be our style, every man a king and no man his subject." He was geniality itself. "All equal, catch-as-catch-can, the absolute opposite of royal courts. Let them see the essence of democracy."

Dolley's strength as a Democrat would compare well with anyone's, but she thought this a ridiculous exercise at so formal a dinner and one sure to make eventual trouble among diplomats jealous of rank and prerogatives. But just then Mr. Lemaire appeared in the doorway and Mr. Jefferson said in a loud, warm voice, "Shall we go in?" He turned and offered *her* his arm. Of course she could do nothing but let him lead her in and seat her by his side.

There seemed a momentary confusion as people formed pairs, some matched well and some not, and came into the dining room to find places as chance might direct them. It was not at all elegant, and she thought from the tight line of Mr. Yrujo's mouth that he was offended, though others seemed placid enough. Dolley saw that Meriwether Lewis had snared Anna, led her in as if she were a special prize, and seated himself beside her.

Then, as if pell-mell wasn't distressing enough, came the president's untimely question right at the start when it might better have been reserved for afterward when the ladies separated or later still in some formal diplomatic setting. Not at her dinner! Still, though Mr. Yrujo had come close to disrespect—Dolley had seen Jimmy's frown—the situation seemed to have passed without apparent damage, and she slowly relaxed, looking around the table as she spooned the soup. She saw that her sister was chatting across the table with Maggie Smith; and then she noticed that young Merry, sitting beside Anna, had a stunned look as if he were ill, pale and flushed in alternating waves, seemingly totally unaware. . . .

• • •

In fact, Anna Payne had just placed her foot against Captain Lewis's foot. It was like being touched with a hot coal. Of course he moved his foot, fearful he was intruding on her space, but her foot followed his, found it, pressed intimately against it. Anna was chatting with the publisher's wife across the table, and all the while her foot made gentle movements and pressures against his. It was as erotic as anything he had ever experienced.

She turned to him suddenly, conspiratorially. "Mrs. Yrujo," she said softly, "what do you think of her?" Her foot moved again. "She seems quite painted, don't you think? Do you like paint? Perhaps men do. I use so little. Do you think I suffer by comparison?"

He sat forward, terrified that she would see his tumult if she glanced into his lap. His voice came out as if he were strangling. "I—I think you are quite perfect as you are."

She gave him that flashing smile that itself could stun him and said, "You're a dear man, even if it's not true."

"It *is* true!" he blurted.

She laughed. "That makes you even dearer."

Then, her foot still giving his that sweet pressure, she turned to Mr. Gallatin on her other side with Mrs. Pichon and asked some question about the Alps that turned their attention fully to her. In a moment she was deep in discussion with them, the sweet pressure of her foot still hard against his, the little way it moved, pressed, withdrew slightly, pressed anew, each touch a little shock that made his breath run short. He sat gazing at her profile, the turn of her cheek, the lobe of her ear. Nothing like this had ever happened . . .

She turned, tapped the back of his hand with a pretty index finger, and whispered sharply, "Pay attention, Captain Lewis! This is your subject." She nodded toward the head of the table and removed her foot. For a stupid moment he felt like a child deprived of something precious and he wanted to follow her foot, but then his head cleared and he heard the president talking of the West and all that it meant to mankind. . . .

"So it has always been," the president was saying, "since man's vision reached beyond the distance he could throw his spear, the West has stood as monument to his desires, symbol of his dreams, root of his yearning."

There! The idea straight from Lewis's heart in words he would never have thought to use. The president's voice was calm and conversational, but he spoke with distinct rhetorical flair, commanding an audience, his manner charged with quiet but unmistakable passion.

"Always it has been beyond the sunset that man has placed that mystical land of romance and mystery, where hopes and dreams and ambitions and even immortality itself may be realized. Enchantment lay to the west—and is it so different today?"

Lewis's mouth was open, his breath short, his fork forgotten on his plate. All his life he had known this, exactly if never so expressed, the lure of the unknown drawing him west. Those years as a boy tramping in the woods for weeks at a time, living on game, turning back only when his powder ran short and the cornmeal was gone and the fatback was down to a nub for greasing the pan. And Mr. Jefferson, who'd scarcely been in the woods, who never had crossed the Blue Ridge, could summon the words to tell the rover that the unlocked passions in his heart were universal dreams of mankind. He listened with wonder and yet with a hard edge held separate, for now that boy had become a man with a single driving objective—the expedition.

"Go back to Virgil, Aristotle, Seneca, Strabo, with their tales of the Elysian Fields and the Fortunate Isles. Of course, they placed these wonders only a few days' sail to the west. You'd hardly clear Gibraltar but what you'd be there. So when business developed and medieval merchants found that the tea and spices and silks of the Orient had a ready market in Europe but a dreadful passage by caravan across the steppes of Asia, it was to these ancients that they turned."

The president paused, fully commanding their attention, sipped from his glass, and said, "Now, we say commerce drives the world, but that's only in a surface sense. Far more than gold, much as they're often intermixed, the world is driven by dreams. And the cosmic dream of the West goes back to the beginning. Listen to Homer, the blind poet, eight hundred years before Jesus graced the world. Where does he place the Elysian Fields, the final reward for the heroes of Greece, but in the misty west at the earth's ultimate extremity. And the west, he says, was a place of joy—remember the lines? It's where 'life is easy to man, no snow falls nor rain but always ocean sendth forth the breeze of the shrill west to blow cool on man.' "

He chuckled and raised his glass. "Not bad, old Homer."

"Not bad, indeed, Mr. President," said Ned Thornton, with an easy grace that made Lewis instantly envious. "Our own great Alexander Pope, if you'll permit me, gave us Homer's view of Elysium thusly." His voice deepened and his delivery gave shape to noble words so they rang in Lewis's mind.

> "Joys ever young, unmix'd with pain or fear,
> Fill the wide circle of the eternal year:
> Stern winter smiles on that auspicious clime:
> The fields are florid with unfading prime;
> From the bleak pole no winds inclement blow,
> Mould the round hail, or flake the fleecy snow;
> But from the breezy deep the blest inhale
> The fragrant murmurs of the western gale."

" 'The fragrant murmurs of the western gale.' Splendid!" Mr. Jefferson cried. "I see you in a new light, Mr. Thornton, that you should have committed to memory so salient a passage."

"I fear I can take no literary credit, Mr. President. A kind lady in Mayfair gave me these words on a scented sheet. She was forecasting that I would find Homeric joy in the New World, and I have to say that she was quite correct. So, you see, I have read them many times."

Lewis glanced at Anna. The lady in Mayfair with the scented sheet had seized her attention, but as the conversation went on she slumped back in her chair. He saw that she was interested only in her own immediate, and he imagined that her immediate had a wondrous excitement far beyond his own experience.

Had they ever studied medieval maps? Mr. Jefferson was asking. "Not for geography, of course, since our modern age has so overtaken their knowledge, but for their imagery, all the strange places and strange names crying of ancient tales of sea dragons and castles of gold and races of men immense in size and unholy in beauty, islands of Amazons, those amazing women who, 'tis said, cut off their right breasts the better to draw their bows, who really are an analogous expression in myth of the true power of women. Looking to the west, always to the west. Valhalla beyond the setting sun where Norse heroes go to meet Odin. Mallory placing Arthur at last on the mystical Isle of Avalon where—I remember those words so well—'falls not rain, or hail, or any snow, not ever wind blows loudly . . .' "

Summoning up such images of mystery and romance, Mr. Jefferson's voice took on a hypnotic note. Lewis felt swept along on a wild current, but impatience was rising as well. He knew the immediate west as no one here possibly could. He had soldiered and slept on the ground and faced starving times when acorns were salvation, while these men had slept in feather beds; so while classical imagery was thrilling, he also wanted to cry out that Homer could only dream but we can go!

"Our own Native Americans tell us the great spirits lie beyond the setting sun," the president was saying, "where the souls of the departed return to their maker. The Spaniard, Cabeza de Vaca, wandering lost for months in the American West, tells us that he never lost faith 'that going toward the sunset we must find what we desire . . .'

"So, of course, when Christopher Columbus made landfall in the Americas, so clearly not the Cathay of silks and spices, what could everyone believe but that this untimely land mass blocking the route to glory was a mere shoal, just another obstacle lying between them and that wonderful sea of legend that washed the golden sands of Cipangu?

"And what are they really postulating but the Garden of the World, that place of human joy, that Eden where all cares are lost and innocence can be reclaimed, where man can live in peace and plenty, forever content in gentle sunlight, at one with God or the gods, as the case may be? From Homer on it is the idea of the garden of human perfection that has driven the western image. And can any of us really say that that garden of glory where all good lies doesn't await us today in the far unknown reaches of our own North American continent?"

At some point Dolley stopped listening. Tom could be fascinating, he could spin intellectual castles in the air that swept you away on dreams, but he also could ramble on for an hour or two; and meanwhile Mr. Lemaire was in the doorway giving her increasingly urgent glances. Plates and wineglasses had been cleared, fresh glasses placed but the dessert wine not poured. On a table beyond Mr. Lemaire she could see the dessert laid out in crystal dishes. A specialty of Chef Julien that involved folding whipped egg whites into whipped cream, it was designed to be eaten within a quarter hour.

She cast an imploring glance at Jimmy, who shook his head sharply. One didn't interrupt the president. The three diplomats were listening with apparent interest. So was Albert Gallatin, who was well schooled in the classics, but Hannah wore a look of bored tolerance. Dolley surmised that as a western Pennsylvanian, Hannah felt she already knew more than she needed of the West. Upon reflection, it seemed to Dolley that Mr. Yrujo wore a rather calculating look; she was amused to see his wife stifle a yawn and wondered if the former Miss McKean's new husband was still giving her exhausting nights.

Anna looked as if her mind was far away, perhaps on Mr. Cutts, who now occupied much of her time, but Merry was listening carefully, his earlier confusion gone. Maggie was giving the president rapt attention; her husband took a small book from an inner pocket and wrote a note with a stub pencil.

Mr. Lemaire shrugged and spread his hands. The beaten egg white had collapsed. And Mr. Jefferson talked on and on. . . .

Though memory of that sweet pressure on his foot burned in Lewis's mind, he was drawn ever more deeply into the president's discourse, for now the talk had turned to the desire that he most understood, the simple hunger to know that drives the explorer and the inventor. Myths, dreams, notions of paradise to the west were fine, but it was the beckoning unknown that had called him since he was a boy.

The wide Missouri pouring into the Mississippi from the west, mass of muddy water so large it must drain a range reaching into the heart of the continent—what lay up that river? What lay beyond the Great Bend already known, beyond the villages of the Mandan Indians that French traders had opened, beyond and into the hidden mists? Did it reach clear to the Stony Mountains with their glittering peaks, and were those mountains really no more demanding than the Blue Ridge, a western range matching an eastern range? Wondrous were the tales of distant vastness here on our own continent, and Lewis burned to see them. And the president was circling the same idea in his own meandering way.

"That hunger to know is more, mark you, than mere curiosity, curiosity being no more than the mainspring of gossip. Rather it is the lure of the unknown, the wonder of what might be. Look at the moon, so cold and distant. Our best glasses tell us merely that it has hills and valleys. What mystery! Will man go there someday and perhaps find a new race that has mastered arts unknown to us?"

There was a sudden loud snicker. Lewis's head jerked around, and across the table he saw Mr. Yrujo bury his face in his napkin, his shoulders shaking. It was outrageous. The Spaniard was too handsome, quite beautiful in fact, and the core of dislike Lewis had felt for him hardened.

Mr. Jefferson, however, didn't seem offended. He smiled and said, "Mr. Yrujo doubts such thoughts."

"Well, sir," the Spaniard said, not at all abashed, "it's so patently impossible one can hardly take it seriously."

"But that is the stuff of dreams, my dear Mr. Ambassador. The impossible becomes possible and then feasible and then one day . . . oh, I make no predictions as to the moon, but what interests me is the persistence of dreams and, specifically, of man's dream of the unknown West. For that is what gave the attitude of the Americas, which attitude shapes what we are and what we know today."

Lewis felt a sudden jolting awakening, as if Anna had poked him with a sharp stick. This was the stuff of his own dreams, but more was at stake than any individual. The president was showing them the nature of America, but there was more than that too. The West beyond the Mississippi was Spanish territory. We had a foothold in the Pacific Northwest, but already the British pushed us there. France was reasserting itself, in Santo Domingo and perhaps even on the Mississippi. And here was the president of the United States laying the theoretical groundwork for an American position with the diplomatic representatives of the three critical nations. Lewis cursed his own thickness. This was no rambling monologue; it went straight to the American role on the continent. Pay attention!

"Why did Europeans strike ever westward?" the president was asking. "Why, upon finding the New World, were they so sure that a way west would reveal itself? Dreams, dreams all. The New World presented itself as a barrier blocking the route to our desires? Never fear—straits parting the land mass, as the Red Sea was parted for Moses, certainly would be found.

"Verrazano thought he'd seen the western sea across a narrow spit of land. Cartier sailed into the Saint Lawrence and was sure he'd found the straits. And when no straits were found, then there must be rivers that could be ascended to a vast inland sea that also had western outlets down which vessels could glide straight to Cipangu. And the inland sea, never found, faded to a great lake with outlets east and west, and then to a small mountain lake, and then to what we know today, that great rivers lead us to the mountains of the

West and so it has narrowed down till there must lie our Northwest Passage."

The president sat back in his chair, a wineglass poised in his hand, his voice warm, thoughtful, easily heard but not loud; it were as if he were a teacher, leading an exploration in which he was participant rather than guide.

"And surely," he was saying, "logic tells us that if such a river falls out of the eastern side of those mountains and runs eastward to the Mississippi, then another must issue to the west. And if that is so, the two should be more or less opposite each other, and that suggests we can find a cut in the mountains at elevation sufficiently mild as to allow easy portage between the two rivers, the one on the east, the other that we've long imagined as the Great River of the West, the mouth of which we now know. . . ." He chuckled. "Logic so insists, and if logic doesn't, desire does, and together the two are irresistible."

Lewis had heard of the Northwest Passage all his life. To find it was one purpose of exploration. Yet so firmly was it ingrained in the fabric of American thought that it was almost disorienting to hear the admission that it might not exist.

The president reminded them of Captain Gray, the American who, in 1792, had discovered an immense river pouring into the Pacific, which he named for his ship, the *Columbia*, and claimed for the United States. Lewis knew Gray's story well. His discovery had prompted Mr. Jefferson's long-ago plans for an expedition that Lewis had dreamed of leading.

The volume of the Columbia's water tells you it drains an immense range, Mr. Jefferson said, and hence must be the outlet of the postulated Great River of the West, which flows from those same Stony Mountains that surely feed the Missouri on the east.

So what of Alexander Mackenzie's new book just in from London? This fur-trading captain for Britain's North West Company had tramped the far northwest as Lewis had only dreamed of doing; he claimed he had discovered a water passage to the western sea nearly ten years before.

"Now, with the greatest respect, Mr. Thornton, I judge he did no such thing," Mr. Jefferson said. "Mackenzie says he found a route with an easy portage at a mere three-thousand-foot altitude that connects to the headwaters of the Columbia. But he is very far north and I think it impossible he's on the Columbia, for I believe that river issues directly from the western side of the mountains, and that it is more or less opposite the headwaters of the Missouri on the opposite slope. After all, the latitude of the Columbia's mouth matches that of the Missouri."

"And are all those calculations, Mr. President," asked Ned Thornton with his engaging smile, "based on logic or on desire?"

"Both," Mr. Jefferson said. "Plus a powerful distaste for the idea of Britain having the Northwest Passage via Canada while we are lacking."

Lewis turned a sharp eye on the president. As if light-hearted and casual, he had gone to the heart of the Pacific Northwest conundrum. Such was the way of men of skill in dealing with great issues. For an instant Lewis wondered if he would ever learn, and then his mind darted back to the mix of politics and geography. The Spanish were only a short-term problem; in two or three decades the westward tide of American settlers would cancel the Spanish hold on the center of the continent. But in the far northwest, if the British succeeded in making themselves masters of the mouth of the Columbia, we could forget the dream of a continental nation. It was so clear. We needed to saddle up and get on out there!

But now, with a broad smile, Thornton drew himself up to answer. "With all due respect, Mr. President, Britain controlling the Northwest Passage would not distress His Majesty's government."

Jefferson laughed. "Doubtless. But you see, it wouldn't be fitting, for after all, the United States is the dominant nation, the one, if I may say so, destined to control the continent."

"But, Mr. President," Yrujo cried, "most respectfully, you may *not* say so! Spain is the dominant nation and will remain so. All that territory you've been discussing, the Missouri country, is Spanish territory."

Lewis's dislike for the man was growing rapidly. He glanced around the table. Thornton was watching, eyes glinting and lips slightly parted. It took Lewis a moment to recognize his expression: It was that of a man watching a fight and thinking about taking a hand in it.

But with an easy smile, Mr. Jefferson said to the Spaniard, "Courtesy, if I recall, of the French. I'm sure Mr. Pichon will tell you in detail that it was the French who explored it, Jolliet and Marquette who gave us the Missouri."

"In their day, of course," Yrujo said, "but that is long past. And we have been actively exploring. We have had *Señores* Mackay and Evans through that whole country."

Lewis sat forward in his chair, for now he was close to home. Mackay and Evans were wandering Britons versed in the northern fur country, whom Spain had hired to traverse the West. "But what good are they, Mr. Yrujo," the president asked, "when Spain is so unwilling to share their findings? We understand they concluded the Missouri rises near Santa Fe and runs north for a thousand miles before it turns eastward and becomes the river of Joliet and Marquette. But when will we be told more?"

"My government feels no obligation to share information on its own territory, Mr. President. If the river rises near our most important northern outpost, we fear interest in it masks aims on Santa Fe itself."

"I met Mackay once," Lewis said. He surprised himself, for he'd had no intention of speaking. But his own western passions, coupled with his reaction to the Spaniard's glib rebuff of the president, brought the meeting with Mackay back with special force, and the memory always angered him. Voice tightening, he said, "It was in Saint Louis. He and Evans were just in, and he was explaining his reasoning on the Missouri's course, and he certainly said nothing about a threat to Santa Fe."

Yrujo stared across the table. "Mr. Mackay was a Briton, Captain Lewis. With all respect to Mr. Thornton here, the

Spanish government needs no advice from Britons, or from anyone else, in deciding matters of its own security. If you had talked a bit longer, Mr. Mackay probably would have told you that."

"I would have talked to him much longer, but a popinjay of a Spanish captain came upon us having a quiet drink together and gave such a tongue-lashing as to leave poor Mackay quivering with fear and me—"

"In Saint Louis, you say? Spanish territory. You're lucky he didn't arrest you and send you to Cuba in irons."

This did infuriate Lewis. "*He* was lucky I didn't knock his damned head off!"

There was an appalled silence. He looked around the table, seeing from their faces that he had gone much too far. Only the president looked not unduly shocked but seemed to be waiting.

God . . . would he have to apologize? He couldn't bear the thought.

Yrujo smiled. "Ah, well, frontier officers sometimes are precipitate."

Lewis heard the president's chuckle. His face flamed and the thought of meeting Yrujo on the street outside flashed in his mind. Too precipitate! But then, as the president resumed his monologue, he realized that Yrujo had used officers in the plural, meaning both men. He was blaming them equally for an encounter, and all at once, the table having returned to normal, Lewis realized the Spaniard had given him a lesson in diplomacy and had rescued him from his own excess.

Presently he caught Yrujo's eye and raised his hand to his forehead in casual but unmistakable salute. Yrujo's eyes widened and then he smiled and bowed slightly. Both gestures, Lewis saw, had gone quite undetected.

Mr. Jefferson, apparently unperturbed, was saying that he doubted the Missouri rose near Santa Fe; but irrespective of that, he thought it inappropriate to ascribe geographic interest to international hostility, for the United States certainly had no aims on Santa Fe even if its streets were paved with gold.

"But I will make a prediction," he added. "I believe we

will find the Missouri's source well north of Santa Fe and well south of Mackenzie's position. I believe we will find our Northwest Passage. We will see that we can ascend the Missouri, find a portage sufficiently gentle to be traversed, and descend the Columbia to the sea."

He smiled, looking around the table. "Now, that is based on evidence suggestive but not conclusive, so I cannot deny that it contains a dollop of desire along with logic." Then, without missing a beat, neatly cutting off further argument, which Mr. Yrujo was poised to give, he said, "And now, my deepest apologies to our hostess who, for the last half hour, has been wanting to let me know that my rambling has delayed our dessert quite unconscionably. Is it all spoiled, dear Dolley?"

Oh, Dolley thought, he's so smooth. He had quite disarmed her, and she laughed and put her hand on his and said, "It fell and it's cold, so I promise only that it will be sweet." It was sweet but also watery and flat, nothing like what poor Julien had planned, and the guests quickly laid spoons aside and seemed pleased to have their glasses refilled. Still, this wasn't much of a tragedy. Jimmy looked contented. The president had laid out a strong and determined national position to men who might someday be enemies, and he'd managed it without a hint of confrontation. Which she supposed was why you had such dinners.

She saw that Mr. Yrujo was disturbed, as if he felt challenged; his wife watched him anxiously, and Dolley wondered if he turned ugly when crossed. Anna was looking restless, responding to comments with a smile but initiating none of her own. Ned Thornton was chatting easily, holding the attention of the women to his right and his left, his manner very relaxed. Mrs. Pichon, holding her spoon and frowning, rattled something in French to Albert. Doubtless she knew exactly how the dessert should taste. He responded, his expression ironic, which seemed to go over her head.

It was late, tapers in the girandoles burning steadily, darkness gathering outside the high windows. And finally, thank

God, it was over, the women separating briefly, the men soon joining them, and then they were going. And she knew from Jimmy's broad smile, from the president's pleasure, that her first diplomatic dinner had been a success.

Anna gave Lewis her ravishing smile and moved off without a word. He followed and nearly collided with Mr. Jefferson, who had drawn Mr. Yrujo aside. The president suggested a ride the next day if the weather were fine, and then Lewis heard him say in the same casual tone, "Tell me, sir, how would your government react to our sending a small expedition up the Missouri to test these matters we've been describing in theory?"

"With great umbrage, Mr. President," Yrujo said. "It would be an invasion of Spanish territory." But Lewis scarcely registered the answer, for of course the Spanish would object, and who gave a damn, they were popinjays to a man. What mattered was the question! The expedition of which he'd dreamed for a decade had been broached. It was in the president's mind; it was real! Or could be, which was almost as good. And here was Meriwether Lewis to make it real!

Yrujo and the president moved off. Had Anna gone? No, there she was, by the door. He hurried after her, wanting— he didn't know what, for nothing in her manner now suggested her earlier charm. She seemed a stranger. What could he say that might restore the marvelous intimacy—

"Mr. Lewis?" It was the guard from the front door. "Mr. Wagner, Mr. Madison's clerk, he's downstairs with someone from London; and he says he must see you immediately."

Lewis sighed. Anna was talking to Miss Dolley and seemed not to notice as he followed the guard down the marble stairs.

"Did you do something to that young man?" Dolley asked.
"What?" All injured ignorance. "Me?"

Dolley let her sister go as Jimmy drew her aside. "We're having hot chocolate in the study; the president wants you to join us."

A servant was pouring when she came in. She settled into an armchair with her cup. Mr. Jefferson sprawled on a Chippendale sofa covered in a blue brocade, one leg up on the cushions. He loosened his cravat and gave a long, shuddering sigh, rubbing his eyes with the heels of both hands.

"Oh, my!" he said. "That was exhausting! But it went well, Dolley, thanks to you. I congratulated Mr. Lemaire too. Even the spoiled dessert. I didn't plan it that way, but it was very useful to demonstrate this wasn't idle talk."

"No one missed that," Jimmy said. It occurred to Dolley that sophisticated though she was, she had more to learn.

Mr. Jefferson chuckled. "I thought Merry was going to get in trouble for a minute there."

She liked Merry and said so, adding, "But there's a roughness in him too."

"Well, he's just what Yrujo said—a frontier officer. Gentility is too much the luxury on the frontier."

"Yrujo handled it well," Jimmy said. "I expect he'll be a formidable opponent."

"Still," Mr. Jefferson said, "Merry turned it well too. That little salute, most gracious. For a moment I feared he didn't understand what had happened."

Dolley nodded. "And Yrujo's little bow—all quite nice."

"Diplomacy at work, eh?" Jimmy looked at the president. "What did you think of their answers to the real question?"

"I had a feeling they were taking very careful positions. Not that it isn't so, not even that they know nothing of it, but that they, at least, have had no definitive word."

"That makes sense," Jimmy said. "But it simply means that if France does plan to take Louisiana, it's doing so quietly. Which is what you would expect."

"Intend to present us with a fait accompli, I expect," the president said, "when it's too late to counter."

"Yes . . . an awful lot of smoke for no fire."

The door opened and Merry came in, followed by a

stranger. He was a slender man about thirty. His clothes were rumpled, and she thought he looked tired.

"Mr. President," Merry said, "this is Sanford Erskine, legation secretary under Ambassador King in London."

Erskine bowed. "Mr. President." He extended a packet sealed with red wax. "Mr. King said you'll recognize this."

"You may hand that to Secretary Madison. Tell me, son, how did you make the trip?"

"By British frigate, sir. Mr. King said it was urgent. A warship leaving on the flood for the American station was by far the fastest. It delivered me to Annapolis."

The president thanked the young man and Merry led him out. She watched Jimmy break the seals and extract a long document festooned in red. "Yes," he said slowly, scanning the first page and flipping to the second and third, "it's a true copy of the actual treaty between Spain and France so long rumored in London, as Rufus has been telling us. Let's see . . . for various considerations, none onerous, Spain agrees to retrocede the province of Louisiana in its entirety, New Orleans, of course, and all to the north and west up the Mississippi, out the Missouri to some indefinite point that matches all that France ever claimed and any claims that Spain may have added. In short, France takes everything beyond the Mississippi."

"So it's true," Mr. Jefferson said in a low voice, "Ah, God, think of that. Napoleon astride the Mississippi. I prayed it wouldn't be so."

"But believed it would be."

"Yes, but believing and knowing are very different."

She had a leaden feeling, the weight of very bad news pressing her chest. This meant trouble on a gargantuan scale. She glanced at Jimmy; his face was smooth and hard.

"We can't allow this to stand," he said.

The president sighed, pinching the bridge of his nose. "I can already hear our western friends caterwauling, can't you?"

"Mr. President," Jimmy said, in that same hard way.

She saw Tom's eyes pop open. "Of course you're right, Jimmy," he said. "We cannot allow it to stand."

21

She awakened suddenly, alone in the big bed. There was a moon, and by its reflected light she saw the clock he had ordered from Paris, gold hands on a ceramic face. Two in the morning. The streets of Washington were silent. The fireplace had burned down and the room was cold. He was in a chair drawn to a window, motionless, staring out into the bare branches of the oak that had been there years before their house was raised. His hands were locked together.

"Come to bed, Jimmy," she said.

He turned. She saw his smile in the faint light. "Soon," he said.

She got up and wrapped a blanket around his shoulders. He touched her hand. She lay awake a long time thinking of the French and all it might mean. Eventually she dozed; it was much later when she felt the feathers sag beside her. She sighed and put her hand on his shoulder. At first light she opened her eyes; he was dressed, sitting in the chair.

"Oh, Jimmy," she said, "didn't you sleep at all?"

"A little," he said.

She went downstairs. Sukey was stirring a fire under a kettle and presently there was tea and a hastily warmed plate of muffins made with honey and raisins. Teapot and bread in their cozies, she started up with the tray; but on the landing above the first floor she paused, rested it on the windowsill, and looked out on the bare oak's heavy trunk.

A tremor ticked in her temple. She was frightened and, she realized with faint surprise, very angry. She'd always liked the French. They'd been with us in the revolution when it mattered so desperately. She would never forget the raw emotion in the voices of her girlhood as Tarleton's Raiders in their red coats swept ever closer, and it was the French who'd stood with us when we stood alone. And their glorious revolution had sprung right out of our own, the same desperate yearning of plain people for freedom, democracy aborning, and you had to love them.

She was stunned when their revolution imploded into chaos to the guillotine's clatter, when the fat little general's coup made him a dictator. But their language still was threaded with music, and their music was threaded with joy.

And then this . . . even as the meaning of the treaty had dawned on her the night before, she had seen that smooth, hard quality on her husband's face, the look that told her instantly he was not to be trifled with just now. She'd glanced quickly at Tom and seen mirrored there the same look that cried crisis more clearly than words.

But she could see it all herself. Like her husband, she hadn't been abroad or even over the Appalachians, but she knew Americans well. A French invasion of the western regions would stir them to frenzy, east and west alike. And that was the other side of the French too, wasn't it, the thread of arrogance, the conviction of superiority, the inability even to see, let alone care, how Americans would react?

Jimmy had poked the fire into life, and the bedroom was warming when she returned with the tray. He took the cup gratefully, waving away a muffin, drank the tea in silence, held out the cup to be refilled.

"It's going to be dangerous, isn't it?" she asked.

"Yes . . . ," he said. He gazed at her over the rim of the cup with concern but with appreciation too, so she thought; and she was glad she'd decided not to press him for details.

"I thought as much," she said. "So you'd better eat the muffin. You'll need your strength."

He walked rapidly along F Street toward the mansion, dodging puddles, mud spattering his white hose above the line of his boots. Shoes with silver buckles were in the case of state papers slung over a shoulder. Tom would be waiting for him, and Albert Gallatin would be along shortly—a message had gone to the Treasury secretary the night before.

The more he considered it, the more appalling it became. Look at the sheer contempt in the French manner. Not a word to the nation most affected, all in secret, rumors denied, Pichon sitting there last night blandly saying his government had not instructed him, butter wouldn't melt in his mouth. It was disgusting.

And if he'd spoken accurately, if his government really had excluded him, that was worse. Didn't tell their own man or their man lied—either was reprehensible. The only reason we knew it now was that the British had sources in Paris and gladly dug it out and threw it in our faces. And when would the French have told us? When their police seized our boatmen on the river?

He stepped around a puddle and into a pile of fresh horse manure, paused to clean his boot, and hurried on. The irony of it seemed overwhelming. They were just over a constitutional crisis, that rotten scoundrel Burr willing to shatter the new democracy for his own selfish dreams. Oh, how the Federalists had crowed over that, the crisis they had predicted all along coming before we'd even taken office! And we'd settled that, things holding steady on a middle course, confounding Federalists who'd expected us to tear things apart, confounding our own radicals who'd demanded the same, smooth sailing at last, whereupon our erstwhile friends raised a danger ten times as great—for this could be fatal.

He felt a sudden boiling in his stomach, a nauseous wash of fluid in his mouth, and he stopped short. In a moment he recognized it as fear taking him by surprise, and he didn't like it. He straightened and calmed himself before he went on. Panic was the unforgivable indulgence.

In control again, he hurried along, reviewing his analysis. What was the aim, the purpose? What did the little dictator who'd seized power out of the agony of self-destructing democracy really intend? Not just to correct an old loss. Men of power did things for real reasons. Why bother to return to Louisiana just now when, after years of war, he had a moment of peace? He had fought his neighbors to a standstill, seized much of their territory to give France what he called its "natural frontiers," and even the British seemed ready to strike an armistice. So now he decides to invade Louisiana? Why?

Not just to continue Spain's weak, hesitant control. Sitting through the dark hours of the night, the oak branches' fantastic shapes against the moon, Madison had found it beginning to make sense. Taking New Orleans, ruling the Mississippi, seizing the great wilderness to the west of the river would be just a start for a man of Napoleon's scale. Next he would move north to attack Canada, transferring the war of Europe to North America. But even that was only a start. Once he had gone so far, why would he turn back?

Slowly, sitting in the silent dark, Dolley's even breathing a rhythm to his thinking, Madison had grown convinced that the Frenchman's ultimate aim was to seize the western United States, Tennessee and Kentucky and Ohio soon to be a state, the Indiana and Illinois country, the forests of Mississippi, and the lands watered by the winding Alabama River, proud American westerners made into reluctant Frenchmen. It made perfect strategic sense. He would convert the great heart of the continent into a French breadbasket, a food empire that would feed his armies as he went on to conquer the world. And the United States would be reduced to a vassal state hugging the Atlantic, forced to serve French needs at whatever price France set. . . .

But we would die before we let that happen, which had to mean—but now he was at the mansion gate and he knew what they would have to do, and the terrible question growing in his mind was this: Would the president see it so clearly?

He nodded to the guard at the north entrance, ducked inside, sat on a marble bench with a crimson cushion, and wiped the mud from his hose. He replaced his boots with the buckled shoes he'd packed in the case, left boots and case by the bench, and climbed the stairs. In the president's corner office a fire was crackling and the room was warming. Leather-covered books with paper strips marking places were stacked higgledy-piggledy on every surface, and even in the midst of crisis it struck him that this was a gentle-hearted room.

Gallatin had already arrived. The president sat in his deep Queen Anne chair cradling a teacup in both hands. His face was sagging and pouchy, as haggard as Madison felt. Gallatin was at a table pouring tea, and he set out a cup for Madison.

"Welcome, Jimmy," the president said, his voice tired but light and relaxed. "I've just been acquainting Albert with the terms of Napoleon's deal with Spain; for returning Louisiana, he swaps them a hunk of Italy that he stole."

"That does put it harshly, Mr. President," Albert said.

Jefferson had a lazy, amused look that Madison didn't like. That damned whimsicality of his, popping up at the unlikeliest moments!

"It's a harsh situation, Albert," Jefferson said. "I know you've admired Napoleon—"

"Well, he is a man of extraordinary power, a genius on the battlefield, an executive of exceptional talents—"

"And a seducer and destroyer of democracy," Jefferson said, still with that easy manner. "Let's not forget that he stole the French democracy with a military coup and has been reveling in power ever since."

"Well, I suppose," Albert said, and sat down with a thump.

Madison felt anger stirring. "He's drunk with power if he thinks he can handle us so cavalierly," he snapped. Let's get down to what matters! Would he have to bring them to order himself and show them the dangers ahead?

"Unfortunately," Gallatin said, "most Europeans haven't the least sense for this vast continent. What is it—four hundred miles across France? Five? Here that just takes you down to Carolina. Napoleon has no idea what he's trying to bite off."

"More than he can swallow," Madison said.

But then the atmosphere changed, as suddenly as a spring sky can clear. The president stood, tall and lean, towering over them both. "All right, gentlemen," he said, "to business." With sharp relief, Madison saw that his face had hardened and the easy-going manner was gone. He walked to a window, walked back, clearly in command. Madison waited. This was the Jefferson he wanted to see, the basic man, strong, stern, very tough, who he always knew was there when you cut through the idle talk, the spray of ideas, the erratic focus on anything and everything, the extraordinary capacity to deceive himself and to believe whatever he wanted to believe, the wild stories he told, the encyclopedic interests and knowledge, all these the reasons men and women who didn't know him well gushed and called him a genius. But Madison knew none of this would matter tuppence if at bedrock there wasn't a man of power, hard as stone.

Madison had spent his adult life as junior partner to Jefferson, who was nine years his senior. Dolley resented it, but Madison saw it as the natural order. They'd done well together—junior didn't mean inferior—and Madison had been content to follow. Only on the Constitution, written while Tom was in Paris as ambassador, had he broken with Tom and gone his own way. He'd seen what must be done, and while the document's writing was a group effort done in convention, he knew he had had more to do with the key points than anyone. And then he'd beaten Tom into support too. For he knew the Constitution was the most important thing that had happened in America, more than Tom's own great Declaration of Independence, more than General Washington as the first president holding the nation together when it wanted so much to fly apart. This was the document that told the core value of the American people. And Tom had seen that in time and come along. . . .

So Madison waited, confident on the one hand, terrified on the other, for what the leader would say.

The president leaned against his desk. "Now, let's start with the basic fact. Ipso facto, who occupies New Orleans and controls the Mississippi becomes our enemy. To control the river is to strangle, or threaten to strangle, half of our country. That is the single point that must guide our every move. We cannot tolerate—we *will* not tolerate—any nation taking that position." A wintry smile flashed and disappeared. "Spain, of course, has held it only at our pleasure. France on the Mississippi we will not accept. Is that understood?"

"But—" Gallatin said, and stopped before the president's raised hand.

"And you gentlemen are quite right. We *are* too big a bite for Napoleon to swallow, let alone digest. The problem is that he doesn't know that. Not yet. Our task is to educate an ignoramus. We must show him his plans are unworkable."

No one spoke. Jefferson walked the length of his office and back. He folded his arms.

"Now, gentlemen, Napoleon, conqueror of all he has seen, doesn't strike me as very susceptible to reasoning. Power is his mode, and I doubt he respects anything else. So he must be made to understand that we will fight, and that in the end we will win. When that recognition penetrates, he will be open to reason."

"But, Mr. President," Gallatin bleated, "how can we fight? We're broke, we're reducing the army, we're laying up ships—"

Again a raised hand stopped the Treasury secretary. "First things first, Albert," the president said. "First, we must make the tyrant understand the danger in which he places himself."

He glanced at Madison. "Mr. Secretary, I will count on you to find ways to do so."

"Yes, Mr. President," Madison said. "Starting with the premise that we will fight."

"Exactly."

"We can raise a hundred thousand militia in the West."

"More. Two hundred, I would say. I know westerners. Every man from twelve to ninety will pull down his rifle."

"But, but—" Gallatin was sputtering. "Militiamen, no matter how many, against highly trained troops, blooded in years of war, supported by countless cannon, supplied and resupplied and reinforced and—"

"We'll need some help," Madison said.

"Well," Jefferson said, "this mad French dreamer has a limited future. His dream of conquering the world is too big a dream. He has absolute power, and absolute power is cruel to its holders. It first seduces and then destroys them, and sooner or later his dreams will destroy him. But meanwhile, if he presses on until we must fight or submit, then certainly, we will need help. From, to get it said, the Royal Navy."

Madison couldn't restrain a great sigh. He knew his face had cleared in relief. Tom had followed the same course of logic through the dark of the night to this same cold conclusion. He saw reproach in Jefferson's eyes. You doubted me?

"The Royal Navy!" Gallatin's voice squeaked.

"Napoleon's days will be numbered if we join the British," Jefferson said. "We're already the largest neutral shipping nation in the world; together we would rule the seas. Britain would be glad to blockade the Gulf Coast while our militia cleared out the French if we were its ally in the world war."

It all sounded cool, no raised voices, no emotional cries—the language of disaster, Madison saw, was not much different in tone from that of ordinary life. But this was disaster.

"That's just what the Federalists want!" Gallatin cried.

Yes, exactly what those who dreamed of conservative rule by the better classes had wanted for years, war with republican France, the little United States curled up between the paws of the British lion, an end to Jeffersonian democracy.

"But it would be to British interest to keep the French out of North America," Gallatin said.

"Well, Albert," the president said, "they wouldn't do it if it weren't in their interests. But every encounter with the British over the last quarter century says they'll make us pay."

Madison saw this as simple logic. And payment would be to join the world war on their side, put our shipping at their disposal, bend our trade to their advantage, perhaps assume the defense of Canada to free their troops for the Continent. Our import-export duties—the government's only source of income—would pour into empty British coffers. Our food-stuffs would flow to their armies with payment when and if and how they said.

"That's the reality," Jefferson said. "Underneath a little face-saving cover they would grant us."

"So the Federalists would win after all," Albert said.

"I assume so," the president said. "They've wanted alliance with Britain against France for years. Surely they would argue that only they have the stature to bend British protection to our ends without losing our own sense of nationhood."

"If we did what they've wanted all along, of course the people would turn back to them," Madison said, "and there go our dreams—back to the old autocracy, Hamilton in the saddle again, bending the economy to serve those who have the most, aristocracy coming, monarchy in the wings."

So defeating France by force would give us a very costly victory, but Madison felt better with the peril laid out on the table. They had decided, they were together, they could fight in lots of ways.

"Remember," he said, "the only thing worse, more dangerous, would be not to fight. A democracy that can't defend itself must fail by definition." Still, he *was* feeling better, and he cried, "But maybe standing strong would save us, prove that freedom works. What do we argue, after all? Only that the common man has the courage, the self-discipline, the control, the collective wisdom to govern himself—that he doesn't need rich men or aristocrats or a king to guide him—" He saw Jefferson's smile and stopped himself, then added, "Well, soldiers of democracy must be preachers too."

The president nodded. "Well said, Jimmy. Preachers must believe, and we must too. We set out the worst, the ultimate disaster. But long before we come to fighting, to rallying militia, let alone appealing to the Royal Navy, we must try to head them off. So, Mr. Secretary, it's in your hands. Take it one step at a time."

Madison stood and squared his shoulders. "Mr. President," he said in his most formal tone, "I will operate on this basis: We know we can drive them out and we will if we must."

"Quite—destroy them by destroying ourselves. Bit of a bad joke, eh? So, Jimmy, I leave it in your hands."

"I'll need some presidential weight, I expect."

"Oh, I'll be available."

Well, Madison thought as he snatched up his boots and case and bounded out into the cold morning air, at least the president was strong, no matter Dolley's reservations. Anyway, what really lit Dolley's anger was the feeling that Madison worked and Tom got the credit. But Madison was full ready to cede credit, for what did it matter? Dolley wanted him to be president someday, that was the core of it, and the idea was taking on a certain appeal to him at that, though his instinct told him he would never be a man to leap to saddle and lead his people. But neither he nor Tom would be president if they couldn't handle this thing, though he knew the difference between talking a fight and fighting it. He must walk that narrow line between showing them we can win but not having to prove it, and he didn't know if that line even existed. . . .

22

As Madison emerged from the mansion deep in thought and hurried along the brick walk toward the little State Department building, Johnny Graham assailed him with a cheery good morning. Johnny had returned from the Madrid embassy. Finding him a bright and capable young man, Madison had pressed him into service and by now had grown fond of him. The talk with the president was reverberating and his shoulders ached from tension, but he smiled and greeted Johnny. A long road lay ahead, and he would do well to hold things in proportion.

Johnny was pegging the State Department nag to graze on the mansion lawn. Every morning he went to the stables on G Street to fetch the horse on which the nation's diplomatic errands were run. A stalwart man still under thirty, with a shock of carroty hair and fists like hams, he'd grown up on the Ohio near Cincinnati and acquired a legal education before he found he didn't much like the law and didn't want to practice. Among Madison's clerks, the Nothingarian had departed; and while he regretted losing a man with such an appellation, he had to admit it was justified. Johnny had leaped at the chance to replace the Nothingarian.

The Mississippi, for which the Ohio was the great feeder, was on Madison's mind. It was the lure and the key. Remembering Johnny's background, he asked what he knew of river trade and traffic.

"A good deal, actually. My uncle's in the business—runs twenty, thirty flatboats out of Cincinnati every year. I went down with him one year."

"That many boats, eh?"

"More going every year. Pa said in a letter they're saying maybe five thousand hit New Orleans this year."

"Really? So how does it work out when you get there?"

"First off, it's a long float. You're mighty happy to see civilization again. And the Spanish? Well, they make some trouble, but you know, my uncle has sixty, seventy men and most of 'em, the bark's still on. They wanted, they could bump up against the handful of Spanish soldiers, take their pieces, and—well, put them someplace that my uncle describes somewhat indelicately. So the Spanish don't push the rivermen too far."

"But suppose they clamped down? Shut the river."

"Shut it?" Johnny laughed. "Western folk wouldn't tolerate that."

Madison walked into his office pondering the image of flatboatmen with the bark still on as an element in the international equation.

He gestured the chief clerk into his office and warned him that the French move must remain a secret. Mr. Wagner hesitated, swallowed, said, "I don't suppose we'll be disputing it. . . ."

"What in the devil gives you that idea?"

"Well, it's just that many people felt the Democrats were—"

"Captives of the French? Many people, eh?" His temper was fraying. "Federalists, you mean." He stared at Wagner. "You'd be wise to see less of your Federalist friends."

But with vulnerable expression Wagner said his friends—former friends—shunned him or pumped him for secrets. "I suppose you find out about people when circumstances change."

"Probably just as well." Madison was calmer now. In fact, he had come to depend on Wagner; but if the clerk let information slip, the hue and cry from radical Democrats would be deafening. Still, that Wagner was only learning this late in

the day that most friendship is shallow made him wonder a
bit about his clerk. Madison had found many a false friend
among Federalists, though he supposed that's how they felt
about him. . . .

"As for the French," he said, "we favored their revolution as
they had ours. But it imploded, and Napoleon jumped in and
bent French hopes for a better world to his own corrupt ends."

"Yes, sir, that's the Federalist view."

"No!" Madison snapped. "The Federalist view is that
without controls by the better classes, democracy will degenerate into mob violence. Now that's poppycock. All
Napoleon says about democracy is that it's always at risk
and always must be guarded. As for us, we'll maintain neutrality in the European squabbles, but we'll tolerate no dab-
bling on this continent. Understood?"

"Yes, sir."

"Now, you know Mr. Pichon quite well, don't you?"

Wagner massaged his chin. "When he was here before as
secretary of the French legation we were more or less coun-
terparts, and I saw a good deal of him. Now that he's back as
chargé d'affaires it's different."

"Why do you think they named him just a chargé, not an
ambassador?"

"A mark of contempt to the host country, I would think."

"So would I, unfortunately," Madison said. "Now just last
night Mr. Pichon denied knowledge of this Louisiana matter." Actually, he had said he had no instructions from his
government, but that amounted to denial. "Do you think he
deliberately lied?"

Wagner sighed. "I'd guess his government didn't tell him.
He's a decent fellow, always seemed honest and straightfor-
ward, as not all French diplomats are. Plain potato, really.
Mrs. Pichon, too. She gives the impression of a milkmaid
who'd really rather be back on her father's farm in Provence."

Plain potato? Well, this was the instrument through whom
they must reach the strongman of the French.

Wagner cleared his throat. "Spends too much time with
the Federalists though. They've got him thinking the De-

mocrats can't survive, that the people'll turn on 'em before long. He's in Gouverneur Morris's Senate office nearly daily."

Madison sat a long time gazing out on the mansion lawn where the department nag cropped a circle. Then he told Johnny Graham to ride up to the Hill, keep an eye on Morris's office just off the Senate floor, and hurry back when he saw Pichon go in.

"I'd like to catch him coming out of that office."

Meriwether Lewis was in a state of wild turmoil. He saddled his horse and set out for the Capitol bearing a message binding the chairman to secrecy on the French move. Of course, the speaker was in charge, but he preferred to do business through the energetic Ways and Means chairman. This time Lewis had specific instructions from the president to place this in Mr. Randolph's hands—personally. So much for the pale clerk.

He was barely aware of the chill morning, the big gelding frisky and rambunctious under him. He hadn't slept the night before, burning as he was with excitement: The expedition had been broached at last! The talk at the diplomatic dinner had been especially charged, Mr. Jefferson expressing precisely what Lewis had always felt—the wondrous sense of the West beckoning like the Golden Fleece.

And he was utterly ready to go! He had armfuls of plans, charts, lists. Nothing more had been said, but it was, after all, only the next morning, and this damnable French business had intervened. Which could ruin everything. If we had to fight the bastards, of course he would revert to the army— with a command, surely, or maybe knowing Mr. J's attitude toward favoritism, not so surely—but the expedition would be shot to hell, about like putting a charge of grape through a paper target. It would be another dream crashing against reality; wasn't that the very nature of life?

He rode on, jaw clamped in his urgency. Yet after a couple of blocks, at Fourteenth and F Streets, he dismounted and continued on foot, leading the gelding. The message he carried was imperative, but the clerk would keep him waiting a half hour—that seemed the way Mr. Randolph wanted it—so he might as well take a moment now.

It happened that Mr. Secretary Madison lived on F Street between Fourteenth and Thirteenth and it happened too that Miss Anna Payne lived with her sister and brother-in-law. Of course he didn't expect to see her and he certainly didn't intend to knock on her door, but just the sight of a window behind which she might be drinking her morning tea would be balm to a ravaged heart.

His foot still burned from the sweet contact of the night before. The erotic force of that touch amazed him—certainly he'd never considered a foot in quite such terms. And she had just *done* it. *She* had put her foot there, he had moved away in courtesy, and she had followed, she had moved and touched and rubbed, all the while talking to someone else. It was *that* that made it so devastating, the secrecy, the intimate touch hidden from the world, her conversation with someone else a sham to cover the blazing center of the whole incredible experience!

When he was before the house, only covertly glancing toward its windows, the front door opened and Anna came running down the steps. She'd seen him, come out to greet him, she'd expected him, perhaps he should have called, perhaps any gentleman would have known enough—

"Oh, hello," she said, obviously surprised. And then, "Good morning, Captain Lewis." She stepped right in front of him to a landau drawn by two smart grays with both its hoods rakishly down that he now saw had pulled up behind him. It held two young men and a young woman. One of the men jumped down to hand Anna up. She waved and in an instant they were gone, carriage wheels rattling against dried ruts, a little dust cloud drifting over him.

He walked on, feeling as if she'd slapped him. Still, he told himself, it wasn't her fault, she hadn't expected him, it meant nothing. But that old darkness was crowding the edge of his vision. He mounted and rode on.

• • •

From an upstairs window, Dolley observed this tableau.
She'd been glancing out from time to time, wondering if she
would see Jimmy. If the meeting with Tom went badly, he
might come home to brood alone in his study. But it was late
enough now so he'd be here if he were coming, so probably
he'd been satisfied, meaning Tom had buckled down to it as
she knew he could when he chose. Still, she'd bet a dollar to
a doughnut he'd laid the main effort off on Jimmy. One more
glance from the window and there were Merry and Anna.
Something was going on, and she'd warrant it was Anna up
to some devilment.

"Thank you for seeing me on such short notice, Mr. Secretary," Ned Thornton said. He eased his fawn-colored
breeches and flicked a dust mite from a polished boot. That
fine blooded mare of his was tied to the rail before the department.

"It's always a pleasure to see His Majesty's representative," Madison said. Again he noticed that calm in the
man, with its air of self-assurance and strength. Speaking
formally, Thornton described the great pleasure that Whitehall, that august heat of the British foreign service, felt in
having been able to deliver the French treaty on Louisiana to
Mr. King and to have provided passage to America on a warship for Mr. King's man. Of course, Whitehall had sent a
dispatch to him on the same ship with a copy of the treaty
and note of instructions.

He was to report, therefore, that Britain would look with
much disfavor on the idea of French penetration of the North
American continent. Should the matter come to extremes,
Britain would consider taking New Orleans itself to keep it
from French hands. But it felt that such action might more
appropriately be taken by the United States.

Cautiously, Madison said, "Perhaps Great Britain would
even lend a hand under the right circumstances."

Thornton nodded. "I have no specific instructions, of course, but indirect commentary makes it clear that is a safe assumption." He smiled warmly. "After all, we are locked in a death struggle with the same tyrant, who now reveals himself as the enemy of the United States as well. Our common interests"—he put delicate emphasis on the phrase—"urge that we smite him wherever and however we can." He paused. "Of course you know that Britain looks upon the United States as a very close friend."

"Really?" Madison asked.

Thornton colored slightly but didn't waver. "It sees the United States as related, as is, say, a man by marriage. It would want to assist in time of trouble, and I suppose it is only natural that it would look for some degree of reciprocity."

"Ah . . ."

"There are so many ways to deal with an enemy in world war terms—trade, for example, and the movement of foodstuffs and other war materiel—and then, we are both great maritime nations. Together we would command the world's seas and none could stand against us. We feel that such a connection, Britain and the United States, would flow as easily as spring water gushing pure from the ground."

Spring water . . . purity . . . interesting formulations. Madison gazed at the handsome envoy. There would be no help from Britain but on Britain's terms. And what else could he expect? That was the way of nations.

"Thank you for this information," he said. "It is most reassuring."

Thornton did have the grace to color again. As he rose to go, Madison heard Johnny Graham arriving at a gallop.

Captain Lewis was at a small desk he had rigged in the unfinished East Room where he had partitioned a sleeping cubicle for himself in a corner; the partition's walls of canvas fluttered when the wind blew. He was still unsettled over the encounter this morning. Afterward, the meeting with the pale clerk and Mr. Randolph had gone predictably badly. He had restrained himself, but it had left him feeling disheveled as if nothing in his life was within his own control. Now he was laboring over the paperwork he hated. Mr. Jefferson did write his own letters as promised, but there seemed countless lists, reports, presidential directives to be written and social activities to be recorded. He was working on a list of diners at the presidential table to be sure none were slighted whom Mr. J didn't want to slight when a slender young groom came in looking agitated.

"Mr. Grumby, he calling for you, Cap'n—he got somebody out there he holding."

Grumby was the guard on duty at the front door. Lewis was almost finished with this damnable list and he didn't welcome the interruption, but he capped the inkwell and wiped the quill.

He found Grumby planted in the doorway, cudgel in hand, and heard him snarl, "Mister, you're fixing to get yourself a sore head, you keep on like this." Lewis had a confused impression of a heavyset man rushing the guard. Grumby hurled him back, so he fell on his seat, and charged him with the cudgel raised.

"All right, Sam," Lewis said. "I'll take over."

Face red, breathing hard, Grumby said, "You do that, Cap'n. Leave him to me, I'll split his damned head."

The intruder scrambled up, turning his back as he did so, and it took Lewis a moment to recognize Mr. Callender, the Richmond editor with all his mad grievances.

"Aha! The soldier boy," the editor squalled. He laughed. "Soldier boy, errand boy. Here's your errand: You get your ass up those steps and tell the great president that James Thomson Callender is here and he's wore out waiting, and he wants what the man can give in a stroke of the pen and he wants it right now!"

"Mind your tongue, Mr. Callender," Lewis said. His voice shook in his rage, his fists so tight they ached.

"Don't you use that tone on me, Mr. Soldier Boy. I tell you, I've waited long enough. I suffered for the Democrats. They were happy to use me when I was winning elections for 'em. I went to jail, I lost my press and my paper—well, Democrats won like they wouldn't have without me, and now I want mine! I want that postmastership at Richmond. It's mine by right, and I want it! You go tell him!"

For a moment the image of this impossible man in hopeless love with a society belle in Richmond softened Lewis, but sympathy fled as Callender continued his obscene caterwauling. Lewis took him by the arm and marched him down the gravel path toward the iron gate. When the editor lunged about trying to break free, Lewis lifted him almost off the ground and said in a venomous whisper, "You scurvy bastard, you give me trouble and I'll beat you bloody!"

Callender's head whipped about. He looked at Lewis wide-eyed and made no further effort to break away. But he gave a low moan and then, with his voice a compressed hiss, said, "I'm warning you. I know everything about this holier-than-thou, this oh-so-important man, whole country looking up to him, thinking he's just the most noble thing, when all the time he's rotten to his heart. You can drag me around and threaten me, you can get away with it now, but I'll win in the end 'cause I'm going to tell the world. Tell the whole vile story. I've got it all, every bit, names, everything. Whole world will know . . ."

His voice rose to a kind of howl as they reached the gate. Lewis restrained his impulse to kick the bastard into the street. Instead he growled, "Walk on, Mister, while you're still able to walk." Callender scuttled away.

At a safe distance, he turned and shouted, "I'm going to tell! The great man, he won't be nothing but dirt when I'm done with him. You wait and see!"

Samuel Clark was standing in front of the carriage, holding the horses while Miss Danny was in the office over the wharf doing business. The square-rigged brig *Sallie Mae,* arriving the night before from Santo Domingo, was off-loading cargo; and what with the stevedore yells and the creak of the windlass and the cracking whips of carters backing their trucks into place, the horses were restless. Samuel held their bridles and talked to them, voice low and soothing. Now and then he rubbed their noses, one and then the other. Presently he saw a big black man in seaboots with a slouch hat pulled low, a red feather in his hatband, come down the gangway.

"Hello, Tinker," Samuel said, his lips scarcely moving. Tinker didn't break stride. "Come see me at Miss Molly's," he said from the corner of his mouth. Samuel watched him go and shook his head—those seaboots, that red feather, that swagger, someday they would fetch the man a load of trouble. Tinker was a free black, and he never let anyone forget it. Bo'sun mate on the *Sallie Mae*, bossing black and white alike, they said he could bring a ship through seas that made the captain piss his pants and ashore he would kill any man who fooled with him. Fighting knife a foot long tucked in his boot. Samuel admired him but from a distance because one of these days Tinker was going to get killed himself.

That night Samuel left the house about eight.

"You going to get in trouble, black man walking the streets at night. You don't know what—"

"Ain't nothing going to happen. Ship in from Santo Domingo; he wants to see me? He's got something for me. Got word from Joshua, I'll warrant. I bet that rascal really did get there!"

No reason he shouldn't walk at night, he was a free man, but he kept his eyes open all the same. When he turned down the alley that led to Miss Molly's, he looked around first; and when he got to her door, he opened it just enough to slip through and closed it quickly. Smoke was thick enough to cut and a banjo was playing somewhere and the odor of rum and beer was strong. No white faces. Good-looking black girls with their gowns cut about to their navels and their waists snugged in so that a man's hands could near encircle them moved about with trays, bringing drinks and eluding patrons' slaps and tickles with practiced laughter.

Miss Molly's was a nice little whorehouse that paid the constable in various ways and kept things quiet, and it was Tinker's place of residence when the *Sallie Mae* was in port.

Samuel saw the big man at a table in a far corner, an absolutely beautiful woman with breasts like melons snugged under his arm. He felt a lift in his own groin at the sight of her. 'Course, he had a fine wife and he didn't patronize fancy women, but a woman like that, she looked like she'd turn a man every way but loose.

Just then Tinker saw him and raised an arm. Samuel sat at the table and called for rum, tossing a coin on the girl's tray. Up close the woman with big breasts looked like she'd kill you for a couple of coppers. Tinker rummaged around in his pocket.

"Feller in Santo Domingo come up to me, asked did I know you?" From the pocket came a small packet of papers, and Tinker sorted them out. "I said maybe I did and maybe I didn't, and he pulls out this and asks me to give it to you." He handed Samuel a crumpled, sweat-stained paper folded small. A letter! By God, Joshua had sent him a letter!

"You know this feller, eh?" Tinker asked.

Samuel smiled. "Maybe I do and maybe I don't."

Tinker laughed. "I ain't asking no questions and it don't pay to talk much about no slave revolt in this town; but fact is, now that I see your ugly face again, that feller could have been your brother."

"You don't say," Samuel said. He slipped the letter into his pocket. "I'm much obliged to you, Tinker. What say I have Miss Molly set aside a couple of bottles for you, my treat?"

Tinker grinned. "Make it four."

"Done!"

An hour later he and Millie were reading the letter together by the light of a single candle. She was a better reader than he, but even she had to work hard to get all the words straightened out. It was written with a stub pencil and looked like it had been wetted through more than once. But the meaning came through loud as the exultant shout that Joshua used to give when he figured he'd beaten Samuel at something, a loud, yelping bark of triumph that Samuel could hear right now in their room.

For he'd made it—he'd reached Santo Domingo, and it

was a paradise! Black folk everywhere with their heads held high! Nobody shuffling and ducking and pulling off their hats and saying, Yassuh, Yassuh, none of that. Wasn't many whites and the ones he saw were mighty polite. They were the plantation owners who once had owned the slaves, and now it was all turned around. Plenty of whites had been killed, good riddance, and the few who were left had mighty little to say and that was just as it should be, for this was black man's land. He'd dreamed of freedom all his life, and now he had it and he'd never let it go. He had come expecting the French to return and fighting to resume, but such was the genius of Toussaint that the French had welcomed him. Santo Domingo was still a loyal French colony, and Toussaint was its ruler with official rank of captain-general in the French army! So he was figuring now on how he could get Junie and the children and bring them down. He begged Samuel to come on, bring Millie, they would all live free with a lifting spirit that he knew a mere set of papers couldn't give in the United States. Come on down! He was alive as he'd never been before.

Samuel felt as if he'd been holding his breath, and now he let it out in a gasp and couldn't stop himself as he cried, "Isn't that wonderful! God, I'd like to go there, see—"

But Millie was on her feet. "Don't you take the Lord's name in vain," she napped, "and don't you go to talking about going yourself! Someone in this family has to have a little sense, and that's surely not that miserable brother of yours."

"Miserable!" Samuel was outraged. "He's a hero."

"My foot, he's a hero! Goes off and leaves his family untended, he going to get himself killed, and what good does that do them? How's he going to get them out of those Louisiana swamps? How? You tell me that. What kind of hero is a man goes off and leaves his family?"

"But think, Millie," Samuel said softly. "Think about walking around with your head up, not bowing down to any man or woman, no slavers with their whips and clubs, no one asking for your papers. You don't think you'd like that?"

For a moment she hesitated and he saw a look of hunger flash over her face, and then she shook her head. "It ain't going to last," she said, her voice a whisper. "Joshua, he'll be lucky to get out alive, and you and me, we'll have to see to Junie and the children. Your brother ain't going to do it."

Her face was set in stone, and he knew better than to argue with her. But he lay awake a long time thinking about what it would be like to be where most everyone was black and they were free and proud and they didn't truckle to every white face they saw. Someday . . .

After a while he realized Millie was crying and he got his arms around her and held her, she as little as a bird against his chest, and he stroked her hair.

Aaron Burr stood high on an upper terrace outside a row of windows on the east side of the Capitol, taking the sun and the brisk air, comfortably out of the wind. The Senate had gone into recess, and as it turned out in this most bitter political season of his entire life, sitting on the dais as president of the Senate was the sole duty that the vice presidency of the United States allowed him. He was empowered to vote only to break ties formed by men clashing in debate, men who were alive, active, living lives full of meaning. He was the third occupant of his august office; the other two had gone on to the presidency, while the third seemed destined for the ash heap. Or so the Virginia cabal was intent on placing him.

He long since had stopped imagining that Jefferson and Madison meant him anything but malignancy. He had liked them too, supported them, worked for them, seen to their great success. He had sewed up New York and handed it to them in a basket. Just as he had presented little Madison to his bride—he often thought of that day, Dolley an extraordinarily fine piece, radiant in full bloom, the little man gaping at her like a desert wanderer beholding a water hole.

And they had all turned on him, though Dolley was friendly when she saw him. She was still a damned fine-looking woman too, if heavier now and a little worn about the edges. But the betrayal that her husband and his Virginia friends had worked on New York's thoroughbred prancer showed how little honor was to be found below Mason and Dixon's line. Of course, the contretemps over the election was just a ruse, for Burr had examined his conduct again and again and found it spotless. He hadn't raised a hand in his behalf, not a hand. It didn't matter that the Federalists' call for him to come and take the place by storm would have done no good; the point was that he had resisted that call, he had shown no sign of grasping desire. Just a ruse. The Virginia cabal would do anything to remove the New Yorker who stood as its greatest rival, the great threat to its dominance.

He swallowed. It all made him a little sick. Everyone knew he'd been shorn of power—was emasculated too strong a word? Castrated? Were they laughing in the streets of New York? In the past his voice had cracked like thunder there; how loud would it be today? He took a deep breath, steadying himself. The story wasn't over yet, not at all, and his enemies might find the chapters to follow much less satisfactory. Mr. Burr wasn't finished, not by a long shot.

A horseman rounded the corner at a canter, riding a good-looking beast but moving too fast for a city street. Abruptly the rider reined up, and Burr saw with surprise that it was none other than the object of his ruminations, Mr. Madison. The little man proceeded at a sedate pace, slowly dismounted, and tied the horse to the hitching rail next to an iron gray on which Burr had seen that French diplomat, Pichon, the day before.

More and more surprised, he saw Madison tie and untie his horse three separate times. He'd forgotten how to tie a horse? Then, from the corner of his eye, he saw Pichon emerge from the Capitol. Pichon seemed about to turn back into the building, but Madison raised a hand in greeting and Pichon came slowly down the steps. So, something going on with the French.

But what? Thank God for a devious mind—Colonel Burr had a strong capacity to look beyond the immediate. It was Federalist dogma that the administration would be subservient to France with its noble-sounding revolution already collapsed into the arms of a tyrant. But Burr was a Democrat, or had been; he had no thought the idea was true.

But why a meeting with the French so carefully staged to appear accidental? Immediately the rumors current on the New York waterfront flashed to mind. The French were taking Louisiana back from the Spanish. Burr had dismissed it as too casual a rumor until now, but something was afoot with the French and what else could it be?

What a delicious prospect! Of course, Jefferson and Madison would have to resist, and of course, they would fail—imagine that pair of bumblers locked in combat with the mighty Napoleon. Oh, my, this might change everything, for they must surely lose Louisiana and then—

But then he had a sudden feeling he was being watched, and he spun about to see that inadvertently he had stopped outside the chairman's office. And there was Mr. Randolph standing inside the tall window watching Burr watch the man who had stolen his power and all that mattered to him. He was suffused with shame, and ignoring the chairman's cruel salute, his ironic smile, Burr stalked away. His hands were shaking, and he thrust them into his coat pockets.

Things were askew, the world off its axis, and it was time to set it all straight—go back to New York and reclaim his ground and refurbish his power.

Madison was sure that Pichon had started to duck back into the building, but the quick wave stopped him. He came slowly down the steps.

"How nice to see you, sir," Madison said, bowing.

"And you, Mr. Secretary. An unexpected pleasure."

"Glad I bumped into you," Madison said. "There was a point I wanted to bring to your attention." He leaned against the hitching rail and spread both arms. "My, isn't this sun splendid? Fairly shows off a building that's quite fine in its own way." He gestured toward the gleaming stone. "Nothing like Versailles, of course, but a building of such magnitude rising in a new city demonstrates strength that older nations should consider. Neither arm nor will is lacking."

Pichon gave him an uneasy glance. "Certainly, sir. I'm sure that is so." He was a slight figure in a plain black suit with white stock. Present problem aside, Madison liked him; there was a steady strength about him oddly combined with a wistful quality, as if he'd once dreamed dreams that were not to be.

"Yes, a handsome building. As much so inside as out. I suppose you've been in with my old friend, Gouverneur Morris." Pichon shot him a startled glance; oh yes, hand in the cookie jar, all right. Of course diplomats spoke to the opposition, but they were expected to be discreet.

Madison smiled. "Gouverneur's a charming man, very able. Unfortunately, he has a terrible blind spot on Democrats. Believes in his heart that we're going to wither and fade into nothing." He laughed. "No evidence I can show him will persuade him. That's the way with blind spots, don't you find?"

His tone had been light and genial. Now he turned to stare directly into Pichon's eyes and hardened his voice. "No one should base his perceptions of America on Gouverneur's opinions. He and his friends are uniformly wrong; they represent the past, the Democrats the future."

"Of course, Mr. Secretary, I don't—"

Madison waved this off with a careless flick of his hand and said, "Now, sir, I have on my desk a true copy of a treaty between France and Spain that details the retrocession of Louisiana to France. What is your explanation for this?"

Pichon went pale. "I—I would want to see that, sir."

Madison took a step back. "Sir! Do you doubt my word?"

"No, no." Pichon shook his head, rattled. "Forgive me, sir. An ejaculation of surprise, nothing more."

"Very well, sir." Madison cooled his voice further. "Did you know about this when the president asked you last night?"

"Certainly not!"

"Then this whole matter was held secret from you as it

was from us. We, who are most affected of all. I find an incredible hostility in that act, Mr. Pichon. Incredible."

"Sir, I—"

"You understand that our vital interests go directly to the Mississippi. It waters the center of our continent, it gives half our nation outlet to the sea, it's central to our commerce, travel avenue for our western people."

Madison saw that as planned, the news flung suddenly in the Frenchman's face in this most nondiplomatic of settings had quite disconcerted him. Plain potato, Wagner had said, and honest; Madison agreed with both.

But he thought Pichon would stiffen, which he did. Perhaps, the chargé said, his nation felt no obligation to inform nations not involved. Not involved? It was an unfortunate phrase and Madison used it to beat him about the head.

"But surely," Pichon cried, "you can't object to France recovering what was taken from it forty years ago?"

"The world has changed in forty years; the United States most of all."

"But what's the harm? It's not yours now. What difference whether we hold it or Spain?"

"Collisions, sir," Madison drew himself up. "Collisions between citizens of both nations are certain to follow, too far from the seat of either government to contain in time to prevent very serious consequences. It is incredibly dangerous."

"But why? Rivers in Europe are jointly navigated by different countries all the time."

"There, sir! You reveal the ignorance that lies behind this mad move—equating a raw frontier a thousand miles distant with the close confines of Europe. 'Pon my word, this suggests criminal ignorance of American terrain in your government."

"Well, Spain holds it now, and you get on with Spain."

"Spain is weak and pliant, sir. And if it weren't, we'd seize Louisiana. Throw them into the sea. It's easily in our power and threatened constantly by our western hot sparks. Does 'pliant' describe the imperial armies of Napoleon Bonaparte?"

Pichon shook his head, his face flushed.

"Now, sir, please mark my words well. The fact is that if France were to take Louisiana, it wouldn't last long. The force of nature will make that country ours in due time. *We* have the settlers flooding westward, advancing mile by mile, a rising tide. In the end they'll absorb and control by the force of numbers. It's the *American* West, you see—a ripening apple poised for the autumn drop. No nation, France nor Spain, can resist the American tide."

The next day Madison issued written protests to France and to Spain. It was plain that neither Pichon nor Yrujo had been informed, which was the most ominous point of all. Yrujo tried to bluster a bit, and Madison shut him off with a glance. Then the secretary went home exhausted. Both France and Spain had been put on notice that the United States intended to play a hand in this game. Now he must set about devising that hand.

23

BOSTON, EARLY 1802

A heavy, blustering fellow with red face and a ruff of white whiskers, wearing a coat that looked slept in and gave off a rich odor, lurched up the stairs to the cubbyhole office over the print shop.

"John Quincy Adams? Good! They tell me no one goes to law better'n you."

The flattery chilled Adams. The fellow seized his hand and pumped it, crowding close as Adams backed almost into the corner.

"Name's Silas Barnstover and I aim to sue my neighbor. Son of a bitch poisoned my cow."

"Can you prove that?" Adams said.

"Why, hell yes. Everyone around saw the dead cow—"

"I mean that your neighbor poisoned—"

"Well, what else could it be, cow swole up and died overnight? Cows don't just die, you know."

"They get sick though."

"Sick? Why, old Boss never had a sick day in her life. Gave milk every day for ten years."

"Ten years? Maybe she died of old age."

Barnstover's face went several deeper shades of red. "You ain't working for my neighbor; you're working for me! And I say the son of a bitch poisoned her, and I want him to pay! So let's get busy."

"I'll need a retainer of twenty dollars," Adams said.

"Twenty dollars! I ain't got that kind of money. We gotta get it out of the hide of that bastard next door."

"I can't start without a retainer."

Barnstover stared with palpable contempt. "Got your palm out first crack outta the box, eh? What the hell kind of lawyer are you anyway?"

As the failed client went down the stairs cursing out loud, Adams sat at his desk and held his head in his hands. God, he did hate the practice of law. What kind of a lawyer are you anyway? A failing lawyer, that's what kind. A lawyer who, in his day, had spoken to kings and dined with dukes and represented his nation all over Europe and now couldn't handle a client with a cow that probably had blown her belly with the colic.

With a start he drew the turnip watch from his waistcoat pocket. Ten in the morning! Court would be opening, and he needed to be there in case a judge tossed a stray case his way. It was exquisite humiliation for the former ambassador, son of the former president, heir to one of the great names in America, to stand in the well of the court where all could see him waiting for a morsel tossed like a scrap to a hound; but he had no choice. He was slowly going broke, savings eroding, cases rare, and winning cases even rarer. Well, it was his own fault too. He spent little or no time with fellow attorneys who were dolts and buffoons, he avoided the clubs and coffeehouses where judges lounged. They were dolts and buffoons too, and politicians were worse. He couldn't even talk to such oafs, found nothing to say, and sounded stilted and unreal when he tried. He disliked his office full of ink odor and the squealing of the press screw from below and he had little to do there anyway, so he walked, miles and miles every day, around the Boston Common and up and down the hills and through pastures, walking and thinking. . . .

At least the house he'd purchased on Hanover Square was finished, and Louisa was beginning to return to life. The time with his parents in Braintree had been hard on her; his father had welcomed her warmly, but his mother had gazed on her new daughter-in-law with reserve if not disdain—seemed to say, let the girl prove herself over the next few years. A rough beginning . . .

Then those long sessions at Braintree, the whole family debating how the brilliant scion, whose star now seemed so dim, should support himself. The law, his mother said to general agreement, there was no other answer, and he supposed them right. Certainly not politics; politics had betrayed the Adamses. The rise of parties with their ugly partisanship had destroyed the purity of public service. Parties so tarnished all they touched that confused voters had turned on the leading man in the nation, a man who towered over others for probity, wisdom, intellect, decency, who had honed himself for leadership over a lifetime. Rejected for a slick talker, a Frenchified dreamer. Yes, once the Adamses and the Jeffersons had been the closest friends, but that was before the French Revolution had seduced the Virginian. And even back in those days, they now could see, there had been a lightness, a curious frivolity that allowed the man to embrace the strangest ideas! And strangest of all was this idea of universal democracy, the common man on a par with those who really count in any society, those on whom a nation's solidity rests! Democracy, the former president sagely observed, was like a rake full of fine promises who seduces a trusting maid. . . .

Yet walking briskly along the Common, circling the long way to Hanover Square, using his stick to thread his way through clusters of sheep who would move after a sharp rap on the nose, circling carefully around obviously truculent goats—goats were true Bostonians, not to be fooled with—Adams remembered his years in public life with nostalgia. A regular income, important work that mattered in international context, a gentleman's existence that allowed ample time for the study that Adams knew was his real vocation—those had been glorious days! Of course, the family was right, for the only entry into public service today was through party, and it was clear there was no party an honest man could join without blushing. Adams was a Federalist but his own party was a disgrace, the other an abomination.

He was thus ruminating when Timothy Pickering came bearing down on him with a loud hail and raised arm. He bowed stiffly but Pickering seized him in warm embrace and half led, half dragged him to a nearby bench surrounded by biscuit crumbs where someone had been feeding pigeons. Seated, Pickering was scarcely taller than Adams, meaning his height was in his legs; for some reason Adams didn't bother to analyze, this pleased him. Pickering sat hunched forward with his elbows on bony knees, eyes deeply set in his slender face glowing with fervor.

"My dear fellow," he said with a warm smile, the rancor of their last meeting forgotten or dismissed, "it's good to see you home where you belong. We need you, you know."

"Oh?" Adams said, more grunt than comment. Pickering headed a radical group of Federalist congressmen called the Essex Junto that was determined to regain power—or separate.

"Yes, great things are afoot." He lowered his voice and glanced around the deserted common as if he sensed spies everywhere. "You more than anyone understand the nation's danger—the administration is a disaster, the coward wretch at the head of it all, he's like a Parisian revolutionary monster prattling about humanity, but truth is he would feel utter pleasure in destroying everything. Handmaiden to the French, sir. Can you believe the process of handing our country over lock, stock, and barrel to that dissolute nation has already started?"

Adams's expression must have reflected his doubt, for Pickering said, as if anxious to persuade, "Captain Sinclair of the brig *Sweet Lily,* out of New Orleans five weeks ago, couldn't wait to bring me the news. New Orleans is alive with a rumor—the French are taking over!"

"Rumors. A penny a bushel."

"But this has the smack of truth. France taking control from the Spanish, reclaim what it lost fifty years ago, rebuild its empire, it makes perfect sense. And not a word from the administration, not a word! And you know why? Because it's part of the plot, let the enemy in the back door, say nothing until it's too late."

Adams didn't answer. He distrusted rumors, but could this be true? A disaster if it proved so. France dominating the Mississippi Valley sooner or later would shear off the West and cripple the country. The habit of thinking as a diplomat in international terms had never left him; at last he murmured, "Very dangerous if true."

"Well," Pickering said, "at least it bells the cat. Tells us what that benighted man really plans—make us a mere province of France."

"Or force us into war."

"Oh, he don't want war. And we won't fight over that river. Why should we? The West means nothing to us. No, no, Mr. Adams, the West's importance is as proof of perfidy, nothing more. That's the real core issue, you see—just how much turpitude must we accept before we act, how much?"

"Turpitude?"

"Of course. His cruel removal of faithful officers, the substitution of corruption and baseness for integrity and worth—." Pickering appeared ready to go on at some length and Adams settled back on the bench. Of course, the man was a famous hater, but his vehemence was surprising. Adams had been reviewing the administration's early record, and he found it surprisingly good. The only removals of office holders for reasons other than cause had been among magistrates and marshals, and almost apologetically Jefferson had explained that some of their own in these ranks really was the only protection Democrats had against the more aggressive Federalist officers. Adams suggested as much to Pickering, reminding him that his own chief clerk, Mr. Wagner, had been kept on. Surely that was a favorable sign—

"That oaf," Pickering snapped. "A traitor! How could he live in that administration and carry out its benighted policies. He's disgustingly loyal to his new masters—won't say a word of the awful scandals we know go on every day."

The former secretary of state continued in this vein for some time, but the more Adams listened the more it seemed to him that all we had here was a different philosophy of government. Yes, Jefferson was economizing brutally, when it was the dictum of Alexander Hamilton that a big and expensive government with its consequent need for borrowing bound together government, business, and high finance, solidifying and empowering each. Jefferson was whittling down the massive public debt that had soared to eighty million dollars under Hamilton, promising to halve it by the next election, with consequent reduction of the power of the moneyed, while Hamilton saw that big anchoring debt putting good interest in the pockets of the wealthy as a fundament of his kind of government. The new men did seem obsessed with democracy—take this foolish "pell-mell" admission to presidential events, no protocol, no ranking by diplomatic standing, just a race for the gravy bowl. The old diplomat in Adams rebelled at such crudity. Naturally the diplomatic establishment was in an uproar. That was carrying things beyond reason. And the Democrats were even more obsessed with making sure that wealth alone gave an American citizen no greater political power than that possessed by the common man. Adams didn't approve of all this and his father sharply disapproved, but both agreed it was a difference in approach rather than a manifestation of evil.

Jefferson was cutting army and navy; Adams disagreed on the question of the navy, the only real protection of our coasts and trade in a world torn by war, but he had to admit that Hamilton's plans for a large army were pointless if not dangerous with no war to fight. Democrats said the real aim had been to control the citizenry; Adams could hardly credit that, but reducing the army's size didn't dismay him. What did dismay him was closing so many embassies, including Berlin and the Hague where he had served so faithfully. Did we care nothing for the people there?

Choosing his words, he said that while he disagreed with administration's aims, he found it moderate in execution. Pickering reared back on the bench as if stung. Head thrown back, he glared at Adams and snapped, "My God! Don't tell me you're taken in by that! Of course he's moderate now. He's luring the people, trying to prove all their fears are groundless, before he unveils his revolutionary aims. Don't you see? He's waiting until he can turn us over to the French revolutionary party! That's what you call moderation—it's simple trickery!"

He leaned close. His stock was twisted on his neck, and Adams caught an odor of garlic. "Study it, my boy, you'll see that it's all flummery. Oh, I pray the people will recognize the dupery in time." He paused, staring with glittering eyes, and then whispered with another conspiratorial glance around the empty common, "But if they don't, we have plans to save ourselves and save all that's dear to God-fearing New England folk. Here in New England, you know, is the locus for all that is pure and fine about our country, the last bastion of decency against the imperial pretensions of Virginia to rule or ruin. Don't think the slave-holding South and West don't intend to crush us to their ends, don't think we won't see niggers as president, niggers in control of Congress. That's what's coming!"

Again that conspiratorial glance all around. "But that part of the country is worthless anyway! *Here* is where all good is centered. And we can save it."

Adams had a sudden feeling he should get up and walk

away right now, but there was a fascination to this ranting too, and he said, "What do you mean?"

He saw that Pickering had taken his response for more than it was worth. The former secretary of state rolled his shoulders in a little shiver of enthusiasm and inched closer on the bench. It was this expression of complicity that reminded Adams that here was the man who had betrayed his president while sitting in his cabinet. Pickering's voice sank to a confidential whisper. He hoped administration excesses would bring people to their senses before the next election and they'd hurl Democrats into outer darkness. But suppose the great villain didn't reveal himself in time and the people remained as duped as they were today. Then it would be time for men who loved their region to separate and go their way alone.

Separate?

A broad smile swept Pickering's expression, and he rubbed his hands together. Adams felt a dismaying heaviness of heart. Radical Federalists intended to peel off New England into a new nation and call on Britain to assist and protect them. They would shake free of democratic nonsense. Let the Virginians sell themselves to France, as they so obviously planned, and the devil take them!

It sounded feckless, the five states of New England—Massachusetts, Connecticut, Rhode Island, New Hampshire, Vermont—forming a viable nation, but Pickering hadn't the slightest doubt and his argument did make a certain sense. New England had the bulk of American trade, most of the shipping, more than most of the manufacturing. But to seal the deal, he added with a sly grin, they would bring in New York. New Jersey certainly would follow, and then they would have all that was worth having and Virginians could go peddle their tobacco.

New York? Alexander Hamilton was part of this plot? Hamilton was no friend of the Adamses—it was on his behalf that Pickering and other cabinet officers had undermined their president, his brutal letter against President Adams that had shattered the election, but you couldn't help respecting the man's intellect. Pickering frowned. Obviously feeling he'd admitted a flaw, he said that Alex had not yet seen the wisdom of separation—he still mouthed platitudes about the integrity of the country when any unbiased man could see there was no integrity and scarcely any country left.

No, he said, Mr. Burr was their man. Burr? Yes, he was more than available. Everyone knew he'd been frozen out, the second office in the land reduced to empty mockery. Burr was a ferret in seeking his own advantage, and he would see immediately that the separation plan would create a compact nation actually stronger than the nation he would be leaving. And what sweet revenge it would promise against the villain who'd so abused him! Burr was certain to return to New York soon to seize the reins. He was a political genius; he'd have no trouble ousting Governor Clinton and Clinton's lickspittle nephew, DeWitt. And he wouldn't hesitate over secession.

Struck between horror and awe at the sheer effrontery of such a plan, Adams said, "You'd make Burr your—what, president, leader, ruler?"

Pickering grinned. "At first. For the time being. When he was no longer needed, then we'd have to see, wouldn't we?"

He inched forward on the bench, drawing closer, voice dropping. "Now, Mr. Adams, here's the point. Your father is too mired in the ways of the past to recognize new opportunity. But you're young and vigorous. We believe you'll recognize the stark sound of reality knocking. In short, I'm authorized to reveal these matters because we want you with us."

"You're authorized?"

"The group decided. I told 'em I knew you. So I extend warm welcome—"

Adams knew the blood had drained from his face. He was being asked to betray the country he and his father and his family had served most of their lives in a plot that could tear it to pieces. It crossed his mind to slap the man's face at the insult, but even in Boston that could lead to a challenge and it wasn't worth it. He stood suddenly. Pickering's mouth went slack in surprise.

"Mr. Pickering," he said, "your plans are rotten to the core, and I, sir, shall fight them in every way I can. Let me tell you this, too. Asking me join in the betrayal of my country is an insult that I shan't forget."

Pickering bounded off the bench. "Now, hold on!" Adams turned and walked away. "You're making a big mistake, young man, and you'll pay for it—I'll see to that."

Adams walked on, feeling soiled and disgusted. Yet within a quarter mile he realized his feelings were more complex; he was also excited and engaged. They had been talking real issues, something to fight, something that mattered, magnitude to engage a man of range and scale. How different Barnstover's cow!

That New Orleans rumor. His diplomat's mind was at work. It had a certain smack of authenticity. He'd had too much experience with the French dictator not to know that such a move would fit Napoleon's thinking perfectly. He began running over the issues that might arise, the variations that could unfold. What would he do if he were in the cockpit when such a rumor matured into fact?

The thought brought up an idle dream that had afflicted him with a curious hunger on his long walks. He was an intellectual to his core and politics was vile, but sometimes he could imagine himself at the helm in stormy seas, wise, magisterial, a philosopher king far above the roiling waters of politics. Just a dream, but still . . .

Could the family be wrong? Did he perhaps owe it to country and community—and, yes, to family too—to take a hand in vital issues wherever he could? But that meant politics and partisanship and soiling himself as he'd sworn he never would do. Yet the Adams name stood for something. The radicals wanted him, and clearly he'd be even more valuable to moderates. Still, he couldn't *seek* office, manipulate and maneuver and promise. He wouldn't stoop to politics, but if the people asked him and he made it plain that he

would be guided only by honor and never by expediency . . .
if the people asked.

Then he stopped abruptly. They had asked! Anthony
Markley, representing Federalists alarmed by Essex Junto
vitriol, wanted to support him for an open seat in the state
senate. Sitting in the senate, speaking his mind on real issues, having a place where he belonged, receiving a small
but helpful stipend . . . it was newly attractive. He turned
abruptly and cut down a side street toward the Sword & Anchor where Markley was to be found each afternoon. He felt
more alive than he had in months.

A bit later Adams found himself in the distinctly unfinished
new city of Washington where forsythia made yellow explosions and the air felt like spring, while in Boston remnants
of snow still lay undisturbed in shadow. On the other hand,
Boston was a fine city with cobbled streets and brick houses
wall-to-wall with little iron fences separating small yards
and alleys leading to the barns in back, while Washington reminded Adams of a man who had only a tooth or two left in
an empty mouth, so widely scattered were the occasional
buildings linked by weed-strewn roads of mud.

He was prowling the unfinished Capitol Building and at
French doors that opened onto a terrace below which a long
staircase fell he paused to gaze on a bucolic scene. Members
and clerks, he had no way of telling them apart, lounged in
the sun on the steps eating sausages wrapped in buns and
emptying mugs of beer bought from hawkers in the rotunda.
Somewhere Adams could hear children laughing; a group of
women hesitated at the sight of so many men on the stairs,
then with resolute shakes of parasols started up as men hastened to make way for them.

He felt oddly at home here, though he knew no one and
doubtless no one knew him. But this was the center of
things, national things. The voters of Boston had welcomed
him as their state senator and were allowing him to feel that

he honored them by serving as their representative. A state office had limited range, of course, but nevertheless had worked wonders on his mood. Even his law practice seemed less onerous now, and the stipend, though small, certainly helped.

Now, more flattering still, crowds were urging him to run for Congress. He must take care not to seem to want office— he was nothing like your usual politician slathering for power—but if they sought him out, don't you see, if they presented a need that only he could fill, the office might have its compensations. A decent salary . . . a return to public life that clearly was his real calling . . . a hand in national affairs and perhaps a voice in braking the mad rush of the Democrats toward disaster with the French. Yes, it could be attractive, provided it was clear he didn't seek it.

He was in Washington despite his duties at home because Louisa's father had died. Poor Joshua Johnson had never been the same since losing the American consul's position in London; he'd been quite lordly when Adams was in his townhouse there courting Louisa, but he'd gone steadily down since, from a broken heart, Louisa was sure. Having made all the proper observances, Adams felt he might as well visit the Capitol where, after all, he might himself soon be installed. And so, having walked the marble halls and purchased himself an egg custard in the rotunda; he had wandered down an empty corridor to these French doors. The sunny scene outside was appealing, but he had passed an open door and seen books lining the walls of a small room and the student in him demanded investigation.

The room, the door open but no one in attendance, clearly was the Library of Congress, composed mostly of a collection of volumes purchased from Mr. Jefferson's fine library. Adams walked about looking at familiar titles; during a period of his youth in Paris, when Mr. Jefferson was almost his mentor, Adams had read his way through much of his patron's already extensive library. There was a tactile, physical pleasure, almost sensuous, in opening the very books he'd read long ago; eventually he settled on an atlas bound in leather that covered the shape of Europe before Napoleon began rearranging it.

Someone entered the room but hunched over the atlas, and resenting interruption, he didn't look up. The newcomer moved about the room pulling down a book here and another there.

"Mr. Adams?" Startled, Adams looked up to see that the newcomer was the secretary of state. He leaped to his feet. "Mr. Madison," he said, bowing deeply. Yet there was something desultory in the other's manner, and Adams had the odd thought, immediately dismissed as totally unlikely and quite self-serving, that Madison had sought him out. That could hardly be.

Sitting across the table as if time was of no consequence, Mr. Madison asked after President and Mrs. Adams, were they well and please convey his greetings. He went on to congratulate Adams on his state senate seat and suggest that he might find happiness here in the national capital. Presently Adams had the curious sense that the man was waiting for something, and finally it dawned on him that Madison waited for him to speak.

So he said, "Sir, in Boston ships from New Orleans are bringing distressing rumors—that the French are reclaiming Louisiana, or at least New Orleans, from the Spanish."

The secretary didn't answer, but his eyes brightened. Adams added, "It would be extraordinary dangerous if it were true."

"Yes . . . if it were true and if it were realized." He gazed at Adams and then, as if making up his mind, said, "Now, you're a seasoned diplomat. I believe you are a man of intense patriotism. I know your father is, and I doubt you've fallen far from the tree. Hence, I think you understand diplomatic discretion. Now, sir, these rumors are worthy of discussion . . . as rumors."

"Yes, sir," Adams said, slightly abashed. The secretary would admit nothing but might discuss matters hypothetically. It was a courtesy, more than he had right to expect.

The secretary was folding and refolding a piece of foolscap; from it he fashioned a small paper boat that he placed on the table between them. "Now, suppose for a moment that any country—France, Germany, Britain—were to act as the rumors suggest; we would want to persuade the offender to change its plan."

"If Napoleon were the offender, he doesn't persuade easily."

"Yes," Mr. Madison said dryly, "but no one is immune to reason, and I think we could demonstrate the reason of our position." He paused and then added almost casually, "In the end, of course, in the hypothetical we're building, we would have to meet force with force."

The words, rich with the clash of arms, had an unlikely sound in this quiet room of books. Both men were speaking in soft voices designed not to carry, and Adams noticed that the secretary sat with chair turned so that he could see the door and anyone who entered. They were almost . . . conspiratorial.

Force with force when the army was shrinking and naval vessels were being retired? What force? Was this just brave talk? Yes, state militias would be mustered, troops willing but raw, but could they stand against a seasoned army? Then, thinking far ahead of the little secretary, he saw the answer. An army lived by its supply chain. Cut that chain and—

"You'd call in the Royal Navy, wouldn't you?"

Madison laughed out loud. "Your Federalist colors are showing, sir! Hook or crook, the Federalists want us under the British wing—or should I say between the lion's paws?" But before Adams could protest, Madison continued, "You see that what would be the Federalists' first move would be our last—for to call in the Royal Navy would reduce us to a British pawn."

Pawn? My, my, my. He wondered if the secretary might be a bit more naive than he had at first supposed. After all, the man had never been outside the United States and knew nothing firsthand of the courts of Europe. To Adam's experienced mind, remembering the long, gloomy corridors of

Whitehall quartering the Foreign Service, London skies leaking rain outside, it was obvious that Britain would react violently to the idea of France trying to restore the empire that Britain had taken from it forty years before.

Look at the threat the French in the Mississippi Valley would pose to Canada; see the way it would challenge Britain's open interest in the Pacific Northwest. Why, Britain tolerated the independence of the United States only grudgingly a quarter century after the fact. That it would tolerate a French move on North America seemed ludicrous. On top of all else, the American breadbasket would give Napoleon the fuel to conquer the world.

Couching these thoughts with elaborate courtesy, he went on for some time, adding, "Now, sir, perhaps Napoleon's dreams are feckless, though can one be sure of anything in this modern world? But one thing I do know, Britain will never acquiesce in France reentering North America—"

He broke off as Madison raised a hand. He felt oddly abashed. Something his father once said came to mind, that many men underestimated Mr. Madison and most learned to regret it.

Gently the secretary said, "Your point is well taken and, I think, accurate. But it overlooks another aspect. You would agree, I think, that Spain, though under Napoleon's thumb, is at best his reluctant ally?"

Adams stared at him. He felt his cheeks turning red. Confound his ready tongue! He'd forgotten that if anyone took Louisiana, the taking would be from Spain, and Spain was in the French orbit only by coercion. When the wars of the French Revolution began, Spain had turned to Britain. It was with Spain's help that Britain had seized the major French naval base on the Mediterranean, at Toulon, and it was Napoleon's thundering guns driving those forces out that set him on the career that made him ruler of France.

Raw force kept Spain in line now. The last thing Britain would want as it faced France in a death struggle on the Continent would be an infuriated Spain converted into a willing ally to Napoleon. His cheeks were aflame; he had grossly underestimated the little man.

"So you see the equation," Madison was saying. Unfortunately, Mr. Adams thought wryly, he was seeing it rather too late. Apparently unaware of his chagrin, Mr. Madison continued in a placid voice, seeming merely to chat about national matters. But a clerk walked in with an armful of books and Madison broke off. Startled and suddenly aware of the silence, the clerk backed out with apologies.

"Of course, these are just rumors from a city famous for gossip," Madison said, "but if there were something to them, doubtless Britain would be concerned. But wouldn't they immediately face two crucial decisions?"

Alternative courses . . . first, they certainly could seize New Orleans and Louisiana themselves. That would infuriate Spain—Mr. Madison nodding to himself thoughtfully—but then there would be consolations, wouldn't there? They would possess the very empire that rumor says France covets. The American breadbasket would feed British rather than French soldiers. At the same time, they could incorporate the vast ranges of Louisiana—right out to the Stony Mountains—into Canada and anchor forever the Pacific Northwest. Why, in effect, it would give them the continent, the upstart United States limited to the eastern seaboard. For such a prize, he supposed they could risk the wrath of Spain.

For a moment Adams thought the secretary would make sport at Federalist expense, since cutting off the West had great appeal to some in Adams's party. But he went right on.

"Or the next alternative: They help us take it. Now, that solves the problem of the French, but it enrages Spain and leaves Britain with a fierce new enemy. And the United States has the West. Canada will be a chilly waste up around Hudson's Bay, and the Pacific Northwest will more likely finish in our hands than in theirs. Were they to enter such a bad bargain, I'd guess they'd want some compensation, don't you suppose? You know they've been urging us to join the war on their side from the start, saying it's our duty to mankind and all that. And it is obvious that together we would rule the seas, our merchant ships feeding their troops and starving their enemy."

Oh, yes, now Mr. Adams could see the equation. Britain's price for snatching our chestnuts from the fire would be to plunge us into the endless European war. He knew how implacable Britain's thinking had become as it fought for its life; let the United States enter that alliance and Britain inevitably would squeeze it dry.

But now Adams found his chagrin was fading into exultation—what a joy to be here at the nation's center talking of vital national concerns to a man of power! It had been months since he'd had such talk, and he could feel the last vestiges of his reluctance to run for Congress melting away. This, not the law in Boston, was his natural milieu!

Yet this was a strange encounter, the secretary going to such lengths on so thinly disguised an account. It seemed something had happened or threatened in Louisiana—he remembered his initial impression that the secretary had sought him out . . . or followed him. He couldn't believe that Mr. Madison spoke so to everyone he met. Could he possibly be interested in the former ambassador's opinion? It was tempting, but he must not make himself foolish again. Yet . . .

Tentatively: "I suppose comment would be inappropriate—"

"I would welcome your comment, sir. You've had a dozen years abroad; you know many of the figures involved."

Yes, that might be Adams's value, not the broad picture about which the secretary had thought much more deeply than he, but the specifics. "Well, sir," he said, "Napoleon, now, I suppose I've talked to him, oh, a half-dozen times. He's brutally strong, rough by nature, not highly intelligent, but supremely canny. Perhaps he's a military genius—I wouldn't know—but the dominant impression he leaves is that his mind is very tough, his will is imperative, and his conscience scarcely exists. But he is absolutely not a fool. In your hypothetical, I think he would be open to reason."

Madison was listening. So far, so good. "I spent three months in London once trying to make headway in the foreign office, and I can assure you that no nation is more assiduous in pursuing its own interests. It does feel desperate and rightfully so, fighting for its life as it is. Yet it is a strong country and even in war thinks long term. It would be fully capable of taking and maintaining Louisiana if it decided to do so; if it were to help someone else do so, it would have to be shown how its own interests were served and it would drive a very hard bargain. So I think the hypothetical makes sense."

He hesitated. His next thought was more personal; would that be appropriate? Still, it could be helpful. "Also, sir, I know Louis Pichon well. Once we made a three-month holiday tour together. It was Pichon that the Directory sent to me with word that France really didn't want war with the United States. I suppose you know it was on that basis that my father sent a new delegation to strike a peace treaty?"

"Your father demonstrated a nobility of nature in that decision. I'd be pleased if you conveyed that thought."

"Thank you, sir; he'll be gratified. As to Monsieur Pichon, he will cleave to the interests of France, but within that context he can be trusted fully. I hope to dine with him before I leave."

"Really? Then let me charge you with a mission. Tell Mr. Pichon, from the highest authority, that the United States has profound affection for France, but that its defense of its own integrity is without limits."

It was wonderful! Like old times at the diplomatic center of things. "Thank you, Mr. Madison; I will convey that."

The secretary stood, stretching. "I must be along," he said, and then, looking into Adams's eyes, added, "You know, you would make a good Democrat. My guess is you will find yourself too often out of step as a Federalist. You're too sensible; you see too clearly. Your fellow Federalists would distrust you. If you reach such a decision, I assure you a warm welcome in the party of common sense."

Well! Ten minutes later Adams was skipping down that

long staircase in a fever of enthusiasm. He wouldn't be leaving his father's party, but as for stepping onto the national stage, he was more than ready! He smacked fist into palm and trotted on.

24

WASHINGTON, EARLY 1802

Johnny Graham brought in the packet bearing Mr. Livingston's report from Paris and squared it neatly on Madison's desk. Mr. Wagner was right behind him.

At last! Their ambassador had long since departed for France with orders to seek out the truth of the early rumors on Louisiana. Since then just a note that he had reached Le Havre. The packet was wrapped in oilcloth, tied with diplomatic red ribbon, and sealed at every possible opening with gobs of red wax impressed with the embassy seal. Something about this fussy wrapping, sealed as if for a trip to the North Pole, brought Robert Livingston forcefully to mind—tall, slow moving and slow talking, long face, long nose, gazing serenely about with an expression Madison read as profoundly self-satisfied. He came from one of the great landed families of New York State, was chancellor of New York for many years, and once was secretary of state himself—secretary for foreign affairs it was called before the Constitution drafted a new form of government.

He shook his head, lips pursed. The truth was he simply didn't like the man.

Whereas young Mr. Adams had been surprisingly pleasant the day before. He had spied the president's son in the rotunda and followed him on impulse. Here was a man with more recent diplomatic experience than anyone Madison knew and engaging him had proved valuable. That he had offered no aspect they had not considered was reassuring; indeed, faced with the realities he seemed to endorse the Democratic view. Clever fellow and certainly no roaring Federalist; but then, the Adamses were always patriots and at their core sensible, though the old gentleman did fly into dreadful fusses to no very useful end. John Quincy might make a good Democrat yet.

Ruminating thus, Madison tore the last of the wax-festooned oil paper off the packet. Of course the letter would be anticlimactic in a sense—it would describe the treaty they already possessed—but it should add details and sort out the aims behind the radical French move. He drew forth the report, a dozen sheets written in an angular, upright hand that seemed somehow to reflect Livingston's proud manner, started reading—

"Good God!"

He looked up. Wagner and Johnny were staring at him.

"He asked about the rumors, and their foreign secretary—Talleyrand—simply denied them. Said there was nothing to it, nothing had happened, nothing to talk about. Waved Livingston off—but we have a copy of the treaty!"

He gazed at them. "Incredible! Talleyrand was simply lying."

With growing anger he read through the long, tedious letter searching for answers that didn't come. When he put it down, his hand quivered. His glance fell on the oilcloth wrapping festooned with all that ridiculous wax—the man must have used three sticks!—and he cried, "And in the end, Mr. Livingston did nothing about it whatsoever. Nothing! He should have challenged that arrogant Frenchman to his face!"

"But, sir," Wagner said, "if he doesn't know what we know, he has no basis to challenge."

"Well, damn it, he should have done something!"

He ran down the letter again. "Oh, my, look at this. Says he's not satisfied, says Talleyrand's manner suggested subterfuge, as if he didn't expect to be taken seriously, says he

really was quite flippant." He slapped the desk furiously.
"Hurrah for our envoy's perspicacity! He actually thinks
there's something odd about all this! Says he'll nose about."

With a bad metallic taste in his mouth, Madison dismissed the clerks. Presently he wadded up the oilcloth and
hurled it into the waste bin. All that wax, those silly seals,
when he had nothing to report but that he'd been bamboo-
zled.

"Anna," Dolley said, "what's going on with you and
Merry?" They were in Dolley's bedroom; she was pinning a
gown to fit her sister's slender hips. It had grown dark outside and two sperm oil lamps glowed.

"Why, nothing." Anna had a quizzical, amused expression.

"You've been encouraging him, haven't you?"

"What? There's no need to encourage him; he just seems
attracted to me. Men are, you know." She shrugged. "What
can I do about it? Anyway, who are you to talk? Men have
always been drawn to you. They used to follow you around
in flocks, and they still look at you all the time."

"But Merry's an innocent, and I think you've been playing games. He's too nice a young man to break his heart."

"Oh, pshaw!" Just then Jimmy came in. Anna ran to kiss
his cheek and vanished down the stairs.

"What got into her?" Jimmy said.

"Oh, I was taking her to task. She's been flirting with
Merry."

"Well, what's wrong with that?" He frowned. "Merry's a
fine young man, I suppose he'd make a good husband—"

"Oh, Jimmy, she's not going to marry Meriwether Lewis!
She's in love with Mr. Cutts."

"Oh," Jimmy said. He sat down, shaking his head.

From a glance at him she braced for bad news. "So," she
said, "how are things?"

He sighed. "Well, I think we've made a terrible mistake in
posting Livingston to the Paris embassy," he said.

What? She liked Mr. Livingston and admired him as well, as much for his urbane, confident manner as for a genuinely kindly nature. She'd known him for years and she'd renewed the acquaintance in a long talk at the President's House just before he went abroad. He'd come to Washington without Mrs. Livingston, and when Tom gave him a small dinner, he'd asked her to join them. Good thing, too, for their guest had scarcely arrived before Tom and Jimmy were called away on something and she had entertained him. Mr. Lemaire sent in a plate of little ham tartlets, the wine was excellent, the talk genial.

Merry appeared after forty-five minutes to express further regrets, saying it was just one of those minor crises.

Most gallantly, she'd thought, Mr. Livingston had said, "Please tell the president that I'm more than pleased for the chance to visit with the charming Mrs. Madison." And to her, with a trace of anxiety, "I hope you won't think me forward, my dear, if I say I expect I'll enjoy this quiet chat with you a good deal more than talking to Mr. Jefferson or even with your esteemed husband." And he'd reminded her of a cotillion in Philadelphia where he'd been her partner while Mr. Hamilton paired with Mrs. Livingston.

"Of course," Jimmy said, "when we named him we had no idea the French would make such an insane move." Listening, she could see why the letter disappointed him but not why he blamed the ambassador. Talleyrand seemed the one at fault.

"I never cared for him," Jimmy was saying, "but we pretty well had to offer him something. He's very prominent—delivered the oath at President Washington's first inaugural, for goodness sake. And New York is important, especially since we dropped Burr."

She still thought Tom and Jimmy made much too much of Burr's apostasy. Aaron hadn't been trying to betray the Democratic Party; he was just being his usual greedy self.

"We needed something good for Livingston, but we'd closed the other embassies, just London, Paris, and Madrid left. Wanted to keep Rufus King in London and Livingston had no Spanish, so that left Paris. And I suppose he'd have been all right if this crisis hadn't arisen."

"But all he did is report this Talleyrand person's answer. Isn't that what you'd want him to do?"

"He should have found something to do."

"Oh, Jimmy, you're too critical. I thought he was charming and quite able, a man of considerable vision. Anyway, I don't see what he could have done; this Talleyrand must be a monster."

"I certainly am not too critical! I know what I expect in an ambassador. My, God, any fool can go to diplomatic parties; you have to *do* something when you get there."

"Isn't Talleyrand the one in the XYZ Affair?"

He glared but she didn't care. Of course the question discomfited Jimmy. This was the same corrupt foreign minister who'd sent three flunkies—Messrs. X, Y, and Z—to demand a bribe as the price of the French government even deigning to talk to the American peace delegation. Disgusting man. But she knew what really burned Jimmy. When the delegation broke the contact and hurried home, the Democrats suspected a Federalist plot to justify war with France and demanded the story be made public. President Adams explained it all, the American public was furious, the Democrats looked like fools and lost ground. Then, when the Democrats had been properly abused and the groundwork for Alien and Sedition was laid, President Adams had turned the knife by sending a new delegation that quickly arranged the peace treaty that still held. Credit for that bright idea, demanding it all be made public, belonged jointly to Jimmy and Tom. Not that she had grounds to feel superior, she hadn't seen the trap either, but still . . .

Jimmy's head drew down in his shoulders as it always did when he was angry.

"Really, darling," she said more gently, "with such a man anything could happen, don't you think?"

"It's the job of diplomats to overcome such problems. That's *all* he has to do—get a single question answered."

"All? Just turn the man who has conquered Europe from his aims?"

He sighed. "You're an able advocate, Dolley, but that doesn't mean you're right." Then, still cool, he changed the subject. Would she preside at a tea Tom intended to give his old friend Pierre Du Pont, whose brother was just in from Paris with fresh insights?

Choices of gowns ran through her mind.

Head still pulled down, he said, "Maybe we can get more from Monsieur Du Pont than our envoy could manage on the scene."

"Oh, Jimmy, sweetie, that's not fair."

"At any rate, I'm hungry and tired. I'm going to find a bite downstairs and go to bed."

"No, you're not," she said. "First of all, you're going to give me a kiss." And she placed herself on his lap. "You can't kiss me and still frown like that. Come on, now . . ."

Mr. Lemaire was beside himself. The visitors, Monsieur Du Pont and his estimable brother, and doubtless his son as well, the latter the chemical industrialist opening a gunpowder plant in Wilmington, certainly were the cream of Paris, doubtless dined with the nobility or what was left of it, and were sure to be men of taste. He would surpass himself. Tea would be splendid, sandwiches trimmed in narrow wedges, smoked turkey with chutney, and then perhaps fine-cut tenderloin in a mustard dressing, and, yes, peppercress in cream cheese with cucumbers, and then sweets, say lemon curd tartlets, neat little discs with scalloped edges, and mincemeat tartlets, with two wines and two teas from China, perhaps three—

"And scones," Dolley said.

"Scones?"

"With a dash of butter."

"Oh, madame, scones are so, so—mundane."

She looked at him without answering.

"Scones . . . ," he said. "They'll give variety, won't they," windmilling his hand, "a sense of, how you say, abundance, yes, reflecting this extraordinary country, no?"

"I think so," she said.

She wore a gown of plum-colored velvet with two broad white panels. Reviewing the tea, she hoped the elegance of the food might compensate for the shabbiness of the mansion walls, with their streaked, unfinished look. The roof was leaking. There were tubs in some rooms and soggy spots on the walls. The tea would be in the Blue Room, so called for its blue-covered furniture, its walls an unappealing pasty white but still presentable, if dingy. She really must talk to the president soon—surely they could find the money for roof repair, paint, wallpaper, perhaps wainscoting, all little enough.

With these blemishes glowing like so many sore thumbs, the Du Ponts trooped in, murmuring pleasantries. Pierre looked about sixty. Louis was younger and junior in status; she sensed something sleek and slippery in him. The son, Eleuthère, wore a velvet suit with fountains of lace at throat and wrists, shoe buckles that looked like gold, each with a glittering little diamond, loosely clubbed hair heavily powdered.

He made an elegant leg, held her hand overlong, gazed deeply into her eyes. His glance flicked to Jimmy and back to her with the faintest lift of an eyebrow and seemed to say what a pity to waste a pretty young wife on an old man. It was all so insulting, so quiet and yet so obvious—she saw Jimmy giving him a speculative look—that she couldn't help being amused. He took her smile as response and, well satisfied with the impression he'd made, seated himself.

Tom had known the senior Du Pont for years; he was economist, philosopher, statesman, long close to royal circles. He'd been an ardent revolutionist, but it had turned on him and he'd fled the guillotine. Now the first consul—the title Napoleon had chosen for himself—had decreed he

might return. This was the happy news his brother had
crossed the Atlantic to bring him.

But he was leaving part of himself here, his son, a chemist
of international standing who had trained under the great An-
toine Lavoisier, would stay. She saw Tom's eyes widen at the
name and Jimmy seemed impressed; she herself had heard it,
though she couldn't have said where. The young man talked
vigorously of the chemical empire he planned, starting with
his plant at Wilmington, which would turn out gunpowder of
such uniformity as to end forever the military problem of
cannon fire flying overlong or falling short. . . .

Breaking this flow at an opportune moment, Jimmy told
Louis Du Pont that his arrival was fortuitous since the
United States had new interest in French affairs.

"Over Louisiana, I suppose you mean," Du Pont said.
Like his brother, his English was accented but polished.

"You startle me, sir," Tom said. "Is this widely known?"

"Through Talleyrand's entourage, certainly. Frankly, I
warned them the United States wouldn't take kindly to the
idea."

"And how did they take that?"

She saw a glint in his eyes that was less respectful than his
tone. "Unfortunately, they didn't seem to care. I'm afraid
they don't take Americans as seriously as they should."

Dolley was serving the tea, arranging the sandwiches on
small china plates. When she presented a plate to young Du
Pont, he turned so that his body blocked the other's view; his
hand, taking the plate, contrived to touch hers in a swift ca-
ress, his fingers sliding across her palm. The touch, so sly, so
unexpected, so unwanted, infuriated her. She drew an explosive
breath, glaring at him, fighting a wild impulse to hit him. He
leaned back, smiling, more pleased with himself than ever.

When her heart slowed and her vision cleared and she became aware of the conversation again, she heard Tom saying
it was odd that Talleyrand's entourage should know all about
the Louisiana move, for he had denied it to Livingston.

Again that little glint, that touch of self-satisfaction she'd

noticed in Pierre as well, as Louis said, "Oh, that's just Talleyrand playing with Livingston. He hates Americans, you
know. Everyone finds him baffling, frustrating, confusing—
ha! Lying to Livingston would just be his idea of sport."

"Yet we did welcome him," Tom said, his voice mild,
"when his compatriots were ready to put his neck under the
blade."

"Well, Mr. President," Louis said, "good deeds are rarely
appreciated."

But of course, Dolley thought, after XYZ everyone knew
Talleyrand was a monster. Defrocked bishop, strange,
twisted, crippled little man hobbling about on a destroyed
foot and possessed of such surpassing intellect and useful-
ness that his greatest excesses were readily forgiven, serving
the king and then the revolution and now the dictator with
equal skill, his appetite for bribes insatiable.

Pierre Du Pont cleared his throat. "But actually it's not
just Americans; he hates everyone."

"Exactly," Louis said. "There's an amusing story. Your
man Livingston was being presented, and Napoleon told
him he had come to a corrupt country and then asked Talleyrand, as a master of its practice, to explain corruption to
the newcomer."

The three Frenchmen laughed heartily. Jimmy watched
them, his expression cool but unreadable.

"And then," Louis said, his tongue darting out to wet his
lips, a small smile playing, "I must tell you, court circles in
Paris are little impressed with this Livingston person. His
French is only adequate, he doesn't hear well, he misses
most of what's said. Apparently he didn't hear the first consul's sally when everyone else did, which, of course, doubled the humor of it."

Dolley was growing steadily more angry as she absorbed
the blatant contempt for things American that these men expressed, each in his own way. Mr. Livingston was a man of
plain dignity and plain American views and somehow the
image of him abraded by the corrupt wit of a corrupt court
sickened her.

Tom, sitting deep in his chair, twirling his wineglass, said, "Tell us about the first consul, gentleman. He must be quite the extraordinary fellow; he's made such swift strides."

"To suggest he moves too rapidly denigrates him, sir!" Louis snapped. Tom flushed at the tone, and she saw Pierre cast an anxious glance at his brother, who blared on. "Sir, understand that in his time he has made a mark on the face of the world that will never be eradicated!"

"Louis," Pierre said in a low voice.

His brother colored. He looked around the room. At last he said, "Forgive me if I seem overvehement. Napoleon Bonaparte has saved France from chaos and ruin. He stands for all that is good, he has brought decency and honor, not only to France, but to all of Europe that he has touched. He is a genius of law, of government, of education. He has wiped away royalty on every side in a way that Americans surely must admire. If I speak too strongly, my apologies. I love that man."

"You speak well, Monsieur Du Pont," Tom said. He smiled. "Of course, the first consul is a man of power too."

"Ah, Mr. President," Pierre said, raising a hand to silence his brother, "Napoleon Bonaparte is a unique figure. I knew him when he was a penniless lieutenant from Corsica, and Corsicans are not highly regarded in France. You didn't see his genius then, his uniforms frayed, he thin as a rail and looking hungry, but he knew guns. And in the wild days after the Terror, he made his mark with artillery. There was a rebellion; his guns settled it. He became a brigadier, but only a little brigadier then.

"But there is a certainty in him, an instinctive sense for what to do in every instance. Skinny little lieutenant from Corsica—and somehow, he *knows*. Knows what the rest of us can't know—is it instinct, intuition? Certainly it's genius. He's barely schooled, often he's as innocent as a boy, he's forever being surprised by things we treat as common knowledge.

"And yet that Italian campaign, my God! A marvel of speed and slashing attack that left his opponents stunned, quick marches to slash again, four major battles in ninety-six hours, his men marching demonically, sleeping on their feet, he sleeping in the saddle but never pausing, and arriving to strike again and again. He sweeps around forts, he flanks them, renders them useless, marches on. Corporals become generals if they have courage and intellect and the instinct for attack. He takes Milan, takes all of Lombardy, enters Florence, defeats the Austrian army, then turns north and plunges into Austria proper, destroys its army, makes it beg for peace.

"Yet his army was never larger than 44,000! And he destroyed armies four times his size: Four times!

"And returned to Paris to find the revolutionary government in collapse. Of course he took over. He saw the way, knew what was needed, acted out of that same sure instinct that made him understand war as no man before him has understood it—out of, in short, genius."

There was a moment of silence. This image of a simple man possessed of the capacity to shake the world was overwhelming.

At last Tom said, voice lazy and unconcerned, "You picture him beautifully, Pierre. And he is, as I said, a man of power."

"Yes, Mr. President, but in the most benign sense."

"Oh, I'm sure. And personally? He's sort of an innocent?"

"Well . . ." Pierre hesitated. "Yes, in the sense he's not highly educated. But he knows his own mind. He can be implacable once he decides what he wants. Nothing can shake him. Ferocious temper too. I'm told his explosions are legendary. Of course, it's because he's so impatient of inefficiency—"

"And of opposition?" Jefferson asked.

Pierre colored. "Well, when opposition gets in the way of his great plans. Still, I've been in a large room when he exploded at some underling and—well, you know that he comes out of the barracks. He can be quite brutal. Charming one moment, ferocious the next."

"That usually frightens people," Tom said, in that easy way.

"Oh, indeed. He terrifies those around him. Everything rests on his favor, you see. You're in if he nods, out if he doesn't. Just like that. No argument, no appeal." He paused, as if seeing where this had taken him. "Of course, in a democratic nation like yours that may have an ugly sound, but believe me, France was desperate when he took over; it needed his discipline. And so does Europe. And Napoleon Bonaparte is the man to give all Europe what it needs—an end to kings and royalty, freedom well backed with discipline."

"French discipline . . . ," Tom sounded half asleep.

"Yes, French—" Pierre stopped abruptly. "Well, you make it sound bad, but—"

"No, Pierre," Tom said, *"you* make it sound bad."

"I don't mean to," Pierre said. And then, as if making up his mind and plunging, "Mr. President, I love this country of yours. It is a refuge for the hunted and the abused of the world. It has been a refuge to me. My son dreams of an empire of chemistry here. Now this country has differences with a man whom I know to be unsurpassed. Permit me to warn you, he is a hard man. He is dangerous. No one knows how his mind works; no one can guess what he will do next, except that it will be what no one expected. He cares absolutely nothing for human life; he cares only for his aims. They are to serve humanity as a whole; whom he may crush to accomplish that is immaterial.

"Please, Mr. President, do forgive me when I say, proceed with great caution. There is no more dangerous man in the world than Napoleon Bonaparte."

And Dolley gazed in horror at the bleakest possible picture: Little Jimmy Madison in hand-to-hand combat with the most dangerous man in the world.

It was dark and a fine, cold rain was falling when they left. She and Jimmy rode home without speaking. In their bedroom she stepped out of the plum gown, noticing a mustard smear on one of the white panels. Jimmy emerged from his dressing room in slippers and a blanket robe. The silence held; apparently it was to be one of those evenings.

He set aside the fire screen and poked and poked until the fire was blazing. His jaw was set, his lips pulled down.

"Jimmy . . . ," she said.

He turned to face her, still on one knee, poker in hand. "Well, whatever else we learned, we learned it was a mistake to send Mr. Livingston to Paris!"

"What?" she cried, suddenly as angry as he. "From those oafs we learned? Laughing up their sleeves at us—"

"Oh, were they?"

"Laughing, snickering inside, at Tom, at you, at me. The sneers of the haut monde of Paris for poor Mr. Livingston, whose French is not up to debating a tyrant. Well, neither is mine, neither is yours. Oh, the *arrogance* of those men—"

"You're angry because the son tried to flirt with you."

"Don't be silly. It's never offensive when a man thinks of flirting. The offense is when he assumes it will be welcome. I was furious, and you should be too!"

"Oh, I saw, all right. I just didn't choose to have an international incident in the president's drawing room. Anyway, what do you want? Call him out? Pistols at dawn?"

"Oh, for God's sake, what a ridiculous thing to say, James Madison, and you know it!"

"Yes, yes, I wasn't serious. But it is true that you wouldn't be half so riled if they hadn't made Livingston look the fool after your fervid defense of him."

"I thought Mr. Livingston came off very well. We should lose faith in him because Napoleon and this creature, Talleyrand, lacked the courtesy and respect to deal properly with him?"

"But why do you defend him so?"

"Because I talked to him—two hours or more—and I judged him a solid man with integrity, a very firm sense of himself, certainly a high confidence that you seem to view as arrogance, but I wouldn't want to send a man into that French snake pit who wasn't sure of his own position in the world and not likely to let others devalue him in his own eyes."

"And on that basis—"

"Yes, on that basis. What other basis does one have? He's distinguished enough; you yourself said you pretty well had to offer him something. I'm not a fool. I've been watching people a long time. You're deep in the intellectuality of government, but I look at people and sometimes I see more than you do."

He stood abruptly. "I'm going downstairs."

"Jimmy," she wailed, "I *talked* to him." But the door had closed. Well, she *had* talked, and it had been very pleasant. She'd been wearing the brocaded gown of sky blue silk, the burst of lace hardly concealing her ample bosom, of which he'd taken appropriate notice and then ignored. Some men seemed never to look at her above the level of her chin. He'd proposed a toast and touched his glass to hers in honor of Virginia and New York, which he saw as the poles of American excellence.

He'd asked her about Virginia and especially its agriculture, querying her closely about Jimmy's plowing and fallowing methods, and soon was talking easily of his own estates in New York grouped for miles around the stone mansion he called Clermont. His voice was warm and musical, and as she asked a few questions she could see him with his huge and far-flung family, tenant farmers and slaves working acres as far as the eye could see. Of course he was confident, standing as he did at the center of a rich, well-regulated world. . . .

Suddenly he was telling her of a discovery he'd made, watching her closely to be sure she wouldn't laugh. On the Hudson flats one day he'd spied a weed in wild profusion, and upon examination found it had many of the qualities of paper, lacking only paper's strength. Its proper name was *conserva,* but the locals called it "frog spit," which gave you an idea of its delicacy; and he'd seen instantly that it might be a new primary ingredient for making paper. You can see, he continued to her willing nods, that with a cheap ingredient the United States could become the paper supplier for the entire world. So he'd had his men gather eighty pounds of the weed—amazing the volume of eighty pounds—and they'd put it through someone's paper plant in New York

City and it had almost—*almost*—worked! That close! Oh, it had been frustrating, but he hadn't given up on it, no, sir!

Nor had he given up on the steamboat, no indeed. Steamboat? Yes, he was leading a group of men who were determined to have a steam vessel on the Hudson, and soon. She listened, fascinated, for while everyone knew that steam would never propel watercraft, there was a core of belief in this man that had to be taken seriously. She knew the problem well; steam engines were so huge that one big enough to propel a vessel must sink it, let alone leave carrying capacity.

But to her surprise, he actually had built a boat with a small steam engine. He had designed a paddle wheel on the bottom of the boat that hadn't worked very well. But now he'd found a man who understood the new lightweight engine James Watt had designed in Britain, and he was thinking of wheels on the sides of the vessel. All this must hold till he returned from Paris, of course, but then he would start anew, for he'd been talking to a man named Robert Fulton who had the most interesting ideas. . . .

Of course, she'd been leading him on. She knew there was nothing like a pretty young woman's smile to draw an older man into revealing his dreams. But through unhappy experience she also knew that most men, given that opportunity, turn into colossal bores, harumphing away, laughing at their own jokes, telling more and more that was less and less interesting.

So in a sense, at least, she had dug a pit into which he might fall, and he hadn't. He was always aware of her rather than of himself, casting what he said to interest her instead of fluffing himself. Perhaps it was that, finally, that anchored her conviction that here was a man of worth.

She had a powerful image of Paris from the novels she read, the streets always shady and musical, strollers on the banks of the Seine, little tables and chairs under graceful elms, the easy laughter, the warmth of lovers—and in her mind's eye she saw Mr. Livingston strolling, dignified, a little austere but warming, bowing to an occasional woman in his path, as content with himself as when he sat telling her his steamboat dreams—

The door opened. Jimmy walked in with a tray. "I thought we might have tea," he said. It was a peace offering. He poured and she took the cup. "We may not be so far apart on Mr. Livingston," he said. "You believe he'll do well. I pray he will."

She smiled and put her hand on his.

25

WASHINGTON, EARLY 1802

Madison heard footsteps behind him. At first he thought it was his own boots scuffing the gravel walk and bouncing off the front of dark houses. But no, someone behind him, quite close. It was cloudy, no stars or moon, the black of night like ink. He'd known he should stop work while there was still light, but there was always more to do; and so again he was last out of the little square building by the mansion. His dispatch case was slung over his shoulder, and he was feeling his way with his stick for the stumps here and there that no one had bothered to pull.

The steps came closer. Secretary of state of the United States of America wending homeward in the dark, alone, a damned blackguard footpad creeping up on him. He reversed his stick, the heavy knob out, and turned with the stick springy in his hand, raised, ready—

The steps stopped.

Silence. Madison could hear his own breathing.

"Got something for you." A man, much closer than he'd expected. There was a faint odor—rum. The voice was a rasp, ruined by drink and smoke, low, a little threatening, utterly confident—and familiar. He knew he'd heard it before.

"This here is information you can use. But it'll cost ye."

"Well, I don't know about that." Madison's breathing slowed.

"I say it's worth a twenty-dollar gold piece. You agree, you wrap the piece and have it delivered to the Broken Goat Tavern for General Sudsbury. It don't come, I'll see you don't value information none and I won't trouble you no more."

"Sudsbury?"

A rasping laugh. "It'll do good as any."

There! Madison had him now. The hunchback. He peered through the dark and made out a bulky figure. His heartbeat was back to near normal; he'd been frightened and now he was angry.

"Are you peculiar looking in daylight?"

"I'm a Goddamned hunchback—that what you mean?"

"That'll do. So what is this information that brings you skulking after me like a miserable footpad?"

Sudden raw fury in the voice. "You like it better I come to your office and put my feet on your desk? You're mighty damned particular for a man who don't know what the hell's going on! I've a mind to walk off—"

"But you won't because you want that gold piece. Now what is it; then I'll decide if I'll pay."

A low chuckle, fury gone. "Thought I'd see if you push easy." The sound of a man spitting. "You know how them niggers done revolted and took over the island of Santo Domingo down in the Caribbean?"

"Of course." He waited, still on edge. The French were worried about Santo Domingo. Pichon had raised United States acceptance of the slave revolt as a continuing point of contention, though nothing concrete had happened. In fact, the success of the revolt raised serious fears in the slave states for reasons that Madison understood only too well. There had been an abortive slave rising in Virginia only two years ago. It had been nipped in the bud, but it could have been bad. He still thought a revolt unlikely, but if the blacks on his own Montpelier were to rise he shuddered to think of the carnage. All the same, he didn't intend to let that fear dominate American foreign policy. Trade with the island continued.

"Now," the voice said from the dark, "you know how when he declared for 'em the Frenchies said that boss nigger was one of them? Made him captain-general, told him to get him some plumes and dress up like a French general? Well, now they're sending an army to crush him. I mean, a *big* army—twenty-five thousand. Under a general name of Leclerc. You heard of Leclerc? Seems he's the fair lad since he married Napoleon's sister."

Standing in the dark, Madison had a curious sense that a bright light was shining on new problems. He'd understood that Paris wasn't entirely happy with its Caribbean colony, but serious French military action in the Americas raised a whole new specter. Again he was slapped with the sense of moving from the abstract to the concrete. Every day the French threat became more real. Still . . .

"How do you know?" His voice was low and taut.

Again that chuckle. "Thing about information, Mister, it stands alone. You don't get no proof with it. Still, I'll tell you I know a lot of folks, and one of 'em come out of France, landed this week, and I've never known him to be wrong. Now, you and me, we've had dealings. You decide if likely I know what I'm talking about.

"Anyway, that ain't the news. French cutting up niggers on some island, I ain't going to hang around in the dark to tell you that. The news is that when they're done there they go on to Louisiana. Orders to occupy it and bring its people under control. That's the news . . ."

Madison heard his footsteps receding. From a distance, the raspy voice, "General Sudsbury, Broken Goat Tavern. Barkeep'll hold it for me."

Madison detested big parties and here he was in the drawing room of the new British legation surrounded by a hundred guests, feeling a fish far from water, hearing his voice grow more leaden with every response to every clever sally. There was Dolley on the other side of the room, bright as a pin, laughing and admiring the faintly beige offsets in the white wainscoting, Ned Thornton eagerly pointing out this and that. She was even more beautiful than usual—Madison just liked to look at his wife—her black hair wrapped in a dark green turban that she said was perfect with her sea green gown. Doubtless the colors did fit together, not something he would know in his plain black suit, white hose, shoes not unduly scuffed if not superbly brushed, gentleman's garb. Dolley supplied the family's fashion. . . .

The place smelled of paint. Thornton had miscalculated, planning this opening reception on the naive hope that the building would be done when promised. He was a precipitate young man. The party could just as well have waited until the paint was dry and Madison could be back in his office, and his champagne wouldn't taste of paint. He switched to whiskey punch, an indulgence he rarely made, and looked around.

Well, well, there was Mr. Pichon, alone by a window, looking the fish out of water that Madison felt. Of course he'd come as a protocol matter, Britain and France now being officially if uneasily at peace, which condition no one expected to last more than a year. He strolled up to the Frenchman.

"Ah, Louis," he said, "paint does give champagne a certain aura, don't you think?"

Pichon smiled. "A piquancy of flavor, Mr. Secretary." He lowered his voice. "Dare I say in these hallowed precincts that it has a certain British quality?"

Madison chuckled. He put a hand on Pichon's arm. "Louis, I hear that France is putting troops into Santo Domingo."

Pichon's head snapped around. "Where did you hear that?"

"An army, really. Huge, twenty-five thousand—and under the famous General Leclerc. They do mean business, don't they?"

Pichon appeared to be having an attack of nausea.

Madison said, "I see from your face it's true."

"I was told in utmost secrecy—no one to know."

"Ah, Louis, haven't you learned by now there are no se-crets? I understand they go on to impose military rule on Louisiana."

"No, sir! I don't know that."

"But it makes such sense it can hardly be denied."

Pichon didn't answer.

"Can it, Louis?"

"No, sir, I suppose not."

"It's really quite vile to bring an army into our sphere of influence in secrecy. Do you wonder we resent it? That we question your aims? Your motives? When you are instructed not to present it to the government most concerned and attest to its innocence, but instead you are to hold it in—how did you put it?—yes, 'utmost secrecy'?"

Pichon didn't answer.

"These are thoughts you would do well to convey to your government."

Back in the blessed sanctuary of his office, Madison heard a spattering of cold rain lash against his window. Thunder rolled in the distance, the interval between flash and sound shortening. He threw another log on the fire and stood look-ing out. The mansion was blurred through wet glass.

So why did France bother with Santo Domingo? The question produced the answer. The importance of the Caribbean island lay in the fact that they were coming to Louisiana in force, as his own instinct had told him. An army of size demands massive supply—in his mind's eye he could see a chain of square-rigged ships, sails gleaming, rolling on brilliant blue swells across the Atlantic, through the straits between Florida and Cuba, into the last long reach across the Gulf of Mexico to the mouth of the Mississippi. But at the hinge point, the Florida Straits, the chain was vul-nerable to British frigates based at the Royal Navy station at Jamaica that could readily sail up the slot between Cuba and

Santo Domingo and fall on French vessels bound for New
Orleans. A French naval base at Santo Domingo, scarcely a
hundred miles from Jamaica, would neutralize that threat.
France didn't care about Toussaint or his island. It cared
about the Royal Navy. The island hadn't mattered till plans
for Louisiana as part of a French empire matured. So the
whole point of Santo Domingo was Louisiana.

But despots are never satisfied. Let him anchor Louisiana
and Santo Domingo as his hinge points and he almost certainly would take Cuba from the Spanish, give them a mite of
face saving by swapping another duchy stolen from the Ital-
ians as he'd done for Louisiana. With Cuba in hand, the
Caribbean his, the next step would be Mexico with its limitless
silver and gold mines. It already was on the edge of revolt and
would fall like a ripe fruit. Powered by Mexican gold, what
would keep the French despot from driving up the Mississippi
and making most of North America his own? What but the tat-
tered militia of Tennessee and Kentucky and the tiny Regular
Army and submitting ourselves to the tender mercies of the
Royal Navy?

After a while he called in Johnny Graham and handed him
a package. "I want you to deliver this to a tavern called—
um, the Broken Goat, I believe it is."

Johnny's eyes widened.

"You know the place?" Madison asked.

"Yes, sir! I . . . ah . . . it's just not the sort of place I supposed you frequented."

Madison smiled. "I'm glad to surprise you," he said.

26

It was still dark when Meriwether Lewis stepped out of the mansion from his canvas-partitioned chamber in what Miss Dolley insisted would someday be the beautifully appointed and highly ceremonial East Room, though you sure couldn't tell it now. The habits of the early riser, alert and ready before first light, the time that attacks would come boiling out of the woods if they were going to come, went straight back to the frontier. The cold was bracing this morning, and he pulled his coat tighter.

"Mornin', Captain." The guard's voice sounded sleepy; he was wedged into a corner behind a pillar, shivering.

"Wake up, Sam," Lewis said. "Tea kettle'll be on shortly."

The night was starlit and he walked swiftly, boots loud on frozen ground. At the stables his big buckskin gelding nickered softly as he lifted the bar on the stall door. As he dropped the saddle on its back, the horse turned to nip at his arm. He rapped it sharply on the nose.

"Where the hell did you get that mean streak, Buck? Not on the plantation." He'd brought Buck from home; Ma said the horse was all stamina and temper. "You nip me good and one of these days I'll beat you bloody. Understand?" He swung into the saddle. Puffing, snorting, the horse wheeled in a tight little circle, but he didn't buck; he'd tried that once and now he knew a whole lot better. They started down the dirt street and soon the horse settled into a steady trot.

The president wanted to see him at ten; didn't say for what. Every time Mr. J. called him, he imagined, hoped—

dreamed, it was beginning to look like—that they would discuss the expedition or at least mention it. But doubtless this
French business had knocked it all to hell anyway. No one
would plan things with war looming. He felt the familiar
darkness crowding around him as he contemplated this
blasting of his dreams. Bastards. They would never get away
with seizing the West and the river; that would never pass
with westerners. Could anyone imagine Tennessee men
kissing the French ass?

A horseman turned onto Pennsylvania Avenue and
waved—Johnny Graham. They often rode together, though
more by chance than by design. He liked Johnny, who was
one of those men you knew right away could take care of
himself. Johnny lived with a number of congressmen and
clerks in a boardinghouse on G Street and kept a horse in the
stables next door. He too liked to shake out in the dawnlight,
and soon they were trotting up the trail along Rock Creek.

Lewis had met Johnny soon after he arrived, on the day, in
fact, that he had clashed with Mr. Randolph's pale clerk.
He'd come boiling out of the chairman's office and bumped
into Johnny, who had a clutch of papers in his left hand.

"Stand clear there!" Lewis was still furious.

"Well, hold on, friend," Johnny had said, quite mildly
considering the provocation. *"You* bumped into *me."* Lewis
noted he had both hands up, the right a fist, ready to drop the
papers and move.

"Humph," Lewis said. "Guess I did. Sorry."

Johnny glanced at the chairman's door. "Simon Pink giving you trouble?"

"A little skinny whey-faced bastard—"

"That's Simon Pink. C'mon, I'll buy you a cup of chocolate and tell you about the first time *I* met Simon."

They'd spent an hour together and become friends.
Johnny had what Lewis thought of as rather a joyous turn of
mind as compared to his own darkening moods, but they
were comfortable together. Lewis was usually easier in the
company of westerners after life on the frontier as boy and
soldier. They seemed more open, less formal, more direct,

said what was on their mind, you didn't like it, make something of it. You were a sight more likely in Cincinnati than in Baltimore to see a couple of bravos go for each other with ten-inch blades, left hands crooked for gouging an eye.

He liked the trail up Rock Creek, winding among rocks and small boulders, coming up above to a marshy meadow where impromptu races often arose. But the trail was hard packed and beaten, and it was a long, long way from the kind of trails, faint and little trod, he'd known in the West. All his dreams were of open country. There was still land available in Kentucky and in Indiana territory, and he aimed to have some of it someday. That and the great trek to the Pacific.

He was a soldier but he wasn't a warrior. Not afraid of combat, mind, he reckoned he'd give as good account of himself as anyone; but open country was his real interest, not the army. He knew the wilderness, and now, tired and disgusted with waiting, doubting himself and Mr. Jefferson as well, he thought about those days when he was just a lad and yet had made himself a self-taught botanist of unusual skills, roaming alone and living off the land, new camp every night, tracking game or going hungry, bathing weekly in a stream with a sliver of soap.

The far beyond, the uncivilized, the unexplored always drew him. His appeal to Mr. Jefferson as a boy—let me lead the expedition—had seemed totally reasonable to him and still did. He remembered Mary Beth Slaney's doubts, but he'd known then that he could do it; and if he'd been allowed, if the plan to trek to the Pacific hadn't been dropped, how different the world would be today. Now—now he was more than competent. He was trained in command, practiced in the military march, used to thinking in terms of a small body of men traveling light on foot or horseback or out for weeks with pack animals or wagons, day by day finding campsites on water, dealing with food, setting up a latrine away from camp even for one night, doctoring sick men and lame horses, monitoring supplies, all the myriad little management details an officer learned. The very idea of

taking a body of men across a whole *continent* thrilled
him—all the details magnified, all the problems and stresses
and unforeseen needs and sudden crises coming up like
storms, the men looking to him for answers. . . .

"Say, Merry," Johnny said, reining close, "cheer up! You
look like you've lost your last friend and plan to break
someone's head over it."

Lewis forced a smile but it wasn't all that easy. His face
felt stiff.

"Tell you what," Johnny said. "Way back, we'll stop at
Absalom's, get one of his big breakfasts."

Absalom Jones ran the Red Fox Tavern and had a bounti-
ful table, but not for the likes of young clerks.

"Dollar breakfast?" Lewis cried. "Rich for our blood,
boy."

Johnny laughed. "Stop for a cup of coffee anyway. We can
smell the food and dream of being rich." And he loped off
with a bright exuberance that Lewis knew he never could
master, not that he'd want to, understand.

It was just that Washington galled him so and yet, he
would never learn—hell, he couldn't even beat down the
hope that today's summons would be different. Though
he knew it wouldn't. He'd sit down in Mr. Jefferson's big office and get some instructions to take to Mr. Dearborn at the
War Department, something designed to foil this latest
French move, maybe, stop 'em at Santo Domingo. They
want to reclaim their island, fine, let 'em do it and drink coconut milk for the rest of their lives, but stay out of Louisiana.
And let Captain Lewis get on with his real mission.

It was like a prize dangled before his nose but never
given. Why bring him here if not for the expedition? He was
the last sort of man to make a natural presidential secretary.
It took a Simon Pink to revel in clerkhood. Meriwether
Lewis didn't care all that much for awaiting the great man's
beckoning finger, even when the man was Thomas Jefferson.
Oh, it had been an interesting year, all right, he knew infinitely more now than he had at the start, not just about how

things worked at high levels, but about himself too. Learned, for example—

The trail bent and up ahead he saw Johnny had reached the meadow and was talking to a rider. Drawing close he saw it was Jim Ross, the senator from Pennsylvania. Jim was a good fellow, albeit a Federalist. He was from Pittsburgh, which put him nicely out to the west, where Lewis had had frequent dealings with him in connection with his old paymaster duties—back when life was still simple! Indeed, Ross was the westernmost member of Senate or House who clung misguidedly to the wrong party.

"Mornin', Senator," he said. It looked as if Ross and Johnny had been arguing about something.

"Merry!" Ross said. "Nice to see you, son. You better pound some sense in your pal's head, here. Johnny's been telling me he thinks that plug of his can beat my Sally Mae."

Ross was a smallish man with a sandy beard now grizzled and a wide, expressive face that smiled easily but, Lewis knew from experience, could darken in a flash. He was on a sleek bay mare, slender and without stamina for the long haul, but swift on the short. Still, old Buck, here, now settled into a comfortable pace, was no slouch either, and he said so.

"You too?" Ross cried in mock amazement. "Well, let an old horseman give you novices a lesson. Here to the woodline, bet you a dollar each I can whip you both."

Lewis read it a quarter mile. The bay was fast, but maybe not quick on the start, and Buck was explosive. Still, a dollar was a dollar, and he said so.

Ross laughed. "Tell you what—make it a quarter pot. Everyone puts up a quarter, and when I win I'll stand us all a big breakfast at Absalom's."

All right! That was a bet you couldn't lose. They lined up carefully, Ross called the start, and sure enough that sleek little bay of his pulled ahead with a long, effortless stride that made her seem hardly working but nevertheless had her three lengths ahead at the woodline. They paid over their losings and the senator led the way to Absalom's.

The tavern was booming. A buxom waitress, face flushed, hair tendrils flying from under an embroidered cap, sleeves of her blue gown thrust up on muscular arms, threaded through the crowd with a heavy tray balanced overhead. Lewis was surprised so many men seemed able to afford a dollar breakfast. But Ross appeared to be an old hand; maybe he came here every day. Lewis remembered the senator had a half-dozen flourishing businesses in Pittsburgh—by far the largest distillery, a rope walk, a small foundry.

"Ab!" the senator roared, "got a couple of hungry lads here."

The proprietor, a saturnine-looking fellow with mustaches that turned down to his jawline, a stained apron wrapped around his middle, whisked dirty dishes from a table and seated them.

"These young fellows thought they could beat Sally Mae," Ross said. "Big mistake."

"So they're buying?"

"Nah! I collected my winnings. I'm buying, and winning always gives me a hell of an appetite, so lay it on! Bacon, sausage, venison, eggs, grits, flapjacks, biscuits, big pot of honey, coffee—you got coffee, don't you, none of that weak-assed tea—"

It was about the best meal for a quarter Lewis had ever seen and from the way Johnny was putting it away, he'd agree. Of course the talk turned around politics, but Ross softened his Federalist rhetoric in deference to his democratic guests and Lewis squelched his own natural inclination to tell the senator a thing or two. Johnny was listening with a tolerant grin.

At last Ross smiled and said, "Letting me rant, eh? Well, you gentlemen have good manners, maybe better'n mine. But here's something we can agree on—the French. They think they're going to take over the Mississippi Valley, they better ponder that a long time. So tell me—any truth to the rumors we've been hearing about Napoleon making Spain retrocede Louisiana?"

Lewis saw Johnny nod and open his mouth. He kicked

Johnny's ankle. "Well, Senator," he said, "you know rumors."

There was something watchful in Ross's eyes. "I do indeed know rumors," he said. "Some false, some true. But there's a lot of smoke around this one to be no fire. So what do you know?"

"Really!" Lewis exclaimed. "What a question!"

Ross smiled. "I take that as an affirmative."

"No, sir! Take it as a reprimand!"

"Reprimand?" Sudden anger slashed across this mercurial man's face, changing it almost totally. "I don't often get reprimanded."

Lewis felt good. He was used to dealing with men ready to quarrel. "Well," he said, "what it means is, I don't talk out of school. Nor Johnny neither. What it means is, you shouldn't ask us to do that."

Ross picked up a piece of crisp bacon and ate it bite by bite, his stare focused on Lewis's eyes. At last he smiled. "Well, Merry, damned if you don't have a point at that."

It was half after nine when Lewis returned to the mansion. He and Johnny tied their mounts to the rail—too late to stable them. On impulse he followed Johnny into the State Department. Mr. Madison was in his office.

"The senator tried to worm some information out of us," Lewis said, explaining the circumstances. "When he couldn't, he gave quite a speech on how the West would react if the French were to move in. Sir, do you know him well?"

"Not well," Madison said. "A few encounters. He seems a bit shifty, to tell the truth."

"Well, he's changeable. Hot one minute, cold the next. I thought he'd blow up when I sauced him pretty hard, but then the sun came out. He's forceful. They listen to him in West Pennsylvania, I can tell you that."

Johnny nodded. "Ohio too. They don't care for his politics, but they admire him."

"Johnny and I talked it over on the way back," Lewis said. "Ross made a lot of the West not standing for any European foolishness. Point is, when the time's right, we have an idea Ross could be a big help. I know he's a Federalist, but he's with us on this and maybe his voice would be the stronger for being one of them."

Lewis could see the secretary's brain churning. He was an exceedingly smart fellow—Lewis long since had lost the impression that Madison was a dried-up little wisp—but he rarely let you know what he was thinking.

Now he merely said, "Thank you, gentlemen. I'll think on that."

As Lewis emerged from the little brick building, he saw Miss Dolley approaching on the graveled walk. He liked her and he recognized a strength in her that somehow made him think of a ship under sail. He bowed. "Morning, ma'am."

They chatted a moment. Then, without warning, she said, "Merry, tell me, has that little sister of mine given you—oh, I don't know, some sort of sign—"

He stared at her in horror. "Oh, certainly not!" he cried. He knew he must be crimson; his face was hot as with sunburn. He shook his head wordlessly. Miss Dolley hesitated, then smiled and nodded and went on toward her husband's office. He was deeply embarrassed. She knew something and he wondered if Anna had talked about their encounter and perhaps made more of it herself than was there. For his infatuation for Anna, beautiful through she was, now was fading rapidly. He felt a bit the fool for having taken her so seriously, but she really was a high-impact young woman. Sometimes he wondered if she herself understood the effect she had; but then he would realize that of course she did, that's what it was about, all quite calculated. So she'd been playing with him and it had hurt at first, but it was all right now. He shrugged. He was a grown man and he'd survived plenty of hurts, and this one already was passing.

Though it was always possible she'd liked him and then had had a change of heart. That often happened, and he couldn't say why. He'd meet a woman and she'd seem drawn to him and he'd get interested and they'd talk and laugh and maybe take a turn or two if there was dancing, and then next thing you know she'd be avoiding him, all stiff and formal when they met. . . .

But what it told him was the same old story: He didn't belong in this setting. He didn't understand these people. Didn't fit. Didn't want to fit, either. Set him on a horse and point him toward the setting sun, and by God, you'd find he fitted just fine. And as for the president, thank you for the honor, but Captain Lewis was just about full up of toting messages over to the Hill—

He paused outside the president's office door, took a deep breath, composed himself. Mr. Jefferson was smoking a long clay pipe, his feet in old carpet slippers propped on his worktable, a book on his lap, two open on the table, a dozen others stacked with paper slips marking various places. As Lewis slipped into a chair, it crossed his mind that he might have been a whole lot smarter to have talked Ross over with the president before taking the idea to Madison, so he made haste to report.

"Tell me about it," Mr. Jefferson said. "What he said, what you said." He smiled when Lewis reached the reprimand he'd given Ross. "That's rather good," he said. "Makes the point without ruffling him unduly." He studied Lewis a moment and then, as if making up his mind on something, said, "You've come a long way in a year, Merry. I'm not sure that riposte would have occurred to you when you first joined me."

Lewis couldn't help being pleased. He'd just about given up on Miss Dolley's optimistic idea that the president had wanted him to learn his way around at high levels, but maybe she'd been right. Mr. Jefferson rambled on to the ef-

fect that leadership turned on self-control and balance, on
the capacity to see broadly, to anticipate pitfalls, to think under pressure, to rise to the need but not exceed the need. This
encounter with Ross, in its way, demonstrated such qualities, so he said.

The president didn't complain often, but he wasn't lavish
with compliments either. So Lewis enjoyed this, conscious
his face was reddening, but it wasn't lost on him that, leader
or no, he was more errand boy than army officer these days.

He was trying to keep a sudden downturn of mood out of
his expression when the president said in the same rumina-
tive voice, not the slightest inflection change, so smooth that
for a moment Lewis didn't grasp the momentous bridge
crossed, "So I suppose we should be talking about the expedition. No hurry, you understand. If we have to fight the
French, that will delay everything. But how big a party do
you suppose a march to the Pacific would require? Optimum
number, so to speak."

The expedition . . . just like that, after a year of hungering, hoping, dreaming, despairing, it came as suddenly as a
thunderclap. Elation snatched his breath away, and he
seemed to be choking as he struggled to keep an opposite
surge of joy from his expression.

"Remember," the president said, "it would be penetrating
vast territory unknown to white men. A balance of numbers,
I'd think. Enough to discourage attack, but not so many
they'd appear an invading army."

"Fifteen, perhaps," Lewis said, getting control of his
breath, "even a dozen."

"Dozen sounds right, at least to start." The president was
talking of costs and the problems of getting a funding bill
through Congress. Lewis was struck by how prosaic this
momentous conversation really was. They might have been
discussing improving a strain of cattle or locating a drainage
ditch. How much time did Lewis suppose such a march to
the Pacific would take? Two thousand miles or so, calculating the longitude of Saint Louis against that recorded by
Captain Gray for the mouth of the Columbia when he'd dis-

covered the river, named it for his vessel, and claimed it for the United States. How long?

How utterly incredible and fantastic to march across two thousand miles of unknown terrain and then march back! Who in the world could possibly say how long it would take? But this was no time to raise doubts. Why, said Lewis, a year each way, estimate ten miles a day, seven months for travel, lay up for the winter, and march back. The president seemed to like that, keep it all manageable; maybe there would be narrow places to cross later, but let's wait till we get to them. Well, after a year's experience in Washington, Lewis could see the wisdom in that!

It must be a military expedition, Mr. Jefferson said, soldiers or men sworn into the military and led by an officer with the authority to enforce discipline. It would leave U.S. territory at the Mississippi and cross terrain claimed by Spain and, perhaps, in the northern reaches, by England, so it must have official imprimatur. Long term, he added conversationally, he knew all this country would end as American, claimed by force of the westering tide of settlers. But for now they must tend to the international amenities. After all, Ambassador Yrujo had already said in so many words that his nation would take umbrage at such an expedition.

"Speaking of that, if Spain did send a party to intercept such an expedition, what chance do you think they'd have of finding our people?"

It was at just this moment that Lewis noticed that the president was speaking in an abstract, theoretical fashion. He wasn't asking what chance the Spanish would have of finding *you and your men*—nothing he had said suggested he intended any role for Lewis beyond offering insight on frontier travel! The initial rush of joy was passing rapidly.

The president unrolled a map of Spanish Louisiana, the vast territory covering the central third of the continent. It stretched along the Gulf of Mexico roughly from Mobile Bay in West Florida to New Orleans and down the Texas coast to the Rio Grande, beyond which you could say Mexico began. Northward, it ran all the way to some point at which it merged imperceptibly with British territory and became more a part of Canada than of Louisiana, though of course no one knew just where that point might be.

The eastern flank of this vast range was marked by the west bank of the Mississippi. On its western flank it ran northward from the Gulf along the Rio Grande, through lonely Spanish outposts at El Paso del Norte and Santa Fe, and on to the north along the eastern flank of the great range that some called the Stony Mountains and some the Shining Mountains. Louisiana, in short, was the central wedge against the United States to the east of the Mississippi, the Pacific fringe to the west, beyond the Stony Mountains. There Spanish California, as an extension of Mexico, ran up the Pacific shore to another indeterminate point at which the Northwest began, where Captain Gray's claim of the Columbia River was more or less in conflict with the British claims made by Captain Cook and Captain Vancouver.

It was this whole central wedge for which the French now hungered, though as a practical matter New Orleans, with its control of the river, was all that really mattered.

Within this wide outline on the map were huge stretches of unmarked white space across which a few wriggling lines represented the sum total of geographic knowledge of the center third of the continent. Lewis brushed his fingers along the wandering line representing the Missouri River, which he knew from hard experience in the field probably ran in some totally different way.

"That's a wonderful stretch," he said. "Spanish patrol would play the devil trying to find—an expedition. Pure chance if they did." He had stopped himself just in time from saying "find us." His mood steadily darkened. What irony that after ten years of dreaming and a solid year of waiting, when the absolute heart of his own dreams appeared to be coming true, he should find himself discussing them as a mere advisor. He kept his voice even, his expression interested but not eager.

Mr. Jefferson dug in a drawer. "You know we planned an expedition in ninety-three?"

Lewis stiffened: Did the man play with him? "I remember, sir."

"Oh, yes, of course. I believe you wrote me about it. Well, these are the orders I drafted for Monsieur Michaux, the French naturalist who was to lead it. Then it turned out he was a subversive agent of the French government, and that was the end of it. But these stand as a model for what I would issue now. You might want to review them for an idea of what will be required of the expedition."

The expedition. Not "of you." Very well; so be it.

These instructions, the president was saying, would be inadequate today, but they did cover the basic ground. There would be many objectives, but the overriding purpose must always be finding a water route across the nation—the Northwest Passage. The president paused. He had a somber, pensive look. Find it and anchor it as American, find it before the British went further in establishing themselves in country that ultimately must be ours. They were already hungering and on the move, and—again that somber look, a deepening of his voice—he thought that someday far down the road we would be at loggerheads with them over this country in the Pacific Northwest. That could be extraordinarily dangerous. It would be on some future president's watch, but let's do that gentleman the favor of getting our claims solidly set now. Put us on sound ground when we face them.

So, the expedition would run up the Missouri to the Stony Mountains, which doubtless were more or less a match for the Appalachians in the East. There the expedition would search out the height of land that logic said must be nearby, and from which there must flow a westward river more or less matching the eastward Missouri. That westward river, surely, was the Columbia, the mouth of which they already knew from Captain Gray. It just made perfect sense.

Thus the Northwest Passage, water route to the mountains and an easy portage to another direct water route to the Pacific. And from there, straight on to the China trade: Direct, simple, logical, and, Lewis suspected, having traveled in rough country and knowing you never find what you expect to find, much too easy. But he said nothing. The president was a theoretician, an idealist, a dreamer of great dreams and vast constructs, not concerned with the mile-by-mile details as one traversed strange country, the fading trails, the search for water and grass, the need for game, the alerts against attack, the stony, steep climbs and the perilous descents with animals slipping and falling and loads spilling . . . but this was no time to challenge his president's most firmly held dream.

He saw Mr. Jefferson was running down. He'd said what was on his mind, said all he wanted to say. The president picked up his book, gentle sign of dismissal. Lewis stood to go and then stopped, irresolute. He felt crushed. But Goddamn it, he wouldn't be much man if he let this go by; he'd deserve to be crushed. He simply must get it out in the open. But how to put it? Don't whine, don't mew like a damned pussycat, don't crawl—put it positively.

So, face hot and doubtless gone scarlet, the president now looking up in faint surprise, he said, with his voice sounding like a frog's croak, "Sir, is it your intention that I—that I won't be accompanying this expedition we discuss?"

Something like chagrin flashed over the president's mobile face. "Well, I'm sorry, son," he said. "Obviously I should have clarified it earlier. You are to command it. . . ."

Sudden tears he couldn't control stood in Lewis's eyes.

Mr. Jefferson rose, now obviously concerned. "I should have said it clearly at the start of this talk. It's what I'd always planned, you see. But you know, Merry, I had to be sure too. You'll be taking a body of men over two thousand miles of terrain unknown to anyone but the tribes that live there, terrain claimed by other nations that are jealous of their prerogatives. You'll be on your own, out of reach of either help or advice. Of course you must be able to command men, but that's just the start. Any good company commander, any good foreman, can command men. I wanted to see how you handled a strange new situation—which Washington certain is—before I decided."

Abashed, Lewis simply said, "Yes, sir." But he saw the president wasn't finished.

"One other thing," Mr. Jefferson said. "I know you're subject to fluctuations of mood. You seem in a bit of a downturn today. Still, I've watched this ebb and flow for a year, and I conclude that you will be able to hold your moods in control. It's not bad to have moods, but you must control them, not let them control you. I judge you will be able to do so, and it is on that basis that I give you the command."

"Thank you, sir," Lewis said. He felt like saluting. He left with the profound feeling that he had walked in the office a boy and emerged a man. The expedition was his—thank, God!—but Mr. Jefferson had made him see that it was a vast task that would take careful planning and preparation. At any time in the past, given this news, he'd have thought of clicking his heels; now he thought he'd better get to work. . . .

27

WASHINGTON, EARLY 1802

Lewis long since had perfected his expedition plans, but now that it was a reality countless new issues of supply, manpower, route, information, maps, armament had arisen, all complicated by the dark probability that war with France would knock everything into a cocked hat. Daily he was at his desk in his little canvas-walled chamber, developing contingency plans and laying out new lists. He was thus deeply engrossed when a steward in a white jacket appeared to say that Mr. Smith was at the door.

Puzzled, Lewis followed him to the entrance hall with its marble benches. Samuel Smith, who was roughly Lewis's age, ran the *National Intelligencer* and was a warm sup-

porter; indeed, Smith had opened his paper at the express
urging of the president. His wife was a pretty woman whom
Lewis seemed to remember had had a part in resolving the
Burr crisis.

He found the editor obviously agitated. "Ah, Captain
Lewis, I must see you in private." Clutching his case, he
looked about guardedly, though Mr. Grumby was outside
watching a grocer's wagon turn into the drive. Lewis led him
to the little chamber, where he opened his case and spread
a Richmond newspaper across the expedition lists on the
desk. "Look," he said, tapping an article headed THE HERO
UNMASKED!!!! It was a broad smear against the president,
and Lewis saw it was the work of James Callender, the disheveled Richmond editor who'd been jailed, fined, and
cruelly abused under the Alien and Sedition Acts for his par-
tisan Democratic screeds and was demanding the Richmond
postmastership in recompense—and in hopes it would make
him acceptable to a high-society belle, the very same man
whom Lewis himself had ejected bodily from the mansion
when last he'd visited. Guilt settled on him in a dark cloud.
Had his own temper been the trigger that had fired this
bombshell?

The piece was scurrilous and even ridiculous in places,
but he saw it possessed an undeniable power. The president
of the United States, it shrieked, keeps a black concubine,
a helpless slave who must submit on command to his foul
advances; in tears she comes to his bed at the crook of his
finger to yield herself to his lust. Yet the dexterous author
managed to present her also as a sable Venus ruling a black
seraglio at Monticello where unspeakable excess was daily
fare, where decent men averted their eyes and no editors
dared take readers lest sensibilities be shocked beyond
recovery.

And who is this African goddess? Black Sally, she's
called, Nigger Sally, one Sally Hemings, who has been
forced to occupy the great man's bed since she was but a
child. And on her our president, who poses as a man of such
nobility, has gotten a passel of little half-breed children who

frolic through his house like innocent mice, never acknowledged by their natural father.

As Lewis sagged in his chair, stomach churning, he saw the attack was curiously contradictory, filled with hateful contempt for the black wench, but offering alligator tears for the slave child given no choice but to submit to naked lust. Thomas Jefferson poses as a nobleman, the servant of the people, the reluctant owner who opposes slavery—but absent the institution, where would he find his lush bedwarmer? Sally seemed to be both a black Venus yielding her favors and an innocent child condemned to a life of shame by the man of power with his perverted desires and his evil dominance.

And so forth for a few thousand words.

In a frightened-sounding voice, the editor said, "You understand, papers all over the country will take this up. Federalists will gloat and sneer and slather, but so will Democrats. No one will leave it alone. Best friends will snigger behind their hands."

"Why," Lewis cried, "people won't really believe it. The editor is a scoundrel, has no reputation. Have you seen him? Disgusting specimen of humanity."

"True, but few people will know that. And yes, they will believe. They'll *want* to believe."

Of course Lewis knew he was right. And in a moment Smith added uncertainly, "It's not true, I suppose. I mean—"

Lewis withered him with a glance. "Of course not!" But just the same he remembered Miz Hemings's beauty and her impact on him. If ever there was a woman to play such a role . . .

"You'll have to present it to him, won't you?"

"I suppose," Lewis said. His heart sank.

"Remember," Smith said, "it'll be in every paper in the country, friendly or unfriendly. Everyone—*everyone*—will know about it." When he left Lewis folded the paper. It lay on his desk like a bomb. After a while he walked across the lawn to Mr. Madison's office.

• • •

"You showed it to him, Jimmy?" Dolley asked. They were in the drawing room; Jimmy had come home early looking very tired. He had handed her the paper wordlessly, and she had grasped the gist of it in moments. "How did he react?"

"He read it. Then he handed it back. His expression never changed."

"He must have said something though."

"He did. He said, 'My, the depths to which the human soul can sink.' "

"That's all?"

"That's all."

"Jimmy, he can't get away with that. He'll have to speak, deny it, something—"

"I doubt he'll say a word more. Ever. So I would recommend too."

Yes, maybe that would be best. "It must have been a tense moment," she said.

He chuckled sourly. "To say the least. I waited till he handed it back. Utter silence. So I said, 'Good afternoon, Mr. President.' He didn't answer and I left, glad to be gone."

She returned to the article. "Could it be true?" She was thinking of that afternoon when Sally Hemings slid the wineglass under the bottle's mouth.

"Of course not!" He glared at her, but she thought the whole miserable situation including Tom opening himself to such an attack was what bothered him. As to the charge, Jimmy might be sure it was false, but she certainly wasn't. "She's a very pretty woman," she said tentatively.

"Really, Dolley, that's quite outrageous! To suggest—"

She shrugged.

"What's the matter with you? This suspicion—Tom simply wouldn't use his people that way nor would any decent gentleman. Tom least of all."

"Many slaveholders do."

"Well, we don't. No man on Montpelier abuses a woman. My father wouldn't have permitted it and neither will I."

"But, Jimmy, if it were true, maybe it wouldn't be abuse." She thought again of how confident and at home Sally Hemings had been that afternoon. This was no cowering slave. This was a woman, her birth and bondage merely an accident. But of course it did go to the core of slavery. A woman of that bearing and aplomb could have her pick in a free society.

That was the point Dolley's Quaker father had made when he freed their slaves—put them in a free society and they'd do as well as anyone else. Poor Pa—he had folded up and gone to bed till he died when his business failed in Philadelphia and Ma had taken in boarders, but it struck her now that Ma had never said a harsh word about her husband. Not a word. And Dolley realized her mother had simply recognized her father's quality. Somehow it had taken her ten years to reach that understanding. . . .

Images of Sally sliding that glass away . . . If Tom used her, Dolley thought, it was not against her will. Late on a chilly night, the woman drifting into the bedchamber when the house was quiet. Quite plausible. But she saw that she had angered Jimmy. She wondered if she had inadvertently tickled his own suspicions.

"All right, dear," she said. "I'm not accusing Tom of anything. But you know there's talk. Sally's children do bear a resemblance to him—remember that beautiful little boy?—and she keeps right on having them. But that doesn't prove—"

"Stands against the allegation, actually. The idea that he's impregnating a slave woman in the very house that his daughters frequent—Lord, you know how he feels about them, sun rises and sets—now that just defies imagination. Or at least, *my* imagination. As to the children—well, it's a big and tangled family."

She listened carefully as he laid out some of the interwoven Jeffersonian skeins. Most of it was new to her; Jimmy had been close to the family for years. Tom had married and been deeply in love with Martha Wayles. Her father, John Wayles, was said to have taken one Betty Hemings as concubine after his third wife died. Betty had been the daughter of an English sea captain and a full-blooded African woman, and she'd borne John Wayles six children, so the story went. When he died his estate, including Betty and her children, went to Martha Wayles Jefferson. Sally and her sister, Betsy, were toddlers then.

Dolley's mouth fell open. "My goodness," she said. "Then Sally was Martha Jefferson's half-sister?"

He nodded. "If the stories hold up. That's another reason I don't think Tom would—"

"But that rationale would work in reverse too." Tom had adored his wife and been devastated when she died. A half-sister might have an attraction no slave woman could match. Nearly twenty years had passed since Martha's death, a long time, which could be all the more reason that he . . .

Jimmy frowned. "Really, Dolley, this suspicion ill becomes you." Well, she thought, he's right. But the resemblance . . .

She saw an odd look sweep Jimmy's face. Tom, he said evenly, had a sister who also was named Martha. She had married Dabney Carr. A good fellow, Dabney Carr, before Dolley's time. Dabney and Martha had had six children before he died when still young. Martha Carr had brought her brood to Monticello, including her sons, Peter and Samuel, who were still there. Tom's nephew Peter had become his favored protégé.

"The story," Jimmy said, "like it or not, is that Peter Carr is the father of Sally's children. And that his brother, Samuel, keeps Sally's sister, Betsy, as his concubine."

She stared at her husband. "And Tom condones this?"

Jimmy shrugged.

Oh, Pa, she thought, at this new evidence of the tangled evils of slavery, you were a great and decent man. . . .

It was an immensely painful time, Madison thought. Over the next two months he noticed every condescending smile, every sneer, every wink and chuckle. In the halls of Congress one day he encountered Burr, and that worthy bowed to him with a look of absolute glee.

"My sympathies, sir," said the gentleman from New York, with a deep chuckle. "She's said to be a fine-looking piece; why, I might have trouble resisting her myself!" At which he laughed out loud.

Hurrying on, Madison rounded a corner to find four congressmen shouting with laughter as they topped each other's ribaldry. They lapsed into embarrassed silence at sight of him. He bowed. "Gentlemen," he said, putting what he hoped was ironic emphasis on the word; but if they understood his meaning it wasn't evident. Each bowed, murmuring, "Mr. Secretary."

Dismayed Democrats from Baltimore to Maine wrote that Federalists were making hay over the spectacle of Sable Sally and the great man. It all went to prove, so Federalists said, that the leader was a licentious devil steeped in sin, a natural follower of the libertine French with their mad revolution. That he would despoil an innocent slave child only demonstrated what the American people could expect as he prepared to spring them into French slavery.

Danny Mobry came for tea, and Madison felt that her big, black coachman looked at him with an open sneer. Dolley said he was imagining things, that in fact Samuel Clark was a good man who was careful not to sneer at anyone. Madison wondered if he were approaching a point where every glance carried a message.

He noted sourly that there was scarcely an editor across the country who resisted the temptation to lapse into doggerel, printing other excesses, then topping it with his own.

> *Of all the damsels on the green*
> *On mountain or in valley,*
> *A lass so luscious ne'er was seen*
> *As Monticellian Sally.*

> *Yankee Doodle, who's the noodle?*
> *What wife were half so handy?*
> *To breed a flock, of slaves for stock,*

A blackamoor's the dandy.

When pressed by loads of state affairs,
I seek to sport and dally,
The sweetest solace of my cares
Is in the lap of Sally.

That epic ran thirty-two stanzas and it was lack of space
rather than of inspiration that ended it.

Letters poured in from loyal Democrats. Take heart. Ignore slings and arrows. No sensible person listens to trashy
gossip. Be strong. Hew to the course. Confound the Federalists. Madison took it as sure sign Democrats were worried
sick.

All the while the president never said a word.

A report came from Boston. John Adams was saying that
while he would not suspect President Jefferson per se, he
was only too aware that southern slaveholders used and
abused their female slaves as a matter of course, hence all
numbered their own children among their slaves.

Someone sent a letter that John Quincy Adams had written for a newspaper to lament the tasteless excesses of press
and Federalists. He doubted the president would stoop to the
actions charged but used the situation to launch a cogent attack on slavery, urging support for the nascent abolition
movement stirring in Boston. The paper said Mr. Adams was
a state senator contemplating a run for Congress.

Madison's eyes widened at that information. Young
Adams had been saying he was above politics as practiced
today, that only a scoundrel could support either party. Now
he intended to run as a Federalist. Evidently he had conceived a need to save the nation. Doubtless the story of Sally
Hemings had energized him—and perhaps, Madison
thought it not too cynical to wonder, it had struck him that
Democrats were reeling and Federalists might storm back in
the next election, now only two years off. Ripe pickings
might be in the offing.

The titillating aura of sexual play seemed to reopen the attacks on Dolley. She stopped looking at papers. Her beauty, her sense of style, her vigor were all used against her. The whispers and hints in the papers said she was too much for her feeble little husband, her hungers drew her readily to other beds, the Democrats swapping her excesses for political favors. Such was the licentiousness in Washington, now proved by the revelations of a leader who would force a black concubine to submit to his illicit lust. And so forth.

Dolley took on a worn, sharp-featured look. Madison realized what he was seeing was the absence of her usual smile. One night when they were in bed with the candle snuffed, her voice a whisper, she said she thought it was a disaster, that this story would attach to Tom and all of them and drag on into the future, living still a hundred years after they were all dead and buried. For all their splendid dreams, she thought this is what people would remember. He rocked her gently, whispering that it would pass in time. There were tears on her cheeks.

Gradually the furor did seem to pass. No new information appeared to refuel the story and it slowly went stale. But Madison knew that things were changed forever. The episode made the administration seem light and weak and foolish, and he knew that their margin of error on the Louisiana question had shrunk. So much already depended on securing New Orleans—the tender plant of the people's democracy, holding the nation together, fending off the dangers of the British connection. Now retribution for failure would be swifter and more certain, for their operating room had narrowed.

The president never commented. But one day at the end of a long talk on dealing with the French problem, he sighed and pressed the heels of his hands into his eyes. His voice came small and muffled. "I think everything is tighter now, James. Wouldn't you say?"

"Yes, sir," Madison said. "I think that is quite so."

28

The wind was still and a winter sun warmed the front of the blockhouse where Rachel Jackson sat coring and slicing apples for a pie. She worked steadily, hands quick and sure, gaze roving over her well-tended acres. Maybe she missed Hunter's Hill and the elegant frame house a little, but this simple log blockhouse—so like the one Pa had built when they first came out to the Great Bend of the Cumberland—really suited her nature and she was content.

And then Andrew was to home. She could see him through a front window that was hardly wavy at all. He had had new windows cut into the log walls and had ordered the big panes from a superior new glassworks in Knoxville and in a near miracle only one piece had broken as it came by wagon over a trail that could hardly be called a road. He was pacing before his desk, studying briefs; the next court season was near and he'd soon be gone. And she would be bereft again, desperate, breath short . . .

Two riders in the distance. She watched them, remembering how in the old days Ma would be reaching for the rifle standing ready inside the door. As they grew closer she saw one was Jack Coffee. Jack was good; he steadied Andrew somehow. More and more she feared that her husband's fierceness in the face of scandal would lead him into terrible trouble someday. Sometimes she thought his need to defy was as strong as her own need to anchor to him. It was all so confusing!

Andrew came out and Jack presented the stranger as Nathan Fosby, from over in Sumner County, Sam'l Fosby's son.

"I thought his son had run off," Andrew said.

"Yes, sir," the stranger said, "But I'm back now and got it fixed up with Pa, and he told me I'd better get on over here, you'd be the right man to hear about it. See, the French—"

Oh, the French, my goodness, rumors like crazy but no one really knew. She went to tell Hannah they'd have guests, shifted tea kettle from hob to grate, and stirred the fire. She was slicing a cake made that morning when she heard the young man say, "General, they really are coming—"

"Hold up, there," Andrew said. "I'm not a general."

"Pa says you're going to run for the militia command, and he's bet a hundred dollars you'll win."

Andrew laughed. "He's a good man, your father. But I haven't been elected yet. Judge will do for now."

The militia . . . her mind wandered. He was thinking hard on the election but General Sevier, he'd already said he wanted the post for himself. The old military hero acted like it was his due, and he wouldn't lose easily. There'd be trouble and here was Andrew already on a hair trigger.

Then she heard Mr. Fosby say, "French army's coming and I believe we gotta get ready for them."

Andrew had that steely look. "Rumors," he said.

"No, sir! This ain't no rumor. See, I just come from Santo Domingo and—"

"All right," Andrew said. "Start at the start."

So this Mr. Fosby told a strange and terrible story. She forgot all about coffee and cake and drew up to listen. He'd crossed his daddy and gone flatboating down the river, and at New Orleans he'd shipped on a schooner that went tramp trading through the Gulf. Till he shipwrecked on a reef off Santo Domingo and tried to swim for it, and both his legs was broke when waves threw him agin rocks. He was drowning when a black man and his son pulled him out and took him home and—well, here was the strange part, gave her an odd feeling but she knew a lot about love and Mr. Fosby's face was full of honest love—

The black man's daughter nursed him to health, and they fell in love and her father said they could marry. Her name

was Marie and she was beautiful, and again Rachel felt that
jolt of surprise. She knew black girls could be beautiful, but
she didn't think of them that way. Mr. Fosby had learned
some French by then and they stood up in the little village
church with frangipani and bougainvillea in bloom, the
comfortable sound of rectory hogs snuffling around outside
the door, chickens pecking and cackling, and the parish
priest had married them, all legitimate if you could call anything papist legitimate. Drumming and dancing went on all
night, which sounded mighty pagan to her, though you could
see how he loved this woman and how kindly her family
was, and maybe it didn't make any difference at all that they
were black folks—

But then the French army came back, twenty-five thousand strong, column after column of soldiers filing off the
ships with slung muskets and grenades, winches swinging
cannon ashore.

"Under a big general, name of Leclerc."

She saw Andrew's eyes widen at that. "Leclerc, eh?" he
said. But she was struggling just to keep up. She knew
blacks had revolted in Haiti and it seemed Haiti and Santo
Domingo were one island. There'd been some fighting, but
things had settled down with a black leader, Toos-ant his
name sounded like, and as far as the people could tell the
French accepted him all right.

She was caught up in the story, found she was holding her
breath, and consciously expelled it. Everything changed
when the army came, the people restless, voices high, eyes
shifting, nerves showing. Soldiers began arresting men,
working from lists. Toos-ant wore his French uniform and
tried to put himself between the soldiers and the people, but
the old fear and hatred of whites was surfacing and strangers
in Mr. Fosby's village would finger their machetes at sight
of him.

There wasn't a sound but his low, steady voice. They were
sitting in frame chairs with deerhide seats around the stone
fireplace, and Mr. Fosby sat far forward like he was straining
to make them see the beauty of the place, brilliant flowers

and birds flashing in the sun and storms sweeping in from
the sea. He'd been happy there, she could see that. She had
the sense that he hadn't intended to talk this way at all, but it
filled him and had to spill, like a milk pail you fill too
full. . . .

It was as if he'd been too happy, in love with the island
and a woman, didn't care if she was black or blue, and in a
moment it all exploded. Life will do that. . . .

Marie, perfectly good Christian name too, went to market
with her sisters one day, carrying produce on her head and
then laying it out on a coconut cloth in the square, and he'd
followed with the men. Folks were buying and selling and
swapping and there were dogs and children and burros and
chickens pecking dung apart and mangoes, whatever they
were, stacked on cloths in golden piles and a fiddle was
playing and everyone was talking and laughing when the
soldiers came.

French troops in their fancy uniforms, bayonets on muskets carried at the ready. They were chasing a tall, skinny
man with frantic eyes who plunged into the market crowd.
The soldiers followed, knocking people aside with rifle butts,
and then someone yelled and he saw two of the soldiers fall
and the others raised their muskets. He ran toward them, crying out, heard the roar of firing, saw them reload and fire
again, and there were half a dozen people fallen, and he saw
Marie on hands and knees with blood pouring from her
mouth. He picked her up and watched the light fade from her
eyes and then the soldiers were jostling him aside, and still
holding his dead wife in his arms, he cried, "Why? Why?"

And they laughed at him. He cursed them. Their officer, a
little major with pointed mustaches, slapped his face and
said—he stopped, glancing at Rachel, and she, caught in the
horror of the story, said very steadily, "Go on."

—Slapped his face and said, "You like dark meat, do
you? Look around. There's plenty more where that came
from."

She was horrified. You'd think he would want revenge, sin
though it would be, but something in his face decided her

not to ask, and into the silence he said, "They're coming here, Judge; you understand that, don't you?"

She looked at Jack, who was watching Fosby intently, his face noncommittal. Jack could be tenderhearted but now he was listening as a soldier listens, and so was Andrew.

No white man could live in the village after that, and Mr. Fosby's family, loyal to the end, smuggled him down to the port city of Santo Domingo that night and he found a ship for New Orleans. But it didn't sail for two weeks, and he decided to learn what he could. Every night he was in the taverns talking to French soldiers sodden with rum.

"Everyone—soldiers, sergeants, officers, everyone—understood that the goal was New Orleans. Bring the blacks to heel in a month or two, then on to Louisiana with fixed bayonets."

"Bayonets?" Andrew said. He glanced at her. "An army? Talk here is they'll just replace the Spanish."

She'd heard Andrew say often that such talk was wishful thinking in the extreme; he was simply drawing Mr. Fosby out.

"That's not what the army thinks. They believe they go to conquer. I figure that's right too, 'cause one night I met an American mercenary, a colonel, he was pretty far along in his cups, and he laughed out loud when I asked the question. Don't be silly, he says, these Frenchies intend to take over the continent. Everything west of the Appalachians, Tennessee, Kentucky, the Ohio River, all French. Said this Napoleon was a pistol, got whatever he wanted, no one could stop him."

He cleared his throat. "So what I figure, Judge, the point of that big army, it's to conquer us."

Jack Coffee had to own up—Fosby's story had impressed the hell out of him. First time he'd seen what all the rumor about the French could really mean. Imagine those bastards in the square at Nashville shooting down women and children!

The judge had been affected too, though you never could

be sure what that canny man was really thinking. Anyway, Fosby's story had strengthened his decision to go after the major generalcy, when everyone knew challenging Sevier was no small matter. But Jackson was a natural commander; you could see that in his response to crisis. It would never occur to Coffee that it was up to him to rally the state, place himself at the pass, defend the nation. Oh, he'd volunteer, do his duty, die if necessary—but see himself as the key to it all? Great men had that image of themselves, and it was ever more evident to Coffee that Jackson was a great man.

So he was thinking when he walked into the Nashville Inn where the field officers of West Tennessee militia had invited Jackson to what amounted to a final judgment dinner: Should they elect him their commander? Eastern regiments would vote for Sevier, so Jackson must carry these western regiments. Coffee stood in the doorway of the small dining-room and spotted his own commanding officer, Col. Robert Hays of the Davidson County Cavalry, under whom as a captain he commanded a company. Hays was talking with Col. Sam Farrow, who ran the regular militia of Davidson County, of which Nashville was county seat. He saw Bob Weakley from over at Lockland and Jake Hemphill of Sumner County, Dick Childress of Murfreesboro, and Dave Phillips from Lebanon, and the others, twenty or twenty-five all told. Just about everyone from the Mero District, westernmost in Tennessee, and some from the middle district too. Jim Scorsby, their brigadier, had been called to Louisville, but he was a Jackson man. Coffee waited till he caught Bob Hays's eye before entering; the militia was democratic and all that, but the CO was still the CO. Coffee was only here as a courtesy to Jackson. He would keep his lip sealed; no one wanted to hear his views.

Hays was an old Jackson friend; indeed, Jackson's whole military career had started with him, when he'd been appointed judge advocate of Hays's regiment. That was ten years back, before statehood, before Nashville had turned into a real town, when the Nashville Inn was still one big room with logs unpeeled on the inside. Of course, that did

point to Jackson's main weakness: he had never really commanded troops and now he wanted to command them all as
major general.

There were three districts; each constituted a brigade, a
regiment for each county plus one cavalry outfit like that of
Bob Hays's. Regimental officers were elected by their men;
field-grade officers elected their brigadier, who joined with
them across the three brigades to elect the major general.
The governor would decide ties. It was a funny kind of election, when you got down to it—so few voting, so much at
stake. That was what the judge had to make them see, that
this mattered. . . .

The odds were agin him, no doubt about that, for Sevier
was the military man; but then the door opened and Jackson
came striding in, the very picture of a commander. Tall, thin,
whipcord strength as obvious as if it were written on his
forehead, wearing a fine suit of black broadcloth with new-
style pantaloons loose over well-brushed boots, a glowing
cigar jaunty in his left hand, circling the room, shaking
hands, a quip, a question, a word of recognition for each
man and his regiment, the whole room glowing with his
presence. Coffee knew him well, and yet this seemed a new
Jackson, lifted by some inner fire, rising to the need—another mark of a natural commander. Immediately Coffee's
optimism returned.

All these men knew him, supreme court justice riding circuit in their counties, already a power by virtue of his office, widely recognized as the civil leader of West
Tennessee—but civil was one thing and military another.
Someone put a glass of whiskey punch in his hand and they
stood close, chatting not with each other but with him, talking hunting, horse racing, a new bull someone had imported, a stallion likely to tear up the track at Clover
Bottom, a new plowing technique someone was trying
down toward Murfreesboro, a bear that mauled three men
before they put him down. They had dinner, venison with
pork sausage to spice it, and ale from Bob Hays's brewery:

and cigars were lighted before the judge turned serious and said it was time to talk.

He laid it out straight. The rumors of the French were true; they were coming and we had to get ready for them. Said Nathan Fosby had come to see him.

"No!" Jake Hemphill cried. "Nathan Fosby's back? Why, I grew up with him. Good man too. In love with Julia Fairchild, Judge Fairchild's oldest? And she up and married Sam Griswold, the one the bull killed later, remember? And Nathan said his heart was broke and he went down the river and never came back. I'll be damned."

"Well, he's back and he's rendered us a service," Jackson said, and took them through Fosby's story with neat efficiency, senior officer talking to other senior officers.

"Everyone Fosby met—he'd learned passable French—said they were going on to Louisiana and couldn't wait to get there. Now, gentlemen, I think you'd agree that among soldiers the rumor of the day is usually wrong, but they pretty well know what's going on. Correct?"

There was a burst of laughter. "Correct," Colonel Hays said.

"And then consider," Jackson said, "twenty-five thousand troops to quell natives armed with machetes? Fully equipped artillery units? More on their mind than Santo Domingo, I promise you. And their commander is General Leclerc."

Coffee had never heard of Leclerc, and from the blank faces he suspected no one else had either.

"Napoleon's favorite and evidently the very devil of a general officer," Jackson said. "Those lightning marches that gave Napoleon the Italian campaign, there was Leclerc always in front. And it was Leclerc who led troops into the Chamber of Deputies in what they call 18 Brumaire—the coup that put Napoleon in power. And to top it off, he married the dictator's sister. You don't think Napoleon would send such an officer just for a miserable island? More to it than that, gentlemen."

They were looking at each other, reflecting the surprise

that Coffee felt. How the hell did Jackson know all this when Coffee figured he was pretty well informed and he'd never heard it? It was those newspapers—they came in from all over the country, stack you couldn't see over on his desk, he'd come off the circuit and spend days poring down those narrow columns. Coffee had been studying Jackson a good while now, and what surprised him most was Jackson's capacity to surprise him. Just a plain man a lot of the time, interested in what interested everyone else, loved a good cock fight, cheered his horses at Clover Bottom louder than anyone, liked a joke and a glass of whiskey and a pipe, and could gossip with the best of them; and yet he had a quickness of grasp about him and a way of seeing things that other men didn't see. He'd be thinking way out ahead of you—well, Coffee couldn't explain it exactly, but this was a worthwhile man. One place he went off the edge though was that temper of his that could right easily get him killed one of these days. Coffee knew Aunt Rachel counted on him to keep the judge on track, and he tried.

"So why is the dictator sending his favorite general? Because, gentlemen, he wants what we've got. What we've built over these years. Look at us! Look at our own riverfront, half a mile of docks, boatyards, ropewalks, hauling yards, hoists and lifts and more warehouses going up every day. No wonder General Scorsby was called to Louisville; same kind of growth going on there. Cincinnati—I was there three months ago—every time you go it's like they tore it down and started over, it's so new looking and big.

"Look at the new glassworks at Knoxville. Gins sprouting all over the country. I've got one myself, ginning cotton for twenty neighbors, and I'm small. We'll have a real road connecting us to Knoxville one of these days soon, and I hear they're working on the Lexington road now. I'll warrant we have a hundred thousand population right here in Tennessee, damn near double our statehood figures, and growing every day. They say Kentuck's over two hundred thousand. Ohio a state now, means at least sixty thousand but probably it's a hundred. We're talking half, three-quarters of a million, put 'em all together. And you know what kind of folks they are, hard-driving men out to make their fortunes, willing to risk, willing to fight; they'd have stayed back in Carolina and Virginia and Pennsylvania if they wasn't. I tell you what you already know, gentlemen, but think about it—we have made this country the garden of the nation and we've done it by our hard work.

"So why are they coming here just now? Because we have built it so. Because that dictator of theirs dreams of empire, wants to conquer the world. Such a man looks at us—why? Because in his pride he believes he can have an American empire too, use us to feed his troops while they take over the rest of the world. Oh yes, they'll squeeze us, allow trade on their own terms, and finally, the way they see it, they'll take us over, vassals to a French dictator!"

His fist crashed down on the table and dishes jumped. "And by God, we won't let that happen! We'll fight!"

Well, they liked the sound of that, Coffee saw: Build our fortunes and defend them like we've done from the start. Looking around the table he saw no doubt that the French coming meant war, and he sure never doubted it himself.

Then Jackson was talking military affairs, but at a whole different level from what they expected. Talking inspiration, really, how you made men want to follow and obey, how you could discipline the very men who elected you, the shooting competitions with real prize money he'd like to start, forced marches called suddenly to get the boys used to the idea that military service could ask everything of you and that was its glory, and then he was talking about supply, the obligation to see that men were well armed and well fed and well led if you were going to ask them to follow you into enemy fire. . . .

"Gentlemen, the French come, and we'll be on the front lines. Meet 'em on the river or in New Orleans, and we'll want the rest of the West behind us. We need immediate liaison with military leaders in Kentucky and Ohio; we need to get ready to beat the drum for volunteers in the Carolinas and Virginia and Western Pennsylvania. One of their senators, Jim Ross—Pittsburgh man, Federalist, but a good man all the same and strong in the militia—I knew him in ninety-eight when I was up there, and we can count on him when the time comes.

"We need to get up to Washington and build a fire under their tails. I wouldn't want to bet they understand the danger. Let's see the secretary of war, get chains of supply moving, get eastern gunsmiths busy—God Almighty, American military is using mostly French muskets and we can't look to France now. All this is well and good, but remember, on the front lines you count most of all on yourself. The U.S. Army's but a handful, now cut in half, scattered all over creation and led by a scoundrel."

"Wilkinson's already sold out to the Spanish," Weakley cried. "I expect he's down kissing some French ass right now!"

When the laughter passed, Jackson headed right into the wind. "Gentlemen, I'd like to be your commanding general. I believe I'm the right man at the right time. I believe I have the vision to see what we must do and the energy to do it. You elect me and I promise you you'll have strong leadership, the kind you and your men can believe in and follow."

There was a long silence. Then an officer Coffee knew only by his last name, Stone, who lived considerably toward the east, said, "I don't know, Judge. Sevier, he's pretty strong in my part of the state. Been a general, made himself a hero at King's Mountain, just stepped down after six years as governor. You can't say he don't show leadership."

For a moment Coffee feared Jackson's temper would rise, but then low and even, the judge said, "I don't say that. I say he's offering the wrong kind of leadership, yesterday's leadership. I believe I represent today's and tomorrow's. General Sevier led 240 men to King's Mountain, and they saved the West from the British and they were heroes all. I remember it from my boyhood, how we cheered. But that was then. Now we're talking thirty, forty, fifty times those numbers. We're a new country in a new age. General Sevier thinks small and local; I think big and national. He was right for then; I'm right for now."

No one spoke and at last Colonel Hays stood and shook Jackson's hand and thanked the others for coming, and thus the die was cast. Next the election. Jackson had done well and Coffee thought he'd carry the West. But what about the East?

They walked out together. Jackson was calm. "We'll see," he said.

So the day came and Jackson was fit to be tied. Rachel understood how much he wanted this, but he prided himself that his avid hunger never showed, not even to Jack Coffee. It was as if wanting would shame him, he who'd faced the worst and never flinched. The governor was at Gallatin this week, twenty-odd miles away, and the vote would reach him there. Coffee was there now, standing by to hurry the result over, a mere two-hour ride if you trailed a spare horse.

He was pacing outside, waiting, the day growing late. He ordered the bay mare saddled, mounted, and rode a hundred yards, changed his mind, had the horse stabled, and paced back and forth through Rachel's garden all banked for winter.

Dear God, he wanted this!

His very gut told him he was a leader. He had an instinct for the thing to do and countless times had swayed men to his bidding. There was a greatness in him, he'd always felt it, but you have to find your way to greatness; it doesn't just come.

He'd tried the U.S. Congress, the Senate. Hell, he'd never make a legislator, single voice in an echoing chamber, parsing issues down to slender advantage. He'd never be governor, kissing the cheeks of babies and the feet of voters. He liked the court, it was command, but only on the case before him. Anyway, a judge has little future; he would quit before long. The military was the answer. Real command—there a man could have impact. He'd loved the military since boyhood.

And then Sevier slapping him down in ninety-six, that still rankled. Not qualified! Goddamned dog in the manger! His breath went short at the very thought of it, and it

wasn't just ambition either. Fosby's story had confirmed
what he already knew, and it made his blood run cold to
think of such men in Tennessee. Everything he'd said to the
officers was true. Tennessee was the front lines of a war that
would come from the south. All that he'd described could be
underway now.

He had a sudden burst of nausea and slumped on a bench,
head in his hands. He was there when he heard hoofbeats
and saw a skinny lad he didn't know with a second horse on
a lead rope.

"Message from Captain Coffee," the boy bawled, "but I
can tell you what it says. Votes seventeen-seventeen with
two to General Winchester. One vote still out."

Winchester? A solid Tennesseean but never in contention.
Throwaway votes.

"One vote still out?" Jackson said. "From where?"

"East Tennessee—over in the Smokies, east of Knoxville."

"Thank you, son," Jackson said, his voice carefully calm.
"Stable your horses and go inside. Mrs. Jackson'll give you
some dinner, and you'll stay the night."

He turned and walked away, shoulders sagging. For a moment he thought he would fall and then he straightened—no,
he would not bow. But it was the worst possible news. The
Smokies—King's Mountain country, Sevier country—Jackson would get no mountain votes. That delayed last vote was
Sevier's, the tally eighteen-seventeen, Jackson's chance of
glory gone, and Tennessee to face an uncertain future under
an uncertain leader.

It was almost dark when Jack came at a lope.

"It's a tie, Judge," Jack bellowed. "Seventeen-seventeen."

"But the last vote?"

"Vote from the Smokies." Jack was boiling with laughter.
"Came in for Winchester. Gave him three. Some son of a
bitch over there hates Sevier, wouldn't vote for his rival but
wouldn't go for him neither so he threw away his vote."

He swung off the big horse and wrung Jackson's hand.
"Fit me out a couple of fresh horses, grab a couple yourself,

and let's ride! Governor wants to see you. It's his call now, you know. He's holed up in Judge Dalrack's chambers. Says he'll wait for you till you get there. Let's ride!"

Jackson felt as if his heart would burst.

Jackson and the governor were closeted in Dalrack's paneled chambers; a portrait of Dalrack's wife hung on the wall, her bossy determination coming magically through the brush strokes.

He had known Archie Roane for years. Archie and David Allison, who had caused such grief before dying in a Philadelphia debtors' prison, had been partners, working for territorial Governor Blount when Blount had been Jackson's great friend. Jackson and Archie had been fellow delegates to the statehood convention when they'd rammed Tennessee into the Union whether the Union liked it or not.

Archie was a good fellow, in fact, convivial, relaxed, not unintelligent—a better dinner companion you could hardly find. But—and this was what Jackson had focused on during the long ride in the dark—you didn't think of courage when you thought of Archie Roane. He'd just sort of slid into office when Sevier stepped down, there being little competition just then.

Now, Archie in Dalrack's chair at Dalrack's desk, Jackson in a side chair done in blue leather and brass studs, a glance at Archie's troubled face told the problem; Archie was going to have to make up his mind and he hated doing that.

They spent maybe ten minutes on polite chat, queries as to their families, recollections of the old territorial days under Governor Blount, and then Jackson put it squarely. "We've got a tie here that you must decide, so let me be frank: I'm by far the better candidate."

Archie swallowed, blinking. He flattened his hands on the desk. "You know how much I respect and admire you, Andrew, but Sevier does have more military experience. More reputation—for the military, that is."

"He's yesterday's general, Archie. But this is today, and tomorrow is the problem. Let me sketch the situation."

He laid out the French threat, the need to rally now and prepare, the frontline equation, the pressure to be ready to march, the flatboats needed to transport troops, the urgency of liaison with Kentucky and Ohio and with the national government. . . .

"Well . . ."

"Don't forget, it'll be the governor's duty to call out the troops. Don't you think I'll be more help when you"—he saw Roane slump in his chair, face slack, and realized with a start that the man was a coward—"have to make that decision?"

"Oh, I don't doubt you would be the better commander. I hoped you would win, but that's the trouble—you didn't."

"But I didn't lose—"

"Yes, that's the problem, all right."

"A problem for you to set right."

Archie sighed. "Sevier is very strong. There would be a tremendous outcry, given his reputation is so high."

"I don't know about his reputation. He's been involved in all manner of shady things."

"Yes, but that was long ago. Everyone on the frontier was involved in—well, odd dealings. Hardly any law or rules, land titles a crazy jumble. You know that. Be fair, Andrew."

So, yes, it had come down to this, here in a paneled office with a bossy woman's portrait staring down accusingly, that he must plunge into the deepest water. He had a sense of the oddity—the irony—that you could decide the whole tenor of your future in an instant, with a phrase precipitate a battle that could have deadly consequences. Roane would make the move on his own if he had the balls of a rabbit, but he didn't.

Jackson said, "There are serious questions about Governor Sevier's reputation now."

"Now?"

"Now."

"Whatever do you mean, Andrew?"

Jackson saw the hunger in Roane's face and wanted to

boot his ass. But it's not unusual for contemptible men to hold the keys, and one must deal with the keyholder.

"You remember the giant land fraud I uncovered last year?" Using the powers of his court, Jackson had exposed a huge ring using forged titles ostensibly from old North Carolina land records to claim—and sell—land in the Tennessee wilderness.

"Remember that I named names, and one of 'em was Rachel's brother? Near broke her heart, but I had to do it. But there was one name I didn't release for the good of the state."

"And that was . . ."

"Governor Sevier."

"You're telling me Sevier was party to that land fraud?"

"Yes. On the edges but definitely in."

"You can prove this?"

"Of course."

"I mean in writing, Goddamn it! Something that will hold up in court. Not some damned jackleg whose testimony will change in a flash."

"I can prove it, Governor. In writing."

Roane stared at him.

Jackson said, "When your two-year term is up, you'll run again, won't you?"

"Of course."

"Well, Sevier is free to run for another three terms once he sits a term out. My understanding is he intends to do it. He'll be a formidable opponent."

Roane licked his lips. "You can prove it, you say? I call on you, you can come forward?"

"Yes."

"In public, understand?"

"Yes. I can prove what I say."

Roane smiled. He slumped in his chair, breathing a great sigh. "I agree with you, Andrew. Sevier, fine man though he is, isn't right for the terrible threats now facing the state of Tennessee. We are thrust into the cockpit of international affairs. It is my judgment, sir, that you are better suited to the modern role of Tennessee commander."

He came out of his chair in a bound and thrust out his hand. "May I be the first to congratulate you, Major General Jackson."

Jackson took his hand. "Thank you, Governor."

29

New Orleans, Mid 1802

No sooner did Danny Mobry walk into Daniel Clark's house on this last urgent errand than Zulie demanded, "Have you slept with Henri yet?" Then, laughing, "No, I see from your face you haven't. Foolish girl!"

Oh, was that so! But maybe Zulie was right.

She was an extraordinarily handsome Frenchwoman well into her forties, the widow of a French cavalier. Madame Zulime des Granges was Uncle Daniel's mistress. She was also well advanced in pregnancy, which seemed to improve her mood. She patted her bulging belly with satisfaction. Once Danny had asked why she didn't marry Daniel, and she'd laughed. Her late husband's family was content for her to sleep with him, which kept her out of trouble, and after all, a woman needs a man. At this Zulie had paused and added thoughtfully, "As do you, dear girl; it sticks out all over you." But it seemed that if monarchy returned to France, her grown son would be a prince, and of course, a prince's mother has obligations. "Meanwhile, Irish seed plowed into a French seedbed—its ecumenical, international, and highly satisfactory."

"But do you love Daniel?"

"Do I love him, does he love me? We make love, my dear. Isn't that enough?"

"Well . . ."

"Danny, of course I love him. But that doesn't change the realities of our lives. You love Henri—don't deny it—at least enough. But that doesn't change your realities."

She clucked her tongue. "And now you leave in a week."

Three months had changed New Orleans, air soft and warm, explosions of flowers, the sultry weight of summer blessedly holding off. Danny had moved to a comfortable pension on rue de Chartres and sent Captain Mac north in the *Cumberland Queen* heavy laden with sugar for the Boston distiller; he had just returned with hardware to Daniel Clark's order, word that her other ships were en route, and a letter.

She'd been busy touring plantations with Henri, assuring herself of the quality of the sugar she would be purchasing. He would serve as her agent when she was gone. Day by day, in his carriage drawn by a handsome pair of matched bays, they rolled down level dirt roads between fields of green shoots. At each plantation they went into the sugarhouse to see the big vats for cooking cane juice down to raw sugar, hogsheads in which sugar the color of a fawn's coat was packed, carts with wheels higher than her head, and arched frame centers that could lift the massive casks and, creaking and swaying, tote them down to a river wharf where her vessels could tie up and winch them aboard.

Henri drove well, his strong hands as delicate on the reins as a pianist's fingers. At noon he would produce lunch and a bottle of wine from a wicker basket. Often they would stop by the vast rolling river, boiling water that had scoured the continent coming now the color of mud and laden with the debris of a million square miles. Looking at that water you had to recognize that who controlled this river's mouth controlled the continent. Whole trees spun slowly in the current, sometimes pegging into the bottom and then rising into the air like ponderous ghosts, to fall back with a splash and vanish around a bend en route to the sea. After the meal they sat quietly, watching brown pelicans scooping fish from the river and screaming at the gulls that drifted in from saltwater. If such sweet days could go on forever—but then she would remember Carl and the ships and a waiting distiller. . . .

Well, perhaps she was falling in love, but what did that mean? Henri wanted a wife, here, a mother for his children; Danny lived in Washington. More important, the law was such that if she married, her husband would take legal control of the business Carl had built, and she would never tolerate that. She reminded herself that she was vulnerable, far from home and lonely, but there was more to it than that. Pulling herself out of grief to seize control of her business had somehow restored her to life and vitality, and with life came all its thrusts and urges. There would never be another Carl, but he had died and she was alive and must go on.

Zulie said she needed a man. Was that all there was to it? She refused the thought, but God, Henri *was* attractive. Sometimes, lying on a blanket with a straw hat over her face after a lunch, she would study him from under the hat brim, intensely aware of a force and power vibrating in him. She hadn't forgotten that first night when Clark had told her the French were coming and she'd seen both men enjoying her dismay. She knew them well now; she always would be cautious with Clark, but her trust in Henri had grown, at least as much as she was willing to trust anyone.

Now, impulsively, she hugged the bulbous Madame Zulime des Granges and kissed her cheek. "You're a sweetheart," she murmured, and then, straightening herself, squaring her shoulders, marched into her uncle's study and closed the door. She placed a large envelope squarely on his desk. It was addressed to her and the red wax seals were broken. She tapped it with a fingernail. "Read this, Uncle," she said.

The door opened. "So serious!" Zulie cried. "But I will help you keep him in line."

"Now, Zulie," Clark said.

She settled herself determinedly, peered over his desk and said, "A letter! To Danny, eh, but intended for you. Do open it, my dear."

The letter was from Dolley Madison, entrusted by hand to

Captain Mac, to be handed to no one but Danny. She had studied it for hours, pacing the quarterdeck of the *Queen* while chanting hands turned the winches that hoisted cargo from her hold.

She watched Clark draw out the two sheets, one a letter to her, the other a commission naming Clark U.S. consul in New Orleans. He tossed the commission aside, glanced at the letter, looked up at her.

"They want me to go to America on your ship?" he asked incredulously. "Impossible—ridiculous!" He flicked the commission to the floor. It was no surprise. He'd been told of it the year before. But it meant nothing, he said. The French were taking command, and Louisiana's future would rest with them. An American connection would be an embarrassment.

"Uncle," Danny said, "are you willfully obtuse? Or just naive?" She watched anger flash across his face. "Can you be so unattuned to nuance?"

" 'Unattuned'! I'm attuned to the fact that you're a damned impertinent young woman!"

"Perhaps, but listen to me. This is an informal letter from the wife of the secretary of state of the United States, and I promise you she has his full confidence, as Mr. Madison has Mr. Jefferson's confidence. She says informally what he chooses not to say formally."

"No, Danny," he said, words clipped and hard, "it is you who misunderstand. Look at me. I'm an Irishman educated in Britain who lives in a French community that's ruled by the Spanish. I have nothing to do with the United States."

"Your loyalty, you're saying, is to yourself?"

"Of course. Why not?"

"Have you met Monsieur LaFarge? Recently arrived?"

"I've met him. French, an envoy of some sort, I expect."

"He arranged an introduction to me," Danny said. "He seems to find me attractive."

"Aha!" Zulie said.

And, Danny said, Monsieur LaFarge boasted a bit and revealed more, not an uncommon trait in men around a pretty woman. She heard Zulie's low chuckle at that. And it turned out that Monsieur LaFarge, in fact, was Colonel LaFarge of the French army, and he was surveying New Orleans as one huge military base, an army staging ground for the advance up the river. She laid out the facts with the cool efficiency of a business report in detail that her uncle could not doubt.

"My business will die," she said. "that goes without saying. But yours will too. Think about that."

He stared at her but didn't answer. The silence stretched. She heard a dog barking somewhere in the distance.

At last she said, "Uncle, do you expect people at this level to spell out precise meanings in a letter that could fall into anyone's hands? Really! Here, let me read it to you again." She paced her voice, reading slowly.

Dearest friend, Jimmy joins me in hoping that all goes well for you. Captain Mac tells us of your sugar arrangements with your estimable uncle. As you by now know, great events are in the offing. Doubtless you are considering your own position in swirling and rapidly changing times. I think you can feel confident that the ground you tread is solid and that no untoward events beyond those in your own control will disturb your plans.

Enclosed please find Mr. Clark's commission. Mr. Madison sends with it his congratulations and felicitations. Please ask Mr. Clark to accompany you when next you return to Washington; there is much to be discussed and it is of great importance. Do not fail in this mission, dear Danny.

Clark did not speak and Danny waited. The dog was still barking but with an aimless note now. Zulie chuckled and Danny saw sophisticated comprehension on her face. "Very interesting," she said. "Daniel, darling, don't be difficult. It's not fair to your niece—nor wise. The letter tells you the Americans will not let the French take New Orleans and control the river. Otherwise, such a fine lady as Mrs. Madison would never tell Danny her commitment to New Orleans sugar is safe."

"Umph!" Clark said. "Perhaps. But I have no interest in going."

"My dear, dear man," Zulie said, "that you'll be gone when our little newcomer arrives will break my heart. But consider, you man of no state. The first paragraph says that if the Americans will not let France control your future, then certainly they will control it. The second says the president of the United States wants to see you on a matter of high importance. Do you really imagine you have a choice?"

The silence stretched again. As if Danny weren't in the room, Clark took Zulie's hand. "Ah, Zulie," he said so softly Danny almost missed it, "you are my woman." Then, briskly, to Danny, "I can't leave for two weeks."

"I'll wait, Uncle. Sail in two weeks."

"Done," he said, and stood, dismissing her.

Henri was waiting in the main salon. It was late now and the city was silent. He escorted her to her pension. They walked in silence, the air between them charged. At the pension door he took both her hands and held them, hard. She saw a nerve flutter in the corner of his eye. The tension became unbearable, and then she tore a hand free and with the other led him inside and up the stairs. She took the huge key from her reticule, unlocked the door, stepped inside, and turned. He didn't move. Her lips parted and she nodded. He came in and closed the door, and she folded herself into his arms with the feeling that she was plunging off a cliff with no idea of what lay below.

30

Samuel Smith, the *National Intelligencer* editor, came clattering up to the mansion on a sweating mare whose iron shoes squealed on cobblestones as he tossed the reins to the guard and called for Captain Lewis. After a moment's explanation, Lewis hurried him to the president's office. Mr. Jefferson, talking with Mr. Madison, looked up in surprise, but this could not wait.

"Sir," Mr. Smith blurted, "the French aims on Louisiana, they're popping into the open. You must position yourself."

Mr. J. stared at him. "You're printing this? Sir, we made you privy to these matters because we trusted you—"

From deep in a wing chair, Mr. Madison said, "Secrets, sir, should remain secrets!"

"No," Mr. Smith said. "Cat's out of the bag. It's in the Richmond papers, Baltimore, Philadelphia. We have no choice."

Their protests died. In fact, Lewis knew they long had expected it to become public. The weight of rumor grew, people had friends in New Orleans and Paris and London, merchant vessels from the Gulf called at ports from Charleston to Boston—how could you keep it quiet? Too many people knew and the pressure to talk became overwhelming. The stories editors wrote turned from speculation to assertion, and since editors all borrowed freely from others the word spread rapidly. Within a month or two it was everywhere. Look how the Hemings story had traveled.

"It's a difficult piece of mischief," the president said. "Now there'll be a public uproar, positions will harden, rhetoric will be more extreme, people will question whether a government responsive to the common people can react with strength, they'll wonder if we're facing war, they'll put more credence in Federalist blather that we intend to turn the country over to France, they'll postulate this is our way of doing so . . ." His voice trailed off and he sighed, then said, "I suppose Mr. Smith needs a statement he can publish. Mr. Secretary?"

There was a quicksilver quality in Mr. Madison that often surprised Lewis. He could shift not only ground but emotions as well, a capacity that quite eluded Lewis. Now he stood and with an easy smile said, "It's even simpler than it seems, Mr. Smith. France is a friend to this country and so is Britain—but to neither are we subordinate. I believe both value our friendship, and it's clear that France cannot keep that friendship *and* take control of the Mississippi River. I think, therefore, that it soon will strike France that some alternative is necessary, some shared ownership or relinquishing the east bank of the river or—well, there are many possibilities, but what is clear is that we will not be losing the Mississippi."

"Well said, sir," the president said.

As Lewis escorted the editor out, he heard Mr. Madison say, "Well, now everything gets more difficult, doesn't it?"

Aaron Burr gave a copper to a boy hawking the *Intelligencer* and opened the newspaper with a sense of dread. He spread it on a marble balustrade and read, letting the finality of its personal meaning sink in. He was in the cavernous space that would be the rotunda of the Capitol; the day was mild, the windows open, the big fireplaces empty, the temporary canvas roof quivering in a light breeze. Vendors awaited the session's end, which would come soon. Weary of stuffy air and stuffy debate, Burr had surrendered the president's gavel and fled the Senate chamber.

The paper had detail upon detail that couldn't be denied: after all the talk, the hints, the whispers, the wild rumors,

yes, the French were taking Louisiana and, as any fool could
see, next would steal the great heart of the continent. That
the vice president of the United States should get this confirmation from a newspaper was the ultimate demonstration of
where he stood. But it also freed him, and he realized he had
crossed some inner bridge to calm, new acceptance, his way
to response now clear.

And he was not without weapons. New York was vital to
any future election, and Burr had little doubt of his capacity
to dominate the state. Governor Clinton, a fool personified,
was acting cock of the walk now, but he and his pecksniff
nephew, DeWitt, could be demolished as soon as Burr put an
effort to it. It was time to get started. He decided to ask reliable old Peter Van Ness, who could thrum the strings of New
York politics with a concertmaster's skill, to come to Washington and lay plans. It was time to crank up their forces and
prepare for battle.

Now he leaned on the balustrade and folded his arms, his
expression carefully serene. A bell rang somewhere, and
members flowed into the rotunda-to-be like schoolboys
flooding an exercise yard, senators and congressmen and
clerks intermixed. The newsboys sprang into action and men
snatched up copies to stare at the front page, rising hubbub
of voices threaded with anger. They bought hot sausages on
buns, mugs of tea and coffee, sweet rolls, Madeira from a
man with a feather in his hat and a carved wooden cart, beer
from competing brewery men with kegs on sawhorses only
ten feet apart who glared at each other while the newsboys
jostled and squalled, racing for the raised finger.

Burr watched them as they stood braced, food and drink
clutched in one hand, shaking the newspaper for emphasis,
faces red, mouths open, voices the roar of the sea as they
reeled before shocking news. Of course it shocked them.
The hints and rumors had never carried real weight, but now
it was fact that the nation was in the most serious foreign
policy crisis in its history. The president and the secretary
acknowledged it!

What now? Could they trust this feckless, ambiguous man

in the president's house to deal with it? Would he yield to France? Could that be what he'd planned all along, this to be his excuse? Secret deals signed and delivered before Congress could intervene? What was their duty in the face of presidential intransigence, evidenced by his failure to take Congress into his confidence? A sphinx until the weight of evidence literally forced it into the open, and then the administration had made only a pro forma statement. We're everybody's friend and we trust our friends! What kind of a statement was that? He should be up on the Hill reporting to a joint session right now!

There were shouts outside. Burr went to the door. At the bottom of the long staircase, he saw a growing crowd that looked ready to storm the Capitol. The news was spreading and its danger was as clear to the man on the street as to the men in these marble halls. Guards holding the crowds back were being jostled and pushed. There was a sudden scuffle, two guards had a man down, then his friends rushed in to throw the guards back and the rescued man melted into the crowd. Over their heads, far down Capitol Street, he could see more crowds gathering, men and women pouring out of houses, responding to the French bombshell.

Jim Ross appeared at his side. Burr liked the Pennsylvanian, who was one of the few men in the Senate who had treated him unfailingly as a gentleman. Ross even had offered apologies for his party after that terrible night at Stelle's Hotel.

Now he put a hand on Burr's shoulder. "Aaron, you've been a friend of the West. By God, my folks out in Pittsburgh are going to take this hard." He gestured toward the crowd below. "Look at 'em—stunned, dismayed, enraged. They understand, you know, nothing innocent in this French move. It's an invasion and it's aimed squarely at *us,* and people know that by instinct."

He slowly raised one clenched fist. "French bastards. My people depend on western trade, Ohio River is their main concourse, and the Ohio's no good without the Mississippi. But any fool can see that sooner or later the French will shut it down and try to take it over. My folks'll have a delegation here hammering my head quick as they can travel, and I'd better have answers. This ain't party either, Aaron. I'm a good Federalist, but that don't mean a thing when chips this size are down!"

There! Ross was speaking the American truth to which the sainted Mr. Jefferson must answer. He and Madison would lose Louisiana. They lacked the lion hearts that holding it would demand. They would yield to the French with weak excuses; and when Louisiana was gone, the people would never forgive them. He smiled; everything plays to someone's advantage.

He shook Ross's hand. "Perhaps we should confer from time to time; I sense we have mutual interests," he said. Satisfied, he walked briskly from the Capitol, threading his way through the crowd. He was nearly clear when he heard his name called and turned to see two men he recognized vaguely as congressmen, Federalists, he thought, hurrying after him. When they were near they gave their names: Josiah Simcoe of Massachusetts and Samuel Baker of Connecticut. Burr bowed.

Simcoe was a heavy man, face red, a sour cast to his mouth. Trotting across the yard had left him gasping. Burr was drawn to the other, Baker, a slender fellow patrician in appearance and manner, light brown hair tossed elegantly to one side, his linen sparkling.

But it was Simcoe who spoke first. "We was at Stelle's that night," he said, still breathing hard. Burr froze. He barely noticed a look of consternation on Baker's face. The invitation to a high Federalist dinner had come from the sort of men you should be able to trust, and after all, he was through with the Democrats. But the moment he'd entered the banquet room, the consternation of the guests had told him everything; it was a humiliating trick to set Democratic tongues wagging. Still, Aaron Burr was not a man to be abused lightly. He'd seized a glass and into the silence offered a toast, "An union of all *honest* men." There was a moment of silence and then a deep voice called, "Hear! Hear!" and there was a rustle as men stood. He held his glass high, let the moment stretch, then drank it down in a swallow and strode from the room as if he owned the hall. But he wouldn't soon forget that night.

And this puppy was reminding him!

"What can I do for you?" he asked, ice in his voice.

Baker held up a hand to restrain his friend and in a low, melodious voice said, "I think what Josh meant was that we date our admiration for you from that night."

Oh?

"In fact, it was a rotten trick," Burr snapped.

"Yes, it was, but you carried it off brilliantly."

Mollified, Burr let his expression ease.

"Now, sir," Baker said, "the point is that we hope you are going to return to New York and restore your position there." This was striking rather close to home. Burr waited. "It's entirely clear that you have been used most shamefully by the administration. As we understand it, Governor Clinton is your enemy to say nothing of his nephew, DeWitt, Democrats though they are. Logic suggests that with little here to hold you, you probably will return to wrest power from your enemies."

"And why does that interest you?"

Baker smiled. "The Federalist Party values you highly, sir. I have authority to say it would look with pleasure on supporting you in a campaign to recapture New York."

Burr gave him a skeptical look and didn't answer.

"Of course you question this," Baker said. "But it makes sense. Many in New England believe this nation cannot—should not—hold together. The current administration is sure to yield to the French. Probably this is just a ploy to give it an excuse. And I can assure you that New England will not remain under French dominance. It will break away, ally with our natural friend, Britain, and leave the rest of the country to Virginia—and to France. Now, sir, the true interests of New York fit those of New England much better than those of Virginia, with its slaves hoeing tobacco. We believe were you to be in command in New York the logic of that position would be unassailable."

My, my. They were suggesting treason to the sitting vice president of the United States. We do live in interesting times, he thought. He frowned. "I think you must know, gentlemen, that this is not an appropriate conversation."

"Ah, doubtless so." Baker smiled easily. "We'll say no more, but after today we did want you to know our feelings."

Burr walked on, swinging his stick. Very interesting. . . .

In the distance he saw two women approaching. His mood always improved at the sight of women. These were trim and good looking. Then up close he saw it was Dolley Madison walking with, yes, that Mobry woman: Darnelle, Dahlia, Danny! That was it. Lost her husband—

He greeted them with a graceful bow. Dolley had the good taste to blush and he the gallantry to leave their differences unsaid. If she knew of administration distress at the turn of affairs in Louisiana, she said nothing of it. In a cascade of small talk, she said Danny was just in from New Orleans. He restrained the impulse to ask if New Orleans was celebrating the news and merely observed that his friend General Wilkinson spoke of that city with much affection. Something crossed the Mobry woman's face at the mention of Wilkinson, with whom he was to dine in the next hour. Interesting; Jim's reputation was always at issue. Mustering his most soulful look, he offered condolences and saw that shadow again. Curious and very interesting. He knew women well, and he knew she had responded to him. He walked on, pleased; my, a pretty woman responding does smooth the hurts.

Dolley had asked after Theodosia, which had let him wax eloquent on his darling daughter, now about to make him a grandfather. The baby would be named for him, boy or girl, Theodosia had promised and young Alston had agreed. They had married and Alston now was entering politics in South Carolina; quite ignobly, Burr had to admit to himself, he'd feared marriage would turn Theodosia's heart to her husband and reduce her father to just an old affection. But no, she loved him with the same fierce passion she always had. She would be coming north soon, ostensibly to avoid the dangerous heat of summer in the Carolina lowlands but really to see him. He had tried to shield her from his humiliations, but she'd read between the lines and condemned the Virginians with fury that warmed a father's heart.

But in another block, as if to deny him even these moments of pleasurable reflection, Simmons McAlester came bearing down on him. What the devil was Simmons doing in Washington? Burr hated to meet his creditors, of whom there were so many with claims for so much money. But if a man wanted to live well . . .

"Aaron, why didn't you tell me?" Sim shouted before Burr could duck into an alley. "You know I don't expect a lot of favors, but if you'd told me you'd have saved me thousands. That's not too much to ask, is it? I'd never have invested in Mississippi trade if I'd figured the French were going to seize it—" He stepped close, a hand on Burr's forearm, his voice sinking to a whisper. "Tell me, is there trouble? I'm hearing bad rumors, that you're being pulled down. You know I'm always your friend, but it's, well, disturbing to hear—"

"Oh, Sim, it's just talk." Burr made his voice easy. "You always hear it around politics. Who doesn't have enemies, but they'll pay in due time."

McAlester nodded eagerly. "That's the talk, Aaron." But Burr saw the doubt in his eyes. Another danger point. A year ago McAlester would never have asked such a question. Burr had lost track of exactly how much he owed, but it certainly was in the tens of thousands. The money came so easily. They were glad to loan to a man of influence. But what if he were revealed as without influence? If they all called, it would mean debtor's prison . . . and debtor's prison would mean death.

He shook that from his mind and walked on, thinking of the women. But the Mobry woman's reaction to Wilkinson's name was as interesting as the look in her luminous brown eyes. Burr would not raise again the rumors that Wilkinson was in the pay of the Spanish—he hadn't forgotten the general's rather frightening reaction the last time he'd done so—but he had an idea this French business was bad news for his friend.

He had ordered a fat duck and two bottles of wine for dinner at three in his rooms. He found Wilkinson waiting, fat and jowly in that ridiculous uniform. Burr glanced at his own trim form in a mirror with easy superiority, a feeling he needed.

The duck was excellent, the Madeira like honey, and soon they were well into the second bottle.

"What a good fellow you are," Wilkinson said, holding his glass toward the light to admire the color. "Able, superb political instincts, capacious of mind, grasp of the large view—and how disgracefully they abuse you, my dear friend. As, I might add, they do me too. We are victims together."

"Oh?" The wine was sweet on Burr's tongue, its fumes strong in his mind. "I don't think of you—"

"Held to this miserable rank, sir. Brigadier! When every leader of the army before was a major general. Mad Anthony Wayne, whom I succeeded, a major general."

Of course, Burr thought, but didn't say, Wayne had been one of the great officers of the Revolution and the period following, and Wilkinson had wormed his way into second in command and was well on his way to cutting his superior's throat when Wayne conveniently died. It was an irony that Burr could appreciate that Wilkinson should then have stepped into his shoes.

"The rank is mine," Wilkinson was saying, anger reddening his face, "and they deny me." Then, as if regretting yielding to emotion, he smiled and went on, "Just as they deny you. Oh, don't pretend, Aaron. It's to your honor, as it is to mine, that such men should abuse us."

"You do have a way of casting things, Jim."

"I think about such things, sir. I care about justice, propriety, decency. I resent its denial, to me and to a man of great worth. Is it any wonder that I dream?"

Burr sipped his wine. This was getting interesting. "Of what do you dream, my dear General?"

"Of the West. You should go there, Aaron. You would find a paradise. Full of strong people, rich fields, vast forests, a river network coursing like veins of gold, all athrob with trade for which the world hungers. Of course the French covet it. But they are fools!" He emptied his glass and refilled it. "Fools because they imagine they can bend westerners to their will. Easier to get a mule to cooperate. The western American will never be a Frenchman. But what he will be is the progenitor of a new nation."

He smiled. "I see you're shocked. But reflect—do present leaders have the courage to defend? I think not. They're in thrall to Federalists, and those idiots hate and fear the West. Westerners know this. You'd be amazed at the spirit of revolt burning there—revolt against the East. It's an empire, Aaron. And it awaits the man who has the range of vision to lead it to its natural future—independence. That man, supported by military force, can know greatness."

Wilkinson's lips were parted, his breathing heavy, his gaze fixed on Burr. "An empire . . . for remember, just down the road a thousand miles or so lies Mexico, vulnerable, defenseless, its mines pouring out their golden stream." A long pause. "Mexico yearns to be taken as a woman hungers for a man. . . ."

Then he relaxed, smiling. "That, you know, not New Orleans, is the real French goal. And maybe they'll take Mexico if more enterprising men don't get there first."

Did the French news discommode him? The answer came in a flash. A man who had maintained a treasonous connection with the enemy for twenty years while rising to the command of the American army would have no trouble making a French connection . . . indeed, he probably had done so already.

"You should go west, Aaron," the general said. "See for

yourself. Drift downstream and absorb possibilities. Forget this French thing; it will come to naught. You should go . . ."

Maybe I will, Burr thought . . . someday. But now there were more immediate prizes at hand, and their taking infinitely more pleasurable. He intended to be president of the United States yet, and in his estimate there was naught to stop him. Doubtless Wilkinson was right that ultimately France would have its hands full in Louisiana, but nothing could stop it from taking the province initially and it was obvious that the nobleman from Virginia could not survive the loss of half the country. The election of 1804 would be wide open, and a new champion would arise. Peter Van Ness would be here in a fortnight; it was high time to start planning.

Peter Van Ness, rail thin as always, pale hair and pale eyes matching his personality—though on paper his words sparkled and sang—was nearly a week on the road from New York, jouncing through holes that sometimes seemed deep enough to swallow the stage. Burr listened until the tedium of travel became too tedious, then brought Peter to attention. It was high time that they took control of New York City again and then of the state. Let Burr sit as governor and the obvious next step would be control of the nation—the presidency.

They had a decent light supper in his rooms and then talked over cigars.

"This fellow Cheetham," Peter said, his voice an uneasy whine, "what a scoundrel! I'm still ashamed that I—"

"Ah, Peter, you know there's no gratitude in politics."

Still, Cheetham's case was startling. He was a London journalist whose string ran out in ninety-eight. He came to New York, met Van Ness, and the upshot was that Burr helped him buy a half-interest in *The Argus*. Maybe that was where some of Sim McAlester's money went, who knew? Through 1800, Cheetham had been subservient and loyal. His coruscating denunciations of Federalists in general and

Alexander Hamilton in particular had no little to do with the victory that put that paragon of ingratitude, Mr. Jefferson, into office.

But ever since, such was his hatred of Burr, the Virginian had been pandering to old Governor Clinton, building him as the chief Democratic voice in New York. The old fool on whom senility appeared to be advancing rapidly was flaunting that damning letter from the president saying there was no opinion in New York he valued more than the governor's. His finger always to the wind, Cheetham switched to the Clinton camp, merged the paper Burr had bought for him with Clinton's *American Citizen,* reprinted the letter and began lauding the governor and damning Burr. He'd even written the president, and sure enough the gentleman from Virginia had responded with warm letters, letting New York know that Burr had the stature of an ant in Washington.

Burr long had refused to read Cheetham, but for months Peter had been urging response. "He's hurting us, Aaron. My, God, it's time we began to remind people what scum he is. Look at this." He pulled a thick pamphlet from his bag. It was titled *A View of the Political Conduct of Aaron Burr, Vice President of the United States.* Burr thumbed it briefly—full of old charges, trying to steal the presidency, doing nothing for New York, on and on. Peter said it was vile, filled with plain lies and slippery innuendo. All to laud old Clinton and denounce Burr.

"They say Mr. Hamilton reads Cheetham religiously," Van Ness said. "His own newspaper wouldn't stoop to such trash, but I've had a dozen reports of him reading this tripe in the coffee shops—seems it's regular entertainment at the Royalton."

Burr digested this without comment, but it was as disturbing as anything he'd heard. Why was Alex attacking him? Of course each had attacked the other during the campaign, but that was just the nature of politics. He and Hamilton long had been friends, more or less. Never close, granted, they were quite different, but both were leading attorneys and had tried cases together. But when Burr was tied with Jefferson

and holding himself to the highest standard of conduct,
Hamilton had campaigned against him among Federalists,
whose votes should have put him into office. And now he
was attacking again.

Was he afraid Burr would return? In a flash, Burr saw it
was exactly that. There was talk that he wanted to return to
public life. That meant the governor's chair, which old Clinton certainly would vacate at the end of his term, and here
came Burr ready to upset Hamilton's fondest dreams. So
maybe it was just politics, but there was a malignancy in
Hamilton's manner that was making it deeply personal.
Well, if he wanted a fight, Burr was the man to give it to him!

"Tell me what you plan, Aaron," Van Ness said. "Any future we have will be gone soon. There are terrible stories
about your being out of favor—"

"Why, Peter, I expect to be elected president."

"No! You do?"

"What's so surprising? Don't you see, this Louisiana
business will destroy the administration. What lovely
irony—Bonaparte putting Aaron Burr into office. But the
French won't be deterred. The present weak administration
will fold up and whimper, and the people will tear them
apart like mad dogs."

"But the Federalists—"

"The Federalists are a spent force, Peter, impotent, frozen
into old dreams. No, the people will be looking for someone—"

"Ah," Peter said, "someone familiar but not tainted!"

"Someone," Burr said, "who can deliver the great state of
New York. So that is how we must position ourselves."

They laid plans. Clinton must be their first target. He was
allied with old Dutch money, the Livingstons, patroon of
whom was the same old gaffer now in Paris about to surrender to Bonaparte and catapult Aaron Burr into office. They
all were out of touch; a new wave was coming and Burr
would ride its crest.

Get Cheetham's lies answered, then start on Clinton. They
needed a paper of their own and Burr must finance it. He

sighed: at least he would have something to show McAlester.

"Peter Irving wants to start a paper."

"Irving? I don't know him."

"Well, you know his little brother, Washington Irving. You financed him for a while, didn't you?"

Yes, by George, Washington Irving was one of the various writers and artists Burr had underwritten on borrowed money, acting less for them than for his own image of himself as a patron of the arts. That was an important distinction because it meant he had no reason to regret his largesse. And he remembered young Irving as a lively man with a pen.

"Good enough," he said. "If he can promise that Washington will write for him and if you'll give him a solid piece every week, yes, I'll underwrite him. Tell him to get started within the month. And give us a pamphlet that will unmask Cheetham and tear that senile old governor to pieces."

He felt a thrust of sheer joy. For too long his enemies had had their way, but now it was his turn. He clapped Peter on the shoulder. "We'll give them no quarter, my friend!"

31

WASHINGTON, SUMMER 1802

Mildred Samuels was playing erratically, Dolley noticed, forgetting her turn one moment, slapping down a card the next as if each winning trick paid off some angry old debt—or hurt. She was a tall woman, deep lines in her mottled face, hair quite gray. She sat to Dolley's right. Maggie Smith had set up two tables of whist, and the eight women playing were a cross-section of Washington society, among them Mrs. Secretary of War Dearborn; Pirette Pichon, the French

ambassador's wife, now quite pregnant, her face pale and a
bit strained; Dolley's close friend, Hannah, married to Treasury secretary Gallatin; and Mildred Samuels, who was that
rarity, a congressional wife with her husband in Washington.
Silas Samuels, a ferocious Federalist, represented an upstate
New York district. It was as well, Dolley thought, that the
women had a rule against political talk. She noticed Mildred
holding up her glass for a fourth sherry.

It was the decisive game and Dolley held the spade ace.
Twice Mildred led spades and Dolley held back, letting Mildred assume her partner held the ace. At the crucial moment,
she placed the crowning card on Mildred's king, took the
trick, and laid down the last five cards, all commanding dia-
monds.

"Oh!" Mildred slapped the table so hard the glasses shivered. Her eyes were wild. "How did you get that ace? I
thought Susan had it. If you had it, why in God's name
didn't you play it?"

"Why, Millie, it made tactical sense—"

"Tactical! You—you took *advantage* of me—"

"Really," Dolley said, "it's just a game—"

Play at the other table had stopped. Maggie was standing.

"A disgusting democratic trick!" Mildred shouted. "It's
just as Silas says—you can't trust Democrats—look at the
terrible mess you've gotten us into now. Silas says we'll
have to fight the French and it's all your doing!"

"Millie," Maggie said, "our rule—"

"Oh, bother the rule! Facts are facts. The Democrats are
ruining this country. They've gone out of control just the
way we knew they would. Look at that nasty Burr person
trying to steal the election before you even got in office; you
call that self-control? We saw what happened to democracy
in France, they went crazy, and now it's happening here.
Everyone knows the French wouldn't have dared take
Louisiana when *we* were in office!"

"Mildred," Dolley said, "don't be an ass. They won't take
Louisiana while we're in office either!"

"Ass, am I?" Mildred downed her glass in a gulp and

glared. "Well, you listen to me. We saw the French were the enemy years ago, and you Democrats fought everything we did. And now you've gotten us into this terrible mess and you won't have the pith to fight—yes, pith, plain old backbone. You won't stand up; everyone knows it. Everyone says the country's ruined!"

Into the stricken silence, Maggie said, "Please . . . I'll pour the coffee now . . ." The women sought their wraps as soon as they decently could.

Dolley hurried home with bootheels scuffing briskly on gravel walks. She shivered. All the hatred of the election was loose again. The Federalists were shouting, their papers were full of their wildest invective, the Congress in turmoil, everyone bending the crisis of the French to their own ends. Mildred Samuels was just parroting that extremist husband of hers—*we* knew all along, *we* understood the French, *we* wanted to lay down lines and challenges years ago and now nothing has changed but you've cut army and navy in half and what did that do but embolden Napoleon, show him we're spineless, free him to steal our territory from under our noses. Oh, yes, *we* understood, but the people were seduced away. Now they'll take their revenge, you'll see, they'll turn back to us, return control to men who know how to use it. . . .

The new explosion began when a merchant brig moored at Baltimore and Tobias Lear limped ashore. General Washington's former private secretary now was the U.S. consul to Santo Domingo, and French troops had ejected him at rifle point! The storm this news started was the worse because a French trooper had smashed Lear's knee with a musket butt when he was slow in moving, and he'd been in pain ever since. It was a diplomatic affront of the first magnitude, the sort of thing that started wars. Madison didn't intend to let it start a war, not yet, but it made everything worse.

By the time Lear reached Washington, limping and leaning on a cane, his story was radiating up and down the East Coast. Baltimore papers hurried copies off by express to other papers that quickly reprinted, north to Wilmington, Philadelphia, New York, south to Richmond, Charleston, Savannah. In Congress the Federalist big mules, Bayard, Gouverneur Morris, Fisher Ames, were fighting for the floor to denounce Democratic-Republicans. Madison sat in his office listening grimly to Johnny Graham's report. Calling us weak and floundering, saying any fool could see the French intention to split us apart, strip us of the West, dominate the continent, make us a vassal state. Saying the Democrats were in thrall to the French, beholden to them, in love with their revolution, blind if not criminally uncaring of our own national rights. And so forth. That idiot Silas Samuels was braying like a jackass after a mare in heat. The Democrats weren't even trying to respond. Chairman Randolph sent word they wanted to see some action from the other end of Pennsylvania Avenue.

War was what they all were shouting for, enough emotion flying around to fill one of brother Shakespeare's plays chock-a-block and plenty of posturing to go with it. But pin anyone down and he'd suddenly want to go slow. They wanted action, all right—so long as it came from *this* end of the avenue. And yes, this new French intransigence did bring war closer. Lear came hobbling into Madison's office and told a story that was as infuriating as it was discouraging. We struggled to present reality to the French dictator, but he seemed blind—and his army seemed a little crazy.

Imagine, coming to Santo Domingo with empty larders expecting the United States to refill them on demand. There was ample American trade with Santo Domingo; but since French credit was worthless, merchants insisted on gold. Leclerc simply seized the goods—emptied warehouses at musket point, impounded American ships and cargoes. Two ship captains were imprisoned, one because he had spoken critically of the French—not there but at home in Baltimore!—the other because Leclerc thought a ship named *Santo Domingo Packet* probably was a rebel vessel. Lear, as consul, finally secured their release, but it was the vigor of his representation that had led to his expulsion.

Crazy . . .

Naturally American commerce to the island stopped.
Meanwhile the French were finding the black rebels in their
vast numbers to be formidable fighters.

"The troops are hungry, and I think frightened too," Lear
said. "There's a fury in the blacks. Troops say it's like nothing they saw in Italy or Austria." Heavy foliage made fighting sudden and close. A soldier barely had time to snap off a
single shot without aim before he was under a slashing machete blade that could decapitate a man in a stroke. Off-duty
ranks talked constantly of finding stacks of heads, mouths
stuffed with severed penises. "Worse, of course, since they
took Toussaint."

"Captured him?"

"No, no—tricked him. Told him they considered him a
Frenchman like themselves and accepted his command of
the island. Set up a big formal conference to honor him: and
when he came in they seized him, executed his lieutenants,
and shipped him off to France. He'll die in some icy dun-
geon in the Alps, poor devil."

Crazy . . .

"The tropics aren't kind to Europeans," Lear said. "Too
much sun, too much rum, snakes and bugs and poisons,
fevers floating on deadly night air. And the yellow fever season hasn't even started."

But it was more than that. Madison saw the dice rolling
for a continent. The westering tide of American settlers
would fix North American as American, but France aimed to
block them with what Talleyrand called "a wall of brass."
Leclerc had come to seize a continent, and Madison thought
this was was his opening gun. So maybe it all had a purpose,
the mad flailing, seizing property, ejecting the American
consul, even the casual brutalization by a trooper with a
musket butt. Maybe this was Leclerc's message, telling
Americans what they could expect in Louisiana.

Pichon arrived wearing a haggard look, face hollowed, eyes
shadowed. His wife was approaching labor and increasingly

ill. Childless himself, Madison felt an odd mix of regret for his own state and impatience with the envoy's problems.

Perhaps that intensified anger already real as he laid out the high displeasure of the United States with General Leclerc's outrageous violation of all diplomatic norms. Pichon, more hangdog than ever, made comforting murmurs. He said he already had written General Leclerc pointing out the grossness of his error.

"I'm sure when Mr. Lear returns there'll be no problem."

Madison studied the Frenchman. That wistful quality was strong in his expression. Perhaps he found himself squeezed between an aggressive leader who was willfully ignorant and his own sense of reality. Yet America's best defense was to make that leader see that his plans must come to grief, and Madison had only two official avenues—Mr. Livingston, who couldn't get a civil word from Talleyrand, and this sallow man with his mind pulled to his pregnant wife.

He judged a soft tone would be most effective. "Ah, Louis," he said, "you can see this sort of thing only serves the Federalists, and they'll never be your friends. Can't you make your government understand that the Federalists, in the minority at the moment but very sizeable, would like nothing better than war with France, the United States tucked under the British wing? My God, Louis, isn't that self-evident?"

He threw up his hands. "Why, even the president—and you know his underlying affection for your country—was saying the other night that if such treatment continued, it must end by making union with Britain. I believe 'universally popular' was the phrase he used, and I must say, I think he's quite right."

He made the case again—Mr. Lear's expulsion, American merchants and ship captains abused, the constant threats and strident condemnations of American democracy made by Leclerc and his officers, the secrecy, the denials, Foreign Minister Talleyrand's refusal of common courtesy, the coin of diplomacy, to Ambassador Livingston . . .

Created awful misunderstandings, he said. The idea that

France could separate western Americans from eastern was ridiculous. No chance whatsoever. Americans were one people. The real loser would be France itself. Britain would take over French island colonies the moment it united with America. Everyone understood the current lull in European war would end, and then union with Britain would be simple to arrange, with any slight embarrassment, since Democrats once had opposed it, quickly dissipating.

He leaned back in his chair, hands laced behind his head, an easy smile on his face. "You know, Louis, France made its real decision years ago. Now it should have the wisdom—dare I say courage?—to live with that decision."

"I'm not sure I understand, sir," Pichon said cautiously.

"Well, why did it back our revolution a quarter century ago? Because it was our friend? Many Americans assumed its motive was utterly selfless, but a man of the world such as yourself will hardly be taken in by so patent a fiction."

Pichon didn't answer.

"We know—and I know you'll agree—it was in the interests of France to help us. It was obvious then that America would in time be a great power. How much better for France for America to be independent than for it to be an appendage to your deadliest enemy. Now you know we've grown tenfold since those days and are well on our way to realizing our potential."

Again Pichon didn't answer and Madison said, "You see the obvious answer to the equation, I'm sure. Having made its decision then, France now should be cultivating us, not forcing us back into Britain's arms."

"I suppose that is so, Mr. Secretary," Pichon said politely.

Madison smiled. "Plain simple truth." Yes, but would Pichon dare report the argument with its fundamental logic? Would he have the courage to make points that neither Talleyrand nor Napoleon wanted to hear?

"Mr. Yrujo, you would do well to position yourself and your nation in this matter," Madison said. He had summoned the

Spanish ambassador peremptorily and now gave him no chance to speak. He was boiling over with Spain's intransigence.

"Let me point out to you that Spain will continue to have great interests when we have settled this Louisiana matter. Florida, Mexico, Cuba—all will be open to question if we are to move into a state of war, a state of mad freebooting by piratical nations on this continent. I assure you, such action will not go unpunished."

"Mr. Secretary," Yrujo squalled, "I protest—"

"That will do, sir. You are not here to protest. You are here to be informed what to tell your government. Tell your masters that the United States is deeply displeased with Spain's secrecy in this matter, its arrogant retrocession without information to us, consideration for us—abominable, sir. That a great nation would act so boggles the mind, calls into question whether the nation is, in fact, great.

"Remind your masters, Mr. Yrujo, that much is at stake here. Our western regions hunger for Florida, and they see no reason that Mexico should be Spanish. Is that some matter ordained from on high? I think not. So be warned, sir."

"Mr. Secretary, I—"

"I am not seeking your response, your excuses, sir. I am telling you what to report to your superiors. Good day, sir."

Yrujo stood, biting his lip, and for a moment Madison thought he would cry. Then he bowed. "Good day, sir."

So, Madison thought, I've made another enemy. So be it. Spain has acted the poltroon and we shan't forget it.

Johnny Graham had just returned from an errand to the Hill. He was feeling good, which he did most of the time. He'd collided with Simon Pink in the chairman's office, and the little clerk had been so outrageous Johnny had burst out laughing.

"Simon," he'd said, "go blow your nose. You're snotty beyond belief today."

That got the little devil's attention. Johnny was still

chuckling as he led the department horse to the watering trough and snapped on the grazing line. He'd just turned the critter loose when he saw the most vividly caparisoned fellow you'd ever want to meet come striding across the lawn looking as if he was pretty sure he was in command of the whole damned world. Grinning, Johnny admired his uniform, festooned with bars and stars and rosettes, effusion of lace and ruffles at the throat, high dragoon boots, lacking only a saber, and at least as bright as what the doorman at Stelle's Hotel wore.

At the street he saw Mr. Pichon arguing with a new guard who didn't recognize him and was demanding he move his carriage. He was about to go to the chargé's assistance when, apparently having convinced the guard, Mr. Pichon came hurrying toward them. But just then the fellow in the uniform, pointing at Johnny with a small, polished stick, barked in heavily accented English, "You, there, direct me to the secretary's office!"

Well, that tone was enough to get Johnny's hackles about straight up, and he said in his most deliberate western accent, "Well, now, he don't see just any old Tom, Dick, Harry comes walking in off the street."

Still, as Mr. Pichon cried breathlessly that he had sent Mr. Madison a note, Johnny got a better look at the stranger and almost regretted his own tone. This was a man of consequence. He was of medium size with rigid military bearing, a carefully barbered beard, and strikingly pale blue eyes that gave him a bleached look despite his deep tan. Perhaps the self-importance of the uniform and the coldness of the eyes combined in some evil way, but Johnny felt a momentary shiver that quite surprised him. Was he intimidated? No, sir, he was not! A surge of anger tightened his face as he led them inside. Still, that shiver, that flash of concern, stayed with him. There was a force in this French officer. . . .

He stepped into Mr. Madison's office. "Sir, there's a fancy fellow out here to see you—you don't mind, I'll stay in the room. This one, you might want me to throw him out on his

ear." The truth was he didn't want the little secretary left at
the mercy of this somehow threatening figure.

But before Mr. Madison could answer, the door opened
and the soldier pushed past Mr. Pichon, clicked his heels,
and cried in a parade ground voice, "Major General Felix
Montane of the French Expeditionary Force to Santo
Domingo!"

Johnny, closing the door, had a sudden insight that if you
met this man in combat you'd need to be handy to finish
alive. He glanced at Mr. Madison: How would he, the least
warlike of men, react? The secretary was small, kindly,
courteous, and quiet, above all a man of books and ideas, the
sort who just needed protection, to put it plain.

Mr. Madison bowed perfunctorily. Without inviting them
to sit, he said to Pichon, "My, Louis, you could have loaned
him a suit of clothes." General Montane's eyes widened, his
mouth sprang open, but before he could speak Mr. Madison
said, "General, things may be different in France, but in the
American democracy, uniforms are totally inappropriate at
diplomatic conversations. Mr. Pichon probably told you as
much—"

Johnny saw Pichon's involuntary nod, at which the general turned on him with such force that poor Louis stumbled
backward.

Immediately Mr. Madison went on, "Well, well, very
poor taste I must say, but let's get on with it. I'm quite busy;
it would be next week before I could spare time for you
again. Sit down, General, and tell me what I can do for you."

Well, goodness gracious, that pretty well said whether Mr.
Madison was readily intimidated.

Johnny watched the French officer seat himself stiffly,
plucking his breeches into proper folds before saying in accented but accurate English, "I, sir, am second in command
to General Leclerc himself. You know of General Leclerc?"

"Of course. The first consul's favorite."

Montane flushed. "A standing he earned, sir, through the
exigencies of war!"

"And of marriage. But what do you seek, General?"

"What I seek, sir, is your guarantee that you will require the United States to support France in Santo Domingo as an ally and a friend should. We have urgent need of supplies. Mr. Pichon has the list"—again that curious glowering glance at Pichon—"flour, salt meat, powder and lead, cloth, medicines—"

"American merchants can supply all that quite readily." Mr. Madison glanced at Pichon and added, "Why don't you send him to Philadelphia or Baltimore—better selection there." He started to stand as if to terminate the talk.

"One moment, sir," Montane snapped. "Your merchants demand gold."

"Of course," Mr. Madison said, looking surprised. "Since French credit is rarely honored."

The general snorted. "That is your problem, not mine. You owe us support. Order your merchants to comply or pay them yourself. Who cares how it's done?" He threw up a hand, radiating anger. "Finances are no concern of mine. No man who risks his life daily on the battlefield stoops to counting coin. It is a matter of military honor, sir."

"Analogous, I suppose," Mr. Madison said, "to the honor with which you dealt with Toussaint?"

The general leaped up at that. Johnny stood, fists doubled, but the Frenchman said, "I will not lower myself to answer that, nor will I waste more time. I am simply telling you that we expect you to discipline your merchants."

"Well, General," Mr. Madison said, "we don't do things that way. So sit down and calm yourself."

After a moment, Montane did so, arranging his breeches once again. "In France, merchants toe a very careful line. They pay attention to government—indeed, they leap to obey."

"Yes, but you see, we are a democracy."

The general shrugged. "Getting around that should be no problem. It's a weak and foolish form, one that wise men already are abandoning."

"Really, General?" Johnny was proud of Mr. Madison, who managed to sound politely bored.

Montane flushed. "Yes, really! It is a spent force, sir, a failure, a refuge of weaklings and fools. The world knows what a disaster it made in France and now the same is happening here."

There was a long silence. Johnny saw Mr. Madison glance at Pichon and raise his eyebrows. Pichon flushed.

Then, voice newly cold, the secretary said, "Let me tell you, General, that when the time comes you will find us not nearly so spent as you imagine."

"In that case, sir, you should have no trouble in meeting our needs. Supplies *must* flow to our forces. If you can't order compliance, then pay from your own coffers. You will be repaid, in gold at some point in the future, in good will immediately. And that should be more important to you than gold."

Another long pause, a crackle of tension, all four men on their feet. Mr. Madison stark and cold. "Please explain yourself, General. Why should the good will of France matter more than that of any nation?"

"Because from the island we go on to Louisiana."

The words hung in the still room. "Sir," Mr. Madison said, "do you threaten me?"

Montane smiled, as if he felt the force of his position was only now being recognized. "No, no—just a statement of facts. We will come to Louisiana, come up the river, take control as Spain with its army of gutter sweepings could never manage. Of course we will encounter your citizens, and our manner of dealing with them will depend on whether you prove yourself friend or enemy. It really is up to you. But I should warn you, in General Leclerc's name, if you choose to be our enemy we will take your so-called American West and make it our own. Change those foolish names, Kentucky and Tennessee and the like, to proper French names—"

Mr. Madison raised a hand to stop him. "I have a message for your General Leclerc. Please deliver it exactly as I give it to you. It is, sir, that the United States will never permit a hostile nation to stand astride the Mississippi River."

General Montane stared. At last he said in a strangled voice, "You have a great deal of nerve, Mr. Secretary."

"Not really. I merely speak the facts. See that you convey them. And now, good day, General."

Johnny opened the door and stood aside to let the visitors pass. He started to speak but the desolation on Mr. Madison's face stopped him. As if he were alone, the secretary murmured, ". . . getting very dangerous . . ." He turned to stare from the window. Johnny went out and closed the door.

32

WASHINGTON, SUMMER 1802

The air was getting bad in Washington. Samuel Clark could tell it early—black folks, free or slave, knew what white folks were thinking. They paid attention. Every hint, every glance, every little shift in tone told a story of growing tension. No one talked about it much, but everyone knew it. Black taverns were full of whispers; Millie heard it every day from women in the market; Samuel heard just the same from other coachmen, free and bound. The white folks were nervous, uneasy, suspicious, and that meant danger for black folks.

Wasn't much doubt as to the source. Black men, slaves till not long ago, were holding off the French in Santo Domingo, those glittering machetes catching the sun as they took off the heads of French boys far from home. It unsettled white folks here. They'd been so relieved when the word spread that the French had sent an army to deal with those uppity niggers on their foul little island, and all they wanted to hear was success.

The French would soon enough kill that nasty little spark of freedom, that madness that said black men could stand against white men and win. Damned dangerous business, way it gave local niggers new ideas. The papers were full of it and some of the black devils could read, more's the pity; and they spread the word that the French weren't finding it as easy as expected. The slaves down there were putting up a fight. Of course the French would win, but it was taking too long and they weren't prepared. That's how come they didn't have much in the way of supplies. Figured they wouldn't need that much, the blacks would fold up and hold out their hands for the manacles and get back to work in the fields, but that wasn't happening. No one doubted the French would win, but what outraged 'em was the idea that the blacks were putting up a fight at all. They were making the French come out into the rain forest and take them one by one, and they weren't being taken easily.

Everywhere Samuel went on the box of Miss Danny's coach he saw white men eyeing him speculatively. Slavers took to carrying second and third pistols and a surprising number of them had a fellow with a double-barrel nearby—well, slavers didn't pay extra for guards without a good reason.

The news came in the slightest whisper. "You heard about Tom Jenkins?" Samuel had the carriage in a line outside the president's house, where Miss Danny was attending a tea. It was already hot and he rigged a canvas over the horse's heads to protect them and sat in the shade under the boot of the coach ahead. That driver joined him there.

"What about Tom?" he asked from the corner of his mouth. He had formed a light friendship with Jenkins in just such lines as this, not too close; it didn't pay to get close to anyone in this town. Anyway, free man talking to a slave man, you had to look out what you said. The other driver— also a free black, though Samuel couldn't remember his name—was slight with owlish eyes and an eager manner. He wanted something and that made Samuel uncomfortable, and usually he avoided him. But now he listened to the low whisper. The fellow's lips scarcely moved.

"Massa flogged him. Say they caught him reading a paper, tells about slaves carving up those French bastards. Damn! Tom ought to know better than that! Now they say he can't hardly walk and Massa talking of selling him."

Samuel turned a harsh stare on the other. Without a word he stood to adjust the canvas over the horse's head, and when he had it set, he took the shade at the rear of his own coach. Didn't need to sit around with talk like that! But he was sick at heart. He liked Tom, who was honest and decent and had an easy laugh, and the image of him screaming and finally fainting as the lash fell like a hammer pounding nails, well, that hurt plenty. Yes, it did.

This town ain't good for us, he thought. He must get Millie thinking on it, start bringing her around. She didn't want to hear, but it was staring them in the face. Somehow she still saw Miss Danny as the child of long ago; but fact was, Miss Danny was a growed woman looking out for herself and it was time he and Millie looked out for themselves. He had a hidden bag of gold that he'd strained for over the years and it was building up pretty good. Enough to see them all the way to Maine. Of course that scared Millie, but with money you can make your way in this country. He'd have enough to see them a year or even two without work. It would be fatal to go with less because he had no idea how blacks would be received in this northern tier of Massachusetts. It wasn't slave country, but that didn't mean white folks would welcome blacks. You take what happened to Tom Jenkins and the fear that the slave revolt seemed to inspire in the white folks and Miss Danny likely as not to marry Mr. Henri. My goodness, it was time to look out for themselves!

He waited till that night to tell Millie about Tom, after she'd served Miss Danny a lonely dinner and then had taken a pot of hot chocolate to the bedroom. She came back with tears in her eyes. "She up there with a candle reading another book on seafaring and shipping and I don't know what-all when what she needs is a man in that big, lonely bed."

Proving Samuel's point exactly! They had to move on. He didn't quite say it—told her about Tom Jenkins instead and she began to cry. Said she knew Samantha Jenkins from market days—she was cook when Tom was coachman—and she'd never heard Samantha say nothing good about their master.

Well, Millie understood too. She saw the new guards around the marketplace, the suspicious looks, the way whites were ordering blacks about. "Here, you black bitch, why you talking to that wench? You move right along now, give you a rap up side of the head you don't watch out." Millie had been asking after Mary Kelly's sick baby, but she let it go. White folks were scared; that's all there was to it.

Still, he went out after he'd eaten, ignoring Millie's protests. Taking Miss Danny down to her office after the tea he'd spied the merchant brig *Sallie Mae* at a new dock and learned it had landed the day before. Now he must see if Tinker had had any word of Joshua. He slowed till he was walking in a lazy shuffle as he approached the alley leading down to Miss Molly's, but all seemed quiet. The alley itself looked all right, but he hugged the wall going down to where the candle flickered in the red lantern over Miss Molly's door.

He slipped in the door smooth and easy; and when his eyes adjusted to the light and the smoke, he saw Tinker across the room standing before some poor bastard on his knees with blood running out his nose. Looked like Tinker was going to kick his chest in, but then he didn't. Someone who patronized Tinker's woman when he was at sea, Samuel supposed. He swallowed and walked steadily to the big man's table. The woman gave him a hard look, but he ignored her and asked Tinker if the voyage had been good.

"Better than good!" Tinker said, and slapped the table so hard the glasses jumped. Samuel saw he was drunk but with that edge of physical alertness that can make drunks dangerous. "And you know why? Because black brothers down on that island, they ain't laying down. They're fighting! Hard, too, my friend. They killing Frenchmen right and left." His voice was loud and Samuel felt a shiver of apprehension. The room had quieted; he realized others were listening to the sailor in from the sea, freshly come from the place of slave revolution.

Tinker's eyes glittered and he tossed back his tumbler of rum and the woman leaned forward to refill it. Her gown sagged and Samuel could see her big, brown nipples. He looked away.

"Any man says black folk can't fight, he should go to Santo Domingo and get his eyes opened." Tinker gave a big laugh. "He'd find you put a machete in a black man's hand, he sure as hell knows what to do with it. French troops go out every morning and every evening they come in with bodies and every morning the bugle plays and they put some more of 'em in the ground. God Almighty—it's something to see!"

He peered owlishly at Samuel. "That feller could pass for your brother, he gave me something for you. You ought to see him now. Got him a sword he took off some French lieutenant, two pistols, he's some kind of general or other, got a couple of hundred men answering to him. Says he's running the French ragged."

Joshua a general! Samuel didn't doubt it. There was a power in his brother that Samuel lacked and just as glad he did, the same power that had driven Joshua to Santo Domingo in the first place. He remembered Junie's terror when he and Millie had seen her on their last voyage south. Wept the whole time they were there, which was just an hour, all Miss Danny's brother would allow. Junie was convinced she would never see Joshua again, and you could see the love for him pouring right out of her eyes. Like to broke Samuel's heart, and Millie's tears were like her sister's. Junie was scared for herself and the children too, but he could see that the real fear was that her man wouldn't come back. He'd die in some way and some place of which she would never know nothing, and she'd have naught but silence.

"You brought me a letter then?" he asked Tinker.

"Naw. Better'n that. A present. He said to give it to you. Said to tell you if he didn't get out, to remember he was fighting and this would prove it." He sighed, gazing at Samuel. "Damn!" he said, "I wish you'd come in last night; you'd have had it. But see, I put it up in a dice game against a huge wad. It felt like a sure shot, felt like I couldn't miss, but the dice did me wrong."

"So you lost it."

"That's right. Sorry." He gave Samuel a look that asked if he wanted to make something of it.

"Maybe it doesn't matter," Samuel said. "But what was it?"

"An ear."

"Ear?"

"White ear. Taken off a Frenchman. Now, generally, to get a man's ear you pretty well got to kill him first."

Samuel was dismayed. An ear, a human ear? That didn't sound like Joshua. But Tinker read his expression and said, "I see you don't really understand what's going on. Way I hear it, back up in the deep woods they're knocking down Frenchmen, cutting off their balls to feed to the hogs and their whacker to stick in their mouths like a seegar, give the French boys something to think about when they find their friends treated so. What I mean, this ain't no place for the fainthearted."

Well, maybe Joshua did have that capacity. Maybe that was part of the power that sent him out to fight, not for himself, but for what mattered.

"Do you mean we're winning?" he asked, in an awed whisper, scarcely aware he had placed himself with the rebels.

"Naw," Tinker said. "Blacks, they'll lose in the end. French got all the power, guns, cannon. They'll win, but point is they ain't finding it easy—"

The door opened with a bang. A half-dozen constables, big, burly white men carrying heavy cudgels, the leader with a whip coiled in his hand. Silence swept the room. The white men didn't speak, just stood there, and presently there was a rustling all over the room as patrons stood and slid away from the tables toward a back door. The white men began a slow march around the room, still not a word spoken, and Samuel got up and joined the movement; and when he reached the door and stepped into another alley still no word had been spoken.

Millie was asleep when he came in and he didn't wake her. An ear, a white ear. Samuel was repelled and yet excited. His little brother a general, two hundred men following him, taking orders, standing toe to toe with white men. Little brother, grown up, become a man—yet that ear betokened a taste for violence unsuspected in his brother till now, that he knew far surpassed anything in his own nature. Were he in Santo Domingo he would be fighting too, but that ear told him his little brother had grown far beyond him. And suddenly it came to him that he would not see Joshua again. His brother would die in that rain forest. His certainty was stunning; tears filled his eyes as he lay in bed aware of his wife's gentle snores.

The next day the talk was all over the black community. Tinker had been found in an alley about six blocks from Miss Molly's. He'd been beaten to death.

This ain't a town for us, Samuel told himself. This ain't for us. We got to get out, got to go north. And he had enough gold saved to do it, too. . . .

Madison was early. He sat alone in the cabinet room, well down the table, fingers drumming on the arm of a chair covered in red leather with brass studs. The president and the others were coming; now he relished the time to think. The steward, a tall black man with an engaging smile, came in with tea on a tray and a platter of crullers, then left him alone.

The French officer the day before had infuriated him. "Bastard!" he muttered in the silent room. But immediately he was abashed. He hadn't revealed anger then and knew he couldn't afford it now. Self-indulgence is dangerous.

He poured tea and bit into a cruller, mulling as he chewed. It was ever more clear that Santo Domingo was central. Yet there was that crazy strain too, outer edge of control. Crazy . . .

Of course French credit was worthless. They were broke, exhausted from conquering their neighbors. For thirteen years since their own revolution they'd been in near constant turmoil or war. Tax collection had almost collapsed. The court glittered still, but the army was being paid with loot from occupied countries. Indeed, with so many men under arms, who was left at home to pay taxes? So why this rash move on Louisiana at huge new expense, why send his favorite general? For grain flowing from the Mississippi Valley, yes, but beyond that a bigger picture was emerging, clever but fatally unreal, conceived in ignorant dreams.

Maybe a bankrupt nation was more desperate than you'd guess. Clearly they needed Santo Domingo to protect the route to Louisiana and Louisiana to support the island. But look beyond that—the Spanish empire had been dying for years, revolution in the air everywhere. Maybe that was Napoleon's real aim—Cuba with its sugar, Mexico with gold pouring from its mines . . .

Grain and gold . . . fuel with which to conquer the world!

Yet it was feckless, wishful thinking pushing dreams, frantic soldiers colliding with reality. In the end reality controls, and Madison had an idea that disaster lay ahead for Napoleon, though better someone else should administer the coup de grâce. All America need do was show him that the centerpiece of his plan was forever beyond his grasp. Warn him off . . .

Madison stood as the president entered the room with Albert Gallatin and behind them, Henry Dearborn, secretary of war. The president settled himself and looked around with a frown as the steward poured tea. He disliked cabinet meetings—they wasted time, invited posturing, set up quarrels, so he said. He liked to sound members individually, then act on his own.

Dearborn, whose suit looked tighter every time Madison saw him, dragged the cruller platter before him and took three with relish. He'd been on Benedict Arnold's starvation march to Quebec in the Revolution; perhaps something of those terrible days still lived in him. Levi Lincoln, the attorney general, and Robert Smith, secretary of the navy, came in together. Robert was Sam Smith's little brother, without half his ability.

"Damned blackguard," Dearborn growled, when Madison described the visitor.

"He was very explicit," Madison said. "They intend to have a Mississippi empire at our expense." He looked around the table. "Of course, we won't stand for that."

"No, we won't," the president said. He glanced at the secretary of war. "Henry, I suppose this falls to your area."

Dearborn wiped his lips with a cambric kerchief. "Yes, sir, and I hope you won't take it amiss when I point out that we have cut the army almost in half—from six thousand when we took office to scarcely more than three thousand today."

Madison heard an edge in the president's voice. "Meaning," he said, "that now we must deal with what is."

"Yes, sir," Dearborn said. Madison saw a bead of sweat on his upper lip. "As to the state of the army, I asked General Wilkinson to be here. He's waiting downstairs."

When Captain Lewis went to fetch the general, some oddity in his expression made Madison wonder what had gone on between them in the past. As the captain opened the door for the general that oddity had intensified. Seemed strange . . .

Wilkinson bowed when he entered. "Mr. President. Gentlemen." Late fifties, Madison judged, stuffed into his uniform like a sausage, the saber a cock's tail jutting out behind. But overall, his usual gaudy uniforms had been set aside in favor of plain blue with cream facings. Not quite a warrior but businesslike. Madison knew better than to judge on appearance alone, but it did strike him that this was a shifty-looking man. Rumor said Wilkinson had been in the pay of the Spanish for years, feeding them information and misinformation. Was he doing the same with the French? Still, rumor was hardly a creditable source. The man did head the army and they were stuck with him, another reason, Madison thought wryly, to avoid war.

Wilkinson laid out the facts well enough. Army of three thousand men, of whom two thousand could be called effective, and one thousand, roughly speaking, could start down the river to challenge the French within three months. A thousand men; Leclerc had twenty-five thousand. They wouldn't all be available, but he certainly would have ten thousand troops free for combat.

American troops still carried French muskets left over from the Revolution. No replacing them now, but muskets wore out in the field, despite regimental gunsmiths. America had gunsmiths, of course, but few were good for more than fifty pieces a year, each weapon being made individually and fitted by hand. Rearming would be difficult. . . .

Uniforms already were scarce and would wear out quickly on a march. Powder and shot was short. Medical supplies. Shoes. Frontier posts had vegetable farms and raised livestock for meat. But on the march they would need massive supplies of food. Wilkinson seemed to have no idea of the availability of corn and beans, let alone salt pork and beef in vinegar.

Artillery . . . well, three pounders were useful for aweing Indians but negligible against professional soldiers. Even the six pounders were small for serious combat. More clearly than ever, Madison saw that the army was a frontier force maintained to discourage Indian raids and keep Indians and settlers apart.

"Of course," the president said, "ultimately we'll rely on militia. We could rally fifty thousand militia men on fairly short notice, a hundred thousand in a year. Everyone from twelve to seventy. But they're prickly, and they'll take suggestions better than orders. Are you prepared to direct such a force?"

For a moment Wilkinson looked as if he'd peered into an abyss, but then he said smoothly that he would welcome the challenge. With a start, Madison saw that the man was afraid—of war, of field command, of the kind of men he must dominate as commander. He was an arranger, a con-niver, not a real commander. The thought jolted Madison back to the idea that they must do all they could to sidestep war—and his belief that the French would swing to his way of thinking yet.

When the general left, Madison said, "Henry, what about these rumors that Wilkinson is—well, too close to the Span-ish?"

Dearborn scowled. "I've heard them, of course. He lived on the frontier for years before he reentered the army and was an active trader on the river. Still trades, I think. But re-member, nothing has been proved. He runs the army well. He's not popular with his men; he's a cruel disciplinarian and his personality makes enemies. But after all, he is what we have."

There was more to it than that, Madison thought. Even he knew that on the frontier Wilkinson was considered a ludi-crously poor trader whose ventures consistently failed to make a profit but who yet returned from Spanish territory with a profit. The whispers were legion, but they were only whispers, and he knew enough about the frontier to under-stand that it was alive with whispers and that drawing a line between consorting with a hostile power and carrying on trade that only moved with the permission of that power was necessarily narrow. And he saw that Dearborn had, in fact, put his finger squarely on the reality before them: Wilkinson was all they had and seeking out a new commander this late in the game could be fatal.

Dearborn cleared his throat and Madison realized that he felt himself under attack, as if military weakness was all his fault. "Now, Mr. President," he said, "we see it takes time to get ready. I'd say the sooner we tie down that connection with Britain and the Royal Navy, the better."

"Maybe we should hold up," Madison said slowly. "There's something crazy here." He described his thinking and added, "I have an instinct, maybe wrong but strong. Let's risk the wait and see what happens. They're on the edge now; maybe they'll come to grief on their own. Let's see how the story plays out."

"Well, now," Dearborn said, his voice became a rumble, sure sign he was agitated, "that's easy for you to say, but war is my responsibility and we just heard the problems—"

"All right, Henry," the president said. He had a faint smile and Madison saw he already had decided. That was the joy of working with Thomas Jefferson, Madison thought; they were often unalike, their minds usually took different paths, but again and again they came out on the same bedrock of good sense. The president was looking at Dearborn. "We may regret it, but I think we'll pause a little longer. Start war preparations and they're hard to stop. People get their blood up and things can go out of control. Let's not go to war a moment before we must."

Then, with a firm air of summing up, he said, "All right. They do sound a bit off their heads. Certainly their dreams exceed their grasp. But given the costs of tying up with Britain, I'd like to push the French harder. So what progress are we making in penetrating their darkness?"

"Unfortunately, Madison said, "we have a better case than we have means to convey it." He sketched out their avenues, Livingston, Pichon, perhaps Du Pont, even Montane and Leclerc, who for all their bluster understood they were in deep water.

The president nodded. "Livingston's not much help. Pichon is the question. Does he understand? Will he relay honestly?"

"He understands," Madison said. "But I don't know how strong he is. That general seemed to terrify him yesterday. Will he have the courage to say what he knows his leader doesn't want to hear? I don't know, Mr. President. I just don't know."

33

It was near dusk, the day warm and dusty. Madison stood near a side entrance of the mansion, inconspicuous in the shadow of a basswood. A closed carriage drew up, young Meriwether Lewis on the box. When Madison stepped inside he found the rear seat vacant and recognized a mark of courtesy.

"Good evening, sir," he said.

"Good evening, Mr. Secretary," said Senator Ross.

They rode in silence, facing each other, the horses at a walk, the carriage groaning and shuddering over the pitted dirt streets of Washington. Ross was a vociferous Federalist, but Pittsburgh was the starting place for all the commerce that floated the Ohio and on to the Mississippi and no place was more threatened by French invasion plans. Rough-spoken and often brick red with anger, his grizzled hair standing on end, Ross nevertheless was intelligent and his word as good.

Fingering his beard, voice low and reluctant, Ross said, "I wanted to meet 'cause I Goddam don't like the way things are going. Young Merry said it would be in confidence—no gossip I'm consorting with the enemy!"

"Enemies?" Madison said. "Well, if so, we're on neutral ground and all is in confidence." Where had Merry found this carriage? It had little flower vases bracketed beside each door and would have been at home in a mourner's train.

Ross's voice was a growl. "Cards on the table though. Way I see it, the Democrats are a disgrace to this country, full of the same crazy ideas that destroyed France and spawned this mad dictator. And I predict that at the next election the people will recover their senses and send your benighted leader back to his Virginia hilltop!"

Madison waited. Ross said into the silence, "Now, I told Merry, I'd never sit in the same room with that man. Disgusting fellow." Madison let that pass too. Given the wild and vicious attacks on Thomas Jefferson all about the country, it was mild enough. Ross pointed a long, bony finger and said, "You—you're different. I know you to be an honorable man, but—well, you know your trouble, James? It's that you get on the wrong side of the question and you're smart enough to convince yourself it's the right side. But it ain't!"

"Senator," Madison said, "I'm glad we're having this little chat. Otherwise I'd never have known how you felt."

Ross stared at him, then laughed. "All right . . . but I'll be working to end your tenure next time around."

"And we'll defeat you again, for we are the wave of the future and you are the story of the past."

He waited a moment, then added, "But we have more immediate problems, so let me set a starting premise. We disagree on politics, but I hope we agree that we don't intend to let any other country split us in half and make off with the West, where, in fact, our future lies—that, in short, we don't intend to give up the Mississippi River to anyone!"

"Couldn't put it better myself."

"So the question is, what do we do about it?"

"Exactly," Ross said. He had a triumphant air. "Here's what I intend to do. Senate reconvenes, I'll introduce a bill to raise fifty thousand troops, appropriate five million dollars for supplies and arms, and float 'em down to take New Orleans and be done with it! Throw the dons out on their ass and dig in to take care of the French when they arrive."

Madison sat back. Five million . . . the annual budget was only ten Million. Bankruptcy stood in the wings; quietly he said he'd like to find a less expensive way to do it.

"Well, let me just say something here. Problem is, way it

looks to a lot of us, you don't really intend to do a damned thing. You may not like the sound of it, but truth is we don't see a lot of pith on display down your end of the avenue."

Madison ignored that. He sketched out his simple thesis: Napoleon could never hold Louisiana, he must certainly be defeated if he tried, and the point was to make him understand that before he took the plunge. They wrangled a bit, Madison patiently leading him to light. Ross was for calling in the Royal Navy, always a Federalist dream. But Madison rocked him back on his heels with plain facts. Suppose Britain took New Orleans and kept it for itself? Britain helping to snatch Spanish territory surely would drive Spain deeper into Napoleon's arms. Didn't the senator think Britain would want recompense for adding Spain to its list of enemies? And wouldn't that recompense take the form of demanding we enter the war—and place ourselves under Britain's wing?

The carriage creaked and sighed, the horses still at a walk. It was getting dark outside and he could hardly see the senator. There was a crackle of tension in the air. At last Ross said in a strangled voice, "Well, what's your idea?"

"We think Napoleon is blinded by pride, but he's not an idiot. So we think we can get his eyes open."

"In time, you mean?"

"Exactly. Warn him off. Show him he can't win."

"And if you fail?"

"Go to Congress. Ask for a hundred thousand men and ten million dollars. Call in the British and strike the best deal we can. A disaster, you see, but not so great a disaster as Napoleon on the Mississippi."

Another long silence. Then, "That's a guarantee?"

"Solid gold."

Ross chewed on a thumbnail, gazing at Madison. At last he said, "Tell you what. You ought to know where you stand by the time Congress takes up. I think it would do Napoleon a world of good to know Congress ain't going to let this pass. So why don't you and me work together? Let's talk, time to time, and one day we'll put a bee in that bastard's ear."

"I'll count on you," Madison said. He put out his hand and Ross grasped it, hard.

"Tough little devil, that Madison," Danny's uncle said. They were strolling the waterfront on the Eastern Branch of the Potomac well out of anyone's hearing. They'd had fair winds out of New Orleans and made Norfolk in less than four weeks. The *Cumberland Queen* had gone on to Boston with the sugar, while Danny and William Clark took a two-day stage to Washington.

He had been sharply skeptical during the voyage, and indeed, until she'd delivered him to the little brick State Department. He'd grunted when she showed him the president's house, and she had wanted to kick his shins. But he was different when he returned. Since walls have ears, he refused to talk till they were safely in the open, ignored in the midst of hubbub—vessels creaking at dockside, stevedores hustling cargo up long gangways, stockmen shouting at the donkeys that powered winches hoisting bales and boxes, and Mr. Clark in his polished boots and bottle green coat stepping carefully around donkey droppings.

"Tough?" Danny asked. She thought she'd better set her uncle straight. "I don't think so. I see him often and he's always gentle, soft-spoken, quite witty, really, though he does freeze up with strangers. That's probably what you saw."

He turned to her. "I see you don't know him at all."

"But I do. I know him well."

"No, you know his social side. I saw his real side. He's not a man to fool with, not at all." Then, after a silence, "He's sending me to France."

She was amazed. "He is?"

"Unofficially, you understand. I'm to see the men I've dealt with commercially. He wants me to use them to reach their most trusted friends in export-import."

"To what end, Uncle?"

"I'm to let 'em know they can lose pots of money in Louisiana if Talleyrand presses this to conclusion. He seems to think Talleyrand is half mad and half devil, and he's probably right. Anyway, if France goes ahead, the United States will fight. New Orleans will be a battleground, and they'll lose everything they've invested. To say nothing of what I'll lose."

She walked in silence, digesting that. It gave her a new sense of Dolley's husband, which made her think she'd better start looking at people more closely. Know your opponents . . . her lips tightened. It had been a valuable morning.

But inexplicably this made her think of Henri. For the two weeks she had been idled in New Orleans awaiting Mr. Clark, she and Henri had indulged in near constant lovemaking, wild, tumultuous, thrilling. She'd been surprised to realize how much she had needed a man. Zulie told her she was much improved—eyes brighter, complexion clearer, laughter joyous. And she realized that day by day Henri had passed from a tremulous lover as delighted as he was needy to a steady assertion of masculinity.

That first night, after they had coupled and even as they prepared to couple again, he had asked her to marry him and she was plunged back into the dilemma. In the days that followed he insisted that he loved her and always had, that he'd married only because she was gone forever, that life would be empty without her, that he had motherless, children who would love her. . . .

But he lived in New Orleans, she in Washington, he in a society in which a free-thinking wife disgraced a man, she among people who didn't give much to women but allowed them to own and carry on business. Business—there was the rub. Marriage would give Henri the business that Carl had built—and that she was taking such joy in running independently.

Give that up? No, she couldn't do it. And yet, every time he tilted her mouth up to meet his, she thought she couldn't give this up either. They had quarreled the night before she'd left, his worst qualities on display, and then he had wept and begged her forgiveness and said it was love for her that drove him to excess. And promised again that if they married her business would be hers forever—as God was his witness, he would never touch it.

Yet something in his manner tugged at her all the way home. They'd crossed the Gulf, rounded the Florida Straits with a following wind, and plunged into the awful seas off Cape Hatteras, Mr. Clark on the quarterdeck most of every day, ignoring icy spray as he gazed into the distance without a word as if trying to search out a clouded future. He scarcely spoke, which left her time for her own reflections, and gradually she grew convinced that for all Henri said, in fact he resented her business and her success. And that really meant he resented her independence.

It was a bad beginning for a love affair, let alone for marriage, but she didn't have to think about it now. To Clark she said, "The French government, Napoleon's police, will they like this line of argument?"

He gave her the quick, raffish smile of a man who didn't mind combat. "It's not without peril and he's not forcing me to go. But the men I'll see, it's to their advantage that I get home safely. And Monsieur Talleyrand loves money above all else; you may be sure he listens to these men."

They reached the end of a dock and gazed off toward Buzzard's Point, where, for the moment, seagulls dominated. A man in an anchored rowboat fished below them.

"You know," her uncle said, "an odd point. He wants me back in New Orleans soon as I can. Says there'll be work there for the American consul. He seemed to be saying— didn't quite say it, you know, but it was the feeling I had— that no matter how this comes out, the Spanish are finished. I think he wants New Orleans . . . and I guess he speaks for the United States."

"I guess he does," Danny said in a small voice. It had been a day of surprises.

The last guests had left and Jimmy, exhausted, had gone to bed. Dolley, always wide awake after a successful dinner, sat with Anna amid the debris of the table. She refilled Anna's glass and her own; she had already sent Sukey to bed. Now, in the quiet pleasure of relaxing after a party's tensions, they chatted over the evening, Danny unusually tense and tightly drawn. Louis Pichon making excuses for Pirette, whose difficult pregnancy was too advanced to risk going out; Hannah Gallatin easing a tense moment with quiet good sense; Albert going on just a little too long—doubtless national finance was important and perhaps it could even be interesting, but over dinner?

"That Ned Thornton is good looking, isn't he?" Anna exclaimed. Her eyes were bright over her wineglass. "Talks funny, but he's a tonic to the eye."

"Anna!" Mock reproof. "What's this for a girl practically at the altar with Mr. Cutts?"

Anna laughed. "Even when I'm married, I don't suppose I'll stop looking at men. Mr. Cutts looks at women—tries to hide it from me, but it won't hide." Dolley smiled, remembering her faint surprise that Jimmy had noticed Danny Mobry's beauty.

"While we're on such things," Anna said, "what do you think really goes on with Mr. Jefferson and his dusky doxy."

"I think that's not a very nice way to put it, to start with."

"All right, all right, but the story—do you give it any credence? All my friends sniff and say it's terrible, but they all seem to like talking about it. Rabelaisian, you know."

Dolley hesitated, remembering the smooth assurance of Sally Hemmings's manner. Anna giggled. "You've answered it, I think. Anyway, it's quite a story. The president! Who cares if it's true? Everyone's laughing about it."

"Well, don't let Jimmy hear you talking that way."

"Jimmy is sweet, but you have to admit he's the soul of rectitude."

Dolley grinned. "He is that."

"But you know, he told me the other day that Captain Lewis got his expedition after all. I was so happy."

"Oh?" Dolley had wormed from her the story of playing footsie with Merry right at the president's table. "Given your escapade, I'd have thought—"

"Oh, Dolley, really! I wasn't so bad. I had no idea he would take it so seriously. It was just a small flirtation. Not many men in this city would have reacted so. And I was a little attracted to him, at first, you know. And it was such a dull dinner! I thought he'd like a diversion."

Well, it was not nice treatment of a decent young man who obviously found relations with women difficult, but they had been over it at length. With a pensive look, turning her wineglass in her fingers, Anna said she thought the captain would be perfect for the expedition.

"Imagine, setting out to walk two thousand miles where no one has gone before. Oh, I know Indians live there, but if I understand it, they don't travel the whole distance. What he may find!—mountains too steep to climb, wild animals unknown in the civilized world—and how do they keep from getting lost? Why they could starve or break down and get sick or go mad in that awful wilderness. Oh, it's just stunning to think of. But you know, no one would be better equipped to do it. There's a power in him, you have the feeling he could crush you if he wanted to—not physically, you know, he's quite the gentleman with women, awkward, though, clumsy, two left feet and his tongue tied in a knot, but this power, he can go and do and be whatever he wants and you'd better not get in his way."

Dolley was amazed. Her little sister was less fluff-headed than she had supposed. "You seem to have analyzed it—"

"You get that power turned on you, you notice it. It's a bit overwhelming. Well, honest to goodness, it's frightening; you have the feeling he'll carry you immediately into deep water where you don't know if you can swim with him or not. And you just smiled and flirted a little—playing the game. Poor Merry—he *is* nice, but—"

Dolley emptied the bottle into their glasses. Anna sighed and said, "You know what that man needs? He needs an older woman, someone experienced who can measure him and deal with him and live with that power. But he looks at girls. Poor fellow."

Jimmy was snoring lightly when Dolley entered the bedroom, candle lantern in hand. She told him to turn over; he
did so without awakening. Well, she still felt wide awake.
She lighted a candle in the alcove where she had left a new
novel on her chair. It was from France and she had read
enough already to see it was mannered if not effete. The
night was still and very dark. She sat in her chair, book unopened, and drummed her fingers on the arm. Then she remembered Jimmy had brought home Mr. Livingston's latest
letter. He'd been irritated, as usual, because once again the
gentleman from New York had reported no progress. Jimmy
was strikingly fair minded, forever catching up her rhetorical excesses, and she considered his distaste for Mr. Livingston slightly irrational, more product of his own
frustration than a reasoned critique. He knew how she felt so
they stepped around the topic; but for all that, Jimmy did
value her insights and judgments on people, and he'd
formed the habit of privately letting her read the ambassador's letters.

She drew the letter from his shoulder case and settled in
the alcove. She'd seen a half dozen by now, and they often
had a peculiar effect. Her memory of the man and his capacity to express himself in ways that sharply defined his personality somehow combined with her own imagination to let
her see clearly the events he described. She had read so many
novels set in Paris, with its fairyland palaces and awesome
cathedrals, that the setting was fondly familiar in her mind's
eye. Of course, living distant scenes was just a game; but especially, when she was tired, it could produce a metamor-
phosis that seemed almost alchemical in its intensity.

And so, reading the small, steady hand written on the sort
of fine paper you'd expect from an old-line New York land
baron the memory of Mr. Livingston took hold, his strong
face with its multitude of planes, his low, pleasing voice, his
profound dignity, and even more, his unshakeable assurance,

that sterling sense of his own worth that could have been offensive in a man of less character. Indeed, she supposed only his simple honesty absolved him of the sin of pride.

Soon the pages engrossed her, scenes unfolding in her mind's eye as if painted on a screen, the little brig on which they had crossed the Atlantic rolling and plunging in heavy seas, the sheep and hogs and cow with calf he thought it wise to take with him bawling in their pens, his wife and both his daughters seeking refuge in the coach lashed to the deck that served them as sitting room, Livingston on the quarterdeck studying the horizon through his own glass. She saw the long, trailing clouds sweeping in from the southwest as they approached France, powerful winds driving them toward the rocks of Belle Isle, his two sons-in-law tearing off their coats to seize lines as the crew set and reset the great square sails, the women huddled on deck that they might die in the open, rocks up ahead like the teeth of a monster snapping from the sea—

But Mr. Livingston has not come so far in life to die on some unnamed rock off a French island he's never heard of, and he seizes the captain's arm and tells him to get hold of himself—and the wind swings to the north and, with all sails full, they run out of danger. Mr. Livingston never doubted that the problem would solve itself appropriately.

General Lafayette awaits them at L'Orient when they arrive; Lafayette, the great friend of America who only through American intervention had himself escaped the Terror when the Revolution crashed into excess and paved the way for Napoleon. Their carriage, their livestock, the twenty wagons needed to carry their baggage will come on later; now they race toward Paris in two large coaches, six-horse teams often changed, drivers cracking their whips with ostentation that quite pains Mr. Livingston as windows are thrown open and women gape in wonder. Through Nantes at a gallop, iron tires thundering on cobblestones, and on to Paris. All quite unnecessary, the democratic master of Clermont feels; when he goes to town for his mail or to Albany or even New York City, he conducts himself like any other citizen—at least, any other prominent citizen. But Lafayette tells him the imperial age is upon them.

And into Paris as it formed in Dolley's imagination, cobbled streets wide and grand with circles marked by arches and statues, over the fabled Seine on an arched bridge of hewn stone, fine town houses on broad avenues with spiked fences of iron and imposing gates, and then they plunge into narrow streets where houses are four or five stories of brick and stone lodging any number of families over a bewildering variety of shops, wash fluttering from balconies above. He sees urchins, bootblacks, newsboys, baker and butcher apprentices with trays overhead, drays and carriages competing with cracking whips and cries of rage, men mincing along in fine dress, women on their arms with great sweeping hats with ostrich feathers, musicians in bandstands filling the plazas with melody, catching that kinetic spark that flashes between male and female at all ages. Mr. Livingston is entranced; immediately he loves this place.

They go to the Tuileries, the palace Napoleon has made his own, where an apartment is reserved for them until they shift to their embassy. From the windows they see the great man himself as he reviews his palace guard, the troops moving with exaggerated pomp to music rather too imperial for Mr. Livingston's taste. And there is the little dictator, fatter than Mr. Livingston had expected, in a gorgeous red coat festooned in gold, on a white horse with flowing mane, hoofs blacked and polished, black saddle and bridle chased with gold—but this is a display horse, unfortunately light in the barrel to Mr. Livingston's practiced eye. Give out after the first few miles, a useless beast altogether too beautiful.

Then in rushes Francois Barbe-Marbois, Mr. Livingston's old friend from the days when the faulty original American government was in New York and he was chargé, speaking for the French government. Now he was gray and looked rather haggard, which Mr. Livingston took as the cost of staying alive in a highly fluid situation. Dolley remembers meeting Marbois once when he was the chargé; now he is minister of finance, testimony to his agility. He sweeps Mr.

Livingston into warm embrace, bows gracefully to the women, and rather casually tells Mr. Livingston that the first consul will receive him within the hour. The gentleman from New York leaps into what must pass as a democratic version of court dress, more elaborate than anything he'd wear at home but plain plumage beside the bright birds of the French palace.

He supposes it will be an audience and wonders if Monsieur Bonaparte will be on a throne. Hastily he informs Marbois that he will not kneel, he is from a free nation, he'll bow, yes, that's common courtesy, but—and Marbois chuckles and assures him all will go well. They enter a huge room in which two hundred people mill about. Dolley can see it clearly in her mind's eye: sweeping red drapes at windows that reach to the twenty-foot ceiling from which crystal chandeliers hang, plaster walls shaped into the images of kings and princes and grand dames of the court. The crowd grows more dense, moving in a swirling pattern, buzz of voices rising and falling, men in ruffles and lace with rapiers at their sides, women in lavish gowns that reveal as much as they hide, whom even Mr. Livingston, naive though he doubtless is, understands are as likely to be mistresses as to be wives. Slipping through the crowd are servants in extraordinary uniforms with exquisite morsels on trays and tall glasses of champagne. Mr. Livingston suspects his stomach won't handle the morsels, but seizes the champagne gratefully. It is the best he has ever tasted, though surely not superior to the best produced in New York State. Not at all.

A stir: Napoleon has entered the room. Marbois touches Mr. Livingston's arm: hold here—he will come to you. Slowly the center of all attention circles the room, men quivering with eagerness for a word, women jostling to touch him, their eyes inviting. He glances here and there, smiles faintly, allows his hand to be kissed, moves on. When he's close Mr. Livingston sees that he's a small man, pale, suety, only superficially handsome, though he moves with an intensely physical, catlike grace; in his face and eyes Mr. Livingston sees a hardness that says immediately that he is a dangerous man. Cold; if thousands or scores of thousands must die to accomplish his ends, so be it. After a glance Mr. Livingston has no trouble imagining the wild rages that are said to terrify those around him. Yet this instantly produces a resistance in the gentleman from New York; in this room he stands alone as representative of the United States of America, a member in full standing of the family of nations, and nothing will intimidate him.

Marbois's whisper identifies the smallish man beside and one step behind the dictator: Talleyrand. Charles-Maurice de Talleyrand-Périgord, foreign minister; the bishop of Autun though hardly religious, a chameleon able to assume the visage of whatever government is in power, a man so valuable for his brilliant ability that his absence of discernable belief in anything but himself doesn't matter, corruption set deep in a face that once was gorgeous, growing stout now, walking with a limp carried from childhood for which he demands payment from God and fate and mankind with a legendary appetite for bribes. He is the man with whom Mr. Livingston must deal.

Mr. Livingston's French is adequate but not polished, and his hearing is poor. An interpreter stands by. Napoleon pauses before him and Marbois presents him. All the earlier impressions are doubled: This is a deadly man, unshakeable, implacable, a man of range far exceeding that of anyone in the room, anyone Mr. Livingston knows. Which is not to say that the gentleman from New York feels in the least lessened.

He bows, as befits his station; the first consul nods and asks if he has been in Europe before. No, sir, he has not had that pleasure. Ah, Napoleon says, you have come to a very corrupt world. He turns and says something to Talleyrand that Mr. Livingston misses; later he learns that the ruler simply said to tell the American that the Old World is very corrupt and added with a sneer that his foreign minister knew something about that, didn't he? At the moment Mr. Livingston sees from Talleyrand's face that something cruel has been said—and understands from Talleyrand's burning glance of hatred that America will pay a price for that witticism.

It's a month before the foreign minister deigns to see him. His audience lasts three minutes, he isn't invited to sit down, Talleyrand delivers in rapid French a series of cutting little sarcasms that lower Mr. Livingston's opinion of Talleyrand but not of himself, and scarcely having said a word he is escorted out. He returns a dozen times; a dozen times the foreign minister waves a careless hand and tells him Louisiana is a dead subject: There is no treaty, no plans, no dealings, no nothing, so there is naught to discuss. And good day, Mr. Ambassador. . . .

And so he struggles. He goes to every reception hoping for the moment with the great man when he can slip in the crucial word. He sits late at night at his desk in the embassy overlooking the silent garden below, composing memoirs that he knows will disappear forever into the bottomless pit that represents his dealings with M. Talleyrand. The foreign minister no longer bothers to deny what everyone in Paris seems to know, that France has a wondrous new American empire.

In answer to Jimmy's tense demands for information on Santo Domingo, Mr. Livingston reacts with some surprise. Yes, Santo Domingo is well understood here as the logical step in the reacquisition of an American empire. The first consul doesn't care a whit for the island, actually; it all has to do with the American breadbasket and its capacity to feed Napoleon's conquering armies. Of course, no one expects peace with England to last, and there is much talk that they should just get on with bringing all Europe under their dominion. Which, he adds dryly, quite forgets Admiral Nelson and the British fleet.

He meets Joseph Bonaparte, the first consul's older brother, and hopes to develop an avenue bypassing that tower of venom, the foreign minister. But Joseph, though utterly cordial, reveals nothing. Does he even see the first consul? Who knows? Marbois remains a dedicated friend of America, loves to reminisce of their days together in old

New York, but when Mr. Livingston raises the situation here, in Paris, today, Marbois is walking on eggs, skittish as a high-wire man in a gale. It occurs to Mr. Livingston that his old friend has not survived by having a loose tongue or by doing many favors for others.

Weekly he has a new idea for a new memoir, a new approach, a whole new plan that will break the deadlock, and he sits down to compose another letter to Jimmy. And the answers come in, mostly disapproving, denying, forbidding this or that move and demanding that he see the first consul and simply explain to him that he is moving steadily toward a disaster that will destroy him. Mr. Livingston sits at his desk over the garden seething. He seizes paper, writes out his resignation, throws it away, writes an angry rejoinder, wads it and drops it in the basket, sighs, takes another cup of tea, lights a clay pipe, starts afresh. He is doing his best, blocked on every side because—each word fiercely underlined with bold strokes and spatterings of ink—*There never was a government in which less could be done by negotiation than here. There are no people, no legislature, no counselors. One man is everything. He seldom asks advice, and never hears it unasked. His ministers are mere clerks, and none dares tell him his follies. . . .*

This was the man, the most dangerous man in the world, with whom Jimmy was locked in combat. Dolley sighed and looked at her husband's sleeping form. Small, his face peaceful in sleep, the vivid intelligence that glowed from his eyes now masked, he looked like anything but the gladiator who challenged the tyrant of Europe. She shivered at the thought. Still, in eight years of marriage she long since had discovered that her husband was a man with an innate feeling for power, who carried in his slight and often sickly form the instincts of a warrior.

He was just beginning to fight. This thought reassured her and she pinched out the candle, undressed in the dark, and slid under the covers without disturbing him.

• • •

The president was in excellent form, Dolley thought, as she watched him massage Ned Thornton. The handsome Briton was all smiles at the attention, which no one in the room could miss.

The oval salon was crowded with guests; she had played no small part in the reception's planning, and she watched with satisfaction. She had made her role quite satisfactory; it placed her at the heart of things, let her do what she knew she did very well and yet she was careful never to assume too much. But she knew she was greasing the wheels of the new government on a tide of food and drink. No success so far in decorating this house as it deserved, but that would come. Meanwhile, she knew it would hardly function so without her and she was content. Which was not to say that the dream of living here, with all that idea implied, was in the least stilled.

The tall windows were open, the soft air of a rapidly vanishing season seeming the more precious. Most of the guests were men, but here and there she saw the bright flash of a woman's gown. Jimmy was deep in conversation with Mr. Clark by a window. It appeared they'd had a good session the morning before; she saw Jimmy laugh suddenly and noticed Clark had a knowing smile that made her think of the French novel she was reading. Danny, ravishing in a scarlet gown and surrounded now by a circle of men, had described her uncle's French mistress, apparently an extraordinary woman who was busily softening his often harsh exterior.

Senator Smith wagged his finger as he explained why no entertainment was complete without Maryland soft shells. She listened with half an ear, watching Mr. Jefferson's vigorous conversation with Thornton. Louis Pichon bowed to her and nodded to Smith as he seemed to drift aimlessly toward the president.

Mr. Jefferson's voice rose. "Ned, I understand you have a splendid new filly."

"She is beautiful, thank you, Mr. President. Virginia's best, you know, out of Damsel Rose by Charger."

"You won't find better lines." Then, as if struck by inspiration, "I'd like to see her. Why don't we go riding?"

"A great pleasure, sir."

"Splendid. Tomorrow at ten?"

"Thank you, sir. I shall be here."

Pichon's face fell and he drifted off.

"My," Smith said, "that was neatly done."

Dolley smiled. Tom could be smooth as glass when he tried.

"Miz Mobry?"

Clinch Johnson stood in Danny's office turning his hat in his hands. He was a big, stolid man, slow, quiet, English in appearance, with wisps of pale hair standing from each side of his head, his suit rumpled, stained, and too tight. At the moment he looked like a boy caught with a hand under a girl's skirt. She felt a thrust of apprehension—*he wants to back out*—that translated almost instantly into cold anger as she realized she scarcely knew more about the man than on the day they'd met. Things were going well, her ships were busy, the Boston distillery welcomed her sugar, she didn't need more business, she should never have listened—

"What is it, Mr. Johnson?" she snapped.

Her uncle had set it all up—seemed on her side, but there was always that sly quality about him. God! She thought she'd learned her lesson after Carl's death when the shipping world turned against her—

Mr. Johnson had taken a step back at her tone. His mouth opened and shut. She saw she'd alarmed him, which was not politic, and she forced a small smile. If he intended to back out he'd find her hard to handle, it would be head to head in the courthouse, he'd wish—

Mr. Clark had brought her the deal just before he sailed for France. Presented Johnson as a friend, said he imported wine and had located a new region north of Marseilles producing a vintage that had done well in Savannah and Charleston on a small test shipment. Mr. Clark said he'd tasted it and was anxious to market it in New Orleans. What they needed now was the right ship equipped for appropriate stowage to make three runs a year, Marcella to Savannah and Charleston to New Orleans.

Mr. Johnson didn't say a word.

Was she with them so far? Her lips tightened as she nodded. Mr. Clark said there was a schooner nearly completed in Annapolis, right size and speed. Clinch would provide capital for her to buy it, against her note, payable half in two years, half in four, appropriate interest. Two-year haulage contract.

"Really?" She looked at Johnson closely for the first time. "You'd do that?"

"Mr. Clark will endorse the notes."

She remembered now how she'd laughed, flattered that her uncle would go so far in trust. But in the end, it was she who'd gone far. She'd bought the vessel, ordered it outfitted, she was committed beyond recall—

He was fumbling with an inner pocket. "I brought payment for the vessel—draft on the Bank of the United States. I hope that's satisfactory."

She took it, examined it, turned it over. In full. She laughed, feeling a bit the fool; maybe she was on a narrower edge than she'd realized. "Yes—yes, Mr. Johnson, quite satisfactory." Still, he wasn't hangdog because he'd brought the money; he wanted something. But she touched his arm. "Sorry," she said. "Perhaps I'm tense today."

"Yes, ma'am," he said, with a knowing expression. Women troubles, he was thinking. She could have kicked him.

She asked him to sit and he did, hunched forward on the chair. "Over to where I live," he said, "the French legation is next door. Mr. Pichon. You know him?"

She nodded. Some new hitch in French export licenses?

"Sometimes I talk over the fence to Mrs. Pichon. She's a sweet little lady, nigh onto dropping a—" He stopped himself.

What in the world? "She's very pregnant, Mr. Johnson."

"Now, that's exactly it, yes, ma'am, and sick, too, what with the baby and all, and the doctor won't let her go out."

She watched him and in a moment he added, "So she'd like you—she asked me—would you come to tea?"

What a strange roundabout invitation! Helpfully, he added, "Seems like she cries most all the time. Does when I see her. Shakes her head when I ask why."

Danny scarcely knew Pirette Pichon. Language drew them together, she supposed, two Frenchwomen in a sea of English, and they'd chatted at social occasions. Nothing more. Still, this was very odd and something was afoot. And Pirette was likeable, gentle, and even more vulnerable with this difficult pregnancy. Which stirred in Danny that familiar sense of loss; she could expect no children now. Her hand on the draft, she told Mr. Johnson she would visit Mrs. Pichon that afternoon.

"Thank you, ma'am." He squared his hat and left. She watched him walk down the street. So that was it, a favor to a neighbor. An odd man, indeed. Still, there was a dignity in him and, she thought, strength. He was very successful, and she knew many men prized his opinion. She had no idea if he liked her or not, but they were partners and, her hand on the bank draft, she was content. Odd, yes . . . but he would do.

Pirette Pichon herself opened the door when Danny twisted the bell at the legation's family entrance. She looked ready to give birth within the hour, her face white as her blouse, eyes puffy with weeping. She chattered away as she poured tea; and after a bit, Danny said, "Pirette, what's this all about?"

A convulsive sob shook her slender frame. "Forgive me, I know we're not close, but you visit Mrs. Madison often, don't you? You know, you're French; I've always felt I could trust you—" She stopped, peering at Danny, then said, "I *have* to trust you. You see, we're in terrible trouble. They're trying to destroy Louis."

"Who is?"

There was hysteria in her sudden wail. "Oh, I'm so frightened, and the baby's coming, and I don't know—"

"Pirette! What are you talking about?"

"General Leclerc. This awful business in Louisiana. He's trying to blame Louis for everything."

Slowly, midst sobs and tumbling words, the story emerged: Louis Pichon had perceived immediately that French hopes for Louisiana wouldn't work, as Danny herself had known in an instinctive flash. Pichon could see that Americans, coupled with Britain, would be an implacable enemy. He understood Americans, their soaring growth, their strength and determination. He'd warned Monsieur Talleyrand to expect unending resistance. Every week Mr. Madison called him in to make points that Louis had been telling Paris all along.

But now General Leclerc in Santo Domingo was sending furious letters telling poor Louis to *order* the Americans to force their merchants to ship supplies—procure ten thousand *livres* of this, ten thousand of that, ship within seven days . . .

And Louis protesting to Leclerc that there was no ordering Americans and warning that the general was making things worse, his ugly threats, ridiculing American democracy, threatening rough force in Louisiana, jailing ship captains for their language or the name given a ship. He told Leclerc the United States was a nation founded in law, not whims. Just now he'd written Leclerc ordering him to send no more of the likes of some general, who seemed to have made an ass of himself.

Yes, Danny thought, that would irk the general, all right.

Now, said Pirette, balled handkerchief clutched to her cheek, the monster is demanding Louis's recall. Brands him a thief, liar, says he takes bribes, is beholden to Americans, in love with them, forgets he's French, is unfit to serve, sends insulting letters to generals—and, of course, nothing infuriates the first consul more than criticism of soldiers.

Staring at Danny, she whispered, "You know, General Leclerc is his favorite. He's young, handsome, elegant, dashing; he won great victories. No wonder Bonaparte's sister is mad for him, and Louis says she can wheedle anything out of her brother. If we're recalled . . . the first consul already furious, Leclerc certain to hound Louis from any post they give him, what will we do? And the baby's coming and I'm ill, and the doctor says the baby will be delicate, a sea voyage might kill him. And the way things are in France just now, why, they could drag Louis to Dr. Guillotin's dreadful machine. . . ."

What could Danny say? She thought Pirette's fears well justified. Unlimited power leads to unlimited evil.

"Louis must never know of this, but please, please, tell Mrs. Madison that Louis is a friend. See if she won't speak to her husband; see if they won't let us stay here if we must. Grant us asylum. Louis would be furious, but now there are three of us, I have to think of my baby. Don't you think I'm right? Tell me you'll speak to Mrs. Madison, please. . . ."

Dolley called Jimmy in. "Of course," he said, after listening to Danny, "we'll protect him."

Dolley thought this was exceedingly good news and said so after Danny left.

Jimmy had the expression of a man who hopes but knows better than to assume. "Yes . . . it's a relief that he does understand. But it appears he fears losing his head for saying it."

"Or his wife does."

"Same thing, I expect."

"Still," Dolley said, "at least he conveys the facts. Maybe they'll penetrate . . ."

Jimmy looked exhausted. "Maybe . . ."

"Mon Dieu, Thomas! You can't mean this!" Pierre Du Pont looked up from the letter. "Tom—that is, Mr. Jeff—Mr. President—this is terrible. It insults the first consul, it challenges the French government, it denigrates French honor, it will make everything worse. Why, it could force war!"

Well, well, well. Madison could see that the letter was

having the desired effect. They were in the oval sitting room,
Madison, the president and Du Pont, whose long delayed return to France was at hand. He would sail within the fortnight, leaving his son to nurture the chemical company at
Wilmington, and he had come to say good-bye. It was a
golden opportunity, given Pierre's connections in French
ruling circles.

"Ah, Pierre," Tom said, in his blandest tone, "it's hardly
an attack. We seek only peace with France. Why, if anything, the shoe is on the other foot. This General Leclerc is
saying the most awful things about us. But we turneth the
other cheek, as men of peace must always do—until, I suppose, they are given no alternative but to slap back." He was
smiling. "Even Jesus, you know, in the midst of turning the
cheek was willing to lay about him with mighty arm when
his cause was right."

"Yes, but still . . ." Du Pont shook his head, not at all convinced. In short, exactly as planned. They needed something
pungent enough to get past that touch of arrogance in Du
Pont, forceful enough to focus what he would say of the
United States and revealing enough to persuade him that he
stood at the center of national affairs, there and here. Nothing like giving a man a chance to preen to turn him into an
ardent messenger.

Madison and the president had laid it out, working in their
usual easy tandem. It should be on paper for clarity and to
avoid misunderstanding, but should not be written to Pierre.
Don't leave it in his hands to return someday to haunt you.
Address it to Mr. Livingston, let Pierre see it, then seal it and
ask Pierre to carry it to Livingston. Make the letter personal,
informal, friend to friend, and only incidentally president to
ambassador, and hence no part of the record unless one
chose to place it there. The result would be to allow Pierre to
speak powerfully but unofficially on the American mind,
with nothing that others could turn to their own manipulat-
ing ends.

They'd worked it out together in the president's big corner
office, Tom on his feet and pacing, Madison bunched mo-

tionless in a chair, his mind churning. Tom paced and talked, trying and discarding words, scrawling now and again on foolscap at his tall reading desk. His capacity for words was just one of his marks of genius, but he needed Madison's level, steady, analytical mind as rudder while his more untethered mind rode the wind of ideas. Madison never doubted his own crucial value in the shared partnership of ideas that held them together.

The letter must say clearly that France, until now a natural friend, would reposition itself as enemy when it stood astride the Mississippi. "Yes," Tom said, "exactly." Then, pencil scrawling swiftly as he said the words, "There is on the globe one single spot, the possessor of which is our natural and habitual enemy. It is New Orleans, through which the produce of three-eighths of our territory must pass to market, and from its fertility it will ere long yield more than half of our whole produce and contain more than half of our inhabitants. . . ."

Then, a few minutes later, murmuring the coalescing words as he wrote, "The day that France takes possession of New Orleans fixes the sentence which is to restrain her forever within her low-water mark."

He threw down the pencil. "There! Say it square, by the good Lord, no hesitation!"

"And what we'll do," Madison said, "explicitly."

"Yes, you're right—" Writing swiftly, "It seals the union of two nations who, in conjunction, can maintain exclusive possession of the ocean. From that moment we must join— no, wait, we must *marry* ourselves—that's it, marry ourselves to the British fleet and nation."

Madison felt like applauding. "Marry" the British fleet. The perfect term—there was the genius of words and the way they impacted on the mind. Madison would have said "ally with" or any of a half-dozen pedestrian phrases. Tom chose the single word that slapped the reader's face with its meaning.

And now, in the quiet oval room with its pale walls and blue furniture, the tall windows open to the lowering sun,

Madison watched those words impact on Du Pont. As their impromptu emissary raised his voice in angry protest, Madison saw that his sense of French patriotism had been affronted. Good; exactly what they wanted. He said the first consul was no man to be intimidated by threats; that they would only make things worse.

"Oh, Pierre, my friend," Tom now said, "nothing in the least unfriendly is intended." Madison wondered if the Frenchman would swallow that, but it passed unchallenged as Tom added, "It is as if I foresaw a storm tomorrow and advised my friend not to embark on the ocean today. My foreseeing it does not make me the cause of it, nor can my admonition be a threat. It is, in truth, our friendship for France which renders us so uneasy at seeing her take a position which must bring us into collision."

Oh, well done!

"Still," Du Pont said, "it alarms me that you would seem to coerce a man so powerful and so proud as the first consul. Much better, I think, to offer to buy the island of New Orleans."

River, lakes, bayous, swamps surrounded the city; it was literally an island and it did control the river.

"We have raised that thought," Madison said. "Authorized a million—"

"Faugh! A million. What is a million dollars when you talk of empire! Offer five, six, ten! They may listen to that."

Jefferson closed the letter with binding of red ribbon held in place with gobs of red wax deeply impressed with the seal of the United States. He stressed to Du Pont the importance of putting this directly and only into Robert Livingston's hand. The emissary must instruct his wife to carry out this duty should anything happen to him. The solemn tone, the envelope festooned in red, the knowledge that he was privy to the president's most closely held thinking had the desired effect. Monsieur Du Pont assured them that he would carry his new understanding of the American position to the highest quarters.

After he left they sat down to another glass of Madeira, and at last Madison said, "Five million, ten million—it would bankrupt us. Break Albert Gallatin's thrifty heart. But you know, it's an interesting idea."

34

Nashville, Fall 1802

Andrew Jackson was attending a flogging on the square at Nashville when Ed Duggan rode in from the south, blew a great blast on the ferry horn to summon the craft, crossed the river, and led an exhausted horse ashore. The day was bright and fresh, the heat gone, real cold not yet come, brisk and lively; doubtless you could hear birds if this miscreant weren't screaming so loudly. Jackson took no pleasure in seeing a flogging, though a good number of people always gathered to watch, fewer than you'd find at a hanging, but still a good crowd. He was here because he was a judge and he ordered floggings, including this one, and a man who ordered them ought to witness one occasionally.

So here was this burly scoundrel who'd sliced off his wife's ear in a drunken rage lashed to the flogging post, which was next to the pillory in front of the little log jail that itself was tucked around behind the one-room courthouse, which also was of logs but much grander. Back east they had prisons, but here on the frontier, well, you couldn't keep a man for a year or two in that little jail, the sheriff's wife having to cook his meals. Hang him or flog him or brand a big T for thief in his cheek, or maybe give him a couple of hours to get out before the tar and feather crowd got hold of him. . . . The sheriff was swinging the cat right fiercely, each blow now bringing blood, making a solid *thwack* that the crowd echoed with a sort of collective grunt, the fellow screaming and blubbering and calling his *wife's* name.

Imagine . . . he'd accused her of infidelity, she not yet thirty and the mother of seven, poor woman barely able to keep her children fed what with her husband mostly drunk and rarely working, said he'd slice her up so no man would look at her again. She'd come to the courtroom holding a cloth to the wound, likely it would run serum and pus for the rest of her life. Well, Jackson would have hung him if he could, this was a gallows bird for sure, but mutilation wasn't a hanging offense. Too bad, too—would've rid the world of someone the world didn't need. And here he was blubbering and howling, typical coward, what you'd expect, a man beat his wife—

"General, this here's important, I believe you'll want to attend to this—"

Jackson spun about. Colonel Hays was there with a chunky little fellow whom it took Jackson a moment to recognize as Ed Duggan, looking trail whipped to a fare-thee-well. Ed was a riverman—flatboats running downstream all season. On his last run he'd had twenty bales of Jackson's cotton.

"They've closed the river, General. Say we can't trade out of New Orleans no more."

"Who has? What are you talking about?"

"French, I reckon. Spanish'd never have the nerve to do it on their own. There were fifty flatboats moored to the bank when I left and more coming. Spanish say they ain't going to let us land a single pound. Taking their orders from the Frenchies, don't you see. So anyway, I figured I'd better get on up the Trace and see what we're going to do about it."

Do? Jackson's mind was churning. Somehow, he'd expected this—known in some way that sooner or later it all would boil over, the Spanish overstepping, French moving in—why, it was certain. And he realized he welcomed it. This meant war and it was high time Americans went down and made New Orleans their own. He didn't know a lot about international doings, but he knew there was a time in any set of affairs, man's life, his courtship, the deals he strikes, the growth of his state—well, the moment comes when you're on the flood and it's time to storm ahead, time to act, seize the high ground, win your woman or your plan or your state. He reckoned it couldn't be so different when nations tangled.

War . . . and overdue at that, way overdue. The damned dons had been lording it over us for years, stifling our trade, claiming the river because they controlled its mouth when everyone knew it was *ours!* And the French would be a hundred times worse, and this was just the action to prove it. Spanish knew better than to go too far. This was a French trick, them pushing the dirty work off on the Spanish. Close the river, then when we take over we can claim we're just holding the status quo. Well, by God, we'll see about that!

"Bob," he said to Colonel Hays, "better start getting your regiment ready. Get hold of Brigadier Scorsby—he should be alerting all the regiments. Send word to the eastern regiments too. We need to be moving. We'll need Kentucky and Ohio in on this. I'll see the governor in the morning, then head right on up north, start lining it all up. Tell everyone you talk to, we ain't going to stand for this."

"Yes, sir! General, you talking full mobilization?"

Jackson hesitated. It would take awhile to put everything together. "I want 'em to know likely there'll be fighting before long. They want to put their affairs in order where they can go off and leave 'em, families and everything. On a week's notice, say—weapons, powder and lead, blankets, set to go. Talk to Nat Fosby—let's see about flatboats to float us downstream. Better set up some drills, too, firing practice, moving through woods, taking cover. Remind 'em they're soldiers. . . ."

Rachel Jackson knew there was trouble the moment she saw him coming up the column of yellow poplar saplings he'd planted, saw it in the set of his carriage, the rigidity of his shoulders, that brush of hair now so gray standing up flaglike . . .

She put the kettle on as he waved and passed on to the barn, and when he came in the tea was ready. Of course he tried to soften it, he always did, but the evidence was stark. The French had closed New Orleans, it was the first step to conquering the West, of course we'd have to fight, he was leaving in the morning—

Leaving! Not next month or even next week, tomorrow at dawn! She saw his hand shake when he lifted his teacup. He was drawn up like a fiddle string, and all at once she forgot her own dismay and the agonies of loneliness that lay ahead and was seized by a boundless dread. That fire always in him, always ready to erupt, was burning brighter than ever.

"Andrew," she said, but she stopped, swallowing.

"No cause for worry," he said, watching her. "Governor's over to Gallatin, by chance. I'll ride over and see him and then get on up to Lexington and talk to General Sanford about coordinating with Kentucky militia, and then—well, I don't know, but I'll be back before you hardly can miss me. . . ."

But that wasn't it at all, and she said so. It was his temper, always ready to boil. Sooner or later it would pull him into terrible trouble. His frown grew deeper as he listened to her tremulous expressions of her fears. He said it was his temper, his speed of reaction, his refusal to let a single jack-anapes scoundrel traduce him or, God forbid, his wife, *that* was what had saved them.

"Wasn't our fault we had a scandal, but we had it. You can't live with scandal, not in this country. You can't bow down to it. You have to fight and fight, *defy* them. They have to know when they go to smirking that you'll *punish* 'em. . . ."

He went on in this vein for some time, growing hotter by the minute. She didn't answer. At last he ran down, breathing hard.

"We're beyond that," she said, keeping her voice a bare whisper so he leaned forward to hear her. "Hasn't anybody raised that in the longest time. But I'm afraid you're so ready to fight—well, General Sevier, they're saying—"

"Who's saying?"

It was a shout and he leaped up. The idea of anyone talking about him drove him into a frenzy, but she didn't intend to have him shouting at her and she told him so. Who had mentioned Sevier? She hadn't the slightest intention of telling him. In fact, as he well knew, the old general had been in a loose-tongued fury ever since Andrew had, as Sevier saw it, stolen the command of Tennessee militia from under his nose.

All at once Andrew's anger collapsed. He sat down and waved a hand. "Oh, Sevier. Forget Sevier. Old fool. I'll deal with him one of these days. I'll pinch his nose."

He would, too, that was what she feared; it could lead to pistols. And now he was going off to Kentucky and, knowing him, to points way beyond, he'd be meeting all sorts of folks and they wouldn't all be full of respect. . . .

"Oh, darling," she said, "please, please keep a rein. Up yonder, they don't know anything about our affairs; maybe they'll cross you but it won't be because of us—"

"Well, I know that, but—"

"You've grown beyond that; judge, major general, whole community looking up to you. You don't let a horse run wild. Rein yourself, Andrew. Rein yourself."

And he came over and drew the pipe from her mouth and lifted her and held her hard to his chest and kissed her—and with that she had to be content.

At Gallatin the next day the governor was a mass of nerves. His very voice shook. "I don't know, Andrew. We'd have to hear something from Washington, wouldn't we? We couldn't just go off and attack France all on our own, could we?"

"Archie," Jackson said, "it'll be all right. Thing now is to get ready. Then when the word comes, we'll be all set. We don't want Tennessee to be caught short, comes the call, do we?"

"No, you're right about that."

"I'll just ride on up and take some soundings. Get things lined up. I come back, we'll sit down together, you'll see what needs to be done. It'll all be clear then."

He rode off thinking that Archie Roane was almost too easy. Sevier, now, when he'd been governor and when he'd commanded militia, he was a much tougher nut. Jackson had heard he'd been mouthing, pretty much the talk of a man disappointed and offended, but staying away from the personal. Still, one of these days Archie would use the information on Sevier that Jackson had given him and it would go off like a charge of black powder in the old man's face. Then, Jackson figured, he would have to deal with Sevier. But he'd known that when he gave Archie the information.

He swung north out of Tennessee toward bluegrass country, making good time, a valise lashed behind his saddle with his blanket roll. He remembered the road when it was just a hard-beaten path through the forests; now it was twenty-odd feet wide, brush chopped away, trees felled to eighteen-inch stumps that wagons could clear, only the largest trees left standing in the roadway and them easy enough to step around. He'd picked up a small group, of course, all heavily armed—nobody traveled alone in country where you might go most of the day and hardly see a soul, where those you met probably were salt of the earth but could just turn out to be thieving scum who should be stretching rope. To say nothing of the occasional band of warriors who still roved this country.

There were a lot of folks up in the bluegrass country, where most of Kentucky's population was concentrated, but southern Kentucky was still pretty much forest, though more and more farms were being chopped out. Before dark they would stop at a farm and contract for supper and a night in the barn rolled in a blanket on a bed of hay and up before dawn.

He made constant notes with a stub pencil as he rode, lay-

ing out a campaign and drafting orders to send back to
Brigadier Scorsby. Figuring the numbers he could raise, the
supplies they would need, the boats to haul them downriver
to Fort Adams just below Natchez. It was coming on winter
and he knew from experience that New Orleans could be
damp and cold, so every man should have a good coat, a
change of clothes, a blanket roll. Gourd canteens too, powder horn, bullet pouch. They could run ball from bar lead on
the way down, make paper cartridges, deck over part of the
flatboat, and hold drill on the deck. Then medicines, ample
viands, chaplains and doctors. . . .

He rode into Lexington somewhat trail whipped, awed despite himself at its size and extent. Nashville, Louisville,
even Knoxville would have trouble mustering up five hundred souls, but they said Lexington was already over two
thousand and sprouting up like a weed. Courthouse of brick
and frame houses all neatly planked with iron fences and
gates, half a dozen churches, worship any old way you
wanted, sheds with cotton bales stacked and squared, wagons loaded with bar iron, distilleries and breweries, grist-
mills and potash yards. He saw a tailor's shop, a cobbler,
even a cabinetmaker—high cotton indeed! Still, you were
looking at Nashville; give it another few years.

It seemed the news had just hit. Boys were hawking three
different sheets. He bought one of each and scanned them—
essentially what he already knew. Clumps of men stood talking in loud voices that said rage on the surface, fear
underneath. When he dismounted at the hotel, a crone with a
huge wad of snuff bulging her lip glared as if it was all his
fault and shouted, "My man and my three boys are down the
river with everything we own. I'll tell you, Mister, we ought
to go down and clean them dirty devils out like we'd sweep
out a barn!" No answer seemed needed, and in a moment
she shot a burst of brown spittle into the dirt at his feet and
stormed away, shouting at someone else.

He had a bath at the hotel, ordered his trail clothes
washed, brushed out a fresh suit, and made for General Sanford's store, marching along dirt streets where that same

mixture of rage and fear rang in passing voices. He found
the commandant of Kentucky militia leaning against his
counter in earnest talk with several men. Sanford proved to
be a bear of a man, sixty or so, who moved in a shambling
walk that bespoke power and authority.

He ignored Jackson till he finished his conversation and
the men left. Then he looked him up and down and said,
"Doubtless you want to know, will we fight over this? The
answer is hell, yes. I've already ordered all regiments to
muster. Governor wants every man on standby. What's your
regiment?"

"I'm Major General Andrew Jackson, commanding Tennessee militia." He put out his hand, but Sanford stepped
backward.

"Tennessee? Then what're you . . ." His voice trailed off.
"Oh," he said. He leaned on his counter, knuckles pressed to
the wood. "Oh." He didn't offer to shake hands. "State your
business," he said.

It was a long way from the reception Jackson had expected, but he held his temper. He said he too had mustered
his troops and looked upon it as his duty to think of coordinating plans.

"I don't know as I need any instruction in my duty."

It was so hostile that Jackson paused. Carefully, he said,
"I mean no offense but if we're going to fight for the
river, and surely we must, then I suppose Kentucky and
Tennessee and Ohio troops will be operating together, and I
figured—"

"Yes, yes, but I doubt we'll be looking to you for much.
U.S. Army will take the lead; General Wilkinson will command."

Jackson felt his control eroding. "Not of my troops, by
God! We know General Wilkinson." The villain had been
sucking the Spanish tit for years, taking his payment in gold.
Everyone downriver knew it even if they couldn't prove it.
Wilkinson gave him any lip, he'd pull the scoundrel's nose
right out of his face. Might do the same for General Sanford
too the way things were going, but he figured this was the

place to rein himself, like Rachel said, so he contented himself with adding, "General Wilkinson's much too close to the enemy."

Sanford glowered. He said Wilkinson had moved to Kentucky these twenty years past, long before he'd reentered the army, lived in Louisville and Lexington and had a host of friends in both, among them Sanford himself. . . .

Well, Jackson hadn't come here to quarrel. It felt like he was rolling over and playing dead, but he said in an even enough voice, "He's your friend, General, I'll say no more. But in any event. I suppose we'll be operating together some way."

"Well, that times comes, I'd expect Tennessee to turn right back to John Sevier."

Jackson stared at him. The man seemed intent on provoking him. Controlling his breathing, he said, "That's not likely. I hold the command."

"Well, a peacetime election is one thing, but it's another when men look to you to lead 'em in war. Then they want experience. And John said—"

"John said?"

"Him and me're old friends. We was at King's Mountain together. He wrote me about you, had plenty to say."

So *that* was what this was all about! Jackson's voice was soft. "What did he have to say about me, sir?"

Sanford paused. His eyes flicked about. He seemed aware for the first time that he'd been . . . impolitic. "I ain't called on to say what others may say."

"You raised it. *You* said you were basing your opinion on what he said." Jackson was stepping slowly toward him. The skin on his face felt tight, a vein was throbbing and pounding. "Now, sir, you'd better speak up and damned quick!"

Sanford ducked behind his counter. "That you're a lawyer," he said in a burst. "That you had no military experience beyond Indian skirmishes. No command experience. Says he figures you'll fold under pressure."

"What else did he say?"

"My, God, ain't that enough?"

"What else did he say?"

"Nothing else! What's the matter with you? He don't think you're fit; thinks the boys made a big mistake. God Almighty!"

Jackson stepped back, momentarily dizzy. His heartbeat slowed, the very skin of his face seemed to ease. "Well," he said, "you're General Sevier's friend and I know he's not happy; but count on it, you'll deal with me when the time comes."

The older man gave him a long, speculative look, then nodded as if to himself. "All right. John Sevier is disappointed and maybe that's all there is to it. My governor orders an attack on New Orleans, we'll be ready, and I'll expect to work with you. We shouldn't have no trouble."

They shook hands. There was no warmth, but it was proper. Still, walking away, thinking of Rachel's admonition, he felt the failure. He'd come with big plans for mutual mobilization and had to fight even for minimum respect. Now, clearly, he would have to go on, to Ohio and probably Pittsburgh as well. He sat at a desk in the hotel lobby and scratched out a careful letter to Rachel.

He went on to Maysville, port town on the Ohio, and found the waterfront in a howling uproar. Merchants with flatboat loads of produce they were afraid to send but knew would rot if they didn't beseeched him for information, advice, promise of action. Half the town already was out of work, men lounging in the streets, fights more common every day.

"Hell to pay, General," the mayor told him. "I hope you can do something."

He rode up to Chillicothe in Ohio and found the militia commander dithering and humbly grateful for advice. Jackson spent half a day sketching procedures to lay before Ohio's governor, then caught a stage to Wheeling and on to Pittsburgh. The moon was full and the stage ran day and night in this emergency. In short order he was in Pittsburgh, a night in a hotel curing his exhaustion. Next morning he called on Captain Frobrisher, who'd supplied him merchandise for years.

"God, Andrew," the paunchy old man cried, "you're a sight for sore eyes. Tell me you can do something about this outrage."

"Whole West is pulling together, Captain, everywhere I've been."

Plugging the river stopped everything. Frobrisher's clients were stores in the West, in Maysville and Lexington, Louisville and Nashville and Natchez down on the lower Mississippi. They paid with the proceeds of the sale of produce that they took in swap from their customers. The only market for produce was downstream, wagon freight eastward being much too dear except for hauling grain in its compact form, good drinking whiskey.

Should Captain Frobrisher supply those downstream merchants knowing they couldn't pay—and knowing his own suppliers would put him in bankruptcy and debtor's prison if he failed his accounts? Yet how long would he last with transactions stopped? How long would his customers last? How long could Andrew himself keep his trading post open? The captain was almost in tears.

"We've got to *do* something," he whispered.

Jackson wanted to see Jim Ross—a Federalist, yes, and correspondingly misguided, but a man who knew his own mind and was quick to action. Jackson had known him during his own brief stay in Congress. Ross, Aaron Burr, and a few others had taken the Tennesseean, rawboned in appearance and somewhat in manner, under their various wings. They were men he could trust.

"Senator Ross is in Washington," Frobrisher said. "They tell me Burr's gone back to New York. They've abused him terribly, you know. He stubbed his toe when he went against Jefferson, granted, but they're after him with heavy artillery."

Jackson didn't like to hear that. Aaron was a gentleman and a good friend, and Jackson didn't forget friends. And then, Ross being off in Washington was more bad news. Jackson was feeling a powerful urge to get home, put Archie

Roane on course, make sure troops and supplies were coming together as they should. A commander's place is with his men. Still, he'd come this far and he needed to be sure that men like Ross and the others understood the urgency.

A week later he was in Washington, marveling as he walked into the Capitol. The great building was years from being finished, of course, but what a change from the modest house of brick Congress had used in Philadelphia. He was asking a guard where to find Ross when he saw the senator bustling down the hall at a half trot, bent forward at the waist, armful of papers, grayer and heavier than Jackson remembered, but unmistakable.

"Jim!" he roared.

Ross spun about and stared, then advanced slowly. "As I live and breathe, Andrew Jackson." He hesitated, blinking. "And I guess I don't need to ask what brings you. It's a damned outrage—that river is ours!"

Congress was boiling, he said, men vying to see who could sound most belligerent. Mail was pouring in from constituents. Not just from the West, either; everyone in the West had family in the East and they were writing too. For once Federalists and Democrats seemed in total agreement.

"So we'll take action?"

"Congress is raring to go. The administration, though . . . tell me, do you know Mr. Madison?"

"Know of him, but he was out of the Congress when I was in."

"C'mon—you need to see him; he needs to see you."

A hack dropped them at the mansion gate. Impressive place, Jackson thought, but he had barely taken notice when Ross pulled him toward a little brick building to their right. There he met a bright-looking man named Johnny Graham who was maybe a bit older than he looked, a Maysville boy, he said, and then they were in Mr. Madison's office.

It was odd. The place was almost bare, simplicity carried to a fault, a table serving as desk, a bookcase, a bust Jackson didn't recognize on a shelf, a couple of straight chairs for visitors. The man himself was small, his hand light and soft

in Jackson's, his face that of a schoolmaster or even an elderly student, his voice pale if not weak. He glanced up at
Jackson with an odd flash of expression, not anger, certainly,
but some sort of discomfort. Jackson wondered if his arrival
had interrupted something. But the little man proved cordial
and deeply interested in the West. Indeed, he plied Jackson
with questions that kept him busy thinking of answers and
explaining, and in short order he lost any feeling that he was
dealing with a graduate student. This was a man of power,
his mind forceful and very quick, information folding
swiftly into ideas and conclusions. Jackson was not slow of
grasp himself, given his intuitive capacity to vault forward to
solutions, but Mr. Madison was every bit his equal.

And the secretary won his heart when he said the West
would always be American; he'd known that for a quarter
century. Now, by God, that was well put! Having queried the
visitor, Madison took the floor. The burden was exactly what
Jackson wanted to hear—that they would open the river by
force, if necessary. The little man said the president would
never accept France on the Mississippi. Amen, said Jackson.
Furthermore, it was too late now to return to the status quo,
Spain in control. The United States must have sovereignty,
the secretary said, it must *own* a chunk of land, perhaps a
square mile or two, from which upriver produce could be
transshipped with full rights guaranteed, perhaps the island
of New Orleans itself, perhaps the whole eastern bank.

Well, now we're talking!

If it came to fighting—and it would if we didn't get our
way right quickly—they would count on western militia
backed by eastern volunteers, and if necessary they would
call in the Royal Navy, which was more than ready to
oblige. But it was his opinion—from the corner of his eye
Jackson saw Ross nodding agreement—that the price of
British help would be plunging ourselves into its war with
France as an exceedingly subordinate partner, and that we
could only accept as a last resort.

Jackson was shaking his head. No, he understood that
danger. He knew the British, that scar on his forehead to

prove it from the days when Tarleton's Raiders had swept into the Carolina uplands, and he didn't want the British to get their hooks into his country. It seemed there was a whole lot more to this than he'd understood.

So, Madison said, they needed time because he believed the French still could be brought to reason. If they would just pay attention long enough to see that they couldn't win a war, they would come around. They were arrogant, but he judged them not insane.

"I hope you're right, Mr. Secretary," Jackson said. "But you want to move right along. Way things are in the West, we're facing ruin, and we ain't going to wait forever. I know my people; and if this ain't settled soon, they'll go down and take New Orleans themselves. That time comes, you'll find me leading the way."

35

WASHINGTON, END OF 1802

The fire, flames leaping over treetops, roar you could hear at this distance, awakened them. Low clouds that had blown in after dark were crimson with madly flickering light. He and Dolley knelt by a window.

"The town's on fire," she whispered in awe. "Will it come here, Jimmy? We'd better—"

But it didn't seem to be advancing. "Hold on," he said. Then he realized it was a towering bonfire hurling sparks into the air six or eight blocks away. It was Federalists clamoring for war while Democrats lay low. The flame roar was pierced by orator's shouts in unintelligible fragments. They watched for a long time and then went back to bed.

In the morning he found Johnny Graham and Meriwether

Lewis at his gate. He was walking to the Capitol and they said they would walk with him. "Thing is," Merry said, "this ain't a good day to be out alone. There's a fury running in the streets." He smiled, a certain light of combat in his eyes. Merry was a changed man since the expedition had been authorized—that tightness around his eyes mostly vanished.

Madison was glad to have an escort. At Sixth and Pennsylvania, work crews were shoveling up ashes from the bonfire. Someone shouted an obscenity that he realized with a start was meant for him. It made him feel naked and exposed. Johnny was amused, but Merry's face tightened and he turned in that direction. Madison caught his arm.

He was surprised to find that both young men had been at the bonfire and both had had fights. Merry said, "Quite a night, in fact. Must have been a thousand or so, plenty of bottles, speakers giving them red meat. That Griswold of Connecticut—you want to watch out for him, sir—he was saying things to curl your hair. And you know that little devil works for the chairman, Simon Pink? He was right up against the speaker's stand taking notes! And I slid up to him and I said, 'Simon, you're going to get yourself killed.' And he says, 'Nah! Chairman'll want to know what they're saying. And these scoundrels, they can kiss my bum.' And I said, 'Simon, you've got more pith than I ever figured,' and he gives me a big smile, looked pleased as punch."

Madison smiled. It didn't pay to dismiss small men too quickly. He asked about the crowd. Were they riffraff?

"Working men, out of work or soon will be," Johnny said.

"Baltimore too," Merry said. "I spent a day there, got back yesterday. Waterfront looks deserted, businesses shut down, especially those dependent on western trade. Food costs already up. Grain houses standing empty, teamsters looking for fodder, teams slowing down. Hungry animals won't work, and that means everything else is crippled. That big candle plant up from the bay, it's closed. Taverns full of angry men; it's as good as your life to go in some of those Baltimore saloons."

• • •

"I saw it from the mansion roof," the president said. "Spectacular, to say the least."

"Metaphor for the white heat out there," Madison said.

"Oh, yes." Mr. Jefferson sighed and slumped into a chair. "Pressure everywhere. Letters pouring in. Every editor in the country with his war drum going. The West ready to march. Another letter from that Tennessee firebrand, Jackson his name is, wants to go take New Orleans. Give the word and he'll command. But all this bubbling; dare we wait much longer?"

"But isn't the real question, dare we not?"

The State of the Union message, which the president must write and send to the Hill to be read to a joint session, was only a week away. Everyone expected it to take a definitive position. But what position? Stand by for war?

God knew there was support for it. The commercial East—not the part that dreamed of cutting off the West to leave a tight little seaboard nation prospering on its shipping—was as militant as the West. Connecticut and Massachusetts were becoming manufacturing states, stationary steam engines huffing away, mechanized looms thundering, new cast-iron implements appearing every year. The West was the market that took these goods in return for the corn and wheat—shipped via New Orleans, mind you—that fed the workers. The nation's economy was more tied together every year; everyone saw that to shatter part was to shatter the whole. Foolish the Frenchman who couldn't grasp that.

Plunging ahead would be safer. Seize New Orleans before the French arrived. Satisfy the American clamor for action. But in the end that would finish common man democracy. It would prove the Federalists were right all along. They would say, and people would believe, that it was democratic weakness that had made war inevitable. And the people would turn back to government that was strong and reliable, and the democratic dream would die as aristocracy rose and monarchy loomed ahead. So Madison foresaw the ominous possibilities.

Yet holding off was dangerous too. It would take time to raise an army and rally the Royal Navy, and if Leclerc struck in force, they might not have time. Still, seven hundred regulars were posted on the lower Mississippi, with two thousand militia standing by and the Tennessee militia ready to move on short notice. So they weren't entirely defenseless.

The other side of the gamble was that if they held off, things still might break their way. Leclerc was beginning to sound a bit mad, and the yellow fever season was sure to trouble the French troops. Reports from Europe said France and England were edging toward war again, which ought to keep Napoleon occupied. And their arguments—in which they had great confidence, given they were so patently true—might penetrate at last to find some few grains of common sense.

The president was at his standing desk. He sighed and wiped his quill. "Do you consider yourself a gambling man?"

Madison hesitated. He was sunk in a deep chair by a window. Morning sunlight glowed on the walls and made everything seem brighter than it was. A gambling man . . . was he? They were talking of gambling the nation's future.

It was a desperate crossroads, either turn a potential disaster. "I've played a few hands of whist."

"And won?"

"More often than I've lost, yes." His mind flicked back to those comfortable days at Princeton in the college Aaron Burr's father had started. "I rarely had to ask my father for more money at college." Aaron had been a young student then. He'd bullied the college into admitting him at fourteen and had been glad to team with Madison at whist. In retrospect, even with the Revolution raging, those had seemed joyous days full of bright hope.

"Then we're agreed," the president said. "Give 'em a State of the Union message with no more to hold onto than a greased pole. And take the consequences."

So in the end, Madison told his wife, they were gambling

men: They would wait a little longer and risk being caught
with preparations yet to be made if Leclerc struck soon.
Troops, weapons, dealing with the British . . .

Dolley said, "That's not gambling; that's making a judgment."

"I like that," he said. But he knew it was a gamble.

The clerk of the house had been droning on for twenty minutes, reading aloud the president's message. Madison sat
hunched inconspicuously in the gallery of the temporary
oval chamber in which the House met, already dubbed the
Oven for its shape and atmosphere on warm days. There was
palpable tension in the crowded room, every congressman
present, senators crowded around the edges, men sitting
with hands cupped to ears, listening for what everyone in
Washington expected. The administration had scarcely admitted there was a crisis, but now it could dodge no longer!

Gradually a murmur started to run. Would the president
still refuse to admit anything was wrong? At last the clerk
reached the single paragraph on the subject—slanting reference to the French, no mention of the crisis on the river. So
they gambled, walking armless up to war in hopes of staving
it off.

Into the silence a single piercing voice: "My God, is that
all the craven scoundrel will say?"

Madison slipped out but not quickly enough. Roger Griswold of Connecticut pinned him between a bench and an
awful statue as members streamed around them. Griswold's
leonine face was red, and he was shouting.

"A disgrace, a rotten disgrace, bereft of courage, mouse of
a man lying about with his nigger mistress, afraid to act—
and why? Because he's in thrall to the French! Loves their
sick, soul-rotten revolution, their murder of those who knew
how to run the country, who had tradition and position and
authority, turned everything to the rabble and that gave us
the tyrant who abuses us. And you too, you miserable little
scoundrel, tail tucked before the mighty Napoleon—"

Roger must have had garlic sausage for breakfast; the evidence was on the air.

"War is the answer," Roger cried. "It's common sense, common decency, national honor. Seize New Orleans and fight them when they arrive. Stand up like men. The Royal Navy would be at our service; they'd relish the chance to thwart the tyrant. Are you blind, for God's sake? We'd welcome alliance with Britain, they're our friends, our brothers, not this mincing Frenchman drenched in the foul perfume of tyranny!"

He jabbed a finger into Madison's chest. "So you'd better tell that effete master of yours—"

Madison caught the finger and bent it back.

"Ouch! What the hell are you doing?"

"I'll break it off, you jab it in my chest." Madison bent the finger farther and Griswold cried out, his knees bending to accommodate the pressure. He backed away and Madison released the finger.

Griswold stood there rubbing his hand. At last he grinned. "Jimmy," he said, "you've got a touch of the terrier in you, I'll give you that. But I'm right in what I said and you know it."

And as Madison caught a hack back to his end of Pennsylvania Avenue, he had to admit that while Griswold was not right and his idea of policy was a paradigm of Federalist fears and dreams, most Americans would be cheering him on.

This clamor for war, Jimmy told Louis Pichon, should alert the powers in Paris as to how united—how very determined—the Americans were. France must see that it courted war. . . .

The Pichons had come to dinner, Pirette with her new babe asleep in her arms. Dolley made over the child with abandon, knowing no excess would be too much for Pirette, but it struck her the little form was very small and disturbingly still.

Louis raised a fresh concern. Philadelphia papers were quoting the president as saying he would put the nation under the protection of the Royal Navy.

"Thus the extremes, Louis," Jimmy said easily, "to which the first consul drives us."

The next day, taking tea at the mansion, they described the encounter.

"Will he dare report it, do you suppose?" Tom asked.

"I was watching Pirette," Dolley said, "and from her expression, yes, he still reports. She's terrified."

The Frenchwoman's hand, at rest on the table beside her plate, had started to tremble. The quiver had grown more and more pronounced, and her lips had drawn down in a grimace that became painful to see. Louis, looking at Jimmy, hadn't noticed; then Danny put her hand on Pirette's and held it until it was quiet. Pirette looked at Danny with a tremulous smile of gratitude. It hurt for a woman's agony to be a matter of state. . . .

Then the president, standing with an elbow on the mantle, snapped her back to what mattered. His face had a thin look, nostrils drawn in, lips tight. "We're cutting this very close," he said. "How much time do you think we really have, Jimmy?"

"Three months," Jimmy said. "Not much more. Depends on when Leclerc can clear Santo Domingo, and he may have to delay. Persistent rumors say he's having trouble."

Three months . . . Dolley suppressed an involuntary shiver.

Pirette Pichon's quivering hand had had a profound effect on Danny too. Placing her hand on Pirette's had been an instinctive gesture born of a woman's sympathy for another's terror. But that terror had communicated, and Danny found herself worried—indeed, frightened—as she had not been

before. Suddenly war was real and imminent. She had listened to Mr. Madison spell what plainly was the truth to
Louis Pichon, and somehow that Louis so clearly understood it and despaired of his own inability to open his blind
and reckless government's eyes had finally opened her own
eyes. Of course she had understood it was serious all along,
but it had not been imminent and now it was and she could
see her own ruin looming ahead.

Henri wrote of New Orlean's joy—soon it would be
French again with all the vast superiority that that status
conferred. The Spanish would be gone, the great leader
Napoleon Bonaparte would make Americans pay through
the nose for the massive benefit the French river conferred
on them, honest Frenchmen would come at last into their
place in the sun. Danny, of course, he hastened to add,
wasn't included in this wholesale condemnation of the rude
nation to the north; she was a Frenchwoman to the core and
would fit perfectly into the new New Orleans.

She knew better; she had made herself an American and
was pleased that her accent had almost vanished. It struck
her suddenly that Henri was obtuse—handsome, clever,
witty, elegant, but blind to reality. And the reality was that
the French were implacable and the Americans would fight,
and she and her business must surely be destroyed in the
clash. She could get her ships out, but the sugar business and
even the little wine business that interested Clinch would be
instant casualties of war and she would be back in the desperate times she faced when Carl died.

Yet the sudden pain of it went far beyond her own affairs.
American though she was, she hadn't lost her love for home.
Oh, she could readily summon up the summer heat, the in-
sects, the snakes, the mold that forms when humidity is
high, the prideful self-satisfaction of individuals, the arrogance of the men—of whom Henri was an example—but
that's not what the city on the great crescent of the Mississippi meant to her. It meant the soft air in spring and fall, the
gentle winters, the explosions of flowers, the gaiety and the

music, the calls of men and sometimes of women in the market place furiously cajoling dice flung across a canvas sheet with an air of challenging the world.

As fresh in her mind as yesterday, she could see, hear, smell the market, all hurly-burly and laughter and sharp dealings and fierce bargaining and half-serious threats. The endless festivities, the cotillions, the Quadroon Ball that drew the men and alarmed the women, the theater, the opera from Paris playing to packed houses, the shrieks of laughter at musical comedy. New Orleans was a tenth the size of Philadelphia, but in such matters it far outstripped the largest city in America and, as for Washington, don't even attempt comparison. She could see the cool interior gardens, goldfish fat as catfish in the ponds, house fronts flush with the street as anonymous on the outside as ranks of soldiers, while the interiors were all tile and plaster and brilliant colors and burgeoning greenery and lavish ballrooms. The people there boasted they knew how to live, and they were right. . . .

It would all be destroyed, it would not survive as she knew it, what followed would be all different and foreign to her. She knew the Americans—once aroused they would fight to the death and nothing around them would survive. What would happen to her? To Henri? To whatever they meant to each other? Henri was foolish, but it wasn't really his fault. He was inexperienced. He'd never left New Orleans but to hunt in the swamps. A wave of tenderness overtook her; she saw she was more than half seriously in love with this stirring, invigorating, downright exciting man, who was exasperated her beyond imagining with his demands and insistence and assumptions, preening his feathers of masculinity like some barnyard cock—

Her office door opened a little and Clinch Johnson gave a tentative little knock, looking as if he would flee if she frowned. So she smiled and waved him in and watched him seat himself with his suit encasing him like a sausage and his yellow hair standing up. She told him she was afraid, and soon she was pouring out the whole range of her fears for New Orleans and for her business and for her adopted country as well, how Pirette had trembled and Louis had looked near tears and Mr. Madison was implacable and friends in New Orleans—Henri really was none of Clinch's business—showed a mad arrogance that ultimately must work evil on them.

"Well, Miss Danny," he said, with such easy calm that she instantly felt soothed, and she cried, "Oh, Clinch, just 'Danny' will do—we're friends, aren't we?"

He smiled with infectious pleasure. "I do hope so, Miss D—ah, that is, Danny. Yes, ma'am."

"Tell me it's not as bad as it looks. I need cheering."

"Couple of things. I do business with some British houses, and I hear tell the French ain't having that easy a time in Santo Domingo. And the way the British tell it, they're ready to crank up their war with Napoleon again."

Britain had struck a truce with the French back in March, which was universally assumed to be merely a momentary cease-fire sure to collapse soon. But meanwhile it made things worse in America, freeing the French as it did to pursue their dreams of empire.

"Way I hear it," Clinch said, "British ain't willing to give up Malta, and Napoleon says he must have it. In London they figure the Frenchman wants it as a stepping stone to grabbing Egypt again and maybe going on to India, and they don't intend to make that easy for him. Rather fight than do that, so they say."

She liked the sound of that. Santo Domingo, an essential stepping stone—and Malta, an equally essential stepping stone on the other side of the world—both making trouble that could only benefit the little United States. Clinch chatted on about what he'd heard in that easy voice of his, and after a while moved on to business talk and soon they were swapping gossip of the shipping world and laughing over some buffoon's marvelous faux pas and presently she took a bottle of Madeira from a cabinet and poured two glasses, and altogether, she felt much better.

· · ·

In Boston, John Quincy Adams agreed to stand for Congress—and he lost! It was devastating. The Democratic incumbent, likeable Dr. Eustis, squeaked through by scarcely fifty votes.

The blow was made worse by his family's elation. Since his father's defeat, his mother felt politics was an evil field beneath an Adams. She wanted John Quincy to be pure, whereas he saw the world turning and wanted to be part of it. Dutifully he said, and sometimes even half-believed, that being spared a political future relieved him. But then Jonathan Mason and Benjamin Foster of the U.S. Senate said they were quitting. Both Massachusetts Senate seats open!

John Quincy stopped talking to his family and started talking to State House leaders, where new senators would be elected. Timothy Pickering, leader of the Essex Junto with its plans to make New England and New York into a separate nation, demanded the first seat. It would serve six years; the second was for two years. Pickering haunted the General Assembly. Mr. Adams couldn't bring himself actually to politic, but he was available day and night to the members. Pickering, glaring often at Mr. Adams, kept his loud voice ringing in the halls.

Shouting, gesticulating, spittle flying, he denounced the Adamses for traitors, the old man for his craven failure to fight France, the son for seducing the old devil into seeking a peace as dishonorable as it was disgraceful! And the outcome today—now we have a lascivious whoremaster in command, a man so pitifully in thrall to Parisian doctrines of revolution and murder that he sounds no alarm as the French prepare to make us their slaves. On the eve of invasion that can sweep our entire nation under the rug of history and make us a mere satellite to the French empire, he fears even now to confess to the Congress. But lo!—at this moment a French army is subduing the blacks of Santo Domingo and preparing to invade Louisiana! But does this lecherous master of lewdness raise the alarm? No . . . He raises not even his voice. What is the State of the Union in the face of the

most serious crisis the nation has ever faced? Why, it's just
fine, just what he wanted, as he planned it. You read that
message, all of you read it! Don't you see? We are doomed
with this lecher in command. We must fight and fight even to
the last ditch to hold on against him long enough for our citizenry to wake and see the clear path and understand the
danger and hold to the true faith. Oh, my friends, I implore
you, send a man to the Senate who will fight the evil conspiracy to his last breath! Don't saddle us with one whose
pretense of fairness covers the nature of an arrant coward!
The truth is before us all and to that we must hew. Give us a
man who will fight the good fight under the nose of the
whoremaster!

It flirted with the stuff of challenges, though of course
John Quincy would never so lower himself. But he was very
receptive when Dock Bartlett herded him into a corner of the
lobby. Dock was short and heavy, soup stains usually on his
waistcoat, hank of gray hair tousled awry, but he was a party
kingmaker, his power unquestioned.

"Tim spits all over you when he gets really excited," Dock
said. He talked around a toothpick in his mouth. "Makes it a
little hard to take him seriously. And then, him and his Essex
bunch, they want to split off from the rest of the country and
go it alone. Cozy up to Britain. But that talk's too easy; I
don't trust it. Yes, it might come to that someday—national
Democrats keep on this mad submission to the French—but
I think we need a calmer voice in Washington than ol' Tim
will give us."

Dock was a good Federalist, as John Quincy knew himself to be, but he wasn't a mad dog. He removed the toothpick to fire a gout of brown juice into a shiny brass spittoon
and moved closer, voice sinking to a confidential whisper.
"But Tim, now, he's right on this French invasion business. I
read that State of the Union message in the Boston *Tran-
script,* I wanted to puke. This is serious—I need to be sure
you're right on it. You're an independent cuss, all right, I admire that; but on this one you ain't getting my vote, nor nobody else's, if you're not right on that."

John Quincy swallowed. This was gut politics. His mother's image flashed in his mind; but then, she wasn't here. He weighed his answer. He wouldn't stand supinely while the administration gave away Louisiana, but he remembered his talk with Madison and felt confident that neither he nor Mr. Jefferson would do any such thing. Indeed, he had the feeling that we were much closer to war than Dock, along Pickering, understood. The French must give up their mad scheme or we soon would be fighting with whatever weight we could muster.

"Let me be clear," Adams said. "If you elect me, I'll disagree with you at times and I'll follow my own counsel. But on this question of Louisiana, we're agreed."

Dock gave him a long, level look. "Betray me on this," he said, "and I'll never forget it. And neither will you."

"Fair enough."

"All right. Now, Pickering got to the boys early and some of 'em pledged. But pledges are only good for a couple of votes. After that, he don't make it, they'll swing to you."

Adams nodded. It was an arrangement and arrangements were keys to politics. But he saw Dock wasn't finished.

"Now, Pickering has friends. He can't just be whupped and tossed aside. He loses the first seat, he'll want the second. I want your agreement you'll support him in that."

Deals didn't get any more crass and direct. Pickering was an enemy. Henchman to Alexander Hamilton in trying to destroy President Adams, he had undermined everything John Quincy's father had done. He would be an awful senator. But supporting him was the price of victory. "I understand," Adams said.

A slow smile settled on Dock's face. "You'll do, Mr. Adams, he said softly. "You'll do."

Montane . . . Felix Montane, the card said. Could it be *General* Montane?

"One and the same," Johnny Graham said. "In civilian clothes, clean shaven, but the same man all right."

Yes, there was no mistaking the general with his pale, icy eyes, though now he wore a well-cut suit with snowy hose and wide lapels, doubtless the fashion in Paris. His slender form was neat and trim, and there was assurance and, indeed, authority, in the very way in which he took the unadorned wooden chair to which Madison gestured him. Yet he seemed different too, and it was not just that his manner was absent the old arrogance and suggested he wanted something. Slowly Madison concluded that the difference spoke of sadness and pain and perhaps even a new understanding of how hard the world could be, an insight that was prerequisite to wisdom.

He drummed his fingers on the plain table that served him as desk. "Well, General, what brings you now?"

" 'Monsieur' will do very well now, Mr. Secretary. I am no longer a general. But I am here, sir, to offer my services. To put my sword at the service of my new country."

Madison allowed his surprise to show.

"I wish to be an American," the general said. "This is the land of people from elsewhere, is it not? People who come for freedom, to escape oppression?"

Madison studied him, something liquid in his eyes. Yes, a man in pain. Could he be a spy? Possible, of course, though there was little to learn about the government that wasn't already in the papers. He put his chin on his hand. "Why don't you explain yourself, sir."

The story that emerged was surprising, Madison supposed, but only superficially. It was full of the muddled thinking, the maneuvering of power, the failure of heart and honor, the betrayal that marred so many human enterprises. It seemed that Leclerc blamed Montane for failing to force aid from America. Eventually Napoleon had choked up enough gold to feed the men, but by then they were in trouble and Leclerc needed a scapegoat. He broke Montane from general to captain and denounced him to Paris. Napoleon replied personally. For destroying the French campaign in Santo Domingo, Montane was to be cashiered, and if Leclerc chose, placed before a firing squad.

Hope fluttered in Madison's heart. "The campaign destroyed, you said?"

"Certainly, sir. And for that someone must pay, and I was chosen."

He fell into a silence that he somehow made dramatic. Then a bitter little smile flickered and disappeared as he said that Leclerc had been his idol and had turned worship to hate. Of course the first consul loved Leclerc, they were peas from the same pod, hard, ruthless, cruel, supremely confident, ready to crush all who stood in their way. Once he had admired that. . . .

With this verdict from on high came impassioned letters from Montane's family in France. His perfidy had brought them under suspicion, and they were being watched. If he returned they would be destroyed, and he would be a marked man. Stay away . . .

So the man's pain was genuine. While Madison could sympathize and so forth and so on, what stirred him was that magical phrase, "destroyed campaign."

Montane, after a suitable pause, for effect or to regain control, Madison didn't much care which, said in softened voice, "So, sir, with humility, I wish to be an American. I proffer my sword because I believe you will have need of it before long."

"General Leclerc is coming then?"

"Oh no, sir, General Leclerc is dead."

"Dead? What do you mean?"

"He died of yellow fever. You understand, do you not, that the French army in Santo Domingo has been destroyed? It doesn't exist as a fighting force. You hadn't heard?"

Madison's heart was hammering. "Tell me . . ."

The slender officer then unfolded a disaster of such magnitude as to leave Madison stunned. First, the fighting grew worse and worse. When the French seized Toussaint and declared slavery reinstituted, every able-bodied man and many women took to the brush. Leclerc issued obscene extermination orders. It was no quarter and no prisoners for both sides. Armed with machetes and muskets taken from the French, the rebels slowly ground the invaders down. Growing fear, fueled by constant evidence of grisly death by torture and mutilation, crushed French morale.

Did Madison know Santo Domingo? No? Dense tropics, incredibly beautiful, vivid green against vivid sky, flowers that burst from every plant in explosions of color, beauty to make the heart ache, beauty that mocked the horror. That was in the winter. But in the summer . . . under relentless sun, air steamy as a farmwife's wash tubs, mosquitoes in droning clouds, a Frenchman understood what hell might be like.

Soldiers in tight uniforms pushing through heavy brush that itself snarled bayonets, listening for the slither of feet on grass that said the enemy was out there somewhere, drawing nearer, nearer, tensed for that sudden slithering rush that meant they were coming, about to burst from hiding in an insane screaming attack, swinging blades glittering in the sun—or sometimes the rush started and then stopped, the silence eerie, nothing happening, and you push on a hundred yards and it comes again, and finally you can't trust your own senses. You hear the voodoo drums at night, and you come to believe that spirits really can leave their bodies and invade yours and eat your heart from within. You push into a clearing and find another stack of heads, and you march always with a shovel so you can bury what you find and keep the wild hogs away.

"These are my men, do you understand," Montane cried, real tears now in his eyes at the memory, "nice young French lads, the tough old sergeant prodding them on, their eyes rolling, starting at every sound—ah, God! Your heart ached for them. Every patrol I lost a few, and they knew in advance when they set out, some wouldn't be coming back; and they'd look at each other and not talk much because the man you talked to might be dead in an hour. Young, you see, most of them had never known love, never had a woman. Their hands shook, they screamed at night in their dreams, and those Goddamned awful drums beating and beating through the night, their spirits come to steal your soul—"

He broke off, staring, then slumped in his chair, blinking, as if surprised to discover himself here with the chill of winter outside, so far from what haunted him.

"Forgive me, Monsieur," he murmured. He wiped his forehead with a kerchief. "They were good boys and almost every one is dead now. Almost every one . . ."

And then the yellow fever came. Madison knew the fever from its visits to American cities. The great epidemic in Philadelphia in 1793 that took Dolley's husband with seven thousand others had started, so they said, after the arrival of ships from Santo Domingo. Probably just coincidence, since it was widely understood that the cause was poisonous night air rising from fetid swamps.

It struck with such awful blinding speed, Montane was saying. You're healthy in the morning, dying in the evening. It's the mosquito season, droning clouds that envelop you and drink your blood till your skin is raw. The disease struck down his emaciated, exhausted, frightened young soldiers as a farmer scythes hay, laying them out faster than those who remained could bury them. Ghastly deaths. Temperature soaring, skin hot to the touch, blood seems to boil. You vomit black bile full of blood, your guts turn inside out, the lining of your stomach comes out of your throat. You're on your knees choking and gasping for air; you try to stand and you fall into your vomit and retch again and again. Then the bowels explode, streams of foul water, fountains of slime and filth geysering, men screaming for water, their systems expelling faster than drinking can replenish, men crawling about naked, out of their heads, blind, crying for mothers and wives and stopping on hands and knees to vomit into the slime someone else left. And those of us spared trying to save them, wash them, get them water, until the best you could do was try to give them a decent death, not covered with excrement. And much of the time even that was more than you could manage. And if you sent a party down to the stream for water to wash them, the enemy would come out of the night . . .

The fever spared the blacks, understand, maybe because they were used to it. It spared some of the whites too, and some who contracted it recovered. But the plain fact was that the disease started in June and by August men were dying by the hundreds. By late September, the army of twenty-five thousand was down to fewer than four thousand effective; and they crouched behind barricades, fearful the hordes would overrun them.

"But you survived."

Montane shrugged. "Yes. I have no idea why. I prayed, of course, everyone does. But after what I saw in Santo Domingo, no, I don't believe God watches over us. I saw too many good men, young men, praying men picked off like snapping flowers for bouquets in heaven."

"And General Leclerc?"

"Lived long enough to know the despair of utter failure, I'm happy to say, then died in twenty-four hours covered with his own shit, not different in the end from the lowliest of his young soldiers."

This account was ghastly, and Montane's grief was too stark not to be real. Still, after pausing in deference to horror, Madison cut to what mattered. "What will happen now?"

Montane hesitated, then said, "I'm afraid they'll be back. The first consul wants Louisiana, and I don't think disaster on a faraway island will stop him."

Well, maybe not, but it would slow him! Madison told himself that he could take no pleasure in the deaths of twenty thousand men, but the rising of his spirits that had started with the first mention of a destroyed campaign continued until they were soaring. What precious time this gave them! Napoleon would need a year to overcome this disaster and any number of things might intervene, chief among them resumption of war between Britain and France, which should carry the French dictator's mind far from America.

He stood. "Welcome to America, Mr. Montane. In peace

we will consider you an adornment; in war we most certainly will call upon your sword."

Actually, if war came, they would be in desperate need of trained officers. That they would give a French officer much authority in a war with France was laughable, but it was all academic: Madison intended to avert war and with this stunning news from Santo Domingo it seemed ever more possible to do so. He hurried to report to the president and then hurried home, shockingly early really, but too pleased to restrain himself. He would have clicked his heels but that it would be inappropriate to the dignity of the secretary of state.

36

WASHINGTON, EARLY 1803

You could feel the tension all over Washington, at least the black community could. Samuel Clark could. Slave or free alike, black folks kept their ears open, they listened to the whites, their expressions as inattentive as so many sticks of wood, which was how the white folks took them. But they knew . . . and it didn't augur well for them.

War was coming. All over town Samuel heard more and more agreement on that, white men wondering why the administration didn't say it out loud, call up the militia, get the Royal Navy to help, get *ready,* for God's sake. The French hadn't turned around yet, and it didn't look like they ever would. It wasn't Napoleon's way to back off; everyone knew that.

So the disaster in Santo Domingo, if you wanted to put it that way, came as a mixed blessing. It would slow the

French some—but it meant the niggers had won. Oh, the French would settle it soon enough, get a new army in and clean 'em out, but it gave America a breathing spell, time to get ready and all. But the thing was, it also gave the niggers ideas. Made slaves wonder if they couldn't do the same.

Most whites pretended they couldn't see blacks, treated them like so much furniture. But low-class whites, one glance told you who they were and you wanted to watch out for them. They were getting more and more on edge and off balance, and sometimes they looked downright scared. And a scared white man was a white man thinking about killing you. It paid to stay out of his way. Made the whole community tense though—there was talk of a lot more floggings in slave yards, and two freedmen had been left in the woods dangling from trees. White people didn't talk much about it, but blacks knew. Whites talked about war and how we'd have to fight the French, but they looked at blacks when they talked that way and they didn't look good.

One day, when he'd delivered Miss Danny to the pier where Mobry vessels moored, she told him to go home and dig in the storage room for a file box marked thus and so. Two hours later he was back, the box heavy as he carried it along the pier to the shed and up the narrow steps to her office. Her door was ajar and he was ready to knock when he heard Mr. Clinch's voice.

"Do you know," he heard Mr. Clinch say, "those blacks in Santo Domingo, they saved America's bacon." He wasn't from hereabouts, Mr. Clinch, he was from up north somewhere, New York maybe, you could hear it in his voice.

Miss Danny said something, Samuel couldn't distinguish the words, and then Mr. Clinch said, "Yes, ma'am, the French can send a new army, but will they? War in Europe seems about to start again. I don't know . . . but just think of the courage of those black men standing against the mightiest army in the world. Why, we'd have expected them to run like rabbits; but no, they took their machetes and fought and won! We think our blacks here are passive, don't care for ought but food and sleep, but can they be so courageous there and so different here?"

Again Miss Danny's voice, a murmur, and Mr. Clinch laughed and said, "Well, I know, but you have to admit it's ironic that the courage of far-away black men saves us . . ."

The box was heavy and Samuel had been eavesdropping too long, someone below would notice, so he knocked lightly and pushed the door open. He made haste to place his burden where Miss Danny pointed. There was a heavy silence as he hurried out.

But when he was safely back on the box of the carriage, he smiled quietly, inside, not exposing himself to watching whites, and he thought on what Mr. Clinch had said—this nation saved by the courage of black men. Slaves. Men who would fight and die to rid themselves of the French. Men like Joshua.

With a wave of exultation like nothing he thought he'd ever experienced, he thought, we won! Joshua won! He was right to go, right to risk, right to stand for freedom!

But the very thought, joyous though it was, unleashed a despair that he saw now he had been holding out on the edge of his mind for days. What had been concern and then open fear now became conviction. He would not see his brother again. Joshua was dead. He'd had no word and expected none, but he knew. It was as solid a conviction as that the sun had risen in the morning and would set in the evening. Joshua was dead. He had died doing what he'd known he must and he'd won his battle, and his life meant more than all the years an old man might live.

He'd seen his duty and he'd gone to fight.

Well, duty took many forms, didn't it?

A dray drawn by a worn gray cut in front of him, and he had to draw the matched team back so hard the horses almost reared. A surly white man at the reins of the dray glared at him and reached under his seat for an oaken bat. Samuel occupied himself quieting the horses, and after a while the white man clucked the gray into motion and drove away without looking back.

This was a dangerous town, more so now, and sure to be worse when the inevitable war started. The French had fought at Santo Domingo till they were mostly dead; they weren't going to give up now. They would be back and the blacks of Santo Domingo would fight them off again; but would the whites in the lower Mississippi have that same courage? He didn't know, and while he knew it meant a lot to Miss Danny, he didn't really care. The question was whether low-class whites like that scoundrel in the dray would take out their fears on blacks.

They should long since have taken their little horde of escape gold and gone north, where whites didn't hate blacks so. . . .

But duty takes many forms. . . .

Was it, then, at last, beginning to break in their direction? Madison had steeled himself for war for so long, walked the narrow tightrope of hope for so long, that he was quite unprepared for the possibility that the French might actually start listening to reason.

So as he sat in the president's office looking at Pierre Du Pont's letter from Paris, he felt dizzy with disbelief and joy and fear that as a magician waves his wand, it might all disappear in a flash.

Pierre said he had information that the first consul was open to the offer by the United States to *purchase* New Orleans!

Think of it! The whole island of New Orleans, which really was the city and its surrounding swamps separated from land by lakes and water courses all around, would solve the whole problem. With the city in our hands the French could do as they liked with the rest, for they could not close the river then, and that was the sine qua non of the whole crisis. If they couldn't seal the Mississippi, our whole central section was safe. The rest of Louisiana was mostly the terrain Meriwether Lewis would be crossing soon; we could worry later about the ownership of that vast stretch. Indeed, Madison was supremely confident that ultimately the tide of western settlers would make the continent American, since neither France nor Britain brought new homesteaders, while the flow of Americans across the Appalachians and westward was constant year by year.

He handed the letter to Albert Gallatin. The president had summoned them both. Mr. Jefferson paced the office, looking as exuberant as a boy. The room was flooded with glowing late winter sunshine, matching their moods perfectly. Albert blinked and shook his head when he came to the basic point.

Of course, Pierre Du Pont had presented this information as all his own doing, a conceit he probably believed and that Madison felt he'd earned. His advice was terse: First, abandon threats. Conciliate. No belligerence. Then petition to buy, not just the city, but the entire east bank of the river, from the Gulf of Mexico to Natchez in Mississippi territory, which included New Orleans. Foreswear any interest in terrain west of the river. Guarantee France full commercial rights. And make a serious offer, one that would command instant respect.

The Treasury secretary frowned. "Of course, Pierre doesn't care if it breaks us. What does he propose?"

"Six million dollars."

"Six million! More than half a year's budget. It would shatter our finances, Mr. President."

"Jimmy?" Tom had that easy smile; he'd already decided.

"Oh, we must do it, of course."

"But not for six," Albert said. "Three, even four . . ."

There was a long silence. Madison would sound off if necessary, but better it came from the president.

"Well," Tom said, his face radiating amused pleasure, "I was thinking of a nice round figure—say fifty million francs how much would that be in U.S. dollars, Albert?"

In strangled voice, Albert said, "Some $9,375,000 that, I must remind you, Mr. President, *we don't have!*"

"Then we must find it, Albert. Scrape it up, you know. I'll leave the details to you, but yes, fifty million francs. That should get the Frenchman's attention."

He popped his hands together in infectious joy that mirrored Madison's mood as well and cried, "We'll drink a glass of Madeira and toast a radiant future!"

When Madison got home he broke out champagne and he had Dolley got well into a second bottle, dreaming aloud about the pleasures of life absent the threat of war.

A week later Jimmy came home in a totally different mood. The very set of his shoulders told Dolley something was wrong. He scarcely touched food and responded to the bits of gossip she offered for entertainment with flickering smiles and monosyllables. Then he said he would lie down a bit.

So she asked, and for answer he drew a letter from his shoulder case. With dismay, she recognized Mr. Livingston's spiky handwriting on fine vellum. Jimmy went to the bedroom and she retreated to the study to sink into the corner of the sofa and open the letter.

She began reading, slowly, with frequent pauses. It was odd how the gentleman's words drew her in so, stirring the already vivid images of Paris that so many French novels had built in her mind. Discursive as always, Mr. Livingston said he had been trying to draw attention to American demands, and she could see his tall, spare frame marching about the Paris of her imagination . . .

Talleyrand proves a total waste of time; Mr. Livingston suspects he has been bribed by British agents to follow his natural inclination to abuse Americans. Britain's ends are served if the first consul's mind remains fixed on an empire on the Mississippi instead of resuming war over Malta. Meanwhile, the supreme leader doesn't deign to answer

missives Mr. Livingston sends directly. Marbois is friendly
but paralyzed by fear he'll make a wrong move. In desperation Mr. Livingston turns to Joseph Bonaparte, the older
brother, to whom the great man may or may not listen, if he
listens to anyone.

The news from Santo Domingo strikes Paris a savage
blow; newspapers are edged in black; portraits of General
Leclerc appear in windows swathed in black crepe. At the
cathedral a memorial mass for the general and his men
draws fifty thousand. Common folk weep in the streets. Of
course, many are the families of the young soldiers swept
away by the disease, but Mr. Livingston still is startled by
the official outpouring.

That the loss of an army under ultimate orders to oppress
the United States doesn't strike Mr. Livingston as truly bad
news is a thought he keeps to himself, especially when he at-
tends a vast reception at which the first consul is expected.
As always, the big room is crowded—Dolley's imagination
has clothed it in grandeur—a thousand sperm oil lamps
blazing in chandeliers, double girandoles on walls between
tall windows that are draped in crimson, waiters threading
through the crowd with trays overhead holding flutes of
champagne in rows as orderly as soldiers' ranks, the whole
room a display that offends Mr. Livingston's democratic
sensibilities. . . .

And then a stir, a tremor—the first consul arrives! But this
time, instead of circling the room and allowing his hand to
be kissed as his cold gaze flicks about, he forges straight toward Mr. Livingston, waving courtiers out of his way. He
wears a black band on his arm, his face is more than stern,
and Mr. Livingston sees that he is angry.

This is a man whose anger shakes the ground around him,
but Mr. Livingston remains composed. He bows and says,
rather gracefully, he feels, "May I express my nation's condolences, to yourself, sir, to Madame Leclerc, to the people
of France—"

But Napoleon is glaring. "Your condolences are neither
needed nor desired." His French is rapid, slurred, guttural. "I

wish to tell you, Mr. American Ambassador, do not flatter yourself that General Leclerc's tragic demise changes anything. Nothing, sir!" Mr. Livingston notes that the first consul speaks like a barracks room sergeant when he's angry.

Then, as if somehow the dictator feels he has lost ground in a contest of wills, he snaps, "Two points, sir. Hear them well, memorize them, take them back to your masters. First, do not disturb me further with offers to purchase Louisiana. Only spendthrifts and fools sell land, and I am neither. Sale is out of the question.

"Second, I am sending a new army immediately under General Victor. He will go with twenty thousand men to Santo Domingo and send two thousand on to take immediate possession of New Orleans—two thousand should be ample to deal with the American rabble there, including scum floating the river."

He gestures to a heavy man standing directly behind him. "I present General Victor. He will leave within the hour for Holland where even now his army is embarking on ships heavy-laden with supplies." He glances up at his general. "You tell him, Victor, tell him what he may expect. And then go to your men."

Dolley dropped the letter in her lap. Her hands were quivering. Again she had that odd sensation of words flying across the sea to deal her a visceral blow. Purchase out of the question, a new army coming—all their hopes for avoiding war were fading. . . .

The candle was guttering down and she lighted a fresh one and set it in its stick. Then she took up the letter and again was immersed in the vivid scene. The first consul, having delivered devastating news, wheels and marches out as forcefully as he entered. General Victor stands with legs wide, head thrown back, looking down a long, slender nose with eyes almost hidden by grizzled eyebrows. A formidable man, his voice an angry growl.

"We will bring a new order to America. Before I'm done your people will be as quick to heel as my wolfhounds."

"Americans don't heel, General. You are sure to be disappointed," Mr. Livingston says, managing to sound relaxed. This oaf is not going to unsettle the gentleman from New York. "And we have treaty rights on the Mississippi that are being violated as we speak. We will expect you to correct that promptly."

The general raises both hands, palms out. "None of our doing. That was the Spanish. But convenient—means we take it with the river already closed."

"Be careful, sir. We have treaty rights on that river—signed by Mr. Pinckney in Madrid in 1795, terms perfectly clear. I will send you a copy."

"Hah! Treaty—it's so much wastepaper—use it to wipe your bum; it's worth nothing more!"

"Sir!" Mr. Livingston lets his voice rise. "Is that French honor? To violate sworn word between nations?"

The general's voice goes soft and silky. "Do not dare mention French honor in my presence or I may feel compelled to uphold it."

"I am at your service, sir," Mr. Livingston says. Dolley's eyes widen as she reads this. The gentleman from New York is placing himself in terrible danger. He makes it clear he is no duelist, but he is not prepared to be backed down by this French scoundrel. He decides to buy the finest dueling pistols in Paris and practice for an hour each day.

The general looks as if the water has suddenly become deeper than he expected. He draws himself up. "Easily said, sir, when you know I must depart for Holland within the hour."

"Whenever you find time, I am at your service."

The general gives him an evil grin. "Perhaps I will avenge your impertinence on your countrymen." He slaps his gloves against his palm, bows, murmurs, "Your servant, sir," and is gone.

The letter ended there. She was in tears as she refolded it. Nothing had changed after all. The sale that Mr. Du Pont envisioned was a feckless dream. The French were still coming with a massive army under a general fully as ferocious as Leclerc. They would crush the blacks at Santo

Domingo and come on to the Mississippi, and we must rally an army to meet them with all our recent hopes gone glimmering.

Then it struck her that Victor and his army were already in Santo Domingo. They would have sailed as rapidly as the ship that brought Mr. Livingston's letter. Why, they might even be in New Orleans now, at this very moment!

In the bedroom she found Jimmy lying in the dark with his eyes open. Without a word she lay beside him and put her head on his shoulder.

A week later another letter from Livingston: Ice had trapped General Victor's fleet in Holland. He couldn't sail until March. A breathing space, that's all.

Things were coming down to scratch. Madison had one real card left, and it was time to play it. After that, war, which probably would leave us tied to the British empire and mark the end of our brilliant common man democracy.

So at dusk one afternoon, with storm clouds roiling on the horizon, Madison watched a closed carriage stop on Pennsylvania Avenue. Young Lewis, sitting his horse nearby, gave a slight nod. Madison opened the carriage door and stepped in.

"By God, I was glad to hear from you," said Jim Ross. "My people are demanding I speak out and I've been holding them off, but I can't no longer. So . . ."

Madison admired the Pennsylvania senator's fortitude. As the westernmost Federalist, Ross was his party's designated speaker to demand forceful action against the French while denouncing democratic failures. The folks at home in Pittsburgh were pushing him, but so were his party chiefs.

"Let's pour it on," Madison said. "Stronger the better. Let's show the world your party is ready to fight."

"Hell, yes, we're ready. We're sick to death of this piddling and hoping and waiting. It's beyond time to fight!"

"Exactly. So lay your bill out. We'll debate awhile, and then of course, we'll have to defeat you."

"Oh?" Ross was suddenly wary. It was too dark to see in the closed carriage to be sure, but the senator's round, red face probably was going purple.

"Then," Madison added, "we'll pass a bill that will be stronger still. Let the world see we're united on this."

There was a long pause. The carriage lurched into a mud-hole. A passing carriage—Madison heard horse's hoofs—splashed mud that he heard spatter against the side and Merry yelled something. At last Ross wagged his finger, a white flicker in the dark carriage, and said, "Listen to me now. You betray me, you beat me and don't pass a bill of your own, I'll make you pay and pay. I'll shout these meetings from the housetops. Do you understand?"

"Fair enough . . ."

So Ross took the floor in the Senate chamber with its carved panels and draped flags to offer a bill raising an army of fifty thousand men and appropriating five million dollars for an immediate attack on New Orleans.

"Let's go *take* the place!" he roared. "Make it our own in fact of occupation when everyone knows it's ours by right of reason, by right of the rivers that flow past our doorsteps and collect in a single mighty stream at New Orleans. Our lifeblood runs down that river. Who can say it's not ours!"

Madison was delighted. He sat listening in the gallery with Harrison Smith, Maggie's husband and editor of the *National Intelligencer.* Smith's pencil was flying as Ross shouted, "For years we've acquiesced in Spanish control, letting them have what we so easily could have taken, and what has it gotten us? Abuse, insult, pecksniffs thinking they can slam the door in our faces, baiting us to do something about it.

"Our people clamor for war. No damned evil foreign power will dismember the fairest land under God's sun. And who is this evil power? France, once our friend, now corrupted, with all its noble hopes destroyed as unfettered democracy ran amok and gave natural rise to the dictator who brings order out of chaos by crushing freedom."

Cries from the floor, "Hear! Hear!" Federalists were overjoyed to hear their core beliefs so clearly stated. It was just as Madison had hoped.

"Oh, our blind friends on the other side of the aisle!" Ross shouted, glaring around the chamber. "Remember that *we* saw the danger, *we* said join our British brethren and destroy the usurper of liberty before he usurps world liberty. And so it has come to pass, democracy without restraint spawning the man who would dismember our nation. But we'll never allow it, never! We must march on New Orleans and take it once and for all!

"The time is now! Not a moment to lose. We must have courage, be daring, show the fortitude that made this country great—we must take our destiny into our own hands. . . ."

Perfect! Every time Mr. Smith's flying pencil flagged, Madison nudged him. Get it all, sir, get it all. Madison had posted Pichon outside the chamber, and Ross hurried out and gave the whole speech again for his benefit. Inside, Sam Smith of Maryland, that darling of the radical Democrats, shouted that he believed a state of war with France already existed! Madison couldn't have put it better himself. The Democrats finally defeated the Ross bill. Breckinridge of Kentucky offered a substitute bill—*eighty* thousand men— that passed in a roar.

Madison accompanied Smith to the *Intelligencer*'s office and waited while Smith set his story, flying fingers pulling letters from the type case as the words formed. They wrapped the first dozen copies in oilskin, and Johnny Graham galloped toward Annapolis with the packet. He would cover the thirty-odd miles in under four hours, changing horses every few miles.

A swift merchant brig lay on the hook off Annapolis, its longboat at the dock. A lieutenant took the packet, and Johnny watched the boat pull for the brig, oars flashing. It lay alongside and was hoisted aboard, men ran aloft, the anchor windlass cranked, the big square sails shook out, and the brig took the wind, running down Chesapeake Bay toward the sea.

So went the last great effort. Robert Livingston's most significant contribution had been a bit of gossip: Napoleon read *The Times of London* daily, had it sent over in the diplomatic pouch, lay soaking for several hours each day in a vast marble tub thinking and conferring with his courtiers and reading history—and reading *The Times*.

The brig would cross the Atlantic and run up the Thames, and the captain would hurry the packet to the American embassy. Rufus King would take it to the editors of *The Times*, who would find the American shift toward war with France welcome news well worth splashing. And two or three days later the first consul, who listened to no one, who ignored Livingston and Pichon, Clark and DuPont, and all who'd tried for his ear, would have the message laid in his hand in columns of hard type.

The Americans were united and gearing for war. Was that really what Napoleon Bonaparte wanted?

37

WASHINGTON, EARLY SPRING 1803

The note a steward handed Lewis when he returned to the mansion late in the afternoon was brief.

"Pls. see me at eight in the morn. TJ"

Why did it have an ominous ring? Such a summons meant it involved him directly rather than just requiring his services to deliver something to the Hill, like the glorified errand boy he really was. As the administration had grown ever more preoccupied with the French crisis, Lewis had found himself taking ever longer walks, eight, ten, fifteen miles. Toughening himself for the expedition, he told himself, but knew better: He was walking off frustration lest he blow right there in the mansion like a bottle of cider fermenting in the sun.

The president had been that close—that close!—to turning him loose to start the great adventure, and then the French business had shut everything down. But this forever waiting abraded his nerves and there were times he was close to marching into the great man's office and . . . but then, there was a quality in President Jefferson, and in Mr. Madison too, that made it not that easy to get up on your high horse. Something in their faces, in their manner, gracious and courteous as they were, told you to walk softly. There was a power in both of them that no one with any sense would cross lightly.

Anyway, he had to grin at himself a little: if he really were so ready to beard the man in his den, why did the summons have an ominous ring?

"I think it's time we got on with it," the president said.

A candle flickered under the silver coffee service. He had poured his clerk a cup and urged a sweet roll on him and there had been a desultory moment and then it was to business.

"I've been pondering this for some days," Mr. Jefferson said. "Yes, it looks like war, but a dozen men won't make that much difference. I want this expedition to go no matter what."

That was good news! And how like Mr. J. to ponder it for days, then slap him with the decision.

"Now, you have crucial study yet before you from men who can better teach you than I can. Botany, medicine, celestial navigation, taxidermy—and that's just a start on the essentials. I've already written Mr. Ellicott and Dr. Rush and Dr. Bartram, and the others, told them to expect you in

Philadelphia momentarily. Also, that's the place for the supplies you must begin gathering now. So can you leave today? Or in the morning?"

"Mr. President, I—"

"I'd like the expedition to push off this year and get on up the Missouri a ways and at the crack of next spring be ready for the great assault on the mountains. We have initial authorization from Congress now; best to strike before minds change. Looking at the maps, you might be able to get eight hundred miles or so upriver before winter catches you. What do you think?"

He saw that in Mr. Jefferson's mind the expedition was akin to strolling the banks of the Potomac.

"We might get that far, yes, sir," he said slowly.

"Well," the president said, "not if you don't get started. Can you leave today? Tomorrow?"

"Sir, I'd like to go first to Harper's Ferry. Gather weapons from the United States arsenal there—and then there's the boat idea—"

"Oh, yes, the boat . . ." The president had been enthusiastic when Lewis had first described the idea, an iron frame carried in parts that bolted together and, covered with waterproofed skins, would give them a vessel wherever they found a body of water in the mountains. But now he was frowning. "I'd really like you to get on with the study we've outlined. And gathering your supplies—I know you have lists and plans but it'll take time actually to purchase everything. The Schuykill arsenal in Philadelphia can supply weapons, surely, and as for the boat, I suppose any competent smith could—"

"Sir, pardon me, but the rifles we carry will be at the heart of the expedition. You live or die by your weapons in the field, for defense, for impressing the Indians, for hunting. I want to be sure of the best, I want weapons made to my order."

"Well, that makes sense."

"As for the boat, I disagree that any competent smith—it's

full of complex curves. They're specialists in iron at Harper's Ferry—best in the country—"

"All right, Merry. You're the better judge of what you'll need, I suppose. How long will it take?"

"I should be through there in a week."

"A week . . . well, that's not so bad." He smiled. "All right, son, you're off. And great good fortune to you."

It was eighty-odd miles to Harper's Ferry where the Shenandoah met the Potomac and carved a great gash in the mountains for its race to the sea. After Leesburg the passengers had to get out every half mile or so in ankle-deep mud and push the stage out of mudholes and up hills. It was late the third day before they arrived. Wrapped in silence, Lewis reviewed everything as the stage lurched and the whip popped like pistol fire. The thing about Mr. Jefferson; he was a scientist. A philosopher. An international tactician, a student of government, an authority on liberty, ranking intellectual—but he'd never been on the trail beyond the occasional hunt.

The president had always been an enthusiast for western exploration, but it had taken Mackenzie's book to jar him into real action. They'd known for a long time that the British North West Company traveler had gone down a river that clearly wasn't the *Columbia,* abandoned it at impassable rapids, and gone overland to the Pacific. Indeed, the president had mentioned it that night he talked of exploration.

But the book seized his attention for what Mackenzie said he had written on a rock in paint of vermilion and hot grease: "Alexander Mackenzie, from Canada, by land, the twenty-second of July, one thousand seven hundred and ninety-three."

By land! Instantly, the president had decided that time was critical and pressed Lewis into a fresh study of botany that he might be fully attuned to new plants he'd find in a march across the continent. This was last summer at Monticello, and each day they'd walked for miles examining foliage, the president lecturing. Lewis was a good self-taught botanist after those years prowling the Carolina wilderness, but the old man was a professor. Plants, their form, their infinite distinguishing marks, the subtle differentiating points in similar species and in variations within a species, the differences accountable to soil, water, location, and light, the way plants could fool you, Latin designations and why they mattered, and every time Lewis decided he'd learned it all, the old man unfolded a new wrinkle. No wonder they said he was a genius! On top of everything else, he was a botanist of a range Lewis knew he never would obtain.

All this with the French doing their damnedest to crowd him into war.

The stage crept into Harper's Ferry at near midnight. In the morning, boots newly blacked, he set out for the U.S. arsenal. The town consisted of a single dirt street running along the river. He supposed Mr. Harper was long dead, but the three-way ferry crossing into the western wilderness of Virginia and into Maryland was the main industry after the arsenal, which he found in small brick buildings along the river, its basic power source. He saw forges glowing in several buildings. This, with a similar institution in Springfield, Massachusetts, was the supplier of weapons for the United States government.

The superintendent spent a long time examining the letter of authorization from the secretary of war that Lewis presented. Joseph Perkins was tall and lean, with a mustache that looked chewed on and a nervous tremor around his eyes. Lewis would have preferred something a bit more emphatic than the single sentence Dearborn had written instructing Perkins to cooperate with Lewis. Made you wonder how warmly the secretary endorsed the expedition.

Perkins looked up with a frown. "I know nothing of this," he said. He seemed to bite off his words.

Lewis said it all had come up suddenly, and there'd been no time to forewarn. Perkins seemed not at all mollified.

"Nothing in here modifies my basic orders," he said.

"Sir?"

"We're working desperately to rearm the army for war. You understand that, don't you, Captain? You *are* aware that war with France threatens?"

A fire began to burn in Lewis. He was under a little too much pressure to enjoy sarcasm. "Yes, sir," he said, "I'm aware of that, and of course the president is too. If you find the orders of the secretary of war insufficient, I'm sure the president would be glad to write you more specifically. Take a week round trip, I suppose, but—"

Perkins's voice rose a couple of octaves. "I said nothing of the sort, sir! Nothing! Of course I will obey the secretary's orders and I resent suggestions—"

"I meant no suggestions," Lewis said smoothly, and went on to cite his needs. The weapons needed would present no problem, Perkins said, but an odd distaste swept his face over the boat.

"My men are gunsmiths, not blacksmiths," he said.

"But you have the stock, the forges, your men work in iron. Granted it's a new idea, but I have complete plans."

Long silence. Then Perkins sighed. "I have a couple of men who might take it on. They make different things—replacement parts for wagons and gun carriages and the like. I even catch them making toys sometimes. . . ."

"They sound ideal," Lewis said. But it was clear he would have to press for whatever he wanted here. Perhaps Perkins would have warmed if he'd known Lewis's plans, but they were still secret. He would be crossing territory of France or Spain, one or the other, and there was no need to advertise it. So his story was that he planned an upper Mississippi trek, and everyone yawned.

A foreman named Jennings led him down the line of buildings. At a smaller one to which an oversized forge was attached underneath a shed, Jennings thrust his head in the door and shouted, "Jimson!"

"He's in the privy," a voice said.

"That you, Little Bit? Tell Jimson to get his ass in here. Man wants to see him."

A small, slender man with a huge beard bobbed up from

behind a counter. "Captain," Mr. Jennings said, "this here is Little Bit Jones," Mr. Jennings said. "Bit, Mr. Perkins, he says you and Jimson are to give Captain Lewis whatever he wants."

There were several anvils in different shapes mounted on rounds from a big tree trunk, iron of all shapes and sizes piled in a corner, hammers and tongs and all sorts of smithy tools hanging from pegs on the inside log walls over a heavy bench supported in front by smaller logs. Everything was massive and spoke of strength. Which applied as well to the man who now bounded through the door, dragging up his pants and hitching suspenders into place.

"Bit," he shouted, "what you doing yelling at me? Man taking a crap don't like to be disturbed." He had black hair that fell to his shoulders and his face was red. His shirt of homespun looked ready to tear on his massive shoulders. Little Bit jerked a thumb toward Lewis.

"Oh," the big man said. Then he extended a hand. "Jimson Cotton," he said.

"Meriwether Lewis." He took the proffered hand, wondering if his would be crushed, but the other's touch was light. He explained himself, Little Bit confirming their orders.

Jimson leaned on his bench. "I bet ol' Perkins was right happy to see you."

Lewis hesitated. "More or less," he said.

Both men guffawed. "He's on us all the time, get this done, why ain't that done—but we don't let him fuss us."

Lewis described his boat concept. It would mean fifty or sixty iron rods rigged to bolt together in the shape of a boat, which then could be covered with waterproofed skins.

"Why you want to do that?" Cotton said.

Lewis explained the idea of portaging, of reaching a point at which regular boats must stop, marching overland with packs on their backs, finding a new body of water, and having a boat that could be readied in a few days. He unfolded his plans.

"Gor!" Bit said. "A portable boat."

But Cotton shook his head. "Naw. We can't make nothing like that. Can't be done."

Lewis smiled. "Why not?"

" 'Cause I ain't never made nothing like that. Never even heard of the likes of it."

"You can get rod iron, can't you? See, it's really just a series of rods, fifty or sixty, with flanges to hold bolts."

"Why," said Little Bit, "ain't that smart? Look, Jimson, you just bolt all them rods together and it's in the shape of a boat." The big man was frowning. "Cover it in skins like the cap'n says, get them all tarred, oughta float like a cork."

"Maybe . . . ," Jimson said doubtfully. "But look at all them curves. How we going to match those?" He dropped a heavy finger on bow and stern. "Curves on paper, that's easy enough. But putting them in iron—what are you going to do, hold 'em up against the paper?"

"Templates, maybe? Wooden templates?" Bit's voice was small.

"Shut up, Bit! I'm thinking." A silence. "Well, Cap'n, straight pieces are easy enough, and you got the same curves at each end, right? Now what we'll have to do, we'll build one end in wood, then keep bending our pieces till they fit the wood. What we call templates."

"Sounds excellent," Lewis said. He didn't look at Bit. "Let's get the carpenters in."

"Bit," Jimson said, "go get old Mayfield. Tell him to bring his box; he'll have to build it right here off the plans."

They watched Bit scurry out the door. "Straight rods for the length of her, we can start on that now. It's them curves that trouble. I reckon we can get it done, but it ain't going to be fast. Some weeks, at least."

Weeks? After a single week the president expected him in Philadelphia. Yet he couldn't just leave this in the hands of Jimson and Bit. They would have to move along, but he didn't need to say that now.

● ● ●

For two years Lewis and his men must feed and defend themselves solely with the arms they carried. Yet he could hardly come to Indian country looking as if he came for war. Muskets, a couple of blunderbusses firing scattershot, two small cannon that could deliver charges of grape, but the core of his defenses would be rifles crafted to his design.

Mr. Perkins gazed with interest at Lewis's drawings; weapons were his business. Take their standard rifle, fifty-four caliber, barrel hexagonal for strength, highly reliable flintlock, 1803 model standing as tall as a small man. It was a fine weapon and it went against the older man's grain to plan alternations, but he was a professional and he listened.

Shorten the barrel to thirty-three inches. Round the part extending beyond the stock to reduce weight. Weld ramrod holder to the barrel. Cut the stock down to bring overall length under four feet—forty-seven inches to be exact. The result would be a carbine versatile in the close confines of a boat and in dense brush, where hunting would be good and ambush would be a threat.

At last Perkins nodded. "Yep," he said slowly, "I'll put a couple of men on it. Two weeks, say three to be safe."

But he didn't have weeks! Couldn't they use more men?

Perkins gave him a cold look. "If the president tells me to cancel my regular schedules in order to do these chores for you, of course I'll comply."

But the president didn't want him here anyway! Indeed, Mr. Jefferson assumed Lewis was en route now; soon the scientists awaiting him in Philadelphia would be writing the president to ask if his man was still coming. Lewis's breath felt short.

Slowly the bow of a boat took shape in wood before Jimson Cotton's shop. Mayfield proved to be a talented if irascible man of indeterminate age, his shirt stained with the tobacco juice that dribbled from his mouth as he worked. He endured a great many jokes—did Noah chew tobacco? Was that an ark he was building?—but under his skilled hands the design that until now had been only on paper was taking shape, bow nicely curved to a point, ribs rising in a graceful round.

Cotton and Bit laid in a store of straight rods for the long middle section of the forty-foot vessel and devised a light-weight flange at the end of each for the linking bolts. Cotton watched Mayfield's work carefully, offering suggestions that clearly improved the design. It was becoming real before Lewis's eyes but the idea of the president wondering where the hell his wandering secretary had gone still hollowed out his guts.

His supplies were piling up in Philadelphia even as he lingered at Harper's Ferry. Bar lead and bullet molds; fifty-two pounds of the best European powder sealed in lead canisters that when emptied could be melted into bullets; five hundred best rifles flints from England, two hundred musket flints, fighting knives, tomahawks, two espontoons that hadn't been standard since medieval war but would function as pikes—all this just starting the list. Chisels, nails, rope, awls, needles, lamps, cord, fishhooks and line, kettles, axes, spades, files, augers, a vise, oilcloth. He thought of something new every day. Spices, salt, tobacco, whiskey, salt meat, and another invention of which he was proud, worked out with a Philadelphia chef, portable soup, dry matter that would keep forever till boiled in water. Six hundred pounds of trade goods to give Indians on arrival and then swap for food and later, when they reached the mountains, for horses. These were mostly beads, the currency of the frontier, and mirrors, kettles, knives, medals, scarlet cloth, uniform jackets.

He now saw that a single boat couldn't possibly contain all he must haul up the Missouri to keep his men alive. A keelboat and a Saint Louis bateau at the least. That meant he'd need more men than the dozen planned—hunters ranging the shore for game, men on tow ropes dragging the boats upstream, men to handle the sheer bulk of supplies. Thirty to forty would be more like it.

He would name sergeants from the ranks, but he would need a second-in-command. He had just the candidate, too, except that if Will Clark accepted it would have to be as co-commander. Will wouldn't take an inferior position. He had been captain commanding the Mounted Rifle Company when Lewis was a lieutenant, and they had become fast friends until Clark left the army to care for an ailing family. Given equality, Lewis would eat his hat if Clark didn't leap at the great adventure.

The weapons were ready. Lewis had been three weeks in Harper's Ferry. He'd started a half-dozen letters to the president trying to justify his delay but finished none. One by one he sighted in the rifles till they were dead accurate. Only the boat remained. Cotton and Mayfield had dismantled the finished wooden form and created a series of templates against which to measure each curved piece of iron. There was nothing that more men could have done even if Perkins would permit it, and he knew that to ask would insult his artisans. Cotton was hard at it now. But he must heat each piece to a vivid glow, bend it a little farther, and then cool it in water before he could lay it against the wooden template. Might take a dozen fittings to get the final nuances of the curve set. Still, piece by piece, bolt flanges in place, it was taking shape. Then the bow was finished and Cotton started on the ribs. Lewis and Bit bolted the bow together. It looked perfect. He felt a glow of pride until he thought of the waiting president.

He must walk! It was always the cure for his upsets of mind. He primed his pistol, closed the cap, stuck it in his waistband, and set out down the path along the river. He saw only a few men and spoke to none, walking as if he were pursued. Men gave him an odd look and stepped out of his way, and he walked with grim intent, pounding along, eyes locked on the path before him. He couldn't go on with this feeling of guilt!

Well, what of Mr. Jefferson? The president's interest in the expedition was intellectual and scientific. Yes, finding the Northwest Passage was the primary objective, but he also hoped that countless new plants and animals would be found, each to be classified by the methods Linnaeus had devised milleniums past. The expedition commander must know celestial navigation; how else would he pinpoint the

Northwest Passage for others to find? He must know medicine; how else to care for thirty to forty men far beyond the farthest frontier? He must understand ethnic studies and be able to classify and delineate the tribes he met and their languages. All awaited him in Philadelphia.

He had not written nor had the president written him. Now this took on an ominous note. He felt sure the president was furious, his very silence a reprimand. Perhaps Lewis should have written and explained himself, but he hadn't and now it seemed very late to do so. Yet, damn it, he really didn't feel guilty! Botany was just fine, but Captain Lewis was a field commander and he had an understanding of the problems of leading a band of soldiers through strange territory that Mr. Jefferson would never have.

Take the puzzle of the terrain itself. The Missouri would take them far to the West, but no one knew how far. Did it come from the mountains, or did it swing down from mountains far to the north? Or to the south? When the river dried up or took turns that no longer served them, they would have to start overland, with horses if no water was near, by portage if water was within range. The keelboat would be too heavy to move; they would have to sink it where they left the river for use on their return. It might be possible to move the smaller bateau with rounded logs serving as rollers but not very far. At that point, see the incredible value of a boat that weighed under a hundred pounds, that one man could carry in its dismantled state but when assembled could float two thousand pounds! They must run out of river when they came to the mountains, but mountains are full of streams and lakes.

The boat he had devised could mean the real difference between success and failure. Whether a new plant was identified now or at some later day was really small potatoes compared to this. Notice that if in the end the expedition failed, it would be his failure, not Mr. Jefferson's. And that was right too, for he was the field commander, he was the cap'n to whom the men would look, he who would make the crucial decisions.

He tore off a branch, trimmed it with his hand axe for a walking staff, and pounded on. People he met pulled to one side to give him room. Turning over his situation with all its confusions, he had a sudden engulfing memory. His father, who'd died when he was only five, so at that time he probably wasn't over four, had been demanding something of him. He had been desperate to comply but couldn't, didn't know or couldn't find or was afraid—all he remembered now was the powerful feeling, the great figure who he so wanted to please radiating disappointment—

But wait! That memory dredged from deep in his mind was not real or rather, not germane. He was no longer that wistful child. He had grown to take his father's place; the mighty figure in command was he himself!

At once he saw the full reality. So long as he was Mr. Jefferson's secretary, the president was in command. But the moment he moved into the expedition, their positions reversed. Mr. Jefferson had already surrendered command, only he didn't yet know it, for how could he even understand the issue? Indeed, it was not for him to surrender, but for Captain Lewis to *take* command. And that act was overdue and had been for the month Lewis had anguished at Harper's Ferry.

The boat, in his command judgment, was more important than botany. Hence, taking the time to perfect it, putting his men and their equipment before science, was justified. No one else could make that decision for no one else knew, nor did anyone else have the authority. As he had the authority, so he had the responsibility to his men, to the country, to science, to the president. Because he was responsible he must use his own best judgment in responding.

Time for him to write the president and explain—but not to apologize. Describe his own frustration at the delays, not that he understood the president was frustrated. It didn't matter what the president felt; he had become a spectator whether he knew it or liked it or not. If he were angry, now was the time to have it out. But somehow he knew that Mr.

Jefferson wouldn't be angry. This stress and strain had been of his own making, and it was rapidly dissipating.

Yet as he turned back toward Harper's Ferry, walking in ever swifter strides, filled with certainty, he felt he had crossed a great divide, gone from youth to manhood, from subordinate to leader. Everything seemed different now, and it struck him that this transition that he hadn't even understood yesterday had been the remaining essential. He could not lead a great expedition until he was solid within himself.

That evening he wrote Mr. Jefferson explaining that, despite his distress at the delay, he judged the boat worth waiting for. Two days later he had the presidential letter he had been dreading, it having crossed his in the mail. Mr. Jefferson was warm and friendly; he was sure any delays were caused by necessity.

A few days later Captain Lewis covered the finished frame with tarred skins, and she floated perfectly. A boat that in its bare frame weighed ninety-seven pounds would carry near two thousand pounds of supplies. It was a triumph!

The next day he set out for Philadelphia, pleased and relaxed. War now seemed certain—no break had come in the month he had passed at Harper's Ferry—and he would be marching across enemy territory. But he set the thought aside; the chance that French patrols would find him would be like two needles getting together in a haystack. His goal was the Northwest Passage to the Pacific, and he was sure that he would make it.

38

Dolley felt enervated and sad. She was sure she was coming down with a cold or the flu or pneumonia or some dreadful thing but no symptoms arose and after a while she realized she simply was sick at heart. Two months had passed and nothing suggested Napoleon Bonaparte was any the less eager for war.

The embers of his war with England and its allies, scarcely banked during the temporary truce, flamed into the open again. Malta or war, he had told the British envoy; but the British knew if they gave up the Mediterranean island, it would become the staging place for a new French assault on Egypt and after that on its empire in India. To force the United States to join the war on the British side seemed foolish, but they waited in vain for any sign that the man heard or cared. Their every move was another head butted into a stone wall.

The president named Gov. James Monroe of Virginia as envoy extraordinary and dispatched him to Paris to support Mr. Livingston. Support? What did that mean? Dolley thought it pointless and a reproach to Mr. Livingston, who had given it eighteen months of heroic effort. But Jimmy snapped that effort without results didn't mean much, and anyway, this was another signal, once more to the French but also to our own West, showing them we were doing something, anything.

The Monroes weren't *her* idea of diplomats, certainly. Elizabeth's restraint, if that was the right word, was often mistaken for hostility, and her husband's manner was scarcely better. He was intelligent, able, unfailingly decent, and always ready for public service; but he also was hungry for fame and position, and in personality was vain, proud, and almost totally humorless. Of course he must collide with Mr. Livingston; each would bring out the worst in the other. What could he accomplish that the New Yorker couldn't?

But she said nothing for she knew Jimmy would scent out her real motives—which she was quite willing to admit to herself—and declare them ignoble. The truth was that she had been watching the question of who would succeed Tom in the President's House. It already was being debated in the party, so vigorous was Tom's insistence that he couldn't wait to get back to his farm on the Virginia hill. The radical Democrats, Chairman Randolph and their old friend Sam Smith in the Senate, had never gotten beyond their fury when they found the administration wouldn't give them the clean ideological sweep they had expected. Now they couldn't wait for Tom to go so they could install one of their own to work the revolution they felt he had denied them, and James Monroe was the horse they expected to ride into office.

But when Tom did step down, not soon, she hoped, she wanted Jimmy to step into his spot. Was this ambitious and self-seeking? Absolutely, and why not? Didn't everyone seek for himself? Hadn't Monroe accepted in the full knowledge that success in Paris could make him the next president? But Jimmy would pish tosh the whole idea. Jimmy was a darling and brilliant, but sometimes he was just too noble!

Or was she ignoble and perhaps foolish to boot, worrying about succession when war with the French and consequent submission to Britain would ruin them anyway, providing new life to old Federalist claims and make Mr. Hamilton and company, the darlings of the day and arbiters of the American future . . . which, in her view, would be the ultimate disaster of war.

Monroe departed late and there had been no word from him. Their last shards of time ran out. The president called a cabinet meeting to approve seeking alliance with Great

Britain. We would make ourselves junior partner to the mistress of the seas, ready to jump when she cracked the whip. There was nothing the British knew better than how to crack the whip.

It meant war within weeks and the very thought took away any desire to socialize. She canceled a game of whist and waited at home for Jimmy's return, knowing he would be sore of heart and would need her. Her windows were open and the drifting scent of some flowering tree came as a mockery in this season of despair.

She saw Mr. Cutts approaching the house and heard Anna clattering down the steps, off to still another party. "Don't wait up for me, Dolley." All this youthful exuberance made her think of Merry, who was just back from Philadelphia, different now, somehow—he seemed older or perhaps stronger in some way. Thank God she had abandoned her feckless idea of forcing an apology from Anna. It would have been presumptuous.

It came as a surprise to realize that when war came Merry would be crossing enemy territory—and her surprise told her she still had not grasped the harsh reality of war, which in turn suggested how ill prepared Americans in general would be despite the war talk they flung around so casually. Talk is so cheap. . . .

Apparently the expedition would be going, war or no war. Merry had joined her briefly one day when she was sunning herself on the mansion's south terrace, and she'd been impressed by the extent of his tutoring from Dr. Rush and the others in Philadelphia. She knew Dr. Rush well—a strange, romantic figure and a superb physician, who responded unfailingly to a pretty woman. Merry talked on and on about celestial navigation, quite losing her in the process, but it all emphasized the chilling fact that they would be on their own in the wilderness for two years or more—what a grand and awesome venture!

She knew privately that he'd had another romance too. Poor Merry didn't find women easy. A letter from Millie Sandwich in Philadelphia said that Merry had cut quite a swath with the Landros girl, and then it had all collapsed and June Landros went off to an aunt's in New York City. June's mother said that Merry had become very interested overnight, which had been startling and even alarming, given his force and intensity. Apparently June had been— well, frightened was not too strong a word, so said Millie. Dolley thought of the way Anna, now about to marry Mr. Cutts, had recoiled; there *was* something frightening about Merry. Perhaps it would take a real woman to handle him, while he, defeating himself, turned to girls like Anna. He'd need luck to find the right woman.

The contemplation of which, she supposed, was as profitable as thinking about war.

Jimmy came home exhausted. Yes, the cabinet had met and Tom had asked for and been given a vote for war. We would petition Britain immediately for alliance and support, which would put the Royal Navy behind us. Did we know what terms they would exact? Jimmy shrugged. Petitioners take what they get.

Meanwhile, our forces were preparing. Jimmy said Jackson's Tennessee militia and troops in Mississippi Territory were ready to move downriver, some four thousand men, Kentucky and Ohio troops to follow. They'd look to the Royal Navy to blockade the mouth of the river and the Mississippi Sound, stretching along the coast to Mobile. The ice in Holland long since had melted, and General Victor must be in Santo Domingo by now; so the troops he was sending to New Orleans could well be waiting there when our men arrived. But after the British sealed the coast against reinforcements, we could grind them down.

"How does Tom take it?" she said. They were in the bedroom by the open window. A flowering tree somewhere near gave a pungent odor and a mocker sang.

"Very hard, I think." They were silent a moment before he added, "He wants us to come for tea."

She was surprised, but he said, "We're the only guests. When things are bad you want to be with people you care for. We're about the only family he has; the girls come so rarely."

Well, Patsy and Polly were married with homes of their own, and she also suspected that with a widower's obsessive attention to his grown children, Tom wasn't an easy father.

"He cares for us, you know, both of us," he added. Yes, he did, and she cared for him, too, this tall, strange, fascinating man—she's often irked, she feels that Jimmy works and he gets the credit, she hears him say things that are weird, things she doubts he believes and knows she doesn't, and yet she knows that he has a profound philosophic grasp and immense insight into the nature of government, which, he's fond of saying, is just a framework in which humans may interact without killing each other.

And yes, in this moment of despair, it would be good to be with a friend whose feeling equaled theirs, just to sit together and warm each other. . . .

At dawn the next day Madison mounted the bay mare and set out for a brisk canter up the Rock Creek Trail. At the meadow he saw Senator Ross letting his horse crop dew-soaked grass and reined up.

"Good morning, Mr. Secretary," Ross said, mounting and turning his horse. He leaned on one stirrup to shake hands. "May I be so bold as to congratulate you? You're a fighter and you've fought the good fight. And now you've lost, and that's as it should be. You know what the cabinet meeting really means?"

"It means war," Madison said.

"Yes, sir, tomorrow or the next day. But today it means decency, for it shows love of country overcame ideology, this mad foolishness about common man democracy." He smiled, ebullient and pink-faced. "No offense meant, I assure you, but I think it really does spell the end of those faulty ideas. The people will turn back to us—we're not undemocratic, you know. We honor this republic. You don't see us trying to seize power. We'll seek the vote and abide by the result. But we know that a firm hand on the passions of the mob, a strong cadre of leaders to whom the common folk can turn, a structure that can keep folks from running wild, a financial structure that supports the controlling structure—"

"A hereditary aristocracy, in short."

"Of course—men who are born to position, who train from birth to the responsibilities of their mature years—where else can sound leadership come from?"

Madison didn't answer. It was pointless to debate after fate had betrayed them. It wasn't democracy's fault that a bullying tyrant assaulted them, but that could be enough to shatter them. He was sure that Ross read the voters correctly. Fate had produced Napoleon Bonaparte at the moment the new democracy in the young American republic was coming to full flower. Give it another decade of peace, and he believed it would be fully capable of standing alone; but fate had denied it time.

Ross smiled and Madison heard something gentle in his voice. "Come on, Jimmy, we needn't debate ideology. Let's go have a big breakfast at Absalom's."

"You go ahead, Senator," Madison said. "I don't have much appetite today."

39

WASHINGTON, LATE MAY 1803

The president received them in the oval parlor. Distress over war didn't keep Dolley from noticing how shabby it was, the walls a uniform dull oyster, nothing to set off molding and wainscoting, streaked where the leaky roof had dripped in little rivers right down the walls to strain the floors, the blue-covered furniture pedestrian at best.

Then Mr. Lemaire wheeled in a handsome cart—two kinds of tea, coffee, clever little sandwiches, and, to her surprise, a plate of fresh scones. And she understood all at once that the chief steward was fond of her—in a terrible time, he had offered her the only comfort in his power.

The president sighed and she was struck by an infinite sadness in his expression. "I suppose I'm naive," he said, but somehow the magnitude of sending young men out to die hadn't quite struck me before. General Washington knew all about this; I imagine he'd be amazed by a successor who came to understand with—well, surprise."

She wanted to pat his hand. "He wouldn't be amazed. I think he felt just the way you do, the way we all do, sad and horrified and not quite believing, even now."

"Yes," he said, "not wanting to believe. But you know, we'll leave widows and orphans at home, and some of the men who do get back will be minus arms or legs and how will they tend their farms?" He gazed from the window for a long moment and then said in a voice so low she barely caught it, "I'm learning the truth of the old cliché, that war means old men sending young men to die. Beside that, perhaps the death of a great movement loses some of its importance."

But that stirred a deep resistance in her and she said, "No! It's just a different kind of death, death of hope, death of a chance to build something new in the world. The French strangled their hope at birth, and we stand alone in the world, and now we're caught in a whirlwind that is none of our doing."

She was on the edge of her chair. "This *robs* us—steals hope and glory and possibility. And when the day comes that we have a nobility, name more important than intellect, when who you are depends on who your father was, then we'll see—" She stopped; she was telling them what they knew perfectly well and suddenly she felt foolish and she didn't like the feeling at all, even though what she'd said was the truth and worth pounding into everyone's head with a mallet. Wildly, she looked about. "Tom, why don't we make this house beautiful? You can see how much it needs loving care."

He and Jimmy were both smiling and she had the curious sense that in some obscure way they were proud of her, which pleased her and yet diminished her somehow on this very confusing day, and then Tom said, "Well, we did put on a new roof."

"Oh, really," she said, voice softening, "fixing the roof isn't loving care." But then the door opened and Mr. Wagner stepped in. He bowed to the president. "Begging your pardon, sir, but there's a message from Mr. Livingston I think the secretary will want to see. . . ."

She watched Jimmy open the packet as Wagner retreated. His eyes widened and with odd formality he said, "I believe you'll want to see this, Mr. President."

Tom scanned the first page, shuffled the others, and looked up. She saw a rush of emotion in his eyes. "Why don't I read this aloud," he said.

For once Dolley couldn't divine her husband's expression, let alone the president's. She knew they were surprised, but were they pleased, displeased, alarmed, excited, dismayed? She started to ask, but Tom was reading in a slow, measured, somehow relishing voice and she settled back to let her imagination give form to the villa on the rue Tradon that served as the American embassy and to the palace called the Tuileries, which she knew only from drawings, and the streets and the villas and the rustle of carriages at night and the crowds and the hint of music always in the distance. Paris as she dreamed it.

A great tension obviously has grown in Mr. Livingston, cold awareness that the last grains of sand are tumbling from the glass. He is growing desperate. His whole mission is to make the single man in the French government who matters see that he can only lose in Louisiana. But how to crack through arrogance?

All he can do is ingratiate himself in French society, at the salons and dinners and receptions where all diplomatic business is done, and he works with a will. His command of the

language has improved sharply, and his honest affection for
Paris and its people wins them over. The very fact that he is
well accepted tells him he is not out of imperial favor, for
society would drop him if he were.

So it's to Madame de Forza's on Monday and receptions
at the second and third consuls' on Tuesday and at Monsieur
de Talleyrand's on Wednesday and a grand circle at the second consul's on Thursday and on Friday a reception at his
own legation. He's with the minister of war on Saturday and
the next day plays chess at General Berthier's, and always he
talks in his mild way of the growing power of America. Lord
Whitworth, the austere British ambassador, tells him that
Britain is America's friend. Rumor says that Whitworth has
offered Talleyrand a huge bribe to press ahead in Louisiana
to give Britain further breathing space before war resumes.
Still, the last year has taught Mr. Livingston that all is fair in
love and diplomacy.

He hires a fine chef and builds an excellent cellar; his dinner invitations are rarely declined. Sooner or later he guides
the talk around to America and its surging growth, three
states beyond the Appalachians and more forming, the rivers
crowded with traffic, factories springing up in Massachusetts and Connecticut that will make the United States a self-
sufficient.

Bears on Chestnut Street in Philadelphia, madam? He
raises her hand to his lips. No more likely than on the
Champs-Elysèes. But further west—he glances around the
table—the people themselves are bears, for the men who
commit themselves to wilderness life are hard, strong,
brave. Their table manners are weak, but they are devils on
the barricades. There is no coercing them; you must kill
them to control them. The table is silent. He sees Marbois
nodding in confirmation, the Treasury minister remembering the happy time long ago when he had the French legation back in the days when New York was the American
capital.

So Mr. Livingston rams his head against the stones of

French indifference. He peppers the first consul with memoirs incorporating all Mr. Madison's points with imaginative twists of his own. He dilates on the American fury when their route to the sea was closed, on Senator Ross's speech, on the ominous bill to raise eighty thousand men, on the unanimity between Federalists and Democrats in their determination to resist the French, on the natural fit between the British and Americans, two seafaring peoples, on the enthusiasm in much of America for such alliance if the French press madly forward.

Mr. Livingston makes sure all this reaches the first consul. What he can't tell is whether the great man listens. His carefully drawn memoirs disappear unacknowledged into a bottomless well of silence, but he knows from the way he is received that he is respected and he knows that Napoleon, blinded by pride though he may be, is not a fool. And so he pounds and pounds. The great man is known to do much business while in his bath, lying there three and four hours a day in a marble tub as servants pour in more hot water scented with attar of roses, and it is to this scene that the gentleman from New York believes the message from the United States finally will penetrate.

But will it penetrate in time?—that is the question keeping Mr. Livingston awake at nights, for the crisis obviously is approaching, General Victor ready to sail before long, the occupation of New Orleans an apparent certainty, all their diplomatic efforts for naught.

Then *Le Moniteur* publishes a stunning article by one Colonel Sebastiani, whom Paris seems to regard as an oracle. It creates a sensation. The colonel says that Egypt, which France once held and was forced to vacate, is again ripe for the taking, and from there he sees the route open to the east clear to India, that British pearl. To that end France must have the island of Malta on the Mediterranean route to Egypt. But the British still hold Malta despite having agreed to give it up, and there is much gnashing of teeth and beating of drums for war. Lord Whitworth becomes haughty; Britain

won't even discuss Malta so long as France continues to occupy Holland, where General Victor's fleet is boarding
troops for Santo Domingo and Louisiana.

He predicts that by the time they read this, Britain and
France will be at war again.

Listening here in Washington, a sparrow pecking hope-
fully on the terrace outside, the impact of this was startling.
It was like awakening from a dream; so deeply had she
imagined herself into the story that it surprised her to remember the letter had been written nearly two months ago.

Yet with the next words the narrative swept her back into
the story. At the next reception, Mr. Livingston positions
himself near Lord Whitworth, and he hears Napoleon say to
the Briton, "I find, my lord, your nation wants war again!"
"No, sir," says Whitworth, "we wish for peace." Napoleon
draws himself up. "We will have Malta or we will have
war!" He stalks away. The story radiates across Europe and
the nations prepare. Can they really think of Santo Domingo
and Louisiana at such a time? General Victor is ready to cast
off, but Britain fears that the talk of Louisiana is a ruse and
that Victor's real aim is invasion of Britain. The Royal Navy
throws a blockade across the English Channel and locks his
fleet in Holland.

That is something, at least; the fearsome general and his
troops won't be going to New Orleans, at least not now.

Napoleon is said to be the most brilliant general since
Alexander, which Mr. Livingston has no reason to doubt, but
even he will have his hands full at war with the British. This
is no time to embark on American adventures that are sure to
be fatal. Mr. Livingston rallies new arguments, papers, as-
sessments, reports of America's growth and its arming itself,
and the fury for war possessing the American people and
hurls them over that stone wall to the great man in his rose-
scented bath. Blow by blow, paper by paper, he believes they
are penetrating.

So he stands on the cusp of success when the diplomatic
packet from Washington delivers a staggering blow: James

Monroe of Virginia has been named envoy extraordinary and dispatched to Paris to support him.

Support! How perfectly outrageous!

The most casual glance between the lines makes Mr. Livingston's feelings clear. The plain fact is that alone he has piloted the ship of state to within sight of the dock, and then they send a new pilot to seize the success for himself. Why, this would enrage a saint! Doesn't it speak to that old rivalry between Virginia and New York that is so evident in the way they abused Aaron Burr? Not that he cares much for Burr, but can anyone believe that two Virginians sending another Virginian to take New York's triumph is just an accident?

But lamentations are beneath a man of his caliber. He came to serve his country, not himself. Yet serving his country is the point of his dismay too, for step by step he has built the American case, he has made the haut monde of Paris respect him, he has shown American reality to the dictator in his tub—and now Monroe will have to start over. Everything will stop for another year while the newcomer establishes himself. And this at just the moment when crisis could open the door to success. Nor is it all that clear that Monroe can establish himself, for he's hardly popular here. He's a radical Democrat when democracy is newly out of fashion in France. On a prior tour he was a rapt enthusiast of the French Revolution, an attitude drawing chilly frowns in the current imperial climate. In short, forgetting personalities, the appointment is an American disaster.

Unless . . . *yes*! If he can strike now, generate movement, bring this to conclusion, win his case *before* Monroe arrives, he can yet save his nation. And drop a memorandum of agreement into the Virginian's hand when he arrives. . . .

But Talleyrand throws renewed overtures back in his face. No word comes from the great man's tub. Napoleon's brothers, Joseph and Lucien, cut Mr. Livingston on the streets. He scents British gold wherever he turns. March bends into April and Mr. Monroe is due soon. A message flashes by semaphore telegraph: The new envoy has reached Le Havre.

Then, on the morning of the day before Mr. Monroe is to arrive in Paris, a message from Talleyrand: See me at once. Mr. Livingston presents himself and ignores the usual sarcasms. The minister limps to the window, foot dragging, adjusts the glass, and stands looking out, talking over his shoulder. Meaningless chat for a quarter hour, Mr. Livingston still seated, and then with no change of inflection, Talleyrand says, "On New Orleans, now, you're always harping on the subject. I suppose you know how tedious you are? No? Ah, well, be that as it may—"

Afterward, Mr. Livingston will have trouble remembering how it struck him, so momentous, so sudden a turn, so swift the switch from dark to light, despair to hope. For Talleyrand, who has sneered at the idea of selling an inch of New Orleans, who had laughed at the thought of American rights, now says without the slightest change of inflection, "Would the United States want the whole of Louisiana?"

Mr. Livingston is struck momentarily dumb. His throat feels swollen, his tongue out of his command. "The whole?" he croaks. "All of Louisiana? You mean . . . all?" Even to himself he sounds stupid. He flounders on. "No, not really. We seek to buy New Orleans, the island, the town, you see. All? West of the river too?"

Talleyrand gives a low, sardonic chuckle. Mr. Livingston feels his face flaming. He has sounded the fool, and the Frenchman is rubbing it in.

"If we give New Orleans," the foreign minister says, "what good to us is the rest of it? If I let part of it go, I'll let it all go. So tell me, what is it worth, what will you give?"

Mr. Livingston is so flustered he quite forgets the 50 million francs he's been authorized to offer and stammers that he supposes they could manage 20 million.

"Faugh! Ridiculous. No, my dear sir, you are not thinking clearly. Take yourself off and return tomorrow with a sensible offer."

Outside Mr. Livingston walks dazedly along sundappled flagstones under a canopy of chestnuts.

The whole!

Good God—the range, the extent, the idea of vast empire, the whole middle of the continent! All they'd ever sought, even imagined possible, was New Orleans and perhaps just a sliver of that. Fifty million, he now remembers, for New Orleans alone—

Clatter of hoofs, a drayman cursing in gutter French, a horse down in the traces. The American ambassador to France has stepped blindly into the street and the enraged drayman extemporizes at a shriek on his blindness, his idiocy, his imbecilic desire to sleep in the streets, the failure of his heritage, the moronic qualities of his father and grandfather, his doltish children, the bad seed of the whole family—

"Pardon! Pardon!" he mutters and hurries along, face aflame once more.

The whole!

He scarcely sleeps that night. In the morning he goes to Talleyrand with offers prepared and is kept waiting half an hour. Mention of Louisiana produces a sneer.

"Talk to Spain; it belongs to them."

"So," says Mr. Livingston, suddenly ferocious, "you'll have no objection to my government seizing New Orleans by force," and has the satisfaction of seeing Mr. Talleyrand choke.

He reels away, dizzy. They dangle the prize, then snatch it away. What did it mean? Toying with the American? But the American had seen the tightness around Talleyrand's eyes and sensed a new strain in this imperturbable man. Something was going on; this wasn't over yet.

Mr. Monroe is to arrive this day. The thought gives him heartburn and emphasizes the irony, that on the very day the man arrives, things begin to break as Mr. Livingston has known must soon happen. Still, Mr. Monroe must be presented and accredited before he can act, until then it is more or less as if he hasn't arrived, and so it may not be necessary to describe this latest development. Not immediately, anyway.

Mr. Monroe arrives; tall, not a bad-looking chap, courteous, of course, with that odd accent you notice in Virginians, a little too proud, a bit too authoritative given that Mr. Livingston is, after all, ambassador-in-fact whether Mr. Monroe likes it or not. And when Mr. Livingston toasts his arrival with a pleasant little bon mot of the sort much favored in Paris with a double pun, one turning in on the other, Mr. Monroe appears not to understand. At least, he doesn't smile. Humorless man, perhaps—or could he be feeling superior? Mr. Livingston's manner congeals.

He gives Monroe dinner at three on this Tuesday afternoon with his senior assistants, and as coffee is served he's startled to see none other than Monsieur Marbois pacing in the legation garden. Another sign in this exceedingly strange day! Of course they're old friends, but a visit from the Treasury minister on such a day as this merits attention.

Invited in, Marbois seems tense and distracted. He draws Mr. Livingston aside: Great things are afoot and they must talk, but there are too many here today. Livingston must come to his office tonight—any time before eleven.

Monroe, no fool, sees something is going on. Livingston tells him about the abortive offer, no clear idea of what it really means. Now Marbois wants to meet at the Treasury. Monroe says he will come along. No, Monroe is not accredited. Monroe says that's only a formality and they'll be stronger as two. But Livingston has built a pattern of trust with Marbois and the minister asked for him, not for both of them. No, he says, no! He sees rage mount in Monroe's eyes.

At the Treasury Mr. Livingston describes the talk with Talleyrand. Marbois snorts. "That Talleyrand! A marplot!" He says they now have proof that the British have offered Talleyrand a million pounds to persuade Napoleon to plunge ahead in Louisiana, in hopes the Americans will keep him too busy to attack Britain until it is ready to attack him. This doesn't really disturb his excellency; to thwart it he need only ignore Talleyrand's arguments. In calling in Livingston, Talleyrand was merely hoping for something, anything, that might unhorse the first consul's great new design.

Marbois then tells Livingston an extraordinary story. It is past dark on Tuesday as they speak. It seems that on Sunday, after Easter mass at Saint Cloud, Napoleon called in Marbois and the minister of marine. Deep in his steaming bath, he said he had been thinking seriously. War is near. The intransigence of the British over Malta is intolerable. It thwarts French destiny, which is to make the Mediterranean a French lake. Now—raising a dripping finger—he likes Americans. Admires them. Believes they are a nation with a great future. He wants their friendship, and he believes it is worth more than a distant province.

Further. It has come to his attention that the Americans are distressed at the retrocession of Louisiana from Spain to France. He can understand that. Spain is a pussycat among nations, France a tiger. A tiger in your backyard is unsettling. He can see that. So he considers yielding to their requests, so respectfully tendered. He thinks of turning the whole province over to them. Furthermore, when war with the British resumes, marines on Royal Navy vessels in the Caribbean might well seize New Orleans before General Victor's troops could arrive.

In such a calamity, the generosity of the French would be compromised, for he would be passing what amounted to an empty title. If he decides to move, he will move immediately. He invites comment. Marbois congratulates his excellency's astute foreign policy. The minister of marine, anxious to have naval bases in the Caribbean, protests. The first consul bids them sleep on it and return with recommendations. But the glint in his eyes tells Marbois he already has decided.

On Monday morning Napoleon calls in Marbois alone and tells him the decision is made. "I relinquish Louisiana. I will sell it to the Americans. Their friendship is the greatest value."

Mr. Livingston sits there listening with his heart hammering. And sums up in a single breath his powerful sense that all of his work, his arguments, his memoirs hurled over the stone wall, all the points from that doughty little Mr. Madison, all of Mr. Pichon's courageously forwarded reports, why even—Mr. Livingston suddenly charitable since he can't stand Pierre Du Pont, the amateur diplomat—even by Mr. Du Pont scratching around aimlessly on the periphery—

And he whispers, "We won!"

Marbois frowns. "The first consul made a distinguished decision based on the needs of France."

Livingston smiles. "But of course. Isn't that just the point we've made all along? The best interests of France are served by passing New Orleans to us."

Marbois gives him a long look. He rises, opens a cabinet, extracts two crystal snifters, and fills each to a third with a fine cognac.

He reseats himself, lifts one of the glasses, smiles at last, and says, "All right. You've won. But you are dealing with a very mercurial man in the first consul. He presents Louisiana as an act of generosity symbolic of lasting friendship between our nations. If the corollary of you won is that he lost, I assure you he will never let Louisiana go. Do you understand?"

He raises his glass again. "So here in this room drink to triumph—and then expunge the idea of triumph from your mind and focus on the magnanimity of a great man, a nation that looks upon you as a brother."

Livingston bows. "It shall be exactly as you say."

"You understand, of course," Marbois says, "that such largesse is not without cost." He says Napoleon has instructed him to conduct negotiations, cutting Talleyrand out entirely. He quotes the first consul as saying, as they strolled in a garden, "Well, you have charge of the Treasury, let them give you one hundred millions of francs, pay their own citizen claims, and take the whole country."

Now Mr. Livingston was not born yesterday. He's one of the biggest landholders in the state of New York, and he has bought and sold more land than Marbois has even seen. Is this Napoleon or Marbois speaking? His old friend is minister of an empty Treasury; what would be more natural than trying to milk the Americans a bit?

The claims of American citizens against France for various seizures of goods and depredations, including those of Leclerc against the American merchants, amount to 20 million francs. So the total under discussion is 120 million, which translates into a bit more than 22 million dollars and in any language that is a lot of money. Especially since he's been authorized to offer 50 million but francs. He digs in his heels to bargain.

It is near midnight and both are reeling with exhaustion before Marbois reaches what he insists is a bottom figure, 80 million francs, including the American claims—call it 15 million American dollars. Mr. Livingston says he must think it over and at midnight, trembling with excitement, he bolts to his waiting carriage and sits drumming his fingers as hooves on the cobblestones of Paris echo in the silent night.

At the legation he goes instantly to his desk and begins the letter of report to Mr. Madison that the president of the United States is now finishing, and Dolley hears in its measured, diplomatic phrasing the cry of triumph of a man who knows he has won a great victory. Mr. Monroe doesn't yet know of these developments, he says casually, because it is now three in the morning and it seemed essential to get this report straight on its way to you. Then he sealed the purchase: This letter will be a month or two in transit with equal time for reply, and Marbois makes it plain that they must move now before the great man has some new idea that changes everything. And so, Livingston says in the closing sentence, "We shall do all we can to cheapen the purchase, but my present sentiment is that we shall buy."

As the president's voice died away, no one spoke. There seemed a roaring in her ears, and she heard a bee buzzing against a windowpane. Then the spell broke and she leaped up.

"Oh, thank God!" she cried. "Thank God! Thank God!"

She seized Jimmy's hand and then the president's and

IV

TRIUMPH

40

There was just one painful thing left to do, and he knew it wouldn't be easy. Otherwise, even now, hours later, the celebration having gone on and on, the Madisons staggering with exhaustion as they climbed the stairs to their bedroom on the third floor, he still thrilled to the incredible news. In a stroke, their problem with France solved and a vast new empire purchased for a song—why, the purchase in whole must double the nation's size. In a finger snap. Just like that!

Dolley emerged from the dressing room in her nightgown and robe and sat before her mirror, spreading an unguent scented with lilacs on her face. She was sure the ointment gave her complexion the smoothness that Jimmy thought nature provided, but he liked its odor.

He rolled down his hose and wiped his buckle shoes and put on his robe and, damn it all, he could prolong this no longer. Should have spoken hours ago.

"So," he said with a note of belligerence he hadn't intended, "time for me to eat a little crow, don't you think?"

She turned on the bench and looked at him with a slight smile, indulgent somehow. An image of his mother coming into the nursery after some great clatter flashed across his mind.

"Why?" Dolley said. "Because of Mr. Livingston?"

He shrugged. "I was hard on him, and in the end he did well."

"He did, didn't he?"

"Not only solved the problem, he got more than we'd even dreamed."

She laughed out loud. "Why, Jimmy, he didn't do that; you did."

She was making it easy on him. Why had he thought it would be painful? But he shook his head.

"Mr. Livingston took the surrender, that's all," she said. "Jimmy, I like him and I defended him, but you don't really think that Frenchman who went from corporal or captain or whatever he was to imperial ruler in three or four years was swayed by what anybody said at parties, do you?"

He smiled, feeling better, wanting to hear her say it.

"So let's not hear any more talk of eating crow. Napoleon Bonaparte was responding to the case you made—words you put in Mr. Livingston's mouth, arguments laid out for Mr. Pichon, sending Mr. Clark to the moneymen of Paris, putting Senator Ross's speech into the great man's hands, playing the flirtation with Ned Thornton and the Royal Navy right up to the end—you did it, darling, *you* did it."

He loved hearing it . . . but he knew there was more to it than that.

She wiped the last unguent from her face. "Don't argue with me, sweetheart. I know what I know. Now for goodness sake, kiss me good night and let's go to sleep."

And so the Louisiana Purchase came to pass. Livingston and Monroe dickered hard, but in the end they agreed to pay the Fr 80 million or $15 million. Of that, Fr 60 million or some $11,250,000 went to France to restore its battered Treasury and Fr 20 million or $3,750,000 went to American claimants bruised by France in one way or another.

Albert Gallatin pulled himself together and issued bonds for the full amount payable in ten years, and Baring Brothers of London snapped them up. No one doubted the capacity of the new republic across the Atlantic to make good on its debts.

Federalist assertions in Congress that we already had plenty of land were drowned in a chorus of national approval. Word of the deal completed arrived on the third of

July in the fateful year 1803. It was in the papers on the fourth, a date everyone agreed was appropriate and many took as a benediction from on high.

In a stroke we had acquired an unbelievable garden, everything between the Father of Waters and the far mountains, from the Gulf of Mexico north to British territory, wherever that might turn out to be when diplomats sat down to draw lines on maps. Infuriated Spaniards—they had taken seriously Napoleon's promise not to let anyone else have the territory—claimed that Texas was not included, but at the moment that was a matter of small concern.

Every Fourth of July was an extravaganza, but this time the bands playing, townsfolk swarming on every square, militia marching, ranked musketmen and riflemen firing salute volleys, cannon booming for emphasis, outdid themselves. Overnight the country had doubled in size and in roaring possibility, and there would be no war and the French threat was gone and the flirtation with the Royal Navy was over and it was just a time to throw up your arms and shout, *Hallelujah! Praise the Lord!*

They had earned a little holiday, and Dolley was determined to have it. Before long they would go to Montpelier as Tom went to Monticello, and she would watch the magical effect on Jimmy of his own soil under his feet, tension draining away, color returning to his face. So today on this Fourth of July, with so much to celebrate, she planned a picnic for two at a favored place on the river where an oak leaned over the water and laid a carpet of shade on the bank.

The horses were brought around about ten. She had her saddle baskets filled with picnic food, while Jimmy had packed fishing line and hooks in his saddlebag. The step was set and she climbed up to mount her bay mare, hooking her right knee firmly around the saddle horn and arranging her skirts with proper decorum. They trotted toward the mansion on streets rapidly filling with horses, vehicles, and families on foot, many with picnic baskets. At the President's House people wandered over the lawn, children dashing about in loud games, families laying out dining cloths, four or five choosing places on the mansion steps.

Tom was at the door greeting visitors, and she saw that many were already inside sampling punch from a large tureen. Doubtless they would wreak additional damage on the shabby interior, but visits on every holiday and certainly on the Fourth were every citizen's right. Officiating would become her duty if she ever lived here, which looked much more likely now (though the purchase was rapidly making James Monroe a man to be watched, which to her irritation Jimmy seemed to feel was beneath his dignity, meaning *she* must be the more vigilant). She waved and Tom waved back, already looking dispirited.

A clatter of drums and the dancing sound of fifes came ahead of a column of marching militia that turned smartly up the driveway and stopped before the mansion. They stood marching in place to a solitary drum as the president came down the steps to take their salute. Flags dipped, muskets came up to present arms, and their captain threw a fine salute, which Tom answered with a bow. They fired a salute volley followed by a lusty, "Hip-hip-hurrah!" another volley, another hurrah, and a third, at which everyone within hearing seemed to be cheering and Dolley had to admit it was exciting, though she had to struggle to quiet her horse; and then they turned and marched off with packs of children hard on their heels, parents calling them back.

Scarcely had this martial display ended, when Senator Ross reined that sleek little mare of his up beside them. She frowned. At this rate they'd never reach the river, and while the senator's fiery speech certainly had been important, Jimmy also had reported his boorish assertion that Democrats were finished and she hadn't forgiven him. Not that it hadn't looked to be true—she'd had to admit that to herself, like it or not—but it was boorish to say so.

But he lifted his hat gracefully. "Miss Dolley," he said, with a little bow from the saddle, and then leaned over to shake hands with Jimmy. His grizzled hair stood out from his ears, and his face was reddened by too much sun.

"I hoped I'd see you, Mr. Secretary," he said. "Last time we talked, memory tells me I did a little unseemly gloating. So now, the way it's worked out, I reckon it's your turn to gloat. You won fair and square, and it looks to me like your party's future is assured. That don't make me too happy, but I gotta say I'm glad we don't need to fight a war; and believe me, my folks out in West Pennsylvania are feeling good. You Democrats have won, and all I can say is more power to you."

Jimmy smiled. "We won't disappoint you, Senator."

"Maybe I was wrong all along," Ross said. "I always said you put things in the common man's hands and he'll blow up. We saw it in the French after their revolution."

"But we're not French," Dolley said.

"Yes, ma'am, we ain't, and maybe my fear was unfounded. When I think about it, I find that folks in Pennsylvania are smart and sensible. They don't run very wild; keep their eye on what's good for them." He shrugged. "Anyway, risky or not, it's the way the country's going. We'll see what happens."

"You'd better join us," Jimmy said.

Ross laughed. "Oh, doubtless I will. I'm a practical fellow. But you know, it's kind of chastening to see how narrow a cut can decide the future. Think of it. If Napoleon had forced our hand, I'm convinced you Democrats would have been finished and the American future would be Federalist. But he didn't force our hand, and so the opposite is true. Maybe it's the way of fate."

At which he gave them a curious little salute and touched heels to his horse. They watched him go, raising his hat to women, turning the horse out to avoid a child who'd darted into the way. "The way of fate?" she asked. "Maybe it's the way of God."

He smiled. "Do you think God takes a hand in politics?"

"I hope He disdains politics but cares about nations' destinies. Good nations, anyway. This was noble work."

• • •

She rode in silence, thinking about it. Ross was wrong to equate freedom with license. Freedom was opportunity, the realization of possibilities. Yes, Britain and France were the great powers now, but already American craftsmen had cracked the Industrial Revolution's secrets, and history insists that empires must ultimately die of their own weight. The Spanish empire was moribund now, Napoleon's hopes had just come to grief, and Britain's would too, in time.

"Jimmy," she said, "will steamboats really ply the rivers someday? Is that practical?"

He shrugged as they swung their horses aside to avoid a carriage. "In time . . . well, our position on the Mississippi assured, there'll be demand and demand stimulates achievement, that's the story of modern industry—look at the new spinning mills in Massachusetts, turning out cloth, I guess by the millions of yards."

"In other words," she said, "progress follows freedom to seize opportunity. That's why we're right and Mr. Ross is wrong."

"Ross sounded like a convert."

She laughed. "Or a recruit. For after all, we are soldiers of democracy, are we not?"

He bowed in his saddle. "Yes, madam, we are surely that—soldiers of democracy."

He looked at her, poised on her sidesaddle; this last month of relief had taken years from her face and made her fresh as spring. Soldiers of democracy . . . yes, he'd say so, crashing through barriers, carrying the assault, planting the flag on the highest peak. Yes . . . this was triumph almost beyond believing.

It was so much more than they had dared to dream. They had asked for rights on the river—to purchase New Orleans or a part of it or a terminal, three or four acres with the promise of American sovereignty—and they had acquired an empire, a continent. To seek a sliver and gain a continent snatched them ahead by years, by decades. It was triumph, for it made real the continental nation that had lived in their dreams. Soldiers of democracy . . .

41

WASHINGTON, JULY 1803

"Hold up, Miss Dolley! Mr. Madison!"

They reined up their horses. Again! They'd never get to the picnic on the river at this rate. But then she saw it was Meriwether Lewis, tall and lean, loping long-legged over the mansion lawn.

"I'm leaving," he cried. "I'm off today!" His face was shining.

"On the great adventure?" she cried. "Oh, Merry, we didn't know you'd go so soon. We'd have had a party, a farewell party, a bon voyage—" She moved her horse to a convenient step and slid down as Jimmy dismounted.

"That's mighty nice, Miss Dolley," Merry said, "But I'm on my way. High time too." His mouth drew tight as string. Poor Merry, he would never relax. "It's July and we're just starting. Why, in three months snow will fly on the plains. I'm way behind—"

She cut him off. He was darkening before her very eyes. What a way to start! "Merry, dear," she cried, "I envy you so. You'll see wondrous things. Why, the president says he expects you'll find a live mammoth waving those big, curved horns."

"The president has very rich hopes," he said, voice gone suddenly dry. She wondered if he'd seen through her concern.

"But there's a core of instruction too?" Jimmy said.

"Exactly, Mr. Secretary. I'm to find the Northwest Passage. All else subordinates to that—examine terrain, identify flora and fauna, analyze the country's receptivity to settlers." He smiled. "And look for mammoth sign."

Finding the Northwest Passage would be wondrous enough, the route to the spices and silks and tea of the Orient that men had been seeking for five hundred years. She said as much, nattering on a bit. Columbus sailing west to reach east and bumping into the Americas, the long, fruitless search for the strait that must split the Americas to let the ocean through, and now the conviction that rivers must be the avenue to the Orient. She ran down, wondering if her enthusiasm sounded girlish.

The captain's smile was ironic but kindly. "We know the Missouri runs out of the mountains to the east. We know the Columbia runs westward to the sea. The president is quite convinced that they rise near each other with an easy portage between. I'm to learn whether conviction equals geography."

Again she had that odd sense of strength or focus or command or some distinct change in the young man. That he was finally going had to mean a lot, but she thought there was more to it. He'd always been strong and rather rough, nothing new about that, but this was different. It was mysterious but quite real.

It also struck her as he talked that what really interested her was not mammoths or even the Northwest Passage, but how it would *feel* to step so boldly into the unknown. Would they be awed or frightened? Or would it be mile by mile just another wilderness trek? It seemed so vast an undertaking, leading a handful of men over two thousand miles of terrain unknown to white men. But she knew such thoughts would embarrass him, and she didn't voice them.

"Oh, Merry," she cried, "God speed to you, dear," and she threw her arms around him and hugged him. When she stepped back, he caught her hand and held it a moment.

"Thank you, Miss Dolley," he said. There was something

in his eyes and then he turned abruptly to shake hands with Jimmy.

As they remounted and turned their horses toward the river, she asked Jimmy if he had noticed that difference in Merry. "Yes," he said, "subtle but there, all right. He seems a little different around Tom too. Respectful as always, of course, but—I don't know—I have a feeling something happened when he was gone, in Harper's Ferry or Philadelphia."

Early the next morning Captain Lewis was on the stage for Fredericktown, Maryland, two heavy seabags with his gear lashed to the top of the coach, first leg of the run to Pittsburgh. In Fredericktown that evening, forty miles on and making good time, he slept with other passengers on the dirt floor of a tavern and was off to Harper's Ferry the next day.

He rode in silence, answering fellow passengers in monosyllables, buried in thought. He'd seen the way Miss Dolley had cut across his worries as if to deny them; she thought he was a pessimist when he knew better. It was very late in the year, and everything had conspired to delay him—the boat in Harper's Ferry, the extra training in Philadelphia, the supplies and the need for maps traced on oil paper reflecting the best rumors of the West—and then the incredible news from France.

The Louisiana Purchase changed everything. Suddenly the vast range of country wrapped in mystery from Saint Louis to the Stony Mountains was U.S. territory. He would march as the representative of the new nation, not as an intruder dodging enemy patrols. As a practical matter, yes, a Spanish patrol finding him would have been two needles mating in a haystack, but the assurance he now felt was surprising and made him realize how much enemy territory had weighed in his thinking. He had a new mission, too; tribe by tribe he must present himself and his country to the Indian inhabitants.

The water passage he sought through the far mountains would open the nation to direct China trade, not immedi-

ately, of course, but in due time. Now the way from the East
to the passage would be clear—and the chances of beating
the British in the area beyond the passage had increased a
hundredfold. He doubted the British would even contest seriously, for the Pacific Northwest—what some already were
referring to as the Oregon country—had become a natural
extension of the United States.

Which meant we were well along to being a continental
nation, the Atlantic washing one shore, the Pacific the other.
The purchase made all the difference. But hold up! This was
thinking for Mr. Jefferson and Mr. Madison over fine porce-
lain teacups. It was drawing room thinking, with a nice comfort that really had little to do with the man who still must
find his way across two thousand miles of territory unknown
to any white man. And that man, truth be told, was cutting it
very close. Too close. He thought he still could get on the
Missouri this year, but how far could he go before winter
trapped him? He had hoped to reach the Mandan villages
eight hundred miles or so upriver. The Mandans were the
trading tribe of the northern plains, dealt with Indians all
around, and factored the results off to British and French
traders who came down from Canada. Unlike most plains
tribes their villages were permanent, with structures that
protected against the cold, which commonly dipped as much
as forty degrees below zero on the high plains, or so traders'
tales claimed. They needed to be moving. Get on down the
Ohio and up the Mississippi to Saint Louis and the great
juncture of the Missouri from the West. . . .

July already . . . now he must detour to Harper's Ferry to
be sure the teamster bringing his supplies from Philadelphia
had paused there as ordered to load weapons, tools, and the
iron boat. Everything should be in Pittsburgh now, ready to
be loaded aboard the keelboat he had commissioned Samuel
Hawkins, by reputation the master boat builder of the West,
to have ready for him. Another week to reach Pittsburgh,
then draw army boatmen from the cantonment and start
down the Ohio before the river got too low, all with fall approaching. And Miss Dolley thought he was a worrier!

But thinking of her brought back forcefully the surge of feeling when he took her hand. He'd betrayed nothing, but suddenly she had seemed supremely desirable. Older than he and safely married and she'd always been pretty, but this was different. The way she'd looked at him, kind, sweet, generous, open, understanding—oh, all the things you'd want in a woman. Maybe that's what he needed, an older woman. He wasn't making much headway with the pretty girls who drew him.

June Landros in Philadelphia, she'd seemed head over heels in love with him. He'd visualized going off on his great adventure with a miniature of her face and a curl of her hair in a locket on a chain of gold. And then she'd gone off to New York without a word. He suspected her mother—maybe a soldier wasn't good enough for her family—but you'd think June would have found a way to get a note to him if she'd really cared. He sighed. Maybe an older woman, maybe a widow . . .

Jimson and Bit greeted him as a comrade in arms at Harper's Ferry. Mr. Perkins seemed pleased to tell him the Philadelphia teamster had judged the load too heavy for his team and had gone on to Pittsburgh without it. Another day to find a substitute. He reached Pittsburgh a week later at two in the afternoon, dashed off a letter to Mr. Jefferson for the five o'clock mail saying he would load and depart the next morning, and then went down to the river.

He came to Hawkins's boatyard—and stopped in sheer horror. There was his keelboat still high on the ways, keel laid, ribs in place, and some planking on the port side of the hull but none on the starboard, no deck planking, no sign of special equipment he had designed. It looked weeks from completion. A half-dozen men were working in desultory fashion on a couple of punts.

"Where's Mr. Hawkins?" he asked.

One of the men jerked a lazy thumb toward a shed with the door closed. He wore an ugly grin. Lewis knocked on the closed door, then opened it. A man was asleep, head flat on the desk, snoring loudly.

Lewis prodded him. "Mr. Hawkins? Mr. Hawkins?" After a while the fellow raised his head. His cheeks were veined, nose bulbous, eyes bloodshot. The smell of whiskey filled the shed. He held up a trembling hand.

"What—what d'ye want?"

"I want my boat, damn you. I'm Meriwether Lewis."

"Oh, my God." Hawkins stared at Lewis, mouth twitching, then slowly stood, wiping his lips. "We've had some problems, going slower'n I expected, but we're getting there. And I been sick—"

"You've been drunk. You're drunk now."

"Now you're right about that." He gazed earnestly at Lewis. "I'm one hundred percent teetotally drunk, and I'll tell you what, mister, I don't sit down, I'm going to fall down."

A workman put his head in the door. "Let him sleep it off. He'll be all right in a couple of hours." Lewis stepped out and looked at the river. A marker showed it had dropped an inch overnight. Soon commerce would stop moving until late fall.

It was too late to go to another builder, and anyway, a few questions in town told him that Hawkins was the best, though yes, he did like his glass and little work was done when he wasn't in shape to push it. Anyway, starting over would be ruinous for this was a very special boat created to Lewis's own design. It was oversized at fifty-five feet with an eight-foot beam, carried a mast jointed to fold that would support both square sail and foresail. Ten feet fore and aft was decked for quarters, eleven benches centered had space for twenty-two oarsmen and left space on each side to pole her forward. He had designed storage lockers that could be raised to form a barrier against Indian arrows, should any fly. It was a superb boat; it just wasn't finished. Lewis set out to drive Hawkins and the workers by combining threats, pleas, and promises of rewards; and plank by plank the boat advanced as inch by inch the river lowered.

At last a ray of sunshine: a letter came from Will Clark far down the river at Clarksville in Indiana territory. The president had immediately approved Lewis's choice of Clark as co-commander; he knew George Rogers Clark, Will's older brother, very well. The elder Clark, as a young warrior, had saved the Far West during the revolution, and Jefferson had called on him more than once. So Lewis had posted his invitation with instructions to answer to Pittsburgh.

Lewis's hand trembled as he cut through the sealing wax and opened the letter. He had an alternative candidate if Clark refused, but for a trip that was shaping up as monumental indeed he wanted a man he trusted implicitly at his side.

And Clark agreed! With the same high enthusiasm that Lewis himself felt, he wrote, "I will cheerfully join you. My friend, I do assure you that no man lives with whom I would prefer to undertake such a trip as yourself. My friend, I join you with hand and heart."

Almost a month passed before the boat was finished. The river fell steadily; old hands said it was no longer passable. Lewis said they would try it anyway. He bought a pirogue to carry some of the load and sent part of his supplies on by wagon to Wheeling, where the water deepened, further to lighten the keelboat. Then he set out with eleven oarsmen from the cantonment; they would get him downriver, where he would gather soldier-volunteers for the great adventure.

It was the last day in August in 1803; sassafras leaves were turning, he saw a gum tree with flashes of orange, the buckeyes showing color. Winter was coming and now he knew the great trek could not begin this year. He would push on to the Mississippi, hook up with Clark, and gather his men, add to his supplies, winter near Saint Louis, and start up the Missouri in the spring: 1804 instead of 1803. So be it.

Off McKee's Rock he saw a ripple in the water and a moment later the boat grounded. He leaped into the water, the men after him. For twenty minutes of agony they dragged and lifted the heavy boat over the shoal. When she floated free, he was gasping and his legs trembled. He hauled himself back aboard and helped others. At Little Horse Tail Riffle, she grounded again and he waved them over the side. He was on his way and going through, take whatever it took; the Pacific Ocean glimmered in the distance.

42

WASHINGTON, AUGUST 1803

The sale of Louisiana was a blessing for Danny Mobry. It solved all problems but those of the heart. Her shipping business would prosper, sugar exported freely, finished goods returned, the wine runs from the south of France. It was more than rescue; it gave her enormous advantage over shippers who hadn't deigned to speak to her, a woman in a man's business. The New Orleans trade set free would surely boom. American vessels would flock up the river, but she was already there.

The Frenchmen greeting these captains from Baltimore and Boston would be angry and suspicious, but they would feel good with Danny, no matter her sex. Men who had been reluctant to deal with a woman would be delighted to deal with a *French*woman who spoke their language, knew their customs, understood their worries, carried the family imprimatur of Daniel Clark, and had made herself a success in the land that now governed their future. She must go immediately to capitalize on her advantage.

Yet business issues were the least of her elation. She was an American, but the thought of her home country as enemy had been heartbreaking. She had understood as most New Orleanians could not that the United States would never have tolerated France on the Mississippi and that the resultant fighting would have left the graceful city on the river crescent a smoking ruin and a people so bitter that she could never go home again. But in a stroke this smiling place of blossoms and flower odors filling the night and honeysuckle wherever you turned, of languorous air and color and laughter and song and wine and clattering dice, and the unparalleled gumbo that was New Orleans for Carl, was restored and awaiting her return.

The *Cumberland Queen* was just in from Louisiana via Boston, and Danny thought she would be in the owner's cabin on its return. She studied the captain's report with the ship's manifest, an order for fresh supplies, minor repairs, and a new mainsails needed, two hands leaving, one by choice, the other by order. The vessel could sail in four days. The documents included two sealed letters, a single sheet from her uncle, a heavy one from Henri that was full of accounting for sugar purchased, prices paid, quality assessed. This also contained a small and elaborately sealed letter, many additional sheets folded in with the original envelope sheet. A love letter . . . her heartbeat quickened and she thrust it into her reticule. She would read it at home, alone, probably in bed, where she could lie and dream of Henri and the rough feel of his lips on hers.

Still at her desk later that day, she heard the creaking sound of a heavy step on the flimsy stairs to her loft from the pier shed below. Silence, then a tentative knock. The uncertainty of it irritated her, and she said with asperity, "Come in, come in!" The men who worked for her were respectful, didn't last if they weren't, but they knew she was approachable.

The door opened slowly and she was surprised to see Samuel on the landing, nervously rolling his hat brim in his big hands. "Come in, Samuel," she said more gently. "What is it?"

He looked confused and very nervous. "What's what, Miss Danny?"

"What brings you here? Today, now." He gazed at her.

"Samuel, why did you come up the stairs and knock on the door?"

"Oh, that! Well, yes, ma'am, I wanted to ask you something."

"So, ask!"

"Yes, ma'am. What with the news about Louisiana and all, you're going back to New Orleans, ain't you?"

What in the world? Rumors like this were dangerous and needed instant squelching. "We're not leaving Washington," she said, putting a knife edge in her voice.

But she saw immediately she had startled him as much as he had startled her. "I didn't mean nothing like that, Miss Danny. But this big change; you'll probably go down for a look see, won't you? Figure out how things will be? Not to stay."

She relaxed. Should have known better. "Yes. Within a week or two, I think—perhaps less."

"But you'll be coming back? Or the ship will anyway?"

"*I* will. What's gotten into you, Samuel?"

"Millie and me, we'd like to go with you. And come back."

"Well, my goodness, that's easily enough arranged. Didn't need all this special—"

"Yes, ma'am, but there's more to it."

"What?"

"You know my brother, Joshua?"

"I know he's on the family plantation. Married Millie's sister, didn't he? Junie, I think. I asked my brother to give them a family pass to come see you when we were there before."

"Yes, ma'am, that's what you did, so what I wanted to ask this time—"

"Another pass? That should be easy enough—"

"No, ma'am, you see, he ain't there no more. He ran off awhile back. Went to Santo Domingo."

Danny stared at him, shaken. Santo Domingo where the slaves had rebelled, where they'd killed white plantation owners right and left and then broken the French army, black standing against white and winning because they didn't lose. And any fool could see that that had lots to do with Napoleon deciding to sell Louisiana. But slaves in rebellion?

Danny liked black people, sympathized with their plight, agreed that slavery should be abolished; she scarcely knew anyone who didn't agree. Clinch was quite adamant on the subject, though of course he was from upstate New York where there weren't many black people. Danny felt she was on the side of the angels, so to speak. But killing whites, swinging machetes, servants becoming masters, stories of heads stacked in triangles, white faces almost blue after the blood drained out . . . it was one thing when they were faceless savages shrieking out of the brush on some distant island and quite another when it was Samuel's brother, married to the sister of gentle Millie who had cared for Danny since infancy. Very different indeed.

But she saw that these thoughts had communicated themselves instantly to Samuel. He was on the edge of his chair, starting to rise. Blacks in a slave society had to be perceptive, she understood that, but this was more than just keeping his eyes open. Samuel was a very intelligent man. But then, a step further, she realized he'd been waiting for just the reaction she'd shown him. He was already on his feet, hat clutched in both hands.

"I 'spect I shouldn't have said nothing. I'll just be going along—"

"Sit down, Samuel. Please, don't go off."

"Yes, ma'am." He sat on the edge of the chair, looking ready to bolt.

"I was startled," she said. She might as well go head on. "You know, slave revolt terrifies a lot of people. Frightens me, I have to admit it. If we ever had racial war, we'd have a lot of dead—on both sides—don't you think?"

"I reckon. Yes, ma'am."

"So it startled me that someone I know was in that fighting."

"My brother and me, we're not all that much alike."

God, he was quick. He said it so simply, but he'd wrapped her real fear with a ribbon and handed it to her. Smarter than she'd realized, much smarter.

Well, they each had revealed themselves; no point in dwelling . . . "So," she said, "Joshua is in Santo Domingo."

"He's dead."

"Oh, the poor man. Went down and threw his life away—"

"No, ma'am! He was a natural leader. Men followed him. He was a general. He set up ambushes that drew the French in every time. He was a hero!"

He sat straight in his chair and gazed at her, all defiance. This was something he wouldn't hesitate on, she saw; he'd tell anyone and everyone that his brother was a hero. And then she saw it was what he owed his brother.

"I guess he *was* a hero," she said softly, "fighting for his people."

"Yes, ma'am."

"What happened?"

"I don't know. After his first letters, the first reports, we didn't hear nothing more."

"Then how do you know?"

He smiled. "I just know."

"Ah," she said. "Then his family, Millie's sister—"

"Yes, ma'am, that's just it! What I owe my brother. He went off to fight; I owe him to look out for his family. I want to buy Junie's freedom. And the three little childrens. That's what I came to ask; we hoping you'll help us on that."

She hesitated. Her brother had claimed the family plantation when their father died and she was off in America married to Carl. Xavier seemed to live in angry terror that she would demand a share, though in fact primogeniture gave it to him. Perhaps that would give her some weight, and if she had to use it she would. He'd probably want to be compensated for the one who had run away, able-bodied man, but she could swing that. Three thousand, four thousand, a lot of money, but she could find it.

"So you want me to buy them and you work out payment—"

"No, ma'am! Wanted you to talk for us. Figure your brother ain't going to want to talk no slave freedom with a black man and especially not a free black man he once owned. But for the money, I have the money. Four thousand in gold—be enough, don't you think?"

Her jaw dropped. "Where did you get that kind of money, Samuel?"

"Been saving for years, Miss Danny. Had a goal."

"To buy their freedom?"

He looked discomfited. "No, ma'am. See, this is a dangerous city. Slave city and there are folks here who look on a free black as a walking insult. You gotta go soft and careful. Women, too. Millie goes to the market; she never knows when someone'll accuse her, grab her, constables beat her. Happens. White folks don't hear much about it, but it happens."

She felt pain growing in her breast. "So you were saving to move on?" He nodded and she said in a whisper, "You and Millie would leave me then?"

"Oh, no." He had a startled expression. "We wasn't fixing on leaving unless you married, and then we'd be dealing with we don't know who. You can see that, can't you, Miss Danny? We'd be on our own then. Even worse for us if you married Mr. Henri, 'cause he sure don't cotton to black folks having any ideas of their own." He hesitated, gazing earnestly at her. "I hope you don't think I'm talking too much out of turn here, about maybe you getting married and all; but you know, we have to think of these things. But I promise you, we didn't have no thought of leaving the way things are right now."

"So this was a lifeline. In case."

He smiled. "That's exactly it. My Millie, she been caring for you since you couldn't walk. She wouldn't never leave unless everything changed. But I had to have the money in case it did."

"So that was your dream—save yourselves if you had to?"

"Yes, ma'am. I suppose."

"But now you're giving up that dream."

"My brother gave up his life. I reckon I can give up a dream. Duty . . . to him, to family."

"Where would you have gone, Samuel?"

"Maine. We hear common white folks up there don't hate blacks like they do here."

She stood and stretched a hand to him and he took it in his big paw. "We'll get Junie and the children out, whatever we have to do," she said. And then, softly, "You're a good man, Samuel; you're a good man."

Henri's letter lay unopened on the dressing chest; she could see it there and in the mirror. She drew a washbowl full of water from the fireplace warmer and sponge bathed, donned a fresh nightgown, rubbed toilet water on her arms, moved the candle to the table by the bed, and slipped under the covers with the letter in hand. She lay there holding it, a little afraid to open it.

Henri stood glowing in her mind, tall, tanned, not just handsome but craggily, fiercely so, masculine to his core. She thought of the way his eyes crinkled when he was amused, his capacity for surprising wit, the way black hair curled against his knuckles and the strength in his hands when he swung her across a stream or picked her up and laid her gently on her bed and fell beside her. She was more than a little in love with Henri Broussard, and yet there was that anger that stood between them, his needs and his assertions of rights she would not yield, his Frenchness clashing with her deep American nature. "But you're not an American!" he'd shouted one night. "You married an American; that's different."

"I became one, Henri," she'd said, and he'd glowered.

And yet there were wonderful moments when he was sweet and gentle and tender and funny and warm—and then, being around him stirred an excitement in her that she could not ignore.

She settled on her pillow and unfolded the letter. He had written it late at night, and it had a great many tender allusions that she hunted out and clung to, suggestive comments and hints that quickened her breathing, even a burst of wit; but as she read it a third and fourth time, the dominant impression turned out to be anger.

His rage seemed to be focused on America and Americans who had cheated him of what he had wanted all his life, to be a genuine Frenchman, a true subject under a ruler who gloried in the French nation. How dare the Americans insert themselves in what had been a perfect picture? The betrayal seemed to be, not that France had sold, but that America had bought.

Of course she understood his pain and even the consequent anger, but he seemed to be taking it out on her and that was hurtful. If he loved her as he said, why would he let his letter reflect anger instead of joy? Or was he simply so consumed that he was blind to the reality? Or was there more to it?

There was that masculine arrogance that personified the New Orleans male for her and was so different from Carl's open, bluff, hearty masculinity. Of course, Henri wanted a wife, and he wanted a woman who belonged to him or at least with him rather than to her business and who wasn't a thousand miles away. But slowly it came to her with increasing conviction as she read between the lines that his anger was aimed less at America and the turn of fortune than at her . . . at her and her American independence and her capacity to function in a man's world.

As this conviction took hold, her own anger rose and after a time she pinched out the candle and lay there, hostile and yet hurt. But at the same time she also wanted to see him, to hear his voice, feel the masculine vigor in his arms, have him kiss her and, yes, make love to her.

• • •

Danny was reading her uncle's letter the next morning when Clinch Johnson came to visit. He wanted her to join him at dinner with a businessman from Baltimore who was anxious to open a shipping connection with the New Orleans that he visualized as sure to emerge from U.S. possession. She accepted with alacrity and then described Mr. Clark's letter. It was short and said the Frenchmen there had reacted to the news with absolute fury, so he'd have his hands full for a while when he was appointed governor. Governor? He said Zulie told him he was assuming too much, but he thought not. After all, his trip to Paris obviously was the real cause of the French decision to sell—all else was the blather of uninformed men. Like all nations, the French reacted primarily to money, and he had made them see the losses they could incur. And then, who knew New Orleans and its people better and who had served with more loyalty?

"What do you think?" she asked Clinch.

"Mr. Clark is a fine man and a powerful businessman, but the idea that we'll appoint as governor an Irishman who has no knowledge of the United States or of the principles of democracy strikes me as unlikely."

She laughed. Clark would never be appointed, and his consequent anger would be a new problem when she arrived, but—

"What does Mr. Broussard think of it?" Clinch asked.

"Henri? Oh, he—" She stopped, staring at him. His suit was buttoned up sausage tight and his yellow hair stood like horns on the side of his head today, but his blue eyes were very clear. "How do you know about Henri? Surely I didn't tell—"

"Well, Danny," he said gently, "the shipping world really is very small."

She digested that, watching him, and in a bit he asked when she would go to New Orleans to consolidate her position. He had offered her excellent practical advice, and now he added more to which she listened gratefully. She said she would go in four days if the *Queen* could clear that soon.

"Well," he said, "I will be here when you return."

The words remained with her and the image of him with his enigmatic smile, placid, solid, bound tight in his sausage coat with those yellow horns. Whatever had he meant? He was a very odd man, but he was a good friend and she liked him. He was . . . comfortable, and the idea that he would be here when she returned was pleasing. She turned to the paperwork supporting the voyage to come with high good cheer.

43

NASHVILLE, AUGUST 1803

Andrew Jackson was in Nashville when the news came that Napoleon Bonaparte was selling Louisiana to the United States, the whole gigantic kit and caboodle, magnificent empire that it was. New Orleans in possession, the Spanish soon to be forgotten, the French threat but a memory, American to its core!

Of course Nashville had exploded with joy and the boys began planning a celebration, bonfire and speech making and the preacher to put some benediction on them and a big dance and a barbecue to end barbecues, couple of steers and a half-dozen hogs, with tents and awnings to shelter folks who'd be coming from miles around. Men were clustered around the general shaking his hand, and he laughed and joked and slapped their shoulders, but he was making his way to the livery stable and his horse. Rachel deserved to share in this—God knows she'd had plenty of worry over it—and he would fetch her in for the doings along with her niece, on whom Jack Coffee was so sweet.

Rachel Jackson was at a table trimming extra crust from an apple pie before popping it into the fireplace oven. Over the table was a window with glass that scarcely waved at all that Jackson had imported from the glassworks at Knoxville as a promised taste of luxury, and through the glass she saw him coming.

He was much earlier than expected and that was a bad sign. He came at a fast trot, the set of his shoulders saying he had something on his mind, and she felt her heart start to flutter and she stood there, the heel of her hand pressed to her chest.

"Oh, my," Hannah said softly behind her, and that made it worse. Hannah had an instinct about these things; she was only technically a slave—actually this was her kitchen.

He swung down, flipped the reins around a sapling by the door, and was in the house in a couple of strides. He was beaming. She felt balanced on a knife edge.

"It's all over!" he cried, and threw his arms around her. "The French folded their cards and went home. We *bought* Louisiana! It's ours, lock, stock, and barrel. I tell you, Rachel, it opens up the future like cracking the biggest watermelon in the field."

He drew back, peering into her face. "Why the tears? It means the future is ours for the taking. Watch Tennessee now!"

Dumbly she nodded, smiling, her hands on his arms encircling her. No war . . . he wouldn't be rallying Tennessee troops and marching off at their head. There wouldn't be new widows and young men absent arms and legs desperately trying to run their little farms. There wouldn't be the endless worries about a flatboat full of corn or cotton or tobacco that represented your fortune at the mercy of far-away papists who spoke a different language. She kept the books, she knew what commerce meant, she knew how grown men went pale and widows fell to praying when the Spanish closed the river. And Andrew wouldn't be at special risk, leading troops. He'd always be at risk, that was his nature, but not marching into a storm of bullets.

"What wonderful news," she whispered.

Jack drove the ladies in the spring buggy and the general rode alongside on a fresh mount; he was *the* leading figure in West Tennessee and he didn't intend to arrive in a buggy. The women were still chattering about the news, Jack in his quiet way, smiling and once in a while adding something. Rachel said she figured Mr. Jackson had had something to do with the decision in Paris all right, which Jack seconded warmly.

The general dismissed such tittle-tattle with a wave of his hand but privately thought it wasn't so far from the mark. He'd always admired Bonaparte until the Frenchman had made himself a dictator. Napoleon was a fighting man of magnificent instincts, knew what Jackson himself knew so well: If you're going to strike, strike hard and strike first and drive ahead, don't give the other side a chance to breathe, but keep your head clear, know when to advance but know when to retreat toward new advantage. All this Bonaparte had demonstrated in the decision to sell Louisiana.

For surely it was a mark of sheer wisdom that the great man had been able to set aside pride and ambition and recognize the cold reality, which was, plain and simple, he could never have won in Louisiana. The American West, ever growing, ever stronger, would have taken it from him; and General Jackson would have been leading the way. Indeed, he himself had made it clear—to come here would have been to fight forever. He'd told that French attaché in Washington—Pichon, that was it—what they could expect. And that fellow Montane, said he was an American now but he sounded a good deal more like a French general to Jackson. And Jackson had told him too, one fighting man talking to another. He'd understood it all right.

So Jackson reckoned he'd had a hand in making the dictator see the light of reason, and he didn't object when the boys set up a mighty cheer as he rode into the square right ahead of the ladies in the spring buggy. He rode into the crowd, bowing and shaking hands with the men close to him, and didn't dismount till he was on the brick steps leading up to the log courthouse. Then he held up his hands to quiet them and made them a speech at the top of his lungs that had them whooping and hollering for more.

The air was full of the odor of roasting hog and three separate men each brought in a barrel of whiskey and everyone was welcome. A barrel of cold tea for the ladies appeared and floating in it was what surely was the very last piece of ice brought down from northern lakes packed in sawdust. The fiddlers turned out and a banjo picker and Joe Simpson, who could make his mouth organ cry like a baby, and folks went to square dancing and when the sun went down lanterns and torches made it bright as day and the dancing went right on.

Louisiana was ours and the future was secure!

Before you could turn around, things began to boom. War had started up in Europe and both sides were hungry for American grain, and now farmers hereabouts were free to ship to the world via New Orleans knowing their produce would pass. That's why the French had wanted it in the first place; now let them buy foodstuffs like civilized folk. When Spain had closed the river and everyone had gotten ready for war, Tennessee folks naturally held up their shipments. Jackson had built an extra barn to store corn and baled cotton he couldn't sell, his own and his neighbors too.

Now there was a run on flatboats. Nathan Fosby—it looked like running off and falling in love with a black woman and getting his heart broke when she was killed had made him a man of the world somehow—opened a yard on the river and was building flatboats as fast as he could get logs downstream and sliced in the sawmill he'd set up in his yard. There would be a ready market for lumber in New Orleans after the boats arrived now that Americans would be moving in and the population would start swelling. Jackson

heard the price of lumber in New Orleans had already doubled and was on the way to tripling! That money was radiating back to Fosby and from him back to the timber cutters,
and the good times were upon them.

The price of land was rising too. What had been going for
ten dollars an acre cleared and ready to plant crops for the
European market now was fetching twenty and twenty-five.
Men were paying premium prices for lots on the outskirts of
Nashville, as much as ten blocks from the center, planning a
house in town when they got around to building it.

Everywhere you looked you saw something new and
thrilling that told you Tennessee was right on the edge of a
glowing future. That was the idea that old John Sevier
couldn't see. The old general, one-time governor and hungering for old glory, was locked in the past. Maybe that
suited East Tennessee, but it didn't suit the west end of the
state nor the man to whom folks in the west looked. And that
was the root of the trouble.

Archie Roane wasn't a bad governor nor all that good either,
but the problem was he liked the office and wanted another
turn. The Constitution allowed three two-year terms. It also
placed no bar on a former governor running again after a
term out of office. Just what you'd expect; old Sevier filed
for election. So Archie naturally dropped his bombshell. Sevier, he said, was hardly a savior of Tennessee who could do
no wrong. He'd done plenty of wrong; he'd been up to his
ears in the recent land fraud that had rocked the state. His
authority for a statement that most Tennesseans simply
didn't believe: the honorable Judge Jackson, who had uncovered the fraud.

Rachel went pale as paper when Jack Coffee brought the
papers carrying Archie's statement. She pressed her hand to
her chest and would have fallen, but Jackson caught her and
eased her onto a sofa and gave her two tablespoons of Dr.
Simpson's Elixir of Life, which she kept handy as a power-

ful restorative. He spent the next hour assuring her that this was mostly talk, which she finally accepted though he could see she didn't believe it.

It was more than talk, but he didn't think it would involve her. She lived in terror of those awful days being reopened—the run to Natchez to escape her husband, the marriage when news of the divorce came, the crushing ending of adultery that they had lived with ever since. . . .

As for trouble with Sevier, best to go straight in. Jackson laid out the accusation in a letter to the *Knoxville Gazette,* right in Sevier's hometown. In the land fraud, numerous Tennesseeans had bribed the North Carolina secretary of state to accept forged claims. It was over now, the secretary packed off to jail. Sevier had had some land warrants that weren't worth much under an old law but would soar in value if falsely registered under a later law. The secretary of state had arranged the switch, and Sevier sent him three warrants in payment for his services. It was tangential to the main fraud but close enough, Jackson figured. He said the warrants were worth $960, given for a service worth a dollar had it been legal.

Sevier reacted like a bee-stung bull, pawing and roaring that this low pettifogging lawyer who'd had the temerity to steal the militia election from the militia's natural commander now sought to destroy him with utterly false charges. The moment he could lay hands on him, he would give this upstart hard lessons in how a man of honor handled calumniators. As for the charges, what he had done was legal, the fee what he would have paid a lawyer to perfect the transaction.

The people paid little attention. Everyone was dealing in land, plenty of deals were under the table, and Sevier was their old hero. They went to the polls, tossed Archie Roane out, and put John Sevier back in the governor's chair. The problem between the new governor and the state's most prominent jurist festered on. Sevier made no immediate move, and Jackson waited till court took him to Knoxville. So it was cracking fall before the clash came.

• • •

It was a bright day, sun glowing, air still warm, oak leaves orange and gold, when Jackson convened court. Knoxville was practically a city and the courthouse showed it, courtroom paneled, the bench downright fancy. But he brought the vigor of the far frontier to his dispensation of justice and settled half a dozen cases before noon. Gradually he became aware of noise outside, the clamor of voices and hoots of laughter. He didn't doubt it related to him, and so he stepped out to see.

Sure enough, a crowd had gathered on the courthouse green, the governor waving a heavy cutlass as he harangued them. He was a stout and solid figure with a soldier's bearing, handsome enough for a man in his late fifties but of small caliber nonetheless. Jackson felt the people had made a dreadful mistake in electing him.

The crowd went silent as it spotted the judge at the top of the steps and Sevier turned, sword at the ready. Jackson touched the pistol under his coat, powder well set in the pan, .70-cal. ball patched in place, hammer on full cock, and went lightly down the steps, hickory cane in hand. Teach the governor a lesson and do it right now. He darted across the street without looking. A horseman yelled and the beast reared. Jackson had an impression of the animal, white and huge, foam flying from the bit tearing his mouth, and then he was across the street and advancing on the governor—

"Here he is," Sevier roared, waving the sword, "this impudent jackanapes, this puppy who traduces men of honor, throws foul lies thick as falling leaves, snake's tongue wagging in his ugly face, a pitiful boy trying to hoist his own star by attacking a man of consequence, a man of prestige—"

He advanced suddenly, raising the sword, crying, "What have *you* ever done for the people of Tennessee? You, a poor sneaking judge hiding behind your judicial robes, hiding behind your bench, who are you to criticize a man who has served this state his whole natural life! Rotten poltroon scoundrel, what services have *you* ever rendered the people of Tennessee?"

The form of the attack took Jackson by surprise, and he found himself on the defensive. Services? What hadn't he done? Served in the Senate, the House, the bench—

And Sevier shouted, "I know of no great services you have rendered the country, *except taking a trip to Natchez with another man's wife!*"

Jackson's eyes bulged, he heard a roaring, it was as if his very skull would explode. "Great God," he screamed, "do you mention *her* sacred name?"

He dropped the cane and clawed under his coat for his pistol, a hoarse shriek in his brain, *I'll kill him!*

They were a dozen feet apart. Jackson leveled his piece and fired just as someone hurtled into him, knocking his aim askew. Sevier's pistol was out, the cutlass dropped at his feet, and he fired almost simultaneously. Jackson felt a bullet tug at his sleeve and heard someone howling, hit by one ball or another. He lunged forward to pistol whip the governor, and three men held him back while others restrained Sevier.

Jackson was stunned. The unthinkable had happened. Rachel's worst fears had been brought to surface.

He ran to the hotel, plunged quill in inkpot and scratched out a challenge, demanding instant satisfaction with pistols for an insult of unbelievable foulness. Jack Coffee carried it; he would arrange terms. But Sevier caviled. Ducked and dodged. He would fight anytime, but he claimed it would dishonor the state to do so on the sacred soil of Tennessee.

Jackson was amazed. Ink spattering, he wrote, "Did you take the name of a lady into your poluted lips in the town of Knoxville? Now, sir, in the neighborhood of Knoxville you shall atone for it, or I will publish you as a coward and a poltroon." He demanded response within the hour.

No answer.

The base, rotten coward! All right, if he won't fight here, let him choose his place. Jackson also drew up a hasty statement for the *Gazette*: "Know ye that I Andrew Jackson do pronounce, publish and declare to the world that his excellency John Sevier is a base coward and poltroon. He will basely insult, but has not courage to repair the wound. *Andrew Jackson.*"

Now Sevier said he would meet Jackson across the line in Cherokee territory. Fine! Jackson saddled and rode. Couldn't wait. He and Coffee arrived. No Sevier. Not that day or the next or the next.

The coward!

At noon on the third day, Jackson mounted to return to Knoxville. He would cane the governor on the street!

On the road he saw a party of horsemen. Sevier! Coming with his grown son and three others, clear violation of the solemn agreement of principal and second only.

Sevier was a swordsman. If he wouldn't follow the code duello, let the fight be with swords. Jackson's cane concealed a blade. He jerked off the base of the cane, leveled the sword like a lance, and kicked his horse into a gallop. Sevier tumbled off his mount to avoid the blow, but his boot caught in his cutlass scabbard and he fell under his horse. He curled into a ball as the nervous animal danced over him. When he stood he had a pistol in each hand.

Jackson jumped down and drew his own brace of pistols. That gave each man two shots. Sevier leaped behind a tree. Jackson leveled pistol sights on the governor's arm stretched around the tree aiming his pistol.

Young Sevier trained his weapon on Jackson.

Coffee aimed his at young Sevier.

Thus they stood, poised, motionless.

One of the governor's party, a man Jackson didn't recognize, darted forward, though standing carefully out of the line of fire. "For God's sake, gentlemen, everybody'll be killed and nothing'll be settled. Please, *put up those pieces!*"

Slowly, each man did. Sevier emerged from behind the tree and slipped the pistols into saddle holsters. Jackson sheathed the sword cane.

"Goddamned jackanapes," Sevier cried, "blackening the name of an honest man!"

"Why," Jackson roared, "you rotten Goddamned scoundrel who would pollute the name of an innocent woman—by God, I'll break your head!" And he lunged with the cane held high.

Sevier ran backward and snatched his cutlass from its scabbard. The rasp of steel on steel startled his horse. It bolted with his pistols still in their holsters. Sevier advanced with the heavy sword in hand, and Jackson drew his pistols and again the peacemaker cried, "Gentlemen, gentlemen, my God, that's enough! Put down your weapons!"

All at once Jackson's mood shifted. The rage drained out of him. It was ludicrous, ridiculous. The leading jurist of Tennessee, commanding general of militia, and the governor of the state standing on a dusty road shrieking curses, weapons checkmated. The orderly processes of a decent duel, a man seeking satisfaction for a gross insult to his wife, had degenerated into a common brawl.

He turned to Coffee. "I think we have no further business here." He mounted his horse. "Governor," he said, "I've posted you in the public prints for the coward I believe you to be. I shall be at your service should you summon the nerve to call on me. Meanwhile, stay out of my way."

He turned the horse and, with Jack following, rode slowly toward Knoxville. And with sudden striking insight, he understood the reality: This will hurt me. It went to no one's credit. We were equally ridiculous.

Everyone was talking about her, Rachel was sure of it. Andrew said no, it had passed, and at least his fight with Sevier had reminded folks of the peril inherent in a loose mouth.

"But that's it," she cried, "I don't want them *afraid* of us. I want them to respect us."

"They do, by God, they do!" he said, but she heard the belligerence, the threat in his voice.

"Oh, darling," she said, her voice a whisper, "we can't live at people's throats. You said yourself the West is changing, getting Louisiana, New Orleans ours, everything will be different. That's what you said and you're right. I hear it everywhere I go even if most folks don't think to put it that way. I don't think you can make your way in that bright future fighting every step of the way. I think the future needs you to be more than a fighter. It needs wisdom and strength." She hesitated, then plunged ahead. "I think it needs restraint. Restraint . . . I fear for us if we lack it . . ."

She let her voice trail off. There, she'd said what needed to be said and maybe he would hear her.

And then, the most remarkable thing. He said he agreed with her! She'd never heard him say that before, not on this issue that had stood between them for so long. Said he thought the fight with Sevier that had grown out of his most basic instinct had hurt him, made him ridiculous, made him seem a man out of control when he had thought he was at the heart of things. Said it was as if the times had swept by him when he'd thought of himself as the most modern of men, swept by him and left him locked in a little backwater with John Sevier.

As she stared openmouthed, he said, "I don't intend to be anywhere with Governor Sevier. You're going to see a new man. It'll take awhile for folks to understand that, but they will. It'll be all right."

Praise the Lord!

Jackson made himself live up to his new resolution. He stayed close to home, didn't go to the taverns, drank very little whiskey, took his birds out of the Saturday cockfights, went to the races and hardly spoke, tended his courtroom with care, authority, restraint, dealt hard with scoundrels but let his feelings show in his sentences, not in tongue lashings given from the bench.

The Louisiana Purchase had changed everything. The river was, or soon would be, open to New Orleans. This young fellow, Meriwether Lewis, and Clark, who was George Rogers Clark's little brother, and from that you knew he had to be all right, they were prepared to walk across the whole new territory and make it our own. Settlers were pouring over the Cumberland Gap, so he heard, and while many turned north into Kentucky or south into the Holstein Valley, plenty took the pike to Nashville and points beyond. This was still the frontier, but the town was full of new men and instinct told him that Sevier was of the past and he was of the future.

The West was opening. The settlers, the flowing river, the explorers ready to track the setting sun across the unknown all told him the East was losing its weight, that power was transferring over the Appalachians. Finance and manufacturing would remain in the East a long while, but this was a country built on land and land lay to the west. Mr. Jefferson understood that with his common man democracy, yeoman farmer at his plow; as long as new land lasted, the nation would grow and grow and Jackson couldn't see any end to it. No end—and he would be growing with it.

Thus his frame of mind after the purchase when all that he expected was coming to pass. He was a new man, calm, collected, magisterial, temper not dead but restrained. Rachel was delighted.

And then on a warm and dusty day in Nashville, when he had disposed of the last case a bit early, he stepped into the taproom of the Nashville Inn for a glass of ale. As he walked in, he heard a voice he recognized immediately as that of Cant Cantwell say, "Well, I don't know. Way I heard it, the governor threw his marriage up in his face and the governor's still alive. So maybe—"

Silence fell across the long, narrow room. Jackson heard a ringing in his ears as he walked to the far end where Cantwell stood before an empty fireplace. Cantwell started to speak but didn't, as if what he saw in Jackson's eyes stopped his tongue.

He was a big man, not as tall as Jackson but much heavier. Now he seemed to shrink a little. When the silence became unbearable, Jackson struck him backhanded in the mouth so hard he was knocked into the dead fireplace. He lay in the ashes staring at Jackson. He didn't move.

"If you want me," Jackson said, "you'll know where to find me."

He turned and walked out of the silent room. The Louisiana Purchase had saved the West; it would make the Mississippi Valley flower as only the infusion of money and people could do. It had changed everything, but perhaps it had changed nothing too. The West was still wild and rough, and a man still had to kill his own snakes.

44

WASHINGTON, FALL 1803

About dusk on an early fall evening, John Quincy Adams, senior senator from the State of Massachusetts, drove into Washington in a barouche with a coachman at the reins. The twenty-day trip from Boston had exhausted them all; Adams, Louisa, and even the little boys, George and John. Everything had gone wrong. They'd set out for New York by ship and found Long Island Sound thunderous with shipwreck weather. They held in New London, and when the storms abated a little and Adams pushed the captain to start again they were violently seasick. In New York they found people fleeing an outbreak of yellow fever. They hurried across the Hudson into New Jersey where Louisa fell sick. Yellow fever? He was terrified until she recovered a few days later. On, finally, to Washington.

Despite their weariness, he asked the coachman to drive slowly; he wanted to savor this raw, rude hamlet with its occasional magnificent building. For he was here now as an official, not a visitor; it was his place and already he knew that

the policy questions he would face as a senator would fasci-
nate him. He was equally sure that his fellow senators would
disappointment him. On Pennsylvania Avenue a small carriage leaving the president's house held up to let them pass.
But when they were close, the driver hailed him by name.

"Why, Senator Adams, welcome to Washington!"

In the pale light it took him a moment to recognize an old
Massachusetts friend, Samuel Otis, now secretary of the
senate. Otis leaped down, bowing to Mrs. Adams.

"Please, Johnny," Louisa whispered. She was exhausted
and still half sick. But he couldn't ignore Otis, so he clam-
bered down as the secretary said, "I've just delivered the
Louisiana treaty to the president; I'm afraid we've bought
the benighted province whether we want it or not."

"It passed without opposition then?"

"Not without opposition. Seven against, twenty-four in
favor. Every Federalist present voted nay, ranks unbroken."
He ticked off on his fingers. "Hillhouse and Tracy of Connecticut, Olcutt and Plumer of New Hampshire, Pickering of
Massachusetts, Wells and White of Delaware. Ross of Pennsylvania was absent. I, of course, as a mere functionary, have
no vote. Pity you weren't here; we'd have made a little better showing."

"No," Adams said, "I'd have made it twenty-five."

"Sir!" Otis stared at him. "You favor this mad acquisition
of Louisiana?"

"I do. It strengthens the whole country. Isn't that what
matters?"

"I see, sir, that you intend to stand alone."

"I hope not alone but certainly on principle."

"I expect that will mean alone then," Otis said slowly.
"I've known you and President Adams so long, I'm really
not surprised. But Democrats will despise you, and you'll be
a pariah among Federalists."

Well, Adams thought as the barouche went on toward
Stelle's Hotel, a man could do worse than that.

· · ·

Timothy Pickering's tortured smile suggested he was trying to be cordial. He had arrived the week before to take his seat, and he waylaid Adams in the members' lobby. The sleek vice president swept into the lobby just then. Adams bowed, which Mr. Burr returned with a courtly sweep of his hand as he hurried into the chamber and mounted the dais.

"We must talk," Pickering hissed. "Mr. Otis tells me you will support this Louisiana madness."

"Yes," Adams said, maintaining a steady smile, "I'd have voted aye yesterday had I arrived in time."

"I had hoped it was a jest," Pickering said. Plumer and Hillhouse and the other Federalists joined them.

Plumer spoke in an angry growl. "We can caucus in a corner, so few are we. Why we must stand together. But see here now, let's have this out immediately. It's downright sinful to encourage this Louisiana insanity. My God, sir, have you no common sense?"

They struck from all angles with a litany of fears and outrage, insistence that adding so much territory would destroy the Union as they knew it and New England in particular. Countless new states would be carved from the vast territory, each eager to plunge a spear into New England's heart. Slave states, they would make the nation a slavocracy, decent people outvoted and ruined, the last vestiges of all that was good and right about America swept away in a tide of mongrel variants.

"Don't you see?" Hillhouse cried, veins standing out on his forehead, face purpling. "This means the end of the Federalist Party, and that means the end of all chance of rule by the well-born, the wise, the good. Make us a mongrel people—"

"Oh, God," Pickering cried, "will you and your fatuous father never understand? Your region will abandon you, it will repudiate you, finally it will destroy you. We won't stay in a Union that sweeps in all the trash of the continent to drown us in common-man scrapings. We will separate, sir, and New York will join us. Great things are coming, and you, sir, you would do well to listen to your peers and abandon your arrogance and save your skin while it is still savable by voting as you should vote, as your people elected you to vote, as common sense and decency demand, as duty instructs—"

"Thank you for these insights, gentlemen," Adams said. "Shall we go in? I believe the Senate has come to order."

So they had declared and he had declared, and he would stand alone. As if to drive home the point, he attended a Democratic banquet celebrating the acquisition of Louisiana and drank to the toasts without offering one himself. He voted with Democrats to provide the funding that paid for bringing the vast new territory into the Union. He voted for a bill that not only admitted Louisiana but left the way open for acquiring other territory. Senator Ross voted with him on occasion but was full of Federalist rhetoric; the Essex men forgave Ross since he would have been tarred and feathered in Pittsburgh if he'd voted against Louisiana and an open Mississippi. Alexander Hamilton approved the purchase too, but he could be forgiven anything; he was the Federalist darling.

Not so Mr. Adams. "Curse on the stripling; how he apes his sire!" Theodore Lyman shouted. "He is a kite without a tail," Stephen Higginson announced to a rapt audience in his Boston bank, all reported to Adams as rapidly as horses could carry mail, ". . . violent and constant in his attempts to rise, lunging right and left but never truly up, ambitious to a fault even for the chair of state, and doomed to everlasting failure."

At parties, which he didn't enjoy though Louisa did, he played chess with the secretary of state. Mr. Madison was a strong, solid player, very hard to corner; Mr. Adams was quicker, lighter, swifter to strike; they were a good match.

"I expect a place could be found for you in the party of the future," Mr. Madison said one evening.

"Among Democrats?" Adams smiled. He was carefully polite, but he spoke his mind. "Never, sir. Never."

• • •

Adams had an analytical mind and was well versed in European affairs after nearly a decade there in the diplomatic service, so the question came naturally: why had Napoleon agreed to sell Louisiana after he'd gone to such trouble to batter Spain into releasing it? He put this to Madison over the chessboard.

"We made it in his interest," the secretary said.

Adams was horrified. "Surely you don't mean you . . . you bribed him?"

Anger flashed on Madison's face; an abrupt hand movement scattered chessmen. Adams had a sudden feeling of danger; he was seeing a much different Madison. In a low, compressed voice, the secretary said, "Certainly not, sir! I take the very question as highly offensive."

Adams heard a tremble in his own voice and stiffened himself as he said, "I meant no offense, but you said 'in his interest.' "

"By that I meant we demonstrated that the cost of his enterprise was more than he could afford. Gave him an interest in pulling out. In short, we showed him he couldn't hold Louisiana and would destroy himself if he tried."

They righted the chessmen and started a new game, but when it was done neither was interested in another.

But Adams found that too easy an answer. Napoleon often said that nothing was impossible. Experts told him he couldn't cross the Alps in winter, but he'd taken his army over with heavy artillery and descended on the Italian states to crush them in lightning strokes. That Louisiana was beyond him didn't sound like Napoleon.

So Adams waited until he and Louisa dined with his old friend Louis Pichon and his pale wife. Through a good dinner and into a second bottle of wine, he and Louis regaled the women with stories of the three-month holiday tour they had taken together, Italy and the Greek Isles and back via Barcelona, with its theater and street music and booming opera. But Pirette wasn't well and when it was time for the ladies to withdraw, Louisa, who was kindness itself, said, "Johnny, Pirette needs to rest; I'll take the carriage home and send it back for you." When Adams saw her out, she whispered, "Don't stay too late. Her baby's dying and there's nothing she can do to help the poor little thing. She'll need her husband tonight."

When he returned Louis had set out cognac and cigars. Adams asked if he should stay. Louis nodded. "Please. It's very hard on Pirette . . . our little boy. Better she sleeps now. . . ."

So Adams asked, Why did Louis think Napoleon agreed to sell? Mr. Madison seemed to feel the United States had bullied him into the move; but knowing something of Napoleon, he'd been doubtful.

"Perhaps you misread Mr. Madison. Bullied isn't right."

"So I suspected. But what is the story?"

Louis drew on his cigar, watching Adams. At last he said, "On what basis do you ask?"

Adams stiffened. "I need a reason?"

"John, I am a diplomat. You are an official of the host government—"

"No, I am a U.S. senator with a free voice, answerable only to my constituents."

"Whom, if gossip be trusted, you don't spend much time pleasing."

"I must please my own conscience first of all. If that doesn't please them, so be it." He waved a hand, dismissing a petty issue. "To respond to your concern, I ask for no purpose beyond the inherent fascination of the question, and I will make no use of what I may learn."

Louis had a faint smile. "Thank you for the assurance. I felt duty required my query, and I too respond to duty."

Adams smiled and touched the back of the other's hand. "So, my friend, answer me or tell me duty instructs you not to."

Louis laughed. "All right, all right, let us not become ridiculous. You misread Mr. Madison in using the term 'bullied,' but the essential idea is correct. The Americans demon-

strated that Louisiana could not be held. I flatter myself I
played no small part in getting Paris to understand that
point."

He described the brutal events in Santo Domingo, the
pressure under which Leclerc had put him, the first consul's
fury at his even questioning a favorite general, the fear he
felt for his own head as he continued to report what neither
Leclerc nor the first consul wanted to hear. With a start
Adams realized his friend was a truly brave man. Louis
added, without inflection, that he thought it was Pirette's
worry in this period that had contributed to their baby's failing health since birth.

"Every week without fail Mr. Madison called me in and
made a new argument, most of which I already had mounted
to Paris. He sent a New Orleans merchant to make the moneymen in Paris see what they had to lose, he enlisted the
whole Du Pont family in America's behalf, made them feel
they were prime negotiators on whom everything depended,
and by accretion, so to speak, water wearing down stone,
made Paris see that it would have to fight forever to hold the
province."

He ran through the rest of it, most of which Adams already understood, boiling down to the assurance that
couldn't be doubted that the United States would ally with
the Royal Navy and join the continental war against France.
Add France's disaster in Santo Domingo and it all tipped the
weight against. Adams marveled at the courage of slaves
standing against a major power and winning. He said he
doubted many of his countrymen understood what they
owed those black patriots. A sour look crossed Louis's face
and Adams remembered it had been young French troops
those blacks had been killing, and his voice trailed off.

"And then, you know," Louis said, "the American frontiersman has quite a reputation in Europe. Ferocious, deadly,
implacable, rides alligators for sport and wrestles bears, rivals
the wild Indians in bloodthirstiness . . . overdrawn a bit,
doubtless, but I think real in essence. A fellow came through
here from Tennessee—Jackson, I think his name was, Irish

ancestry out of Carolina, apparently—quite ferocious. I didn't take him entirely seriously, but then he talked to Montane. You know Montane?"

As Louis described him, this General Montane sounded interesting; he had opened an export-import business in Baltimore to which he was applying the same ability that had brought him a general officer's rank in the army.

"It seems this Jackson was not just a pioneer, he was a commanding general of the Tennessee militia, and he and Montane spoke the same language. Later Montane told me to take him very seriously indeed, and I paid attention to that."

So it was just as Mr. Madison had said, all American pressure? Adams said he was surprised.

Louis smiled. "Of course, that's not all of it."

"Ah. So I had supposed."

Long silence while Lewis drew on his cigar. "How well do you know the first consul?"

"Don't know him at all. I've spoken to him two, no, three times, at receptions. Awesome every time."

"Those of us whose careers and sometimes lives depend on his whims, we get to know him quite well." Even here in America, he added, he had kept up—had a friend well placed on the general staff who kept him abreast of things, all very sub rosa.

"First, understand that when Napoleon seized power four years ago, France was in a desperate condition. Ten years of revolution had demolished almost everything and had led to such violent excesses the people were frantic for relief. There were explosions of joy when he announced the revolution was over."

"And they got in its place a dictator."

"Yes . . . but this is no return to the absolutism of monarchy, no raising of nobles. His Legion of Honor, it alarmed a lot of French democrats, but entry to it was by merit not birth. Countless parts of French society have that same openness to the common man. The national university, the system of lycées he established, every scholar accepted on merit, the ten thousand special scholarships so no outstanding student can be denied. Even opened national schools for girls, three schools—*everyone* to be educated." Adams could see that his friend was a little shocked by this outbreak of equality, and it surprised him too.

Louis rushed on in full voice. The man establishes the Banque de France and stabilizes an economy that had been out of control for a decade. He establishes hospitals, medicine open to every citizen. He sets up a new legal code, civil, criminal, regularizes what has been chaotic, unjust, ridden with favoritism in which little men are given the most barbaric sentences and rich men and nobles walk free. Already some of the new code had taken effect; it was promised in full for the next year.

"So you see," Louis said, "he has brought order, confidence, stability back to France; he has greatly improved the society; he has rejected monarchical forms just as fiercely as the revolution ever did, if not so destructively. In short, he is a great man, no doubt the greatest of the age. He has put his stamp on France, and France has put its stamp on everything from the Atlantic to the Urals. Europe will never be the same, believe me, no matter what happens to Napoleon."

"But there's a price for all this, I suppose," Adams said.

"Of course. The secret police are ever vigilant." He looked ready to say more and then stopped himself. Well, it didn't matter. In today's France loose talk probably was dangerous, even for a diplomat, perhaps especially for a diplomat. The secret police were always the key to despotism, monarchical or otherwise. The torturers of the tzar's secret police were notorious. Adams already knew that in France everyone guarded his tongue. Open debate was rare, though it had been rare under the revolution too, after the first thrilling days of liberty and equality and fraternity, ironic words today.

As on Napoleon's bright side, you saw his genius on the dark side as well—the amazing energy, the single-minded focus, the implacable certainty, the capacity to see deeply

into every situation, to leap ahead as needed, to confound his
enemies at every turn, on the battlefield and at home.

Napoleon himself was the chief censor. No book could be
published in today's France, no play presented without his
approval. He demanded uniformity of ideas—his ideas, the
only right ones. Work was for the common good, which he
defined. Views different from his own were degenerate, dissent was not tolerated, every block had spies reporting all
that was said, fodder for the secret police, the knock in the
night, the victim dragged away. History was being rewritten
to reflect only French glory, blemishes ironed out. Perhaps
that last bothered Adams the student and scholar more than
anything. Yes, France was paying a price for the stability
given it by Napoleon Bonaparte.

"Still," Adams said, "you'd think that an overweening
pride would hold him to an American empire."

"But that's exactly it," Louis said. "Things weren't working well in America. Between black rebels and yellow fever,
he'd had an army destroyed, so he must send another. Of
course he could occupy and hold New Orleans, but he'd forever be fighting a man far different from the masses in Europe, a free man willing to die for his freedom, a man trained
in the rough and tumble of the frontier. And while his armies
faced this rather ferocious figure, his supply vessels would
be under attack by Royal Navy ships. Not a very comfortable picture.

"And then, quite separately, the slavery issue. In today's
republic, hangover from the revolution, you know, slavery is
anathema. If he left it intact in Louisiana, he'd have an uproar at home. If he banned it there, he'd have an uproar
there."

"But offsetting that, the great American breadbasket
would be his—corn and wheat pouring in from the Mississippi Valley."

"Yes . . . but if he had war again, he'd have client states all
around that could be milked for the gold to *buy* American
grain . . . and maybe that was one more attraction."

"You're saying he wanted European war?"

Louis shrugged. "You know as well as I do that it had never really stopped. The pause was no more than that, a truce."

"Agreed."

"You understand—Napoleon, France itself, always had one great enemy, and it was never little America."

"Britain the goal, eh?" Adams was smiling.

"Exactly. Gone on for six hundred years, that rivalry . . ."

And then, Adams thought, that pride that seemed to underlie all that Napoleon did. How can you be *the* power if there is another power? And Britain with its dominating fleet was very much another power. Napoleon had conquered Europe essentially, all but Russia, and there was Albion on its little island defying him. And see: Europe at peace gave him subservient allies; Europe at war meant client states that could be bled for treasure and troops. For Napoleon Bonaparte, war was natural: He was first of all a soldier.

"Apparently he was hungry for Egypt again," Adams said. "The Sebastiani article—they say it had huge influence."

Louis gave him a skeptical look and didn't answer.

"Who is Sebastiani, anyway?"

"An old diplomat cum soldier or soldier cum diplomat. Deeply involved in Egypt when the British trapped Napoleon there and he had to duck out and abandon his men."

Adams smiled. "I understand when he came home from that debacle, he seized power in the coup that gave him his office today. An odd reward for losing an army in Egypt."

Louis's eyebrows rose. "A subject I don't discuss."

"Of course. I shouldn't have yielded to temptation." He heard Louis's soft chuckle. "But the Sebastiani article arguing that Egypt is ripe and the road to India clear—it's a chance to avenge Britain ejecting France from India so long ago."

Louis smiled. "But where did it run? In *Le Moniteur*—Napoleon's paper. Nothing goes in it without his approval. Sebastiani influencing Napoleon? No, I think the first consul told him what to write."

"But Napoleon told Ambassador Whitworth that France would have Malta or it would have war—that's well documented."

"Quite so."

"And Malta is a way station to Egypt. There'd be no chance of conquering there with Malta in enemy hands. And Britain will fight to hold it for just that reason."

"Makes a perfect case for war, doesn't it?"

Adams gazed at his friend. "You're saying—"

Louis shook his head. "I'm not saying."

"No, of course. But one could surmise that the man wanted war for another reason, and Malta was a handy excuse."

"I suppose one could so surmise."

"Now, see here, Louis. You've brought me this far, you can't just leave me here."

Louis gave him a long, level look. He went noiselessly to the door and opened it suddenly. The hall was dark and empty. He left the door open but drew his chair close to Adams. "The servants are asleep." He was whispering. His voice sank further. Adams could scarcely hear. "He intends to invade Britain directly. Across the channel."

"My God! Against the Royal Navy?" Adams whispered too.

"He wants to mount a fleet of a couple thousand small boats and send them over in a storm. That or build the French fleet till it can keep the British busy. He needs war to rally all the forces and extract plunder from client states and drain the national treasury for so extraordinary a plan. Finally, war lets him stitch together a continental syndicate or system to destroy Britain economically. Deny it all trade."

Yes, Adams could see that that could be devastating. Britain lived on the value added to the raw material she imported to make the finished goods she exported. If Napoleon could make such a scheme work, he could weaken Britain until she was gasping and then some dark night two thousand boats would start across a channel only twenty-four miles wide at its narrow point. And Napoleon would be ruler of all he saw. Knowing the man even from a distance, it was easy to imagine him so dreaming.

"There's a story," Louis said, "perhaps apocryphal, perhaps not, that the first consul told his secretary rather sadly that for all his accomplishments, if he stopped now world history would give him half a page. And he wants a chapter."

"Then Mr. Madison was wrong. The decision really had little to do with us."

"No, no, no, John—you draw the wrong conclusion. The first consul's decision resulted directly from the campaign Mr. Madison waged, just as I said. He made Napoleon see that America was more trouble—would cost him more of his real interest—than he could afford. He could never have realized his dream of conquering England if he were in a slogging match in America. In short, Mr. Madison won the battle that he was waging."

There was a long silence. Louis emptied his glass and said, "Yes, perhaps the first consul's interests were larger. But Mr. Madison fought his own war, and he did it brilliantly. And very successfully."

Adams stood to go. "Thank you, Louis," he said.

45

NEW YORK AND WASHINGTON, LATE FALL 1803

For Aaron Burr the French offer to sell Louisiana was the worst possible news. He remembered as in a sick nightmare the day the page galloped into the senate chamber waving a communication from the president. Burr was on the dais, eyelids sagging as Sam Smith of Maryland droned on about something the point of which the senate president already had forgotten. He was struggling not to disgrace himself by

falling asleep with his head flopping on the desk, and he was
scarcely aware as he unfolded the message.

But the contents jerked him wide awake. France to *sell*
Louisiana to the United States, settling the whole issue in a
stroke! So completely did this ruin his hopes and plans that
he felt a wave of nausea and feared he would vomit on the
desk. In a croaking voice, he summoned the majority
leader. "I believe you'll want to present this to your colleagues." And he'd sat there, contemplating the death of
dreams.

For now the Virginian would be unbeatable. Whatever the
mad and foolish reason behind the French decision to sell,
Jefferson would get the credit. Had Napoleon stuck to his
plans and put troops on the Mississippi, the sick weakness of
this politician manqué would have been instantly exposed
and the people would have driven him from office at the next
election and might have tarred and feathered him as well.
The whole world would have learned of his imbecility, and
by the very force of nature the man Jefferson had reviled and
abused, the New York alternative to the Virginian, would
have been lifted to the heights.

He hammered the gavel, declared the senate in recess "to
digest this momentous news," and hurried off to his rooms
where he threw himself down on his couch with an arm
across his eyes. He awakened an hour later calm and clear-
headed. Yes, it was distressing, but all it meant was that his
plans must change. Jefferson could not be deposed in 1804;
so be it. But 1808? All his political instincts told him the
story would be utterly different by then. This bit of good fortune the Virginian had encountered through no effort of his
own would soon be forgotten and the man's ineptness would
be clear. Democrats would turn readily to the powerful governor who controlled the second largest state, the only man,
indeed, who could draw votes from both sides of the spec-
trum for overwhelming totals!

He had counted too much on the Louisiana loss, that was
all. That in itself was disturbing. He wouldn't want to think

of himself as a man who lived on dreams. He prided himself on realism, which he regarded as the sine qua non of politics. But actually, this news meant very little. It said he must do immediately what he long had been planning—hie himself back to New York and prepare to take up the reins again. What he had expected in 1804 would come in 1808, and for the sheer unadulterated pleasure of taking the office from the sainted Tom, he could readily wait four more years. Nourish himself on anticipation. He would make travel plans tomorrow. And he slept again, sweat slowly staining his linen.

"Know why Governor Clinton ain't standing for another term in New York?" Senator Pickering asked.

He had proposed the dinner in a private room at Stelle's and the Federalist powers were there, Hillhouse and Tracy of Connecticut, Plumer of New Hampshire from the Senate, Roger Griswold and Samuel Baker of Connecticut from the House.

"You tell me," Burr said.

" 'Cause he's going on the national ticket next year with Jefferson." When Burr didn't respond, Pickering added, prodding him, "In your spot, Vice President, cutting you out."

Burr chuckled and said, "You called a meeting to tell me something so obvious?"

Pickering colored and Hillhouse said smoothly, "We were reflecting our own surprise—and the sense of opportunity it opened to our hopes and, we believe, to yours."

Ah, now they were coming to it. Pickering was clumsy as always, backing into the point. Burr had accepted the reality—or so it now seemed to him that he had done—when the Virginians began courting the old governor and his sycophant nephew, DeWitt. Now DeWitt had given up his Senate seat and gone back to become New York City's mayor. The Clintons supposed that gave them the city, but Burr knew better.

Peter Van Ness had established a new paper, the *Chronicle Express,* to counter the poison in the Clinton attacks on Burr. He'd written a series of scathing articles signed Aristides after the famous Greek who'd been known as "the Just," which was exactly how Peter saw his patron and himself. He'd written a book too, putting a permanent cap on what had come to be called the Pamphlet War, throwing Clinton slime back in their faces. So the Burr forces had not been asleep. He had been slow to acknowledge the governor's attacks, yes, because he didn't want to elevate them from the gutter. But when they did answer they were ferocious, battering Clinton hip and thigh. Of course these Federalist leaders knew all this.

Burr was enjoying himself, subtly dominating a dinner that the blustering Pickering supposed was all his. The food was good, the wine excellent, though he continued to take it sparingly, and the scene was radically different from the humiliation the last Federalist dinner at this same hotel had worked on him.

"Do you have any idea how disastrous this Louisiana madness really is?" Pickering asked. Hillhouse raised a hand. "I'm sure so astute an observer as Mr. Burr is fully aware, Timothy," he said. "A slavocracy in the making, endless territory to be carved into states that must in no great time overwhelm the original states. What happens then to the fine blood stock that made this country great, the ideals and genius and nobility that mark the true American? All to be overrun by men who traffic in human chattel, a party and a people led by a man who beds his own slaves and breeds his own slave stock. Oh, sir, you know and I know this is not what the people of New York intended when they gave this Virginia mountebank their votes. Isn't this the final straw? Isn't it the ultimate signal that says New England and New York must look to their own interests and prepare to stand alone?"

Burr saw a mad cast in his eyes and realized he was just as wild as Pickering, with somewhat smoother mien. But the texture of confederates doesn't really matter, only what they can do for you. On the other hand, there was no need to commit to anything nor, most certainly, to respond to rhetorical questions. He kept his silence, allowing a faint smile on his face, waiting.

Nothing new in a sense. They were talking secession, outrage over Louisiana just another string in a harp they long had been plucking. *Sep-ar-ray-shuuun* . . . Was he interested in secession? Who knew? He was interested in a commanding position in 1808, interested in demolishing Jefferson and Madison, in being president of the United States. But if that didn't come to pass, then command of a new country—small, compact, rich—that might be considerable compensation.

Actually, it was Plumer and Griswold, practical men, who took over when the talk came to cases. They assumed Burr would run for the governor's chair that Clinton was vacating, which was so obvious he didn't bother to nod. Therefore they wanted to put real money behind him. They wanted him to stage a couple of big steer roasts in every county with barrels of whiskey and kegs of beer and all the trimmings that go with savory beef and roast hog and lamb, with red-blooded speakers to present the benefits of Governor Burr in the statehouse and local leaders to add their endorsements, and then a separate doing for the ladies, with sewing bees and canning contests and preaching for those who sought it because ladies don't vote but you'd be surprised how many tell their husbands how to vote. You'd just be surprised.

Wanted him to put on half a dozen such extravaganzas down on the Battery in New York City and have emissaries wandering Peck's Slip with a bucket of beer in each hand, walking into taverns and shouting, "On the house and vote for Burr!"

All this would take money, real money, and what they wanted to do, they wanted to put the resources of New England commerce and banking and manufacture and shipping behind him.

"And," Pickering growled, "when you're elected—"

Hillhouse cut him off. "I think Mr. Burr knows our interests, Timothy. Mr. Burr is a great modern gentleman; I think he'll remember us at the appropriate time."

Burr smiled. Didn't say a word, just smiled, and that was all it took. A very satisfactory dinner.

Burr knew how to wait. It was one of his great strengths and he guarded it carefully, ready to squelch impatience the moment it reared its head. He kept his people going slowly, talking up a Burr candidacy now and again but always with an indefinite air. The Democrats were looking over candidates to replace their titular leader, who was going on to the vice presidency. Of course, DeWitt was the real leader.

Meanwhile several local Democratic groups met and nominated Burr. It wouldn't mean much after the DeWitt machinery took hold, but it told him he was still strong among garden variety Democrats, the folks whose votes told the story in the end. Then the DeWitt Democrats fixed on John Lansing. That disturbed Burr. Lansing was a good man, serving as chancellor, the post Robert R. Livingston held before he went off to Paris to buy Louisiana. He worried a bit. Lansing might prove a difficult man to unseat. Still, he reined in impatience.

A half-dozen different Federalists called quietly on Burr. Was he interested? He told one after another to show some patience, wait, lie low. Then, so the talk around the state went, Lansing was told he could be governor in name, but DeWitt would wield the power. Lansing was too big a man for that. He withdrew, and the DeWitt forces centered on Morgan Lewis, an old-line judge of no great dash noted for being quick to do exactly what he was told.

Burr relaxed. Morgan Lewis should be downright easy to take.

When it was too late for the Democrats to shift to a stronger candidate, the Federalists met. Their disadvantage in numbers was offset by the Democratic votes Burr could expect to draw. Alexander Hamilton mounted a battle against nominating Burr, which certainly was galling. Burr lodged it carefully in memory, but held his peace. For now.

Numerous convention speakers sang to a single tune: Yes, yes, Alex was the father of the party and must be reckoned with, and yes, he certainly didn't like Burr but this time the aim was not niceties of ideology—they wanted to *win* and Burr was the man who could add Democratic votes to his total. They refused to nominate a Federalist candidate for governor of New York and made it clear that Federalists should vote for Burr, standing as an independent.

The virtues of patience. He stood against a rival he couldn't help but beat, being more popular with Democrats even as an independent than was Morgan Lewis, the Democratic candidate. He had ample wherewithal to make sure that every voter in New York was courted with beef and booze, the essence of political campaigning. Keep 'em well fed and well-likkered and in his view you could hardly go wrong.

Pleased and relaxed, he returned to Washington for the final weeks presiding over the Senate. He felt his future was as assured as it can be in politics. As governor of New York he would wield the state as a club in national politics. By 1808, the Virginia cabal would have shot its bolt and exposed its emptiness to everyone, and it would be New York's turn on the carrousel. The beaten Virginian would step down; the New Yorker would step up. He would say something about his old rival in his inaugural remarks, something gracious but neatly condescending—he would have to craft the remark with careful thought, but he had plenty of time to work out something brilliant.

And should perchance something go awry in all this, there was always Senator Pickering and his friends waiting in the wings. All told, Burr had every reason to feel at the top of his form.

46

Jimmy came home exhausted but elated. He had walked he said, his cheeks stung from the cold. He threw off his coat and stood with his back to the glowing fireplace, bouncing on his toes and looking ready to laugh. Dolley sat in her Queen Anne chair, a shawl pulled around her shoulders. Sukey brought in the tea tray and Jimmy took a cup, holding it against his palms to warm them.

"Message from New Orleans came in today," he said, beaming. "It's done. Louisiana is ours—stars and stripes aloft." He said the message had been written the same night and sent by special messenger, who'd made it in seventeen days flat, horseback all the way, up the Natchez Trace, over the Knoxville Pike, up the Great Valley.

She felt a surge of relief. "No trouble then?" That had been the question. Would the Spanish, enraged by the French move and still in control, actually surrender the territory? Would the people, French to the core and even by Danny's admission having no love for Americans, accept this change in status without question? Or would it trigger revolt?

They had sent General Wilkinson with four hundred troops to be sure matters didn't get out of hand, and doubtless that accounted for some of the quiet, but Jimmy said the letter made it clear there was no real opposition. In a fit of peevishness, Spanish officials insisted on turning the province over to the French prefect who had been sent to receive it in the first place; an hour later the prefect surrendered it to the Americans and up went the flag. Next, in six weeks or so, a similar ceremony would pass St. Louis to the United States and the great transaction would be complete.

"The tightrope walker in the circus?" Jimmy said, drawing an ottoman close to the fire and sitting with elbows on knees. "Don't you suppose that when he's on the rope he just goes ahead with his balance by feel and doesn't think about where he is? And afterward, well, he's a professional, so maybe not, but you'd think he'd look at that wiggling rope and the distance down and he'd think, Oh, my word, what was I doing? Or at least, I would, and Dolley, that's how I feel about this Louisiana thing too. Calling in Pichon every week, conceiving of new ways to tell Napoleon we'd beat him while not admitting that to do so we'd had to destroy ourselves or close to it, change the whole nature of our history anyway and our very concept of ourselves."

He threw out his arms, swelling his chest. "How wonderfully it's all worked out, but it wasn't complete, you know, things could still have gone wrong, till the actual transfer."

Apparently he and Tom had talked at length. Everything seemed to be going splendidly. Maggie's husband at the *National Intelligencer* said papers coming to his office from across the country were uniformly lauding the Democrats. Even New England Democrats were gaining strength, and papers from Massachusetts and Connecticut made that clear, even if in the form of editorial denunciation. The party couldn't yet carry either state, but in both it grew stronger every day. Jimmy said even the Essex Junto seemed to be drawing in its horns; day by day young Mr. Adams distanced himself further from the Federalist radicals.

Of course the West was delighted and throbbing with new activity. Possession of the river solved the West's deepest concerns for the future; Senator Ross reported that hordes of people were pouring through Pittsburgh and launching themselves down the Ohio. Said he himself had new status; he could do no wrong in his people's eyes. And as for the president, why, in Pittsburgh they figured Mr. Jefferson walked on water. After the final transfer at St. Louis, western settlement would be as an arrow released from the bow.

Nor was this just from Ross. Reports flowed in from all over, a merchant in Lexington who appeared to be a militia commander too, that volatile Tennessee general and an equally volatile judge, maybe one and the same, the covey of Americans in the Natchez colony, Captain Lewis reporting from his winter camp near St. Louis that folks on both sides of the great river were delighted.

But if success hadn't come, if the pressure Jimmy had applied to the Frenchman hadn't been enough, if Napoleon had decided to skip European war in favor of western empire— if, in short, we had had to fight, everything would have changed in a finger snap. Then Federalists would have been triumphant and Democrats condemned as weak, clumsy, unfocused, without strength or power, lovely in theory but failing before the world's brutality.

"To think," she said, "it could have died in its infancy, written off as one of those wonderful ideas that aren't strong enough to stand on their own, and we'd never have known for sure if we'd even been right at the start." She hesitated and then spoke her mind. "I think God was watching over democracy."

Jimmy smiled. "You do, eh?" Well, Jimmy was an eighteenth-century rationalist; his view of God was somewhat remote. "Think He shines on Democrats too? We're the personification of democracy?"

Nettled, she said, "Yes, I do!"

"Apparently the president does too," Jimmy said. He had moved to a chaise and tossed a throw over his legs. He was favoring a cough she didn't like. She heard a touch of asperity in his voice. "Seems he's a rationalist but not that much of a rationalist."

"Really? What did he say?"

"We were talking about how well the Democrats are doing after Louisiana, the West all enthusiastic, the East almost as eager, commerce picking up, not a cloud in the skies— suddenly it seemed a little too euphoric. Just as that thread of uneasiness tickled at me, he fired a cannon. Said we were so strong that he didn't need to run again. You know he hates the job and can't wait to get back to Monticello. What with all this popularity, says anyone can win: why does he have to endure another four years?"

Her stomach lurched. "Who—whom did he have in mind?" She thought her voice sounded like a croak.

He looked at her. "Me," he said. "Said I should stand in his place."

She felt a mad surge of joy even as every instinct shouted that it wouldn't work. And at once she realized as she had not quite realized before, not fully, just how ambitious she really was—for him and for herself and for what they could do in this country. And she knew it wouldn't work. She stood to put another stick on the fire and stir it with the poker.

"What did you tell him?" Her voice was nicely even.

"That it was madness. That it would destroy all that we'd gained. That the people associate him with the revolution we've worked and him with the Louisiana Purchase, him and no one else."

"You had as much to do with both," she said.

"Oh, yes. He agrees with that, you know, doesn't deny me an ounce of credit. But the people, they see these things as his doing, with a bit of assistance from his lieutenants; and in the midst of adulation, if he stepped down they would be disoriented and God knows where they might turn."

That was the cold fact of it all right.

"Might well turn to Monroe," he said.

Now, *that* was an infuriating thought! Even now Monroe was fighting bitterly with Livingston, trying to seize credit for the great purchase. It seemed ridiculous to her since the agreement was struck the very day he arrived, but he claimed it was his coming that made the French see that now they must toe the line because the Americans were sending in their heavy artillery, and so they had timed their offer to his arrival. Livingston was fighting hard, drawing on his wide strength in New York and his connections with Governor Clinton and his nephew, DeWitt, the same whom it appeared Aaron was preparing to challenge right now. Tom and Jimmy were carefully staying out of the fight.

But what disturbed her most was that the radical Democrats were talking to Monroe as their candidate for the presidency, and he was listening! He was the darling of Sam Smith and John Randolph and the rest of the radicals, who felt that Tom and Jimmy were knuckling under to Federalists they should have cleaned from the government in one wild sweep, their prime example that Mr. Wagner hadn't been fired even though Federalists now denouncing the poor man as an apostate were outshouting the radical Democrats. Yet Monroe had just stepped down as governor of Virginia, he was well-regarded in the West, he was staking a claim, valid or not, on the Louisiana triumph—yes, just at the moment he might be a formidable candidate.

"What did Tom say?"

Madison tossed off the throw and crossed the room to pour two glasses of their best Madeira and then positioned himself, standing before the fire again. "You know," he said, "I couldn't tell how serious he was in the first place. You never quite know with Tom. Maybe he just threw it on the table the way he does so many things, though we know he does hate the job and can't wait to go home. He's never equivocal on that. Maybe the sheer brutality of the dusky doxy story made him hate it even more. But I'll tell you, the idea of Monroe taking over sobered him in a hurry. Said with the radicals in control, the Federalists would win everything back at the next election. No question—we all see that extremes won't work. That's why the Essex Junto is in trouble—perceived as extremes that only prosper in desperate times."

Yes, yes, Jimmy did natter on sometimes.

"So what did he say?"

"Oh, he agreed readily enough. Said all right, he'd stand for another term. But he said he was putting me on notice now—next term will be his last. Says I must be ready to take over then."

There! That was what she'd been waiting to hear. What

she'd been dreaming of for years. In fact, truth be known, she'd had this in her mind before Tom was elected, back in Virginia when she was imagining the future unfolding.

Her lips were dry. "And what did you say?"

"That I didn't think I was the right man for it."

"Jimmy! You didn't!"

"Well, yes—"

"Whatever possessed you? Of course you're the right man for it. Who else is there? Monroe? Aaron Burr? Hamilton? Who—young Adams? Some illustrious senator wise as Solomon? Who, for goodness sake?"

"I'm not a leader, Dolley. I'm just not."

"Then you must become one. Anyway, you are. You are! You led the whole Louisiana campaign, you worked it like a field general, you made the most powerful man in the world come to you, who in the devil are you to tell me you're not a leader!"

He had to laugh at that. "But all the same, darling," he said, "I don't *feel* it."

"Oh, Jimmy," she cried, and let the tears flow. They were real but not without calculation. This was madness, and he had to be brought to see it.

Tears didn't work this time. "Now, Dolley," he said, "let's not get carried away. We'll see. Maybe in time I'll develop some leadership. Meanwhile, war is blazing in Europe and we are sure to be caught in its backwash, impressment by the Royal Navy, Napoleon trying to force our support. That'll keep me busy—"

"I don't doubt you'll be busy—"

"Well," he said with an air of ending the conversation, "there's no rush. I have four more years to decide—"

"No!" Danger loomed as an open pit ahead. "No, that's just it. You can't wait. If you don't decide you want it right now, that you can do it, that no one else could do it as well, that you'll fight and fight, then . . ." She let her voice trail off; she thought she'd never felt anything so passionately.

"Then what?" He was glaring at her.

"Then you won't get it."

He didn't answer and she said, "It'll be denied you, be taken from you, some miserable lesser person whose only asset is that he really wants it—Mr. Monroe, for example, or Aaron—will get it. And you'll be out."

"Dolley, that's not—"

"Jimmy, think about it! Don't answer me for a moment. Just think. Then tell me you think I'm wrong."

He sat still on the ottoman, watching her. The French clock of brass on the mantle ticked loud in the silence. She heard a carriage drawn by a team go by with a clatter of hoofs. Snowflakes clicked against a window glass. The silence stretched. Would he see it? Could she be wrong? But she knew she wasn't wrong, and in a moment she knew that he knew too. You can't reach for the heights without wanting the heights with all your soul. Even under the most favorable conditions, the climb is too arduous and painful, pitfalls lurking at every turn.

He smiled slightly and sighed and tension seemed to flow from him in a stream. His very shoulders relaxed and at once he looked comfortable, less with the idea than with himself. "Well," he said, "that's the question, do I want it or don't I? Because you're right—if you don't know what you want, you send signals—and others *do* know what they want. Aaron, for example—in his sly, sleek way he thinks of nothing but what he wants for himself." He stood and poked at the fire, still looking very relaxed.

"Cast against some abstract ideal, General Washington or even Tom, I don't feel much like a leader. But against Aaron or James Monroe or Colonel Hamilton or Rufus King or anyone I can think of, I'd choose myself. Honestly, I know no one who would do it better than I, and it would break my heart to watch someone throw it all away."

"Abstract ideals aside, then, you do want it," she said.

"I do." Then, with gathering force, standing straighter, hands on hips, "I do. I really do."

"So?"

"So we'll see, four years from now, but I don't think I can

be beaten if I start now. It's a matter of posture and positioning; that's your idea and I think it's right."

He had it now—not campaigning, of course, to present
himself as hungry for office would be fatal, even Aaron up in
New York insisted he was merely willing to serve on the
people's call. But letting those who count, those on the inside, know that he is the natural successor. Let him stand
ready, the goal always in mind; if he knows it, everyone will
know it.

Then he laughed out loud, rubbing his hands together.
"And the mansion will be yours, and you can repair it to
your heart's content. I'll authorize anything and everything."

She jumped up and into his arms. "You are a darling," she
said, and kissed him. She felt their future was settled.

They had dinner, whatever the cook had prepared in the separate kitchen out back, and were well into the second bottle
of wine before they went upstairs. There was a lot of laughter and reminiscence and easy talk about easy things and
snippets of gossip interworked with observations on the
foibles of their friends, and in the whole time Dolley didn't
mention what she would do with the big white house in
which the president lived and worked.

Jimmy was tired and went to bed, but Dolley was boiling
with energy and she donned a blanket robe and fur slippers
and kissed him and pinched out the candle and sat in the alcove formed by the bay window in their bedroom, where
moonlight was bright enough to read by and the stars were a
glittering swath across the sky.

It would be unseemly to talk overmuch of the great
house's possibilities, perhaps even courting misfortune in
the future. But Dolley had a new friend, one Benjamin Latrobe, an architect from England whom Tom had engaged to
design a drydock that would lay up the Federalist frigates.
She thought the frigates hadn't really gone out of service
and the dock probably hadn't been built or at any rate fin-

ished and she wasn't interested enough to ask. She had found herself next to him at a presidential dinner one afternoon. He was rather a handsome fellow with tousled brown hair and light eyes and a very English look, whatever that meant, and in fact she wasn't sure except that he fitted her sense of the English, who were pleasant enough when they weren't impressing our seamen and coercing our trade. There was something poetic in his speech and she liked him.

She'd scarcely noticed him until she turned to him out of courtesy and he said in his soft voice, pleasing her with the use of the honorific, "Doesn't *madame* think this gorgeous building deserves more attention?" She stared at him as he spoke her thoughts aloud. "The walls, so shabby. Water damage not recent—the roof's been fixed, I take it, but the interior ignored. In fact, you know, the interior rivals the exterior in importance, in meaning—a building's soul is on the inside."

He paused, wide-eyed. "But perhaps *madame* does not agree, perhaps she thinks a foreigner's criticism rude and unseemly, which indeed it is, and yet—"

She put her hand on his to quiet him. "Perhaps you are a treasure, sir. Tell me, you seem conversant with the interior arts—is that a matter of taste or of experience?"

He drew himself up. "I am primarily an architect, but I have decorated some of the great homes of England."

She made up her mind. "Why don't you come here for tea tomorrow. Mr. Madison and I will give you a tour." Mr. Madison so no errant thoughts would strike the architect and because it would do Mr. Madison a world of good to see the house's faults through a professional eye.

Mr. Latrobe rose fully to her hopes, discussing wainscoting styles with much expertise and moving on to the blending of colors and their multiplicity of shades and the use of their contrasts, the technique of faux marble, the use of rough stone for effect, the kind of windows that made a plain room gracious, a gracious room glorious. On the spot she decided that he would be her consultant and confidant when the time came. Since then he had worked on the Capitol and other buildings, but he had never lost his interest in her project.

"I want this to be a great house for the people of America," she told him one day. "I want it to stand for the richness of our democracy."

She remembered how he had bowed. "It will be a great honor to assist." Now the day when she might tell him to start seemed measurably nearer.

So she gazed out into the starry night, comfortable, warm, wine still swirling in her head, and let her imagination soar. If she could fly to the glittering carpet above or even over the trees and the houses gleaming all around in the moonlight, if she could soar high over the Appalachians and pick out the Ohio, a silver ribbon winding through the dark, if she could go on and on and spy the great silver streak running southward down the center of the continent and draining east and west, and on over the ground across which Merry and his men soon would march, what would she see?

She smiled, enjoying the fantasy the more because it was so unlike her. If she could fly into the future, what would she see? Farms replacing forests, towns with churches and schools rising along the rivers, southbound flatboats dark specks on the rivers from the Appalachians to what Merry called the Stony Mountains, and it would all be American. They always had known that ultimately American settlers would control the West, but now the process had been wildly accelerated. But out beyond, still further . . . Jimmy said we would be a continental nation, different oceans washing our shores east and west and maybe you could say the south, except she guessed the Gulf really was part of the Atlantic. . . .

Well, no matter. A two-ocean nation, that would do. A continental nation. Merry's expedition surely would make what had been hope become real expectation. Already the public folklore had leaped to the assumption that the purpose of the exploration was to explore the new possession. Of course, maybe out in the future the British and the Spanish would have something to say about our west, but then, the

French had thought to take a hand in the American game and we dealt with them. We'd deal with the others too.

Because we were strong. We had come through a great crisis. We had settled forever—or at least, for as long as the blank future allowed you to guess—the issue of democracy. Anyway, freedom is for each generation to preserve and protect, each generation facing the risk of its loss. We were the *only* democracy in the world, but we wouldn't be the last. For we had just proved the strength of the democratic form, proved it against all the naysayers and sad doubters.

And we had opened the West as it never had been opened before; the continental dream beckoned with the glittering stars.

We've done well by the country, she thought, she and Jimmy and all the others. We've done well.

She was riding the dream now, eyes shut, and the edge of sky behind her went pale and the sun rose and glinted against the river and far overhead, above her, below her, she didn't know and it didn't matter, an eagle wheeled, its harsh warrior's cry that of a king, lord of all it surveyed. . . .

She opened her eyes onto the blanket of stars, the image of the great bird vivid in her mind. She was supremely happy.

Cold had overtaken the room. The fire was down, and she stood and gazed once more at the sweep of stars brilliant as daisies crowding a field. Then she slipped off her robe and kicked off the slippers and slid into the warm bed. Jimmy muttered something, and she touched his cheek and he sighed and was gone again in sleep.

AUTHOR'S NOTE

On Methods and Sources

Eagle's Cry is a novel. Yet it is in general accurate both as to the history of the events it chronicles and as to the character, personalities, and conflicts of the historical figures. To sum up in a phrase, this is *the imagined inside of a known outside story.*

So I believe that with a few exceptions, most listed below, the novel is a close account of what happened and why, and of the individuals involved. I base the words I put in their mouths on the records they and their contemporaries left and my own estimate of how reasonable men and women might reasonably respond. One immediate variance from rigid fact, however, is that I frequently put people together for direct dialogue when in fact they communicated by letter; what I have them say, however, is fully consistent with their positions and attitudes.

History strives for what is documentable and provable. My books strive for the story that underlies reality, what I see as an imagined reality. To clarify that reality, and to give the reader information not readily delivered through a historical character, I have used a few fictional characters to interact with real characters and thus illuminate their views. The biggest fictional additions are Danny and Carl Mobry and their servants, Samuel and Millie Clark. But all that I have them say and do accurately reflects the historical events in which they were involved. In matters such as the Louisiana Purchase or the Jefferson-Burr tie, it must be assumed that much of what passes is not laid out in the record. An example of this is the contact I postulate between Madison—through Dolley and Danny—with Bayard of Delaware; some contact was made, and I supply a version that could have happened but that would never have been recorded. In my view, the important point here is that all that I have Bayard and the two women saying accurately reflects the situation and attitudes.

Danny's contact with Mrs. Pichon is fictional but clearly represents Pichon's position. Though John Quincy Adams and Pichon were friends and their conversation represents historical truth, it is not documented. General Wilkinson is an odd figure, thought then and known now to have been a traitor—the Spanish listed him as Agent #13. His connection to Burr is well documented.

Meriwether Lewis's trail adventure when we meet him is fictional but consistent both with the times and with his nature. His seizure of command is accurately presented. Dolley's sister Anna was a real person, but her flirtation with Lewis is fictional; it accurately reflects, however, the trouble that Lewis did have with young women who drew his attention. The reasons I advance for that trouble are not documented, but I believe they are reasonable speculations fully consistent with the known biographical facts. Mary Beth Slaney is fictional, as are the other young women whom I show Lewis meeting. His application to Jefferson for command of a transcontinental expedition when he was nineteen is factual. Mr. Lemaire is a real figure, and Dolley's relationship with him is accurately portrayed; an initial clash is assumed but not documented.

The strange tale of Andrew Jackson's marriage and the scandal that followed is fully accurate. The violent response to scandal he presented, and his wife's crushed nature, are accurately portrayed. The quarrel with Governor Sevier is presented almost word for word as those who were there recorded it. I believe my account of Jackson to be highly accurate, both as to events and as to his personality and nature; the only place I have purposely exceeded the record was in bringing him to Washington when the disaster of the Spanish closing of the Mississippi inflamed the West. The story is accurate as to the West's violent reaction, but I have no knowledge that Jackson left Tennessee at this time.

Did Aaron Burr plot to bring about the election tie? He denied it, but Madison was convinced to his death that it was true, and this is Madison's story. My portrayal of Burr's character may offend his ardent apologists, who are numerous even today, and while offending anyone distresses me sorely, I do believe a case can be made for my portrayal. Burr's bitterness over being excluded after the tie is well documented.

General Washington's last hours were as I portray them, and he was being importuned to return to the helm. Danny's lover, Henri, is fictional, but her uncle, Daniel Clark, is a famous figure in New Orleans history who did, in fact, undertake a mission to Paris. How the U.S. government recruited him for this mission is not recorded. His mistress, Zulie, is a historical figure. The DuPont family, in the process of starting the great firm we know today, played exactly the role I describe. Senator Ross's part in persuading Napoleon is accurately stated, but the extent to which and the means by which he and Madison communicated are not documented. I find it impossible to believe that his great speech, put so neatly into Napoleon's hands, had not been arranged. A splinter party led by Timothy Pickering did for years lead a secession movement in New England which the Adamses, father and son, rejected. The personality of the Adams family and its bitterness are accurately drawn. The Sally Hemings story is accurately drawn, as is, I believe, the character of James Callender, who shortly after this book's period fell drunk into a shallow ditch in Richmond and drowned. Federalists' stunned disbelief at losing the 1800 election is accurately portrayed. The unfolding French decision to sell Louisiana is well documented.

Language in the early nineteenth century was more formal than we use today, but I'm sure thoughts were as fluent, tempers as quick, analyses as surefooted as they are today, and that all were rendered from person to person just as fluidly. My aim is to create for modern readers the intimacy of decisions and pressures then affecting these individuals, and so, while avoiding modernisms, I have chosen language that sounds more formal than modern usage but that probably is somewhat less formal than what actually was used then.

Political parties can be confusing to modern ears. As the opening chapter makes clear, at the start there were no parties. As the democratic spirit rose, reaction to elitism took the form of the first Republican Party under Madison, Jefferson, and others. Almost immediately, this opposition group became known as Democrats, and I have used that term to avoid confusion with the modern Republican Party, which was formed in the 1850s with John Charles Frémont its first presidential candidate. Adams and the old guard took the Federalist label.

The sequel to this novel, now in preparation, will undertake to finish stories that could only be started here. We see that Burr clearly was destroyed by the tie that we chronicle in *Eagle's Cry* as we watch him play out his fate—the deadly duel with Hamilton, the flight, the attempt to steal the West, the trial, exile.

Meriwether Lewis, set on the path to greatness in this book, makes his monumental trek to the Pacific and returns to his own tragedy. Madison and Dolley persevere against the machinations of radical Democrats and the challenge from Monroe here set up, ending in triumph with election to the presidency in 1808. Dolley can begin her ardent and quite famous refurbishing of what a few people by then had started calling the White House.

The trouble with the British becomes increasingly volatile and dangerous. The possibility of war with England becomes a constant pressure. Madison must walk a narrow path resisting that pressure and holding national pride and position while staving off a war we were too weak to fight, a war that holds off until 1812, which story I have already chronicled in my novel *1812*.

Of course, *Eagle's Cry* depends heavily on research; this is to express my appreciation to the Butler Library at Columbia University, the New York Public Library, the Library of Congress, the library of the Century Association, and the library of Greenwich, Connecticut, one of the finest and busiest community libraries in the country.

I relied heavily upon Irving Brant's six-volume treatment of the Madisons and Ralph Ketcham's single volume. Dumas Malone's wonderful six volumes on Jefferson are superb, and so is Merrill Peterson's single volume. *The Age of Federalism*, by Stanley Elkins and Eric McKitrick, sums up the 1790s beautifully. For General Washington, I relied on James Flexner's fine four-volume treatment and on the more recent treatment by Willard Randall. Stephen Ambrose's treatment of Meriwether Lewis is definitive, but earlier works by David Lavender and Richard Dillon are useful. Robert Remini's three-volume treatment of Andrew Jackson is excellent, following Marquis James and James Parton. I relied on Milton Lomask's two-volume work on Aaron Burr, though my impressions of Burr are different from his very favorable treatment. My portrait of Robert Livingston is drawn from George Dangerfield's fine biography. Finally, of course, there is the brilliant *History of the United States During the Administrations of Thomas Jefferson and James Madison*, by Henry Adams, its ten volumes available in full today in a magnificent two-volume edition from the Library of America. Adams is splendid, sometimes biased, sometimes off-base in the view of some modern scholars, but unfailingly interesting and often very wise.

In the end, however, I based much of my estimates of how politics and human nature really work (they are, of course, intertwined) on my own substantial experience with politics, Washington, and the White House as a national journalist.

—DN

Look for
David Nevin's

TREASON

Available October 2001
from Forge Books

1

This was the way she remembered it—memories cherished across thirty-five tumultuous years when the world turned upside down and she moved to the center of the nation's affairs—this was her story:

She was born in `Sixty-eight and that meant she was—let's see—eight when the trouble started. She remembered her father's distress there on the Virginia plantation. He was a Quaker strong in his faith and he held against war. But Millie Esterbridge, who was a year older and lived on the plantation next to theirs, said General Washington would lead the American troops and everyone knew—well, everyone in Virginia—that he was a great man. It would be all right with General Washington in command. Of course, at eight you take a lot for granted and later she'd marveled at how ignorant they were of war. Everyone, grown-ups, too. At first it had just been the awful splitting between patriots and loyalists, Millie's father selling out and moving her best friend off to Canada. Later they understood that dislocation and dissolved loyalties hardly mattered against the deaths and the aching widows, the hunger and pain of folks at home and men in the field alike, the men who returned absent arms and legs, their eyes hollowed out like melon husks, and the men who didn't come home at all. Maybe it was in reaction to the war that Pa decided that his faith required him to free their slaves, sell the plantation and move to Philadelphia, the Quaker center that only incidentally was America's largest city.

She was fourteen when the Revolution ended and the last British soldiers boarded ships lying against the wharves in New York City and went home. General Washington mounted a big white horse and led his ragged troops into the city the enemy had held so long and the whole country erupted in joy, bonfires and parades and martial music and speechifying to numb the senses.

The nation was free. There were people who said it would sink right out of sight without British leaders to direct it or war to hold it together, but that made no sense to her. She said so, too, plain and clear, and presently the Quaker elders called to tell her it was unseemly for a mere lass to talk so. But she snorted when the trio departed, austere and unsmiling in their black garb and coarse woolen hose and flat hats—she had a mind of her own and didn't need anyone telling her how to use it.

She was fifteen and then sixteen and when she turned to the mirror she liked what she saw, and from the way young men looked at her and boys stared and Quaker matrons frowned, she came to understand she was not just beautiful but fetching as well. Bright colors weren't the Quaker way but she managed always to have a red ribbon in her glossy black hair or a sash of vivid green on a white gown or the bootlaces of purple silk she once wore, creating a minor stir.

By then everyone in Philadelphia was talking about the way the post-revolutionary government was falling flat, imploding, no head and no real body, no resources and no authority, no direction and no aim or intention or purpose, every state in the confederacy standing alone and for itself. Seemed we weren't Americans at all but Pennsylvanians or Virginians or what-have-you. But shoot, she was both Pennsylvanian and Virginian!—and hence hardly could be one or t'other. By 1785 when she was seventeen and fresh as a rose in bloom, Pa said the country was going to ruin and the elders blamed the slight attention paid the Lord's word and she thought it was high time someone did something and wasn't backward about saying so.

And sure enough, as if he'd been listening, General Washington called a meeting for right here in Philadelphia over to the State House that aimed to straighten it all out so the blood and pain of the war wouldn't be wasted. Every day she got out her parasol against the sun—oh, it was hot that summer of 1787!—and put a ribbon in her hair and with a half-dozen Quaker girls went to stand along the brick sidewalks and watch the delegates enter and leave. Ah, frivolity!—the girls along the sidewalk like so many flowers wanting to feel part of a great day, or at least to be noticed. The delegates looked toilsome and dour and they danced on the hot brick because the slippers they wore with snowy silk hose were so thin. It was said that they were talking themselves blue, sitting at little tables covered in green felt while General Washington looked on from a small dais. He hardly said a word, so it was remarked, but his stern look held them to the task.

Everyone talked about it on the street and they said the brightest man in the Constitutional Convention was the smallest and the quietist with ideas that thundered but a voice that could hardly be heard. His name was James Madison and he was a fellow Virginian. She saw him one day, pale, wizened, looked old, forty or so, and my goodness, you could just see he was smart. She watched him, wondering if he would look up and see her and look at her the way everyone else did, but he walked along with hands clasped behind him, head down, probably thinking great thoughts right before her eyes!

Gossip said the delegates fought like dogs but by summer's end when blessed fall swept away the miasmic heat they had created a new government. Pa said the Constitution they'd written was a magnificent document that would last into the ages and though it had been threatened a few times it was holding right to this day. This was about the time Pa lost his business and the Quakers read him out of the Society for debt. He went to bed and turned his face to the wall till he died while Ma took in boarders. That was how Aaron Burr came into her life, he a congressman and then senator from New York and a boarder at Ma's house when Congress was in session. Even as a girl she'd recognized what an elegant fellow he was. Handsome, smooth, courteous, usually smiling, he seemed to say that this was how life should be led among men of power. In time she wondered if her own sense of elegance, ribbons and all, had been modeled on the image he presented.

They held elections and of course General Washington took the presidency and she knew everything would be all right. Electing anyone else would have been unimaginable then, though in later years there were plenty of harsh attacks on the grand old man. Everyone said this thoughtless brutality had broken his heart, though he was never one to show pain—maybe to Aunt Martha, but not to the world.

Not that she was calling the president's wife Auntie in those long ago days or, indeed, anything at all. She was far removed then, jostling on the sidewalks with everyone else to see the parades. John Adams of Massachusetts who'd been a great patriot for as long as she could remember became vice president. Secretary of State was Thomas Jefferson whom she'd heard Pa denounce often enough when Jefferson was governor of Virginia. Little Mr. Madison was in Congress and everyone said he was the General's right-hand man. But none of this really touched her. What mattered was the Quaker elders after her again for those ribbons and the glow in her eyes and the way her figure was developing now that she was in her twenties. That surely wasn't her fault — what should she do, hide in her bedroom?

So when a handsome Quaker lawyer named John Todd asked for her hand she married, had two beautiful babies and was prepared to be a Quaker matron, biting her tongue and going easy on the ribbons. But when she was twenty-five the great yellow fever epidemic of 1793 spared her and little Payne but took her husband and new baby along with seven thousand others, one out of ten Philadelphians. She'd never forgotten the malevolent horror of that terrible summer, no one knowing where the disease came from or how to treat it, who would be stricken and who spared—and what a ghastly way to die, black vomit spewing, black water bursting from bowels. One matured overnight.

The grief-torn days that followed seemed blurred later; she seemed hardly aware of day turning to night and night to day. And in that terrible period, it was her mother's boarder, Aaron Burr, who came to her rescue. The New Yorker had turned something called Tammany Hall into a political force and was said to be a power in New York City. He took her quietly in hand in the midst of her grief, gentle sympathy mingling with easy practicality. He saw to her business problems, liquidated her husband's law practice and invested the results, saw to funerals and estates and probate matters. She even drafted a will naming him guardian of her child should the terror sweep them again. But even then, she recognized that it wasn't so much what he did as the way he did it. He was smooth and patient and looking back it seemed that somehow it was his steadfast presence that brought her through those dark days. She owed him a great deal. But she was strong too, possessed of a deep inner resiliency, and gradually her sparkle returned. In time she found herself pondering what life might hold for her next. And Aaron reassured her then in a different way that told her he knew the ways of men and women and of the world: she was a most eligible widow, he said, beauty making up for lack of fortune.

Aaron's elegance, his dress so beautiful, his manner so graceful, to say nothing of that certain quickening in his eyes produced an equal quickening in a great many women, so the talk went. She well understood the feeling; it wasn't that he was so handsome, though he was, or that his charm was beyond resisting, but all together he produced an undeniable pull. She was grateful that in her vulnerable period he had seized no advantages. Later, as she recovered, she was grateful that in due time he did advance himself, suggesting a willingness to service other needs that absent a husband she might now feel. A bit of nirvana, he said. Somehow, it pronounced her ready to meet the world.

Oh, Aaron . . . she was so fond of him and so definitely not in love with him and held such a clear vision that yielding to the temptation he offered—and temptation probably was the right word—would be to throw away her future that she laughed out loud.

"What," he cried, laughing with her, recognition of failure bright in his eyes, perhaps somehow liking her better for her refusal, "dost thou cast nirvana to the swine?"

"You darling man," she said, "you are a caution." She kissed his cheek and told him to sit in the chair in the opposite corner, and it was then that he told her that his good friend, Mr. Madison of Virginia, had asked to be presented. Presented . . . that had a serious sound.

The famous Mr. Madison, a smallish man somewhat shorter than she, gazed at her like a tongue-tied ox when Aaron brought him around but she found his very hesitations endearing. They were the honest product of obvious inexperience with women. But then, she was none too experienced with men, either—or with the national affairs that presumably dominated Mr. Madison's life, right hand man to General Washington as he was. And for all his fumbling, when he did open his mouth it was to reveal intelligence of a very high order. He said his friends called him Jimmy. She gazed at him. Jimmy . . . for a man so distinguished? But she didn't voice this—she knew he would hear it as mockery. Jimmy, she said . . . it has a gentle sound. And he smiled. Silence overtook them and she rattled on a bit and when he rose to go she was sure that would be the end of it. Instead he asked if she would accompany him to a small dinner General Washington was giving the next evening, and to a reception the evening following. He was forty-three and had never married; Aaron had told her his heart had been broken by a callous lass eleven years before and he'd never recovered.

The table of the President of the United States was rarified company for a Quaker miss without experience; she decided that intelligence must take experience's place. Before they reached the main course she had come to understand that she would get just one chance at this level before she was written off. Her solution, reached as she finished the turtle soup, was to keep her mouth shut until she had something to say that she knew she could defend and then say it well. Two such occasions arose before desert; the second time the General smiled and nodded, whether to her or to Jimmy she couldn't be sure, and Mrs. Washington gave her a conspiratorial wink that was as surprising as it was thrilling.

That spring of `Ninety-four there were balls and dinners and he saw her every day, sitting in her mother's parlor, anything but tongue-tied. Ideas poured out and she responded and he accorded her respect, agreeing or explaining disagreement. If his heart had been broken—she didn't inquire—he seemed to have recovered. But when Mrs. Washington—Aunt Martha as she instructed the younger set to call her—asked if he had proposed yet she could only answer, no, not yet. I'll speak to him, the great lady said.

They were married in the fall. She was twenty-six. The Quakers expelled her for marrying outside the faith and she bought handfuls of ribbons and wore vivid sashes and startling turbans—oh, she was bright as a parrot! And her husband's spirits opened like a flower and he laughed and danced though he still was frozen in social groups of any size.

By then the great schism was shredding the government and she was startled to find how bitter and personal it became.

"I mean," she said, faltering, "you and Mr. Hamilton, you were friends, weren't you? Together on—"

"Friends?" said Jimmy, as his friends did indeed call him. "I suppose. When we still saw eye to eye."

They had collaborated on what came to be called *The Federalist*, a series of cogent papers that as she understood it had pretty well put over the new federal government, gaining the nine states needed to give the new constitution effect.

"But Alex changed," Jimmy added, and that was how he characterized the fight. Alex was a handsome fellow fully as irresistible to women as they were to him, famous for it, in fact. She remembered an explosive evening when she had danced with him in one of those intricate quadrilles. It was at a ball the Washingtons gave when she and Jimmy had been married a year or so. The music was gaily rhythmic, the dancers dipping and swirling, and responding to Alex, she couldnt deny that he had a certain magnetic pull. But it seemed aggressive, an invasion that alarmed and then angered her. She was just sorting through these riotous feelings when he said in a low voice, "I wonder that you dare dance with me."

She stared at him. Her face felt hot as it did when she bent over a cooking fireplace. Had he read her mind? Her hand came up—later she realized she'd been close to hitting him—and he added smoothly, "Given that your husband finds me so detestable."

The music ended and his words fell loudly into the sudden silence just as Jimmy, partnered with Hannah Gallatin, stopped beside them. Of course Jimmy had heard and as Hannah gave her a conspiratorial wink he said with a smile, "I don't detest you, Alex. I detest your ideas." All good humored, but she saw by his expression that he wasn't joking.

"Because I want the economy solid and workable?"

Jimmy hesitated; she knew this was tender ground, because the new nation had been flat broke and a country that can't pay its bills, international or domestic, has little standing in the family of nations. But Hamilton as Treasury Secretary had put American finances on a sound footing. Jimmy said Alex was a financial genius, which was the more amazing since his only financial experience had been keeping books in a country store in Jamaica, he the bastard son of a minor Scottish nobleman. Hannah patted her arm and went off somewhere.

"No," Jimmy said, "because you want to feed the rich at everyone else's expense."

"Oh, Jimmy," Alex said, carefully smiling to show this was all in fun, "next you'll be prating about the bank!"

"Yes, I will, now that you raise it. Bank of the United States. Functions as a treasury of the nation, doesn't it?"

"Well—"

"It's where government stores its money, deposits taxes collected, disburses as necessary?"

"Exactly—and—"

"And three-quarters of its assets are in private hands and hence the owners of those monies are in position to manipulate public funds to their own advantage."

Alex's smile was gone. "You will never understand, James. Of course our bank favors the wealthy. Their capital is power and we need them with us, not agin us."

"So you shape law and government and power to their interests."

"Of course—and the bank is a fine example," Alex said, now looking quite self-satisfied.

Then, quite surprising herself, seeing a startled look flash over Jimmy's face, she said, "But won't that build an elite class, the wealthy over everyone else? They hold land, hold commerce, hold politics—they'll have it all, won't they?"

She found herself holding her breath in sheer fright and let it go with a rush. Without a thought she had inserted herself into a complex argument that she was suddenly sure a wiser woman would have avoided. Alex hesitated as if arguing with a woman unsettled him and then Jimmy said in an easy voice, "She does sum it up well, doesn't she?" She felt a flash of gratitude as he went on, "Control by the right people over the rest of us, that's what you're saying—and Alex, isn't the next step logically to make control hereditary and doesn't that suggest nobles and princes and such and doesn't that—"

"Damn it all, Jimmy, you can't believe I want a king when we fought a war to free ourselves of a king!"

"I don't think you want a king. But I think your attitude takes us in that direction—"

"Faugh!"

Jimmy colored. "Faugh, my foot! I could see the reality as soon as the debt question came up."

She knew that was a true sore point with Jimmy. At war's end the nation had countless small debts—soldier's mustering out bonus, the paper given a farmer for a couple of hogs and a sack of oats, payment to gunsmiths and powder dumps and lead mines, all given on a promise of someday, if we win. Well, now someday had arrived and Alex's plan was to float long-term bonds that would pay these debts all at once and clear the books. Debt management, he called it, and yes, it did make fiscal sense.

But who was holding these slips of paper given across the war? Not the soldier mustered out, the farmer for his hogs and oats—no, they long since had been forced by need to sell that scrap of paper to a speculator at a dime on the dollar. Jimmy still got red in the face when he talked of this—he said that piece of paper was a sacred debt of the United States given in honor and taken in the belief that the nation would survive and prosper and honor debts.

But when Alex prepared to pay these debts—and then, quite suddenly as one awakens from a dream, she realized that the music had not resumed and a small crowd had gathered around them. They had interrupted the whole entertainment! She saw Mrs. Washington frowning, the general striding toward the musicians—

And Jimmy cried, voice rising, "I saw it when you rewarded the speculators and froze out the little men, the veterans, the farmers, the small debt holders who'd long since lost their paper. You paid the speculators and devil take those whose suffering had won the war!"

The musicians were lifting their instruments and the general was coming toward them when she heard Alex snap, "Talking of the plight of veterans ill-behooves a man who sat out the war."

The first violinist sounded an A and the general had turned and was coming toward the disruption as she saw her husband go pale at this sally. It was his point of vulnerability. Even today his health was delicate and he was often ill. While Alex had been a dashing officer on General Washington's staff Jimmy hadn't been physically fit for the field. He knew that made sense but it still bothered him. As he stood ashen and silent she was moved to a mighty rage.

"Sir," she cried, "surely a man boasting of his war exploits is at his least attractive!"

At which Alex's cheeks flamed deep red and he turned away. She took her husband's arm and turned him into the dance and in a moment the Washingtons passed. The general looked stiff and cool but Aunt Martha glanced at her and with the faintest smile inclined her head in clear-spoken approval.

The next time she saw Alex he smiled and bowed but didnt approach her, and it was just as well. Of course he hadn't been boasting of his exploits, but he had been positioning himself against Jimmy and that had brought up in her a willingness to fight that she found startling—and exhilarating too.

Jimmy didn't say much afterward. He made it clear he was pleased with her and she realized on her own that he didn't need his wife to fight his battles. Yet things seemed different and after a period of reflection it came to her that she had somehow advanced on that day from the Quaker miss feeling her way to a woman who had legitimated her place in a new world.

But certainly the exchange stood for the schism that was dividing the country. It was philosophical, she supposed, though she didn't spend much time in philosophical musing. Anyway, the basic argument was pretty simple. Are you for entrenched power regulating life or for free people finding their own way on their strengths and instincts? That was simple enough so that left to themselves Americans would have come to satisfactory answers—but then the French Revolution upset all the balances in America.

So it was that on a sunny day in Philadelphia a week or so later she heard someone calling her name as she strolled near the Statehouse. It was a woman's voice, high and urgent with a little note of hysteria. She turned to see Charity Jester almost trotting toward her, wearing an expensive gown of crimson velvet, her pink parasol stabbing the brick walk like a cane. They had been girls together, sharing a reader under some dreaded schoolmaster they both preferred to forget.

Charity seemed to be having trouble getting her breath. "Oh, do you remember that nice Mr. Fournier, Jacques Fournier, I think, he was with the French embassy or some such? Remember how he would smile and correct your French without making you feel a silly goose? He was the count of—oh, I don't know what he was count of, but something, he was somebody, don't you see? And Mr. Jester just learned today that they cut off his head with that terrible slicing machine in Paris. Imagine, murdering a wonderful person in the name of their democracy!"

She stopped, staring, head thrown back, the parasol gripped in both hands. "This democracy business, it's terrifying! I know you believe in it, Mr. Madison and Mr. Jefferson its promoters, I hear the talk, but it'll fool you, it'll turn on you, wait and see! Common folk go mad, give them a chance, that's what France proves. Your followers'll turn on you too, on all of us—you'll see, the ravening mob in the streets, the good people hanging from trees on Chestnut Street. Oh, how can your husband endorse this madness?"

She bristled, ready to leap to Jimmy's defense, but Charity patted her hand and went hurrying down the street as if she feared democracy would consume her right now. But democracy needn't lead to chaos, though Jimmy always admitted that its success did depend on the capacity of free people to control themselves. Frenchmen, breaking out of centuries of feudalism into anarchic revolution had lost that control. But there was a vast difference between France and America; here revolution had been for liberty, there it was for equality. As the search for equality darkened the nobility was executed in ever greater numbers, Dr. Guillotine's grisly machine snicking and snacking and Guillotine square slick with blood. Then the revolution turned on its own and the Terror began when no one proved sufficiently poor and equal. Finally the guillotine was too slow for the killing ordered and crowds were gathered and taken down by cannon fire or burned alive. The dead numbered tens of thousands. And the mob chanted slogans that once had defined American patriotism and democracy.

No wonder Charity Jester in her fine gown was terrified—so was everyone else of position and wealth. These pressures led to a seismic shift in American affairs that was itself revolutionary. Until now there had been no parties; leading men simply stepped forward to take the reins. But the growing schism led automatically to two parties evolving into the two-party system. The old line wealthy elite were Federalists, personified by Alexander Hamilton. For the moment they had the government and were turning toward coercion and control of the little man, driven by the fear that what they saw in France must follow here. Opposing them were Democrats, first called Republicans, then Democratic Republicans, soon shortened to the Democratic Party. Thomas Jefferson led, Jimmy provided the intellectual power and her old friend Aaron Burr of New York was a rising star. They stood for the little man and the tighter and meaner things grew under frightened Federalists, the stronger the Democrats became.

And she, herself stronger and more confident each year, marveled at how often great events and national movements and crucial decisions turned on the same human emotions that children in a nursery will exhibit—rage, fear, greed, hunger. . .

Thomas Jefferson was Jimmy's best friend and the three of them were often together. She liked Tom no matter what Pa had said. He was clever and witty and very gentle, an innately decent man. His mind ranged all over the place with bewildering speed and she often stopped trying to keep up. Yet in the end she thought Jimmy had greater weight which was another reason she rather resented the deference he showed Tom, a decade his senior. Settled in marriage now, she handled herself well and people listened to her with real interest.

Things were changing rapidly. General Washington retired to Mount Vernon. John Adams succeeded him. Tom had stepped down as secretary of state and was at his estate at Monticello. Jimmy left the Congress and they returned to the Madison estate, Montpelier, in sight of the Blue Ridge.

Living in a mansion in which Jimmy's family made her welcome, she nevertheless had a full taste of life in a house not her own.

The national atmosphere darkened steadily. Rank fear seemed to guide Federalists as if they saw hordes of common men advancing on them. Laws became abusive. Every time she and Jimmy went to Philadelphia, still the capital though the new capital on the Potomac would soon be ready, things became more volatile and dangerous. And then Congress passed the Alien and Sedition Acts.

On one of their Philadelphia trips she went on to New York with Hannah Gallatin to visit Hannah's family. New York was booming, soon to overtake Philadelphia, she was sure. Aaron Burr gave them dinner and a tour, bursting with pride. Then, afternoon shadows lengthening, she and Hannah strolled down Broadway.

They were near the Battery when they heard hoofs clattering. A wagon fitted with benches and bearing a half-dozen men in dark coats stopped across the street before a print shop. Carrying oaken clubs the men jumped out to kick open the shop door.

The two women stood frozen, gazing across the street. They heard shouts and a crash within the shop and then a scream. An upstairs window popped open and a woman leaned out.

"Jeremy!" she yelled. "Come quick! They're after Paw, they'll smash the press—"

The press? A sign hung over the door, *The Peck's Slip Tattler*. A newspaper! The men were constables after an editor who'd spoken out of turn.

A dark-haired young man in breeches and buckled shoes and a white shirt with bunched sleeves burst from a next-door tavern, dashed into the shop and was knocked senseless by a constable's club. Then a skinny, gray-haired man in his fifties was led out with hands bound behind him. Crying and cursing at once, he stepped over his son's inert body. Two stalwarts hurled him face down into the bottom of the wagon. When he sat up the side of his head was bloody.

The woman in the window poured invective on the constables, their ancestry and parentage, their sexual proclivities, their dietary habits—it was thrilling no matter how rough, for in the most direct way at her command this woman was making her stand. But without even looking up two of the constables took sledge hammers from the wagon, strode into the shop and from the sound were beating something to pieces.

"God damned scoundrels," a tall man in a sailor's cap snarled. "Busting up poor Jethro's press. The only man in New York with the guts to tell the truth, pin the tail on those donkeys in Philadelphia, damn president don't know his right hand from his left and here they are smashing Jethro's press!"

He stood poised on the balls of his feet, fists clenched. "You know why they want to crush Jethro, don't you? 'Cause the truth scares the shit out of them!"

At which the leader of the constables turned with eyes red and club poised and said, "Maybe we'll take you too, you seditious son of a bitch!"

The man in the cap laughed. "Try the Alien and Sedition Acts on me, will you? Well, you can kiss my arse!" With another loud laugh he turned and fled into the warren of streets that led to the eastside docks.

"I expect we'd better walk along," Hannah said, voice trembling. It was deeply disturbing—this was the Alien and Sedition Acts in action and it was sickening. It had become a crime to criticize the government. Speak your mind on the capabilities of the president and look for the constable to snatch you from the tavern and into jail you went. Troublesome aliens who arrived under the illusion that democracy meant democracy were easily deported. Print a letter in your newspaper that said the government was a donkey and draw a couple of years in prison, your press destroyed.

They walked on, neither speaking, and it struck her suddenly that her view of everything had changed. A slightly abstract view of politics had shifted in her mind to something visceral and direct. "It's all real, isn't it?" she said to

Jimmy on her return. "This printer, editor, this Mr. Jethro, doubtless still in a cell somewhere, probably in the same bloody shirt—"

Of course she had known that politics affected people's lives but never again would she see issues only in the abstract.

"What about the First Amendment, free speech, free press?" she demanded of her husband.

"Oh, yes," he said, "violates the Constitution, all right. But who's to stop the Congress? The Supreme Court is powerless, scarcely functioning, really—government can do as it pleases."

"That's outrageous!"

"Well, maybe it'll make common folk see the danger."

One could hope, anyway. The Federalists were squabbling among themselves while Democrats were coming on strong. The election of 1800 was nearing and Tom was making a serious push against John Adams, while Aaron Burr stood for vice president. Adams had New England, Jefferson the South and West; they counted on Aaron for New York.

Not long before the election she bumped into Aaron by chance on a Philadelphia street and let him give her tea in a sidewalk café. He was remembering life in her mother's boarding house and the day he brought Jimmy to call and what an innocent naïf she was then. Well, she was a far cry today from that long ago Quaker miss. And the times had changed with her. Imagine—through Tom they might sit in the august General Washington's seat yet.

With a little smile that she took as introduction to a witticism he added, "Though it might just as well be me."

But he wasn't joking and she said rather sharply, "No one sees you there, Aaron."

"Oh, I don't know," he said, all geniality. "Try that in New York—you'll be surprised. There's little sentiment there that I am in any way inferior to the sainted Virginian. Stranger things have happened, you know."

She snorted. "Horse gives birth to a goat, that would be stranger."

Something sparkled deep in his eyes and he said with what she saw was utter seriousness, "You underestimate me, dear girl." It unsettled her; Aaron had a profoundly devious mind.

So the election of 1800 came about and the Democrats won with the help of New York and poor John Adams was sent home to Massachusetts with a broken heart just as the government moved into the new capital on the Potomac.

It was no less, as Tom put it, than a second revolution! The people had turned from the old way to the new, from privilege and control and coercion to the belief that free people could find the self-control to govern themselves. Magnificent!

And then Aaron sprang his dirty trick. For a terrible few weeks he seemed in position to carry out what she had first taken as a bad joke—with Federalist help, to exchange places with Tom and make himself president, Tom vice president.

She was enraged at this sudden scandalous turn—my word, Aaron seemed to be confirming the Federalist fear that the agony of France must play out here. Charity Jester's worst dreams ready to unfold—Democrats attacking each other before they even took office! Oh, but she was far from Ma's boarding house now. She watched the country boil toward civil war, Virginia and Pennsylvania preparing militia to march on Washington to enforce the Constitution. Responsible Federalists began to back off. Hamilton put country before politics and argued for Jefferson over Burr as a man of quality. More Federalists abandoned Burr and his dream collapsed.

So the crisis passed, and with it her anger. For after all, she could see that this really had just been Aaron being Aaron—greed and cavalier willingness to strike for the main chance was an indelible part of his nature. That and his pride and his unshakeable confidence—he would have made a good pirate.

Democrats remained enraged and so did Jimmy. But Aaron had been a real friend when she needed one and that she could not forget. And wouldn't, and that was that. Anyway, it was settled after a few alarming weeks and no great harm appeared done. Things went on, Aaron as vice president presiding over the Senate with his usual panache, graceful and smiling. Really, it struck her as a triumph of democracy that it had responded to crisis with such vitality.

But she saw that Tom and Jimmy intended to punish Aaron, strip him of power and deny him victory's rewards. She knew he'd assumed that once it was settled they'd all be friends again. Punishing him struck her as small, unproductive, even dangerous. Of course they shouldn't trust him—he always would be drawn to the main chance. But to strip him of power and position, bare him to the world as a shattered man—all aside from cruelty, she saw no profit and much risk in that.

Jimmy remained adamant and finally it became one of those subjects best left alone in a marriage. But in the act of differing from her husband, of questioning his judgement, she realized that in some subtle way she had come of age.

Now Tom was president—she had decided that "Tom" would do perfectly well—and Jimmy was secretary of state and they were presiding over a great success. The people loved them and Federalists crept around like whipped dogs. By this time they had moved to the new city on the Potomac and built a handsome home of brick, three stories with cupola and porte-cochere. It stood a few blocks from the President's House where Tom, the lonely widower, pressed her into service as official hostess. She took over presidential entertaining and invitations to the mansion became wildly sought after; the town was still a social wilderness, few congressmen brought their families, and everyone was hungry for a kind word and a good meal. Jimmy was at the heart of everything as secretary of state, but she felt she wasn't far behind him, so central to Washington affairs did her dinners become.

Her ambitions grew. If Jimmy succeed Tom—and who would be better?—she would be the president's wife. Her social mastery would matter more than ever and she would be in a real position to complete this magnificent mansion. It was glorious on the outside, if a little boxy, its yellow sandstone walls painted white, but it was scarcely finished inside and in desperate need of decoration which she quickly found that Tom intended to ignore. But just wait!

Year by year, adventure by adventure, she and Jimmy grew closer; once she had amused him and then she pleased him and then she interested him and now he depended on her. When they were apart they were equally stricken. He was a darling man.

And then a terrible whisper came up the Mississippi from New Orleans. Napoleon intended to reclaim the province of Louisiana from Spain, to whom France had surrendered it long before. Napoleon? Napoleon Bonaparte, dictator of France, the most powerful man on earth? He who had whipped the British to a standstill, who controlled most of Europe and obviously intended to rule the world? He wanted Louisiana?

Yes, as a matter of fact, the whole vast territory, New Orleans to Canada along the Mississippi and westward to the Stony Mountains. The day he took possession Jimmy's dream of a continental nation would be dead. But Napoleon wouldn't stop there. Soon he would want American territory too, Appalachians to the Mississippi, including the new states of Tennessee and Kentucky and Ohio. The United States would be left hugging the Atlantic shore. And it would kill the new democracy—voters would cast the new form into the dustbin.

Yet how could the embryo nation stand against Napoleon's eagles? Only by subordinating itself to Britain in return for a Royal Navy blockade to seal the coastline and starve French troops. But subordinating itself to Britain, a Federalist dream, would destroy the new democracy just as quickly.

So they must make Napoleon see he could not win *before* they reached that point. What could she do in this crisis? She could stand by, and she understood how important that could be. When he talked all night of possible approaches, she listened. When he went silent she awaited his return. When he drew his chair to the window and stared into the dark she draped a blanket over his shoulders. She fed him and cosseted him and fussed over him; one day he told her—voice casual but eyes fixed on her—that he doubted he could get through this alone. That was worth a very great deal to her.

Two years passed without French response. They had done all they could and Jimmy drew up a proposal to the British that would save Louisiana but destroy the new democracy. And then one day as they took tea with Tom in the mansion the message arrived: Napoleon Bonaparte had offered to sell all of Louisiana to the Americans! We had asked for the city of New Orleans or the right bank of the river or even a square mile above New Orleans on which the American flag could fly as guarantee of free trade on the river. And Talleyrand had said, what would you give for the whole?

The whole? The country rocked with joy. Negotiations finally settled on fifteen million dollars and the deal was done. Jimmy told her poor Albert Gallatin, treasury secretary, was horrified at the price—and Hannah told her later that Albert muttered in his sleep—but Jimmy said someday it would be regarded as a great bargain. It saved the new democracy—that was bargain enough for her.

Oh, the vast and wonderful change—the nation more than doubled in size, its future as a continental nation assured, the threat of Napoleon removed forever. And she had changed with it. She was thirty-five years old and she had grown up too, faced tragedy and been made stronger; she had entered national life as an innocent and grown wise in experiencing democracy's birthing pains. She had focused ambition and she felt complete as she had not at any time in her thirty-five years; and she supposed that is what maturity meant.

But more immediately, she grew uncomfortable with the wild celebration of the vast Purchase. Everyone said Tom was a genius for mastering Napoleon and with sublime contradiction said how lucky that the Frenchman decided to sell. And with growing outrage she began to ask where in all

these salutations was credit for her darling little husband
who had taken on the most powerful man in the world in
hand-to-hand combat and won? While he, modest man that
he was, generous and decent, his voice light, his manner
quiet, watched credit being taken by most everyone when it
was plain to her that he and he alone had stood as Horatius at
the Gate. Carefully she sharpened a fresh quill and unfolded
a clean sheet of vellum and began to write:

Mr. James Madison, Esq.

Sir: Permit me to inform you that in the opinion of
all right-thinking Americans the credit for the late great
triumph of Louisiana rests squarely on your shoulders,
as did the weight of the equally great campaign that
achieved the triumph. And who, dear sir, should know
this better than the undersigned?

Your loving wife,
Dolley P. Madison